THE AGE OF SCORPIO

Also by Gavin G. Smith from Gollancz:

Veteran
War in Heaven
Crysis: Escalation

THE AGE OF SCORPIO
Gavin G. Smith

GOLLANCZ

LONDON

First published in Great Britain in 2013 by Gollancz
An imprint of the Orion Publishing Group
Orion House, 5 Upper St Martin's Lane,
London WC2H 9EA
An Hachette UK Company

A CIP catalogue record for this book
is available from the British Library

ISBN 978 0 575 09475 8

3 5 7 9 10 8 6 4

Typeset by Deltatype Ltd, Birkenhead, Merseyside

Printed in Great Britain by Clays Ltd, St Ives plc

The Orion Publishing Group's policy is to use papers
that are natural, renewable and recyclable products and
made from wood grown in sustainable forests. The logging
and manufacturing processes are expected to conform to
the environmental regulations of the country of origin.

www.gavingsmith.com
www.orionbooks.co.uk
www.gollancz.co.uk

To Evelyn & Grant Smith (or Mum & Dad as I like to call them)
without whom none of this would have been possible
(though someone had better tell Mum about this as she
doesn't like Science Fiction very much).

1

A Long Time After the Loss

The deep-space salvage tug looked like it was made of hundreds of years of patched-together scrap parts. The original parts of the ship were buried underneath layers of barely functioning detritus. It was a scavenger ship, a space-going parasite that fed on the misfortunes of others. Just like everything else in Known Space.

Forward was Command and Control, the crew area, workshops and a small internal hold, but much of the rest of the craft was exposed to vacuum. The massive towing apparatus, tools for use in vacuum, rolls of high-tensile net to carry externally salvaged cargo, detachable boosters to attach to towed hulks and hangars for the various drones, including Nulty's own hangar. The rest of the crew had long since given up trying to guess Nulty's original race and gender. A long time ago Nulty had uploaded himself into a deep-space salvage drone and chosen to live in a machine body in the vacuum.

The tug was called the *Black Swan*. Few names could have been less fitting. None of its current crew knew what a swan was and none of them had the inclination to find out.

The oversized engines, used for towing hulks many times larger than the *Black Swan*, were on heavy-duty manoeuvrable pontoons that looked like muscular arms reaching out from the tug. The engines were old and didn't function optimally, like everything else on the *Black Swan*. Only the bridge drive was new. This was because of all the captains based out of Arclight, only Eldon Sloper was desperate enough to agree to a salvage job in Red Space.

'Where are we?' The question irritated Eldon. Most things had for many years now. It was the irritability of your life not working out the way you wanted it to. He hadn't asked for much, he thought, just a thriving salvage business, but that had been too much apparently.

'Space,' the small weasel-looking man with the pockmarked face and thinning hair answered. Eden had often wondered why someone who looked like that hadn't had themselves extensively redesigned a

1

long time ago. Nulty, during one of his rare fallings-out with his captain, had suggested that Eldon had been sculpted, but his personality had bled out and turned him back to his original form.

Eldon didn't have to look at Eden to know his sarcastic answer to her question had irritated her. It had been designed to. After all, she'd had neunonic access to the co-ordinates since they'd left Arclight.

The tug was old enough to still have manual displays and controls, though it was, like nearly all spacecraft in Known Space, piloted via neunonic interface. The pilot and co-pilot/navigator's seats were raised to give a better view of the subjective front of the tug, which the hull's smart matter had rendered transparent, providing them with a panoramic view of outside. Information cascaded down the vista of black and pinpricks of light. The view was repeated in the minds of each of the crew along with pertinent information for their specific job roles.

'We're not quite off the charts but this is pretty much the edge of Known Space. Much further and I expect we'd have to explain ourselves to the Church.' The cheerfulness, implying as it did that Brett felt this was some kind of adventure, further irritated Eldon. It was symptomatic of his overall irritation with the handsome younger man – life hadn't ground the hopes and dreams out of him yet. Well that and the way that Melia looked at him.

'Eden, wake up Melia,' Eldon said.

'Oh, is kitty going to do some work for a change?' Eden said, not even trying to hide the acid in her tone.

Eldon turned in the flight chair to look at the engineer. He had always assumed that the glorified mechanic was jealous of Melia, though why she didn't just sculpt herself to look more pleasing to the eye he had no idea. It wasn't as if he didn't pay her enough and she didn't have the crippling financial responsibilities of trying to run a ship, well, a tug anyway. Eden was neither one thing nor another. He was pretty sure that her base uplift was human, though she'd had some lizard DNA in her somewhere along the line as much of her visible skin was scaled. She'd obviously had both soft-machine biological and hard-machine tech augments, whereas most people tended to go for one or the other. Eldon wasn't even sure of her gender: he was pretty sure she was base female but from one of the more masculine female genders.

'Eden, just for once could we pretend that I'm the captain and we're about to do something really—'

'Fucking stupid?' Eden asked. Eldon felt a vein on his forehead start to twitch as Brett laughed, good-naturedly, of course.

'Eden, Melia's our bridge drive specialist – we'll need her,' Brett said. *Oh go and fuck yourself, you supercilious little prick*, Eldon thought. But it didn't matter, Melia was all his, a fully bonded concubine bought and paid for. He'd paid for her training and neunonics so she could help with the ship's systems. So she wasn't just an ornament and sex toy.

Eden glared at Eldon. He was just as capable of waking the fucking cat, she thought as she ran through the pod's shutdown sequence on her neunonics. Strictly speaking, as the ship's engineer the pod's systems were her responsibility but Eden was pretty sure that Eldon had just got her to do it because he knew how much she hated the cat.

The pod creaked open. It needed maintenance but Eden was putting it off as long as possible in the hope that Melia died in a horrible cryogenic accident. Eden had sent the cursory, bordering on rude, wake-up call to the cat's neunonics. Melia hadn't responded but the pod's systems reported that the cocktail of drugs required to bring the cat to fully functioning consciousness had been administered.

Melia sat up in the pod and made yawning a performance that allowed her to show off all her sculpted assets. Eldon turned to watch the show. Even Brett, healthy polysexual though he was, looked around briefly.

'That is so fucking demeaning,' Eden muttered under her breath.

'And yet everyone does what I want,' Melia said, smiling. The lightly furred feline humanoid's smile was of course predatory.

'Only because you pander to some xenophile pornographic fantasy hard-wired into the wannabe masculine since before the Loss.'

'Come on, Eden.' Brett said. Eden normally liked Brett, but his want for everyone to get on was starting to irritate her as well.

Eldon was looking at Melia with an expression that bordered on worship. His adoration was shattered by the grateful smile that Melia shot Brett.

It was short walk from the pod to Eldon's flight chair, but the naked feline made a performance of that. Eden tried not to grind her teeth as Melia put her arms around Eldon and jumped into his lap.

'We're in space, baby?' Melia said, rubbing against Eldon and purring gently.

'Oh put some fucking clothes on!' Eden said. Melia bared her teeth and hissed at the human – mostly – woman.

'Go and fuck yourself, you puritan bitch!' Eldon snapped at the engineer.

'Eden, you know that they have different social mores to us,' Brett said in a conciliatory tone.

'Would those social mores include manipulating the fuck out of every halfwit with a penis?'

'They like being looked after,' Brett said.

'They like other people doing shit for them, you mean.'

Eldon's mood had improved with Melia waking up but was now beginning to sour again. He needed to replace Eden but needed to find someone of her calibre that came at her price. He tried his best to ignore her. Instead he focused on the wriggling naked feline in his lap.

'Will we be docking soon so we can go and do something fun?' Melia asked.

'Baby Doll.' Eldon ignored the gagging sound that Eden was making. 'We need you to do some work.' Melia pouted. 'Did you look at the data packet I 'faced you?' Eldon had to suppress his irritation as Melia shook her head.

'I figured that if it was important you'd tell me when I woke up.' Melia concentrated for a bit. 'We're in the middle of nowhere, baby. Why'd you want to go into the Red here?'

'We've been given a tip on a some salvage, Baby Doll.'

'In Red Space?' Melia's purring baby talk had gone; now she sounded more businesslike. 'Isn't that like, really dangerous?'

'Yes. There's a reason the Church has us stay on the routes marked with the beacons,' Eden snapped.

'They're paying a lot, Baby Doll – they even installed a new bridge drive,' Eldon continued. Greed and the need to be safe warred within the feline.

'Enough money to have fun?' she asked. Eldon nodded. 'A lot of fun?' Eldon looked pained but nodded. Eden groaned as she saw her bonus getting smaller. Melia smiled.

'I'll go and put some clothes on before what's-her-face expires in a puddle of jealousy.'

'While you're at it, why don't you fuck yourself?' Eden suggested.

'Only with Eldon watching, darling.'

Nulty didn't want to miss this. It had been so long since the *Black Swan* had gone into Red Space. His hangar door slid down as he disconnected himself from his immersion link. In aperture configuration, Nulty scuttled out of the hangar on deceptively spindly looking insectile legs. Even living as a machine he felt the vertigo of being alone out in the stars and embraced it. He hoped he never grew tired of it. Though he had to cut off the comms chatter from the rest of the crew. He wondered how they could just bicker at times like this.

In front of the *Black Swan* space was ripped open, though Nulty did not appreciate it as violence. To him it looked like a tear lined with a silk ribbon of blue pulsing radiation. Through the tear it looked like space was bleeding, the bright crimson of Red Space. As incredible as this sight was, there was something about the fabric of Red Space that made him feel uncomfortable. He knew Red Space was dangerous. He knew much of it was uncharted territory, and in his several hundred years of spacefaring he'd heard all the stories, though like most people he'd never seen anything. Deep in his metal shell he just couldn't shake the feeling that it was wrong at a fundamental level. If he were forced to put a word to it, the word would have been vampiric, though every time he thought it the rational part of his brain scoffed at him.

As they moved through into the eddying, seemingly living crimson smoke of Red Space, Nulty retreated back into his hangar. Reconnecting, Nulty went looking for solace in immersion fantasies.

'Sorry, boss. Nothing but glitches,' Brett told Eldon.

'Baby, I'm bored,' Melia said. Her tone suggested that she wasn't just bored, she was more than a little worried.

'Wow, so this is what Red Space looks like,' Eden muttered to herself sarcastically.

'Everyone fucking shut up!' Eldon shouted. He was trying to concentrate. He even ignored Melia's pout, which this time wasn't just for effect. They'd been in Red Space for the better part of twenty hours, running every conceivable sensor sweep they could. Different rules applied in Red Space, though none of them had ever thought to investigate those rules and find out how they worked. Normally it was just enough to know that some things worked, others didn't, and stick close to the Church beacons so you didn't get lost. Those different rules, however, were playing havoc with their sensor sweeps. They had been chasing glitches and sensor ghosts, some of them terrifying in scale, for the last twenty hours.

Despite the uppers, most of them were tired. Because of the uppers, most of them were jittery and even more irritable than normal.

'What's that?' Eldon asked, sharing information with Brett.

'Another glitch,' Brett answered wearily. Eldon sighed and then highlighted more of the sensor information. 'Okay, so it's a repetitive glitch.'

'If it's that regular then there's a reason. Nulty?'

Nulty had been quiet but he'd been monitoring the sensor sweeps through neunonic interface with his own liquid-software brain.

'That's called cause and effect,' Nulty said over the interface.

'The signal's so weak,' Brett pointed out.

'Baby, are we moving?' Melia practically mewed. She sounded frightened.

'It's okay, Baby Doll. The Red plays tricks with your perception, just like with the sensors. We've got the engines compensating for a stationary position.'

'Does it play tricks on the bridge drive as well?' the feline asked.

Normally Melia liked it when she was the centre of attention. She did not like it so much this time as they all turned to look at her.

'What do you mean?' Eldon asked. He wasn't sure if it was his mind playing tricks on him, but now Melia had said that, it did feel like the *Swan* was moving.

Melia shared the pertinent bridge drive info over the neunonic interface.

'Shit,' Eldon said simply.

'That's weird. It looks like something's pulling at it,' Nulty said over the interface.

'Ever seen anything like that?' Brett asked.

'No, never even heard of anything like that, and I thought I'd heard every bridge drive tale going.'

'We could be about to start one,' Brett said, his curiosity overriding his concern.

'Maybe our mysterious benefactor gave us a dodgy drive,' Eden said.

'If something's pulling at it, then there has to be some kind of measurable force or transmission,' Nulty said. The rest of them just looked at each other blankly. Nulty had left human mannerisms behind a long time ago. He found himself missing sighing. 'We've been looking for something solid, a wreck. Reconfigure the sensors to check every conceivable spectrum capable of carrying a transmission, then check the rest.'

Much to Eldon's irritation the others didn't even check with him; they just followed Nulty's suggestion.

Eden didn't say anything, but her expression changed to one of shock.

'What?' Eldon demanded. Eden shared the link. Over the 'face the transmission took life in the centre of their minds. At first it just sounded like a deeply unpleasant discordant noise that put them all further on edge. Then with the help of their internal systems they started to discern a pattern.

'Is that a language?' Brett asked. Even his normally positive attitude was being overridden by wariness bordering on fear. It felt like an ancient fear, like something he knew at some base instinctual level as an uplifted ape. One thing was clear: if it was a language then it was from a species very alien to any of the known uplifted races.

'It's singing,' Eden said. There was something about it, drawing her to it.

'Turn it off! Turn it off!' Melia all but screamed. Melia could break the link any time she wanted and had in fact already done so. Eden just shook her head at the performance, but the others had broken their link to the horrific sounding 'music'. Eldon was hugging Melia.

'Boss, this is getting a little fucking weird,' Nulty said.

'I don't like this. Let's go back,' Melia said.

'We can't, Baby Doll. We need the payoff, we really do.' Eldon's tone was pleading for understanding.

'Shine any light on this, Cap'n?' Brett asked.

'Just these co-ordinates. Find the hulk and take it to a rendezvous point.'

'Not back to Arclight?' Nulty asked. Eldon shook his head. Nulty saw the gesture through C and C's optics.

Nulty ran some diagnostics on the signal, which was coming in from some exotic part of the EM spectrum. Eden had to scrub out the background noise of the Red to isolate it. Nulty shared the information and then did some further checking. That part of the EM spectrum matched some of the emissions produced by the bridge drive.

'It's talking to it?' Brett asked when Nulty shared the information.

'Don't see how, it's a drive,' Eldon said. At this Nulty would have laughed but as an electronic uploaded consciousness it would have been an affectation.

'No offence, boss, but the Church keeps their manufacture so secret we can't really say anything about this for sure,' Nulty said. 'It might well be talking to something.'

Even Brett looked horrified. Melia bolted away from Eldon and hissed at him, all submissive coquettishness forgotten now.

'No way! Fuck that! I am not getting involved in any Church shit! You can take my contract and use it to sodomise yourself for all I care.'

'Are we working for the Church?' Brett asked more reasonably.

'I don't know, not as far as I know,' Eldon said, as confused and frightened as the rest.

'If this is to do with bridge drives then more likely it's a Consortium bid to break the Church's monopoly on their manufacture,' Nulty said.

7

'You fucking moron!' Melia screamed at Eldon.

'I didn't know,' he said defensively. 'We're jumping to conclusions.'

'But that doesn't make any sense,' Brett said. 'I mean, why us? After all we're a bit ...'

'Crap?' Melia suggested.

'Rough and ready, I was going to say.'

'Deniability and expendability,' Nulty answered.

Melia turned on Eldon. 'That's it. Contract's null and void. Get us out of here.'

'But, Baby Doll—'

'Don't Baby Doll me, you repellent, cockless fucktard. Get us out of here before a Church cruiser turns up, kills us, destroys our backup and murders everyone we ever met. I may be the cheapest clone possible of the original, but I have no wish to wake up in one of their immersion interrogations!'

Eldon seemed to deflate. He'd lost his big score, through that probably the *Swan* and his only real pleasure in life in one brief moment. Brett's look of sympathy wasn't helping either. Then he realised that Eden had been uncharacteristically quiet throughout Melia's outburst.

'Are you still listening to that noise?' he asked. Brett turned to look at Eden. Melia did as well, an expression bordering on horror across her feline features.

Eden just shrugged.

'Shut it off, now,' Eldon said. Eden did so.

'There's another signal,' Eden said. She tried to share the second signal. She found that the others weren't so swift to interface with her.

'You'll want to hear this.'

'She's right,' Nulty said over the interface. The others relented. This message was much weaker, broken. 'What the fuck is this? A radio wave?' he mused to himself.

'What's a radio wave?' Brett asked. Nulty ignored him.

The language was unknown but sounded like one of the uplifted races, probably human. Eldon started to ask if it was live but stopped as it repeated itself. It was some kind of recording. His neunonics searched for a translation program but came up with nothing despite the thousands of variant uplift languages and dialects in his systems.

'I've got it,' Nulty said over the interface. His voice didn't sound right. 'It's a mayday signal in human common.'

'Bullshit,' Eldon started.

'From before the Loss.' The four of them on the bridge just stared at each other. Eldon was the first to smile. He looked over to Melia to see the cash signs mirrored in her eyes.

Nulty lived for extravehicular activity but he still wasn't loving Red Space. Space should be really big. Somehow the strange gaseous-like nature of his surrounding environment seemed to be bearing down on him, making him feel claustrophobic. The living smoke effect of Red Space that he was used to was so much thicker here than on the normal Church-approved routes.

'You got it?' Eldon asked as Nulty scuttled over one of the detachable boosters, sending a diagnostic check as he did so. He'd sent some of the vacuum drones out but didn't want to let them get too far from the drifting tug as he wasn't happy with the 'face connection.

He reached the final spotlight and snaking tool limbs rapidly began repairing the 'non-essential system', as Eldon had called it when Nulty had suggested repairing it the last time they were docked at Arclight. He jury-rigged it and then stressed the repair by increasing the power output. The billowing red clouds were so thick here that the sensors were now next to useless, too much interference. It had rapidly come down to just what they could see with the optics.

They were letting the bridge drive pull them to wherever it was apparently going. Melia was running complex intelligent navigation programs that they hoped would be able to take them back to their initial position, or close to it, because they had no idea where they would end up with even a small amount of movement in Red Space.

The spotlight's beam stabbed out into the living smoke with enough power to put some laser weapons to shame, illuminating swirling eddies in the red gases.

It appeared through the smoke like some primal leviathan.

They weren't used to Nulty screaming. He just didn't emote that much.

'Turn on the engines! We're going to hit it!'

Eldon and Brett reacted with a thought. It was a simple matter to swing the engine arms around to point subjectively forward and trigger the engines, halting and then quickly reversing the gentle forward momentum of whatever had been attracting the bridge drive.

Eldon was about to reproach Nulty for his overreaction, but Nulty chose that moment to trigger the rest of the spots and bring them to bear. Eldon saw just how close they had got to the other ship – thing – whatever it was.

'How did we miss that?' Eldon asked in awe. It was at least the size of a capital ship. He was pretty sure he'd seen smaller habitats.

'Even now it's barely there,' Eden told him. She was just staring at it through the transparent smart-matter hull. All of them were using the ship's sensors and feeds from the drone, Nulty and the external optics to get a more complete picture in their minds via their neunonic interfaces.

It was massive, dwarfing the *Black Swan*. The smoky Red Space seemed to stick to it somehow, helping to conceal it.

'That's not right,' Melia said.

Eldon and Brett worked in conjunction to manoeuvre the *Swan*, tilting it subjectively downwards so they could get a better look at their find as they travelled down the length of it.

'Can you clean up the resolution on the lenses?' Eldon asked Nulty. 'I think the gas is messing it up.'

'No, you're seeing what I'm seeing,' Nulty said.

The hull of the ship, if that's what it was, seemed to be made out of some kind of thick heavy-duty material which looked like the rubbery flesh of some sort of abyssal sea creature. It was so large that it was difficult to get an idea of its shape but it seemed aerodynamic enough for atmospheric operations. What he could see of the shape reminded Eldon of marine life, or maybe a seed pod. Then he saw the hull of the ship move. Like it was breathing. Melia, noticing this through one of the drones' optics feeds, let out a little gasp.

'I don't like this,' the feline said.

'Can't you say anything else?' Eden demanded. 'Very little heat bleed. If its internal systems are working then they are very efficient – fuck all is penetrating its hull. Also getting some very strange energy readings from it, in weird spectrums. Like it's generating a field of some kind.'

'Be more specific,' Eldon snapped.

'Can't,' Eden said, sharing her readings with the rest of the crew.

'It's a Naga spore ship,' Melia said.

'There's no such thing as Naga,' Eden scoffed. Melia looked like she was about to argue.

'You know what it looks like, don't you?' Brett asked. 'A colonial carrier.' Eldon started laughing; he liked it when Brett said something stupid.

'Except they were made of metal. We've all been in one: they're museums and churches now.'

'Actually I grew up on habitats,' Brett said. Eldon rolled his eyes as if that explained everything. 'But I've seen pictures, and if they had been made of some kind of flesh then that's what they'd look like.'

'He's got a point, boss,' Nulty said over the interface. 'Knew this guy once who claimed that all the museums and the churches that we supposed were in the hull of old colony carriers were actually fakes. 'Course he also said he used to be one of the Lords of the Monarchist systems.'

'Nulty, what do you make of the composition of the hull?' Eden asked. She knew but she didn't want to be the one who said it.

'That hull's alive,' Nulty said, the first to give words to what they'd all been thinking. 'That's Seeder biotech, that is.'

On the bridge the four of them glanced at each other. They knew that managed correctly this could be worth a fortune, if they could hold on to their claim. The Seeders were the semi-mythical progenitor species of the uplifted races as well as the inspiration of worship for the Church. Most of the uplifted races having long abandoned the idea of actual supernatural gods.

'Why's it speaking monkey if it's Seeder tech?' Melia asked before remembering everyone else on the *Swan* was either human or started off that way. Brett looked at her reproachfully. Eden just glared.

'I don't know. I'm not getting anything through the hull. Eden?' Nulty said.

Eden went through the sensor suite, but a combination of the Red Space environment and the craft/thing's hull/skin was blocking even the harshest of active scans.

Something occurred to Brett. 'Was this the area where the glitch was coming from?' he asked Eldon.

Eldon considered this. 'I don't think so.'

'So what? We tow this to the rendezvous and get paid?' Melia asked, undisguised greed in her voice. She was not very interested in sensor glitches. Eldon seemed reluctant to answer the question.

'What?' Melia demanded.

'We need to go on board,' Eldon said. Melia looked at him like he was insane. Brett was nodding eagerly.

'Fuck that!' Melia said.

Eden was irritated to find herself forced to agree with Melia. 'Go inside what? We don't even know if it's a ship! It could be a fucking animal for all we know, and I don't want to get swallowed. If it is a ship, the environment might be completely inimical to human life.'

Melia was nodding in agreement.

'Then why's it broadcasting in human common?' Eldon asked.

'I don't know, a caught transmission? A lure?'

'How dangerous can they be if they're transmitting a mayday?' Brett asked. Eden just looked at him as if he was a moron.

'He's right,' Nulty said. 'We want to salvage this, we have to check to see if it has crew.'

'The crew of that thing can't be subject to Consortium salvage laws,' Eden said, getting more heated. 'If that's Seeder tech, what if the whole thing is filled with servitors? Have you thought about that?' They gave a shiver. All of them had seen the wedge-headed, multi-limbed, armoured carapace effigies of the last living remnants of Seeder biotech, crucified on the X-shaped crosses in churches.

'Then we can't take it back into Known Space,' Nulty said.

'Look, this is a big fucking score—' Eldon started.

'Yeah, for you. Even with a bonus it's not worth the risk for the rest of us,' Eden said. Eldon was less than pleased to see Melia nodding in agreement.

'But, Baby Doll, you'll get to share in my fortune,' Eldon pleaded.

'Uh uh, not this time. I want an equal share. When I agreed to our little arrangement you misled me into thinking that you were a ship's captain ...'

'I am.'

'No, you're owner of a piece of shit. I want an equal share.'

'Equal share? Are you actually going to do something or just hide in your cryo-pod until it's over?' Eden asked.

Melia turned to glare at the more masculine, scaled woman. 'I'll do my bit,' she answered haughtily. Eden just raised an eyebrow.

'Look. I am the captain, and you will fucking do as you're told or you'll be out that airlock for mutiny!' Eldon screamed at them, visions of his fortune slipping away. Melia, Eden and Brett just looked at him sceptically.

'And how do you intend to enforce that?' Eden asked. Eldon turned to look pleadingly at Melia. He couldn't believe she'd turned on him after he'd treated her so well.

'Oh, grow up,' the feline snapped.

'I think it's time to negotiate, boss,' Nulty said.

'This is mutiny,' Eldon said weakly. The rest of them ignored him. 'We don't even know how to get in.'

Eldon had finally admitted how much his mysterious contact was paying him after Eden held him upside down and Melia threatened to torture him. To make matters worse, Brett had had to intervene on Eldon's behalf, further adding to the humiliation.

Brett was piloting the *Swan* steadily nearer to the craft/thing, trying to get close enough for their active scans to work, when it happened. During a very slow pass, something seemed to grow out of the craft. It looked like a tunnel made of the hull's rubbery flesh.

'What is it?' Melia asked. There was something obscene about it,

Melia decided, and it wasn't as if she had terribly delicate sensibilities. 'Some kind of defence system?'

'I don't think so,' Nulty communicated over the interface. 'I think it's a docking arm?'

Brett swung the engine arms around to bring the *Swan* to a halt. The tunnel seemed to be swaying in the cloudy Red Space in front of them.

'You're going to let that touch the *Swan*?' Eden asked doubtfully, looking over at Eldon. Eldon was crouched in the corner, sulking. He had been trying to work out how get the money for the ship/thing and then burn the rest of the crew. He looked up at the sound of Eden's voice.

'Oh what? Am I captain again? Is there actual work to be done?'

'Take it easy, Cap'n,' Brett said good-naturedly.

'Go and fuck yourself, muscle-head,' Eldon muttered. Brett just laughed as if it was friendly banter.

Eldon had seen the thing in his mind but he walked over to look through the transparent hull.

'Nulty, if it goes badly do you reckon you can cut that thing?' Eldon asked.

'Er ... yes,' Nulty said. He did not sound very sure of himself.

Eldon turned to Eden. 'Sure, why not? A fifth of something is better than nothing and you gotta take risks if you want the pay-off. Besides,' he stabbed a finger at Melia, 'maybe then I can get rid of this bitch and get a decent concubine.' Eldon glared at her. 'You're coming. None of your bullshit. I've got the contract. You don't come, you don't get paid, understand me?' Melia looked like she was about to argue. 'Besides, if it all goes horribly wrong I want to make sure that you die as well as me.'

Melia hissed and made an obscene gesture.

Brett pushed both hands into the ball of semi-solid liquid. The space-suit started crawling up his arms, covering them and then growing down his torso. He held the visor in front of his face and the liquid suit crawled over his head to connect with it. The armoured environment bladders on the suit inflated as they took gas from the surrounding atmosphere. The suit had already connected to his neunonics and Brett adjusted the gas mix with a thought.

He had already adjusted his nano-screen, brought it in close to his body, only leaving a little outside the suit. Whenever he did this it always made his skin crawl but he knew this was psychosomatic. A screen of nanites surrounded Brett, like everyone else in Known

Space, everyone who didn't want to quickly sicken or die and could afford it. The screen prevented him from being attacked by rogue nano-swarms, provided him with a degree of privacy and stopped him from coming down with all but the most sophisticated advertising nano-viruses. Nanite pollution was so extreme in all but the most expensive enclaves in Known Space that without a screen you would be dead within days, or at very best sporting a colourful rash advertising the latest soft drink.

However, for cultures that did not have such a high level of nanite pollution exposure, the nano-screens themselves could be potentially harmful.

'First-contact protocols?' Brett asked. He had just realised that he'd always wanted to say that.

Melia and Eden stopped and looked at him as if he was mad.

'What do you think happens if there's a crew on board, arsehole?' Eldon demanded. Brett was taken aback by the anger in his tone. Eldon was just pissed off that he had to spell this shit out to Brett. 'We get nothing. Reining in our nano-screens is the least of our issues.'

Brett just stared at Eldon as he lifted one foot and then the other so the spacesuit could assemble the hard-wearing soles.

Eldon was holding the quick-release holster for his double-barrelled laser pistol to the thigh of the suit so it could bond, as Eden handed out the double-barrelled disc guns. The disc guns were basically electromagnetic shotguns. It fired solid-state cartridges of smart matter that split into multiple razor-sharp aerodynamic discs. Designed to be fired semi-automatically, the disc guns had a pump-action mechanism to help clear the inevitable jams. Like most brutal close-quarters weapons, they had been designed by one of the tribes of lizard uplifts. Eden held out one of the weapons to Brett. He eyed it through his visor for a while and then took it from her.

'Just so you know,' Eldon said, holding up a hardened biohazard container. 'Just so you're in just as much trouble as the rest of us if this screws up. Just so you can't claim you had no knowledge or rat us out, this is a bucket of the most potent virals I could lay my hands on. If we get in and there's crew, this is for them.' Brett stared at it. He looked like he was about to object but he caught a glimpse of three hard faces watching him through darkening visors. 'In fact, I think you should carry this.' Eldon held the canister out. Eldon was enjoying this, starting the boy down the long road of moral compromises and disappointments that was life. He also thought he was doing the boy a favour. You want to prosper, then people are going to have to die; it was an important life lesson.

'I don't want to—' Brett began.

'Just fucking man up,' Eden snapped at him. Brett had thought they were friends.

Brett swallowed hard and took the canister from Eldon.

'Fuck up, you get left. Don't hold up your end, you get left. Understand?' Eldon was starting to feel more in control again. Also, he was never going to get tired of making this kid miserable. Brett just nodded.

With a thought Eldon fired the *Swan*'s engines gently to spin the ship slowly and match up the end of the tunnel of flesh with the *Swan*'s crew airlock. Compared to the jarring impact of most docking arms, this felt like a kiss.

Eden checked the readings from the sensors on the outer airlock door in her neunonic feed. 'We've got a seal. Atmosphere looks fine, all within uplift tolerances, no discernible exotics, no discernible nano-activity, but I'll run a more thorough check when we're through ...'

'What?' Melia asked.

'Nothing, just it looks a bit moist is all.'

Eldon tried not to think that he'd let his clone insurance lapse. He transferred command protocols to Nulty.

'You've got the *Swan*, Nulty,' he said across the interface.

'Okay, boss. Go careful.'

Eldon sent the command to open the airlock.

2
Northern Britain, a Long Time Ago

The sound of the water lapping against the rocks at the mouth of the cave had pushed through into her dream and gently woken her. Britha opened her eyes. Her lover's silver skin reflected the sunlight that had managed to penetrate the sea cave. The selkie's fine scales turned the light into a glittering rainbow pattern.

'You slept,' Cliodna said.

Cliodna was sitting next to her, naked as she always was, gently stroking the border where the shaved stubble on the side of Britha's head met her long dark-brown hair.

Britha rolled onto her side to better look up at the other woman. The muscles on her back flexed, making the tattoo of a Z-shaped broken spear entwined with a serpent move as if the snake lived. 'More like passed out,' Britha said, smiling up at Cliodna, who smiled back, but the smile looked sad.

The dark pools of her lover's eyes were impossible to read, so different were they from those of Britha's own people, the ancestor folk, the Pecht as they called themselves.

Britha propped herself up on her elbow. 'What's wrong?'

'I ...' the selkie started and went quiet as if she was searching for the words. The last few times Britha had visited her, Cliodna had seemed even more quiet than normal. Britha felt an ache in her chest.

'Cliodna ...' Britha reached for her. The change was instant. Cliodna hissed, the nails that Britha liked to feel across her skin suddenly looked like claws; needle-like teeth were bared, and the selkie bolted for the back of the cave. Britha started away from her lover. She knew that the other woman shared ways with the animals, as Britha did if the ritual required it of her, but Cliodna had always seemed so gentle. Britha angrily suppressed her moment of fear. She bore her scars well. Fear was not something she could entertain even in the face of the Otherworld.

Britha pushed herself up onto her feet and made her way into the darkness at the back of the cave. She was still naked; it did not occur to her to clothe herself. Like many of her people she was more comfortable naked, she was even prepared to go to war like this. Intricate interwoven tattoos of animals whose traits she wanted, or symbols of power that could armour her, covered her upper right arm, across her muscular shoulders and down her left arm to her fingers. More tattoos curled down onto her breasts and ran up her right calf. All of them were various shades of blue, from the darkest midnight to the brightest summer sky. The woad had taken her to many places and shown her many visions when they had pierced her skin with it. She had lost days travelling beyond this land in the waking dreams it brought on.

Cliodna was crouched down hugging her legs, her long dark hair covering her features. Britha crouched down and reached for her, but Cliodna flinched away from her touch.

'Cliodna, what's wrong?' Britha asked.

'I ... we're not like you.'

'Selkies?'

'That's just what you call me. To give me a name, so you can understand ... We have to do things – we're governed by different laws.'

'What are you telling me? That your people wouldn't approve?' Britha asked. She didn't think that the rest of the Cirig would like what they were doing either, but none would dare challenge her and after all, one of her responsibilities as *ban draoi* was to treat with the Otherworld. Though this probably wasn't what they had in mind, Britha mused.

Cliodna's laugh was short and bitter. 'My people ... they would not understand but nor would they care.'

'Then what?'

'I can't explain ... my responsibilities – things that I have no choice but to do ...'

'What are you telling me?' Britha all but demanded. She was not the most patient of people and she was beginning to feel exasperated. Britha felt she was already being a lot more patient than she would have been with a male lover but then something about their pricks turned them into lack-wits.

Cliodna looked up at her, her long black hair parting. The selkie's eyes had never looked so alien to Britha. She could see herself reflected in those deep black pools.

'I'm leaving. I have to go south. I have no choice.'

It was the pain – she actually felt it physically – that made Britha realise just how much she loved Cliodna. At first it had just been for the thrill of it. Then her visits had become more and more frequent. They had swum together. Cliodna had taken her far out into the cold sea on warm days. Guided her through the dangerous currents and fierce tides. The selkie was much more at home in the sea than on land.

Britha hated the tear that ran down her cheek. She could never show weakness. Tears were for the men in their cups listening to laments of ancestors long gone.

'I don't want you to go,' was all she managed.

'You will. I'm changing. Who you know will soon be gone.'

'What do you mean? I don't understand.' Britha hated the desperation in her voice.

Cliodna cocked her head to one side. Her face crumpled with emotion but no tears came. Britha wanted to hate her for the lack of tears.

'I have to go south, far south. The waters have been poisoned. There's something ...'

'I'll come with you,' Britha said, knowing she couldn't even as she said it. Cliodna shook her head, looking frightened. She grabbed Britha's arm, her nails digging in.

'Promise me you won't!' Cliodna all but hissed. Britha looked down at her arm, blood flowing from five wounds where Cliodna's nails had broken the skin. She looked back up at Cliodna. 'See?' Cliodna asked desperately.

'I'll not go where I'm not wanted,' Britha said evenly, trying to compose herself, trying to wrap her pride around herself like armour.

Cliodna took Britha's head in her hands, leaned forward and kissed her. Britha wanted to resist, but she couldn't. She wrapped her arms round her lover and reciprocated. Cliodna tasted the salt of her lover's tears.

'No matter what happens, please remember that I love you, that I loved you,' Cliodna said when they finally broke apart. Britha just stared at her, her face stained with tears.

Cliodna stood up. She jumped from the rock. Powerful legs propelled her through the air and into the pool at the mouth of the cave. Sinuous movements carried her rapidly through the water, helped by the webs of skin between her long fingers and toes.

Britha watched her go.

'Loved?' she asked an empty cave.

Britha cursed herself and turned to look out at the sea. Hoping that the wind and salt spray would explain her red eyes. Normally grey and rough, the sea was bright blue under a cloudless sky today, an otherwise beautiful day. Talorcan was waiting for her. The finest tracker in the tribe, the short wiry man was considerably less full of himself than the rest of the *cateran*, or warband. Even so, Britha did not wish him to see her emotion. She looked out at the sea making sure she was fully composed.

'*Ban draoi?*'

'Do you know what happens to the curious who follow too closely dealings with the Otherworld?' Britha asked.

'The *mormaer* bid me fetch you – it's starting,' Talorcan said. His expression was difficult to read but he seemed to be looking at her as if searching for something. His beard was trimmed, his long dark hair let loose and blowing in the coastal wind. He wore no trews, just his *blaidth*, which came down to just above his knees. Tattoos spiralled up both legs and also ran down from his temple, across his cheeks to his chin. He had his bow with him, but no weapons of war, just his dirk at his waist.

Britha smiled.

'More like Cruibne's worried that I've run off with his horse.'

Talorcan nodded but kept his peace. Britha looked at him a while more; he held her look. There was little scar tissue on him: he fought quickly and cleverly when he had to.

Britha went to one of the powerful heavyset ponies that the Pecht favoured. She called it Dark Cloud because its near-black colouring reminded her of storm skies. Britha wrenched the spear that Dark Cloud had been tethered to out of the ground. She retrieved her iron-bladed sickle. Cliodna didn't like the cold metal anywhere near her. Britha pushed the sickle though the belt that held the rough-spun brown wool robes of her calling closed and then swung up onto the pony, riding it bareback, her legs against the horse's flanks. She pulled her fringed hood up to protect her eyes from the sun and headed south and west down the coast. Talorcan broke into an easy run to keep up with her.

Ardestie was on a flat plain that looked down on the silver water of the mouth of the River Tatha where it emptied into the cold harsh northern sea. It was a large settlement of about twenty or so roundhouses, wattle and daub structures with conical thatched roofs, surrounded by fields of spelt, bere barley, flax and fat hen. The fields had been hacked out of the soil generations before. Fields not used for crops were grazing for horned Soay sheep and the hairy cattle, not all of which they had stolen on raids. Beyond the cultivated fields were the thick woods that covered all but the most mountainous or boggy parts of the land. In the woods the wolf, lynx, bear and spirits from the Otherworld ruled.

The roundhouses lived in the shadow of the broch, a circular tower of stone blocks at the summit of the Hill of Deer. The broch was a watchtower and place of refuge if they were attacked. From it they watched for raiders from the Fib, the rival Pecht tribe across the river, and the blonde sea devils from the sea and ice far to the north. It also provided them with sight up the river over the thick woods to the hill fort some five or six miles to the west. From the broch they could see when the traders came down from the crannogs on Loch Tatha in their log canoes to trade with the foreign merchant ships that came from hot lands far to the south.

The broch was also where the Cirig stored the parts of their war chariots. The small cart-like vehicles could be assembled rapidly for battle. Each chariot was pulled by two of the small, rugged ponies that belonged to the horse-rich Cirig. The chariots' lightweight construction meant that they were capable of considerable speed and were very useful against the northern tribes, who did not use chariots as the mountainous terrain of their home made them useless. They were also useful on the long coastal beaches when the blonde sea demons from the ice raided.

The largest of the houses was the meeting place as well as home to Cruibne MaqqCirig, the *mormaer*, or sub-king, of the Cirig. Ardestie was the capital of the Cirig, one of the seven tribes of the Pecht, descended from the seven sons of Cruithne.

Britha passed the forge set apart from the village, ignoring the fire watcher who gazed longingly towards the village. Britha, like all women, was banned from the forge. It was where the men did their ritual sex magic. As a child in training she had sneaked into the forge, eager to learn the secrets of their magic as well. She had watched them stoke the belly of the furnace, watched the molten metal pour hot from the men's metal vagina. She had not been impressed. They could keep their magic. Later, when she had learned her own sex magic, she had thought it more fun. Yet, like her, the metalworkers wielded magic and like her had to live outside the tribe to serve it.

As Britha rode towards Ardestie, the sun had not yet turned the sky to blood on the western horizon but the feast was already under way. As she rode by the grain pits, already sealed after the harvest, she saw the body. The powerfully built and scarred man had been opened across his chest. Britha did not recognise him but thought him one of the Fib from across the river. She did recognise the cut. Nechtan, Cruibne's champion, had done this. Presumably the man had challenged him for the hero's portion. Britha's smile was without humour. She understood the need for this but always found it wasteful. Still, the ravens and crows deserved a feast too, and he would have died well with a sword in his hand.

She could hear the sound of voices raised in jest and laughter, accompanied by the *crwth* lute, *bodhran* drum, the *feadan* flute and the triple pipes, though they were playing softly. People would be relaxed now. Cruibne would have displayed his largesse but there would still be business to discuss.

Britha rode to where the rest of the horses had been tethered. She did not like that there were not nearly as many guests as she had expected. She dismounted Dark Cloud and slipped the rope off her neck. Talorcan watched impassively as Britha whispered into Dark Cloud's ear. Then she slapped the large pony on her flanks. Dark Cloud was free to roam. She knew to come back close to Ardestie once night finally fell. Even a pony trained for war by the Cirig was no match for a pack of wolves or a bear, both of which lived in the forest to the north and east of them.

Britha turned towards the feast.

'Why haven't the others come?' Britha asked Talorcan, seeking as much information as she could find before she had to join the feast and play her part. Talorcan just shrugged. 'Do you receive many compliments for the way you use your tongue?' she asked. Talorcan finally smiled but didn't answer. Britha sighed and turned, heading towards the feast.

'Look at the size of this head!' Cruibne said. The hulking grizzled old man held up a massive misshapen skull that had been embalmed in cedar oil. Rents and cracks in the skull had been filled with pewter. 'This one gave me no end of trouble, I tell you!' The *mormaer* was wearing his best plaid trews – well, his only pair but it looked like he had dunked them in the river – and a new *blaidth*. He had iron rings in his beard made from the blades and spearheads of dead enemies and a thick white-gold torc around his neck as befitted his position in the tribe. Similar torcs, also of white gold, were wrapped around either arm. Because of his advanced age – he was in his late thirties – most of his skin was covered in the tattoos that told his story, armoured and protected him. What skin that wasn't tattooed tended to be scar tissue. He was missing three fingers from his left hand and two from his right. Part of his skull was misshapen and no hair grew there due to a blow from an axe swung by a sea raider not three years past. 'A sea demon! Allied with the Goddodin!' The Goddodin were a tribe of Britons to the south, constantly warring with the Fib and the Fortrenn.

'Or another small man with a huge swollen head!' Britha smiled. It had been Ethne who had shouted. She was Cruibne's oldest and fiercest wife, a heavyset woman of an age with Cruibne and just as scarred and tattooed as he was. In battle she could be looked for standing next to the *mormaer* or driving his chariot. Like the rest of the *cateran* she wore a thick silver torc around her neck. Ethne had killed more than one of Cruibne's other wives whom she had felt was getting above herself. There was laughter at Ethne's comment.

Good. They were already in their cups. Britha had brewed the heather ale herself, an old and secret recipe. Cruibne had made sure that there would be more than enough of the *uisge beatha*, and he was not drinking as much as he appeared to be.

'Och woman, you spoil all my stories. Well I tell you, it was worth taking his head. Look how much drink it holds!' Cruibne tipped the massive skull and drank deep from it, much of it running down his neatly trimmed beard to the sound of more laughter. Cruibne had a hundred skulls and a hundred stories.

Some of the guests at the feast were starting to notice Britha's quiet approach. Her hood was up. Much of what she did was about performance, a lesson she had learned early in her training. Hush spread across the feast. She had timed it well: the sun was bleeding into the sky and the light was changing. The time between times, a good time to evoke the Otherwold.

The quiet was broken only by the sound of one of the landsmen, who had not noticed the *ban draoi*'s approach, dropping a red-hot stone from the fire into the cauldron. There was a *crack* as the stone split. People would be having stone with their stew, Britha thought. The landsman Britha recognised as Ferchair, a crofter from land to the north of the woods. Britha had delivered his first child, a daughter, in the cold winter. The child had survived, she knew. Spring was the best time for birthing, but at least Ferchair knew his daughter would grow up strong now.

Ferchair turned to see why it had gone quiet. He saw Britha, averted his eyes and made to sit down again far behind the inner circle of the *cateran* and their noble guests.

Looking round the inner circle, Britha saw missing eyes, ears, fingers and a lot of scar tissue. All were ugly enough to be warriors; there were few who looked blade-shy around the fire.

Cruibne looked up and smiled. His two massive deerhounds, lying close by and sporting nearly as many scars as their master, got up as

Britha entered the circle and wandered over to stand by her. Absently she scratched behind their ears.

Britha took her time looking around the circle. She nodded to Nechtan and Feroth, the war leader of the *cateran*. She did not like Nechtan – he was as sly as he was violent, a careful bully – but she had to admit he was a more than capable champion. Feroth was even older than Cruibne and many whispered that his place at the ravens' feast was long overdue. Britha, however, liked the canny old warrior. The tribe would miss his clever stratagems when he was gone and she suspected more would die on raids and in battle. Most of them were too caught up in thoughts of their own personal glory to appreciate what Feroth did for them, but Britha understood.

The meat on the spits was mostly gone but the cauldron still looked full. Still not speaking, Britha made her way to the cauldron, removing her meathook from her belt. She leaned in and hooked a choice piece of mutton from the thick stew. She left it to cool it for a few seconds, then took a bite, chewed slowly and then swallowed.

'Cruibne, I think the belly of your cauldron is pregnant with more meat than you would see on lesser *mormaers*' spits.' There was laughter from the Cirig and most of the guests. Some, however, had heard a slight in Britha's words and were less pleased. 'I also hear that your heather ale's particularly fine.'

'You should know – you made it,' Cruibne said. He then made a show of serving her himself, as he had done with all his guests, including the landsmen and women. However, the skull that Cruibne served the ale in had been taken by Britha. It was not the way for the *ban draoi* to take heads, but Britha had insisted on it. Killing someone in battle was a quick and easy way to get the warriors to listen to her when she spoke.

'Will you sit by my left side?' Cruibne asked her formally. Britha looked to Ethne, on Cruibne's right, for her permission – she didn't need to but respected the older woman. Ethne nodded. Then she looked to Feroth, on Cruibne's left. Feroth moved over, always glad of Britha's counsel and company.

'I'd say you're late,' Cruibne spoke to her quietly, 'but I think you know exactly what you're doing.'

'Don't speak out of the side of your mouth – it makes them think we have something to hide,' Britha admonished him.

The inner circle consisted mainly of the chieftains of the Cirig loyal to Cruibne. He had invited the *mormaers* of all seven of the tribes, but by the looks of it only Finnguinne of the Fib, Deleroith of the

Fortrenn, both southern tribes, and Drust of the Fotlaig to the west had come.

None of the northern tribes, the Ce, the Fidach and the Cait, had sent anyone at all. The Cait Britha could understand – it was a long way to come – but the absence of the rest of them worried her.

Britha saw Finnguinne talking quietly with one of his men. This was a breach of hospitality but Britha let it pass. She assumed that Cruibne, Feroth, Ethne and Nechtan would have noticed as well. They had not achieved their positions without being canny, but they chose not to challenge it. Britha hoped that none of the more hot-headed members of the *cateran* had seen.

'Cruibne MaqqCirig of the Hundred Heads, meat giver, ale provider,' the man Finnguinne had been talking to started formally, 'all of us stand in the shadow of your generosity, but if you will indulge me I have a question.' Britha took a sip of her own ale from her skull. She was pretty sure the man was called Wroid, an average warrior in the Fib *cateran* but known for his way with words. He was called Wroid the Provoker.

Britha cursed the Fib. Cursing the Fib was common among the Cirig, as was the reverse. Living across the river from the Fib meant that the Cirig were the most likely targets for Fib raids. Of course the opposite was true as well, and this summer, as it had been for many summers now, the Cirig were the stronger tribe.

Cruibne's look of irritation was obvious to all. Trying to have the patience to put up with the provocation he knew was coming was Cruibne's least favourite part of being *mormaer*.

'We came because we hoped to see the other descendants of Cruithne. Where are Fergus of the Ce, Oengus of the Fidach and Calgacus of the Cait? I hope it was no mere boast that they would be present,' Wroid said, a smile on his face. There was muttering from the younger warriors in the Cirig *cateran*. Boasting was an inevitable part of being a warrior but Wroid had stopped just short of calling Cruibne a liar.

Britha glanced over at Nechtan, who was still lying looking relaxed, but she noticed that his skull was full of ale. *Drunk champions don't live long*, she thought.

'No boast, lad,' Cruibne said. 'Messages exchanged, they said they were coming. If you look to our cattle pens you'll see more than enough beasts to feed more than twice this number. The Fib can take some home with you if it'll stop your teeth rattling around in your head.' There was laughter from all but the Fib. That was good, Britha thought. *Put him in his place but do so with an act of generosity.*

'They were probably yours to begin with anyway,' Nechtan said, his tone relaxed but promising easy violence as well. Britha guessed that the body she'd passed had been an example to drive this point home earlier in the festivities. This time the laughter only came from the Cirig. Wroid continued smiling but Finnguinne did not look happy.

'Then might I ask where they are?' Wroid continued. Britha could all but hear Cruibne grind his teeth.

'I can think of no reason why they are not here,' Cruibne answered.

'I can,' Finnguinne said. All faces turned to him. Even Nechtan sat more upright. 'Because they will not be ruled by a high king and neither will the Fib,' he spat.

'Who will stand as a champion for the Ce, the Fidach and the Cait, who are slandered when not here present?' Britha asked.

'What?!' an obviously startled Finnguinne demanded.

'You think if my spearbrothers thought that I wanted to be high king they'd be too afraid to come and tell me no to my face?' Cruibne said, trying to sound fierce and not smile into his beard.

'No, that is not—' Finnguinne started.

'Then do not split you tongue; speak clearly!' Britha demanded. Already warriors, and not just those of the Cirig, were offering to stand as champions for the three absent tribes. 'We are not sly southrons who require wriggling serpent words. Say what you mean!'

'I meant no offence,' Finnguinne muttered.

'Good,' Cruibne said, smiling before getting up and grabbing a large earthenware jug of *uisge beatha* and handing it to Finnguinne. 'Drink this and then we can be really abusive towards each other.' There was more laughter as the atmosphere relaxed.

Good, more generosity, Britha thought as she drank more of the heather ale from the skull. *Show them we have nothing to fear and all to give*. Finnguinne hadn't been too far from the truth. Cruibne did not want to be high king. There was no need, no external threat sufficient to require it, and the other tribes would never accept it. What he wanted was to make clear his position as first among the *mormaers*. He wanted to assert the strength of his tribe, their supremacy. He wanted to say that challenging the Cirig, even raiding them, was far more trouble than it was worth. Then he wanted to get on with his real ambition of growing old and fat.

Britha largely agreed with his plan but needed to make sure that the rest of the tribe did not grow fat, lazy and unused to battle. Britha let the circle around the fire lapse into easy conversation. She remained aloof from it, only saying something when directly addressed and then as little as she could. This was a necessary part of her role:

it helped promote the mystery and respect required to do what she did, and she found that the people who spoke the least were often considered the wisest and actually listened to.

When she was able, Britha slipped away from the fire. Walked into the night and looked down at the moon reflected in the Tatha. Looking at the water made her think of Cliodna. Wondering where she was. Had she returned to her cave? Britha was already trying to think of excuses to return there and then cursing herself for her weakness. She could not explain the sudden change in the other woman. Britha knew she was being foolish. Her mother and her grandmother before her, when they were teaching her the secrets that the male *dryw* could not, had warned her against becoming involved with those from the Otherworld.

She felt a large strong hand grab her buttock. Her elbow flew backwards with a satisfying crunch followed by a series of curses. Britha swung round to see which drunken fool wanted to be cursed until his testicles made acorns look large.

She found Cruibne holding his nose and cursing. He was obviously the worse for drink but not insensible. A champion needed to remain sober, a *mormaer* just needed to hold his drink.

'My nose! You scabby—'

'Choose your words, Cruibne. *Mormaer* or no, I will not be man-handled.' She respected the king and would not have struck him in front of others, but at the same time that did not give him licence.

'Ha! I just came to see if there was a ritual we could do to ensure the success of the gathering.'

Britha could not help but smile. She knew exactly what kind of ritual he had in mind. Britha guessed that chancing like this to get what he wanted was probably a useful, if at times irritating, quality in a *mormaer*.

'That is for very specific situations and only with Ethne's blessing. Unless you think I enjoy lying with a stinking sack of pus like yourself?'

Cruibne's expression darkened at the insult. Britha was not terribly worried, but fortunately the *mormaer* rediscovered his sense of humour quickly.

'You always seemed to,' he said, reaching up to stroke her hair. It was true to a degree. Cruibne was not an untalented lover, which was important for the success of the rites, the sacrifice – her sacrifice – the seed they returned to the earth. He'd had to be trained of course. However, all the magic in the Otherworld could not have compelled her to tell Cruibne that.

'Don't make me hurt you and then ask Ethne to come over here and hurt you as well,' she told him. Cruibne gave this some thought. He stopped stroking her hair.

'It worries me that the Ce, the Fidach and the Cait did not come,' Cruibne said, changing the subject, seeming almost sober. Britha nodded. She had been thinking the same. When not thinking about Cliodna. 'Finnguinne's a serpent-tongued sheep rapist, but do you think he's right? That they think I mean to rule them?'

Britha shook her head. 'Can you see Calgacus of the Bitter Tongue not coming here to tell you what he thought of that?'

'Do they plan war against us?'

'Maybe Oengus, for the sake of harvesting heads, but he would tell us to our faces. Besides, things are well now. Why risk that in war? And there are easier prey than us.'

'I do not like this. Have they fallen to war among themselves?'

'It seems unlikely that we would not have heard about it, or that one or more of them would not want to ask for our aid. Besides, even at war they know they could come here safely under our protection.'

'What then? Famine? The Lochlannach?'

Britha just shook her head. Cruibne was more than capable of speculating on his own. He was saying this because he was drunk and wanted to hear a voice. 'I think we should send a—' Britha began, knowing that she would have to repeat herself the following day. She was interrupted by a clamour from the circle around the fire. Both of them headed back.

A landsman stood in the circle of flame-shadowed warriors. Britha did not recognise him but he looked ill-used. He had been beaten and cut. He would have been terrified if he had not been so fatigued that he swayed with the warm summer breeze.

'On your knees!' one of the Fib warriors yelled. Britha was pretty sure he was called Congus and unlike Wroid he could fight. He was Finnguinne's champion and known as a dangerous man. From where he sat Congus knocked the landsman's legs out from underneath him. Britha strode across the circle and kicked Congus in the face. She was not expecting to get away with it but anger overwhelmed better judgement. To her surprise her foot connected and spread Congus's nose across his face. He reeled back even as his hand went to the sword by his side.

'What are you so frightened of that a landsman has to kneel?' Britha demanded. Congus, seeing that it was the *ban draoi*, did not draw his blade though he had hate in his eyes.

'There are *mormaer* present,' Finnguinne said angrily.

27

'So? We'll make our landsmen go on their knees when we learn to eat swords,' Britha spat at him.

'Besides, this is my fire. I decide who gets mistreated,' Cruibne said from behind her as he knelt to cradle the man and gave him ale from his own skull in a bid to revive him.

'The man's clearly a thief,' Finnguinne said. 'He came in riding a horse.'

Cruibne glanced at Talorcan, and the tracker went to check the horse.

'It's a brave woman who strikes a warrior knowing he cannot return the blow,' Congus said. In theory there was a ban against striking a *dryw*. There was also, in theory, a ban on *dryw* taking part in combat.

'It is true,' Wroid said. 'Poor hospitality is this. The *dryw* are not meant to strike warriors.'

'Ours does,' Nechtan said.

'What's your name?' Britha demanded of Congus. 'I do not know you. You could not have done much. Are you sure you received your first meat from the tip of a blade?'

'I am Congus, champ—' he began angrily.

'Are you known as Congus the Timid? Congus the Abuser of Landsfolk?' Britha demanded. It was hugely rude to interrupt a warrior formally introducing himself. There were sharp intakes of breath from all around the fire. Britha knew she was pushing the man hard, but his was exactly the sort of arrogance that she despised most among the warriors.

'You go too far even for a *dryw*,' Congus said dangerously. Behind her she could hear the warriors in the Cirig *cateran* shifting, readying themselves.

'Well, Congus the Timid, you have my permission to return the blow,' Britha said. 'No ban, no boycott or satire. I promise you the only consequences that you will reap will be those wrought by Flesh Render.' Meaning her spear. Then she looked Congus straight in the eye. Britha was a fair fighter but she had grown up training to be a *ban draoi*. Congus had spent his whole life training to be a warrior. She was pretty sure that in a straight fight she would lose, but first Congus had to overcome every bit of inherited dread about crossing a *dryw*. In many ways, to humiliate him publicly and challenge him was not very fair at all. The two of them stared at each other. Congus looked away first.

'Is this the brave Cirig? Hiding behind a woman?' Wroid demanded.

'We are stronger than you because our women fight,' Cruibne said distractedly while he looked over the newcomer's wounds.

28

'And any one of us will fight you at any time,' Nechtan added quietly.

'We are stronger than you because we know enough not to fear our women or our landsmen,' Britha told him.

'The horse is almost as ill-used as he is,' Talorcan said, appearing out of the darkness. 'It's a warrior's mount, but it has been ridden long and hard and I don't like the look of its wounds.'

'See!' Finnguinne spat. 'A horse thief!'

'Hold your tongue, sheep king!' Cruibne spat. There was deathly silence around the fire. Britha closed her eyes and cursed Cruibne for allowing Finnguinne and his people to bait him. 'You should consider yourself lucky I don't take your head for breaking my hospitality. Get from my fire and do it now. Think hard if you want to war with us, and I will think hard on the right compensation for what you have done here.'

There was lots of shifting and muttering from both *caterans*. 'Sheep king' was not an easy insult for a *mormaer* to walk away from. Finnguinne stared at Cruibne.

Cruibne ignored him. 'Britha, he needs your healing ways.' Britha moved to kneel by the man's side.

Finnguinne stood up and stormed away from the fire. Congus accompanied him, quickly followed by the rest of the Fib, Wroid at the rear, raining insults down on the Cirig, many of whom were on their feet.

Feroth prevented the Cirig from responding to Wroid's words with violence. It would look ill if they fought the Fib after inviting them to share their fire. 'They'll have a hard time on the Tatha the amount they've had to drink,' Feroth said. It was a weak jest but he was trying to lower the tension.

Britha was all but oblivious to this. Instead she was cursing Congus's arrogance as she peeled away the landsman's *blaidth* to reveal a horrible-looking wound. She exchanged a look of horrified surprise with Cruibne, who was holding the writhing man.

It was a sword wound. She had seen many before. Except this one looked wrong somehow, too wide even for the thickest blade, and too ragged. Something about it put in Britha's mind that the sword had been hungry.

'That's not right,' Cruibne said. Britha nodded. She had seen wounds this bad, just not on anyone living.

'Who knows this man?!' Cruibne demanded of the remaining people around the fire. Many peered at the wounded man, who was drooling blood. Britha used her fingers to force his mouth open.

'His tongue's been cut ... ripped out,' Britha said. 'He could not have ridden far, not in this state.' Except that she knew everyone for many miles and she did not know him.

One of the Cirig's own landsmen edged forwards. He lived in the northernmost of their lands.

'*Mormaer*, I would not swear to it, but I think he is a landsman from the land of the Ce.'

Britha gestured to two of the warriors. 'Take him to the circle. Go quick and soft – he is badly hurt.' The warriors picked the man up and carried him out of Ardestie towards the woods to the east. Britha walked with them. She had to mask how unnerved she was.

What frightened her the most was that without woad, without mushrooms, she could see the lines of blood within the man's flesh. They looked like they had fire crawling through them.

3
Now

He suspected that the drugs and alcohol made the sea of naked bodies in soft red light seem more erotic than the cold harsh reality probably was, but that didn't matter. It felt good, edgy, exciting, like they were pushing boundaries. Besides, she was beautiful; they complemented each other in both looks and willingness to go forward, to explore. Being inside her felt right, more than just sex. He looked down at her, hair dark, eyes glazed with narcotics and sex, moving against him, guiding him inside her to where she wanted, where he felt good, moaning slightly when he found it.

He'd heard the stories but hadn't believed them, but what mattered was that she liked edge play. He could see the scars on her neck from the bloodletting. The bullshit about people seeing things after tasting her blood was probably just the effects of blood-drinking while tripping.

As he moved inside her he reached for the razor. Pushing deep into her he held it in front of her looking for consent. She didn't say no. Best not to spoil their game with words. He used the razor to draw a line in red on her neck.

He considered himself creative. Perhaps that made him more sensitive, perhaps it didn't. He would never know the latent talent he had and the tiny tear that talent made when her blood sought it out. A single tear of blood ran down his smooth pale cheek, as he became a beacon first. Then a gate as his mind was torn apart. He saw it, briefly, the red burning ghost world.

Then as they came through he felt like he was being torn apart at some base level. His scream echoed in another place. Nothing that heard it cared, or even understood it. It was drowned out by a much louder and all-encompassing scream.

Then there was destruction.

*

Du Bois hated driving through London almost as much as Londoners hated people driving Range Rovers through the tightly packed streets of the city. He fantasised about killing the taxi driver who had seen him coming, seen him obviously in a hurry and had still pulled out in front of him. Pedestrians scattered as he slewed the big four-by-four onto the pavement. He had not hit any of them, not that it mattered – they would all be dead soon. He did nudge the taxi, the impact barely registered on the armoured Range Rover that du Bois had won from a drug dealer playing baccarat in Monte Carlo.

'They got all the crèches?' du Bois asked again. He was talking into the air, but the secure mobile connection easily picked up his words. It was not often he asked for information to be repeated – there was no requirement – but it was not every day you heard the death of hope itself.

'Each was hit simultaneously worldwide and in orbit.' It did not matter that Control was discussing near-certain extinction, the female voice was the same, somehow managing to be cold, artificial, distant and sexy at the same time. Normally it had du Bois musing on how things had changed but not today.

'The souls?'

'They are all gone, the backups as well. They used a virus, a possible derivation of L-tech.'

'Then it's over,' du Bois said quietly.

'They may have stolen the souls,' Control said. That explained the security incident he was on his way to deal with.

'Which is just so much information without the children. Who was it – the Brass City? The Eggshell?'

'All information points to it being agents of the Brass City, but we cannot be sure. We would like the souls back, Malcolm.'

Du Bois said nothing. He had to ignore the hopelessness he felt. More than two thousand years of planning, all for nothing. They had failed.

He threw the Range Rover around the corner and had to brake hard, brought up short by a cordon of flashing lights, vehicles and armed men. He could just about make out the building the suspect was supposed to be in. His vision changed to bring it into sharper relief. He watched the members of SCO19, the Metropolitan Police's specialist firearms unit, hit the front door of the run-down, four-storey building with a battering ram and pile in.

'Brilliant,' du Bois muttered to himself. It was the tiniest of consolations but he had decided that whoever was responsible for this fuck-up was going to suffer.

As soon as he climbed out of the Range Rover he felt the blood-screen. It was like walking through preternatural spiderwebs. He hid behind the door of the Range Rover as he did not want the local police to see him self-harm. Du Bois drew the tanto from the sheath in the small of his back. The blade opened his flesh. He barely felt it, the folded steel was so sharp.

Waiting was the worst thing for Hamad. His first out had been blown: the Circle, with their grip on the security services and their command of surveillance technology, had responded too quickly.

He sat cross-legged in the filthy room in the flophouse. In front of him were the two curved daggers. They were older than any existing civilisation and made from materials that most modern scientists would fail to understand, unless of course they were part of the Circle.

The simple white blade, Gentle Sleep, was not the problem: it killed easily, almost sorrowfully. The other blade, the blade of skeletal black metal, Nightmare, was another matter. It lusted for the killing, whispered to Hamad, drew out the dying and made it hurt for every victim.

Hamad had thrown a blood-screen up, and through it Nightmare was aware of everyone within the flophouse and the surrounding buildings, the street, the station. Nightmare wanted all their deaths.

He had been aware of the sirens from the furthermost elements of the blood-screen long before he had heard them. Nightmare had whispered the joy the sirens heralded. Hamad felt like weeping. When would he finally have killed enough?

Chief Inspector Benedict Appleby did not have time to deal with the special-forces cowboy walking towards him. The man wore loose-fitting, dark casual clothes, his sandy-blond hair down to his shoulders, surprisingly clean-shaven, blue eyes and designer leather jacket, but it was his cock-of-the-walk attitude that gave it away.

'Tell me, Chief Inspector, was one of the group of men you've just murdered fucking your wife?' du Bois asked.

'What? No!' Appleby had been so taken aback by the question he had actually answered it.

'Then why have you sent them all to their certain death?'

'I think we can handle—'

'No, you have shown no aptitude for thinking at all. I need to get in there now.'

'We're in the middle of an op—'

'A very public sodomising – yes, I'm aware of that. Do you know

33

what one of these is?' The man showed Appleby a warrant card. Appleby's eyes widened.

'Yes. I mean, that is, I've never seen one before but—'

'This means I can do as I please. Order your men not to interfere with me in any way, understand?'

'Look, you can't speak to me like that! I will need to check this.'

Du Bois sighed: the whole point of the warrant card was to avoid situations like this. He pulled out his phone and hit speed dial.

Hamad had wanted to run. He really had. Nightmare had not. Nightmare wanted to stay. He heard the door battered open. Hamad thought about the police officers thundering up the stairs. Their families, their lives, the sum of their experiences up to this moment. Were they loved? Did they have children? Nightmare howled in his head. He was not done killing, it seemed. Not that it mattered any more.

He felt the screen snagged, attacked, changed.

The godsware implants were two slits on his forehead. He opened his eyes. All of them. The Marduk implant showed him the ways through. They made a lie of matter. He fell back through the floor.

Hamad emerged through the ceiling above the stairway halfway through a graceful somersault and landed among the armed police officers on the cramped stairway. He pushed gun barrels away from him, the slightest touch of hand and foot sending the officers tumbling down the stairs. He seemed to flow among them, moving to where they thought him least likely to be. Toying with probability.

Hamad crouched low, his leg kicking out behind him. Gentle Sleep cut through a heavy boot like it did not exist. A nearly sentient poison coursed into the firearms-officer's body. He died happy as if in the middle of a pleasant dream.

Nightmare just had to open the cheek of one of the officers and the screaming began. There was panic as the terror-stricken officer tried to flee and shoot his way out of his worst nightmare. The black blade drew blood again and again.

Du Bois shook his head, the sound of screaming and gunfire playing in stereo for him. He could hear it clearly echoing down the street and through the radio tap. Appleby had gone white as he listened to his men being murdered.

'It's me. I'm at King's Cross. I'm being obstructed.' Du Bois offered Appleby the phone. 'It's the Home Secretary. He thinks you're a cunt as well.' Appleby stared at the phone like he was being handed dog shit.

Du Bois was sprinting towards the house. Knowing that it was too late. He drew the accursed .45, ejected the magazine and replaced it with a new magazine of ammunition that probably cost more than any one of the properties lining the street.

He ran up the steps and into the house. He saw the first body lying in a contorted heap halfway down the stairs. The police officer's face was a rictus of agony and terror.

Du Bois took a moment to compose himself. His skill set and experience aside, he was facing someone who could appear from anywhere armed with ancient and potent weapons. Still, he was pretty sure that the person he was hunting was long gone. He could already feel the blood-screen collapsing in the local area, no longer multiplying like bacteria, no longer putting up a fight as his own screen consumed it. Du Bois tried desperately to spoof the blood-screen with disguised tracking elements of his own.

Du Bois left the house. He had been right: whoever had done this was long gone. A number of the armed response team had been killed. They had either died blissfully or in pain and fear. The latter outweighed the former. Du Bois knew he should not be surprised. After all, whoever had done this could steal souls and murder hope itself.

Du Bois looked around for someone to blame. He found Appleby quickly and strode towards him. Appleby was sitting on some steps leading to one of the other terraced houses. He was gazing down at the Euston Road unseeing. He looked broken.

'Was "Don't enter the building under any circumstances" somehow not emphatic enough for you?'

Appleby looked up, appalled that someone would say something like that at a time like this, further angering du Bois, who saw it as self-pity.

One of Appleby's subordinates moved towards du Bois, arm outstretched to intercept him. Du Bois grabbed the man's hand, locked it and then elbowed him in the face, easily knocking him to the ground.

'Stay down there,' du Bois spat as he reached Appleby and leaned down. There were more officers running towards him. 'Tell me—'

'Sir!' an armed police officer shouted at him. 'Get away from the chief inspector.'

Du Bois turned on her. 'Don't make me kill you just for some peace and quiet.' He turned back to Appleby. It was the waste that bothered him the most. 'Tell me. How does a mental subnormal, incapable of understanding the most elementary of missives, rise to such a high position in the Met?' Appleby flinched. 'Are you a Mason or something?' Appleby turned to look at him, appalled. Shock was rapidly being replaced by anger.

'I lost men to—'

Du Bois grabbed him, pulling his face closer.

'Listen to me, you seeping cock-sore. You didn't fucking lose them; you killed them. You killed them because you are a moron, because you are too fucking stupid and greedy to sit back and think, *Hmm, perhaps this position of power and responsibility is too much for my tiny mind to handle. Perhaps I won't risk murdering people because I'm a simpering lightweight vastly out of my depth and lacking the common sense that God gave shrubbery!'*

Du Bois felt a degree of pride as he saw tears form in Appleby's eyes. He worried that people like Appleby would find ways to rationalise what they had done. Du Bois wanted to drive home the man's culpability, hopefully help break him so he would not manoeuvre himself into a position of responsibility and influence again. In du Bois's mind, Appleby's stupidity made him dangerous. Surrounded by nervous police officers, du Bois stared at the man with cold blue eyes. He wanted to see the breaking point.

Beth knew she was ugly. She knew because the cell-block mums had not tried to rape her. She stared at the hated reflection in the small mirror. She knew she was too squat, too brutish, had too little femininity for the rest of the world. No matter how much you try and get away from other people's expectations, reject them utterly, you still ended up feeling their looks, judging yourself through their eyes. Still, she had broken enough mirrors and going down for manslaughter had been her seven years of bad luck, let out early for good behaviour. The only thing she did like was the Celtic tattoo creeping up from her neck. That and, mannish or not, she had kept in good shape. Though she wondered if they would let her work on the doors again with her record. She had been working that night after all.

The slamming of a cell door echoed through the prison. She hated that sound. It had become the soundtrack of her life. The first time she had heard it was when she had known that her whole wide world had been shrunk to four ugly institutional walls. Soon she would not have to listen to it any more.

Not very much money, an old-fashioned cassette Walkman – she was almost touched that they had removed the batteries, though she doubted they would have much charge – charity-shop shirt and tie, the para-boots and her pride and joy, her leather jacket. The interlocking knotwork pattern painted on the back. It was a copy of the cover of her favourite album from her favourite band. It was the outside world.

The sound of the outside door closing behind her for the last time. Beth knew that the long inhalation was a cliché. It didn't matter. Out here the air didn't smell of hundreds of dangerous women in close proximity.

She had known they would not be there, but some part of her had still hoped. She was pleasantly surprised that the batteries still had some charge and tinny music came out of the cheap headphones. Beth zipped up her jacket and started walking. It was going to be a long walk.

'Hello?' Beth called as she entered the house. Beth often knew whether or not someone was in a house when she entered it. This house, nominally her family home, felt empty though the smoke hanging in the air suggested otherwise.

The house had not been redecorated in more than twenty years. It looked like it had not been cleaned in almost as long. In some ways the cramped little house on the Undercliff Road was a microcosm of Bradford. The city had been dealt a death blow in the 80s that it had not managed to recover from.

Beth found her father in the lounge in his chair, smoking, the ashtray next to him overflowing. He had the pipe from the oxygen tank next to the chair up his nose but Beth hoped that it was turned off. She watched the cherry glow as he inhaled shallowly. The resulting cough sounded wet.

'Dad? It's me.'

'Talia?' It was the sound of pathetic hope in his voice that hurt the most.

'No, Dad, it's Beth.' She moved through the smoke. The curtains were closed in the filthy room. He was living in darkness. The little band of pale sunlight that shone through a gap in the curtains illuminated her father like a corpse. He looked awful and he looked disappointed.

'When did you get out?' he asked. Despite the wheezing he still managed to sound disappointed too.

'Yesterday.' She had slept in a hedgerow last night. It had been a very long walk. She had taken a bus when she had got to the outskirts of Leeds.

'Are you staying long?' he asked.

'I was hoping to stay until I can get some work and afford a place of my own,' she said.

'Not much work for a jailbird. Not much work …'

'I'll get something.'

He just nodded. Beth waited, looking for something more – anything. They let the awkward silence grow, then she headed for the door. She turned back.

'When's Talia back?' she asked. It was like watching his face crumple. Tears appeared on his cheek.

'She's gone. Left me,' he said, his voice a wailing rasp.

Beth was by his side, reaching for his hand, but he flinched away from her.

'You! You did this. You drove her away when you killed her man. What were you thinking?'

Beth stood up slowly. *I was thinking that maybe if I left it this time he would beat her so hard he'd finally kill her*, Beth thought. Talia, the pretty one, Talia the popular one, Talia the feminine one, Talia the fucking trouble-magnet. Beth took after her dad and Talia took after some lost dark beauty from their family's genetic past. They had never got on, but Talia was her younger sister so she had looked out for her. Not the easiest of jobs for someone that self-destructive. Beth had lost count of the number of times that someone had come to find her to peel Talia, messed up on drugs or alcohol, off the floor and take her home, or pull her out of some other scrape. Not that she had ever been thanked.

Talia had found Davey with her unerring ability to get involved with the worst guy possible. He was a minor-league dealer with a history of violence against his partners. None of this had mattered to Talia. It had been true love through the bruises. Beth had been pretty sure that Davey was going to kill her that final time. That said, she knew she had lost control. She had not needed to go as far as she did. Even then it had still hurt to see Talia in court testifying against her. Had it not been for that, the sentence might have been suspended.

'How long?' Beth asked.

'Six months.'

'Where?'

'Down south somewhere, where they all go.'

This was the way it went in this house, Beth thought: Talia broke her parents' hearts, back when her mum was alive, and Beth got blamed for it.

'She was going to leave home eventually anyway,' she told the old man. She left it unsaid that Talia had never had anything but contempt for them all anyway. She could not wait to get out of there. Talia had just been waiting for a way to sustain her lifestyle with the minimum of actual effort on her behalf.

Beth stood and headed up the stairs.

Beth had the music on too loud. She knew that, but what was he going to do? He couldn't even shout at her after all. She was doing press-ups, carefully so she didn't make the needle jump on the old vinyl. She was exercising out of sheer boredom. She had done a lot of this in prison.

Beth heard him making his agonising way up the stairs but she did not go to help and did not turn the music down. Eventually the door to her room opened, and her father, coated in sweat, stood gasping for breath in the doorway. His look expressed what he thought of her activity. This was clearly another thing that good girls were not supposed to do. Like beating her younger sister's boyfriend to death, she guessed.

He made his way to her bed and sat down. He used the time he needed to recover the ability to speak to gaze around her bedroom disapprovingly at the posters of the various bands she liked on the walls.

'Go and find her for me,' he finally rasped.

'Dad, she's just moved out. A lot of people do it.' She had known he wanted her to do this downstairs.

'No word, nothing,' he told her. *That's because she doesn't give a shit about any of us*, Beth thought but said nothing. 'She would have phoned – she's a good girl.' He might as well have added 'and you're not', Beth thought. She had heard it anyway.

'Have you tried phoning her?' Beth asked.

He shook his head. 'No number,' he managed. 'She said she would call when she got a phone.'

Beth knew for a fact that Talia couldn't live without her phone. There was no chance she didn't have one. It just wasn't important for her to call her father. After all, what use was a poor, broken-down, dying old man?

'Look, Dad. London's a big place. I wouldn't even know where to begin.'

Beth was surprised when her father reached forward and grabbed her arm. It felt like a skeleton had grabbed her, but for all that his grip was still strong.

'What is it with you? Why can you only hurt this family?

39

And believe me, you have no idea how true that is!' Beth closed her eyes, wondering if this was when her father was going to blame her for her mother's death, but he let go. She opened her eyes and he was struggling to his feet. He brushed away her attempts at help.

'Look, I'm not going to London but I'll phone a few people, okay?' she told him. He just nodded as he made his way towards the door.

Beth was angry with herself. She was angry because she was concerned despite herself. When she had seen Talia's pale, spite-filled pretty face from the dock, she had sworn she was never going to help her again. Let her die choking on her own blood and vomit face down in the street somewhere. But after calling around she was starting to share her father's worries.

Talia had not gone to London; she had gone to Portsmouth. That was good. It was a smaller city and she should be easier to find. She had been in semi-regular contact with her remaining friends in Bradford, those she had not used up, until a few weeks ago. Talia had gone down to meet some goth, or whatever they were called now, a pretty boy called Clark who Beth vaguely knew. She had managed to get his number out of one of Talia's friends and called him. He had given her a mouthful of abuse and hung up, refusing to answer any more of her calls.

However, another of Beth's friends, Billy, who also worked the doors, had said that there had been some Internet porn clip doing the rounds recently. He was not alone in thinking that the girl in it looked a lot like Talia. He had not gone into details and Beth had not asked, but he had said awkwardly it was some pretty raw stuff. Billy had been one of those guys more than a little bit in love with her sister but was too nice for Talia to be interested. Billy had gone round to see some more of Talia's friends in person. It sounded like he had been not quite so nice this time. Two hours later he had phoned Beth back with an address in Portsmouth.

'I have some money saved from my disability,' her dad said from the doorway to the living room. She had been sitting on the stairs talking to Billy on the phone.

'This is it, Dad. This is the last time I try and help her.'

'Just bring her back to me before I die.'

She doesn't care! Beth wanted to scream. *And you've always been dying, haven't you, Dad? It's a wonder that Mum beat you to it. The only thing Talia is interested in is using you in her 'poor me' stories.* Instead Beth just nodded.

*

In her room Beth packed. Clothes, soap, toothpaste, deodorant, ratty old towel, sleeping bag, all went into the army-surplus kitbag with the Celtic knotwork patterns drawn on it with marker pen. It was not much. Beth knelt in front of her bed staring at the kitbag, trying to make a decision. Finally she reached under the bed and pulled the box out. Opening it, she laid each item on the bed carefully. Brass knuckles, not the ones she had used on Mikey, her old ones that had lived in her pocket when she was working the doors. A pickaxe handle, one end with a bike chain wrapped tightly around it. A Balisong knife, often incorrectly called a butterfly knife. Beth had confiscated it from some kid when she had been working. She had kept it because she recognised a high-quality blade when she saw one. Finally she drew her great-grandfather's First World War bayonet out of its sheath and looked at the old blade. She had stolen it years ago because nobody else cared about it, and she had not wanted Talia to sell it. The blade needed work, but that was okay – she would take her whetstone with her.

She packed all of them. If Talia had properly done it this time, was in real trouble, then she would have need of them. She was off to try and help her sister again. She was armed. This was how she had ended up in prison.

Beth put her leather jacket on, slung the kitbag over her shoulder and headed down the stairs. She did not even say goodbye. *Let him hear the door slam on another daughter*, she thought.

She walked out onto wet streets surrounded by grey stone.

McGurk leaned heavily on his cane and looked at the bloody and naked girl lying on top of the rubble, dust still settling on her. He was sure she was still alive: her tits were moving.

'Well fuck,' he said, his strong Portsmouth accent unmistakable. He could hear sirens in the distance. 'Put her in the motor.'

'Boss?' Markus asked. A house blowing up was bound to draw the attraction of the police.

McGurk turned to look at Markus, who looked away from him, unable to meet his eyes. *Total obedience, that's what it's all about*, McGurk thought as Markus went to pick the girl up. Besides, it was his house and he wanted to know what had happened, and he thought that maybe she was the one Arbogast had told him about, the one he had come to see.

McGurk climbed into the back of the BMW and felt the boot slam.

'Before the Old Bill shows up, Markus,' he said, letting just enough impatience creep into his voice to worry the other man.

4

A Long Time After the Loss

It took a long time to convince the *Black Swan*'s systems that the mating with the other ship/thing was safe enough to open the airlock. The docking system was too strange, too organic. Eventually Nulty had to override the system himself.

They were not shy. One of them was waiting in the docking tube for them. He looked like an eccentric soft machine sculpt. Except the alienness seemed less forced. He – they were pretty sure it was a he despite a degree of androgyny – had pale skin with lines traced over it. Eden magnified her vision. They weren't lines but the outline of delicate scales. His eyes were black pools, no visible iris or pupil. His neck seemed to palpate slightly and his head, utterly hairless, looked swollen. Webbed fingers with black sharp-looking nails were wrapped around a staff which looked like it was made of a material somewhere between bone and pearl. He wore a scaled robe of silver-coloured material that seemed to move of its own accord.

When he opened his mouth, they recognised the noises as words; the syntax was familiar but even so it strained their neunonics' translation routines. Behind the strange, nominally human, man they could see a soft pearl-like luminescence. It smelled, not unpleasantly, of the sea, and they could hear the sound of water gently lapping against something. Their suit sensors showed that the atmosphere was apparently breathable. If there were any toxins the sensors couldn't pick them up. The sensors also told them that the atmosphere was warm and damp.

'I am Ezard,' their translation subroutines finally came back. 'I am the speaker. You are welcome here.'

'First contact?' Brett asked the others over the interface.

'He's human, or was once,' Eden replied.

'Follow me,' Ezard said. The translation was coming faster now. He turned and walked down the tube of flesh. With a degree of trepidation, the four followed. Eldon was last. He waited until the *Swan*'s airlock closed behind them and then sent a neunonic command to set off the viral canister that Brett had attached to his suit. He had expected some sort of warning siren and to then be torn apart but nothing happened.

'The environment is clean here. You can take your helmet suits off if you wish, although we will not be offended if you don't,' Ezard was saying when Eldon caught up.

'It's as much for your protection as ours,' Brett was explaining through the translator interface with the suit. 'We come from a culture with a great deal of nano-technology pollution.' They walked out into an open area. 'Seeders.' There was awe in his voice.

Eldon looked around, struggling to cope with what he saw. He did not even notice that they had lost contact with the *Swan*.

It was clear that, allowing for the thickness of the hull/skin, the chamber was as wide as the craft and almost as long, though either end seemed to be packed with interconnected biomechanics that were neither quite machines nor internal organs.

The chamber – Eldon struggled not to think of it as a wet cave with ribs – reminded him of the texture of the inside of his own mouth. The suit sensors told of a warm wind blowing through. The wind seemed to blow one way and then be sucked back. There was no visible floor; it was mostly clear water. The same omnipresent pearl-like luminescence that illuminated the rest of the cavern lit the shallows. There were much darker areas that were obviously a lot deeper.

The water was broken by islands which looked like a mixture of bone and some unknown type of flesh. On the islands there were more people like Ezard. They appeared to have binary male and female sexes and only a very few of them were clothed as Ezard was.

'I assure you it did not look like this when we started. It was far more utilitarian. We sculpted this over the many generations that we've lived within the Mother,' Ezard told them.

'Where are you from?' Eden asked, awe in her voice.

'Earth,' Ezard answered.

'You don't happen to know where it is, do you?' Eldon asked.

'If it exists still it will not be as it was.'

Eden glanced at the others questioningly.

'They could know so much,' Brett said over the interface.

'Yes, alive they would be of incalculable worth to the uplifted races but nothing to us,' Eldon told him angrily.

'Boss, Brett may be right. We can't get away with this.' Eden said.

'Just shut the fuck up and think about the money. Look at them – they're not right.'

43

'They've just evolved to fit the environment,' Eden said.

Ezard turned to look at them. 'I cannot express how glad we are to see you. We have been trapped in this realm too long. We want to meet the rest of humanity. Can you take us out of the red sky?'

Eldon sent the command from his neunonics and his suit visor opened. He breathed in the air. He, like the rest of the crew, had immunised themselves against the particular flavour of viral they were using. If you used virals you hadn't protected yourself against, then you were a fool who deserved to die, in his opinion.

'We'll be glad to help.' He ignored the demands to know what the fuck he was doing over the interface. He knew with his long life he must have picked up all sorts of nano-infections that his cheap nano-screens could barely control. *Time to spread them around,* he thought. A plea of ignorance might help if they got caught.

Nulty was still picking up the sensor glitch. Eldon had been right: there had to be something there. Nulty did not like that and was running the signal through every filter he could think of, but the interference of Red Space was preventing him from gathering any more information. It seemed like another strange field reading, not dissimilar but not the same as the weird readings he was getting off the thing they were docked to. A thing he was more and more sure was some kind of S-tech ship.

He had expected to lose contact with the boarding crew but that did not mean that Nulty liked it. He wondered if they were being torn apart by feral Seeder servitors. He could pilot the *Swan* if he had to, though he was not sure about the bridge drive. The issue was the docking tube. It wasn't a known tech interface. It seemed attached to the *Swan* like a leech.

Eventually they all followed Eldon's lead and opened their visors, making the suits recede from their faces. Melia was the last.

'It smells of fish,' she observed. 'I'm hungry.'

The bio-sculpted inhabitants of the ship/thing Ezard referred to as Mother were all staring at them, their expressions unreadable. Eden could not shake the feeling that they were communicating in some way. She had watched one of them crawl to a swollen nipple-like growth on the wall of the chamber and suck on it. Moments later she had sunk to the ground in what looked like a narcotic stupor.

Ezard had said little. He had just let them wander, as they wanted.

'When you feel safe, when you are happy, we should discuss if you would be prepared to help us leave this place.'

Eldon had just nodded.

'Call me when you need me.' Ezard had then dived off the smooth bone/flesh island into one of the deeper pools. He glided though the water, propelled by a rippling movement in his cloak. Eden was not sure if it was technology, biology or some symbiosis of both.

Brett was looking despondent. Their attempted genocide was weighing heavily on him. He was wandering towards the subjective front of the craft, approaching the biomechanical machinery/organs. In front of the wall of machinery/organs there was what looked to be some kind of web made of a fine, delicate version of the same material as Ezard's staff. In the centre of the web was a cocoon of the same material. It glowed with an inner light and something about it suggested a feminine quality.

Brett stood looking at it for a while. The others were some way back sitting on one of the islands, not sure what to do while they waited for genocide to take place.

'We should be heading back,' Melia said over the interface.

'If it happens it'll happen quick,' Eldon replied, still angry at what he saw as betrayal by the licensed concubine.

'We've no idea what effect it will have on their altered physiology,' Eden pointed out. 'If Nulty's right and this is S-tech, then who knows how they could have augmented themselves.'

'So what? We just make our excuses and leave?' Eldon asked.

'They don't seem armed,' Eden said. 'But I don't fancying holding off a small civilisation with four disc guns, yeah?'

Brett looked down. He was surprised to see a dolphin looking at him, similar to those that worked with the Church. Except it was not quite a dolphin. Where the Church dolphins had waldos, this one had tentacles. Where the Church dolphins used interface to communicate, this one appeared to have a human mouth growing out of its neck. The creature looked old, its skin cracked and covered in growths.

It was staring straight at Brett from about eight feet down in the clear water. A shadow passed over it and with a flick of its tail it dived down into a tunnel that led into the machinery/organs.

Ezard all but leaped out of the water to land on the island next to Brett. The black pools of his eyes made him difficult to read, but Brett was pretty sure that he was staring at the cocoon with an expression of reverence.

'What is it?' Brett asked. He now spoke the same anachronistic version of Known Space common that Ezard did, the translation subroutine having learned it fully and meshed it with his neunonics. Effectively the language had been downloaded into his brain. Though

Brett was pretty sure he had heard the others here speak a different language, one that sounded a little like sea life communicating. He had heard sounds like that in immersion programmes. Brett reckoned it would require modifications to their voice boxes to allow them to make the sounds he had heard.

'She,' Ezard corrected. He seemed to be struggling to explain concepts with the linguistic tools he had. 'She is a conduit, a translator. The Mother speaks through her because she is of the Mother's line. When we are in the real, maybe she will hatch, become like a god. She is the link between them in the past and us now.'

Brett did not understand but found something beautiful in what Ezard was saying. More and more he was sure that he did not want to kill these people.

'Look, Ezard, there's something I have to tell you,' he said. His handsome face was in turmoil as he struggled with his betrayal. He liked and trusted his companions but his loyalty to them was outweighed by the magnitude of the crime they were about to commit. Ezard regarded him with an expression that managed to be both expectant and inscrutable.

Tentacles shot out of the water and wrapped around Brett. He was ripped off his feet and dragged into the water before the others had a chance to respond. Ezard dived into the water after him.

The panic that came from submersion was just an ancient race memory. Brett had more than enough oxygen in his system to survive for a reasonable amount of time underwater. The grip of the dolphin's tentacles was strong but not crushing. Still, as he struggled to get free, the tentacles might as well have been steel cables.

The dolphin moved with incredible rapidity through the water towards the tunnel that Brett had seen him disappear into earlier. Except now it looked less like a tunnel and more like a sphincter.

His neunonics sounded an alarm as the sensors on his skin, which he used to understand pheromones when dealing with insects, picked up an unknown secretion. The sphincter closed behind them.

Brett found himself being dragged through massive and very alien internal organs that seemed to pulse with their own life. There was the sensation of going deeper and deeper, though whether that was real or just fear, Brett couldn't be sure.

He tried the interface and was more than a little disturbed that he could not contact the others. Whatever prevented them from contacting the *Swan* obviously had the same effect between different sections of the ship/thing, whatever it was. Brett did not like the totality of the signal block either.

The dolphin breached onto a small bone-like alcove that looked different to the other areas – dark, lacking in life. The organs around the alcove looking diseased to Brett. The tentacles dragged him out of the water and laid him next to the prone dolphin.

'You carrying violence?' Brett ignored the question. His disc gun was still bonded to the back of his suit and he had a laser at his hip. Shooting was imminent when he got free. His neuronics would replay the way back to the others. 'I'm your only friend here young 'un. Don't worry. They don't know where you are. Mind blind in here. I killed it, whipped up a little disease right here, just small enough for them not to notice.'

Brett wondered how good the dolphin was at reading human expressions as he stared at the grotesque human mouth under the dolphin's main mouth. It just would not stop talking, the ancient common accompanied by a clicking noise.

'They call me Zadok. They say I wasn't grown right, that the template was fucked, but they need the likes of me. All sorts of disease alchemy. I can heal as well as hurt. Put a disease in my tool though, so there'd be no more of me.'

Brilliant, Brett thought. He appeared to have been kidnapped by a disease-spreading mutant dolphin bearing a grudge against their hosts.

'They don't have anything good for you here. They just want to get out of the dark and spread, like a disease. Everyone has to be the same, like. They are no friends to you and yours.'

'Can you let me go?' Brett asked.

'If I let you go, you going to behave? Because I think you're carrying some violence with you and I can't get hurt before I tell you what you're into here.'

Brett just nodded. The dolphin shifted him around in the coils of his tentacles so he could examine him with one crusty eye.

'You got any bottled fun on you, boy? You are a boy, aren't you?'

'Yes,' Brett answered, trying to shift, the coils of tentacle tightening around him as he tried.

'Yes to bottled fun or orifice fun?'

'I'm a boy, man. I'm male. I don't know what bottle fun is.'

'See, they cut me off from the drug nipples, no more mother's milk for me and I'm not an endorphin drinker, otherwise I could just suck it out of you. You wouldn't like that though. It's not fair, is it?'

'Yes, I have drugs,' Brett managed between gritted teeth. He kept to himself that they were part of his internal systems. He did not like the idea of being torn apart by some junkie dolphin looking for a fix. A thought occurred to Brett: 'If they don't wish us well then how come they let you live?'

'Told you. They need me for maintenance. You, you're just spare parts, some new information, maybe a top-up on the old gene pool, but most importantly you're a key to this smoking red prison. I'll be honest. I'd like to see the ocean that my ancestors saw. I 'members it up here.' He tapped his skull with a tentacle. 'But it's far more important to fuck them. Ruin it for them. Just like they fucked me. They took my tool; they can all die.' The little chamber of dead meat resonated with obvious anger and bitterness. Brett grunted as the tentacles started to tighten around him.

'Drugs,' he managed.

'Oh sorry,' Zadok said much more brightly and loosened his grip. 'Where are your drugs?'

'They're in one of the suit's internal pouches. You'll have to let me out so I can get to them,' Brett said in what he felt sure was a cunning manner. 'No violence,' he further reassured Zadok.

Zadok eyed him with what Brett assumed was cetacean suspicion, but he felt the tentacles loosen round him.

'That's good. Just a little something to take the edge off. I've got a lot to tell you, boy.'

Brett stood up among the serpentine uncoiling tentacles and wondered if they were looking for him. The bonded disc gun came off the back of his suit as soon as he touched the weapon. His neunonics sent the safety code to the gun instantaneously. Brett also sent the command to switch the weapon to pump action because he thought it was cooler.

The butt of the weapon was snug against his shoulder. Zadok saw what was happening but obviously did not have the soft machine enhanced reaction augmentations that Brett did. The dolphin was only just starting to move when both barrels of the disc gun went off. To Brett it was like everything was happening in slow motion. The butt of the weapon contracted, cushioning the recoil as solid-state shot turned into razor-sharp, electromagnetically propelled spinning discs. Zadok's flesh spread itself across the diseased chamber. Brett worked the pump mechanism on the weapon, chambering another two rounds from the tubular magazines under the side-by-side barrels. He fired again, just to be on the safe side. There was another display of dead flesh.

'Fuck yeah!' Brett said, trying not to dance a little. 'That's what you get!' Then he remembered where he was. He looked around the chamber for further threats, expecting more junkie, mutant dolphins but finding none.

Brett held the visor in place as he sent the signal to his suit and it grew out of his neck to cover his head the rest of the suit attached itself. He tried the interface again but got nothing. He reviewed the journey to the chamber in the memory of his neunonics. He was reasonably sure he could find his way back.

Brett rose out of the pool with the disc gun ready, scanning from side to side. This was the way the tac program in his neunonics told him to do it; more to the point it was the way he had done it in immersions. Playing legionnaire for fun.

Brett was now sure he was lost. He was not sure how as the recorder facility on the route finder application in his neunonics should have taken him back to the main chamber.

He rose, dripping, into a large chamber with a gently curving roof. The chamber was formed of what looked like thick, smooth, rubbery, but not unpleasantly so, skin. It reminded Brett of Zadok's skin if Zadok hadn't looked diseased and crusty. He retracted part of his spacesuit, which dragged the visor off his face and up onto his head.

The chamber was dimly lit. A warm wind blew though it and he could hear the sound of water gently lapping against the walls. It gave Brett a dimly remembered sense of well-being.

Then he saw the growths in the wall. He waded through the shallow water towards them. Drawn by curiosity, his sense of well-being bled off him the closer he got.

At first Brett thought it was some kind of organic waste sack or tube. Then he realised it was a massive distended pregnant belly, not unlike the ones on the few fetishist weirdos he had seen go in for natural births. Only this one ended in a biomechanical vaginal orifice. Brett followed the tube up. It was part of something that had once been very clearly human – more human than Ezard and his friends in the main chamber.

He/she, gender did not matter, was merged with the flesh of the chamber. No eyes, no ears, these were extraneous – why would it need them? Instead of a mouth there was a translucent tube. Matter could be seen moving sluggishly down it. This was not pregnancy. This was flesh as a material, storage, an incubator. Somehow Brett knew that the Mother and the Father were the ship. He knew that the passengers and crew were raw material. Their minds were only of use as inspiration. All over Known Space, human flesh was used as a raw material in more base ways – labour, sex, sustenance – but this had nothing to do with humanity. To Brett this was abomination. He looked around, his eyes brightening the darkness and magnifying what he saw. The abomination was repeated on either side of the chamber many times. Through the gloom he could see more chambers.

The *plop* it made sliding out of the closest stomach's orifice was almost comical. Brett's features contorted as he looked down at the utterly inhuman thing uncurling in the water in front of him. Even the flesh sculptors on Cyst could not have invented such a departure from humanity using the same basic material. Humanoid disgust overwhelmed Brett as for the first time he was confronted by something that, although hybridised, was genuinely alien and not just another uplifted animal like himself.

He raised the disc gun to his shoulder and aimed it at the newborn crime against human flesh. The safety was already off.

Brett's neunonics recorded the flight of his head through the air, its impact on the surface of the water. As Brett's head sank before his systems registered brain death and became inert, the neunonics recorded the hazy image of a full-grown version of the newborn Brett had just seen, vomiting something onto his headless corpse. The final thing Brett's systems registered was the enzyme breaking down his flesh for the thing to start sucking up his corpse.

Eldon looked down into the pool that Brett had just been dragged into. Melia and Eden appeared on either side of him. Eden had her disc gun drawn and was pointing it into the pool. Eldon glanced between the women.

'Well fuck,' he finally said.

'We need to go after him!' Eden said.

'Fuck that!' Eldon and Melia said simultaneously.

Ezard practically flew out of the water to land next to the three of them.

'What the fuck?' Eden demanded of the speaker.

'I am very sorry. It is a malfunctioning maintenance creature. Do not worry. It should not hurt your crew member. We will find him quickly though and return him to you safely. We are already looking.'

Eldon gave this some thought.

'Well that seems fair enough,' he finally said.

Eden glared at him. 'We need to find him!' she snapped.

'I'm sure they know what they are doing,' Melia said. Though she would miss Brett. On a ship with a crew as aesthetically challenged as the *Black Swan*, he had been her one respite.

Eden turned on the feline, but her angry retort was cut off by a shrieking cry from behind her.

They swung round to see a woman walking towards them and pointing.

'You did this!' She shouted the words as if they were new to her. As if she had not used even this ancient form of common in a long time, if ever.

Her skin was covered in jumbled words and patterns, some of them animated. Others glowed with their own luminescence. Eldon could not keep his eyes off her chest – the flashing and animated images looked like a collision between adverts for a soft drink and an insect brothel. They had apparently carried in a number of nanite advertising plagues. Plagues that their own screens would have stopped but against which those here would have no countermeasures.

Nearby they saw other adverts growing out of the naked skin of the crew/passengers of the biological ship.

'Shit,' Eldon said. Eden was trying to explain the concept of nano-pollution to the angry women as more closed on them. Ezard was staring at them like he wanted an explanation.

'You brought something else ...' Ezard started.

Eldon drew the disc gun from his back and let Ezard have both barrels. Ezard's abdomen almost ceased to exist as he flew back into the pool.

The angry women with the virulent advertising disease grabbed Eden by the neck and lifted her off her feet. Nanites quickly laced through the skin and flesh of Eden's neck, hardening it, protecting her windpipe, but her augmentations were strictly civilian and designed for industrial accidents. The woman's fingers were still crushing her flesh. There was blood running down Eden's attacker's fingers.

Eldon turned his disc gun on the woman holding Eden off the ground. His neunonics warned him that Eden's position was within his field of fire but offered him the best target solution. He pulled the trigger. Both barrels fired. The discs tore chunks out of Eden and the woman. The woman staggered but did not drop Eden. Moments later Eden's head just seemed to pop off. The headless corpse dropped to the ground and the angry and already injured woman turned towards Eldon. Melia's double-barrelled disc blast tore the woman off her feet.

Melia and Eldon moved back to back, trying to cover all around them as they were encircled by a mass of pale flesh sporting multiple adverts on their newly diseased flesh. All Eldon could see were their inhuman eyes, black nails and needle-like teeth.

'What the fuck did you shoot Ezard for?' Melia demanded,

piteously aware of how few rounds the disc guns had in their tubular magazines.

'Panicked,' Eldon answered, thinking that this was not a good time for a domestic.

'And Eden?'

'Same thing.'

'Are you panicking now?'

'Yes.' Though had Eldon been totally honest he would now have told her that panic was warring with irritation.

'You going to shoot me?' Melia demanded. Eldon gave it some thought.

'You hold them off and I'll make a run for help,' he suggested. He looked up at the cocoon. He was surprised to see an ugly wiry-looking man with no hair and green-stained lips climbing around on it.

The man's spacesuit sleeve was halfway up his right arm. Clinging to this arm, its legs digging into his flesh, was an arachnid with pincers and a sting. The arachnid looked like it was made of living brass. The sting had extended and seemed to be deep in the material of the cocoon.

Eldon recognised the man, or his neunonics did. He was famous. But there was something else, something familiar, as if he had actually met him but he could not remember when.

There was a cry of pain from the man as the sting retracted from the cocoon and the brass arachnid sank into his flesh, moving underneath the skin. The man's spacesuit covered him and the visor slid over his face. Then the man hugged the cocoon.

Nulty didn't like this at all. Red Space was starting to clear. The clouds were dissipating as if swept away by wind. Nulty had seen this effect before, watching ships gate from the red into real. Except this much cloud clearing away would mean either a very large ship or a lot of them simultaneously. Neither option seemed good for them.

The repeated interface hail to Eldon and the others might as well have been screaming into a vacuum. He was now very sure that the sensor glitch that Eldon had found was a stealthed ship. It was showing some of the strange energy signature that the S-tech craft they had found was displaying.

The violence done to the very fabric of Red Space was appalling in its scale. Nulty watched from the hull of the *Black Swan*, feeling exposed in the vacuum that he'd thought of as his home. As space was torn open, the craft coming through looked like a massive cliff of armour and technology from his perspective. It moved slowly, gracefully, through the pulsing blue tear, angry ribbons of white energy sparking off its hull. Nulty had the absurd urge to go and hide on the other side of it. Except that the sensor feed from the *Swan* was showing another bridge of similar size opening behind him. For a supposedly off-the-beaten-track part of Red Space, things were getting very busy. The second craft was of about equal size and similarly armoured, but unlike the smooth, angular lines of the first craft, its hull was ornate, even bearing statuary protruding.

Nulty recognised both craft. The first was a Consortium Free Trade Enforcer-class heavy cruiser. The second was also a heavy cruiser but belonged to the Seeder Church. Nulty understood why they were here. Both would have an interest in the Seeder craft, if that was what it was, particularly if it held the secret of bridge tech. To the Consortium it could mean breaking the Church's monopoly, a monopoly that the Church would not want to see broken.

Despite the heavy interference, Nulty listened to threat and counter-threat rage through Red Space as the ships tried to lock weapons on each other through their glitching sensor systems.

The odd thing was that the Church ship was showing the same or similar spectrums of energy that the Seeder craft was. It was similar to some of the readings he'd been seeing from the *Swan* since their mysterious employer had paid to get the bridge drive functioning. Their employer had also apparently paid for some other modification, which Nulty was less than pleased about. The Consortium craft was not showing anything from that part of the energy spectrum. In fact Nulty was getting exactly what he would have expected from sensor readings of a Consortium heavy cruiser.

Nulty found himself praying to the Seeders, something that he had not done in a very long time, that both sides would want the Seeder craft intact. On the other hand, he could not imagine that whoever got the craft would have a good reason for keeping him alive.

Nulty started the ship's systems via interface. He would just have to skip into Real Space and hope he could find a way home. If the worst came to the worst, he could set a repeating mayday, point the craft in Real Space towards the closest planet or habitat and hibernate.

Sorry, boss, he thought. He wasn't surprised when the unpleasantly organic-looking docking tube would not relinquish its grip on the *Swan*. Nulty had already manoeuvred one of the torches into place. Just as he was about to start cutting, he noticed something in one of the optics and, with a thought, magnified it. The skin of the Seeder craft was changing, becoming more mottled, unhealthy-looking, diseased.

Seeder's sake, Nulty thought as the two cruisers began to stab bright beams of energy at each other, *what kind of viral had Eldon taken in with him?*

One of the ship/thing's inhabitants moved too close to Melia and she fired. Eldon also fired as they closed on him. To Eldon it looked like black veins of disease were crawling across the walls/flesh of the ship/creature. Eldon cursed himself roundly. The virals he had brought on board were the most potent he could find in Arclight. He had never imagined that they would be as potent as this. He had killed his prize.

'You've done this!' one of the women screamed at him with a larynx designed for a different language.

'I didn't mean to,' he cried, and then shot her with both barrels. The craft bucked under his feet. It felt like an impact, a powerful one. The ripple that surged through the craft and knocked him off his feet reminded him of dry retching. In the ceiling above he watched as the flesh transformed itself into fire. A chemical reaction as explosives fed on flesh until it reached fusion and breached the outer hull.

Eldon did not see space. It was his torn-up constituent parts that were sucked through the hole in the ancient creature's flesh and into Red Space's clouded starless night.

5

Northern Britain, a Long Time Ago

She felt the heather against her cheek, under her, providing a soft warm bed. Normally bleary in the morning, she was sharp. Britha was aware enough to remember the expectation of being cold and stiff after a night in the heather. She was not. She felt fine though it was a strange awakening. Like she had just woken from a fever to find that it had broken. She felt better than she could remember feeling in a long time – fit, strong, aware and more attuned to her surroundings. However, she had a strange sense of disconnection that she could barely put a name to, let alone explain, and a taste in her mouth that for some reason reminded her of Cliodna.

Britha unwrapped her robe from around herself. She had been using it as a blanket. She belted it in place as she watched the others rise. Talorcan had already been awake. It had been his turn on watch, his features as impassive as ever.

Nechtan sat up in the heather, pushed his arms through the sleeves of his *blaidth* and reached for his sword. He didn't pick it up. It was just an unconscious gesture to make sure it was still there. Many champions were huge muscular men. Britha suspected that they won battles as much through intimidation as skill. Nechtan, though well built, was not overly muscled. He was, however, fast and he practised, a lot; he did not just rely on past glories. Britha also thought larger warriors underestimated him. Nechtan brushed down his short beard with his fingers. Vanity was the enemy of all warriors, Britha thought. She was pleased that Nechtan had managed to limit himself to just his silver torc in terms of decoration. She watched as Nechtan smoothed his dark wiry hair back and tied it into a ponytail with a leather thong before getting up to join the others.

Drest and Giric, the other two warriors, had come from the same womb but not at the same time, although they looked like twins. Both were young, their whiskers sparse, but they had completed the tasks required to join the *cateran* after training since childhood.

They were eager to please. Britha suspected that Nechtan had chosen them as much because they looked up to him as because they needed the experience. That said, Britha had to admit they were both easy on the eye, largely because they had not been in as many fights as the other warriors. They had yet to be scarred; they weren't missing fingers, ears or teeth. She considered bedding them, wondering if both of them would come to her at the same time. Perhaps to celebrate the shortest night, she thought.

Her musings were broken when the most worrying member of their scouting party walked across her line of sight on the way to make water. With him having no tongue and no knowledge of how to make symbols, there had been little communication. He had nodded when agreeing to lead them back to his village. Not even threats of violence had made the man answer other questions.

This was not the most disturbing thing about him. Britha had had no more visions like the one of crawling flame under his skin, but the man's wounds had healed very quickly. If this was the result of her ministrations then she had never been that successful before. Despite the severity of his wounds when he had ridden into camp, most of them were just white scar tissue now. Even the stump of his tongue had healed over and he seemed to move with vigour. The lines of blood were still visible in his eyes, however. Most of the time his features were expressionless, or close to it, but Britha was sure that she saw hunger there, somewhere deep down.

'He did not sleep all night,' Talorcan said quietly, appearing by her side. Normally Talorcan was one of the few that could sneak up on her, but even on the soft heather she had heard him. 'He just stared towards the north.'

'It's his home and he wants to get back,' Britha said, but even she did not quite believe this. The man had had an encounter with something else, something from the Otherworld, she suspected, and it had changed him.

'How far are we?' she asked.

'Half a day's ride, a little more if Ferchair had the right of it.'

Britha knew she had put more time on the ride by insisting on coming through the mountain passes. The coast would have been much quicker, but she did not trust the sea. She hoped it was not just because she connected it with Cliodna, though it could have been Cliodna's words that had put her off.

Nechtan had mocked her, but Talorcan had guided them without a word of complaint.

The champion, three warriors, the *ban draoi* and six ponies was a lot of resources to risk, Britha mused. Cruibne must be almost as worried as she was. As an added precaution she had painted some charm stones as protection from the Otherworld. Each of them carried one. They were as much reminders to tread cautiously when dealing with the Otherworld as anything else. Britha smiled bitterly. She should have carried one when she first visited Cliodna, she thought.

When she had made the stones she had not begged favours from the gods like she had heard the Goddodin and some of the other southern tribes did. The Pecht knew that the gods were no friends to men and women. Instead she had invested part of her will into the stones, her will focused as protection against the gods of darkness and ill will.

They rode out of the pass and down towards the coastal plain. Britha could already see the destruction. Even now, some four days since it had happened, there were still wisps of smoke rising into the air from the ruins of the village.

The village had been of reasonable size, not much smaller than Ardestie. Britha had known of it, though the name of the place escaped her. The Ce that lived here, mostly fisherfolk, had traded with the Cirig.

'I don't think we'll find much life down there,' she said. The warriors gave her a strange look; the man just looked straight ahead and said nothing. 'What?' she demanded, tiring of the four warriors staring.

'Do you not think we should at least look in the village before we make that decision? The smoke could just be from hearths,' Nechtan suggested, just a trace of mockery in his tone.

Britha turned to look at him as if he was an idiot. The village was obviously burned, not a house left standing. She turned back to look at the village. It was still very far away. She lapsed into silence.

Hungry wounds. Like the one the man had been suffering from when he rode into Ardestie. They were definitely sword wounds but ragged and too deep. Like the blades had eaten their way into the wounds. The warrior was scarred, his shield dented and his sword pitted, but both had the look of being well looked after. The Ce were not a timid people, their warriors were capable, but his blade was not even reddened. It was the same with the rest of the dead. They were either warriors, the ruling family of the village, or landsmen and fisherfolk with spears because all adult Pecht could fight. They were all dead with no sign they had wounded any of the attackers.

The village had been put to the torch, the roundhouses little more than smoking ruins, but it did not look as if anything had been stolen. Even the precious livestock had been left. On the stony beach the small fishing curraghs, the skin-hulled, wooden-framed boats, had been burned as well.

'They couldn't have been very good fighters,' Drest suggested, Giric nodding in agreement, but even Nechtan, who was quick to denigrate another warrior, did not believe it.

'Where are the rest?' Nechtan asked.

'Slavers?' Giric suggested.

'Slavers would take things. There's gold round the necks and the arms of the warriors. They wouldn't have left the livestock either,' Britha said from where she was kneeling next to the dead warrior. She used the butt of her spear to push herself to her feet.

It was a beautiful day, fresh; there was a strong wind blowing in off the sea, clouds scudding across the bright blue sky. The wind almost took the smell of burned wood away from their nostrils. It did not take away the smell of five days of rotting flesh. Britha spat at the crows, messengers of malevolent gods. They had disturbed them feasting on the dead. She felt their eyes on her and the others. Talorcan was waving at them from down by the water. Britha made her way towards him accompanied by the sound of stones being moved up and down the beach by the gentle lapping of the waves.

As Britha headed towards Talorcan she glanced back at the man. He had not even got off the pony they had given him to ride. He was among the ruins of his home. He knew the dead and the missing but he did nothing.

Britha was not used to Talorcan looking worried. The hunter was normally very calm.

'They dragged the ships up here onto the beach,' he said, pointing at drag marks.

'How many?'

'Two ships came ashore. Whether or not there were more I don't know.'

'How many raiders?'

'Difficult to tell. The tracks in the village are too confused. I'm guessing they came late and took the village by surprise. There's a watch fire further up the headland. I'd wager that those manning it are gone or dead as well.'

Britha nodded. 'So they killed those who fought, but why didn't everyone fight? The Ce are not sheep people.'

Talorcan said nothing; he just moved further along the beach to an area clear of stones. He pointed to a mark in the sand. Even without bending down, Britha could see the faint imprint of something that looked like an irregular four-pointed star. The sand had been disturbed as if something ran between each of the deeper indents. Though no tracker, she recognised that five nights ago the indents must have been a lot deeper. The whole imprint was about two feet across.

'You'll need to get closer to see it,' Talorcan said.

'I can see it,' Britha said. Talorcan gave her a funny look. 'What is it?'

'It's a footprint,' Talorcan said. Now she understood why he had looked troubled.

Then the screaming started.

The man had got Drest's sword away from him. He ran the boy through. Drest was still standing, shaking from the wound as he soiled himself and drooled blood down his front.

'No!' Giric cried and charged the man with his longspear.

'Wait!' Nechtan cried.

The man tore the sword out of Drest and the boy slumped forward to the ground. With surprising speed he turned on Giric. The man threw a sweeping kick; his foot contacted with the haft of Giric's spear and drove the point into the ground with sufficient force to snap the wood. Giric collided with his own spear. The man was already swinging Drest's blade. He cut the spear haft again and opened Giric's throat. The young warrior staggered away, blood pouring from the wound, bubbling into froth. With his left hand he tried to hold the wound closed and to his credit his right was trying to draw his sword, but before he could he slumped to his knees and then fell onto his face.

Britha sprinted across the stony beach, making for the village. She quickly outpaced Talorcan, but when arrows started to fly past her she realised the hunter was fighting the best way he could. Meanwhile, the man had turned on Nechtan.

Arrows started to appear in the man's flesh. They did not slow him. Nechtan was a judge of fighters. He had to be. The man was not only fast; his technique was nearly flawless. Rapidly the Cirig champion threw one casting spear after another as he backed towards his horse.

The man batted one of them away with the flat of Drest's sword. The other two hit him true and penetrated flesh, but even they did not stop him. Nechtan backed into his pony. The horse was already nervous but trained for war and did not bolt. Nechtan mastered his fear. He grabbed his small square shield from the pony and drew his iron-bladed longsword from its scabbard just in time.

The man swung at him. Nechtan took the blow on his shield, the force of it splitting the thick reinforced wood, making his arm numb and opening a long gash on it. Nechtan used the parry to duck under the blade and dart away from his pony, giving himself more room.

The man swung again and again at Nechtan, the champion having to use every last bit of strength, speed and skill he possessed just to parry the well-aimed, powerful, fast blows. He was aware of Britha sprinting towards him. Some way behind her, Talorcan was doing the same. The hunter could not now risk using his bow.

Nechtan parried again and retreated, changing position slightly so that when the man renewed his attack his back would be towards Britha.

Britha charged the man, her spear aimed at the centre of his arrow-studded back. He struck at Nechtan. Nechtan parried, catching the blade, realising the mistake he had made just before he was head-butted in the face and kicked so hard in the stomach that he was lifted off his feet and the wind driven from him.

The man turned on Britha, ready to receive her charge. Britha leaped. Nechtan watched in amazement as Britha seemed to fly through the air. The man tried to parry the spear but Britha twitched it out of the way of his blade. The tip took him in the chest, and the force of her landing drove three feet of the weapon through him. Nechtan had to roll to the side to avoid the spearhead.

Still on his feet, the man moved towards Britha, swinging at the *ban draoi* as she scrambled out of the way.

'Cut off his head!' she screamed.

Nechtan was back on his feet now. He clubbed the sword out of the man's hand with his own blade and then swung it two-handed at the man's neck. It was like cutting leather. Each blow was more frenzied as Nechtan painted himself with blood. On the fifth blow the head came off, tumbling free of the body, which was still stagger-ing around. From the stump of his neck waved hundreds of rippling strands of what looked like red filigree. In horror, Britha turned to the severed head and saw the same.

'Cut his body up!' she shouted. Nechtan swung at the headless corpse's legs, taking it off its feet. Talorcan slid down next to the flailing body, his hatchet in one hand, dirk in the other, and started frenziedly hacking and cutting. Britha pulled her sickle out of her belt and raised it to strike. It was red work.

*

They had dismembered the body, then burned the still-twitching remains. Now they were looking to her for answers.

'How?' a still shaken Nechtan demanded.

Britha had always hated to give magic as an answer. More often than not, another answer could be found.

'Magic,' she said. 'At a guess the Lochlannach, with help from dark gods.' *The very gods that the Pecht would not bend a knee to?* she wondered.

Nechtan and Talorcan both spat. Britha noticed the quiet red-stained hunter touch the small pouch around his neck with the charm stone in it. The Lochlannach were half men, half demon raiders. People said they came from the hell where the sea freezes far to the north. Britha guessed they had somehow possessed the dead man.

'Can you fight their magic?' Nechtan asked.

'As you see,' Britha said. Nechtan was studying her as if he had just met her anew. 'What?' Britha demanded testily.

'You used magic in that fight,' he said. Britha almost demanded to know what he was talking about, but from experience it was always best to play at being mysterious. Let their minds come to their own conclusions. Still, she wondered what he meant.

Nechtan thought back to seeing Britha leap the height of a man and make a spear strike that he knew in his heart he was not fast enough to have made.

'We travel back,' Britha said. 'Quickly down the coast; see if we can spot the raiders.'

'What about Giric and Drest?' Nechtan asked. He did not like any-one else giving orders, even the *ban draoi*, though they were definitely living in her world now. 'They were warriors.'

'Now they are crow-feeders,' Britha said, but behind her impassive, almost cruel mask she felt sorry for the two boys. She tried not to get close to the warriors or indeed any of the Cirig. Familiarity would have interfered with those times when she had to make cruel decisions. Still, Drest and Giric had been less obnoxious than many of the other warriors and she felt they had deserved to see more of life than they had.

They had left the sweat-soaked, foaming-at-the-mouth ponies behind in the woods. They had crawled out onto the headland, Nechtan muttering all the while that sliding on his belly was no job for the Cirig champion.

They saw the fires first. Out on the sandbanks. They could just about make out the dark figures surrounding the orange flickering flames. There was the smell of meat on the cool night air. It had taken a while for Nechtan and Talorcan's eyes to adjust, but Britha very quickly noticed the black bulks of the hulls against the night sky. They were curraghs like her people used. She had just never seen any so large before. There were two of them.

As Britha looked down at the camp, no more than six miles along the coast to the east of Ardestie, she realised that there was something else wrong here. There was no noise. The wind carries voices, and warriors talk, boast, shout, fight, jest and sing, but the wind brought them nothing from this camp. Nor could she see anything that could have made the monstrous footprint that Talorcan had found.

Britha opened her mouth to point this out, but Talorcan motioned her to be quiet. Then he pointed. Britha cursed herself when she saw the sentry leaning on his spear. She should have expected and then looked for the man. He wore a metal skin like some of the southern tribes and the ones over the western sea that she'd heard of. There was a longsword at his hip and he carried a large oval shield. He was also perfectly still, his cloak flapping in the wind. He did not seem bored nor did he fidget like most did on sentry duty.

Talorcan gestured for them to crawl back towards the wood. Britha started to move but then she heard Cliodna's song. It seemed to come from inside her head. Tears came unbidden to her eyes. Her head was filled with beauty. *Why hurt me like this? Either stay or go, but don't play with me.* She wondered if it was even her will that made her turn and look to the sea.

Cliodna's dark hair was spread out over the calm surface of the water; only the top of her head and her eyes were visible. The eyes were enough. Britha could feel them looking past her skin and deep into her. They had changed though. They seemed colder.

Britha motioned the warriors to go on but Talorcan shook his head and gestured for her to come with them. She gave him a baleful eye and moved towards the cliff. Nechtan actually grabbed her arm, but she gave him an even more baleful look and he shrunk back from her. He had had enough of messing with things that he did not understand for one day.

She made her way very slowly to the cliff. As she did, she was mindful to keep watch on the sentry, but he did not move at all. She made it to the edge and slipped over. Like most of her people she had been climbing these cliffs or ones like them since she was a child. It was no trouble for her to clamber down into the little inlet and crouch by the side of the water.

The reflection of the moon was like a spear of light in the dark water pointing towards her. Cliodna surfaced in that light. Britha recognised this for what it was, a trick designed to awe the watcher. *Is this all I mean to you now?* Britha wondered. *Another mortal to be made to feel small?*

Cliodna remained in the water. Her song was fading. The dark pools of her eyes no longer looked welcoming and soulful to Britha; now they just drove home how different the selkie was from her and her people.

'Listen to me, *ban draoi*,' Cliodna said as if she was addressing any one of the *dryw*. 'You cannot fight this. If you love your people well then you will take them far inland and hide from this. Stay there for twelve nights and then seek passage to another land. Head east over the sea and do not stop; there is much land there.'

The words made sense. Britha even liked what they said. They were good counsel. It was the way they were delivered. As if they were strangers.

'Cliodna, what is this? What do you know? Who are these people? Are they the Lochlannach?'

'The Lochlannach is as good a name as any. They are led by a man called Bress. They are not of your world and they wield magic that you cannot fight.'

'What do they want?' Britha asked.

'A moonstruck world. They harvest pain,' Cliodna all but hissed at her. Britha could make no sense of her words.

'I don't understand.'

'This is not for the likes of you to understand. Run and hide or live like death. That is your choice.'

'My people will not run, you know that,' Britha said. They had not seen what Nechtan, Talorcan and she had seen.

'I know only what you have told me,' Cliodna said impatiently.

Is that it? Britha wondered. *Is it because I would not take you to my people? I thought that was what you wanted. It was not shame that kept the secret; it was wanting a life in which I did not have to be the* ban draoi, *where I could be what's left of the child that was,* she thought but kept her peace.

'You must make them understand or they … you all will be less than slaves.'

Britha knew that there was more to this than simple survival. Even if they fled to another land where their weakness was not known, they would know. They would have murdered what they were. Life is not worth living crawling on your belly.

'What words do you have for me if we fight?'

'You cannot.'

'But if we do?' Now there was anger in Britha's voice.

Cliodna's face softened. It was the first time Britha had seen the woman she knew. 'The leader, Bress, but your weapons ... It is not easy to harm him, nearly impossible to kill him. To your people he may as well be a god.'

'Tell me how to kill him,' Britha said. Even in the darkness, even with how strange Cliodna had become to her, Britha could see the other woman's sadness.

She had not realised that their voices had stopped being whispers some time ago. Britha had time to look up. Her confused mind thought for a moment he was flying. After all, no man in that much armour and carrying a shield would jump off a twenty-foot cliff.

Cliodna disappeared as two casting spears hit the water where she had been moments before.

Britha just had time to roll to the side as the sentry landed where she had been crouched by the water. He kicked her in the side and sent her flying into the rocks. Ignoring the pain, she reached for her sickle as he drew his sword.

Without a spear or Nechtan or Talorcan to help, she did not see this fight going well. The sentry advanced on her, in the moonlight and shadows, his blade already looking red.

Cliodna exploded out of the water, wrapping herself around the man, a spitting, hissing frenzy. Off balance, he toppled into the sea. There was thrashing, then it went still. Britha could see dark clouds in the water. Sickle at the ready, she leaned forward.

Cliodna exploded out of the water again, grabbing Britha around the neck. She was covered in blood, her expression feral, the skin somehow swept back around her mouth. Britha saw the rows of needle-like, red-stained teeth and smelled the meat on her breath.

'You want to die? The weapon you want to kill Bress with, bathe it in your blood.' And she was gone. Again.

6
Now

It took fourteen hours to hitch from London to Portsmouth. Beth had taken the train into King's Cross and been delayed there by some kind of nearby terrorist incident. She had decided to hitch to save some of the small amount of money her dad had given her.

A bored lorry driver picked her up. She struggled to keep up her end of the deal, providing enough conversation to keep him awake. It had looked so close on the map. She could not understand why it was taking so long. They got there in the early hours of the morning. Came in on the M275, drove onto Portsea Island past the rusting hulks of dead submarines and other military-looking vehicles.

The lorry driver was taking a load over to the continent and dropped her close to the ferry port. On the other side of the road was a high wall of grey concrete council flats. They reminded her of the prison she had just left. She turned and trudged towards the town centre, following the signs. Nothing moved. The town seemed as dead as the rusting hulks she had seen on the way in.

It was Hamad. Control had seeded the rats. There were too many eyes in the city. You were never more than two metres away from a grass. They had uploaded the images into his head and du Bois had got to see his old adversary, a man he once wished he had had the courage to call a friend, staggering through the more picturesque of London's Roman sewers.

He thought back to when he had first met the Syrian Nizari. Du Bois laughed at his own naivety back then. He had actually been looking for the grail, fool that he was. He wanted to heal his sister's mind. Hamad had been looking for the milk of Innana. Both of them had been wrong. Hamad had been closer to the truth.

The Hamad he had known had been calm, even tranquil; the Hamad he saw through a rodent's eye looked mad. Du Bois wondered if the madness was guilt over his crime or something else, something ancient and corrupted whispering horrific truths into his godsware.

Du Bois now knew where Hamad was going. It made sense. He could hide there; after all, Hawksmoor had been a rogue and a turncoat before du Bois himself had caught up with him and put a stop to his geometry of violence, ironically with violence. This was after the architect had faked his death and been reborn. He hated the churches; each one was a death trap that knew him.

Beth awoke to judgemental glares from people waiting at the bus stop. She was achy and tired. You never got much sleep on the street; you had to be aware at some level in case someone tried to do something to you. She ignored the glares and the suggestions that she find a job and rolled up her sleeping bag.

She didn't feel much cleaner after a trip to the toilets in a fast-food place, but it would have to do. A little bit more of her preciously dwindling money brought her a map and she found the address. Pretoria Road down in Southsea.

The walk gave her time to think about how much she was not looking forward to seeing Talia. The anger she thought would have died down after years inside came back stronger than ever, and she saw her sister's face crumpling under her fist. She tried to suppress the anger. She could not let her temper go like that again. Lose control and she would be straight back inside. All those years of model behaviour would be worthless. She was not institutionalised, she thought fiercely. It did not matter how shit it was outside, she did not want to go back.

It was unlikely that Talia would want to leave whatever she was mixed up in and return to her dying father and a very still house. Beth did not even really know what she was doing. Maybe she could get Talia to write a letter pretending to care.

Du Bois did not so much park the Range Rover as just abandon it on the side of the road. He checked the accursed .45. He still had the magazine with the special loads in place. He chambered a round and then slid the weapon back into the hip holster, safety off. He hoped it would be enough, he did not fancy taking heavier artillery into a London church.

He glanced up at the pyramid spire, a reconstruction of the Tomb of Mausolus at Halicarnassus and nothing at all to do with Christianity. The statuary – St George, the lion, the unicorn – all made him nervous. Still, at least it was not Spitalfields. He still saw the stream of blood pouring down the red-painted church when he slept sometimes. Even after he had tried to edit his memories.

How decadent Christianity has become, he thought as he headed up the stairs past the bacchanalian porticoes and pushed the door open. When it closed behind him he knew that it did not just lock, it sealed itself shut. The spite with which the tendrils of his blood-screen reaching out towards the building had been destroyed was amplified in the church itself. This building fundamentally did not like him. He wondered if the vicar, staff and any unfortunate visitors were already dead.

The .45 held in a two-handed grip, Du Bois advanced slowly, checking all around. The white of the Portland limestone seemed to jar with his presence here. Even if he had not understood the significance of the architecture he would have been able to see why people connected this with a pale reflection of heaven.

Above the pulpit he saw the hilt of a black dagger rammed into one of the supporting pillars. Du Bois recognised the weapon. He was surprised and more than a little worried that even now the Brass City would let Nightmare out. The dagger was said to be far beyond insane. He did not like the violence it had done to the church either.

'Old friend?' Even with his screen being eaten, there were few people who could hide from du Bois. He spun towards the voice. Hamad had emerged from the nave and was leaning heavily against one of the pillars. He held the curved white-bladed dagger in his right hand. Gentle Sleep was a much more reasonable piece of ancient insanity to be let out, du Bois thought.

Hamad looked awful. Haggard, haunted, fatigue written painfully across his face in a way that should have been impossible for someone augmented like he was. His suit was soiled and stank from his trip through the sewers. His headscarf was long gone and the slits of his extra eyes were plainly visible on his forehead.

'Hamad,' du Bois said carefully. He tried to forget about the magnitude of Hamad's crime but could not. The hopelessness, the destruction of more than two millennia of planning all washed over him. He could not even muster anger; he just wanted to sit down. It had all been too long. 'Clever coming here where we cannot track you.'

'I just wanted to be closer to God.'

Du Bois smiled despite himself.

'Even though you know there is no God?'

'I think that there is. I just don't think it is what we want it to be.' Du Bois said nothing. 'Are you going to shoot me or ask me why?' Hamad said when the silence became too much. Du Bois swallowed.

He had not had time to really think about it. 'Last I heard you were tracking down looted Sumerian artefacts in Iraq.'

Du Bois just stared at the Syrian. 'Why doesn't really cover it, does it?' he finally said.

'All things have a time.'

'Humanity would have survived,' du Bois said, unable to master the anger in his voice. Hamad started shaking his head before du Bois had finished.

'No, not humanity, a perversion. Is it so bad to stay with the rest of us?'

'So spite then. You cannot go so nobody will? You couldn't even leave one bridge, even the cloning information, so something of humanity could live?'

'It wouldn't be living; it would be slavery and hell. The powerful people who out of selfishness made decisions that messed things up down here would have gained even more, perhaps total control. We will not allow you to remake humanity in their ... in your image.'

'Decisions always go to the powerful – that's just the way of things,' du Bois told the Syrian. He saw the guilt dissolve on Hamad's features and for the first time anger appear.

'No! That is an excuse. That was not what the Circle was set up for. The best minds working for the same purpose, and when their time had come they could be uploaded, so you could take them with you, the real treasure of humanity, and do you know what your powerful men did? They erased half of those minds. People who had sacrificed everything for your grand plan destroyed, made nothing with a thought for what? For more storage space.'

Du Bois tried to make his features impassive but the accusation felt like a blow.

'You're lying,' he said. Hamad stared at him incredulously.

'At this late hour? Why would I?'

'Then you have been told a lie.'

'Is it more likely that you, the perfect servant, have been lied to or that I have been lied to?'

'So what now?'

'I will not be going with you.' It was said as matter of fact, calmly.

'The souls?'

'They are all gone. Burned in the fire.' Hamad was a good liar, but du Bois had a lot of help reading the tells of the bluff.

'Give me the souls, Hamad,' du Bois told him.

Hamad's face hardened. 'No.'

'What difference does it make? We're all fucking dead.' Hamad said nothing. 'What? You think the Brass City can protect them? And who will be the lords of your little utopia?' Hamad still didn't answer. 'Hypocrite!' du Bois spat. 'A virtual prison is still a prison.'

'It's another world,' Hamad said with the voice of a true believer. Du Bois knew this was not going to be solved with words.

'Give me the souls or I swear I will tear them out of your head,' he said evenly though he could not help but glance over at Nightmare sticking out of the limestone pillar. It was a matter hack, an ugly one at that. The ancient weapon was whispering its madness to the church. Or rather to the semi-conductor quantum dots that acted like programmable atoms in the smart matter that the limestone was impregnated with.

'The things that I have done this day, do you really think a threat will work?' Hamad asked, sounding genuinely aggrieved.

Du Bois barely had time to register what it looked like as it burst from the matter of the pillar. Part gargoyle, part image of a malign desert spirit, part disjointed, strangely angled alien other, and all madness. Nightmare's hilt stuck out of its head.

Hamad spun behind the pillar. Du Bois might have risked a shot but he couldn't afford to waste a round. He swung round, bringing the gun to bear on the smart-matter monstrosity. He had misjudged its speed. He was too slow.

Nano-fibre-reinforced armour and flesh hardened but not nearly quickly enough. The impact alone felt like it had fractured, if not splintered, ribs. Limestone claws tore open a huge gash in his chest and sent him flying through the air.

Du Bois landed twenty feet away, the air forced out of him, spine hardening to survive the fall. His impact destroyed a pew and sent him sliding into more. The limestone gargoyle galloped towards him on all fours, running through pews, vestigial wings flapping on its back.

Du Bois sat up, shut down the nerve endings that were trying to disable him and forced his body to work. He brought the .45 to bear and got off one shot. The gargoyle slapped the gun out of his hands, breaking them both. Du Bois rolled to one side just in time to avoid a punch that pulverised the floor beneath where he had been.

He rolled to his feet, realising he was going in the opposite direction from his pistol. His body was healing but slowly, his own systems having to fight the little nano-scale surprises that were inhibiting his own nanites every time the gargoyle hit him. He ran from it, trying to gain time. However, the gargoyle was not limited by human physiology. It barrelled into him with all the building's hatred for him.

Du Bois hit the wall and left a red smear on the white limestone as he slid down it.

As his systems were knitting the wounds caused by the impact back together, the gargoyle pounced, landing on du Bois's prostrate face-down body. It could have finished him then, but the ghost of hate that lived in it wanted him to suffer. It flipped him over.

Du Bois's features were repairing themselves. It looked like his face was being inflated. The tanto he had in his hand was forged from folded steel during the Sengoku period in Japan. Crafted by a master swordsmith, it was just about as fine a knife as you could find in the world. It would be of no use against the gargoyle. Du Bois used it to mutilate his rapidly healing left hand. As the gargoyle reached for him, he smeared his blood over its limestone flesh. *If you want to win you have to sacrifice*, he managed to think. He sent the signal to his blood.

The gargoyle's misshapen jaws opened wide in a soundless howl as it picked him up. The tanto fell from numb fingers as du Bois was bashed against the wall. Only just managing to stay conscious, he grabbed the small punch dagger disguised as a belt buckle. He rammed that into the gargoyle's stone flesh. The blade disintegrated into its constituent nanites, flooding the gargoyle's animated limestone. Acting with his own blood and the first bullet he had fired, they replicated like a matter virus. The gargoyle started to crumble, but its free hand swung back to tear open du Bois's skull. Somehow he managed to reach up and tear Nightmare out of the thing's head.

As soon as he touched the hilt of the weapon he heard its whispering as the ancient and corrupt AI nearly overwhelmed his neuralware. He dropped the evil old curved dagger as the gargoyle turned black and continued crumbling, dropping him in turn.

A moment's respite was just enough time for more healing. The white blade opened up his cheek. Immediately addled and blurry, he threw himself to the side, scrabbling for his tanto. He found the blade as his internal systems fought off the tiny ancient machines that offered sleep and a gentle, peaceful end.

On his feet, he managed to dodge more of Hamad's slashes. If the Nizari had had both blades he would be dead by now. He could not afford to get cut again. The nanites made by the assemblers in the hilt of the ancient weapons carried a lethal neural toxin. Anything more than a mild gash from either knife would overwhelm du Bois' own internal defences.

Hamad came at him with the blade, his fist, open-hand attacks and a series of short kicks, each strike calculated to be the most efficient, to cause the most damage. A fighting system perfected across centuries.

Du Bois moved sinuously, swaying, his hands and feet moving to be where they were least expected, blocking punches with raised legs, checking Hamad's blade with a hand to the wrist, slashing his leg open with the tanto when the Syrian tried to kick him, all the while the seductive urge to sleep becoming fainter as the alien nanites were hunted down and destroyed by his own defences.

Hamad was by far the better knife fighter, but mental fatigue had taken its toll. Du Bois never stopped moving, swaying, making debilitating finger strikes to his opponent's eyes, groin, nerve clusters using rapid whipping movements, all the while looking for an opportunity with the blade.

He found one. The incredibly sharp folded-steel blade sliced across Hamad's throat, opening it. Blood surged out. Hamad staggered away holding his neck. Du Bois backed off.

'You fight like one of them!' Hamad hissed when his throat had knitted itself back together enough for him to speak.

I should do, du Bois thought. *One of them taught me.*

Hamad saw what du Bois was slowly moving towards and charged. Du Bois threw himself back, grabbing the .45 from the floor. Blossoms of red appeared on Hamad's soiled suit as impact after impact slowed his charge. He staggered to a halt over du Bois. The bullets' nanite payloads were overwhelming Hamad's own systems. Du Bois was breathing hard. The slide on the .45 was back, the magazine empty. Smoke drifted from the barrel. It seemed quiet and still in the destroyed church.

'Would you do the right thing?' Hamad asked and then collapsed.

Du Bois crawled over to Hamad's body. He looked peaceful.

'Sorry, brother.' Du Bois drove the tanto into Hamad's head, prised off a piece of skull, cut open his own thumb and pressed it against the brain. Du Bois downloaded yottabytes of information just before ephemeral electronic Ifreet destroyed it.

Then he sat back and looked at his friend's cooling corpse. He could hear them if he concentrated. All the souls. He did not concentrate. He did not want to hear their voices.

Southsea seemed still, as if abandoned. It was a grey day. All the colour had been bleached out of the city as Beth made her way through terraced street after terraced street.

It wasn't until she turned onto Pretoria Road that she saw signs of life. About halfway down, it had been sealed off. The middle part of the street was encased in an opaque tent-like structure with some kind of airlock leading into it. Police vehicles and officers prevented people from getting close. There were other official-looking vehicles behind the police cordon and Beth saw people wearing NBC suits going in and out of the airlock.

Beth could not see a connection between this strange sight and her sister but somehow couldn't shake the feeling that Talia was involved. She headed down the street, head down, arms in the pocket of her leather jacket, trying to avoid drawing attention to herself. She did not have to go far before she realised that the address Billy had given her had to be in the tented area.

'Hey, what's going on there?' she asked a slow-moving cyclist being trailed by a scruffy mongrel dog. The guy braked the bike and shrugged.

'Don't know. At a guess it's some kind of terrorist thing. Maybe a germ bomb or one of those dirty bombs. Makes you think though. Be lucky if we don't all end up with cancer or a head growing out of our neck or something.'

He wittered on for a bit as she stared down the street at the tented area. Eventually he said goodbye and headed off. Beth was wondering what to do. The thought of her sister as a terrorist actually made her laugh.

'God is a prude.' The voice was all but a croak. Beth had to replay the words in her head until they made sense, or not as it turned out. Very little of what the bag lady actually looked like could be made out through the layers of clothes, the dirt and the tangled mess of hair. She was crouched beside a nearby garden wall. She could have been anything from thirty to ninety for all Beth knew, and she stank. Beth's initial reaction was to move away. What stopped her was the night she had just spent on the cold concrete.

'He can't stand nudity. Hawkings said that.' The bag lady pushed herself up on the long stick she was leaning on. Even with the stick she was still hunched over.

'Are you talking to me?' Beth asked. She genuinely wasn't sure. The answering dry chuckle sounded like twigs being snapped. The chuckle turned into a cough and the bag lady spat up something red or black that Beth did not want to think too much about.

'God abhors a naked singularity because that's when things stop making sense. Predictability breaks down. That's why the universe takes all its dirty little secrets and hides them in the centre of a black hole.'

The woman laughed to herself and began to shuffle away. Beth watched her go. She turned back to the tented area and found a policewoman watching her. She'd been there too long, she decided, and left. She wasn't sure where she was going.

By the time du Bois left the church it was his clothes rather than himself that were the worse for wear. His phone started ringing the moment he was on the street. In the distance he could hear sirens. They would be intercepted, he imagined, and a clean-up crew sent to the church.

Du Bois ignored the phone until he had changed his clothes in the back of the Range Rover.

'Report,' Control's voice said placidly as soon as he answered. As tersely as possible du Bois explained what had happened, including him taking the souls from Hamad's neuralware. Control asked pertinent questions and even remonstrated with him slightly for wasting resources when he requested a new punch dagger and a magazine of nanite-headed bullets.

'We have godsware that needs harvesting and two L-tech artefacts,' du Bois told Control. Nightmare had tried to hack his systems the moment he picked the evil weapon up. He had locked both weapons in a strongbox. 'Nightmare and Gentle Sleep, assemblers in the handle and AI aware. Nightmare's AI is badly corrupted; both will need containment.'

Control gave him a cache drop where he could pick up what he needed and leave the two artefacts. They would even cut the Marduk Implant, the two extra eyes, out of Hamad's head.

'What do you want done with the souls?' he finally asked.

At first there was silence.

'They are surplus to requirement and may already have been corrupted by the Brass City,' Control finally told him. The pause had meant some kind of consultation, du Bois knew. 'Erase them.'

Du Bois said nothing.

'Du Bois?'

'It's done,' he said.

Du Bois wasn't sure why he'd lied. He would have to find a way to hide them for the next neural systems audit if he wanted to keep them. He was not sure why he would even bother; after all, the Brass City had doomed them all.

'Du Bois, there has been an incursion in Portsmouth,' Control said. Du Bois started the Range Rover's engine as Control downloaded co-ordinates into the vehicle's satnav. He glanced at them before pulling out into traffic.

'Is this the beginning?' he asked.

'No, the evidence points to this being something else.'

As he drove, du Bois edited his memory. Just a tiny bit. He made himself think that he had erased the souls as per his instructions from Control. He was ravenously hungry.

7

A Long Time After the Loss

Scab hugged the cocoon like a lover as he watched Eldon Sloper get torn apart. The crew of the *Black Swan* had played their part. The *Basilisk*, Scab's ship, had tapped into the *Swan*'s sensor data. The suggestion he had implanted when he had meat-hacked them had sent them on board despite the stupidity of such a move, and they had provided a distraction. Now there was a race on to see if they were going to be vented into Red Space or torn apart by the Seeder-augmented human throwbacks.

When they had given him the viral they had described it as some kind of song. The Scorpion, an ancient and very illegal piece of S-tech, had drunk it like it was milk. Scab had felt the weapon's excitement as it dug its legs deep into his arms, making them bleed again. He'd had to reseal the wound before anything too toxic had leaked out of him. As the scorpion had fed the poison into the Seeder ship he had shared the weapon's near-sexual pleasure at the murder. *After all, it wasn't every day you got to kill a genuine alien as opposed to just another fucking uplifted animal,* Scab thought, unable to prevent his lips curving into a smile. Scab wished he were naked. Pleased that the only people who could possibly see this were his soon-to-be-dead dupes.

Scab had absently wondered how old the song the Scorpion was singing to the Seeder craft was. Had humanity's lost sun even been born then? The first stage of the viral song the Scorpion had sung had got him in. It had felt like being pushed back in after being born. Or so he imagined. The second stage had started killing the ancient creature/craft. The third stage had delivered the message to sever the craft's hold on the cocoon as high above him preset explosives fed on the matter of flesh, turning it into fire and force.

There was pain as the Scorpion sank into the flesh of his arm. He was more aware of than actually felt it scraping against bone as it wrapped itself around his radius and ulna.

More pain when he heard the Seeder spawn's death scream in his head as he was pulled into vacuum. Scab felt blood trickle from his ears. It all but exploded from his nose, covering the visor of his suit as he rode the cocoon out into a Red Space strobing in violent light.

'Well shit,' was all that Vic could muster. The eight-foot-tall insect was extensively hard-tech-augmented, initially for work in gravity and then after a stint in the military for combat as well. He looked through the transparent smart-matter hull as he searched through his neunonics for accounts of combat in Red Space. Very few people did it. It always ended badly. 'Well shit,' Vic tried again, speaking out loud to nobody. He then followed that up with 'Fuck.'

He was receiving more information on the full-scale space action from the ship's sensor suite. Both cruisers were ponderous but graceful as they simultaneously tried to use the Seeder craft for cover while manoeuvring for a clear shot on the other.

Laser batteries fired so rapidly that they looked like arcing curves against the black, their beams lighting up energy dissipation matrices like neon. Battery after battery connected the two ships with lines of bright light. Various kinetic harpoons hit armour so hard they heated it white-hot as the reactive plate exploded out, trying to lessen the force of the impacts. Carbon reservoirs fed the assemblers with the raw material to regrow and replace the reactive armour. Broad-pattern DNA hacker beams lit up disruptive countermeasure screens. AG-driven autonomous suicide munitions hunted for each other and openings to the enemy ship. Meanwhile, both craft tried to bring their big guns to bear: the Church cruiser's D-guns, the Consortium cruiser's fusion and particle-beam cannons.

While in the Thunder Squads, Vic had personally carried enough ordnance to severely damage cities and with his team had done so on various conflict resolution worlds; this, however, was on a different scale. Outside everything was fire and force. Night turned to day.

The ship's upgraded stealth systems would keep the *Basilisk* hidden while this mess was going on. However, when one side won they wouldn't be hiding from a beaten-up old salvage tug like the *Black Swan*. Red Space or no Red Space, Vic doubted that *Basilisk*'s systems could hide them from military-grade scanners.

Vic nodded to himself. 'Well shit,' he said again. Yes, Scab had properly fucked them this time. Then he saw part of the Seeder craft's hull burst. *Basilisk* was kind enough to zoom in on the area and pick up the bodies tumbling into Red Space. Vic was peripherally aware of a tiny white light coming from the *Black Swan* moments before the Seeder craft exploded. Actually, Vic thought with a sort of hysterical calmness, it was less like an explosion, more like it had just burst. Vic completely reset his initial estimation of just how much Scab had fucked them both this time. There wasn't enough meat left in his brain to hear the Seeder ship's death scream. Still, Vic thought, the intensity of the fight between the Church and the Consortium cruisers had slackened off considerably.

Vic let off the pheromone equivalent of a human shitting himself when Fallen Angel tore through space. He wasn't sure if the enormous wingspan of the hermaphroditic figure armoured in liquid obsidian was some sort of hologram or shadowy exotic material. Fallen Angel was shorter than Vic, though not by much, but its wings seemed to cast a shadow over both the cruisers.

The Elite were the ultimate expression of armed force. Extensively augmented, each was armed with fully integrated S-tech weapons of near-unimaginable sophistication that allowed them to go toe to toe with entire fleets. There were only six of them in existence at any one time. In part this was because of the tremendous expense of keeping them operational. And in part it was due to the worry of what would happen if one of them ever broke its extensive conditioning and turned against its master. Three Elite served the Consortium and three served the Monarchist systems, and an uneasy balance was maintained. Fallen Angel served the Monarchists. Mostly the Elite acted domestically. For the Monarchists to break the uneasy cold war and utilise one of their Elite against Consortium interests like this was all but a declaration of war.

They couldn't hide from the Elite, Vic knew. If bounty killers were celebrities then the Elite were celebrity killer gods. It wasn't a case of sophisticated sensors. They understood their surroundings on an instinctive level as if they were somehow connected to the very fabric of time/space itself. Vic suddenly found himself envying the human ability to weep. He wanted to weep like the little hairless monkey infants wept. Underneath the panic, the combat veteran of more than a dozen CR worlds and hardened bounty killer had just enough presence of mind through the fog of rapidly administered calming drugs to feel awe, as once again Scab reset the bar on just what a total fucking shit-magnet he was.

Tumbling into a storm of fire and light, at first Scab thought he was seriously ill as a foreign sensation flooded through him. He had forgotten what joy was. Then he saw Fallen Angel. They had actually sent an Elite. He wondered if this would be a good enough death.

The fire from both craft had severely lessened after Scab had blasphemously murdered the Seeder spawn, but now both were trying to fire on Fallen Angel. The exotic, some said dark, matter of the Elite's armour phased the kinetic shots that hit it. An entanglement effect transported the solid-state munitions elsewhere. Lasers hit the armour creating a prismatic effect as the beams of killing light were redirected away from the Elite and back at the two cruisers.

Longing drowned Scab's joy. Once the Elite's power had been his; now he was nothing more than a spectator, soon to be like every other piece of biological waste in Known Space, a victim.

He watched enviously as Fallen Angel lifted its weapon to its shoulder. The smart matter of the spear it held reconfigured into a wide-barrelled rifle/cannon weapon. Scab knew that all the weapon really was, was a conduit for an entanglement effect connecting it to munitions in the Citadel, their hidden base, and also, like the rest of the armour, to the vast network of primordial black holes that powered the Elite's armour and weapons.

Scab's neunonics chose to interpret the focused particle beam from Fallen Angel's weapon as a thick line of blue light. Fallen Angel played it across the Consortium's Free Trade Enforcer-class cruiser. The beam disrupted the craft at its molecular level – disassembling it, changing the signal, sometimes removing molecules, sometimes agitating molecules into an explosive reaction. The result was the craft started to come apart. To Scab it was a slow, ponderous yet strangely beautiful death as the ruptured craft spilt crew out into the swirling clouds of Red Space.

Fallen Angel continued to cut at the hull a long time after it needed to. Scab could identify with that. It wasn't so much that they wanted to kill by the time they were chosen, though most of them did. He had. But once you merged with the armour you felt its need to destroy life. Scab had always been told they were weapons that understood their own nature rather than being just tools for killing. Their ancient creators apparently hadn't been hypocrites. Fallen Angel was painting with the particle beam. Scab remembered what it was to hate life and crave destruction, to be one with a poisoned and violent technology.

Scab was remaining very still. Trying not to be noticed. Wondering how best to get the cocoon back to the *Basilisk*. Then he noticed that the Church cruiser had stopped firing as well. Augmented soft-machine biotech eyes searched space. He only saw the disruption in the Red Space clouds because he knew what to look for. Surprise was another emotion he was unused to.

The CR worlds were a game, nothing more, R & D, a way of keeping score and training executives or minor nobility. When it was serious, when the outcome actually mattered, the Elite were sent. One being sent was rare. The number of times that two were sent in the entire history of Known Space since the Loss could be counted on one hand, even if you were a lizard.

The Monarchists had sent a second Elite. He saw it through the butterfly-wing shape of its disruption of the Red Space clouds. It was squat, roughly cylindrical with various strange technological components attached to its external body, and covered in the same liquid obsidian-looking armour that all the Elite merged with. Ludwig was the only automaton Elite. Ludwig was a supposedly ancient S-tech automaton that had continually upgraded itself from scavenged tech as it had drifted through Real Space. It had been a 'found weapon' during the Art Wars in the Monarchist systems.

Ludwig was heading towards the Church cruiser.

Scab glanced back at Fallen Angel. It had become bored with the particle beam. Fallen Angel's wings were a manifestation of its coffin. The coffin acted as a personal satellite, a slaved extension of the Elite's weapon systems. The morphic nature of the exotic material the coffin was made from could also turn it into what was basically a tiny one-man ship. Fallen Angel had made its wings very sharp and was dancing among the remains of the Free Trade Enforcer-class cruiser. Using its wings to slice through wreckage as it went.

Scab turned back but Ludwig had gone.

They had mostly stopped firing. Ludwig was barely aware of taking hits from automatic close-in weapon systems as it drifted close to the Church cruiser. The ancient machine mind shifted out of phase, vibrating its molecular structure to become intangible. It felt the resistance of some of the cruiser's defensive screens but combat was a bidding war and more resources had gone into Ludwig's creation and augmentation than had gone into the cruiser.

Many options on how to destroy it presented themselves to Ludwig. It was not about the most efficient way of dealing with the cruiser; it was about relieving countless millennia of boredom.

Ludwig dropped into the areas of smart matter in the hull. It became solid again and infected the smart matter with itself. Effectively becoming a material virus.

Most of the crew who weren't extensively hard tech-enhanced were still reeling. Their knowledge and stranglehold on S-tech aside, they had not expected to hear the scream of the dying S-tech craft in their head. Bloody tears leaking from their eyes blinded many. Blood seeped out of their ears and noses.

Ludwig made the cruiser's smart matter grow organically, like a tree, if a tree was made of spikes and edges. The smart matter grew through the heavy cruiser, impaling, rending, seeking out soft flesh and lifting it up into its branches, turning the very ship itself on its crew. Through his new viral smart matter branches, Ludwig got to taste the crew.

When Ludwig rose through the dormant Church cruiser's hull, the liquid-like coating of his armour bubbled with the crew's screaming faces.

Vic was sitting on one of the so-called smart chairs in the minimalist lounge that doubled as the *Basilisk*'s Command and Control, though most of the ship's systems were handled neunonically. After a brief interface squabble with the chair to get it into an even vaguely comfortable shape, Vic was now just waiting for death, his head cradled in his upper pair of arms. He hoped the Elite would make it quick.

Vic was still receiving the external feed into his neunonics. Without using active scans it had taken him a while to find Scab clinging to the package they had apparently been paid a lot to retrieve.

Vic glanced up to the ship's hull and sent the signal to magnify that piece of space. For a moment there was just a spark of hope. Perhaps Fallen Angel would kill Scab but ignore him, Vic thought. Maybe, just maybe he would be free of his insane 'partner'. After all, he was small fry – he didn't matter in the big scheme of things. On the other hand, if Scab was any indication of how the Elite thought – and this was after the neuro-surgical spaying he had relieved upon leaving the Elite – then who was to say what they would do?

Scab stared into the featureless black glass face of Fallen Angel and saw himself reflected. The Elite hung there motionless in front of him. Subjectively below him was the corpse of the Seeder ship. Above him the dead Church cruiser was slowly mutating into another form; the Consortium cruiser was now little more than a field of debris.

For some reason Scab saw sadness in the Elite. Almost like a child's. He wondered if it was because Fallen Angel hadn't been the one to kill the Seeder craft. He also wondered if this death – anonymous, body never found – would be enough.

As Fallen Angel reached to take the cocoon, Scab decided it wouldn't be a good enough death. His employer would have no reason to fulfil his part of the deal. Fighting Fallen Angel would have been foolish, nothing more than an empty gesture, still it galled Scab to just hand the cocoon over. It was the feeling of powerlessness.

With a flap of his wings, an affectation, Fallen Angel propelled himself back from Scab and then soared up towards the Church ship. Suddenly, in a series of jerky moves that somehow looked panicked to Scab, Fallen Angel wrapped his massive wings around himself and they morphed into a rectangular shape that looked like a mixture between a coffin and an arrowhead. Both Fallen Angel and Ludwig disappeared into the clouds.

Scab glanced down as what had looked like a tumbling piece of inert wreckage lit up. The *Black Swan*'s main engines took it quickly away from the hulk of the dead Seeder craft. The tug's bridge drive, that Scab had paid for out of this job's expenses, tore a blue pulsing hole in space as the oversized engines propelled it through the rip into Known S pace.

'Vic, come and pick me up,' Scab said as he re-established the interface connection.

'What the fuck!' Vic screamed at him. 'What the fuck!'

Scab was still wondering if something had startled the Elites when it happened. The holes that appeared subjectively above him didn't so much look like gate rips, more like larvae eating through rotting fruit. More holes opened in space; white lightning seemed to spark and then flicker out as if consumed. The energy involved must have been colossal, Scab thought. More and more holes appeared until Red Space began to resemble a rotten honeycomb.

The things crawling through the gates, dissipating the clouds they touched, were not black. They were the absence of colour – wriggling, hungry, maggot-like voids. Where they touched the debris of the two cruisers, the wreckage simply ceased to exist as if it had been consumed. It was beautiful, Scab thought, utter oblivion. Not just the antithesis of life but the antithesis of everything. Scab could hear their idiot song. An acidic tear traced its way down through the pale make-up, mucus and blood on his face. Then the sleek wedge of the *Basilisk* was in front of him.

'What the fuck!' Vic screamed at him hysterically when Scab was back on board. The tall hard-tech-augmented 'sect was pointing at the external display that took up one wall of the hull. Red Space was still being consumed.

With a thought Scab sent co-ordinates to the ship. The ship's engines lit up as the view changed and the ship headed towards the co-ordinates. Outside, red was becoming black, or rather the absence of colour. If you focused hard enough you could see it wriggling like all-consuming bacteria.

Scab sent the ship into a series of rapid evasive manoeuvres to avoid being consumed, though the ship's anti-gravity field compensated for this and both he and Vic remained comfortably standing.

Scab sat down on one of the two smart chairs, the only real furniture in the otherwise bare room. With a thought he peeled the arm of his spacesuit back. His arm hung limp. The Scorpion had reacted badly to something and squeezed, powdering his radius and ulna.

Vic was watching the screen on the edge of collapse as the *Basilisk* spun and banked, narrowly avoiding consumption or ceasing to exist or whatever was happening out there.

Scab coaxed the Scorpion out of his flesh, grimacing at the pain he allowed himself to feel. The lockbox rose through the carpeted floor at his neunonic summons. The room was suddenly bathed in blue light from the gate rip. In the lockbox was some fluffy, core-world pet creature designed to appeal to spoilt, mid-echelon corporate children. The *Basilisk* had already injected the previously hibernating creature with the wake-up. It looked up at Scab with big soulful eyes. Scab was more interested in the neunonic feed of the very fabric of Red Space being consumed by whatever it/these were. Scab absently dropped the brass-skinned Scorpion in with the pet. The Scorpion immediately reared up, sting coming over its head, as Scab gave the signal to close the box.

Scab had time to light a cigarette with his left arm and they were through the rip.

In Real Space Nulty was dancing on the hull of the *Black Swan*. He'd made it! Somehow, among all that, he had cut the *Swan* free and remained unnoticed until he could get out of there. Sure, he had a long ride home, but the *Swan* was his now!

The modified Corsair-class ship swept out of the rip, its engines on high burn. To Nulty it looked predatory and violent. He couldn't even be bothered bringing the *Swan*'s paltry weapon systems online.

'Bollocks,' the engineer said.

Lasers lit up the darkness; the *Swan* briefly became light before its energy dissipation matrix was overloaded, but it was the kinetic javelins that did the damage. Penetrating the *Swan*'s hull, shredding it, scattering the remains, the vacuum cooling the heat from the friction of hypersonic impacts.

Nulty was still alive. He was damaged, missing limbs, but largely intact and spinning away from the wreckage.

'Bastard!' he screamed at the receding light of the *Basilisk*'s engines.

Scab took a long drag of his cigarette, savouring his retro vice.

'What the fuck!' Vic screamed at him again, spoiling his contemplative mood. 'The Consortium navy! The Church! And ... and the fucking Elite! And what was happening there – it was like space was being eaten or something?!' Vic paused for breath, for psychosomatic reasons Scab assumed. 'What have you got us into?!'

Scab gave the question some thought. 'It's exciting,' he finally said.

Vic stared at him with multifaceted eyes, his mandibles agape. Vic was a humanophile, a worker 'sect who had rejected the tightly regulated, genetically programmed, caste-based social structure of 'sect society and escaped into gravity, augmentation and, somewhat ironically to Scab's mind, military service. Scab's military service had been different. He hadn't volunteered. Before he had been chosen to be an Elite he had been Legion. Offered the choice between serving the Consortium in the CR worlds as one of its most expendable troops or execution for his crimes as a street sect leader on Cyst.

The mandibles-agape expression wasn't quite working for Vic, Scab decided. 'Besides,' he said as he started looking for the portable assembler, using the interface to send it his medical requirements and some more of his debt credits, 'how often do you get to see two Elite in action?'

Vic's mandibles clattered together tightly. 'Oh yes, that was a real treat for me,' he told his 'partner'.

He cast his mind back to one terrifying night in the Abyssal Reaches. The destruction of an entire habitat. Their officers had told them that the subsidiary they had been fighting had gone rogue. However, a rumour had spread that they had found Seeder ruins in the Reaches, the Consortium board had done the maths and it had simply proved cheaper to use an Elite to bring the conflict to a rapid conclusion. Vic had never quite worked up the nerve to ask if Scab had been the Elite that had killed all those people. Women, children, larvae, it hadn't mattered. Then he realised what Scab had just said.

'Two! What do you mean two?'

'Ludwig was there as well. What do you think took out the Church cruiser?'

Vic allowed more calming agent to mix with his neurochemistry.

'But we're out now, done, yes?' Vic asked when the chemicals had calmed him enough. The 'sect was more than a little worried about how Scab would answer. He knew that Scab was psychotic and more than a little self-destructive but you didn't go up against the Elite.

Scab finally nodded. 'We've lost the package and we don't have anything like the resources to retrieve it.' *Once*, he thought, *once I could have done it.*

8
Northern Britain, a Long Time Ago

Surely the body cannot lose this much blood and live? she thought. It had felt painful at first. Now it felt like getting close to sleep. She was weak and tired.

Britha lay naked on the ground among the undergrowth. The surrounding oaks reached above her to form a canopy that the sunlight filtered through. The sunlight had a green look to it. She had been lying there for a while. Night was best for blood magic. She had been drifting in and out of consciousness dreaming of the night. She had dreamed of stars and then what the night sky would look like if there were no stars.

Britha had dug a small pit and lined it with a skin she had waxed to make waterproof. She had placed a framework of trimmed branches above the pit and hung clay pots filled with various herbs that she burned for their fragrant smoke. Then she had opened her veins with the sickle and worked the flow, covering herself in her own blood. She had lain on the cold earth, her arms over the pit in which she had placed the sickle, blood dripping onto the iron blade.

There should be more, she had thought. Normally rituals had various parts to them – words, movements, ingredients each designed to focus the will on what she wanted to achieve. She concentrated on the death of the invaders, who were not more than five miles from where she lay.

When Britha had returned to Ardestie she had found the village in chaos. Many of Cruibne's guests had ridden back to their villages. Those who lived to the north, particularly on the coast or along major rivers, had returned with stories of destruction. There were a lot of very angry, grieving men and some women with swords and spears. Some felt that Cruibne was responsible and had lured them away from their homes; others pointed out that they paid tithes and swore oaths to Cruibne so that he and his *cateran* would protect them from such raids.

Talorcan and Nechtan had returned before her, Nechtan telling of the black curraghs on the sandbanks. Many had wanted to set off immediately to exact revenge. Britha had arrived as Feroth was trying to prevent them moving without a strategy. There was a lot of shouting, anger, posturing and very little getting done.

'Quiet!' she shouted. The cry silenced them. Cruibne's shaggy darkhaired head whipped round to see who was giving orders in his land, immediately relaxing when he saw Britha. 'I will not shout over you again,' she said quietly enough to make them strain to hear her. 'It is the Lochlannach. Demons from the ice and sea. They are hard to kill.'

'Iron will do for them,' shouted Feradach, one of the *cateran* and Nechtan's closest rival. 'My father always told me that iron will do for the fair folk.'

'It has to be cold wrought,' Brude, the smith and a *dryw* in his own right, said. He was a massive man who wore a moustache like those from the western isle, his bright orange hair tied into a ponytail, his right arm much larger than his left. 'There is not enough time.'

'Even with his head cut off he still fought—' Nechtan started.

'If you are too frightened ...' a warrior from one of the northern villages interrupted, his face still dirty from a hard ride, tear tracks streaking the dirt. Britha felt bad for the man but she silenced him with a look.

'Cold iron is not enough. They have fire and metal in their flesh,' she said. Brude looked more than a little disturbed at this. 'They have to be dismembered.' Talorcan and Nechtan nodded in agreement.

'Feroth?' Cruibne asked. The tough wiry old man looked thoughtful.

'We know the terrain and the sandbanks are flat; our people know the ways of them.' There were smiles as people caught on to what he was suggesting. The tear-streaked northern warrior looked confused. 'How do we fight when the northern tribes are stupid enough to fight us on our own ground?' Feroth asked the warrior. Britha watched understanding creep slowly across the man's face. 'We'll need to attack soon or they'll come for us.'

'What about the giants?' Talorcan asked. A number of people spat. They were looking to Britha now for an answer. She tried to remember everything they had taught her in the groves.

'We did not see them,' Britha replied.

'They'll be in the sea,' the hunter said with a surprising degree of certainty. Britha had to agree with him. The sea was the Lochlannach's home.

'Grapples, like you would use to pull down a wall,' said Britha.

There was nodding from some of warriors assembled, doubt in the eyes of others. 'You'll need to work together, bring them to the ground. This is not a fight for glory. There will be no glory if we do not live past this. We either fight together or we die. No songs will be sung of this, and any who seek glory over their duty to the people I promise you now, I will lay a satire on them that will curse their lines down to their grandchildren's grandchildren.' There were mutterings and a few of the braver spat to show their unhappiness.

'Is that all you can advise?' Drust, the *mormaer* of the Fotlaig asked, sounding less than convinced.

'These are creatures of water and ice,' Britha told them. 'We must take everything that can burn – oil ...' There were groans. Oil was expensive. The best had to be traded for with southron merchants from across the sea. '*Uisge beatha* ...'

'You're not burning good *uisge beatha*!' Cruibne cried.

'Shut up, you,' Ethne told him. 'It'll be done,' she told Britha.

All eyes turned to Cruibne. He was nodding.

'Gather the family,' he told them, meaning the *cateran*, the war-band.

When she awoke again she felt better. It was dark now but the cooler air didn't seem to bother her. Britha pushed herself up and looked into the small skin-lined pit. Her sickle was there. Perhaps it was the darkness or her mind playing tricks on her, but the blade looked darker.

All the blood was gone. She would have assumed that it had just soaked into the skin or leaked through into the earth except there was no staining whatsoever. She reached down to touch the skin. It was dry. She touched the sickle. It was dry as well. She picked it up and held it in front of her face. It felt different. Somehow easier to wield. Somehow more connected to her. Britha could not remember her magic ever being this strong before. At some level she knew that the sickle shared her purpose. They would see the entrails of this Bress.

She looked at the wounds in her wrist. They looked fresh but had healed over. Britha had to suppress the fear she felt, fear of herself.

It was an effort to put the sickle down, but she had other preparations to make. She had to make friends with the night and look into the Otherworld. She reached for the clay pot of woad dye.

Cruibne and Feroth had no idea she was there. That was good. Both men were standing just below the peak of a dune on the headland that overlooked the sandbanks. They were watching the Lochlannach camp, using patches of dry sharp grass as cover. Their hundred-and-fifty-strong warband was concealed among the dunes. The war dogs with them had rags wrapped around their maws to stop them from howling.

Of the warband about seventy were warriors, half from the Cirig's *cateran*, the other half from the Fotlaig and the Fortrenn. The rest were landsmen and women, spear-carriers. Those too old to fight and the children had gone to the broch on the Hill of Deer. There the youngest of the old and the oldest of the young would stand guard.

Cruibne and Feroth were wearing stiff leather jerkins with overlapping scales of iron sewn into them.

'Nervous?' Britha asked, meaning the armour. Both the older men visibly jumped; Cruibne reached for his spear.

'Woman! Don't you know that sneaking up on a warrior like that will get you killed?' the *mormaer* demanded in a hissing whisper when he finally recognised her. Britha was naked and covered head to foot in woad the blue of midnight. In shadow she became part of the night itself. The woad was working its mysteries on her. The air seemed alive all around; she could see further; her hearing was sharper; she could smell the sweat and the metal and the meat from the fire of their enemies.

'Or the warrior will get killed,' Feroth whispered, smiling.

'Aye, when my heart bursts. My wife asked me if I was nervous as well.'

'You should have told her you were too fat to fight dressed only in woad. There are enough sickening sights in battle as it is,' Feroth suggested. Britha grinned, white teeth in a midnight-blue face, but she knew this talk was a sign of nerves.

'What are you talking about? I'm a fine figure of a man. For my age.'

'You're a fine figure of a man for a boar,' Britha suggested.

'There's still time for one last rite,' Cruibne suggested, winking. Britha sighed.

'Leave the poor woman alone, man,' Feroth said. 'He's in armour because he's the *mormaer*,' Feroth said seriously.

'I didn't want to,' Cruibne said. She largely believed him. Cruibne felt safer wearing armour but would rather have fought clad in the sky like his warband.

'I'm wearing it because I'm frightened,' Feroth said in jest. But Britha knew he was armoured because he needed to focus on directing the battle. He was also frightened, but for his people, and he would master that fear.

'Nechtan's wearing armour,' Cruibne told her.

Britha cursed under her breath. The fight in the fishing village must have shaken him more than she thought. It was not good for the champion to show fear. Even if she went to him now and shamed him into fighting skyclad, the fear would have already done its damage among the warband.

'They follow gods. They are slaves. Nothing more,' she told them. The two men regarded the much younger blue-painted woman trying to reassure them. Feroth glanced at the sickle she held in her right hand. *It would go ill for someone tonight if they fell under that blade*, he thought.

'Aye,' Cruibne said, 'but there's a lot of slaves.'

'Will you not fight with us?' Feroth asked Britha. 'It would do the warband good to hear you, see you.'

Where you can watch over me, Britha thought to herself.

'I'll harvest this Bress's head,' she told them.

'Bring me his cock and balls so he can have no more children to plague us,' Cruibne muttered.

'He won't be able to father children if we have his head,' Feroth pointed out.

'That's not what I've heard,' Cruibne said. Britha thought back to the fishing village. He was right. They would not want to harvest these heads.

It was a long crawl but the living night kept her company. She heard insects crawl with her across the sand. Listened to owls and bats hunting in the woods. She saw a seal breach out in the distant dark sea and thought of Cliodna. Ghost light traced patterns in the darkness, showing her hints of the Otherworld just out of sight. All of which she could have embraced had it not been for the smell of people living in their own filth and the sounds of whimpering that came from the black-hulled curraghs.

She slithered past charioteers lying flat on their stomachs as they crawled across the sandbank removing stones. They nodded to her but she continued on towards the flickering flames, the dark hulls of the ships and the eerily quiet and still shadows of the people around the campfire.

The spearman was standing just across a shallow channel, a run-off from the burn that ran down towards the sea. Britha was lying in shadow as close as she dared. In the groves they had taught her that it was movement that gave you away. She was waiting for the spear-man to move, but he had remained still for a very long time. Britha was worried that if she didn't move soon the attack would start before she could do anything.

She tried to study the spearman, get an idea of him, but his features were shadowed and he just looked like a normal man. His weapons and armour seemed of high quality but it was difficult to tell in this light. *Why are you doing this?* she wondered.

Caught up in her wonderings, it took a moment to register that he had turned to look at a sound behind him. Crouched low, Britha was across the channel, sickle in one hand. Hearing her or just sensing the movement, the man started to turn.

Britha leaped onto his back, wrapping her legs around him, relax-ing her weight, overbalancing him, making him fall to the sand on top of her. Her hand covered his mouth. He immediately bit, and she felt his teeth against the bones of her hand. It was all she could do not to scream. Turn the pain to anger. Turn the anger to viciousness. With her free hand she arced the sickle towards his stomach. The curved bronze blade went through his chainmail and into his stomach as if it was hungry. The man didn't scream, but as she tore the sickle up towards his chest cavity he bucked violently on the sand. Thousands of strands of what looked like living red-gold filigree whipped around the wound she was making. With her legs clasped around him, muscles screaming from the exertion, she somehow managed to keep hold of him. His struggles lessening, the strands seemingly started to die. She saw the tiny insectile fires in his flesh fade. She felt his death in her core, in her cunt, feeling the pleasure from the blade in her hand, wanting more.

The spearman lay still. Britha took time to smear herself with some of his blood. Then the shaking started.

She hid between the furrows made when the curraghs had been brought ashore and the black hide hulls of the craft themselves. She did not like it here. There was something wrong with the hulls. They seemed to move of their own accord. As if they were breathing or maybe trying to crawl back to the sea.

From inside the ships she smelled the rancid reek of frightened people forced to live in their own muck. She heard sobbing, whimper-ing and whispered prayers to uncaring, malevolent gods long forsaken by the Pecht. *That will not help you*, Britha thought. *Only strength can help you.*

From where she was half-buried in the sand she could see their fire. It was like a mockery of Cruibne's gathering of the tribes. They sat round the fire like Cruibne's guests had, five deep, but it was as if they were dead, all so still, all so quiet. To Britha's eye all their armour, shields and spears looked exactly the same. The men had identically vacant expressions on their faces. Despite herself, Britha felt fear rising in her like a tide. This was potent magic. Regardless of how strong she had become, she couldn't hope to fight this. The only thing that made her feel like she was still in the same world she had always lived in, and not ghost-walking, was the smell of the wood burning on the fire.

On the other side of the fire was what looked to be some kind of temporary hut made from sewn-together skins. Britha had never seen the like before. Through the opening in the skins, the interior of the hut looked very dark indeed.

He ... it – Britha wasn't sure – came stalking out of the tent. He looked very different to the others, a hulking squat brute, his hairless head shining in the moonlight. It was the head that was wrong, or in the wrong place. It was off to one side, almost growing out of his right shoulder, making him look grotesquely lopsided. He carried a heavy-looking axe with surprising ease.

Britha fought down the urge to bolt. It looked like he was making straight for her, but instead he climbed up into the curragh she was hiding next to. She felt it rock slightly, heard scrabbling, then screaming, then begging and a brief struggle.

A young man landed on his side, winded, in the sand worryingly close to her. Britha did not know him but recognised him for what he was by his dress. He wore the rough-spun *blaidth* and trews of a Pecht landsman. One of the Fidach, she reckoned.

She felt the impact through the sand as the lopsided axeman landed next to the landsman. Britha got a closer look at the deformed man. She didn't think she had ever seen anyone so heavily built. Corded muscle was layered on corded muscle. He wore a stained leather jerkin; a variety of knives hung from a belt. The blades looked stained as well.

Gasping for breath, the landsman tried to scrabble away from the axeman, who quickly caught him and started dragging him towards the fire. The man was screaming, begging to be let go. The axeman dragged him into a kneeling position by the fire. He was still begging. Britha watched, knowing that there was nothing she could do.

Britha watched as Bress – somehow she knew he was Bress – came out of the skin hut. He was tall and had nearly bent double to get through the slit in the animal hides. Bress was slender but there was undeniable power in his movements. He was the most attractive man Britha had ever seen, handsome to the point of effeminate beauty. He had smooth white skin, surprisingly delicate long-fingered hands and long pale-blond hair which was practically silver. It was only the eyes that spoilt the picture. They were grey, cold, devoid of emotion, almost devoid of life.

Britha stopped breathing for a moment. How could she make out the colour of his eyes in this light? She looked again. Even with only the flickering light from the flames playing over him, she could make out the colour of his eyes. Again she felt the fear rising. It was as if she was becoming someone else. Was one of the old gods looking through her eyes from their home in the sky of the Otherworld? Was she becoming their slave? Was she by demons ridden? Beneath Bress's skin she could see the fire that burned in his blood.

Britha forced herself to be calm, to focus on what she was doing, to look back at the beautiful Bress and gauge him as a victim. His boots and plaid trews were of the highest quality. The stiff leather armour looked like it had somehow been moulded to his body. There was a circlet of red gold around his head. Across his back he wore a massive sword that would take both hands to wield. Britha had heard Brude and the warriors in the *cateran* talk about such weapons in the past. Brude had always said that iron would bend too easily at that length and it would be too heavy to wield quickly enough in battle or single combat.

The malformed axeman looked at Bress. The tall man's nod was almost imperceptible. The axeman reached into the fire, his flesh blackening and blistering; sweat beaded his skin, teeth gritted, the pain written across his face. From the flame the axeman pulled a chalice of red gold. Inside the chalice was the same red metal heated to a molten state. The kneeling man was screaming and struggling, but the axeman held him with his other hand with ease. As Britha watched, the axeman's burned hand started to heal itself in front of her.

The axeman brought the chalice to the captive's mouth, who clamped it shut, but the molten metal surged out. The man screamed as it touched his face, and the metal crawled into his mouth, lighting it up through his skin. He dropped to the ground writhing and jerking. Britha watched the fire course through his body. Finally he lay still.

Britha had to force herself to look away. All attention was on the man who'd drunk from the chalice. Now was the time to move. She kept to the shadows. The night matched the blue of her skin as she willed herself to be nothing more than a shadow and moved as quickly as she could towards the skin hut. It was difficult to influence someone unseen and unknown but she kept her thoughts on Bress returning to the hut alone.

Britha waited. Her eyes adjusted much faster than she thought they would. But even before she could see, she knew that she was not alone. The skin hut did not feel empty. Her hearing, now seemingly more sensitive, like her other senses, picked up the sound of breathing. She smelled sweat on flesh, mixed with the scent of recently extinguished burning oil in braziers and some kind of incense. The smell of the sea, carried on the gentle night breeze, was the only reassuring scent.

Slowly she could pick detail out of the darkness. She saw the bent tree branches lashed together with leather to provide the framework for the hut. She saw the pallet with fresh ferns and a clean woollen blanket, the urns of wine and very little else.

They were asleep in the corner, piled on each other the way a dog or wolf pack sleeps. The way her people slept if they were caught out overnight during the winter months. It was difficult to make out what they were at once, to even recognise them as human, as children. They were hairless, pale, like they lived in the darkness. It took a moment to realise why. Their physiology was all wrong. These children were built like dogs. They looked like they could move at speed on all fours. Their finger- and toenails ended in sharp black claws. Their hands and feet were all red, marking them as creatures from the Otherworld.

One of them stirred as she watched. Yawned and opened his eyes. They were completely red. He looked straight at her and hissed. The others began to wake. Britha gripped her sickle but she had no stomach for this sickness. They began to move about, growling and hissing. She shrank back as one of them lunged at her. The thick chain around the creature's neck brought her up short. The other end of the chain must have been buried deep in the sand.

Britha backed into the corner of the hut, into the deepest shadow. The pack of children was going mad. All Britha could hope for was that the noise would draw Bress in.

It was the axeman who appeared first.

'Quiet!' he shouted in a language Britha was sure she didn't know but somehow understood all the same. His accent was similarly strange, his voice sounding like it was made for anger.

'Stranger,' one of the children said bestially, pointing into the corner. The fact that one of them had spoke just seemed to make it worse. The axeman turned towards her. Britha readied herself.

Bress ducked into the hut. The axeman was moving. For someone of such bulk he shifted with surprising speed. He was a blur as he grabbed two bronze blades from the front of his leather jerkin. Somehow she was moving faster. The point of her sickle headed straight towards Bress's head. Bress just seemed to reach out and casually catch her wrist.

'No,' he said quietly. The axeman's blade stopped against her skin. A drop of her blood ran down the surprisingly sharp bronze blade.

Britha knew she was going to die. It didn't matter. All that mattered was that she took Bress with her. She kicked out, connecting solidly with his leg. He shifted slightly but showed no other sign of even feeling the blow. She struck out at the axeman, who cursed and grabbed for her other arm.

Suddenly she was lifted high, Bress's fingers wrapped around her neck. She panicked. She could no longer taste the air. There was a sharp pain in her wrist and she felt the sickle tumble from her numb fingers. Bress pushed her down onto the pallet. She fought him, kicking, punching, scratching but never once screaming. His grip never faltered. Her nails drew red lines on his pale flesh, but the wounds quickly closed.

He loomed over her, holding her down, ignoring her attacks, staring down at her like he was confused, as if he was studying her. The pack was pulling at its chains in a frenzy as it tried to reach her to tear her apart. The axeman appeared at Bress's side. He was drooling.

'Let me hurt her,' he demanded. 'I'll wear her head and make her talk.'

'We're about to be attacked,' Bress said. Britha's heart sank even as she fought on. 'Take the pack outside, Ettin.'

'What?!'

'Now.' He said it quietly, but even over the sound of her struggles his authority was unmistakable. The axeman glared at him but grabbed the pack's chains, cuffed a few of the feistier ones hard and dragged them outside.

'If I let you go will you calm down so we can talk?' he asked calmly. Slowly Britha stopped fighting; finally she nodded. Bress relaxed his grip from around her throat. Britha dived for her sickle. Bress let her get her fingers round the grip and then kicked her so hard in the stomach that it lifted her off her feet and sent her flying across the hut. It wasn't the pain of the blow. It was the momentary sensation that she would never be able to breathe again that frightened her, but again she was surprised by how quickly she recovered.

Britha swung at him. He swayed backwards; the curved blade just missed. Britha tried to bring the sickle up into his groin. It was the closest she had got to an expression out of him. Bress stepped back quickly, brought his palm down to block the blow and then cried out, more in surprise than pain, when the sickle bit hungrily into him, the point appearing through the back of his hand. Britha kicked him with all her might. He staggered back crying out, this time in pain, as the movement tore the blade out of his hand. Britha swung at his head. Bress stepped to the side and punched her. She felt sick and the ground seemed to fall away from her as the force of the blow lifted her off her feet. Bress walked quickly over to where she had fallen. Britha was trying to get up. Something in her head felt broken. Her vision was blurry. Bress stood on her hand. He knelt down, warding off her blows, and tore the sickle from her grip. Examined it.

'Where did you get this?' he asked quietly, turning to look at her. The deadness of his eyes aside, his beauty and the intensity of his stare caused Britha suddenly to find herself struggling to breathe for all the wrong reasons. She didn't stop fighting, however. Bress flung the sickle into the corner of the hut and grabbed her around the neck, easily picking her up and laying her on the pallet again.

'You can't hurt me,' he told her. 'Talk to me, just talk to me.' His voice remained quiet and calm, but Britha thought she could hear just the slightest hint of pleading in his voice. She stopped fighting, but decided that if there was to be rape she would not make it easy for him.

'Let go of me. Now,' she demanded. Cursing herself for giving in.

'If you fight again I'll have to kill you.'

Britha nodded. Bress let go. Britha sat up, rubbing her throat.

'You're here to kill me.'

It wasn't a question so she didn't bother to answer.

'Why are you here? Why are you doing this to my people?'

'Does it matter? There's nothing you can do about it so you might as well resign yourself to it.'

'You know that won't happen.'

'I don't know anything. Your people will suffer more if they resist.'

'You didn't answer my question.'

'Because I must.'

'Why?'

'Because I am nothing: less than a ghost, a servant, a mercenary, serving a god I do not believe in.'

'Gods make slaves of people.'

Bress's laughter was devoid of humour.

'And people overestimate their importance in the scheme of things, but I cannot deny your words. What is your name?'

'Britha. They say you will bring madness on the land.'

Suddenly all trace of humour was gone.

'And who are "they"?'

'The spirits on the night wind, the dead who speak to me in my dreams,' she lied.

He stared at her suspiciously. Britha met his eyes. She didn't like how they made her feel, but that feeling subsided as she remembered the pack.

'What you've done here – despoiling, slaving – what you did to those children ...'

'Flesh is a tool, something to shape for the amusement of the gods.'

'Do you not know this is wrong? Evil!'

'Yes, I just don't care.' He wasn't looking at her now. He was looking out through the entrance to the skin hut into the night beyond.

Britha stared at him. He just sounded tired and horribly alone. Britha cursed herself for her weakness, remembered the pack and forced down any feeling of sympathy. He was a monster from the Otherworld.

'I have to kill you,' she said almost involuntarily. He nodded.

'Take your blade and go,' he told her quietly. Britha stared at him. 'Fight and die in the battle if you will, or run and live, but if you ever falter then never forget that I have done this to your people.' He turned to look at her with his dead eyes. It was all Britha could do not to flee. Bress stood up and walked out into the night air. Britha didn't move. Then the deep howl of the *carnyx*, the Cirig's dog-headed brass war horn, filled the night air.

The *carnyx* had sounded at the last moment. The warriors had been, like Britha, painted blue as the night, and had slowly made their way on their bellies across the sand as close as they dared. These were *cateran*, professional soldiers. The spear-carrying landsmen waited in the dunes still.

With a gesture rather than the sounding of the *carnyx*, Feroth had sent the chariots onto the beach, each wood and wicker cart pulled by two ponies straining at their harness at full gallop, driven by a kneeling charioteer. Trying to close with the enemy as quickly as they could before they were noticed.

To Cruibne, the familiar beach was a blur beneath him as he crouched on one knee. Gone were the days when he would stand in a chariot – he didn't feel so steady on his feet these days. He glanced to his right and saw Nechtan in his armour walking carefully out onto the yoke between the two horses – the chariot feat. The champion had his casting spears at the ready. Nechtan, like all the *cateran*, wore a wicker framework headdress designed to look like a dog's skull covered with dog hide. Still, it would have been better if he had gone to battle skyclad like the rest of the *cateran*. Nechtan was lost to view when the chariots drove into a narrow channel in a spray of water.

Cruibne reached down to grab the boards of the chariot as it bounced back onto the wet sand. Ahead he could see the spearmen lying down. They had previously agreed lanes for the chariots to drive through. Ethne, who was the only person he trusted as his charioteer, expertly controlled the horses through the prostrate spearmen. Cruibne heard a scream, the sound whipped away from him by the speed of the chariot: someone had not been as accurate. Ahead he watched as the enemy, seemingly unhurried, arranged themselves into a tightly linked shield wall. Cruibne kept his mouth open – he didn't want to break any teeth as the chariot bounced up and down – and shifted his grip on his casting spear. No shield wall ever stood against a chariot charge.

Behind him the dog-headed spearmen had got to their feet and were sprinting in behind the chariots. The *carnyx* sounded again and the spear-carrying landsmen poured out of the dunes and started their long run across the sand. The baying war dogs quickly outpaced them, the rags that had held their jaws closed had been removed.

As the cart bounced and juddered despite the smoothness of the sand, Cruibne watched as the wall of shields and spears got closer and closer. *They had to break. Everyone did.*

Britha heard the *carnyx* sound again. The attack. Her tribe were about to throw themselves against these creatures and she had not done what she had said she would.

Britha ducked out of the hut. She had a moment to see the back of the shield wall and hear the hoof beats echoing across the beach. The man she had seen drinking from the chalice of molten metal was standing behind the shield wall with a few others. They didn't have armour or spears but were carrying swords. They were for those who got through. Britha moved quickly towards him, not allowing herself to think that he was an innocent victim who had been forced into this by Bress's magic. Britha jumped at him and cleaved the sickle into his neck, driving it down into his chest cavity. She stared at the wound, wet and red, appalled. *How can I have the strength for that?* The sickle felt hungry in her hand. As the man juddered and sank to the ground, Britha noticed that his entire hand was covered in the red-gold filigree – it looked like it had grown out of the pommel of his sword. Then the chariots hit.

They weren't going to break. Ethne slewed the chariot to the side hard, showering the enemy shield wall in sand. Cruibne felt the cart start to turn over and held on for dear life, but Ethne was better than that, forcing the terrified ponies forward through the sand, their speed pulling the cart straight.

Others weren't so lucky. Some tried, like Ethne, to turn at the last moment but lost control, sending ponies, cart and passengers tumbling sideways into the shield wall. Others, their charioteers unable to believe that the shield wall hadn't run, ploughed straight into it in a screaming, tangled, tumbling collision of wood, metal, human and horseflesh.

Britha threw herself to one side as a chariot went tumbling past her in an explosion of sand. She pushed herself to her feet. A figure charged her. He slashed his sword down. She caught the blade in the curve of the sickle blade and swung the sword away from her. She brought the sickle back and into his stomach, driving the curved blade up into his chest cavity. He fell back; the sickle slid out red; the expression on his face didn't even change.

They were galloping along the enemy shield wall now. Cruibne struck out with his longspear again and again. The spear glanced off shields mostly but caught one of them in the head. Cruibne felt the impact in his arm as the spear haft snapped and the man was torn off his feet sideways, his neck broken, head gashed open, skull caved in.

Ahead of Cruibne, Nechtan stood on his yoke and threw casting spear after casting spear at the enemy shield wall. Shields were raised to block, but Nechtan caught more than one of the enemy warriors. A lucky shot took one of them in the face, sending him staggering back out of the line, but the gap was closed quickly by those on either side. At the end of the shield wall, following Nechtan's chariot, Ethne steered the ponies in a long circle to bring them back into the attack.

Britha watched one of the enemy spearmen stagger back, a casting spear embedded in the ruin of his face. He reached up, pulled the spear out and threw it away. *They had to call off the attack.* She had to find Bress and kill him. She reached down and took the sword from the dead man's hand. There was resistance – the red filigree had to be tugged out of his flesh and seemed to come to life. There was a moment of panic as she felt it start to dig into her flesh. She felt heat in her hand, wrist and then arm. Then she felt sick, like a strong fever. Her arm glowed with an inner light. She watched as the filigree on the cursed sword retracted into the blade's pommel. The feeling of heat and sickness passed.

Sword in one hand, sickle in the other, she started towards the back of the shield wall. She glanced down the line and saw Ettin with the pack straining at its chains. He looked back towards her. Even over the distance she could feel the intensity of his stare, the hatred. Then she heard a crashing sound. The pieces of metal in the hollow brass sphere at the base of every one of the *cateran*'s spears were being rattled to frighten their foes. Britha couldn't see it working this time.

The war dogs, massive, powerfully built deerhounds, many wearing their own protective leather jerkins, many of them scarred veterans of other battles, were nearly at the Lochlannach line. Their job was to distract and disrupt the enemy shield wall, make them lower their shields just ahead of the attack of the spearmen. The shield wall took a step forward. Many of the dogs died on the ends of spears, or shields broke their leaps, sent them tumbling back into their own advancing men.

The spearmen hit the shield wall. Britha watched as the force of their charge pushed the enemy back, their feet digging into the sand. The *cateran* battered against the Lochlannach's shields, trying to force them up. Some *cateran* warriors went tumbling over the defenders' shields, their naked, painted and tattooed bodies dead moments after they hit the sand.

Britha ran towards the back of the shield wall but was intercepted by swordsmen. She felt her blood sing as she ducked and parried blows. The sickle and sword cut through armour as if it wasn't there and bit deep into flesh. She leaped and spun; she felt like she was dancing between her attackers. She had never fought like this. Never revelled in it like this. She wanted to see wounds. Feel hot blood on her skin, taste it.

The swordsmen dead, she went looking for Bress. He was pretty, she dimly remembered through her battle pleasure, but she wanted to see what his innards looked like. She thought they would be just as pretty.

The *cateran* had been flung back so hard, many of them had lost their footing and been speared. *Now it would be the grind of shield wall on shield wall*, Talorcan thought as he looked for a target. The advantage was with the Lochlannach with their large oval shields versus the Cirig's smaller square ones.

One of the enemy was looking the other way. Talorcan loosed the notched arrow. The man somehow seemed to know. He ducked down behind his shield and the arrow flew over his head. Talorcan cursed. *They were so fast.*

Ettin released the pack.

Sleek lithe shapes clambered up the backs of the Lochlannach and launched themselves at the *cateran*. They were so quick that Talorcan struggled to make them out. *Demons from the Otherworld*, his frightened mind thought. It was easier to think this than acknowledge how much they looked like children. They tore at *cateran* and war dog alike.

He watched as one of the red-eyed demons threw itself at Feradach. The warrior swung his shield at it, catching it in the head in mid-air with enough force to knock it to the ground. Feradach stepped forward and ran his longspear through the demon, pinning it to the sand, but the creature was still writhing, fighting, screaming. A wild blow snapped the haft of the spear and Talorcan watched in horror as Feradach staggered back screaming, the demon's hands redder now and dripping. There was a gaping wound where Feradach's manhood used to be.

There weren't many of the demons but enough of them to disrupt the *cateran* line. Talorcan glanced behind him. The landsmen were still too far away. As one, and without any order that Talorcan heard, the Lochlannach line moved forward. Spears thrust out. Pecht died. Spearheads embedded themselves in *cateran* shields. The Lochlannach stood on the hafts of the spears, forcing the shields down, and with frightening speed drew their swords and opened flesh. With each step more of the skyclad warriors died. To Talorcan their wounds looked worse than they should have been. Wide gaping red gashes and rips in his friends' flesh.

Talorcan was loosing arrow after arrow, but his targets didn't even seem to notice. It was when he watched one of them draw an arrow from his neck, toss it away and drive his spear through the head of a Fortrenn warrior that Talorcan knew that not only would they lose but they could not fight these people.

Talorcan dropped his bow and shrugged off the quiver. The small Pecht pulled his dog's head on, drew his knife and hatchet, then ran towards the fight.

They had circled the entire battle looking for a place to attack where they would not run over their own warriors. Now his chariot was in the lead. Cruibne glanced behind him to see Nechtan following.

Cruibne could see their leader, the tall one. Even from the juddering boards of the fast-moving chariot he looked exactly like the *mormaer* expected a warrior from the Otherworld to look. Cruibne had shouted at Ethne to head for him. His oldest, and if he was honest, favourite wife had not even acknowledged him – she was too busy. Nevertheless the chariot was heading towards the tall warrior, who just stood there watching as Cruibne's warriors were massacred. Cruibne felt calm. He was certain he was going to die, but he was with Ethne and sure that he was going to kill this man. *So much for growing fat*, he thought, *well, fatter*.

To Cruibne it looked like the giants exploded out of the sand, and they had in fact leaped out of the holes they had been buried in lying down. Cruibne only had a moment to see them – huge, dark, misshapen figures obscured by all the sand in the air. The closest lumbered towards him. Cruibne found himself in the shadow of an enormous foot. It stamped down, crushing wood and horseflesh, killing Ethne. The destruction of the chariot sent Cruibne flying forward. The beach rushed up to meet him. Darkness.

Nechtan soiled himself as the giant stamped on Cruibne's chariot. Screaming, Broichan, Nechtan's charioteer, yanked on the reins, trying to steer the terrified ponies away. The chariot jumped with each one of the giant's footfalls as it swept down one massive hand, hitting the side of the cart and the horses, sweeping them up and sending them tumbling through the air.

Britha was laughing now, now more red than blue, little more human than those she fought. She swayed to the side, avoiding the slash of a sword, cutting at the neck of her attacker, hitting him so hard it spun him round. Ducking and then straightening her legs, she tore the sickle through someone's flesh. She was oblivious to her tribe dying just the other side of the shield wall as she made her way closer to Bress. Excited, eager to do more violence, she wanted to see what this man really looked like on the inside.

The darkness had been good – cool, restful, it smelled of the sea. Not the metallic tang of blood or the smell of ruptured bowels. The sand shook beneath him. Giants walked the land now. Cruibne looked up, his face covered in a mixture of blood and sand. He was broken somewhere inside. He felt it. But he could still move.

Movement was pain. Standing was agony. He stuffed his beard in his mouth so he wouldn't scream – too many years of not being able to show weakness. It tasted of sand and more blood.

Tears sprang unbidden and unwelcome to his eyes as he drew his sword, the blade blue from the forge, not polished like a southron warrior's would be. He looked for their leader; instead he found some deformed but massively built man with an axe stalking towards him. He spat out his beard.

'The gods that piss on you didn't put your head on straight, but my sword will put you out of your misery,' he shouted at the creature. *May as well do this properly*, he thought. He found he couldn't move his left arm – the bone stuck out through his armour.

'I need your head,' the creature said.

Cruibne swung his sword in an overhead arc, bringing it down towards the ugly creature's head, the speed and violence of the blow causing pain to shoot through his body. Ettin had time to step back and then swing up with his axe. Cruibne stared at the stump of his sword hand. The lopsided creature was huge but had moved so quickly, and Cruibne had never known an axe so sharp. He marvelled that he was able to think this as Ettin swung again.

Cruibne was lying in the sand again. He could see his leg. It seemed much further from him than a leg should be. He tried to get up. He felt a boot on his chest, forcing him back down into the sand. Beyond his leg he could see the landsfolk fleeing. He couldn't blame them. *How could they fight this?* The giants caught up with them easily, sweeping down, killing many with each blow. Broken and crushed bodies rained down on the sand.

'Hold still. I want a clean cut,' Ettin said. Cruibne didn't even see the axe as it swung down towards his neck.

He was running, except he wasn't running. It was like he was being carried. He tried to stop running. He couldn't. How could he be running without a leg? Cruibne opened his eyes. To his right he saw the Lochlannach spearmen pursuing the last of the *cateran* and the landsmen. Some were surrendering. Ahead of him he saw the tall man, the one who had the look of a leader, maybe even a high king, standing with his arms crossed watching Lochlannach swordsmen sprinting towards a warrior. There was joy as he recognised Britha. The *ban draoi* had always been a capable warrior but Cruibne couldn't believe what he was seeing.

As one of the Lochlannach charged her, she ran her sword through his stomach and rolled as he crashed into her, sending the already dead body in a clumsy somersault over her. Britha rolled with the momentum, coming back up into a crouch. Her sickle blade went through another warrior's knee and she pulled him off his feet; the sickle tore out of flesh, rose and then fell again as the man's throat was ripped out. She spun round, biting her tongue and spitting blood into her next victim's face before yanking her sword up between his legs. She continued her violent dance towards the tall pale man.

As Cruibne somehow ran towards her, he leaned down and picked up a discarded longspear without breaking stride. Cruibne did not understand. He was about to attack Britha, and the arm that picked up the spear was not his.

'Noooooo!' The scream broke Britha out of her bloody reverie. Her head whipped around. Ettin was sprinting towards her, axe in one hand, longspear in the other. He looked less off kilter. He had two heads now. His original head was laughing. The new one was screaming, begging, threatening. She recognised Cruibne's voice.

'I'll kill you! I'll cut you open and shit in the wound! I'll have your corpse raped by dogs! No please! Don't!' Cruibne begged. Never in his life had he felt so helpless. Ettin just laughed. There was something else though: Cruibne could feel what Ettin felt. The creature's pleasure. He knew things, like that Ettin had an erection and where he came from. He just couldn't understand. It felt like it was his arm that threw the spear. Did he want it now? To see her corpse. No, that was Ettin. Cruibne prayed to gods who had not heard his people's prayers in an age. If they heard, they chose not to respond.

Britha had a moment to wrestle with trying to understand why Ettin wore Cruibne's head and then the spear was flying towards her. She tried to leap it. She had done so many times this night, but somehow Ettin had anticipated this, as if he had known what she would do. The spear caught her in the stomach. It felt almost as hungry as her sickle. She felt it grow inside her like a tree of iron tearing through her body. The force of the blow carried her through the air and she hit the sand hard. She lay still, looking at the spear sprouting from her. The shaft was moving slightly as the head continued to grow through her body.

Ettin appeared over her. Cruibne's head was sobbing.

'I'm sorry, so sorry,' her *mormaer*'s head said from Ettin's shoulder.

It was getting darker and colder, like something wrapping its wings around her. Britha was pretty sure that she was going to like death. She wasn't feeling pain now. It had to be better than this, the death of her people.

Bress appeared over her. *So, so pretty*, she thought, even with his dead eyes.

'I'm going to wear your head so you can see what I do to your corpse,' Ettin told her. There was more wailing from Cruibne's head. *That's no way for a* mormaer *to act*, Britha thought faintly. Bress just shook his head. He grabbed the haft of the spear. Britha actually felt the spearhead contract back to its normal shape. Then nothing.

9
Now

A police officer ran towards the Range Rover waving at du Bois to stop. He understood the necessity for a cordon and supposed that the self-important look the policeman had on his face made him feel he was part of this. Du Bois had to remind himself that this would go more smoothly if he was a little patient and not too rude.

'Turn this round now!' the florid-faced and fleshy policeman demanded when du Bois rolled the window down. He sighed and handed the officer his warrant card. The officer stared at it. 'Right, you stay here, I'll have to check this.' The policeman turned away with the card.

Fuck it, du Bois thought. 'Excuse me, lowly paid civil servant.' The police officer turned around. It took a moment for the anger to come as he processed what du Bois had said. 'Please imagine, if that's not beyond you, that the card in your hand just has the words "Yes, I can" written on it. It is not for you to check that, question me, or even talk to me. You are here only because it is more cost-effective than training a monkey to do your job. A job, that despite its simplicity – keeping the people who are not allowed in, out, and letting the ones who are allowed in, in – you are still somehow managing to screw up.'

The officer's face seemed to lumber through increasingly severe stages of fury. He opened his mouth to retort but du Bois got in there first.

'If someone is to question me it will be the highest-ranked monkey on the scene, do you understand me? Or should I have your extended family murdered for emphasis?'

The policeman snapped his mouth shut. In his heart he knew that the threat was idle but there was something about the casual delivery that made him believe that du Bois was capable of this. Du Bois reached out of the four-by-four, took his warrant card back and drove towards the inflatable hazardous-material isolation tent. He glanced at the near-identical rows of terraced housing on either side of the road. He was already not enjoying being in Portsmouth.

The hazardous-material suit was largely an affectation but appearances had to be kept.

'Brilliant,' du Bois muttered to himself. He was looking at a surprisingly small pile of rubble where a house used to be. The houses on either side looked as if they had chunks bitten out of them as well. The whole lot was underneath a large hermetically sealed tent. The place was crawling with scientists and technicians in similar yellow plastic suits. Most of them, however, were only engaged in spraying the area down with steam hoses and various chemicals.

Professor Franklin Kinick was a distinguished-looking, rake-thin man whose prominent nose and bushy white eyebrows made him look like a bird of prey wearing a hazmat suit. The professor worked for the Defence Science and Technology Laboratory at Porton Down, near Salisbury. Professor Kinick wasn't looking at the hive of decontamination industry going on around him; instead he was looking at du Bois as if he was something to be studied in a lab.

'So imagine my surprise when I was asked to drive all the way down from Wiltshire and bring some very particular instruments designed to measure some very particular things? Particular things that don't tend to be used in a counter-terrorism investigation. And then report all my findings to you, when, despite my clearances, I don't even know your organisation or rank,' the scientist finished.

Du Bois turned to him, smiling.

'How much would you like to know, Professor?'

Kinick just looked at him. Du Bois knew that Kinick, who was probably more than a little curious and whose nose was more than a little out of joint, had been at this game long enough not to push the issue. He had narrowly avoided the purge in the late 80s. Kinick held du Bois's gaze. He was convinced that he was looking at some kind of shadowy intelligence-operative cowboy.

'Well, we found lots of interesting stuff. Pretty much traces of the entire electromagnetic radiation spectrum, dust, energetic charged subatomic particles, beta and gamma radiation. In fact, do you know where we would be most likely to find all these things at this level?'

'Deep space?'

'Yes. You don't seem very surprised.'

There was more than a little anger in Kinick's voice. Du Bois had heard this before. This was people trying to cope with having their world view radically changed in a moment.

'Pick an explanation you like and hold on to it for dear life,' du Bois suggested. *Not that it'll matter*, he thought. On the other hand they were so close to the end that at least Kinick wouldn't be reprogrammed or assassinated, the latter being a lot less resource intensive.

'Want to know something else interesting?' the professor asked.

No, du Bois thought sarcastically. *Please keep all the interesting information from me.* He tried to suppress his annoyance.

'As far as we can tell, there is a lot of the house missing, and if there were people here then I can't find any trace of them at all. It's as if it all just disappeared.'

'How much material?'

'Initial estimates put it at about seventy-five per cent.'

Du Bois nodded. Kinick noted that again there was not much in the way of surprise. Du Bois turned to leave but at the last moment he swung back to Kinick.

'You won't listen to me, but if I were you, enquiring mind or not, I'd try not to dwell on what you've seen here too much.'

Kinick said nothing. He just watched du Bois head for the tent's airlock.

DC Nazo Mossa was not good at concentrating when there was a lot of background noise. This made her singularly badly equipped to work at Kingston Crescent, the main police station in Portsmouth, or indeed any other police station. The mobile command centre that they had set up had been even worse, so she had found an empty house up for rent and had quietly broken in.

As du Bois reviewed the second-generation Senegalese émigré's file, this small crime was enough to endear her to him a little. He minimised her personnel record on his phone and brought up the narcotics and vice file she was looking at on her laptop as he entered the house. Mossa was a solid-looking, athletic black woman, her cornrowed hair tied back into a ponytail. She was sitting at a table in the front room. She looked up as he entered, recognising du Bois as the arsehole who had given PC Danes such a hard time.

'Fuck off, you rude bastard. I'm busy,' she told him, looking away.

'I don't care,' du Bois said, his face wrinkling in a look of mock confusion. With a thought the screen on his phone displayed nine photographs of the inhabitants of the destroyed house and their most regular visitors, all of whom the drugs and vice squads had under occasional surveillance. Most of them were dressed in black, were pale and wore too much make-up. He placed his phone down on the table next to DC Mossa. She glanced over at it but went back to work.

'Who are these people?'

Frowning, DC Mossa looked back at the phone and then her own laptop.

'Did you just hack our systems?' she demanded angrily.

'Hacking suggests a degree of effort,' he told her. 'Look, I don't mean to be rude, which is unusual, but this is going to go my way. How easy or hard do you want to make this on yourself?'

Mossa stared at him.

'You've got a small penis, haven't you?' she finally said.

'Nice,' du Bois said, smiling.

'You like that?'

Du Bois nodded. 'But isn't that just something that people with windsock-like vaginas say?'

DC Mossa stared at him with mock confusion.

'Oh I get it. I insulted your manhood, therefore I must be some kind of crazy slut. That's really clever.'

'Seriously though, I could sit here exchanging crude sexual insults with you all day, but I don't want to get all buddy movie with you; I just want to expedite getting this information.'

'Act and talk less like a wanker then,' she suggested.

'Please, will you answer my questions?' he asked, mildly exasperated.

'Such a pain having to deal with us little people, isn't it? Answer me first. What's going to happen?'

Du Bois looked at her for a while, trying to decide how much to tell her.

'D notice,' he finally said. 'Nothing goes out on the news; a cover story will be found for the locals. It'll become an urban myth.'

'It'll go out on the Internet,' Mossa said.

No, it won't, du Bois thought. The Circle had the resources to police even that. He shrugged.

Mossa pointed at the nine pictures on the phone. 'These kids weren't terrorists.'

Du Bois didn't answer.

'Look. You've got everything on the files, obviously, but that's not what you want. You're looking for a little bit of local info, right?'

Du Bois nodded.

'This wasn't a terrorist incident?'

'It seems unlikely.'

'Then what?'

'Drugs lab explosion,' he told her, failing to sound even remotely sincere.

'With deco? Hazmat? Techies from some agency I've never even heard of? You want to insult my intelligence, you can go and fuck yourself.' She turned back to her laptop.

'You know I'm not going to tell you, right? If it's any consolation, the ongoing investigation is going to have nothing to do with you,' he said impatiently. *Reasoning with people is such a chore,* du Bois thought.

Mossa turned back to face him. 'Fine. Level with me. Is this something I have to worry about?'

Du Bois gave this some thought.

'Yes. However, it's not something you can do anything about. Feel better?'

Mossa studied him for a moment.

'That I believe. They're a group of goths, or emos, or whatever unhappy white kids like to call themselves these days. They set themselves up as some sort of club of hedonists. Sex, drugs, ropey music, that sort of thing.'

'A cult?' du Bois asked.

'Wouldn't know, wouldn't be surprised if they dabbled in that sort of thing, but I think their focus was on exterminating rational thought and getting laid. Though they were into the vampire thing.' Du Bois raised an eyebrow. 'Bloodletting.'

'Why?' he asked, mystified.

Mossa shrugged. 'Fun?'

Du Bois wondered if that was how this had happened. Something in the blood, a sensitive enough mind would act like a beacon.

'Is that significant?' Mossa asked, watching du Bois's reactions.

'Why your interest?' du Bois countered, ignoring her question.

'Minor-league dealing. We were getting close to arresting one of the weaker ones, getting them to turn over and give us someone bigger. Vice caught just the slightest whiff of specialised prostitution.'

'Specialised?'

'Maybe the bloodletting,' Mossa said, shrugging.

Du Bois reached down and touched the centre of his phone screen. The central picture expanded to fill the screen. The girl in the picture was not just attractive, she was beautiful, the sort of beauty that could stop a room and make people either desire or hate her. She was slender, pale, with high cheekbones, dark eyes. Her dyed-black hair was a travesty. Even through the surveillance picture he could see a sadness that was more than a subcultural affectation. This was an unhappy, isolated and lonely girl, and he thought he knew why.

Mossa knew her. 'Natalie Luckwicke, twenty-one, from Bradford. She may be vice's whiff of prostitution. Rumour has it that she does tricks for some of the better-paying and weirder johns in the area.'

Clear all that shit off her face and she could command a high price, du Bois thought. He tried to imagine what she would look like now, but he had no real frame of reference. It could be her. It could be any of a thousand girls her age.

'Pimp?' du Bois asked, still studying the picture as he downloaded all the information he could find about her.

'Nothing so prosaic. Just a friend who knows people, can make the right introductions, that sort of thing. A real sleazy piece of shit called William Arbogast. Mid-level dealer to Portsmouth's great and good, has fingers in some dodgy Internet sites as well.'

He was already downloading all the information on Arbogast. He quickly went through blinds and holding companies, found his connection to online porn sites and did a search through them with tightly defined parameters, found what he was looking for and cleaned up the image. Even with the wig, the make-up and the bad camera work, it was Natalie Luckwicke he saw in his mind's eye. He didn't like seeing her this way. Mossa watched him clench his fist. He cut the feed off.

'Thank you,' he said. Mossa just nodded. Du Bois turned and headed for the door.

'Tell me something.' Du Bois stopped. 'Who do you work for?' When he turned to look at her, Mossa was surprised to see that he was smiling. There wasn't much humour in the smile.

'Would you believe the druids?'

Mossa frowned. 'You're not funny.' She went back to the laptop even as all the information on the Pretoria Road incident was being wiped from that computer and every other computer, regardless of security, all over the world.

Du Bois forwarded everything he had found out to Control. The question was, could she have survived an incursion, even one as small-scale as this?

King Jeremy stared at the manticore through the bars of its cage. It, or rather she, had the body of a red lion, rows of shark-like teeth and a scorpion tail that could fire its sting and quickly regrow it. The bat-like wings had been the most difficult. They allowed it to glide but not fly. It was of little use in the arena but he liked to remain true to the designs in the Shattered Skies Massive Multiplayer Online Role Playing Game.

It was the face he liked the most though. She had been a model once, before she became graft meat. She had made the mistake of laughing at him at some party. It had been a matter of dropping something in her drink and programming her to kidnap herself. No way to trace it back to him. Beautiful face, monstrous body – difficult to imagine how he could be more like God, Jeremy mused. It was the misery on her face he liked. The desperately-trying-to-work-out-what-had-happened-to-herself. It wasn't just her flesh he'd violated; it was everything she knew about reality. Pretty young women weren't turned into monsters and forced to fight in an arena in her world. *Bitch wasn't laughing now*, he thought.

Jeremy realised that he couldn't remember her name any more. He shrugged and looked back at the monitor. He still found it easier to use high-spec monitors than do it entirely in his head. The situation in Portsmouth was very interesting and pointed towards more of the lost tech, as they had started calling it because it sounded cooler than super tech or alien tech. They still had no idea what it was or where it came from, though much of it seemed to be very old.

Jeremy had first heard rumours in the darker parts of the black market that dealt in technology far in advance of what people thought possible. Jeremy had been in his second year at MIT. Hacking, various data crimes and all-out electronic theft had not enabled him to afford the sort of prices that the lost tech commanded. They had, however, provided him with more than enough money to hire military contractors, as mercenaries were called these days, to hit one of the deals and steal the item.

Despite the multiple electronic blinds and go-betweens he had put between himself and the contractors, it had been the most frightening thing that Jeremy had ever done, but he'd hit the jackpot. As far as he could tell, what they had stolen was some sort of miniature nano-machine factory capable – assuming enough energy and raw materials – of producing the tiny machines that could create just about anything and alter matter at its molecular level. He'd named it Cornucopia after the magic item on the final level of Pagan Earth.

Once he had worked out how to use it, he no longer had to rely on contractors. King Jeremy could augment and hardwire the skills he required to mimic most of the characters he played in games. He had done this and then taken out the contractors just to be on the safe side. Since then he had got hold of more of the lost tech. Some of it was spectacularly advanced software, some biotech, but most of it was hardware. He had bought some, though rarely for money; most of the rest he had killed and stolen for, or arranged proxies to do so. In one spectacular case, an entire nanite-slaved battalion of the Chinese army had done his dirty work on a mountain plateau in Tibet.

Then through a series of games he had designed himself to psychometrically and intellectually test other gamers, he had recruited the rest of the Do As You Please Clan.

He was reading a blog about some emo kid with hallucinogenic blood on some vampire wannabe's blog. As he watched, the words started to disappear.

'What the fuck?' he muttered to himself. He had set his systems to automatically save any information he came across on the Portsmouth situation. It was a minor AI search routine. Not only was the search routine violated, but when he checked his own internal systems he saw the scant information he did have being eaten.

'No, no, no, no!' The amount of time it had taken to violate his security, security far in advanced of what modern technology was supposed to be capable of, had been so small it had been difficult to measure. Only someone with access to lost tech would be able to do this, and they would either have to have better lost tech or be more skilled at utilising it than Jeremy was. He had been aware that other groups had access to the powerful technology but had always tried to avoid them unless he was stealing from them. Even then he tried to pick on people on the lower echelons, for example the ultra-rich who had just stumbled on the technology or poorer countries' black science programmes that had found the technology purely by chance.

King Jeremy stared at the monitor, which was swiftly becoming a focus for his rage. The sounds of heavy metal and simulated warfare came from the other room. Dracimus was playing a first-person shooter. This acted as Jeremy's soundtrack as he tore the monitor off the table, flung it across the room and reduced the rest of his immediate surroundings to so much destroyed junk.

Seething, he headed towards the pleasure dome – what they called the main area of the Boston warehouse. They had used Cornucopia to terraform, as they liked to term it, the warehouse.

When King Jeremy had found himself capable of redesigning flesh, he had kept his basic look but got rid of his imperfections, made himself more handsome and a lot more athletic, aping the look of characters he saw in films, games and comics. The irony – that he now looked like the high-school alpha males he hated – was lost on him.

Dracimus was gaming old-style. There was little challenge in gaming now, when you could control the characters with your mind. Besides, they had the capabilities to make the real world like their games if they so chose. At the moment Dracimus was using an old-fashioned controller on one of the intermediate levels on the hardest setting of the Wild Boys FPS. He was playing the hacked game at lightning speed, slumped in his shorts in the middle of their massive line of sofas. The future war played out on the cinema-sized screen that took up one of the warehouse walls.

Dracimus, if anything, looked more like a high-school jock than Jeremy, if the jock had a serious steroid problem. He acted like one as well. What Dracimus wanted he had to have, immediately.

Baron Albedo was asleep, entwined with three of his latest sex zombies. After all, nano-technology was better than Rohypnol. His face was still white from burying it in the small mountain of synthetic cocaine on the table in front of him.

Inflictor Doorstep – King Jeremy had no idea where the name had come from – was looking more and more demonic. His skin had taken on a grey cast and was starting to look more like armour plate. His eyes were black-and-red spirals. He was rendering down one of the sex zombies he had broken. Feeding the woman head first into Cornucopia, something he liked doing. Inflictor Doorstep even scared Jeremy a little.

'We've just been hacked.' That even got Inflictor's attention. 'We're going to England.'

Another night on the street. Despite the warmth during the day, Beth had spent most of the night awake, shivering in her sleeping bag and staring at graffiti. Someone had painted the words THE EMPIRE NEVER ENDED on the wall opposite. Beth had no idea what it meant but had initially thought it a little profound. Now it was just irritating her.

She was going to go back tomorrow. Hitch to London and get a train home. She had no idea what she was going to tell her dad. She could not see her sister as a terrorist. It would have been too much like hard work. Even with Talia's near-suicidal taste in men, Beth still couldn't see her even getting involved with that. On the other hand, Talia hadn't visited her in prison, and a lot could have changed in the years since she had last seen her sister. Maybe she had been unknowingly sharing digs with a bomb-maker, but even that sounded far-fetched. *On the other hand,* Beth thought, *someone had to share digs with terrorists. You just never think it will happen to someone you know.* Her dad was going to have to be happy with what little she could give him. Maybe she should tell him to get in contact with the police.

Every time Beth felt herself falling asleep, the same question echoed around her head. *Who's to blame?* She hadn't liked Talia, but she was family. Beth couldn't accept the pure bad luck of Talia being in the wrong place at the wrong time. Someone had to know more about this than she did. Talia had always been the tragic social butterfly on the alternative scene. Everyone had known her in Bradford. It would have involved a radical change of personality for her not to want to be the centre of attention in Portsmouth as well. If nothing else, someone would know what she had been doing in the run-up to this.

In the early hours of the morning Beth got up and found a place to hide her kitbag. She took an old picture of Talia, the Balisong knife and her brass knuckles, and started to wander.

It hadn't been difficult. The clothes might have changed a little, same with the hairstyles, but all subcultures had their uniforms. She spotted them on a wide street called Elm Grove. Followed them into a narrow street with what looked like some kind of clock tower at the bottom of it where it intersected with another road. Beth was pretty sure she wasn't too far from the sea.

The pub was in the middle of the street. It was called the Colonial Arms and had a late licence. She had heard the bustle and noise as soon as she turned into the street. It had a paved beer garden packed with people.

Inside it was warm and seemed to Beth to be full of light, though the atmosphere was strangely subdued. She wondered if it had anything to do with the terrorist incident. Had these people lost friends? The pub was made up of two large wooden-floored rooms and a smaller area up some steps set back from the bar. The bar was close to the door and it was standing room only. Beth had to push her way to the bar to order a pint of bitter with her scarce cash.

She got some looks on the way in but she had on her leather, her combat trousers and her army-surplus boots. She wore the uniform even if it was an older variant. The bouncers had sized her up on the way in as well. Wondering if she was going to be trouble. Beth hoped not but she was pleased they hadn't searched her.

She took stock of the place and then started showing the photograph around, asking people if they had seen Talia. Beth started with the goth/emo crowd and got negatives. She was pretty sure some of them were lying because they didn't want to get involved but she wasn't going to push it yet.

Eventually she spoke to someone who at least admitted to having seen her. This led to Beth cornering another girl in the bathroom. Beth had put a leather-clad arm in the girl's way and asked her to look closely at the picture. The frightened girl had tried to bluster her way out of it, but Beth had just stared at her. Finally she had given her a name. Jaime. Beth had got her to describe this Jaime. He was in tonight. He was here every night. Where was he sitting? How many people were with him? Finally she'd let the girl go.

Beth found him quickly. She had intended watching him for a bit before going to speak to him. He had a narrow pockmarked face, long lank hair pulled back into a ponytail. Wearing jeans and a T-shirt. She reckoned he was a bit older than the majority of those in the pub, probably of an age with her. He was at a table with a couple of cronies and several girls a few years younger. He had minor-league dealer written all over him.

Beth sighed when he saw the girl from the toilet rush over to Jaime and point at her. He said something harsh to her and the girl backed away. Then he looked over at Beth. She sighed and headed over to his table. He glared at her all the way over.

'You looking for me?' he shouted over the din of the music and people talking. Beth nodded and showed him the picture.

'You know her.' She made sure that it didn't sound like a question. Jaime barely glanced at it.

'She's dead,' he told her. *Nice*, Beth thought. People were starting to listen now. One of the girls at the table, a pretty young goth who had the look of a nice middle-class girl slumming – Beth knew the type – was trying very hard not to look at the photo.

'I know. I'm her sister.'

'So?' She was getting hard stares from the two guys with Jaime.

'Look, I'm just trying to find out about her. Speak to someone who knew her. It's been a long time.'

'Bit late now, isn't it? Should've picked up the phone.'

'I've been away,' she told him evenly, hoping he got the message. He did, and looked at her with renewed interest, maybe a bit more caution.

'That supposed to impress me?'

'I'm not trying to impress you. Look, if not you then point me in the direction of one of her friends, and I'll get out of your hair.' As she said 'friends' one of Jaime's cronies, an ugly skinhead with blue biro tattoos, glanced over at the girl. Beth tried not to let on that she'd noticed.

'Why don't we go and talk about this outside? A bit quieter. Hear ourselves think, like. Delicate stuff this.' Suddenly he was all smiles. *Here we go*. Beth sighed.

They'd come out of the pub and headed down towards the sea but turned off into a parking bay underneath some flats. Beth couldn't help but think that the little block of flats looked like a nice place to live. She couldn't even be bothered to ask Jaime why he needed his two mates for their private little chat. Reaching into a pocket she turned to face the three of them. As she did, he was on her, grabbing her leather jacket and slamming her against the wall. Something about it made her think that he was used to trying to intimidate women – there was a rehearsed familiarity to his actions.

'You're one ugly—' he managed to get out. There wasn't much power in the headbutt but she'd placed it correctly and nobody likes getting hit in the nose. Jaime grabbed his nose instinctively. Beth pushed him back to give herself room and kicked him in the knee, hard. There was a *crack* and he screamed and went down. The ugly skinhead moved faster than the guy in the shell suit. He grabbed for her, but his momentum brought him onto Beth's hook. His nose exploded and he staggered back holding his face. The brass knuckles came away bloody. She hit him again, a fast jab to the side of the head just to discourage him from any more involvement. He sat down hard on the ground.

The *click* of the switchblade opening was unmistakable. Beth turned to look at the guy in the shell suit. Jaime tried getting up. Beth helped him back to the ground with the sole of her boot. It wasn't the first time she'd had a blade pulled on her. Most of the time it was just a threat. Shell suit looked like it was just a threat, like he was used to showing people the blade and getting what he wanted. Problem was, it could be difficult to be sure.

'Come on then,' she said and gave him the hard stare. Even if he went for her she was pretty sure she could take him. He looked like a long streak of piss to Beth.

Shell suit looked at skinhead and Jaime and started backing away. If he left there was always the chance he'd come back with friends, but she didn't think he would tell anyone. When you're a guy you don't expect to see your mates knocked down by a girl, particularly if you think you're a hard man.

Beth had to smile as he turned and tried to walk away casually. She turned back to the other two. Skinhead was trying to get up. His eyes couldn't focus. Beth was a little worried that she had hit him too hard but didn't think he would bother her any time soon.

'You fucking ugly bi—' Jaime started. Beth kicked him in the ribs, very hard.

On the doors she remembered working with another bouncer called Thomas, who had been a member of the infamous Derby Lunatic Fighters football firm in the early 80s. He had once told her that if you wanted to know something and someone wouldn't tell you, then all you had to do was let the tip of your knife touch the lens of their eye. You had to be very careful not to puncture it, though Thomas had been of the opinion that scratching it was okay. That way, every time they opened their eyes they'd think of you.

The Balisong knife opened easily in her hand as she knelt down by Jaime. He tried to get up so Beth punched him in the ribs, the same place she had kicked him. He yelled and she grabbed his face. Seeing the blade of the knife heading towards one of his eyes, Jaime closed them.

'Open your fucking eye or I'll put it out,' she snapped. He seemed to believe her. Resting the tip of the blade against the lens of the eye was harder than Thomas had led her to believe. He kept blinking, but she was pretty sure that he got the point.

'Stop being a prick and tell me about my sister,' she demanded.

'What do you want to know?' he asked desperately. That stopped her. What *did* she want to know? What she had been doing for six years? Had she grown up? Was she happy? Or was she still destructive and miserable? What was it about Beth that Talia had hated so much when all she had wanted was to be her older sister?

'What happened to her?' she asked.

'We don't know,' he finally managed. 'Nobody does. Some kind of terrorist bomb, but there's nothing in the papers. What, you don't think that I ...'

Beth took the blade away from his eye and sat down on the ground. *What the fuck am I doing?* she asked herself. This was a good way to get put back in prison.

'What was she to you?' she finally asked. 'I'm not going to hurt you,' she added.

'We saw each other for a while, you know?'

Yep, you're just about a big enough sleazebag for her to be interested in you.

'But she was just using me, you know? Because I had gear and she liked it.'

She hadn't changed, Beth thought.

Jaime had been in love with her, he said. Beth felt more embarrassed than anything else when he started crying. 'I miss her, I really miss her,' he wailed.

Brilliant.

'Who did she hang out with?' she asked, wondering why she was bothering.

'That goth bunch. They were weirdos. I mean they all are, but they were dead cliquey. Called themselves the Black Mirror or something wanky like that. They said they were like hedonists, like Burroughs – exterminate all rational thought, drugs, orgies, all sorts. Modelled themselves on the Hellfire Club, read de Sade. They all went up in the house.' Then he really started to cry, sobs racking his body.

She believed him. It sounded exactly like the sort of bullshit that Talia would get involved in.

'Was she doing a lot of gear?' she asked. Jaime nodded. 'What?'

'Pretty much everything and as much as she could get.'

Beth grabbed him by his hoodie. 'From you?' she demanded, the threat back in her voice.

'Not after I found her messing with H. I went mental at her.' He started sobbing again. 'That's when she called me a small-minded little man and left.'

'Where were they getting the money from?'

'I don't know.' Beth shook him. 'Really, I don't know!'

'What's going on down there?' The owner of the voice sounded like he had been building up the courage to shout for some time. 'I'm calling the police!'

Beth got up and headed back to the street.

Head down, hands in the pockets of her leather jacket, she walked up the little street. It had started to rain and the lights from the pub reflected off the wet tarmac. It was kicking-out time. Few people spared her a look. If they had seen her leave with Jaime they would have assumed she was buying from him. Only the girl from the toilets who had grassed her up was staring at her. There was no sign of shell suit.

'Excuse me?' the question sounded like it was the third or forth time it had been said and Beth had only just noticed it. She looked round to see the pretty little goth who had been sitting with Jaime.

'Yeah?' Beth was glancing around, eager to get away in case the police turned up.

'You don't look like her.' Beth turned back to fix her with an angry glare, and the girl shrank back. Beth was sick of the comparison.

'What do you want?' she demanded.

'Talia was my friend,' the girl said. She looked like she was about to cry. *Talia didn't have friends*, Beth thought, *just people she could use.*

'You got any money?' Beth asked. The girl seemed taken aback.

'A little.'

'Buy me a kebab and we can have a bit of a chat.'

'You're just like her,' the girl said, smiling. Beth clenched her fists. *No, I'm just skint.*

It had been a bit of a walk to where Elm Grove curved round onto another road with a theatre on the corner. It was lined with shops, closed pubs and open junk-food shops. Beth was tucking into the kebab before it occurred to her to ask for the girl's name.

'Leticia.'

'Really?' Beth asked sceptically.

'Well, it's really Maude.'

'Maude's a nice name.' This time it was Maude looking sceptical. 'Okay, it's really not.'

Beth couldn't believe how good the kebab was. She had been hungrier than she thought. Maude was picking at pitta bread with some salad in it.

'Were you part of this Black Mirror?' Beth asked.

'They were considering me.' Beth rolled her eyes. *Arseholes.* 'But they scared me a little bit as well. Talia was the nicest of them – she was really friendly.' Beth was surprised to hear this. Perhaps she had grown up a bit since she had last seen her.

'She didn't have anything to do with terrorists, did she?' Beth asked. Maude just laughed and shook her head. 'Were they making drugs in the house or anything?' Maude shook her head and looked sad again. Beth was worried that she was going to cry again. Her make-up was smeared enough as it was.

What are you doing here? Beth asked herself. *You're not going to learn anything good about Talia. What you need to do is think of something to tell Dad that isn't going to break his heart.*

'How did you become friends?' The question just popped into her head. She just hoped that it didn't bring more tears. Maude seemed to be struggling with an answer.

'Well, I'd known her to say hi to ever since I came here for uni, but ... well, she helped me through a difficult time.' Maude wouldn't look at her. She seemed embarrassed about something. This was sounding less and less like the Talia Beth had known.

'What?' Beth asked and then groaned inwardly as she saw tears start to well again. *It's a wonder she has any eyeliner left.*

Suddenly Maude looked up at her. 'How much do you want to know?' she asked.

'Go on.'

'I got into something well over my head.' Her face crumpled.

'Look, don't cry; just tell me.'

'Well, he said it was upmarket stuff – tasteful clients who would pay a lot of money, you know, help me get through my course a little less in debt. But then when I saw him and he was old and fat and wanted to do … things … It wasn't like the films, you know, champagne and a few Js.'

Beth stared at her. 'You were turning tricks?'

'Just one. I couldn't handle it. But Talia … she helped me deal—'

'Was Talia?' Beth asked despite herself. She knew the answer but it wasn't real until someone else told her it was. Maude nodded.

'It was horrible, but she really looked after me,' she managed through the sobs and the gulping for air.

'Did she get you into it?'

Maude looked stricken. She probably hadn't thought about it like that.

'She introduced me to William, but only after I asked about it.'

And how did you know to ask? Beth wondered.

'She did porn as well, didn't she?'

Maude looked guilty but nodded.

She actually thinks she's betraying Talia. 'Who's William?' In her mind Beth was screaming *Go home* to herself.

10
A Long Time After the Loss

Arclight was a mess, the result of expansion without regulation. The black market in Arclight, however, was very tightly controlled by the insect-run Queen's Cartel. Originally the hollowed-out asteroid had been a hive ship, and it was still run by 'sects, Vic's people, though he hated dealing with them. Vic had abandoned their caste society a long time ago. In the centre of the rock he knew there would be a metal and hardened carbon-fibre, honeycomb-style construction where the augmented 'sects lived. Once upon a time, steel and carbon fibre would have extruded resin and chitin.

No part of the surface of the original rock could be seen; it was buried beneath layer after layer of haphazardly added habitations forming a massive warren that had been centuries in the making. All of this orbited a distant fading sun that nobody had ever taken the time to name.

There was no traffic control on Arclight; you just tried to find a safeish place to dock and hoped for the best. Almost the entire surface of the asteroid was covered in animated holograms, though few were still functioning properly. Many of them offered safe places to dock, though plenty of those were bottom-feeding wreckers.

The *Basilisk*'s comms should have been flooded with similar offers of safe haven. However, Scab had broadcast the ship's I-dent over the Arclight 'face to let them know who was coming aboard. That significantly cut down on the time-wasters and wreckers. Even the most hardcore hijack crew was going to think twice about taking on Scab, the bounty killer who worked without clone insurance. *It was times like these that Scab's rep paid off,* Vic thought. Besides, when Scab announced he was coming to a place everyone thought the same thing: *Is it me he's after?* After the I-dent they started taking in reasonable bids for docking, security and privacy.

Vic was less than pleased that Scab had decided to fly the ship under his own neunonic control. Scab was stood in the centre of the lounge/main room/Command and Control of the *Basilisk*. He had turned most of the ship's hull transparent and was looking all around as he put on his brown suit and did up his tie. Scab wove his way through the parasitical suburban habitats attached to Arclight, heavily armed industrial assemblers, from one Consortium subsidiary or another, slowly eating away at tethered asteroids, past ships, the lowliest jury-rigged tramp traders to the massive Consortium bulk ore/carbon haulers, past salvage tugs and sleek scout craft belonging to xeno-archaeology prospectors, down-at-heel feline pleasure barges, scrap-built reptile fighting craft – there were even Consortium navy contractor ships and a Church craft berthed there. Scab took his time taking the *Basilisk* in, dancing it through the busy space, flying through the aging hologramatic displays, making them distort so it looked like *Basilisk* was pulling the dissipating light with it.

Vic tried to ignore the 'faced warnings from craft and parts of the habitat they got too close to. It was more difficult when they were flying near enough to see batteries, with sufficient firepower to obliterate them tracking the little craft.

Scab had finished dressing and was pulling weapons more socially acceptable than the Scorpion from the smart-matter storage compartment that the ship had extruded though the floor. He unloaded, checked and then reloaded each of the weapons before holstering them. To Vic's mind this was still, arguably, Scab dressing.

Vic had already done the same, three handguns with seven barrels between them. Light armour was clipped onto his largely hard-tech chassis to augment the built-in protection. He clipped an autonomous blade disc to his armour. It was designed to seek out the EM fields of biological life, and like most brutal short-range weapons it had been designed by lizards. Vic still wasn't sure it was enough, not with the people they'd pissed off. On the other hand, nothing would help if an Elite came looking for them.

The *Basilisk* seemed to give birth to two black globes that floated smoothly on silent AG motors into the air to hover close to Scab and Vic. They had cut right back on the personal satellites' hardware but augmented their sensor packages. The P-sats would need the augmentation to sort through the clutter inside Arclight and provide them with accurate info. Both of them could extrude handgrips, and their AG motors were more than powerful enough to carry Scab and Vic if they had to.

'We going to talk about this?' Vic asked. Scab ignored him. 'Apparently not. Is there anyone we didn't piss off back there? I mean Consortium naval contractors, the Church and the fucking Monarchist Elite?

Not one mind you – one's not enough for Scab – no, two Elite.'

'That's vanity bordering on monomania,' Scab finally said. He made it sound like a sigh. 'None of them have any interest in us. They were after either the ship or the cocoon. The Angel or Ludwig could have destroyed us whenever they wanted.'

'Comforting. You mean they knew we were there?'

Scab just nodded, remembering when he had been reliant on senses unknown to most biological life. Senses that spread out over hundreds of thousands of miles in space. Senses that meant he could feel the slightest movement in the fabric of space/time itself. Not for the first time Scab thought of how he missed being a god of destruction. He preferred myth to what he thought of as the sordidness of flesh.

'Has it occurred to you that the Consortium and the Church might want to know who our employers are?'

'No, I'm a moron,' Scab said.

Staring. In terms of human reactions this called for staring, Vic was sure of that. He didn't blink, but staring he could do. He also let off a little fart of pheromones in surprise. Scab wasn't known for humour, even sarcasm. Vic cursed himself: Scab's soft-tech-augmented olfactory glands would pick up the pheromones. 'I was not apprised of how dangerous the situation was otherwise I would have charged more.' Vic was trying to work out the appropriate amount of time to stare to convey his shocked response. 'Or said no,' he finally suggested forcefully.

Scab stopped loading rounds into his tumbler pistol and turned to fix Vic with one of his looks. Vic didn't like this look. He couldn't quite read the expression, despite his studies and the help of onboard computer systems, but it did unnerve him.

'It was an interesting job,' Scab finally said. Vic did some more staring.

'And the Church! Really?!' Vic eventually responded. Scab had done some truly stupid things, more than borderline suicidal, and pissed off some genuinely dangerous and powerful people, but in Vic's opinion he'd gone too far this time.

Vic followed Scab as he picked up his homburg and placed it on his pale-skinned hairless head. Part of the *Basilisk*'s hull opened and they stepped into the airlock. The hull sealed shut behind them.

'I fucking hate zero G,' Vic muttered.

'You grew up in it,' Scab pointed out.

'I grew up drinking synthetic mother's milk out of a wall nipple; doesn't mean I don't prefer steak.'

'That's just something you heard in a colonial immersion.'

The hull opened out in front of them into what looked like a bunker made of patched and corroded armour plate. They were facing five heavily armed scum. Scab had accepted their bid for docking and security. He 'faced them the amount of debt relief he was prepared to pay along with the obligatory ritual threats that went with doing business.

They stepped out of the *Basilisk*'s AG field and let old instincts and hard-wired zero G routines take over as they drifted towards the ceiling.

'If the Church does take you and torture you, you can feel good about having no actual information to give them,' Scab 'faced over their secure link.

'What is that? A joke?' Vic demanded. *Confusion*, Vic thought, he was pretty sure that Scab's expression was one of mild confusion.

The passageway Vic and Scab took was relatively new and a luxury express route. Scab paid the high price demanded to use it. Vic guessed the fact that the tube was transparent and they could look down on the non-toll routes deeper in the labyrinth of Arclight was supposed to make them feel better. People were packed in so tightly they had to wriggle past each other. Scab could see 'sects, little more than grubs, working the packed passage as his P-sat pulled him along. As he watched, one of them started screaming as some nasty countermeasure took him out as he tried to lift a pistol belonging to a reptile wearing luminescent body-paint gang colours.

'So why come back?' Vic 'faced over the secure link.

'It's close; we're unemployed.'

'We could have looked for bounties from the *Basilisk*.' Vic was starting to sound confused as he watched a fight break out in the packed transport tube below. It looked desperate. Someone had probably panicked and the crowd had turned on them. It looked like he was being torn apart. 'What if Sloper had friends who saw you talking to him?'

'Then I would imagine we'll have to do some free killing, but I chose Sloper because he didn't have any friends and both he and his crew were malleable,' Scab 'faced back.

You mean programmable, Vic thought but said nothing. Then it dawned on him.

'Seeder's sake, Woodbine,' Vic said. Scab looked over his shoulder in irritation at the sound of his first name, but it was one of those moments when Vic just didn't care. 'Are you looking into this?'

'It's interesting,' Scab said.

'Are you fucking mad?!' Vic asked before realising that it was a stupid question. Though it had occurred to Vic in the past that Scab was a new iteration of sanity, a psychological evolution designed to help the naked monkeys cope. Maybe one day all humans would be like Scab. The thought had frightened Vic.

'I was offered a good deal,' Scab said. He almost sounded wistful.

'Debt relief's a bit fucking difficult to spend when some Elite's re-written your DNA to see what you'd look like as protoplasm!' It had taken Vic a while to learn to shout over the interface; it was mainly a human talent though lizards were good at it as well. He had been proud when he'd finally managed it. It was very useful for conversations like this with Scab.

'It wasn't money,' Scab said. He didn't say it over the interface. He didn't even say it aloud. Vic's hearing through his antenna had been excellent before it had been augmented by the 'sect's hard-tech retrofit. Scab had just moved his stained lips as he sub-vocalised it.

'Are you using us as bait?' Vic demanded.

He always becomes difficult to manage when he's frightened, Scab thought.

The Polyhedron Club was specialised: it catered mainly to men of the heterosexual kink and women of the homosexual kink. Most of the six-armed, no-legged, zero-G dancers were either of the girly girl or ladyboy gender. Most of them were human though there were a few felines and one reptile. Whether it had been custom fabricated or originally something else, the Polyhedron was, as its name suggested, an area with numerous sides. The club made good use of all twenty sides of the cavernous red-mock-velvet-lined chamber: each triangle had tables and chairs with micro-hooks that could be neunonically controlled to fasten the clientele to their seats.

The supports for the superstructure provided poles for the dancers' complex, gymnastic and erotic dances.

'So, just to be clear,' Vic asked over the secure interface, 'the plan is to wait here until something bad happens?'

Scab took another suck from his drink bulb and ignored him. Vic went back to watching one of the human dancers. He was pretty sure she was attractive by human standards as he had run her through some comparison routines in his neunonics. On the other hand, it kind of spoilt the thrill of being a humanophile if they had the same amount of limbs as you.

Both of them felt the atmosphere in the room change. Their P-sats rose from where they had been hovering in one of the many faceted corners, and the club's defence systems 'faced automated anti-violence warnings with graphic examples of the consequences to both of them if they disobeyed.

The dancers scrambled and swung out of the way. Vic could understand why as he tried to suppress feelings of hatred, anger and not a little fear. Fully armoured and armed in Thunder Squad gear, he could have taken them, of that he was sure; like this he wasn't so sure. He couldn't make up his mind whether or not he wanted Scab to start on them or not. It would be an interesting death for him and a fight that Vic would want to see. Scab, however, just sat at the table taking the occasional sip from the nipple of his drink bulb and annoying everyone who could smell near him by engaging in his smoking retro-vice, as he watched the two warrior-caste 'sects fly towards them.

Compared to the custom-evolved biomechanical killing machines, Scab looked positively spindly. Overlapping plates of chitin formed armour the match of high-grade military protection. It was rumoured that the armour's energy dissipation matrix was an application of S-tech that had been bred into their line. Their lower limbs ended in bladed legs, the four upper limbs all ended in grafted weapons. Their oversized mandibles were knife-like blades attached to sinuous corded muscles designed for close-quarters combat.

The two warriors propelled themselves across the club on small armoured wings that moved so quickly they were a blur. Ideal for zero-G manoeuvring, they could be retracted into armoured chitinous sheaths. The two warriors held a human between them. He wore a white suit of some rendered linen analogue and a panama hat. Despite an androgynous quality, Vic was pretty sure the human was male. Skin grew across his eyes, adding to the expressionless look on his face.

Vic clattered his mandibles together, wishing he could whistle like he had seen surprised humans do in immersions. Even Scab raised an eyebrow. The warriors were towing a blank towards them. A very rare, very expensive and very illegal application of S-tech, it involved some kind of neural entanglement of identical clones. The neurology of blanks was altered by the ancient alien tech, allowing them to be used as transmitters and receivers. Some even whispered that it was an S-tech application developed by the Naga, the semi-mythical race of serpents, the so-called missing fifth and oldest uplifted race.

'Do you think they could have drawn more attention to us?' Vic wondered. Scab frowned slightly.

The warriors brought the semi-comatose drooling blank to their table as another chair grew out of the floor. Mandibles clattering together produced a series of synchronised clicks accompanied by scents as they released pheromones.

'They feel, quite strongly, that we should talk to the blank,' Vic translated, though he was sure that Scab would have understood. Scab was staring at the warriors. Vic wondered whether or not he should tell him that staring at them or any form of intimidation was a complete waste of time. He also considered provoking a fight just to see who would win.

Finally Scab just nodded. The warrior 'sects put the blank in the chair and retreated slightly to hover in the air. Everything else in the Polyhedron had stopped: the dancers, the bar staff and the other clientele where all staring at Vic, Scab and the blank.

Single-minded, privacy-enforcing nanites went looking for the inevitable surveillance nanites to eat. As the privacy cage grew up out of the floor to encompass them, the last thing Scab noticed was a shaven-headed human woman watching them. There was something about her, something that screamed Church to him. Then the privacy field started up.

The automaton wasn't the Absolute. The Absolute was changed. Human was no longer a word that could really be applied to it. It was a series of complex sense organs with redesigned neural pathways that could process sensations which would destroy a normal human mind and physiology. Its mind was spread holistically throughout its physical whole. It was an organism designed primarily to experience pleasure. Its physical body was buried deep in its home planet's crust, protected by vast amounts of automated security, and provided for by automated life-support systems far from the eyes and touch of other people.

The automaton was designed to look like something from myth, to inspire awe: an idealised body of brass complete with a suitably intimidating phallus, the face of a pre-Loss ancient god made from beaten platinum and gold. It was an avatar, a messenger; it shared a fragment of its creator's intellect and did the Absolute's bidding. It helped keep the signal constant.

The hall in the Citadel was an appropriate place for the automaton. It was a huge, empty, echoing chamber of black marble. It was meant to look like a place where gods walked.

The cocoon lay on the cool marble floor. There was still a blue-white glow from within but it was fading. The automaton stared down at it for a long time. Finally it climbed onto the cocoon and lay down, caressing it.

One of the Absolute's favourite toys materialised from the wall, like the cold dead marble had given birth. The Elite's armour disappeared into his body, its absorption feeling like breathing in. The tall male-favouring hermaphrodite was no less alien and god-like despite his nominally human appearance. Expressionless, he watched the automaton's sensual display as he walked over to the cocoon. Animated shadow followed him, making abstract but somehow terrible patterns on the floor.

'Where is Ludwig?' the automaton asked quietly. Its voice was the result of thousands of years of research by the uplifted races and AIs into trying to synthesise charisma and awe.

Fallen Angel closed his eyes. Sight had long since become an over-rated sense. 'He is drinking a star,' the Elite answered, his voice deep and melodious.

'They know it was us?' the automaton asked. Fallen Angel just nodded. 'Any trouble?'

'Scab's pale reflection was there.'

'It is no matter; he is no longer an Elite. If he comes looking for it then he can play the Game.'

'If the Consortium send their Elite?'

'You'll fight them, and stars will weep, but I don't think they'll risk full-scale war. They don't have our sense of adventure. They like to control and measure their wars. Fight among themselves. That way they can be sure of the outcome.'

'The Church?'

'They would but don't have Elite,' said the automaton.

'They have access to lot of S-tech.'

'Embargoes are more likely, but the Consortium are as sick of their bridge monopoly as we are. We may find they are unexpected allies. No, this was one dice roll and we won.'

Fallen Angel knew that the wants and desires of the Absolute were not necessarily the wants and desires of other sentient life forms. 'What are you going to do with it?'

'It's a toy. I'm going to play with it.'

The privacy field's internal holographic projector was old but service-able. It made them look like they were sitting at their table in deep space looking at a spiral galaxy. Vic liked it. It was retro but evocative.

Despite the Polyhedron's security guarantees, Scab was still running his own checks. Privacy wasn't as dead as people liked to claim. It was, however, very expensive.

'I am disappointed.' The words seemed to crawl across the blank's features as a series of violent tics before they came rasping out of its mouth. Scab was mildly surprised that anyone would think he would care if they were disappointed.

'So this is our mysterious employer then?' Vic said largely for the sake of something to say.

'What happened?' the blank managed after a violent-looking facial spasm that made Vic sit back.

'Doesn't matter. It wasn't viable,' Scab told the blank.

The blank's mouth opened wide. 'I want it,' it finally managed.

'Whoever's running the Monarchist systems these days wanted it more,' Scab told the blank.

'Two fucking Elites!' Vic snapped, his mandibles clattering audibly. 'Not one, because that would have been easy, but two fucking Elites.'

'I want it,' the blank repeated.

'Elites are beyond my capabilities,' Scab said. It sounded matter of fact, and only someone who knew him as well as Vic did could understand how much that admission cost him. 'I would like to be able to kill them but I can't.'

'I want it,' the blank repeated.

'Well at least we finally have a reasonable employer,' Vic said. The 'sect was never one to pass up an opportunity to practise his sarcasm. Only felines were better than humans at sarcasm.

The blank's head slewed around violently to stare at Vic with the patches of skin over where its eyes should be. It turned back to look at Scab with an equally violent motion.

'Fine. Give me back my armour and the rest of my capabilities, undo the neural surgery, but leave me free and I'll get it for you,' said Scab.

Vic turned to stare at Scab. His features weren't designed to convey the horror he felt.

'Tell me this isn't what this is about?' the 'sect demanded. Scab ignored him.

'You would be a monster,' the blank managed through a series of painful facial contortions.

'Which is what you need now,' Vic pointed out. The blank shook its head. It looked like it was trying to turn its neck all the way around.

'Then I can't get it for you,' said Scab. 'Once I had access to intelligence on the possible whereabouts of the aristos' Citadel but not now.'

'We ... will ... provide,' the blank managed. A cold chill settled on Vic.

'Even with the intelligence, the Citadel's going to be high-end S-tech. It could be out of phase; it could even be in Red Space.'

'We will provide.' The repeat message seemed to be easier for the blank.

'It doesn't matter if you give us the tools and the intelligence; we can't fight Elite.' Scab was starting to sound exasperated.

'Proliferation,' the blank whispered. Scab stared at it for a moment, then it was Scab's features' turn to contort. Vic felt like moving away from him. He didn't like Scab having emotions. Particularly negative ones like anger.

It happened quickly. Vic found himself wearing part of the blank. The top of the blank's skull was missing. Scab was holding a smoking tumbler pistol. The sound of the shot inside the tiny privacy cage was deafening but both of their augmentations had coped easily with it. The privacy field that protected them from surveillance also protected them from the Polyhedron's security systems. There was a reason that privacy cages were also called murder cages.

'Impulse control! Impulse control!' Vic screamed at him. Scab's pale face was also spattered with bits of blank. 'The S-tech in that guy would have cost the Cartel a fortune! Have you ever had a queen angry at you! It was just a fucking messenger!'

The 'sect was sure they would now have to fight both of the warriors waiting for them. Even as ex-Thunder Squad, starting life as a member of the worker caste had instilled in Vic a fear of the warrior caste on a genetic level. Vic drew both his double-barrelled laser pistols with his top set of arms. With his bottom right he drew the triple-barrelled shotgun pistol. Scab was placing a new round in the empty chamber of his archaic tumbler pistol. The blank was still opposite them, what was left of his head little more than a red bowl of bone and skin. Scab replaced the tumbler pistol in its holster.

'I mean, what a fucking total waste of time!' Vic continued ranting. The last time the 'sect had been this angry was when Scab had lobotomised the *Basilisk*'s AI because he hadn't liked the ghost's attitude. 'Why aren't you drawing weapons?' Scab ignored him. 'I mean, what is it with you?! You hear something you don't like and someone, anyone has to pay! And I mean what the fuck?! The whereabouts of the aristos' Citadel?! That's either board-level consortium intel or one of the fucking royals turning on their own! A palace coup! Like the fucking Art War! Remember that?! What have you got us into?!'

'I value these little talks,' Scab said, lighting a cigarette. He took a long drag, the cigarette's end glowing cherry-red. Vic stared at him. It was scarier because he knew that Scab wasn't being sarcastic. He probably meant it. This was quality time with another carbon-based life form for Scab.

'We're doing it,' he finally said. For a moment Vic was speechless.

'You're not a fucking Elite any more! We are way out of our league!' Vic's neunonics autonomously took the calm and informed decision to release massive amounts of sedative into his biological systems to calm him. Through the narcotic haze he started to wonder what the blank had meant by 'proliferation'. 'I'm not doing it. It's suicide and since you murdered me I don't have any clone insurance left. So die here, die there – makes no difference to me. This way it's over quickly and I don't have to put up with however many time units of shit-excreting fear.'

Scab nodded.

The warriors were waiting for them when the cage receded back into the Polyhedron's subjective floor. Vic had holstered his weapons, but the 'sect was still seething with anger at Scab. However, he was no longer in control of his body. Scab had slaved him and hacked his neunonics, taking control of his body. Again. Vic was entertaining murder fantasies that he knew he would never have the courage to act out.

Scab 'faced his clean-up bid to the Polyhedron's AI. It was accepted and the club's security systems did not attack him.

'Check with your queen,' Scab told the two warriors. They were radiating impending high-order violence. The dancers and other clientele were looking for cover.

Nothing happened. Locked in his prison body, Vic was shocked. The killing would already be on Arclight's newsfeed, which meant transmission to docked ships, who would send it to the transmitters on Red Space beacons the next time they bridged. The footage of the blank's killing, visual, audio and possibly immersion from some of the witnesses would be available for sale throughout the Consortium as quickly as Red Space travel and light could carry it. Everyone would know that Scab, already a celebrity killer, had, for whatever reason, destroyed a very valuable Queen's Cartel resource. If the cartel did not respond then they would look weak.

Vic experienced a sinking sensation when he realised that they would not respond. He badly wanted Scab dead right now. Instead this was just going to be another story in his partner's legend.

Scab stood up. The micro-hooks in his brogues anchored him to the floor. His P-sat rose to hover over his left shoulder. Vic found himself following Scab as he slowly walked towards the exit.

Vic looked around the club. There seemed to be more people there now. A lot of them sat at the bar, ignoring the dancers, wearing long black coats that could cover a multitude of sins. They had the look of Church Militia. *Brilliant*, Vic thought.

Vic barely had a moment to think that the human male in the button-up black suit who landed in front of Scab looked familiar, before Scab stuck a metalforma blade in the guy's face. It wasn't so much the speed of the attack that appalled him, Vic reflected; he'd seen Scab fight before. It was how quickly he got his bid into the Polyhedron's security systems so they didn't blow him away. The metalforma blade grew inside the man's head, branching out into a razor-sharp, root-like structure. The man swayed back on his anchored shoes, bobbing back and forth in the zero G.

Vic had a second to realise that the dead guy looked a little like his partner before the shaven-headed women landed in front of Scab. She was a monk. She wore brown armoured robes. She was powerfully built but all high-end soft-machine augmentation, S-tech as well if the rumours were true, moving tattoos based on Seeder symbols. She was not carrying any weapons; her hands were open. Scab levelled the tumbler pistol at her face.

'It's stupid to martyr yourself for a faith that doesn't even have an afterlife,' he told her.

'We're just here to talk,' she said.

A Church monk was probably more than equal to dealing with Scab, particularly with all the backup she had. The militants he had noticed were now all turning to focus on them. Nobody had drawn weapons yet except for Scab. Vic was surprised that he hadn't drawn any either. The problem for the Monk and her militants wasn't so much Vic and Scab as the bidding war that would be required to act in the Polyhedron. In that, Scab already had the drop on them, and they would have to fight him and the club's automated systems.

'Stop cloning him,' Scab told her, and with his gun levelled at her continued heading for the door, Vic following him. The Monk just watched them leave.

He had had been waiting for them as they left the Polyhedron. He had the look of home- and ship-less excess humanity. He was someone who had failed in the life of economic Darwinism but hadn't yet got round to dying. The one resource that nobody ever seemed to run out of, the one resource that the Consortium didn't seem to care enough about to control with artificial scarcity, was so-called sentient biological life. *This was presumably why you couldn't use human matter in assemblers*, Vic mused. *Then there'd be no shortage of raw material for the Consortium to control.* However, most of what Vic termed human refuse tended to come with only two eyes. The 'sect was more than a little surprised when two wrinkles on the man's head opened. Vic wasn't sure if they were eyes or not. Each looked like a biotech collection of nerve endings forming sensory organs. Still Vic couldn't shake the feeling that they were staring at him.

'What the fuck?' Vic said, wondering when his capacity for surprise would wear out. The man reached up with a small-bladed, but obviously very sharp, anachronistically-steel-bladed scalpel and cut the two eye-like organs out of his head. Blood poured down out of the wounds into the man's real eyes. All the while he stared at Scab and Scab watched the self-mutilation. 'Street art?' Vic wondered out loud.

Scab looked at the man expectantly as he drew an archaic-looking syringe from his jacket and stabbed it into Vic's armour. The vibrating power-driven needle drove itself through to original flesh.

'What are you doing?!' Vic cried, mandibles clattering together, the panic in his voice belied by his calm, combat-ready stance.

'It's a vaccine. Relax,' Scab said. Vic felt like an animal wanting to bolt but trapped in a cage.

'I've been waiting,' the man said. 'They told me you would come and I was to do nothing but wait.' The ragged, gaunt, dirty nobody finished cutting out the two eye-like organs and handed them to Scab. Scab continued to watch him as he slipped the organs into the pocket of his raincoat.

'I am nothing now,' the man said.

Scab nodded. 'Few people fulfil their dharma,' he said after a moment's reflection.

Vic watched the man collapse to the ground, his flesh slowly being eaten away. Then his virus warning went off, and he turned to look at Scab as Arclight started broadcasting a viral contamination warning. Vic knew if the virus was powerful and new enough to defeat Arclight's countermeasures and most people's personal defences then it would have to have been very expensive.

Scab grabbed the extruded handle of his P-sat and allowed it to pull him quickly towards the ship. Vic found himself doing the same while covering their retreat.

The expressway sealed as Arclight tried to keep some of its wealthier denizens safe. The P-sat dragged them through the lower passageways. They were still quite crowded, but it was easy to push through corpses in zero G, particularly as a lot of their flesh was missing thanks to the nano-enhanced necrotic nature of the virus radiating from Scab like a bad smell.

'They won't let you get away with this,' Vic said. He knew the cartel could not leave this unanswered. 'We're dead the moment we set foot on the *Basilisk*.' The 'sect was quite looking forward to his death. More than anything else, 'sects were about efficiency. They wouldn't make him suffer, just snuff him out. It would be a release, swimming through corpses as a virus ate their flesh was not his idea of fun.

However, Scab had already allowed for this. The *Basilisk*'s recently upgraded sensors had thoroughly mapped their path into Arclight, and Scab had uploaded it into his neunonics. Since they had landed he had been planting the seeds of escape just in case things turned out bad. He had sent out stealth AI programs of his own devising to burrow quietly into the various weapons and security systems that could give him problems on the way out, be they on the station or on other ships.

'You just killed a Church Militiaman,' Vic said. 'They have a frigate here.' He had seen the craft on the way in – sleek, violent-looking, a minimum of statuary on it, the armour engraved with the fall of the Naga. Frigates were fast. The *Basilisk* was faster, but the frigate horribly outgunned them and would be manoeuvring into position at this very moment.

'The *Saint Brendan's Fire*. I saw it,' Vic said as he concentrated on the virtual map in his mind, cracking systems that were readying to fire on the *Basilisk*.

'Fear and desire,' Scab said over the interface. It took a moment for Vic to realise that his partner was talking to the security force where the Basilisk was docked. They would be under a lot of pressure from the cartel to ambush Vic. 'Leave now and you have cartel trouble. Stay now and we'll take you down and take you with us. Your suffering can be my hobby for a week and then I'll turn you over to a house of pain. You won't die so your clone insurance won't be valid.' *And he would do it too*, Vic thought. He would have to, otherwise people would not take his threats seriously in the future.

When they got to the dock the door was open and the place was empty.

The pair of them strode onto the ship. Scab had left both airlock irises wide open. He closed them with a thought and the *Basilisk* began to scrub out the virals, its powerful nano-screen hunting down all the new guests. The *Basilisk*'s skin was hardening so the external feed was coming straight through the interface along with all the sensor data. Sure enough, most of Arclight's batteries capable of a firing solution on the *Basilisk* were aiming at the small craft. The *St Brendan's Fire* was manoeuvring into firing position, its thrusters glowing against a background of black and neon.

'Well, it's been a pleasure,' Vic said, ready to die and yet still absurdly proud of how much sarcasm he had managed to get into what he assumed was his parting shot. The 'sect felt the *Basilisk* disconnect from Arclight.

The night lit up as all the batteries on Arclight shifted to fire at the *St Brendan's Fire* as per their hacked orders. So many batteries fired in such a small area that it looked like a grid of fiercely defined light. The 'sect was aware of the acceleration: constant sensor feed from the *Basilisk* made the ship seem more real than his own slaved body. The burn of the engine, the *Basilisk*'s own batteries firing, the racks of kinetic shots silently emptying. All aimed at the *St Brendan's Fire*. The Church ship's energy dissipation grid lit up, making it look less like a solid, more like a ship of painfully bright light. Reactive armour blew out, trying to dissipate the energy of hypersonic kinetic shots, destroying the engraved scene as the carbon reservoir struggled to replace the armour.

The *St Brendan's Fire*'s manoeuvring thrusters burned bright as it tried to rise above the firestorm. Vic knew that all over Arclight security coordinators, pet hackers and weapon operators were desperately trying to regain control of their weapons. Arclight's PR team and spin doctors would already be apologising to the frigate and assuring them that the Queen's Cartel was not initiating hostilities against the Church.

The *Basilisk* soared through the fire, taking minor hits from a few opportunists in independent craft. Scab made a note of every shot and added the ships to his enormous opportunist kill file. The pursuit craft that the cartel had launched were too far away; however, all the bridge points were covered by picket ships.

'This is Woodbine Scab in the *Basilisk*. If you're going to fire then make sure you get it right,' he told the light cruiser waiting by the bridge point he wanted. A Corsair, even one as high spec as the *Basilisk*, was no match for a light cruiser. The picket ship didn't fire. The *Basilisk*'s bridge drive did violence to the fabric of space/time. The *Basilisk* left Real Space.

Only when Scab had locked the *Basilisk* onto the closest Red Space beacon and linked into the beacon network did he pull out the grisly objects the dead self-mutilator had given him. To Vic they were looking more and more like the eyes of some kind of properly alien species, not those of uplifted animals like themselves.

'How'd they know you'd need that?' Vic asked.

'Are you going to behave if I give you your body back?' Scab asked instead of answering the question. Vic nodded. The human gesture still felt uncomfortable but he was pretty sure that he had it down.

'Who was the Church Militiaman you killed?' Vic asked. Scab was staring at the alien organs pulsing in his bloody hand as he used a sophisticated neunonic surgery program to reconfigure his internal nanites in preparation for a xeno-graft surgical procedure.

'Scab,' Vic said.

'I need to find the template and kill it.' Scab said it in the same tone as everything else he said.

11

Northern Britain, a Long Time Ago

She was moving, floating to the sound of waves gently lapping against the shore. There was a bump as she hit the beach. She enjoyed the gentle movement of the sea. It was a moment of peace before her nostrils were assaulted by the charnel smells of aftermath. Her eyes flicked open. Carrion eaters wheeled in the grey, blank, nothing sky above her. She sucked in air in a long ragged gasp like the first breath of the infants she had delivered. She didn't scream though. Britha just didn't understand why she wasn't dead.

The beach looked red. The sand crawled with flies that rose into the air in thick black swarms when the ravens landed to feast. The carrion that used to be her people had enticed a pack of wolves out of the forest, their maws red now.

Britha's hand went to her chest and she traced the line of scar tissue. It was as if the wound had been received years ago. She understood that her magics were getting stronger, perhaps because of her relationship with Cliodna bringing her closer to the Otherworld and its wellspring of power, but it had been a mortal wound. She had felt the head of the spear grow through her like the sharp roots of an iron tree.

She had dreamed of Cliodna. The selkie had been strange, frightening and hateful. In the dream Cliodna had done cruel and agonising things to Britha's body. Her eyes hurt but felt dry. She couldn't cry. She ached but she could stand, though it seemed like the beach was trying to tilt up to meet her, nausea washing over her. She felt different somehow, hot, feverish.

The warriors and landsmen of her tribe were gone, all that was left was their empty shells making red patterns on the sand. Britha could not bury them all. She would not try. The sky would be their burial place. There was no shame in that. The ravens would carry their flesh there. The beasts of the land had nurtured them and they would do the same for the carrion eaters.

There was a low growl. The wolf pack scattered. Britha watched the bear lumber across the beach towards her, its maw already red from feasting on the dead. Normally all gave way to the king of the forest, but Britha felt nothing. That included fear. The beast got up on its hind legs but did not roar at her. It just stared. It was as if the bear didn't think she belonged.

'Maybe I am just a shade now,' Britha said quietly to herself. She had failed to protect her people. This was the *ban draoi*'s main responsibility – to live apart from the tribe but use her knowledge, wisdom and skills to keep them safe. Britha could not imagine a more complete failure. *But how do you protect against the likes of the Lochlannach?* she wondered.

Among the bodies Britha only found one of their dead. She had killed him, she knew, but she had killed more than one. They must have taken the rest of the bodies with them. As well as the hungry wounds she had drawn on his flesh with sword and sickle, she saw thousands of tiny cuts on his skin.

Britha cut into his cold dead flesh with an iron knife she had found. The strands of filigree were gone. His armour and weapons had been taken as well.

She heard the voice, soft and weak, barely audible, carried to her by the breeze.

He was lying on the beach propped against some rocks. He had stained the sand red underneath him. He spoke the same words over and over: 'I fought well, I deserve to die in battle. I fought well, I deserve to die in battle. I fought well, I deserve ...'

'Feroth?' Britha said softly. He turned to look at her. Tears sprang to his eyes. She could not recall anyone looking happier to see her. He had been old, Britha thought, but always full of life; now he looked all but a corpse. The life had been taken from him by what he had seen. It had left him a long time before he would actually die.

'Britha.' Then he became more guarded. 'Do demons ride you?' he demanded, trying to hold in his guts with one hand and reaching for his sword with the other.

'It's me, Feroth,' she said. He relaxed though more blood ran through his fingers from his exertions.

'Too old and too wounded to take, they told me. The demons would not even grant me an iron death,' he managed. 'Even the wolves wait until I am too weak to fight.'

'I will give you an iron death,' Britha managed, her voice cracking, the tears coming now.

'I saw them leave. The black ships, the demon ships. They grew ... then they sailed against the tide and the wind ...'

'Which way?' Britha asked.

'All the while Cruibne's head was screaming from that monster's shoulder.'

He was just raving now, Britha thought, but then they had all seen things. It must be true.

'Where did they go?' Britha asked again.

'West, up the Tatha.' He was sounding weaker and weaker.

'Hold on,' she told him gently.

She found one of the invaders' longspears. It had been driven deep into the sand and must have been overlooked. She grasped its wooden haft. There was screaming in her head. She felt hot and feverish again as she staggered back still holding the haft. She watched as tendrils of filigree grew, writhing from the spear's silver-coloured metal head and crawling towards her flesh. Britha understood now: all their weapons were alive, prisons for the demons locked inside. She wrestled for control of the spear, knowing that her magics were stronger, that she was stronger. The demon in the spear shrank before her, the fever subsided and the red-gold filigree crept back into the spearhead.

Britha was relieved that Feroth was still alive when she returned with the spear. He made a weak attempt to attack her with his sword as she drove the spear through his chest, burying it in the sand beneath him. She twisted the spear and tore it out. Her eyes never left his. She watched the life leave him, ready for his next journey.

She felt nothing.

Britha woke suddenly, her face raw, sore and covered in sand where she had collapsed face first onto the bloody beach. She felt so weak. She had dreamed of Cliodna again. She had dreamed of being dead, a corpse, and Cliodna making her walk to her cave and laying her in a pool of blood. Then the selkie had danced around her and made her drink blood. Cliodna had been angry. Only the moon had lit the cave, the shadows the moonlight threw were horrible to look at.

Cliodna had looked different: her skin had seemed harder, her features more angular and predatory, her lips peeled back to accentuate her wicked rows of blade-like teeth.

Britha rolled over and sat up. She felt frail, emaciated, all skin and bones, as if she had been feeding off herself just to survive, or her magics had. She used the spear to push herself to her feet. Slowly she made her way across the corpse-dotted beach back towards Ardestie.

Nobody falls further than a proud people. *Were they slaves now?* she asked herself, but she knew the answer.

In the village most of the food had been taken. The stone-lined storage pits next to each house were empty. The salted and smoked meat and fish, the fresh vegetables that had been harvested for the feast, the grain, all had been taken. Britha guessed this was to feed her people on their journey. She wasn't sure, but she thought that some of the sheep and cattle were missing.

All the horses had been killed, presumably to stop pursuit. In normal circumstance she would have mourned Dark Cloud's death but she was already overwhelmed. This and the beach would mean fat ravens.

Still, she knew where more food was kept and she was ravenously hungry. She gorged herself on heath pea, the tuberous root of the bitter vetch plant; she fried up oatmeal with blood and water; she found the last of the meat in the smokehouse that the raiders had overlooked; she raided the salt pits for fish and more meat. She ate more than she had ever eaten in a single sitting before. No matter how much she ate she was still hungry.

She knew that it should all go to her belly, but instead she felt herself start to bulk out again, to return to the shape she had been only last night. It was wrong, unnatural – she knew this – but still she kept eating, enough for five at a feast. She was eating in a way that would have shamed her in front of the rest of the tribe as others would have had to go hungry for her gluttony, but that did not matter now. Something had changed inside her. She felt different.

Finally she was sated. She did not feel bloated or uncomfortable but more awake, healthy; her wounds had healed and the only pain she felt was a dull ache from the branches of scar tissue on her stomach. She had the same heightened awareness of the night that she had felt the night before, when she had thought it was the woad.

Britha went to her roundhouse, set a little aside from the rest to show her position in the tribe. She took the ritual tools and materials, the herbs, medicines and poisons she thought she might need, those that could be carried easily. Her hearth fire was mere embers now. She swept them carefully into a hollowed-out horseshoe fungus and blew on it, letting it burn. It would smoulder for hours and the fungus was proof against water and wind. She found an old robe and hood and put them on. Her usual robe was still back in the circle of oaks in the woods and she did not have time to fetch it now.

Britha took one last look around her home. It felt strange and foreign to her. It was nothing without the sound of her tribe outside.

She made her way tiredly towards the Hill of Deer. Even as she made her way across the fields towards the hill, she knew the broch had not kept her people safe.

The carrion eaters took to the air on black wings as Britha approached the broch. There were only a few bodies, mainly those of landswomen. Grandmothers who had died trying to protect children, Britha guessed.

The broch was sundered. Britha guessed it had been the giants. It looked like they had punched through and then torn apart the ancient moss-covered blocks of stone. She imagined what it had been like for the children inside. Stone walls ripped open, the monstrous heads pushed through to stare at them. Their fear. That was when the pain really hit her. The magnitude of her failure, the failure of Cruibne and the *cateran*. They were gone, all of them. Many dead, the rest taken by an enemy that they, that she, could not fight. They were probably already being ridden by demons. The tears came. Sobs racked her body. Their life, her life, children being born, the old dying, the councils, the harvests and the planting, droving, raiding, battles, feasts, laughter, tears, life – the raiders had taken all that.

'No.' Sharp nails dug into flesh, drawing lines of red on weather-beaten skin. 'No!' Louder, more forceful. Those who were dead had lived and died well; they could not have asked more from life. The memories of them could not be stolen from her even if the demons came for her flesh. This was weakness, self-pity. She still had responsibilities. Some of her people were still alive. She could fight the Lochlannach. She was the only one who could. She needed to find a way for others to do the same.

Britha stood on the shore and watched the fire arrows arc into the night air on the other side of the Tatha. In flight they were mirrored in the black glass of the river before studding the demon curraghs with points of orange and red light. It was a good plan but she knew it would not work. She watched the Fib villages all along the river's north shore burn.

Then because she did not feel tired she turned to the west and started walking. She walked all night, tireless, no pain in her muscles or her feet despite a steady, fast pace.

She passed the black rock on the shore of the Tatha. In the distance she could see the hill fort. The height it sat on was just known simply as the hill. It would be locked up tight but only the younger children and the older landsmen and -women would be there. They were Cirig – their clan elders owed fealty to Cruibne – and all of the elders had been at the feast with their warriors and would have died on the red beach.

Beyond the hill fort were the Sidhe Hills, where the fair folk slept in their mounds and her people chose not to go. Best to leave the Otherworld alone. *What if it would not leave you alone?* she wondered. In the woods just west of the black rock she met some of the older children from the fort. They had chosen to go out scouting. She told them to return to the fort and that if they saw the black ships land on this side of the river they were to flee, with everyone, carrying the old if they had to, into the north and stay away from the coast and the wider rivers. They knew her – she had delivered some of them – and would listen and do as she asked.

Watch fires on either side of the river flickered into red life, Cirig and Fib alike warning of the black ships. Still she headed west. She was sure that Bress would take his people raiding as far up the Tatha as they could get where there were still villages and settlements worth raiding. This time she wouldn't hesitate. She would kill him and that monster, Ettin, as well.

Under the wooded grey cliff-lined hills to the west, the Tatha narrowed considerably and there was an island in the middle. Britha tied her robe around her. She had taken as much food as she could carry – oatmeal, heath pea, salted meat, anything that wouldn't spoil quickly – and wrapped it in hide sacks. She tied the sacks and the horseshoe fungus carrying the embers of her hearth fire to the end of her spear and waded into the cold river.

She had taken off her fur leggings. Barefoot she was better able to grasp the smooth stones on the riverbed with her toes. Even so, halfway across, when the water was over her stomach, she began to feel as if she had made a mistake. The sacks of food tied to the end of her spear threatened to unbalance her. She managed to compensate and then slipped, going down on one knee. The fast-moving current nearly tore her off her feet. She fought to hold on to the spear, dipping the sacks slightly in the water but regaining her balance. Eventually she managed to stagger to her feet and take another step, knowing that if it got any deeper she would have to ditch her food and spear and swim for it. But the water got shallower.

The island was important to the Fib. It was a place of power for their *dryw*. It was said that the Auld Folk had come here to worship their terrible and uncaring gods. To the Cirig it had been a convenient place to cross when they went chasing Fib cattle, though they always had to ford the beasts further upstream on the way home.

From the island she watched another of the Fib's villages burn. She was close enough to hear the screams but it was how quickly and efficiently it happened that got to her. The Fib were not as strong as the Cirig, but how quickly their resistance was dealt with shocked her. Standing on the shore of the island, she watched the Lochlannach, black figures silhouetted against the flames, herd their captives to the curraghs. The black ships were much larger than they had been when Britha had last seen them. If they came further west to make for the settlements on the Tatha further inland then Britha could try to sneak on board, either by swimming or via the branches that hung over the river.

The sun rose. The smoke from the still-burning settlements on the south bank was easier to see now. As were the black curraghs sailing east, back to the sea, their magics taking them against the wind. Britha still did not feel like sleeping. She ate too much, again, watching the huge black ships getting smaller and smaller. When she had sated herself she waded across the Tatha to the south shore and trudged south through the steep wooded hills. Avoiding the cliffs of wet grey stone when she could, losing time climbing them when she couldn't.

Two days of walking. Britha had never been this far south in Fib lands before. She knew she could not be too far from the lands of the Goddodin. A tribe not of the Pecht, they were a weak people who bent their knees to a god of the sea. The only Goddodin that Britha had ever seen had been slaves of the Fib. If they worshipped gods this made them suitable to be slaves, in Britha's opinion. But she knew that the Black River lay to the south – she had heard tell of it from southron traders all her life. If it was, as they said, similar in size to the Tatha, then she was sure the Lochlannach would raid along it for more captives.

Britha's eyes flicked open. Usually a restless sleeper, she had woken from a deep, restful, dreamless sleep fully aware. The sensation that had roused her was a tug from deep inside. Instinctively she knew that something was wrong at a fundamental level with the world around her. She reached for her spear, the demon inside it long since cowed, and rolled to her feet.

She could see it through the trees. A bright, rapidly pulsing, blue and white light illuminated the thickly forested hill. It made the silhouettes of the trees look grotesque and alive. There was the sound of wind rushing through the branches. It tugged at her robes. She had been sleeping with them wrapped around her, although the night cold did not seem to bother her so much now. She realised that the air was being sucked towards the light and that her hair was standing up just like it did before a thunderstorm, but this feeling was stronger than any thunderstorm she had ever experienced.

She retreated and dropped low as she saw lightning play across the trees in the distance. Cursing herself for a coward, Britha forced herself to stand. She had never seen the like but she was sure it had something to do with the Otherworld. It was moments before dawn, and as the pulsing subsided, the forest was lit by the soft grey light of that time of the day and the occasional flash of lightning in the branches of the trees. Dawn was the time between times, the border times when it was easiest for things to cross over.

Britha cursed inventively for a long time for no other reason than to put off what she knew she had to do. As *ban draoi* she had to deal with the Otherworld, though she was of the opinion that Bress, Ettin and the Lochlannach were more than enough Otherworldly trouble.

'Let's just try not to sleep with them this time,' she rebuked herself as she made her way towards where she'd seen the light.

It was a cairn, one of the circles of stones left by the Auld Folk. All the trees within a hundred feet of it had been blown over, their broken trunks pointing towards the circle. Lightning still arced between the stones.

It was known from stories told by mother to daughter and in the oak circles of the *dryw* that the Auld Folk would conduct rites and offer sacrifice in an attempt to appease or even curry favour with malevolent gods. Often the *dryw* of the Pecht would carve symbols of power onto the stones to counter the magic of the Auld Folk and their awful gods. Clearly this had not been done here.

The sense of power was palpable. The feeling of being on the edge of a storm was very strong but even now fading. She could feel the earth moving beneath her, vibrations that grew fainter even as the lightning flickered out. The sucking wind had long since subsided. At an instinctive level she knew that violence had been done to the very fabric of the land.

Britha walked around the stones slowly, looking for tracks, moving in a widening circle. In the soft earth beneath the trees she finally found signs. Two sets of tracks, both men by the length of stride and depth of the imprint, both carrying either spear or stave and, again judging by the depth, at least one of them armoured. One wore boots of a type she was used to seeing, though if she had been forced to guess she thought they looked more like the boots that the southron tribes wore, or even the warriors from the isle far to the west. The other man's boots, the one who was unarmoured, were something else entirely. They had a hard sole of a type she had never seen before. She wished Talorcan were here. He had taught her how to track and hunt and would be able to get more from the tracks. She tried to ignore the tears welling in her eyes. She had to concentrate on what she was doing. Many of her tribe were still alive, though they might be little more than hosts for demons. The tracks headed south and east.

There's no gain in courting trouble, Britha decided. She would continue south but keep away from the direction the tracks were going. Perhaps if she was lucky they were Otherworldly enemies of Lochlannach.

Britha found the first crow feeder some distance from the smoking village. The gaping wound was in his back yet he wore armour, though he had left his shield and spear behind when he had fled. The crows took flight at her approach. She took the time to spit on the coward's corpse. She had a good mind to roll him into the Black River. He had no business being taken into the sky by the crows and the ravens. Then she remembered that these people worshipped a god of water.

'If they are craven enough to bend a knee then this god gets what he deserves,' she muttered, but she did not have the time to carry the coward's corpse to the water, or any of the other corpses she saw.

Britha had seen her first glimpse of the Black River from the top of a cliff in the forested hills overlooking the mouth of the river. She'd only ever heard of the river in stories before. If anything it was larger than the Tatha. The north bank was a series of wooded hills and cliffs overlooking the river, which was studded with rocky islands, though the water did not look particularly black to her. More stone-grey under the overcast sky. She saw no demon ships either, though smoke rose from a number of places along the shore.

It had started to rain by the time she made it down to the village. It was the sort of constant drizzle that soon soaked through and made you feel very cold, though the cold still wasn't bothering her.

The village was a series of crannogs connected by a network of bridges over the water. The crannogs were very similar to the roundhouses that Britha was used to: wattle and daub walls, conical thatched roofs held up by internal pillars lashed together with nettle rope. However, these crannogs were built on stilted platforms over the grey water.

The bridges between the houses and the land were made of strong branches cut to size and could be pulled up to isolate the buildings from the shore and each other. This defence had done little good against ships and giants. More than one of the crannogs looked like the top had been torn open, presumably by one of the giants standing in the river.

The village told the same story as her own and the others on the banks of the Tatha. They had come for the people. They had taken food as well. Those warriors who resisted were quickly killed. The tracks told of people herded onto dry land, along the pebble beach and back into the water to climb into a curragh. If she was reading the tracks correctly, then they had split their forces and only one of the curraghs had attacked this village. She guessed that the attack had taken place at least two days ago.

She looked down at one of the bodies. It was headless. The body was the largest and well fed, covered in patches of scale-like woad tattoos, and was also, judging by its hands, the oldest. Britha reckoned he had been the chief. She wondered if his head now rode on Ettin's shoulder. She hoped that Cruibne was free from that torment at least. The headless warrior's body wore scaled armour, a small fortune in metal, but it had been left. All the scales made him look like a fish, a true servant of their sea god. Judging by his wounds he had at least tried to fight. He had died on the smooth pebbles down by the waterside. He had charged them as soon as they came ashore.

'Treat him well, you bastard,' she told the river.

Britha stood on the platform that circled the furthest crannog from shore. She had had to lay the bridges back down to get there, and more than a few had been broken, presumably by the giants. She stared out across the river and out to the sea to the east, hoping to see the black curraghs but they were presumably long gone.

Sighing, she turned to look through the broken wall and roof of the crannog. The entrance faced to the east, she guessed to greet the dawn. Opposite the opening she saw an altar, carved from driftwood, the crude figure of the sea god, a scaled large-eyed man. Too Britha's eye there was something grotesque and unsettling about the figure.

Britha cast her eyes back to the beach. The smoke had not been from the crannogs. They had left the stilt village but burned the tiny fleet of fishing curraghs and log canoes. Even if they hadn't, if the Black River was anything like the Tatha then the tides and currents were treacherous and she would need the guidance of a local to make a crossing. She would have to head further west, deeper into the kingdom of the sea god's people, to cross. *The Lochlannach would make even more distance, but they had to be going somewhere and the land could only be so big*, she thought.

145

Britha heard movement behind her as she looked over the seemingly calm, grey surface of the river. She loosened the grip on her spear slightly and turned around.

It was one of the Goddodin, of that she was sure. He was no spear-carrier though; he had the look of a king's champion, the kind of massively built man that Nechtan had loved to fight because they always underestimated his speed and size. 'They won because people feared them, not because they were good fighters,' she remembered him telling her before he killed the last champion that Finnguinne had brought onto Cirig land.Britha wondered why the man still lived. Had he been craven? The patchwork of scars that covered his torso showed that he had not been afraid of wounds in the past, but she knew that each man and woman only had so much courage and could reach a point when all of it had been harvested. He staggered towards her, dragging his longspear and shield over the wooden bridge to the platform she stood on.

'I did not do this,' she said. Though he would not know her tongue. The Goddodin shared the same language of the people known as the Britons, who, like the Pecht, were made up of many different tribes. All of them were gods-slaves, to hear tell of it.

The champion was not far from seven feet tall – he towered over Britha. He wore fur leggings and trews, and his naked torso was covered in intricate blue woad scales. The top of his shaved head was likewise tattooed. Britha reckoned that his god made him ashamed to fight skyclad and that the tattoos were meant to make him look like a fish, or maybe it represented armour. The dead warriors she had seen had been similarly tattooed but not as extensively.

'I wish to talk. They attacked my people as well. Many were taken. I am tracking them.' The man ignored her words. He just stumbled towards her, a look of slack confusion on what little she could see of his bovine features.

'Can you hear me? Are you hurt?' she asked, thinking that he had taken a blow to his head that had perhaps laid him low, and the Lochlannach had left him for dead. It was a shame Ettin hadn't taken his head, she mused; the size of it would have unbalanced him.

The man turned to face her and she saw it. His eyes were a solid metallic red, and paths of blood bulged beneath his skin as if he was in the throws of *riasterthae*, the fabled battle frenzy that she'd oft heard of but never seen. She looked hard at him and saw fire crawling like insects throughout his body. Britha cursed.

Then the man was holding his spear one-handed, and the powerful upwards sweep that Britha only just managed to parry with her own would have splintered the haft of any normal weapon. As it was, it sent her staggering back towards the Black River. Whatever he had been, he was one of them now.

The huge man roared as he threw his large oval shield into the air and caught it by the handgrip. He did the same with the spear, getting a better grip. Britha backed towards the river. She was running out of platform, and the shaved, rounded branches beneath her feet were slippery, preventing her from finding a steady stance. The huge man would be used to the shifting platform, however, and if he had been a good slave to his sea god then the water itself could act against her.

The Goddodin warrior stabbed out at her with the spear. She dodged it, darting to the left, exactly where he wanted her to go. His leather-covered oak shield hit her with enough force to pick her up off her feet. She landed hard on the platform, feeling the branches bend beneath her. The impact drove the wind from her but she still had the presence of mind to scrabble for her spear as she tried to remember how to breathe again. Britha rolled to the side as his next spear thrust turned the branches that had been underneath her into splinters.

Grabbing her spear, Britha staggered to her feet and threw herself through the hole in the wall of the crannog. The huge warrior stabbed at her through the wall as he moved around the building to block off her escape.

Britha ran out of the crannog and made to jump into the river but changed her mind. She did not want to feed herself to the Goddodin's sea god. Changing direction, she made for the bridge leading to the next crannog. The warrior made lies of Nechtan's words. He was incredibly fast. The thrust missed, but then he reversed the blow and caught Britha in the back hard enough to take her off her feet and slam her, winded and struggling for breath, again, onto the floor of the bridge.

As he advanced on her, Britha's foot hit him in the groin with a maiden's kick. He barely seemed to notice. From the ground she had to batter aside another savage spear thrust. She lashed out with a foot again, this time at his knee. Her foot contacted with force that surprised her. She heard the knee shatter and the man staggered back. Suddenly he looked unsteady on his feet. With a roar he reached down and grabbed her round the neck. He was too close for Britha to use her spear. Britha beat and clawed at him ineffectively. He picked her up and held her high. The fingers on his massive hand squeezed, cutting off blood and air.

Panic.

Britha reached down and pressed the ragged nails of her thumbs against his eyes. They did not feel like eyes; it was like pushing against bronze. Then she felt burning in her arm and then her hand, a sensation like something moving beneath her skin. She watched in horror as the nails on her thumbs changed shape and colour, turning into sharp black claws not unlike Cliodna's. She pressed them into the huge man's eyes. The nails pierced and Britha felt something wet squirt out over her thumbs. He howled like an animal and dropped her. His hands went to his eyes.

Sprawled on the bridge gasping for air, she tried to crawl away, seeking desperately for her spear. She was trying to fend off the blackness of unconsciousness that threatened to overwhelm her from lack of oxygen.

The man was staggering on his damaged knee. He steadied himself and took his hands away from the red ruin of his eyes. Britha managed to find her spear as her breath came again. She heard the bones in his knee knit together. She turned to face him, calming herself like Feroth had taught her. Even through the blood she could make out the look of feral hatred on his face.

Yanking his sword from its scabbard and screaming incoherently, he charged her. She tried to remember everything that Nechtan and Feroth before him had ever taught her about fighting. Her spear had the benefit of reach over his sword, but as soon as he was past her guard she was dead. However, she was faster than him and, she hoped, more intelligent.

Britha glanced behind herself, making sure she knew the position of the crannog and the network of platforms and bridges, and backed away rapidly. His powerful sweeping blows were designed to intimidate, sunder shields and tear open armour. If you were fast and unencumbered they were easy to avoid.

Britha struck out again and again with the spear. Slower than her he may have been, but he used his shield well. The point of her spear just made deep gouges in its leather covering.

She feinted to his leg and followed up with a lightning-fast strike to the head that surprised even herself. She opened a cut on his face.

Ducking, avoiding and parrying blows with her spear that should have shattered the haft, she kept the perfect picture of the crannog village that she had taken from the quick glance behind her in her head. Britha was trying to make her way back to dry land.

She turned and ran, leaping across a gap that she had thought too far to jump, expecting to find herself in the water. The huge warrior was in the air right behind her. She threw the spear above her head to parry his sword as he tried to open her skull in mid-air. The blow shook the spear's haft, sending painful shock waves down her arm.

Britha landed. The warrior's knee caught her in the back as she did, sending her flying, but she managed to stay on her feet. She spun round to parry vicious sword blow after vicious sword blow with her spear. He was herding her, controlling her movement. This time when she tried to move around the closest crannog, he blocked her. She darted to the right, stabbing out with the spear. Somehow the huge man managed to parry the thrust and hit her with the shield again. The jarring blow knocked her off her feet and slammed her into the wall of the crannog. The structure cracked behind her. Her head lolled as she struggled to remain conscious. She felt broken inside, nauseous, not sure of where she was for a moment and she had dropped her spear.

As he screamed at her, raising his sword, he sprayed her with spittle, his breath smelling of fish, ale and decay. He brought the sword down, moving the shield that was pinning her to the wall aside at the last moment. It was enough. With new-found speed she threw herself to the platform, rolled and grabbed her spear. The Goddodin's sword cut through the roundhouse's thatch roof and wattle and daub wall. On her feet holding the spear, she turned and used the momentum of the movement to help power the spear thrust. The massive warrior seemed momentarily confused as to where she was. He was starting to turn when Britha drove the head of the spear into his side and up into his ribcage.

She cried out as the ash haft of the spear became burning hot. Britha let go. She had felt the demon in the weapon awaken. It wanted to bury itself in flesh and bathe in blood. It wanted to drink the champion's death and revel in it, even if he was one of theirs now.

The man staggered towards her.

'Die!' she screamed at him, putting every bit of her will behind the word. Too intent on the curse, she did not move quickly enough to avoid the powerful backhanded slash of his sword. It drew a line of burning blood up her torso from right to left. She stumbled back, falling hard. Already she could feel the poison on the blade coursing through her.

The light went as he towered over her, dragging her spear in his flesh. He reached down and managed to yank it out, tearing so much of his flesh it looked like his chest had caved in. Even through the pain Britha felt horror at what she saw. The end of her spear was wriggling tendrils of bloody metal. It looked alive. The warrior dropped the spear and tumbled forward like a felled tree, crashing through the

149

platform and into the water. Despite the pain, Britha rolled onto her side to stare into the dark water. She stared for a long time. He did not surface. *He has gone to feed his god*, Britha thought. She felt hot and feverish. Under her skin her flesh burned.

Britha had no idea how long she had been unconscious, but she had woken to find the wound no better, although the cold night air had gone some way towards cooling her fever. She felt like there had been a war and her body had been the battlefield.

The sword wound had been deep but not deep enough to kill. It was puckered, wide, as if the flesh had torn itself open in the path of the sword. She had managed to hold it together long enough to start a fire in the hearth of the closest crannog, using the embers held in the horseshoe fungus. It too had a carving of the fish god. She did not like the way it stared at her. She wondered if it was working against her healing magics.

She had also managed to find some mead and had washed the wound out with the boiled liquid. She had passed out screaming doing this. When she came to again, she knew she did not have much time. She was already having to swat flies away from the gash. The knife she had taken from one of the dead warriors was red in the fire now. She picked it up and felt the heat coming from the blade. At that moment she feared nothing more than the red-hot blade of the knife but she knew she had to do it in one go. If she lost consciousness the flies would get into the wound, it would fester and she would die. Even after she'd cauterised the wound, she knew her chances of surviving were not great.

She tried to surprise herself. Suddenly she pressed the knife to the wound. She wondered if her screams made the sea god himself cringe far beneath the water.

There were no flies, no crow-black wings. Perhaps they felt how unnatural she had become, tainted by the Otherworld in some way she did not understand. She felt exhausted. The wound throbbed but was the manageable side of agony. She was very hungry, frail and emaciated. Looking at her body, she had lost a lot of weight again. Skin was stretched across bone.

She ate what supplies she had left. She scavenged and found more. What she ate she did not think a normal person would even be able to contain. Dimly she realised that she had not shat since before the red beach. She began to fill out again after she had consumed enough smoked fish and salted pork, lamb and beef to feed many people. She had been eating for hours.

A thought that had occurred to her on the red beach came to her again. She had tried to force the idea from her mind. It was the darkest of magics taught in the groves only when winter came, when animal innards festooned the branches of the oaks and blood watered the land.

Britha still knew almost nothing of them. Only what little Bress and Cliodna had told her. That they were slaves to a god and that they brought the madness of the moonstruck with them. It was not enough. She needed more. She needed to know where they were going. It would be more difficult if they were to sail across the sea, perhaps south to the kingdoms of the dark-skinned people the Pecht had sometimes traded with, or north back to their icy home.

She knew a way to steal knowledge but she did not wish to use it. Recovering from the wound had weakened her and these kinds of magics took their toll. They would stain her, make her less than other folk, but it was her people at stake, the people that she had sworn to protect.

Chanting to herself, hoping that her tattoos would offer enough protection to ward away the Goddodin's sea god, she waded into the water. Every time she dived down into the dark water she feared the god of the carved effigies she had seen would find her. Eventually she found the body, her sight better underwater than she remembered. She managed to hold her breath for a long time and tie a rope around him. The huge warrior's body was heavier than she thought, but with strength that surprised herself she dragged it onto the beach.

Naked, so that her tattoos could protect her, she had drawn with woad on her skin. The symbols would tell her body and mind what to do when she was lost in the vision. They were the magics that would steal knowledge from the dead champion. She had made do without the correct herbs to burn but she had said the words. Ancient words that allowed her to force her will on man, woman, beast, the land and the sky.

Her sickle would have been better, particularly since it had been bathed in her blood, and blood magic was the strongest of all, even more so than fire magic, but that had been lost on the red beach. The iron knife that had seared her flesh would have to do. She reached down to the champion's body and cut the first slice of meat off. She held it to her face, steeled herself and opened her mouth. She had eaten raw meat before but it was all she could do not to vomit. She swallowed, stealing some of his power, looking for his knowledge, looking for what the demon inside him knew.

It was like swallowing fire. The fit hit her in a burning wave as she threw herself into violent contortions on the ground, screaming.

12
Now

The young Asian guy staring at her had one of those strange hair-styles that seemed to involve gluing your non-symmetrical hair to your head and, at least in this case, then sleeping on it. It took a few moments for Beth to remember where she was. What she couldn't work out was who this guy was and why he was staring at her so angrily. His shirt and shorts were obviously what he wore to bed, but both came from what Beth vaguely recognised as designer labels.

'Hello ...?' Beth tried.

'So you're a Luckwicke, are you? Gosh, how lucky we are to have another Luckwicke in our house.' His voice full of effeminate sarcasm. Beth was pretty sure he was gay. He was certainly attractive enough. Beautiful skin, sensual dark eyes, slender, almost petite frame. *Typical,* she thought. Clearly he knew Talia and hated her. This wasn't the first time something like this had happened to her. The sensual eyes were filled with anger as he leaned in close to Beth, who was just desperately trying to wake up.

'Listen to me, bull dyke,' he began.

I'm not a lesbian, Beth thought in mental protest but kept it to herself.

'I know Maude thought that Talia was the coolest thing ever and a good friend, but I know that fucking little bitch was trying to turn her out! Try anything like that and you'll have me to answer to. Understand?'

'Er ... yes,' Beth said.

'Now I want you the fuck out of my house and stay away from Maude, you understand me?'

Beth would have liked to say something, to stand up for her sister, to defend herself, but she could see his point. He and Maude were presumably just two more of her sister's victims.

'Fair enough,' she said and sat up in her sleeping bag. It was pretty much the archetypal student flat, patched and worn furniture, a

153

mixture of band and young male heart-throb posters on the walls. Perhaps a bit more effort had been put into decorating the place, a bit of cheap glamour used to good effect. She found her combats and grabbed them. The pretty young man was glaring at her, arms crossed. 'A bit of privacy?' she asked.

'As if I'd be interested in anything you have to—'

'Uday, are you being nice?' Maude said, coming into the lounge in novelty pyjamas that Beth thought made her look like a gothic Dalmatian.

'No,' Uday said pettishly. Maude handed him and Beth cups of tea.

'Thanks,' Beth said.

'She was just going,' Uday said pointedly. Maude turned to Beth.

'Have you got anywhere to go?'

'Home?' Uday suggested.

What a good idea, Beth thought. 'Just got to sort out a few things first—'

'What, because your bitch sister blew herself up?' Uday interrupted. Beth turned to stare at him. Uday, to his credit, met the glare and held it. Maude's face began to crumple into tears. Uday's face softened as he put an arm around her. 'Oh darling, I'm sorry, I didn't mean it, I was just being a bitch.' Uday glared at Beth as if this was all her fault.

'I'll go,' she said and unzipped the sleeping bag, standing up to pull her combats on. Maude reached out and laid a hand on her shoulder.

'Look, you don't have to go. You can stay here for a while.'

'No, she can't!' Uday all but screamed. Maude turned to fix him with a stern glare.

'Uday, you're being horrible. Just because you never like Tal—'

'Because she was a heinous bitch!'

'Uday,' Beth said quietly. He turned to glare at her, daring Beth to speak. 'My sister wasn't a very nice person, I know that perhaps more than anyone. But she's dead, so please don't talk about her like that. I wouldn't do it to you if the positions were reversed.'

Uday stared at her. 'She fuck you over as well?' he finally asked.

Beth thought about this. They both seemed nice. Close. Uday was clearly just a protective friend. Beth had the choice of how much to tell them, but she really didn't like letting anyone in, not when she hadn't known them for a long time. Trust did not come easy to her.

'She testified against me at my trial after I hurt her boyfriend, who nearly beat her to death,' Beth said. It felt like a massive gamble. It felt like she was opening herself up to attack. She decided not to tell them that she'd killed her sister's boyfriend. Maude looked shocked.

Beth didn't think what she had just told her gelled with the girl's image of Talia.

'Okay, you can stay. But just for a little while. I fucking hate freeloaders.' Uday finally said.

'Yaaay!' Maude said. *They were just children*, Beth thought, and *I'm not a freeloader.*

Beth walked over to the window and looked out onto a broad tree-lined road. The houses were all three or four storeys, many of them converted into flats, and she thought it must have been a wealthy area at some point in Southsea's past.

'Do you know where I can get some work?' she asked.

Beth guessed the amusements on the pier looked better lit up at night. During the day you saw the cracks. It was an odd place: a mixture of bright plastic, irritating jingles, peeling paint and frayed, stained carpets, the smell of fried food and brutal concrete buildings that reminded her of home. The main building had what looked like a flying saucer on top of it. Bright plastic pirates and animal-headed characters enticed children onto the rides and parted parents from their money.

The guy she had spoken to was called Ted. A large man, he had seemed cheerful enough, but Beth felt there was an edge behind the happy fat-guy demeanour, that he was not someone you messed around with even if the constant cigarettes he smoked made him short of breath. It made sense if he had been running this place for as long as he claimed. He had clocked her for what she was straight away.

'You've been inside,' he said. Beth hadn't seen the point in lying. She had just nodded.

'Drugs?'

'No.'

'You mess with children?' She just glared at him angrily. He was studying her. Coming to his own decision, looking for the reaction not the words. After all, anyone who had hurt children probably wouldn't admit to it. 'Got a temper?' he finally said, apparently content that she didn't mess with children. Beth gave his question some thought.

'I worked doors. I'm used to putting up with a lot of shit before I blow.'

Ted watched her some more.

'Well, we can always use someone who can look after themselves round here. Thing is, you look desperate to me.'

'I'm not desperate; I need the money. Who doesn't? Look, you don't know me, that's fine, but I don't need much and I work hard.'

'I can't have people sleeping here,' he said, but she knew that meant he would hire her. She could kick in some money to Maude and Uday and get a little money behind her for a place of her own if she was going to be here that long.

'I've got a place. I'm not on the street or anything.'

Ted's face brightened and he shook her hand.

'Start tomorrow. Be ready for long days of screaming kids and longer nights of drunk older kids.'

Beth nodded. It felt good to be working again.

Beth had used a little more of the precious money that her dad had given her to celebrate. She had bought herself some fish and chips and a can of decent bitter and gone down to the empty pebble beach. She looked over the slate-grey water. She could see artificial islands with buildings on them and beyond them, the Isle of Wight. It wasn't the sea proper. She knew that. It was a channel called the Solent. She didn't care. With the ships and the boats it was the sea to her.

A fierce wind caught her hair, whipping it around as nearby a hovercraft swept up the beach to land by a small passenger terminal. She watched as a big passenger ferry left for some place she would probably never visit. She hoped that everyone on board wouldn't just enjoy where they were going, but take pleasure in being able to do the very journey itself. She watched some kind of warship – it looked high-tech to her eyes, violent – coming into the port, disappearing between Old Portsmouth and Gosport into the harbour, presumably towards the naval dockyards.

She liked it here, she decided. Maybe it was because it was a change. Somewhere different where you didn't get to see the same old faces age in front of you. Where everyone didn't know what you had done. Or maybe it was just because it was open: the air could get to you here; you weren't trapped in a valley. Beth had no doubt that this town had its problems, just like everywhere else, but she didn't feel the same air of defeat she felt at home.

Late evening but still warm. Port Solent was obviously a new development. Shops, cafes and restaurants, surrounded by high-rise luxury apartment blocks for whoever passed for the beautiful people of Portsmouth, Beth assumed. She always felt like an outsider in places like this. She had been waiting outside the address that Maude had given her for over an hour, waiting for someone to go in.

Finally a man walked past her, not even registering her existence, and keyed the number into the door. Beth waited until it was just about to click shut and slid her fingers into the tiny gap to stop the door from locking. The guy had his back to her walking down the hall. She slipped into the apartment building.

In the lift Beth tried to get the words of her favourite revenge song out of her head. *This was about information, not revenge*, she told herself.

Beth had chosen the bayonet purely for intimidation. *Size is everything*, she thought. She knocked on the door. It was a secure building, so he would be expecting a neighbour, someone safe; he wouldn't have a chain on the door or check the peephole. She hoped. The door opened.

He was attractive, but it was the sort of attractive that made Beth immediately suspicious. To Beth he was a chameleon, an actor who made himself into whatever was required for him to accomplish his job of getting the young and attractive to service the older and wealthier. The nice clothes were doubtless accompanied by the right words, the comforting smile. He wasn't just a pimp and dealer; he was a pusher. He talked people into the vices that he profited from. There was nothing real about people like this, as far as Beth was concerned.

She saw his look of confusion change to one of suspicion. She had to do this quickly and quietly. This was the sort of place where people would actually phone the police, and they'd turn up, probably quickly.

He started to close the door. She pushed it hard, knocking him back. She was in, kicking the door closed behind her, her great-grandfather's bayonet in her hand. Grab him by the face. Keep moving. Keep him off balance. Let him see the knife, then let him feel it on the skin of his throat.

'Very quietly or I cut you,' she hissed. He looked more angry than frightened. That wasn't what she wanted. He tried to scream through her fingers as she drew a line of red down the skin under his cheekbone. He started to struggle. 'I will fucking stab you!' she told him. He stopped struggling. 'Are you going to keep it down?' He nodded warily. She took her hand away but kept the point of the blade pressed into the skin of his throat.

'I know people,' he said.

'I don't, and they don't know me. They won't know you if I cut your fucking face off.' She had to convince him she meant it. 'I'm Talia Luckwicke's sister.' There was the fear she wanted. It was the start of a very bad night for William Arbogast.

*

Beth had kicked his legs out from under him, taken him to the ground and then straddled him, ignoring his look of distaste, her knees pinning his arms. She kept the blade at his throat.

'I'm just looking for information. I'm going to get it. All you need to do is decide how much I'm going to have to cut you before I find out what I need to know.'

'Look, fuck you and fuck your whore—'

She hit him in the nose, broke it, blood spurting down his face, his head thumping into the tile flooring. Beth brought her fist back. She knew she was just going to keep hitting him and hitting him. It was war. She knew this feeling, Beth was almost gone. She had to get control, had to ...

Arbogast's vision was red and blurred; he felt sick. He shook his head, recovering, looking up at the mad girl with a big knife. He knew that look. Seen it in the eyes of his clients who liked to hurt the merchandise. He'd seen it in McGurk's eyes.

'Okay, okay. What do you want to know?'

Breathing hard. Trying not to kill him. Beth closed her eyes. She needed not to see the world in red right now. She willed herself back.

'You knew my sister, and don't fucking lie. I know you were her pimp.'

Arbogast started to scream, but her hand was over his mouth, gripping it hard as she dug the blade into the side of his head, pressed down until she felt bone and then dragged it down through the skin, blood spurting out of the wound. Head wounds always bled more. Show them their blood, she remembered Thomas telling her. She held up the bloody knife. Showed it to him. Shaking with anger.

'I'm not in control of this. You are. How much do you want to get cut? Are you trying to show me your skull?'

'Please, my face ...' He was crying.

Your face, Beth thought angrily, *and the clothes, the easy smiles and expensive aftershave, the nice car.* All props so he could use people, profit from them. She leaned down close to his ear, intimate.

'I'm going to cut it off.' She thought she meant it. More importantly so did he.

'I remember her. She was a party girl. She wanted to do it all but she didn't have any money, just her looks. Look, she was cool with it. She did some films. Is that what this was about? Did you see her on the Internet or something? Look, I'm sorry but it's a free country. She had a choice!' He was sounding desperate.

'The hooking?' she asked. She was surprised to see him turn even paler. Somewhere at the back of her head a sane voice was asking

158

why she was doing this. She wasn't going to hear anything good, anything that would help, and her sister would still be dead.

'Look, I know it sounds bad—'

'Sounds?' Beth hissed.

'Look, she wanted the money; I knew the people. She made her own decision. All I did was make sure that she was okay. I looked after her ...'

'Like the big brother she never had?'

'She wasn't standing on street corners. It was upmarket clients, reasonable. She was treated nice.'

Beth wanted to hurt him. Despite his words he knew that he had played his part in what Talia had become. She also knew that she was lashing out. Talia was capable of making her own choices.

'She was in demand,' Arbogast said before realising that this might not be the best thing to say in the circumstances. Beth concentrated all her attention on him again.

'Why?' she asked suspiciously.

'She was really pretty, you know. She had the whole goth thing going ...'

Beth didn't doubt that Arbogast was an excellent liar under normal circumstances, but she didn't think this was his normal power relationship with the opposite sex. He was hiding something.

'Tell me.'

'Look, you've got to underst—'

She grabbed him painfully by the mouth again. She could hear him trying to beg through her clenched fingers. She put the knife back into the wound she had made and started to twist the blade. She tried not to think whether her great-grandfather would have approved or not.

'Please,' he was sobbing. 'Blood ...'

'Like this?' She showed him the knife again and he shrank away from her.

'Bloodletting. She and her goth friends were into the vampire thing. They would drink blood from each other. Some of my clients wanted to live that fantasy out ... some of the specials ... but ...'

'What?'

'There were stories, rumours about her, that people saw things when they drank her blood.'

Confused at first, then angry again. She hurt him some more.

'Do I look like I'm fucking around, you cockless little bastard!'

'No, no, no.' Begging. 'Please ... She came back bad a few times, hurt, you know, they took too much. They wanted her blood, I wouldn't tell you this ... I couldn't make it up.'

She could see he wasn't lying. Her anger was as much because she couldn't understand. She had no frame of reference to process this, and people get angry and frightened when they can't understand things.

'Did you ever do it?' Beth demanded. He stared at her terrified through the tears. He nodded. 'And?'

Running, foot on the balcony, into space, travelling forward but in a backwards somersault. Land on the roof of the next building. Nice and smooth, like in PK Killer. Not just a case of augmented speed, strength, agility, but having neurally rewired yourself to remove the fear and inhibitions.

He threw himself off the roof, grabbing his knees, tumbling sideways. He dropped two storeys and grabbed the balcony rail. He pulled himself up with enough force to leap over the rail and onto the balcony. *Upper body strength without tears*, he thought smiling. His clan joined him.

'It was like space, you know, like in a film. It was beautiful. Like heaven. I think I heard God. He was angry.'

Beth stared at him.

'What the fuck am I doing?' Beth said out loud. The anger just drained from her. Talia was gone. All she was doing was trying to put balm on that. Cheapening her sister's death with violence and strangeness. She rubbed her face. Talia was gone. She was starting to feel it. She had often hated her but she was family. She felt tears behind her eyes. She turned away from Arbogast. He couldn't see that. She left him on the floor in his own blood. She didn't even bother with a parting threat.

It took a moment for fear and self-pity to be replaced by anger and self-pity. Arbogast managed to get to his feet despite the pain. He had to see what she had done to his face.

The door to the balcony opened. They were twelve storeys up. It didn't make sense: nobody could have been on the balcony. Dark urban wear, hooded sweatshirts, expensive trainers and monster masks.

The one in the front, flayed skin mask, held a phone in one hand; his other hand was cupped. It looked like it was full of glitter. He held the phone out. Arbogast saw a picture of Talia and dearly wished that he had never even met the fucking emo bitch.

'Look, I know people, right. She's fucking dead.' Every time he

160

spoke it felt like his face would split open; more blood coursed from the wound Beth had made. 'I think she and her friends were trying to cook meth or something. They blew themselves up.'

Flayed skin stared at him. Then he lifted up his cupped hand and blew glitter all over Arbogast. King Jeremy decided it looked as cool as he'd thought it would. He'd seen it in a comic book.

The sun had gone down some time ago but the night was still warm. He had decided to look over Arbogast's building, justifying it to himself as lazy reconnaissance. Actually he had just fancied a cup of tea. Du Bois was sitting outside a cafe opposite the luxury flats where Arbogast lived. He was wondering why, in Britain, he could get just about every type of coffee possible, including some he felt were patently ridiculous, but finding a good cup of tea was becoming harder and harder.

Arbogast's picture was on his phone screen. He could have had it appear in his vision but he was of an age that made him very uncomfortable with that kind of thing. Using the phone to externalise things might have been unnecessary but it helped him feel more human.

He saw the woman leave the building. Leather jacket, combat trousers, boots, all looked well worn. Her long hair was tied back into a ponytail, sides shaved. She had a Celtic knotwork symbol painted on the back of her leather jacket.

She looked out of place. Du Bois decided to take a picture of her. The phone's intelligent graphics software cleaned up the blurry image and ran it through facial recognition software far in advance of what was available to the public. The search was slowed only by having to use police and government databases.

He found the girl. Du Bois read about her. Her sister. Her conviction. That she had beaten someone to death for what he'd done to her sister.

'Shit.' He ran towards the apartment.

Du Bois stood in Arbogast's open-plan lounge. It was mostly white. The sofa had been white. Bits of it still were. Not the bits where Arbogast was sitting, apparently unable to move, though not restrained, his face cut up. Trying to chew off his own fingers. *There was no way the girl had done this*, du Bois thought; someone else had been there. Someone had slaved him. Someone with access to S- or L-tech.

'That would make me the ghost of Christmas future then,' he said. Arbogast was staring at him, eyes full of pain and desperation, but he couldn't say much as teeth cracked on bone.

'You are a drug dealer, Mr Arbogast. Do you have a syringe in the house?'

Arbogast's eyes went wide but he was desperate enough to try anything. There was pointing and searching. Du Bois found the reasonably well-hidden drug paraphernalia stash. Arbogast was a careful man. The syringe was still in its sealed packet. Du Bois walked out of Arbogast's sight. He suspected what he was about to do would give Arbogast hygiene and contagion issues. Du Bois concentrated momentarily, programming his blood. He tapped the vein and then slid the needle in, removing a very small amount of blood. It was all he needed.

Arbogast tried to protest around a mouthful of his own fingers but du Bois slid the syringe into his neck and depressed the plunger. Then he sat down opposite Arbogast, his .45 held in one hand, resting on his leg, pointed in Arbogast's vague direction.

He waited for the nanites in his blood to eat the nanites that had been used to control Arbogast. Someone else was playing. Someone in the know. But who? This wasn't the City of Brass's style and they had more to cope with. All over the world the Circle was mobilising to utterly annihilate them. After all, they'd doomed humanity, so why not use your not-inconsiderable resources with a final act of revenge? The Eggshell was little more than a myth, even by the time he had joined the Circle.

Arbogast stopped trying to eat his fingers.

'I realise you'd probably prefer to die at the moment, but I need you to tell me everything that you told everyone else. Only quicker.'

The stairway was made of glass. It gave him a commanding view of the harbour. He could see the neon-lit Spinnaker Tower, designed to look like a sail. He could see the real sails of historic ships and, as he rounded the corner, the cranes in the naval dockyard.

Du Bois attached the vial containing a sample of Arbogast's blood to the bottom of the phone. He texted the info sent from the nanites in the vial to the phone, which then sent the info on to Control. Then he hit speed dial to Control. The phone ran a biometric check on his fingertip, and one of the most secure telecommunications links in the world connected him to the soothing female voice.

'Kids in monster masks – who else is in town?'

Beth felt like shit. They had let her into their place; they didn't know her but they had shown her kindness. She was repaying them by washing blood off a family heirloom in their bathroom sink. She had to take her madness out of their life.

The bathroom door burst open.

'What! The! Fuck?' Uday demanded. Beth had thought she'd locked the door properly. 'Omigod! Have you actually killed someone?!' He was still too angry to be frightened of the woman with a bloody knife yet.

'I'll go,' Beth said. 'Please don't tell Maude about this.'

She could see Uday lose some of his certainty. The fear start to crawl in.

'What have you done?' he asked more quietly.

'It's Arbogast's. I ... I ... didn't kill him.' *You wanted to*, she told herself savagely, just to lash out.

Uday nodded. He was still not quite sure what to do. He could see Beth's face crumpling. The tears came.

'My sister's dead,' Beth managed before the sobs racked her body. She slumped to the bathroom floor. Uday stared at her, not sure what to do. Finally he knelt next to her and hugged her.

Maude appeared in the doorway.

'What's all the noise?' she asked sleepily. 'Oh ...'

Uday beckoned her in. Maude knelt down and held Beth as well as she cried. She didn't even notice Uday hide the knife.

One of the problems with being a petty criminal is that there are always people higher up the ladder. Still, there were always people lower as well, and the beating he had taken at Beth's hands had not done his self-esteem any good. The likes of Beth were supposed to be prey, not predator. It was thoughts like this that made Jaime think he was quite the street philosopher. However, as the BMW took him closer to Bucklands, self-pity was fighting with fear as the dominant emotion. Nobody in the drugs game wanted to hear the words 'Mr McGurk wants to see you' from any of his large and violence-capable business associates. Jaime just hoped he didn't piss himself on the leather seat. He couldn't see that going down well.

The underground garage under the long wall-like block of flats smelled of sweat. None of the inhabitants of the flats above had been stupid enough to park a car in the garage for years. The vehicles that weren't burned-out husks had come for the fight. Their headlights were used to provide illumination. They cast long and violent shadows from the two combatants.

Even relaxed, resplendent in his shell suit and gold, leaning on his cane, McGurk still had an air of barely contained violence. His constantly moving, sparsely-haired jaw and eyes bloodshot from lack of sleep accentuated his cadaverous, weasel-like features. He was watching, bored, as two desperate young men beat the crap out of each other to the cheers of the surrounding crowd. It no longer even interested him, let alone excited him. It was just a taster for the real excitement. He glanced over at the Transit van parked in the corner.

'Mr McGurk?' Markus said. McGurk turned around. Markus was a solid, slab-like piece of meat and steroids with a shaved head and rings in either ear. He looked away as McGurk looked him in the eyes. McGurk liked that.

Markus had hold of some scruffy-looking ponytailed specimen who smelled of fear and low-level drug dealing.

'I know your name,' McGurk said in his thick Pompey accent, cockney two generations removed. Jaime wasn't sure what to do except stare and try and control his fear. 'Imagine how pissed off that makes me?' McGurk continued. Jaime felt his bowels loosen. 'I mean, you're so down far down the food chain, Markus here wouldn't bother with you, isn't that right, Markus?'

'No, Mr McGurk, I wouldn't,' Markus rumbled, playing his part in the pantomime. McGurk looked at the young man properly for the first time, taking in his bruised and cut face.

'Someone give you a bit of a kicking?' he asked. The kid nodded. 'With knuckledusters by the look of it.' The kid nodded again. 'Who?'

'I don't know her.'

'"Her"? What are you, fucking queer? You got beat up by a girl?' McGurk laughed. It was the kind of laughter that Markus felt he should join in. Jaime just looked miserable. 'Son, you don't ever want to go to prison, let me assure you.' Jaime just nodded miserably. He was so frightened he wanted to cry, but he was pretty sure that would be unacceptable. 'So who is this girl with brass knuckles then?'

'I don't know her name, sir,' Jaime started. McGurk turned to fix him with a stare. Jaime shut up, swallowed hard and pissed himself just a little bit.

'But I know your name, yes? Give me something I can fucking use.' This was punctuated by the flat hard sound of meat hitting meat.

'She was looking for her sister. Talia, she was looking for Talia.'

'What'd you tell her?'

'That we'd gone out together for a while. That she liked gear. I'd binned her when I found her using H, and she liked to hang around with those emo arseholes who blew themselves up.'

'That all?' McGurk demanded. The fight was over. One of the combatants was lying unconscious in a pool of his own blood. The other was standing over him, not looking much better, gasping for breath.

Jaime nodded.

'I swear, Mr McGurk, I didn't know you had any interest.'

McGurk stared at him for a while. Jaime tried desperately not to piss himself further.

'You know how I enforce loyalty?' McGurk asked. Jaime swallowed, nodded and a wet stain started appearing on the front of his jeans. McGurk leaned towards him. 'Imagine how I enforce silence.' Jaime could smell the eucalyptus on McGurk's warm breath. Jaime had his eyes closed tight. 'You say nothing about this, nothing at all. You hear any more, you call Markus and tell him, understand?' Jaime nodded, tears streaming down his face. 'Get the fuck out of my sight.'

Jaime fled. McGurk watched him run out of the underground garage.

'Find out,' he said to Markus. Markus just nodded. McGurk turned to the winner of the bare-knuckle fight.

'Brian, mate, you've made a bit of a mess here.' Brian nodded, grinning savagely through the blood and the sweat. McGurk turned to Trevor, Markus' counterpart muscle, who was standing over by the BMW, and nodded. Trevor leaned into the car, pulled out a briefcase and walked over to McGurk. Trevor opened the briefcase and showed Brian the neat rows of tens and twenties. 'That's ten thousand pounds, Brian. Do you want it?' McGurk nodded to Markus, who started towards the Transit van.

'Yes, Mr McGurk,' Brian said, greed lighting up his eyes.

'But how much do you want it?'

'A lot, Mr McGurk.'

'No holds barred with my man in the van, and I think he's going to try very hard to kill you, yes?' Brian looked nervous but nodded. 'You don't have to win, just fight.' Brian looked unsure but his eyes kept flicking to the briefcase full of money. Finally Brian nodded. The crowd cheered.

'Excellent!' McGurk said, clapping Brian on the back. 'Markus!'

Markus opened the back of the Transit. The van's internal light spilled out of the back of the vehicle. Brian watched with mounting unease. Something shuffled into the light. Brian screamed.

13

A Long Time After the Loss

Vic was no stranger to seeing or causing death. When he had been in the Thunder Squads his job had been property damage on a massive scale. One squad was enough to bring entire city sectors to their knees. He had been involved in the destruction of starscrapers, watching the weight of the buildings tear their top floors out of stabilised geo-synchronous orbit. Collateral damage to sentient biomass had been inevitable but that had been on conflict resolution worlds. Though he had to admit that some of the CR worlds had been newly designated and the new designation had come as a shock to the civilian populations.

As the hard-tech-augmented insect watched his partner cut open the front of his own skull with a beam saw, he decided that it wasn't the number of people that Scab had killed on Arclight with the virus just to get away, it was the context and quality of the killing. The Queen's Cartel had a lot of money. If they let them get away with what had happened on Arclight then the cartel would look weak and their competitors would assume that they were prey. Vic didn't even want to think about the ramifications of killing a Church Militia-man.

Travelling through one of the conduits in the exotic gasses of Red Space, Vic had been searching all the comms traffic on the beacons they were in range of, looking for bounties going down on him and Scab. It was okay for Scab – he would make a pile of bodies of any who came after him – but Vic knew it wouldn't be the same for him. Vic was probably one of the top bounty killers, but the guys who they would send after them were at least his match.

'At least it will be over soon,' he actually said out loud. Then he found Scab staring at him. *Oh now you're listening,* Vic thought.

So far there had been nothing. This meant that someone with an awful lot of resources to throw at this problem was running interference for them. What worried Vic the most, however, was that whoever their mysterious patron was, they had found a way to sufficiently motivate Scab into this insanity.

And this new madness. Despite the *Basilisk*'s excellent life-support systems, the ship could not quite scrub the smell of burning bone and flesh out of the air. The argument had gone on for some time, but it hadn't been much of an argument. It had mostly been Vic screaming at Scab. It was only after he had thought to do a scan of Scab that Vic realised that his partner had been listening to his favourite pre-Loss music on ancient crystal earrings. Scab preferred listening to music rather than downloading it directly into his cerebral cortex via his neunonics. He claimed it sounded better. Vic just thought it showed what a throwback Scab was.

Finally Vic had refused to help. He told Scab that he would have to slave him. Scab had said that he could not risk the drop in performance that came with slaving; Vic had to help him willingly. Scab's idea of willingness was to slave Vic and put him in an agony immersion of his own design just long enough for Vic to agree. Despite his hard-tech augment, Vic had shaken for hours after Scab had let him out of the immersion – the things he'd seen, experienced, the things in Scab's mind. Scab had only ever done something like it once before. Vic realised how important this was to Scab.

Scab removed two slits from the bone in the front of his skull and lit a cigarette, dragging deeply. The *Basilisk* extruded the cold storage drawer with the two biotech organisms in it. Vic had started thinking of them as alien eyes and was more and more sure they were S-tech. He watched, unease trickling through him at some base, instinctual level. Scab lifted the bioware towards his head. Scab's P-sat was hovering just over the hole in the skull, projecting a sterile field, though Scab's own bioware and nano-screen were probably more than enough to ward off infection. Scab took another drag on his cigarette and placed the bioware into his skull.

Vic had to admit that things never got boring working with Scab. The universe might be infinite, though the sparsely starred sky of Known Space had always felt claustrophobic to Vic, but after seeing and doing the things he had seen and done with Scab, he was impressed that he could still feel horror and fascination as he watched the things crawl into his partner's skull. Trickles of sweat made rivulets through Scab's white make-up. Vic realised that his human partner was shaking. The bioware flattened itself into the two slits Scab had made in his skull. Tendrils burrowed into the grey meat. Vic was even sure he had seen sparks of bioelectric energy. *He must be in agony*, Vic thought. *Good, stupid cunt.*

A chair extruded from the white-carpeted floor of the *Basilisk*'s C and C/lounge and Scab sat down just a little too hard to make it look casual. The P-sat moved to continue projecting the sterile field. Scab reached into his suit and removed his works. Another pointlessly retro vice. Vic didn't understand why he didn't just download the drugs he wanted from internal storage. When he had asked Scab about this once, Scab had told him that as a child he had been the leader of a street sect on Cyst, his home planet. When they had captured him and sent him to the Legion, they had done neural surgery on him to remove some of his more dangerous traits. They had cut out the heretically religious aspect of young Scab, but ritual had remained important to him.

Not long after, Scab drifted away on a nod. Vic thought long and hard about extending a blade from one of his power-assisted limbs. Just pressing it into the grey meat. Scab's P-sat would try and protect him of course, but good as it was, it was no match for Vic. Just a simple movement and all the madness and fear would be over.

He didn't do it, of course. He didn't like the way the two eye-like organs on Scab's head above his human eyes seemed to stare at him. He felt like the coward he knew he was. He felt like he understood the politics of fear.

Instead of killing Scab, Vic went with his partner into Monarchist space, looking for the Citadel.

'You didn't kill me then?' Scab asked when he awoke. Vic said nothing. 'Good.'

The Citadel was out of phase. That much Scab was sure of. Entrance had required a different physical state. Technology, alien or not, was just something that made things happen when he wanted them to. The fragment of the god that lived with him in his skull had shown him the way. A different-coloured space. Reality was broken down to the level of subatomic particles, nothing more than a series of interlinked fields. The ancient technology meshed with human consciousness; science became instinct, matter merely vibration, and then his modified brain translated that information into something he could understand – physics as a waking hallucination. It felt like the defences of the Citadel were shredding him piece by piece, as he flitted between existences in different spaces.

He arrived naked, screaming, flayed and bloody on the cold black marble floor. It was like being born except he had been diminished. The powerful biotech implants notwithstanding, it had required every single intrusion trick he had known, and what knowledge of the Elite that hadn't been cut out of him surgically and virally. He felt like he had been peeled back layer by layer to something raw, feral and inhuman.

He lay on the cold marble, regrowing layers of skin. Tiny nanites crawled through the pores in his skin to replace his repeatedly murdered nano-screen. He kept them close this time. This high chamber of marble was like a tomb from some xeno-archaeological immersion. There were only a few distant rays of light from some unseen source, but the light illuminated the motes of dust. Scab knew that much of that dust was nanites far in advance of any in Known Space.

He knew that the empty monolithic chamber masked the vast amounts of tech, Seeder and otherwise, that existed to support the Elite. There would be reservoirs of matter that could feed assemblers and provide solid ammunition to feed their weapons instantaneously via complex matter entanglement. Generators and controls, probably merged into the very matter of the place, to provide the defensive fields and stealth systems. Connections to the network of primordial black holes that powered Elite tech, again through complex entanglement, and presumably provided the power to keep the Citadel out of phase and in a different physical state to Real Space, assuming it was in Real Space. There would also be storehouses of forbidden S-tech, Scab imagined and half remembered.

The Scorpion was agony. It had burrowed deep into the flesh of his left arm, wrapping itself around the bones. Only the top of its back was visible, the sting twitching in and out of his skin. He could have deadened the nerve endings easily but didn't. All sensation was a reminder of existence. The pain would end when he was finished. It was how he would know.

'Are you a shade? Someone I've killed?' The voice was beautiful, deep, resonant and so very sad-sounding. Scab rolled into a defensive crouch. The crouch in the presence of the figure that stood over him made him feel like a feral animal. Scab was fine with that. Sometimes beauty was there just to be destroyed.

The figure had a shock of the blackest hair that Scab had ever seen. Tall and so slender, he somehow looked delicate. There being no fat on him, despite his delicacy his musculature was perfectly toned. He might as well have been carved out of marble. His eyes were dark pools with stars in them. He was naked. *Well, that wasn't entirely true,* Scab thought, *he would have drawn his armour back under his skin.*

Scab angrily drew upon his internal drug resources to subdue the feeling of awe rising in him. He knew that this was a tailored psychological response designed by the AIs and scientists who over the generations of the existence of the Elite had helped mould them into the legendary gods they were. Every movement, every mannerism designed to tell you one thing: there is no hope.

A moment of concentration and then recognition.

'I've seen you before. We slew monsters and you were there.'

Fallen Angel.

'I want the cocoon.'

'I don't really know what that means.'

'The white thing you took off the Seeder ship.'

'It wasn't a ship, but I apologise. I have misled you. When I said that I did not know what that means, I should have said I don't care.'

It was the tone of honest sympathy that angered Scab the most.

'Is it here?'

'Why would it be here?'

'Because you brought it here.'

'If we did, it would be because we are slaves. It will be somewhere else now.'

Scab stared at him. Still trying to shake the feeling that he was a disgusting beast in the presence of something transcendent.

'Then you won't mind if I have a look.'

Scab stood up and made as if to move past Fallen Angel. The Elite took Scab by the shoulder. Fallen Angel held him lightly but Scab could feel the power in the fingers. It was magnitudes above what Vic could have managed with his high-end, hard-tech augments, impressive for what was primarily soft tech. On the other hand, there had to be a price for laying a hand on Scab.

A flat palm to Fallen Angel's wrist to knock the arm away. That almost contacted. The Elite made the moving of his arm out of the way look languid. Fallen Angel allowed the roundhouse kick to land, taking the meaningless impact on the shoulder. With Scab's ability and soft-machine augments, he knew that the kick had more than enough power to powder bone in someone as highly augmented as he himself was. He was reasonably sure that Fallen Angel hadn't even felt it.

Fallen Angel raised his knee level with his chin and then straightened his leg. The impact broke ribs. Scab spat blood in mid-air as the kick tore him off his feet and sent him flying backwards. He landed hard on the black marble. The noise of their violence seemed obscene in the otherwise quiet chamber.

Scab rolled back into his animalistic crouch and bared his teeth. Fallen Angel watched him, his expression a mix of curiosity and confusion. Scab ran at him, launching himself into the air, knees forward.

It was an easy thing for Fallen Angel to roll under the blow.

Scab had known this. He channelled every bit of hatred, every bit of anger at being in a situation where he was so horribly outmatched, where cunning and ultraviolence would not see him through, where he wasn't in control. The Scorpion, ancient and vile, responded.

The sting drew a long thin line of black just under Fallen Angel's eye. This was extraordinary in itself. More extraordinary was the ancient venom in the sting actually giving the Elite's internal anti-virals a moment of trouble.

Scab landed, scampered across the floor like an animal, using one hand for support, and turned to face Fallen Angel again. The Elite touched his face and then held his black-covered fingertips in front of his eyes. The exotic matter looked like liquid as it was sucked back through his skin.

Fallen Angel was starting to look angry. He glanced at the Scorpion dug into the flesh on Scab's left arm and hissed at it, eyes blazing. Scab actually screamed as the S-tech weapon burrowed under his skin, hiding itself completely in his flesh, brass-like living metal wrapping itself around his bones. He had to force himself to ignore the fear radiating from the Scorpion.

Fallen Angel strode towards him. Scab had to put every inch of effort into trying not to get hit. Years of experience, street fighting on Cyst, the planet that most embraced the creed of the cult of Darwin in Consortium space, every dirty trick he'd learned in the penal battalions of the Legion on countless CR worlds and what he could remember of the Elite dances. It wasn't enough. It was a one-sided and short fight. It was like Fallen Angel was dancing with him in his sleep.

He spoke to Scab as he committed violence on him. The Elite threw a punch to his stomach that lifted Scab off his feet. For an absurd moment Scab felt that his opponent was wearing him like a glove.

'You did not infiltrate.'

A casual axe kick fractured his skull despite it being seeded with armoured super-hardened ceramic and drove him to the marble floor again. All happening faster than the unaugmented would even be able to see.

'We may as well have invited you.'

Picked up by the back of his neck and flung against the marble wall. Air forced out of him, replenished immediately by his internal systems, more broken ribs despite the carbon lacing. Fortunately his spine remained intact, though Scab suspected that this was calculation on Fallen Angel's part to prolong the lesson.

'You saw nothing of import.'

Lifted up off the ground by his skull. Both of Fallen Angel's hands, with their long powerful fingers, were wrapped around it.

'I can see the little god in your eyes. Remember that you did not do this; you are only a vehicle.' Fallen Angel pushed his fingers into the alien eyes in Scab's forehead and squeezed. Scab screamed in a way that would shame him when he thought back to it. It was a humiliation in a life largely free of them. The ancient eyes became a sticky mess on the end of Fallen Angel's fingers.

'The Consortium has tipped its hand. Now we know they know where we are. They should have sent their Elite instead of this ghost. We'll move. You're just here to learn what it's like to be helpless.'

Now, Scab thought. It was a coherent energy field weapon, a rod, more commonly known as an energy javelin. It was ancient S-tech and, like the Scorpion, completely illegal. It lived in a hidden sheath in Scab's right arm. He killed with it only on special occasions. A momentary white and orange glow in the flesh as his neunonics sent the order, his hand swinging towards Fallen Angel. The mortal who killed a god. Maybe.

The time between thinking the order, the movement, the glow of the energy field initiating was so small as to be difficult to measure. It was enough. Fallen Angel grabbed Scab's arm at the wrist and squeezed, crushing the sheath. Trapping the energy javelin, which started to cut and burn its way through Scab's flesh. More screaming as flesh smoked and the smell of burning meat filled the air.

'That might have actually hurt me,' Fallen Angel said quietly, sounding calmer now. Scab's right hand fell off, his wrist still glowing as the meat around it cooked. 'But you're not really there again, are you.'

Scab felt sick. Different, somehow less with the eyes gone. He was aware of his wounds, the holes in his skull.

'Will you let him go for me?' asked a female voice every bit as beautiful, resonant and sad as Fallen Angel's. Scab managed to look up from the floor. His nano-screen was all but screaming warnings in his neunonics, his defences were being overrun. Elites fought at all levels of conflict.

Scab felt absurdly gratified that after dropping him, Fallen Angel had shown enough respect to take a few steps away, out of easy striking distance.

She was a female version of Fallen Angel: same black hair, a feminised version of the same build with small pale breasts, same eyes. Tall, slender to the point of fragile while still conveying power. Scab recognised her: she was the third monarchist Elite. She was called Horrible Angel and was said to be Fallen Angel's sister.

Uncaring of Scab, she took her brother's head and kissed him long and deep.

'You know who he is?' she asked when they had finished.

'Another ghost of someone I killed who has followed me into the underworld. He'll seek revenge but in the end just follow me with empty eye sockets and a tongueless mouth. Silent and accusing.'

Clearly to Fallen Angel it was all about him, Scab thought. The idea almost made him smile. He was going to die fighting Elite. He had cut one, and given him pause with the energy javelin. Impossible feats for many. Scab wasn't sure if it was enough. *If he could die now ... No.* He remembered the deal he had made. This way it would not end.

'No,' Horrible Angel said. 'This is Woodbine Scab, bounty killer extraordinaire and ex-Elite. One of us ...' Fallen Angel turned to look at him. Something had changed. It was as if he was regarding him in a new light as he wrapped his arms around Horrible Angel.

' ... now little more than a frightened animal,' Fallen Angel said, finishing his sister's sentence. 'Why did they take your wings away?'

Horrible Angel turned to look at Scab as well. He had managed to back himself against the wall so he could sit up a bit. Trying to ignore his smoking wrist, he was tempted to tell them the truth. That he couldn't remember. That the information was gone after they had mentally spayed him. It was, after all, very difficult to lie to Elite. They were trained and augmented to read people. They had to be able to predict the movements that any opponent made against them. Be it a single opponent in hand-to-hand or an entire Consortium navy battle group. Scab still had vestiges of the talent himself. He wished he had a cigarette.

'I didn't want to be a slave,' he told them both. They both looked impassive. Maybe they believed him, maybe they didn't, maybe he had inadvertently guessed the truth. It was the ultimate irony of the Elite. They were undoubtedly the most dangerous and physically powerful people in Known Space but their masters were not stupid. Their loyalty was conditioned and programmed to the nth degree, it was absolute. The killer gods were the ultimate servants.

'What did you think you could do here?' Horrible Angel asked.

'He fought me,' Fallen Angel said redundantly.

'Did you think to use our arrogance against us?' she asked. Scab couldn't see the point in answering. 'What if it's not arrogance?'

'I just want the cocoon?' He felt the burning itch in his flesh, under his skin, coming from patches all over his body.

'It is gone from here,' Horrible Angel said. Her voice was little more than a sigh. 'We know where and we know why but we will not tell you. As you pointed out, we are all the servants of contemptible gods.'

Scab's chuckle sounded like dry paper being crumpled up.

'Not me, not any more.'

'You more than all,' Horrible Angel said.

'You are the most puppet of puppets,' Fallen Angel said, almost brightly. 'I can see your strings from all the way over here.'

He watched as the first lesion appeared. It looked like patches of skin were caving in. A fast-acting, flesh-eating nano-virus.

'You've made his flesh necrotic,' Horrible Angel said.

'For you.'

'It's beautiful.'

All Scab could do was watch. A guest at his own consumption. Both of them turned back to him.

'It was the connection,' Horrible Angel said. Some feeling prickled Scab. He did not like this, did not want to hear her words.

'At some base level we are attached to creation,' Fallen Angel continued. It was true: the uplifted races understood very little about S-tech except how to use it, but the Seeders must have understood the universe at a fundamental level. The technology the Elite wore connected them to this somehow. Scab remembered Vic describing it as a gun being taught physics. He almost smiled at the memory.

'It's not slavery you fear. We are all slaves, even our shadowed undying masters, the Lords and Ladies of Monarchist and Consortium space,' Horrible Angel said.

'Even the Church. You are still a slave, you have always been a slave; everything else is just so much thrashing around signifying nothing. Little more than desperate cries for attention,' Fallen Angel said.

'You feared the truth,' Horrible Angel said.

Scab wanted to tell her to be quiet. He opened his mouth to issue a pointless threat.

'Don't threaten her,' Fallen Angel said. 'If you threaten her I have to act.'

'And you are more plaything than victim still.' Filed teeth clamped together in Scab's mouth. 'Fear made you lose your wings, not the wish for false freedom,' Horrible Angel continued. Then she stared at the necrotic patterns the virus was drawing in his flesh as if transfixed.

'You cannot remember that destruction is your only birthright. You search endlessly not realising that the only freedom you have left is to come to terms with your slavery to grotesqueries. The freedom to realise that everything is meaningless. You don't fear slavery, you're a more sophisticated version of everyone else; you crave slavery. You were shown the truth and panicked. It is freedom you fear.'

Un-Scab-like retorts and denials filled his mind, but he just lay there and watched them. He could not know if what they were saying was true. That secret had long since been eaten from his mind. Connected though they were, with access to the highest levels of intelligence the Monarchist systems could gather, they could not have known the truth of his expulsion from the Elite. But there was something in their words that Scab did not like at an unconscious and possibly instinctual level. If this was what empathy felt like then he did not like it.

Again it was the sympathy on Horrible Angel's face that got to him the most.

'Throw him out,' she told her brother. 'Ludwig is killing his friend now.' She turned and walked silently away, leaving Scab more than a little confused. He was about to die now but it wouldn't be enough.

'I don't have any friends,' he told Fallen Angel. It seemed very important that Fallen Angel understand this before he died.

Scab liked vacuum – he had been exposed before and felt a kinship with it. He was still alive. The virus had been trying to eat his flesh back to his skeleton when they flung him into space. Somehow the *Basilisk* had found him. The ship's medical systems were able to counteract the virus but only because the virus allowed it. They had tested him but let him live. Scab could only imagine it was because they thought it crueller this way, but he couldn't forget the look of sympathy on Horrible Angel's face.

Vic opened his eyes to the inside of a clone tank in some faceless insurance company laboratory. He had never expected to see this again. Vic had used up the last of his insurance money when Scab had last killed him. More than anything, it annoyed Vic that Scab would not tell him why he had killed him the last time. He said that if Vic knew he would just have to kill him again. So someone else had paid for him to be cloned.

Vic felt the itch of the nano-sculpting of raw flesh as they rebuilt him. This was the cheap part, the flesh. The expensive part would be putting his hard-tech augments back in. The gear fetishist part of his custom-designed humanesque personality hoped that whoever was footing the bill would opt for upgrades. He felt the crawling beneath his vat-grown chitinous skull as neunonic-filled liquid software and hardware was implanted. This comforted him. Soon he would be able to communicate.

He had almost been free, he thought, free of Scab, but someone had brought him back again.

The memory upload of his last minutes hit him. Terror had overwhelmed him. He had been sat in the C and C/lounge of the *Basilisk*, feeling enough tension to make an augmented heart explode. The walls of the ship had been transparent but space was a blank canvas. There had been something behind him. It had ghosted through the hull of the ship. He had done the pheromonic equivalent of shitting himself. He did not want to turn around. He knew the machine was waiting for him.

They had taken everything from his mind, where he had been, what he had been doing. All they had left him with was the memory of the machine's ability to kill him in a moment and make it feel like eternity. A lifetime of agony. That was their message for him.

What he couldn't understand was why he still lived. Ludwig would have sensed the memory download application in his neunonics. Neunonic viruses that could be carried through the download process to wipe the victim's mind utterly were among the most difficult and expensive to create, but an Elite, particularly a machine Elite, would certainly have access to them.

Through the gel he could make out unfocused grey eyes staring at him. Vic ignored his partner and as soon as the neunonics were installed set up a secure interface to the *Basilisk*. Even lobotomised (the ship had lost a disagreement with Scab), trying to talk to the ship's AI felt like trying to coax a frightened animal out of hiding. Ludwig had hurt the ship as well and removed the relevant part of its memory.

Scab's polite request to 'face sounded like someone knocking on his skull. Vic took the mental equivalent of a deep breath and then opened the link.

'You got me fucking killed by an Elite! You don't think this in-over-our-heads overkill bullshit has gone too far now?!'

'It didn't go well,' Scab agreed. He was sitting on a chair outside the tank, hat in his hands, watching Vic in the tank as if looking for a clue or some sign of irredeemable weakness. Vic assumed he was engaging in the retro-vice of smoking just to annoy any of the insurance technicians who had olfactory glands.

'I notice they didn't kill you.' Vic tried to put as much venom into the comment as he could manage. Scab was well known as one of the few bounty killers who never took out clone insurance. Vic was sure

Scab wanted to die but on his own very specific terms. The 'sect was unsure what those terms were.

'I had you cloned,' Scab 'faced, the words soft and quiet in Vic's mind.

'Yes, thanks for that,' Vic spat back. 'You couldn't leave me in peace then? Actually finally let me go?' Vic had often thought that human tears looked very cathartic but were beyond him, and his pheromone-producing glands were not quite rebuilt yet. Scab seemed to be giving Vic's words some thought.

'You like life,' he finally 'faced.

Vic gave this some thought. Scab was right. He like immersions, drink and drugs, partying, sex with experimental female-identifying humans, violence when he was in control; he sort of liked travel but was becoming more and more convinced that everywhere the uplifted races went was a shithole. Maybe it was all shallow stuff but Vic was happy with that. What he couldn't cope with was the abusive, albeit well-paid, borderline slavery that was being Scab's partner.

'I'm seeking an end,' Scab said.

Vic wasn't sure what he meant. 'And you have to take me along with you?' Scab said nothing. 'I take it we didn't get the cocoon thing back?' Vic just about made out Scab shaking his head through the thick opaque gel. 'So we're finished with this now? This is just so beyond us, even for you it's just banging your head on a hull. There's nothing we can do here.'

'I got into the Citadel,' Scab 'faced.

Oh shit, Vic thought. The insect knew this wasn't over. He thought back to human tears. There was enough of Vic to push his way through the gel and press his chitinous features up against the tank's transparent material.

'So all that effort, the expense, the S-tech, the blanks, the viral attack on Arclight, the dead Church Militiaman ... NOT TO MENTION MY FUCKING MURDER AT THE HANDS OF A SICK MACHINE MADE EONS BEFORE MY PEOPLE EVEN FUCKING EXISTED was for nothing?!' He was absurdly pleased that he had managed to convey angry/shouty human across the interface.

Scab considered the outburst as a reasonably asked question.

'I don't know.' He shrugged. He was still both worried and trying to make sense of the Elite's words.

'Look, this is about bridge technology. The Monarchists want it; the Consortium wants it so they can break the Church's monopoly. It's the key to Red Space. This is way out of our league.'

'Fun though,' Scab said. He almost meant it. He was healed, his hand regrown, but he still missed the graft. The eyes. What he had seen with them. 'And you've said that before.'

'We're working for Consortium interests?' Vic asked.

Scab said nothing, which to Vic meant he knew but was not going to say. Scab tried to avoid lying where possible.

'What I don't understand is why they haven't sent their own Elite.'

'Maybe they have. They are capable of acting with subtlety. Or maybe it's a case of mutually assured destruction. The Monarchists are mad, the Consortium greedy. The Consortium know that sending their Elite will lead to a confrontation. A very expensive one.'

'They must have better options than us.'

'And they are probably using them in ways we don't see. The nobody who gave us the S-tech graft for ex—'

'He seemed more like a street heretic,' Vic said. Scab just stared at the 'sect. He hated interruptions. 'Sorry.'

'Despite your whining, self-pity and lack of self-belief, we are two very capable operators.'

'But it's over now, right?' Scab shook his hand. 'You once told me that you were a killer, not detective. They have the resources of the entire Monarchist systems at—'

'They are fragmented.'

Though apparently it was okay for Scab to interrupt, Vic mused. 'Even if it's just one of the kingdoms. We're two people and a ship you've bullied so badly the AI committed suicide.'

'I killed it, well, lobotomised it.'

'Whatever.'

'We're going to Pythia.'

Vic gave this some thought, feeling himself getting angrier as he did.

'Why the fuck didn't we just go there in the first place?' he demanded.

'Intelligence pointed to the Citadel. It would have made sense to hide it there.'

14
Northern Britain, a Long Time Ago

Ysgawyn awoke to the smells of earth, rot, decay and horse. It was a comfort. Once you were dead then nobody could kill you. All his people were warriors and all had chosen to live in Annwn. The living were their victims.

Ysgawyn climbed off his shelf in the barrow that he shared with the bones of many generations of his family. He also shared it with his horse. His horse, like him, was covered in lime, both their eyes ringed with black. Rider and mount had disturbing unnatural-looking symbols painted on the lime.

Ysgawyn took a deep breath and then turned to look at the shelf where his father's decayed remains lay.

'Soon,' he said. He would often speak to his father, his grandfather and ancestors from further back. He heard their replies in his head and often took their counsel, but tonight there was little time. Armour had to be oiled and then limed, weapons honed, his mount prepared. Then he would eat the fungus and ride.

They emerged from barrows all across the plain, white like corpses, some leading their horses, others already astride them. The Dark Man had spoken to them. They would ride for the god of death and they would not stop. It would be an end to the living.

There were no war cries, no *carnyx* sounded, no orders were shouted; there was just the thunder of hoof beats echoing across the flat desolate plain.

Britha felt fire crawl through her, under her skin. Felt the demon in the consumed flesh try and consume her in turn. It burned. Not like a fever but like putting your hand in a fire and holding it there. The burning was pain but the agony was still to come. Her back was arched, her hands claws as she convulsed on the ground. The smell of the river, the feeling of pebbles beneath her, all of it went away as the stars in the night sky went out one by one, leaving nothing but darkness.

She saw a tribe painted white like corpses around a hearth pit, wriggling on their stomachs, so many, so close together, like white worms crawling over each other, in supplication that made Britha sick to see. How could they even call themselves people after such a display? The fire burned cold in the hearth and there was a tall man made of darkness. It hurt to look at him; his shape did not entirely make sense and there was something behind or through him, something she could feel, seething hatred and anger made of nothing. Then the screaming. Eventually, when she felt the blood in her raw throat, Britha would realise that she was the one screaming.

A cage, for people, her people, in the sea. Something inside them, a little crystalline egg waiting to hatch. She sank under the water, still burning, the water bubbling around her. Something came at her, darting through the water, a bestial fury on an alien face.

Then the agony started. It seemed like all the agony, pain and fear. Then she recognised the voice. Her people. Others. Thousands. A sacrifice.

There was too much pain. Britha went away into darkness, her flesh still burning, a cool whisper in her mind promising respite, promising relief, promising freedom from it all. All she had to do was serve the seductive voice. Listen to the blood in her veins. It was the tiniest fragments of a god.

It was all too much. She had failed. Her people would die in agony. If she would serve, what was her could recede into darkness and the pain would end. So easy ...

Almost.

Britha's back arched so violently it almost threw her upright. Violent contortions racked her body, making her writhe across the pebble beach. Her bloodstained face became a rictus mask of twisted facial expressions. The warrior glanced over at his misshapen friend.

'Do we help?' he asked.

The warrior's misshapen friend gave this some thought. It was clear that he wanted to move on. The pair of them had a purpose after all. 'Do we help?' the warrior asked again. His misshapen companion said nothing; instead he knelt next to her, his eyes narrowing as he studied her more closely.

*

Britha's eyes flicked open. The crystalline skull looked down on her, smiling its rictus grin. Roots grew off the skull, blowing in an invisible and disconcerting wind and ending somewhere that Britha couldn't see and was sure did not exist. The face of the skull that wasn't a skull had too many angles. Somehow she knew it existed beyond what she could perceive. The many faceted crystals caught and reflected a strange red light, the source of which was also beyond her sight. Then the crystals seemed to consume the light. Each separate crystal was moving, changing shape as if crawling back into the skull and from there to some impossible place.

Britha started to scream again.

Teardrop held her as she convulsed on the pebble beach. The flesh she had just eaten made her froth bloody. She tried clawing at Teardrop's face. He just moved his head back to avoid it.

'I think she can see me,' Teardrop said. Fachtna glanced over at his oddly dressed, swollen-headed compatriot, then he turned back to look past the distant crannogs at the mouth of the river under the overcast sky and out to sea.

'We are so far behind,' he said quietly and then inhaled deeply. 'I don't like where the sky is, or the sun.'

'You'll get used to it. She's eaten one of the possessed's flesh.'

Fachtna did not grimace. Such practices had long since been abandoned by his people but he knew of them. It was a primitive response to what had happened, but he could understand it.

On his back he felt the spear shake and moan. It would need to be drugged and bathed in blood soon.

'Will she live?' the warrior asked.

'She should, but she could also be possessed. The strange thing is that she is fighting it. He nodded towards the body of the huge tattooed warrior. 'It looks like she killed one of them with their own weapon. I don't understand how she could do that.'

This made Fachtna suspicious.

'Someone else has blessed her?'

Teardrop took an obsidian-bladed knife from inside his jerkin and made a small incision in Britha's cheek. He brought the blade to his mouth, licked it and concentrated.

'I can taste the demon blood but something wars with the demon blood within her.'

'What?'

'Something old and powerful but so faint.' Teardrop's eyes widened. 'I can taste the Muileartach in her.'

Fachtna stared at his companion.

'Where's she from?'

Teardrop leaned in to smell her.

'Local.'

'Sure?' Fachtna asked. Teardrop gave him a look that left him in no doubt as to the stupidity of his question. 'Can you help her?'

Teardrop gave the question some thought.

'It will diminish me.'

Fachtna said nothing. It was Teardrop's decision. More than anything he needed his friend strong, but she might be able to help and he wasn't comfortable leaving her like this. And she looked strong. He would respect whatever decision Teardrop made.

'Even if she wins the war in her blood, if she gets closer to Bress and the Red Chalice their influence on her would grow stronger. She's pretty.'

'For a mortal. Your head is so swollen, but it's still the other one you want to use?' Fachtna asked, amusement in his tone. Teardrop grinned at him. He was happily married; the comment had been for Fachtna's benefit. It was the warrior, after all, not Teardrop who had an eye for pretty 'mortals'.

Teardrop wiped the knife on his jerkin and then brought it up to the side of his oversized head. The black blade pushed though swarthy weather-beaten skin, cutting into it. As the blade broke the skin there was no blood, only interlocking crystalline growth. Teardrop closed his eyes, his features wrinkling in concentration. Something leaked through the dry wound. Some of the crystals seemed to melt into a viscous quicksilver-like liquid and run down onto the knife blade. The drop of quicksilver stayed on the blade. Teardrop forced Britha's mouth open as gently as he could and held the knife over it. The quicksilver hung on the blade momentarily and then dripped into her mouth. Fachtna watched expectantly but nothing happened. Britha continued writhing on the pebbles, staring fixedly. Teardrop started to sing. It sounded like a series of disparate syllables but worked into a soothing melody.

'Will that strengthen the blood of the Muileartach, weaken the demon's blood?' Fachtna asked.

Teardrop looked at his warrior friend, trying to decide if he could be bothered to explain. The warrior didn't really care about these things. He was just talking for the sake of something to say. *That was fine,* Teardrop thought; the older he got the more he did the same thing.

'No, what it should do is give her more control,' Teardrop said and then had to stifle a smile as Fachtna nodded like he knew what the other man was talking about.

Then Britha woke, still screaming. Both of them jumped.

The impossible, painful-to-view crystalline skull faded away, crawling back into the head of the most bizarre man she had ever seen. His skin was dark but looked different from the southron traders her people had dealt with. There was a reddish tint to the brown. His face looked like it had never seen a blade and yet there was no trace of a beard there. Even allowing for this and the strangely bulbous hairless head, the strangest thing about him was his clothing.

He wore a pair of absurdly large trews, with thick red and thin white stripes. These were tucked into a pair of well made high leather boots. He had a white shirt under a stiff-looking leather jerkin, which was fastened with small metal discs that Britha had never seen the like of before. Over that he wore a piece of apparel that looked to Britha to be a cross between some sort of sleeved over-robe and a cloak. The garment was made from some kind of supple hide.

Next to him on the pebbles was a long gnarled wooden staff. There was a large crystal in the centre of the staff. It looked like the staff had grown round the crystal. Another crystal tipped the staff.

- It was clear to Britha that this was some kind of monster. She looked around frantically for her spear but she was not where she had been. She was sore from the battering she had given herself during the visions. It was day now. The night must have come and gone.

'It's okay ...' the strange man started. Britha kicked him in the mouth from her prone position.

'Hey!' Britha turned at the cry and saw another man moving towards her.

She put her hand on Teardrop's staff and flipped over it onto her feet, coming up holding the staff, a feat she was sure that she would not have been capable of until recently.

The other man had his hand on the hilt of his sword and was bringing his shield to bear. The shield was rectangular with rounded corners, leather over oak with complex spiral knotwork patterns ending in three dragons' heads. He at least she recognised, or at least what he was. He was clearly some kind of warrior. He looked like a Goidel, warriors reputed to come from an island beyond the land to the west.

He wore a boiled leather breastplate, and armour covered his upper arms, vambraces his forearms, and he wore thick leather greaves over fine plaid trews. Around his neck was a finely wrought torc made of thick strands of silver twisted together rather than the more chain-like designs of her own people.

Britha had a moment to appreciate how handsome the man was – well built, fine-featured, long reddish-blonde hair, his similarly coloured beard and moustache in a plait. Attractive or not, there was something about him that Britha knew she would find irritating even if they hadn't been about to kill each other. The fact that his armour, shield and face were unscarred gave her confidence that she could beat the pretty young warrior.

'Wait!' the swollen-headed man cried from his bloody mouth. Britha kicked him in the face again and then hit him on his head with his own staff. The man cried out and rolled away from her.

The warrior drew his sword. The blade shone even in the pale light of the overcast day. The metal looked silver. The blade seemed to hum and shimmer as if singing. Britha did not like the look of the blade. She sensed magic in it. She had encountered too many weapons that actively thirsted for blood recently. The beautifully crafted longsword looked sharp enough to cut the air. The last time she had seen a blade that fine, Bress had been holding it.

The warrior was charging her. Britha changed her stance, ready to dart to the side.

'Fachtna, wait!' the other man cried. Britha understood his words, though she was not sure he was speaking the same language as the Pecht, but there was clearly magic in the air. His accent was strange.

The warrior skidded to a halt, keeping his eye on Britha, clearly ready to attack. The swollen-headed man turned to the *ban draoi*.

'Look we're not here to—' he started. Britha hit him on the head with his own staff again. She could not risk him weaving magic with his words. She hit him hard enough to break the skin, but there was no blood.

'Ow! Stop hitting me with my staff. That's not what it's for!'

Through the gash in the creature's head she could make out some kind of crystalline growth. She stared for a moment and then remembered the warrior.

Fachtna made a move towards her. Britha shifted position.

'Wait!' the swollen-headed man shouted. Britha made a move to hit him again, but he scrabbled away from her on the pebbles. 'I said stop doing that!'

'Then still your tongue. There's magics in it.' Britha's voice was little more than a rasp, and she tasted blood from her throat when she spoke.

'We just want to ...' Britha moved towards the monster. So far her attacks had drawn no blood. 'Please listen ...'

'If you wish to talk, then let him talk,' Britha said and gestured at Fachtna.

'I don't want to talk; I want to fight,' Fachtna growled. His accent sounded like what she would imagine a Goidel would sound like.

'Many-Edged Ones, take me now,' Teardrop muttered.

'Are you working magics?' Britha demanded, moving towards him, 'No!'

Fachtna shifted to intercept her.

'Fachtna, stop, please,' Teardrop implored. Fachtna stopped but did not look happy.

'Why won't you let me talk to you?' Teardrop asked and then scrambled to his feet and backed away quickly as Britha tried to hit him again.

'I saw through your glamour,' Britha spat. 'I saw your true face. You're an evil spirit, a demon!'

Fachtna grinned at this, but Teardrop looked thoughtful and more than a bit worried.

'She has you there,' Fachtna said.

'Shut up!' Teardrop snapped. His warrior friend's humour often seemed poorly timed.

'His magics helped bring you back. They fought the demon's blood inside you,' Fachtna told her. 'We only mean you harm if you mean us harm. I will swear by my blood and his if that's what it takes.'

Britha considered this. If he was a Goidel then she had heard that they had their own honour and could be held to an oath. Teardrop was relieved that Fachtna had decided to be diplomatic and found a way to talk to the woman.

'We're here to—' Teardrop started. Britha swung around to face him again. 'Fine, fine,' he said backing away, hands up.

'I don't like that sword,' Britha told Fachtna.

Fachtna smiled. 'You would like my spear even less.'

Britha could see that he had a spear in some kind of leather tube strapped to the back of his armour. It looked like something was struggling to get out of it. Fachtna was right: she did not like it. She felt its malevolence in her blood.

Teardrop was looking bored.

'May I speak now? No ...' Britha tried to get at him again. Fachtna got in between them but sheathed his blade and dropped his shield, holding his hands up to show he meant no harm.

'I will give my oath for my friend as well,' he said. 'He worked magics on you while you were asleep.'

'Oh brilliant,' Teardrop muttered as Britha looked furious again.

'But they were healing magics only.'

Britha still regarded the pair suspiciously.

'Why are you here?'

'I have come to find and kill someone called Bress,' Fachtna said.

Britha looked for the truth in Fachtna. He seemed the archetypal warrior: cocky, boastful, arrogant and not too bright, but with a modicum of charm. Judging by his lack of scars he was untested and therefore vastly overconfident, particularly about facing Bress, but she could see no untruth in him. She nodded towards Teardrop.

'And that? Is it some demon you have bound into your service?'

Teardrop made a small humourless laughing noise. He was sitting on the pebbles now. He had spat on his fingers and was rubbing the spit into the dry wounds that Britha had made by repeatedly bludgeoning him with his own staff.

'No, he is my friend and a wise and powerful *dryw* in his own right.'

'Why is his head like that?'

'Because he has a grand opinion of himself,' Fachtna said, grinning. Teardrop silently cursed another of the warrior's poorly timed attempts at humour.

'It's this shape because I sing the mindsong. It's where my power lives,' Teardrop said, getting to his feet. The previously conciliatory tone had gone. Britha recognised this – she used it herself – it was the tone you used when the tribe needed to listen to her in her capacity as *ban draoi*. 'My name is Teardrop on Fire. Don't hit me with my staff again. In fact, give it back to me.'

'I'll swap you for my spear,' she said.

Fachtna sighed, 'I'll go and get it,' and headed back towards the crannogs. Britha continued staring at Teardrop.

'Teardrop on Fire, what sort of stupid name is that?'

'The only one I have.'

'Then you're brave to let me have it.'

'I have no fear of you. My friends call me Teardrop.'

Britha threw the strange creature his staff back to prove that she did not fear him either, and the more she talked to him the less frightening he seemed.

'Where do you come from?' she asked.

'A place where the ground is the sky and the sky is the ground,' Teardrop said as he grumpily examined his staff.

'The Otherworld?'

Teardrop put the base of his staff on the ground and leaned on it. It looked to be a familiar pose.

'If you like,' he said.

'What tribe do you come from?'

'My friend is a Gael descended from Mael Duin himself. I am Croatan.'

The words were meaningless to Britha. Fachtna was running easily across the pebbled beach back towards them carrying Britha's spear.

'He is *sidhe*?' Teardrop did not answer. 'You were the two that came through the circle.' It was more of an accusation than a question. Teardrop nodded. 'Why do you want to kill Bress?' There was only a small conflict in her voice. Her treacherous fledgling feelings for Bress were a paltry consideration compared to the plight of her people, but Teardrop's eyes narrowed. *I will have to watch him*, she thought. *He is clever*.

'Because even if this story had been long ago told, he does not belong here.'

'That does not make any sense.'

'He is unnatural to this place and means it ill. He is from elsewhere, and his magics were not made for this world.'

Britha gave this some consideration. He spoke in riddles but confirmed what she had thought.

'Why are you dressed so strangely?' she finally asked, more for the sake of something to say. Fachtna overheard as he returned and threw Britha her spear.

'Because he likes to draw attention to himself,' the warrior said. Teardrop gave his companion a weary look.

'Bress has an army. Is there just the two of you, or are you scouts for a great army from the Otherworld?'

Fachtna looked at Teardrop, who just shrugged.

'Teardrop is a powerful *dryw* and I am a mighty warrior.'

It was said in jest but Britha could tell he believed it as well.

'You don't look like a mighty warrior,' she said. Teardrop laughed.

'What?!' Fachtna cried in mock outrage.

'Even in training warriors get scars and wear them proudly,' Britha told him.

'Where I come from, the women train us to fight and they leave all kinds of wounds, but I have lain in the cauldron and that has made me whole again.'

Again Britha was not sure what he was talking about, but cauldrons with healing powers she could understand.

'You will have to believe me that he is a good warrior,' Teardrop said. 'And very, very vain.'

'Besides, we are three now,' Fachtna said, grinning, sure of himself. Britha had decided that her earlier judgement of him was correct. He would annoy her.

'Are we?' she said scornfully.

'Are you hungry?' Teardrop asked with some concern.

Britha had been ignoring the sensation but she realised suddenly that Teardrop was right. She was hungry to the point of being in pain. She felt as if her skin was hanging off her bones.

They were like her, like her people, or at least Fachtna was. She studied both of them, their features bathed in red from the fire they had lit. The smell of roasting venison filled her nose and made her mouth water. Her stomach called to the meat. Fachtna had stripped off his armour and boots and gone into the wooded hills with just three casting spears. He had come back with a roe stag over his shoulders.

Britha had searched the crannogs for food and found some. She had eaten but it had not sated her hunger. The rest she had given to Teardrop, who had returned from the woods with mushrooms, some berries and herbs.

Britha had also found an iron-bladed sickle. It was pitted and rusted but she had scraped off the rust and honed the blade as best she could. When she had the time, she would do the ritual that would attune the sickle to her. Though she would not bathe this one in her blood.

They were like her people but too perfect. Meat filled out their shapes as if they had never known a harsh winter. There were few lines on their skin, though she was sure that Teardrop was older than Fachtna. Their teeth were straight and white, and they smelled like they had washed in a mountain burn just moments before. Their clothes and belongings were well made and showed little if any signs of wear. *Life must be good in the Otherworld,* she thought.

The deer could have fed many. Britha had thought it too much for the three of them, but they had torn into it ravenously. There would be little left for the wolves and the crows. Teardrop was cutting off the remaining meat and putting it into a leather bag. She could see that it contained salt.

'That's no way to salt meat,' Britha said.

Teardrop just smiled. 'We have a way.'

'What did you see? When you ate of his flesh?' Fachtna asked, spearing another piece of meat with his dirk and dipping it into the wooden bowl containing the preparation of wine and berries that Teardrop had made. Britha didn't answer.

'Those are dark magics,' Teardrop said.

'We can eat what we kill,' Britha said haughtily, meeting Teardrop's stare until he turned from her. Britha turned to Fachtna and stabbed her dirk point towards Teardrop. 'I saw his real face, what he is.'

'That is not my real face,' Teardrop said quietly. 'Only what I must be to serve ...' His voice trailed away. He sounded sad. Fachtna was watching him thoughtfully.

'What are you then?'

This time Teardrop met her gaze unflinchingly.

'Would you tell me all your ways, your secrets?'

This time it was Britha who looked away.

'I felt the demon, burning in me, trying to consume me, make me a slave like all the others. I saw people who thought they were dead, who chose to be slaves and a dark man.' Fachtna and Teardrop exchanged looks. Britha did not notice. Tears sprang to her eyes. 'I saw my people caged, in the sea, and felt their fear and their pain as they died by fire ...'

Fachtna was looking at her sympathetically.

Teardrop looked angry. 'To come here ...' he muttered.

'Was there anything else?' Fachtna asked gently.

Britha's head snapped around to look at him. She had disliked the sympathy in his voice. She was angry through her tears.

'There was something under the water,' she said. Fachtna and Teardrop exchanged looks. 'What does it mean?'

'We're not sure,' Teardrop said.

Britha could tell he was lying. If he was a *dryw* then he could lie for what he thought was the best. She ignored him and turned to stare at Fachtna. He felt like her stare was burrowing into his head. *Good*, Britha thought. They obviously had their own *dryw* and knew to obey them or face serious consequences.

'We think that Bress has found an aspect of the sleeping goddess, the Mother to us all, and he seeks to pervert or corrupt her somehow,' Fachtna told her.

'And he will do this by offering those he has taken as sacrifice?' Britha asked.

Fachtna nodded. Teardrop was not looking happy.

'Will you swear by blood that you are here to stop this?' she asked.

Fachtna did not answer. Instead he produced his finely wrought, silver-bladed dirk and drew a line in red across his palm with the blade.

'Wait,' Teardrop said, but he knew it was pointless.

Britha took her iron-bladed knife.

'Use mine,' Fachtna said. But it was too late. She had made a ragged gash in her hand. The leather tube that lay on top of Fachtna's pile of armour seemed to move and make sounds as she did this.

'Look, don't ...' Teardrop started but Fachtna and Britha clasped hands.

'This oath will bind,' Britha warned him.

'By my blood, I bind myself. I, Fachtna ap Duin, swear that I am here to stop Bress from corrupting the Muileartach and to kill Bress and his servant.'

Britha felt a flutter in her stomach when he said he meant to kill Bress.

'Then I will travel with you to get my people back,' Britha said. In the back of her head she heard a voice asking when she would learn to leave the Otherworld well enough alone. Britha looked into Fachtna's eyes looking for falseness. All she found was desire. She let go of his bloody hand and walked down towards the small dark waves of the Black River lapping on the pebbles.

'What is it with you?' Teardrop asked Fachtna.

'I meant what I said. What they are doing is an abomination.'

'I know you thought that was what you were doing, but you always have to try and impress, don't you?'

'I'm an impressive person,' Fachtna said, smiling. Teardrop felt like slapping him for never taking anything seriously.

'In this world, yes ...'

'And in the *Ubh Blaosc*,' Fachtna said more quietly. Teardrop sighed. He hated having to deal with prickly warrior pride.

'I'm not doubting your prowess, but she cannot do the things we do.'

'She has the blood of the Muileartach and the blood of the Red Chalice. That is powerful blood magic and with your help she should be able to harness it. She will keep up.'

Britha was walking back towards them again. Teardrop did not like the look on her face. She was staring at him again. 'Besides, she's too much woman for you,' he said quietly.

Fachtna grinned. 'Such a creature would be a like a dragon. They may exist, but nobody's ever seen one.'

'I am beginning to understand why Uathach beat you so often.'

'She wanted me.'

'There was something else from my dream,' Britha said. Fachtna noticed that as she came to a rest by the fire, she pushed her foot under the haft of her spear. 'I saw them push a seed, like the crystals that grow in the caves, into the heads of my people. These things just seemed to sink through their skin.' Britha waited for either of them to speak. They just watched her. Teardrop could see what was coming. 'It looked like what I saw under the skin of your head when I bashed you.'

'It is similar magics. From the Otherworld,' Teardrop said.

Britha could not decide if she wanted to believe him or not.

'It's a fungus that they grow in his head,' Fachtna said. Teardrop looked furious. Britha had to stifle a smile. If one of her warriors had given away a secret like that to a stranger she would have cursed them until their manhood dropped off. Not that she ever allowed the warriors to learn her secrets. She could tell that Teardrop would be having words with Fachtna in private.

'A fungus inside the head. That makes no sense,' she told them. 'What would this seed do?'

'Enslave them,' Fachtna said.

'No, Ettin makes them drink from a cup of demon's blood for that,' Britha told him.

'It's to hear their mindsong,' Teardrop said quietly.

Britha turned to stare at him. 'When they are afraid, when they are suffering, when they die in torment,' she said. Teardrop looked at her across the fire. She could see new respect in his eyes. She did not care, though she was beginning to think that she wanted his magics. Either learned or taken, they would make her tribe stronger, if she ever found them.

'Now you know my secrets, will you tell us one of your own?' Teardrop asked.

'Unlikely, but you may ask,' Britha told him.

'You have the blood of the Muileartach in you. How?'

Fachtna turned to look at her expectantly.

'I don't know what you mean,' Britha said. 'The gods are cold and cruel and do not mean us well. My people forsook them when my farthest ancestors were young.'

'Have you drunk blood?'

'No,' she said uneasily. She remembered the fevered dream as she lay dying on the beach. The pool in Cliodna's cave. Teardrop was staring at her. It was the truth-finding look; she had used it herself before. He knew.

'Eaten flesh of the Otherworld?'

'No!'

'Some kind of fluid must have been exchanged,' Fachtna said with a leer.

191

He was too confident of his own abilities to think that Britha would attack him. The punch was a solid blow that spread his nose across his face and squirted blood over his mouth and down his chin. The blow had been quick and delivered with a surprising amount of force. Fachtna staggered back, and Britha turned and stalked off, pulling her hood up and wrapping her robe tighter around herself.

Teardrop made enough noise walking across the pebbles to give Britha warning of his approach. She turned to look briefly at the strange creature. He was carrying an earthenware jug. Britha went back to staring at the stars, wondering if she should be insulted that men thought alcohol was the solution to her problems.

'I found this,' Teardrop said. 'What sort of raiders leave the good *uisge beatha*?' he took a pull of the clear liquid. 'It's good,' he managed.

Britha took the jug off him and took a long swig.

'I don't like the sky now,' Britha finally said.

'Your vision?'

Britha nodded. 'It seems angry and hateful now.'

'I think it's like your gods, cold and uncaring.'

'No, our gods hated us. We would give them everything just so they would leave us alone.' Teardrop turned to look at her. 'Or so the stories handed from mother to mother go.' She handed the jug back and he had some more. 'Do you have gods?' she asked. He smiled.

'You know enough of us for one day, I think.' Both of them looked up into the night sky. 'We need to know,' he finally said.

He certainly knew all the masks, Britha thought, just the right word magic to get what he needed. When to be listened to, when to be feared, the caring mask, the one he was wearing now. Was he using this mindsong on her as well, she wondered, because she wanted to tell him. She wanted to tell someone, and he was, after all, from the Otherworld as well. He wouldn't, couldn't judge.

'Fachtna is an arrogant fool,' she said instead.

Teardrop laughed. 'Yes, but you must have met warriors before.'

'Her name was Cliodna,' Britha said. 'She was a selkie.'

'I have heard the name.'

'One of the seal people, skin changers.' Though now that she thought about it, she had never seen Cliodna in her seal form.

Teardrop looked a little confused. 'And you drank her blood?'

'No, I told you. Though she may have used her blood to heal me, or I may have dreamed it.'

'Then ... you were lovers?'

Britha turned to look at him defiantly. People feared those who behaved differently to them. Britha had never been able to differentiate between the desire for men and the desire for women. She could not understand why people would cut off half the oppurtunities for beauty and pleasure. Teardrop looked momentarily surprised but there was no judgement there. Then he looked amused.

'What?' she demanded.

'Fachtna will be dissapointed,' he said.

'She turned different, angry, hateful.' Britha hated that a tear rolled down her cheek in front of this stranger.

'She lived in the water a lot?'

Britha nodded.

'It sounds like she was an elder child of the Muileartach.'

'And the gods are hateful,' Britha said bitterly.

'Bress is harvesting sorrow. Did she push you away?'

Britha nodded again, cursing more tears.

'She was probably trying to protect you. She knew she was changing and there was nothing that she could do about it.'

Britha said nothing. She tried to look at the hateful sky and not the dark waters. Teardrop had learned long ago that the best thing at times like these was to let the tears run their course. He looked out over the waters to the south. He knew that that way lay Bress.

Finally Britha wiped away her tears, took the jug from Teardrop and had another long pull.

'It was a great gift she gave you,' Teardrop said. Britha nodded.

The following day was grey and overcast as well. The rain was light but constant, the kind that soaks through and then chills down to the bone, except today Britha wasn't feeling it. She felt stronger, faster, more aware than she had at any time she could remember. She felt amazing except for the dull ache of loss in her chest.

'Does the sun ever shine in this land?' Fachtna demanded cheerfully as he dragged a log boat he had found in the treeline down the pebbles towards the Black River. Even so early, he was already annoying Britha. The *uisge beatha* pain in her head was not helping her tolerance either.

'Do you know what you're doing?' Britha asked.

'I think I know how to work a boat,' Fachtna said.

'If this is anything like the Tatha, then the currents and tides will be treacherous. We need an experienced boatman who knows the waters. Besides, their god lives in there and he will be angry now his people are dead.'

Fachtna stared out at the water, seeming to concentrate, then he knelt by the side of the river and placed his hand in the water and concentrated some more.

'Come. We will break spears and give them to the river,' Teardrop said.

Britha looked over at him. She couldn't shake the feeling that he was just trying to humour her.

'I know this river now,' Fachtna said, standing up. 'We will be fine.'

15
Now

Maude had held her as she sobbed while Uday, his expression difficult to read, had made her hot chocolate liberally laced with cheap whisky. They were near strangers to her, and her sister had hurt them – Uday certainly had no reason to trust her – but they looked after her. Made sure she was okay.

Later Maude was curled up on the sofa snoring gently, her head in Uday's lap. He was stroking her hair as she slept. Being held had become too much for Beth and had just made her cry more, so she had moved to the ancient but still comfortable armchair, bringing her knees up to her chest as she sipped another Irish hot chocolate. Her face was still streaked, her chest still hurting from crying. *Some tough ex-con*, she thought. Then more bitterly, *If it had been the other way around, the only crying Talia would have done would have been to call attention to herself.*

Uday reached under the sofa, making Maude stir in her sleep, and pulled out the bayonet. The blade was clean. Uday held it in front of her.

'I don't like this being here,' he finally said.

'It was my great-grandfather's,' Beth said. She wasn't sure why.

'I don't want violence brought here. Do you understand?' He was still holding the bayonet, staring at the blade.

Beth looked down. 'I'm through with it. She's dead. There was some weird stuff ... There's nothing I can do.'

'Arbogast,' Uday said quietly, not wanting to wake Maude. Then he handed the bayonet back to Beth. 'I almost wish you'd killed him. Piece of shit.' There was a barely restrained fury in Uday's whisper.

'You knew him?'

Uday shook his head. 'I was just around to try and help Maude pick up the pieces afterwards. Oh, it wasn't rape – too genteel and manipulative for that. May as well have been for what it did to her self-esteem. All the bullshit justifications from your sister dearest.

Look, I'm sorry for your loss, but I'm glad your sister is out of our lives, her and all those other Black Mirror arseholes.' Uday lapsed into a brooding silence. Maude had shifted on the sofa but was still asleep.

'It was bad enough after she turned a trick – days sitting in here just sobbing, a couple of attention-grabbing pieces of suicidal talk, but it was when someone at uni found the film she'd made with Talia. Because of course their Internet porn habits are just a reflection on the dirty girls in the films,' Uday spat bitterly. This was anger that had been stored up and nurtured, Beth thought. 'Of course, Talia revelled in the notoriety. Made it out to be some kind of a statement of how clever, interesting and nonconformist she was.' A tear leaked out of Uday's eye. 'A different story for Maude. All the looks in lectures, in the corridors. The guys deciding she was easy, so they could say what they wanted to her and she would jump into bed with them, somehow forgetting that the porn industry exists because of people like them. All the girls sitting in judgement. A slut to some, a threat to others, or just a poor example helping to objectify the sex. Everyone just so pleased that they weren't the target, and we're supposed to be the clever ones. University's supposed to be a place to experiment. It's the twenty-first century and apparently a gal's reputation is still what matters. What a load of shit.'

Maude was moaning in her sleep. Uday tried to calm himself, stroking her hair as she settled down.

'Nobody?'

'Oh there were some, the understanding ones, as if they knew. Sometimes I think they were the worst. Every sympathetic look a reminder. I know we're all supposed to talk about our feelings, but sometimes you just want to forget about your mistakes and move on. And let's be honest, she's fragile, arguably too easily led, but she is an adult and has to take responsibility for her actions as well.'

Beth tried to imagine what it had been like for them. They had clearly developed something of a siege mentality. In her mind's eye she could see Maude in tears while Uday verbally went for some bitchy girl or sleazy guy who'd upset her.

'They don't give you a chance, you know? You fall down, make a mistake – suddenly you're public property and everyone wants their pound of flesh.' Tears were rolling down his cheeks now. Beth said nothing. There was nothing to say for now; he just needed to get this out.

'That was Talia for you,' Beth finally said after a long silence. Uday looked over at her. 'She was like a virus. Everything she touched got infected.' Beth reached for what she was trying to say, trying to give words to a half-formed thought. 'I think the more people she hurt, the more she thought it meant that she mattered ...' She wasn't sure she had managed to get across what she was thinking, but Uday was nodding. More silence. The pair of them lost in their own thoughts.

'I'm going to have to tell my father that his only daughter is dead,' Beth said. It was self-pity. She knew it was self-pity. It was also true. Uday just looked at her. The silence drew out awkwardly. Beth looked down at the threadbare carpet.

'I know it probably won't seem like it sometimes,' he finally said, 'but your parents don't hate you. They probably just do the best they can with what they know.'

'Parent,' Beth said. 'My mum died when we were both young. What about your parents?'

'What about them?'

'What do they think?'

'About what?' Uday asked innocently. Beth got embarrassed and was not sure what to say. 'What, because I'm Asian and a fag?' Uday started laughing. 'I'm just playing. Mother is in major denial, keeps on trying to introduce me to nice girls. Father's also in denial. I think he'd rather I meet some less nice girls; I suspect he prays that I'm sleeping with Maude.' Uday looked down at Maude, still asleep and looking peaceful. 'Brother and sister are supportive. The problem's cousins and some aunts and uncles.' Uday looked away, but Beth saw the darkness creep over his face. She recognised the sign of old pain.

Maude stretched and opened her eyes, looked up at Uday.

'I fell asleep,' she said drowsily.

'On the sofa again,' Uday agreed.

'I need bed.'

Uday nodded.

'Tomorrow we go to the pub and we can pretend we're normal, as unpleasant as that sounds,' Uday said. Maude smiled and nodded. She stood up and stretched dramatically before giving Beth a kiss on the top of her head.

'I'm sorry,' she said sympathetically.

No, I'm sorry, Beth thought, *for what my family helped do to you*, but she just nodded.

Beth wondered if it was as simple as pretending that you were just like everyone else for long enough that you eventually became so. She sat on the sea wall just outside the amusements, looking out at the water towards the Isle of Wight. To her left along the front was some kind of tower, beyond that was Old Town and then Gosport.

It was ridiculous how exotic Portsmouth felt to her, but then she'd never really been anywhere except Bradford and prison. Well, Leeds as well, she supposed.

It was a cloudless day, bright blue sky but fresh and windy. She had her leather zipped up tight, her hat pulled down over her ears. She took another sip from the mug of hot sweet tea.

This would be okay, this would be enough, she thought. Time for a change. She wanted to get away from Bradford and live by the sea. Stay away from the clubs, the bouncing and all the violence. Live in a place where not everyone knew you and your business.

The work was menial and repetitive but that didn't matter. When she was finished she could see a clean floor, or an oiled ride, or a happy punter, well more or less, and could measure what she'd done.

She would have to go back and tell her dad face to face what had happened first. It would devastate him and he already needed care, but he had made his choice. He had made it clear that he didn't want her around, that he blamed her for something, though she'd never known what.

She heard his huffing breath as he shuffled towards her a long time before he said anything.

'I'm not paying you to eye up the Isle of Wight,' Ted said sternly.

'I've done all the floors in the arcade and the caff before it opened. I helped Jimmy with the ghost train and I've worked the tombola all morning. I was just having a quick tea break.' When she turned around, however, Ted was smiling.

'I know. I know when people work and when they slack. I know everything. It's the rides themselves – they talk to me. I'm like a fairground shaman,' he said. Beth was smiling, trying not to laugh and shaking her head.

'You're so full of shit.'

It was Ted's turn to laugh. With difficulty he manoeuvred himself onto the sea wall and offered her a cigarette. She was about to take one when she realised that she didn't smoke and didn't need them to buy stuff and trade for favours any more.

'It's beautiful, isn't it? The sea,' he said.

'Isn't that the Solent?'

'Have I ever told you about my time in the merchant marine?'

'It's my first day,' Beth protested. Ted's chuckle was a rasping wet noise that threatened to become a cough. 'You shouldn't smoke so much.' *Or eat all the shit you obviously do*. He had the look of someone who had a full English breakfast every day of the week.

'This is what a real man looks like,' Ted said, slapping his belly. It was avoidance but Beth had to grin. 'I heard you had some trouble this morning?'

'Just some kids trying to tip one of the machines.'

'Little shits.'

'Nah, I was worse when I was their age. Just bored and skint. I don't like those tracksuits they all wear though.'

When she looked back up she saw that Ted was studying her intently. Beth wasn't sure why. Ted had worked the amusements for many years. When punters came to the stalls he had learned how to read them. He knew people. Beth didn't realise it, but how she responded to kids was a test. She didn't hate them or resent them, she just saw them for what they were.

'Lot of people try hard their first day, their first week, their first month and then slack off.'

Beth shrugged. 'You don't think I'm working hard enough, just fire me.'

'You keep this up you can stay as long as you like,' Ted told her and pulled out his wallet. He took a fifty out of it. Beth started to protest. 'I told you I won't have desperate people working for me. It comes out of your pay, but it'll tide you over until the end of the week. Understand?'

'Thanks.' She finished her tea and Ted watched her head back towards the amusements.

He hung in the murk, the particulate matter floating all around. He could not imagine how once he had thought that this was not a good place to come. He did not feel the coldness now. He did not care about the lack of visibility. He did not need to see her to know that she was there. He could hear her sleeping song calling to her lost daughter somewhere in the city he and the others had forsaken. Lost for generations but so close.

He was but a child to her. A servant. The daughter would bring freedom. The daughter could wake her. The water felt warm, quiet and subdued like the womb. Everything was loud, painful and so dry on the land, in the city. In the city every street was a reminder, fragmenting memories played out like an old film. They might as well have belonged to someone else. On dry land it felt like you could reach up and touch reality, pierce through it like a membrane to where madness and hate waited.

He swam down. He would do his duty, but first he needed to touch her, be with her, join with her, and inside her he would try to cease to exist so there was only her.

Heavily sedated and on as much pain relief as he was, Arbogast couldn't stop the tear trickling from his eye as he saw McGurk, resplendent in shell suit and bling, the cane, the latest phone in hand, flanked by muscle, making his way through the ward towards him.

The other patients and the staff watched him walk by. If they didn't know who he was, then they knew what he was. The constant chewing and the wild amphetamine stare didn't help.

McGurk walked into Arbogast's room and stood at the bottom of the bed, looking at him with contempt. Trevor remained behind McGurk while Markus went and pulled the curtain shut across the window that looked out onto the ward. Then he closed the door.

McGurk looked down at the bandaged stumps where Arbogast's fingers used to be and then back to the tear running down the pimp's face.

'Do you know what I hate most?' he asked. Arbogast dared not answer. 'Fucking weakness.' McGurk moved quickly but with the jerky movements of a habitual speed freak. He grabbed Arbogast's wounded hand and got up close to the pimp's face. Over the sterile and sickness smell of the hospital and through the fugue of sedatives and painkillers, Arbogast could smell spearmint over something rancid on McGurk's breath. McGurk put his hand over Arbogast's mouth. Arbogast wet himself. He was sure it was over.

'I want to test the limits of modern medicine's ability to relieve pain,' McGurk told the pimp. It was something cool to say that he'd thought of on the way over. McGurk squeezed the stumps of Arbogast's fingers. The dressings turned red. 'Don't you cry! Don't you fucking cry, you bastard! You owe me an explanation.'

McGurk was wiping his hands with a paper towel when the doctor burst in flanked by security.

'It's okay. We're leaving,' he told them.

'We've called the police,' the doctor told him. McGurk turned to look at the whimpering ball of pain on the bed that used to be William Arbogast.

'He doesn't want to press charges, but you do what you think is right.'

Trevor made a path for them through the security and they left.

'You believe that shit?' Markus asked as they made their way through the ward.

'City's getting weirder.'

'What do you want to do?'

'I want to know who the fuckers in the masks are. I don't want any of the cunt with a gun – he sounds like some super-plod, Special Branch, something like that. Find me where the sister is, though.'

Caitlin felt like she had bled onto the page today. Sometimes it just wouldn't come, but today it had been pure stream of consciousness. Poetry wasn't cool or interesting to most people any more. Caitlin felt it was difficult to do well and with relevance to the modern world, but today line after line had come out of the platinum-nib fountain pen given to her by proud parents and onto the yellow legal pads. She felt like she was talking to something else, listening to the beat of the city or the world, channelling the words. Normally she hated her work immediately after she'd written it. Sometimes it was hard not to tear it all up and burst into tears, but not today. Today she even took pleasure from the shape of the words on the page, wishing she could publish them in her handwriting rather than through some soulless word-processing package. She was the biggest critic of her work. If she liked it then she knew it was good.

The inspiration had wiped her. The invitation to go out had been half welcomed and half not. She could do with leaving her flat after such an intense day, seeing some actual people, but she felt drained. The answer had been obvious, a little chemical pick-me-up. After all, she was following a trail blazed by hedonists of all stripes.

Red-haired and unconventionally attractive, a little too tall for the more insecure male, Caitlin didn't stop a room when she walked in, but some attention was inevitable. Single, she was keeping an eye open, but she didn't panic when she was on her own, like some of her friends. Tonight she just wanted to dance but she needed some fuel.

It was something new. Caitlin was initially suspicious as it looked like an acid tab with a dot of red on it. The girl dealing in the ultraviolet-lit toilets had assured her that although it provided good visuals, it was all about the dancing. Caitlin had let herself be talked into it.

Dancing. Moving to beat and bass. Trying to find that perfect moment. The modern shamanic experience. The lights above her becoming stars, light refracting through the dry ice becoming glowing gaseous nebula. Dancing on the edge of a spinning spiral galaxy. Joy. This was why she did it. This was the moment. To transcend the club. The music receding. She felt something wet under her eye, coming from her ear. She tasted copper in her mouth. She touched her face. Her fingers came away wet. She looked at the other dancers. They were covered head to foot in blood. Above her, space started to seethe like angry bacteria consuming everything.

There wasn't even time to scream.

Du Bois lay on the bed in his room in Fort Southwick. He liked the room. It was another faceless barracks room. He had felt at home in places like this since he had lived in his first preceptory. His room was part of the officers' quarters for the contingent of Royal Marines who guarded the facility.

Fort Southwick was one of the grand Victorian forts built on Portsdown Hill at the behest of Prime Minister Lord Palmerston for an invasion that had never come. The huge, squat, red-brick edifice had been used for Operation Overlord during the Second World War, as a NATO communications centre during the cold war and was now part of the Admiralty Research Establishment.

He had the information sent to his phone. He could have had the information downloaded straight into his brain, but he preferred to watch and read and then assign data to his augmented memory. He received the information shortly after he had used his phone's systems to interrogate the control nanites he had found in Arbogast's blood.

He hadn't understood some of the words. Or rather he had understood them but struggled to make sense of how they fitted together. He had learned new terms like RLK, which apparently meant real-life kill. He understood those who killed for belief, profit and pleasure. He didn't understand insanity, but appreciated it as a motivation. What he didn't understand was how humanity had become so jaded. Perhaps they deserved their inevitable destruction. He had never felt so old, so divorced from everyone around him, so out of his time.

They were called the DAYP clan. This stood for Do As You Please. They had taken their name from Carroll. Du Bois was of the opinion they should give it back. He understood their criminality. What he couldn't understand was how it connected to their games. As if it was all part of a computer simulation and they could do what they wanted to whoever they wanted. As if none of it was real and therefore none of it mattered. How had they become so divorced from reality?

They had started life as an elitist gaming clan. Something called an uberguild, apparently. It had taken a while for du Bois to realise that the weapons they were dealing were effectively electronic game pieces for computer games and not real weapons. Even longer to realise that people would pay for these virtual weapons and for high-level characters. This was how the fledgling DAYP had financed

202

themselves. Virtual weapons dealing and organised league game E-sports, where they were known for domination and bullying.

Their first connection to real-world criminality was with a Korean game gang that they contracted out debt collection to. This was also their first connection to offline PKs – player kills.

According to Control, the DAYP recruited from top-echelon game nerds. The super-intelligent, many of them dropouts from top universities. They were recruited online after the DAYP used gameplay to psychometrically measure them, targeting excluded, disaffected sociopaths capable of doing the sort of things that would be required of them. Recently their games had become more sophisticated and capable of influencing people towards such behaviour.

It would almost be funny, except that through dealing in experimental software, hacking, upmarket games discovered via industrial espionage and experimental hardware, the DAYP had come across S-tech and L-tech. Worse, they had learned how to utilise it.

Then the DAYP started seriously hunting for it. They searched the most accurate conspiracy sites, the darkest, dangerous and often most secure parts of the web, looking for info on the tech. Each time they found it, they attempted to replicate it, augment themselves and their technology and then sell it. They were close to controlling the black market in S- and L-tech.

Their dominance of this black market had required a degree of ruthlessness. Initially, influenced by a type of computer game called a first-person shooter, they had used external contractors to do their dirty work and secure the tech for themselves. These contractors were normally security companies who used ex-special forces personnel. However, with access to such a high level of technology, they had started to augment themselves and do their own dirty work with violent enthusiasm.

They were implicated in thefts, murders, rape, slavery and numerous other crimes. Du Bois had seen men given licence to do what they wanted before, but they had not been given the power of near-gods on earth. The DAYP were thought to be based in America, though it seemed that some of them at least were operating in Portsmouth and interested in Natalie Luckwicke.

Du Bois was angry that he had not been briefed on them. Control had told him that his direct experience had made him more useful in dealing with the City of Brass and agents of the Eggshell, though more and more du Bois was starting to believe that the Eggshell was a myth. If they had ever existed they were long gone. It hadn't been so long ago that the Circle would have never allowed such parasites to get their hands on S- and L-tech. He wished that he had been allowed to deal with these spoilt, evil child fantasists a long time ago.

He got up, poured himself a healthy measure of Scotch and moved to the window. He leaned against the frame, his face lit up by the harsh sodium lights that illuminated the wet concrete and brick of the base. He could see one of the later buildings that had been added to the military facility. Despite being a typically ugly utilitarian design, there was something of the art deco about it. It reminded him of a film he had seen many years ago about a failed utopia. This thought made him smile humourlessly. Beyond that he could see the lights of the city.

Did it matter? Yes. What the DAYP did was wrong. He was not a righteous man, not any longer if even a shred of what Hamad had said was true, but even if the Circle was corrupt they were not unnecessarily cruel. There was no pleasure in the suffering of others. Like every animal they did what they had to, to survive. Though it looked like that was over. If the prodigal had been here it looked like she was dead.

Du Bois took out his own phone. A normal phone. This one wasn't filled with liquid soft/hardware many iterations in advance of what was thought to be the cutting edge of computer and communications technology. He knew that Control monitored his 'private' phone as well. It was more a symbol of separation between his work and what he could only jokingly call a private life.

He cycled through the few names on his contact list and stared at Alexia's. He put his thumb over the dial key. His work phone sent the text straight to his internal systems, flagged as very urgent. He narrowed his eyes, his vision magnifying the city below him. He could make out the flashing lights from the emergency-services vehicles.

Some of her co-workers had told her that the fish and chip shop on Castle Street, just down from the Colonial Arms, was the best in the city. Beth had practically run down Elm Grove to Campbell Road, where Uday and Maude's flat was, to stop the three fish suppers she'd bought from getting too cold.

It was a funny thing about Portsmouth and Southsea that Beth was coming to realise. Perhaps it was because it was an island and space was limited, but it didn't seem to be a case of good neighbourhoods and bad neighbourhoods, it wasn't even a case of good streets and bad streets. It was more good house, bad house. Everyone was mixed in together. Students lived next to 'nice' middle-class families, who lived next to drug dealers and other career criminals.

With a can of one of the better bitters, the fish and chips had tasted amazing to Beth. Uday had looked at the greasy food with some disdain but Maude had teased him until he'd eaten it.

Both of them had then taken some considerable time to get ready – much to Beth's amusement. Beth practically had to fight off Maude's attempt to put make-up on her. The getting-ready process had involved booze from the off-licence on the corner of Outram Road and Victoria Road North, because it was cheaper than drinking in the pub, and a volume war between Maude and Uday's disparate musical tastes. Beth tended to side more with Maude but only a little.

Then on to a crowded pub on Albert Road. They had to shout to be heard, and spent the first hour standing up until Beth managed to intimidate some kids off a table, much to Maude's embarrassment and Uday's amusement. Several rounds in, Beth had stopped worrying about how much of the money that Ted had given her she was spending and how she didn't recognise any of the music, and was starting to believe the fiction of normality she was trying to construct.

Beth was studying the wooden panels on the wall, each filled with pictures of butterfly statues, girls with rabbit heads, VW Beetles ... They were odd but Beth was slowly coming to the conclusion she liked them. She liked that someone cared enough to take the time to decorate the pub like this. Though she wasn't sure it justified the price of drinks in the place.

Beth had noticed Maude get a few looks and there had been whispers behind hands. Maude had pretended not to notice. Uday had looked relieved when some drunk arsehole came over to the table and asked Maude if she was the porn girl, and Beth had been the one to see him off with some serious threats. Beth guessed Uday usually had to do that. She suspected Uday's comments would have been more cutting.

'... and then we can find a nice girl for Beth.' She hadn't been paying any attention, but the sound of her name broke into her art appreciation.

'I'm not a lesbian,' she said just a little too loudly, getting some looks of amusement from nearby tables. She was a little pissed off but saw Uday was smiling mischievously.

'Are you sure? Then why'd you dress like one?' he asked.

'Stop it!' Maude scolded him.

'Perhaps clothes and make-up and stuff aren't as important to me as they are to other people.'

Uday clamped his hand to his heart dramatically. 'Oh my gosh, you are so right. I am so shallow. I shall immediately change my ways and start wearing dowdy things. What is that, homeless chic?'

Beth felt herself colouring. She hated conversations like this. She flicked Uday a V-sign.

'Don't mind him,' Maude told Beth between giggles. 'He's just being a bitch.'

'He certainly is,' Beth muttered.

'Oooo! I know!' Maude said, grinning and clapping her hands. Beth was watching the young goth with suspicion. 'Makeover!'

Uday's eyes widened with glee. Beth suspected it was more out of pleasure at her discomfort than sharing Maude's genuine enthusiasm.

'Maude, what a marvellous idea! It'll be like a gruff Yorkshire *Pygmalion*!'

Beth shifted defensively, like she was getting ready for fight or flight.

'I will beat up both of you,' she warned. Mostly joking.

'Darling, not everyone can be as pant-creamingly beautiful as the likes of Maude and I,' Uday began. Maude smiled graciously at Uday, who gave her a mock bow in return. 'But with some effort even the dowdiest caterpillar can become a beautiful butterfly.' Uday considered his own statement while studying Beth. 'Well, a beautiful moth anyway.'

Uday was enjoying Beth's discomfort but Beth didn't like where it was taking her. She had never liked the way she looked. Neither had anyone else, so it seemed, so she had made it unimportant to her.

'Look, the whole being-pretty thing, it's really not me. That was more Talia's kind of thing,' she said, then turned away, taking a mouthful of her drink. Uday looked awkward, apologetic, Maude concerned. Then Maude smiled again.

'I think you're pretty,' she said. Her apparent sincerity almost made Beth believe her.

'And I concur. There is beauty there, no doubt, though we may need to dig deep to find it.' Beth gave him the finger this time. 'But I am, after all, the archaeologist of gorgeousness.'

From all over the pub came the sound of bleeping as people received text messages almost simultaneously. Uday's phone sounded. He took it out of his pocket, a look of concern on his face. He opened the text. In the distance they could hear the sound of sirens.

'What is it?' Beth asked as Uday read the message, his face darkening as he did so.

'Someone's just blown up Weightless,' he said. Horror crept over Maude's face.

'Weightless?' Beth asked.

'It's a club on Guildhall Walk,' Uday said quietly. 'We'll know people who were there tonight.' A pall was settling over the pub.

'It's happened again, hasn't it?' Maude said. Beth looked at her. 'It's like what happened to Talia.'

'Maude, we don't know. Anything could have happened.'

'How do I get there?' Beth asked.

There was rubble and a hole in the shadow of the neoclassical Guildhall where a building used to be. The hole was illuminated by the multiple flashing lights of numerous emergency vehicles and inhabited by police, ambulance people and fire officers, all of them vastly underqualified to deal with the situation.

Was this how it started? du Bois wondered. One small morsel at a time. *No, this was too localised, too specific.* He tried to murder the feeling of hope; he wanted to connect this to the prodigal. It was too much of a coincidence for there to be two incursions in such a short period of time.

He supposed he should do something. Find out who was in charge and throw some weight around. At least get them away from the hole before they dosed themselves with lethal levels of cosmic radiation, though it was probably too late. They were in there because they were hoping for survivors, trying to help people. *Sometimes we seem worth saving,* he thought.

Control would start putting the cover story in place. Another terrorist incident. He felt sorry for whichever community was the scapegoat this time around. There would be response teams on their way from Porton Down to seal the area. He already knew what they would find.

If Natalie wasn't dead, then he needed to find her. He looked around the street. There were a number of CCTV cameras. Du Bois sent instructions to his phone. If the CCTVs were attached to the net in any way, he would be able to download the footage and run it through sophisticated intelligent facial-recognition software. Moments later he received a message saying that nobody fitting Natalie Luckwicke's description had been anywhere near the club for the last week. Du Bois sighed, though he had known that it wasn't going to be that easy.

He turned to look at the crowd. Many of them were drunk or high, clubbers evacuated from the clubs along Guildhall Walk. A lot of them were sailors, du Bois guessed. Something caught his eye – someone backing into a narrow alleyway between one of the pubs and a Chinese restaurant. He wouldn't have thought anything of it except the figure moved furtively, suspiciously, and there was something off about it. Something about the glimpsed figure suggested that it was misshapen in some way.

Du Bois ran to the alley, drawing looks from some of the assembled police. The passage ran for about twenty feet, ending in a high fence with a gate in it. The fence was topped with broken glass. Du Bois tried the gate. It was locked. Feeling slightly absurd, he drew his pistol and kicked the gate in. It led into a small courtyard at the back of the restaurant. Some of the restaurant's employees came out of the open back door to look at him but said nothing when they saw the gun.

Du Bois shook his head and returned to the street. Scanning the crowd again. Disconcerted. Then he found at least one face in the crowd that he recognised.

Uday and Maude had gone home. Maude hadn't wanted to add to the chaos at the scene. They would use social networking sites to try and find out if the people they knew were okay.

Beth had circled the taped-off police perimeter trying to get the best view. She'd ended up leaning on one of the lion statues on the steps that led up to the Guildhall itself. She'd watched the blond man run into the alleyway and then reappear moments later with a gun in his hand. The man had been scanning the crowd. He stopped as he looked in her direction. Beth felt like he was staring at her, though she thought she was too far away for him to make out her features. Nevertheless she ducked behind the statue of the lion.

'I think your sister's been here, don't you?' The bag lady's face was inches from Beth's. Sweat, piss, stale smoke and cheap alcohol emanated from her. Beth's face crumpled in disgust. It was the same woman she'd seen on Pretoria Street.

'What do you mean? My sister's d—'

The bag lady blew smoke all over her. Beth coughed, her eyes watering, and turned away. By the time the smoke had cleared, the woman was nowhere to be seen.

Beth sat down hard on the steps. It was just a weird coincidence, she told herself, the ramblings of someone with mental health problems. Her sister was dead. This had nothing to do with her. She could work hard, get on with her life and be normal. At the back of her mind, the question *What if Talia is alive?* just wouldn't leave her in peace.

'Well?' Baron Albedo asked. Both of them had their hoods up. They liked the look and were only peripherally aware that it would draw attention to them rather than away.

'Our journey might not be quite the waste of time that the pimp made it out to be,' King Jeremy mused. The pair watched the response to the destruction of Weightless. It was kind of cool because it was like a disaster movie, but a bit lame because it was British, which made it look low-budget.

16
A Long Time After the Loss

The flickering black wound in Red Space at the bridge point to Pythia looked soothing to Vic. Scab had made as much of the hull transparent as he could. Vic wouldn't have minded so much but Scab had retracted the walls to Vic's room to make the ship as open plan as possible. Vic's psychotic partner reclined in one of the smart chairs. The light of Red Space made his naked form look like he was covered in blood.

They said that the really damaged could talk to Red Space. Vic wondered if Scab was communing. Vic, on the other hand, had red fatigue. The constant light was making him angry. He had tried to immerse as much as possible. Experiencing his favourite colonial immersions starring his namesake Vic Matto, letting experimental soundscapes wash over him. None of it was really helping.

The bridge point to Pythia was one of the busiest points in Red Space. Ships were queueing at the bridge-point beacon, sending their bids through to transponders in Real Space for their place in the line. Coming to Pythia was always expensive.

Engines glowing, the *Basilisk* flew down canyons of parked ships. There were vessels from all the main corporate interests in the Consortium, each jockeying for more market position despite ultimately serving the same organisation – competition for the sake of it. Odd-looking craft from the various Monarchist systems, part works of art, part throwbacks to eras that were probably mythical anyway, and part external manifestations of decadent and broken minds. Massive military ships, brooding tonnes of armoured potential violence, moving slowly and majestically through the red, the well-armed beacons tracking their movements. It would not be the first time there had been violence at a bridge point. Then the smaller ships, private yachts of the super-rich, broken-down vessels belonging to info prospectors and gamblers looking for their big break, craft so anonymous that they screamed some intelligence agency or company, a heretical sect looking for enlightenment or whatever the opposite of enlightenment was. The poorer ships containing plenty of supplies for the months or years of waiting their turn.

And bounty ships. *People like us,* Vic thought. Small, fast, well armed, mostly ex-military ships. If they could afford what Pythia charged then they were good, the sort of people that the Queen's Cartel might send after them. Even before getting in-system, the Pythia bridge point was a reasonably good place to mine data, and neither Vic nor Scab could find details of any bounty on them. Vic gave this some thought. It either meant that there wasn't one, or it had been done carefully and contracted to professionals.

On the first day they saw some junk ship come apart under the barrage of a garish Monarchist pleasure barge. There hadn't been any reason that Vic could see. It was probably just to relieve the boredom. The Pythia bridge-point beacons responded immediately. An AG-driven autonomous suicide drone was launched. Its AI system had it dancing around the beams of the pleasure barge's defence systems. At the same time the beacons were broadcasting their automated admonishment of the pleasure barge publicly, along with how much property damage the suicide drone was about to do and how much it was going to cost them.

The suicide drone was destroyed as it closed but not before it fired its sub-munitions, clustered high-yield lasers, which lit up the barge's energy displacement grid, and low-yield fusion warheads, which blossomed blue against the red. Massive reactive armour plates blew out. New matter poured like sentient tar from the chagrined pleasure barge's carbon reservoir.

'Thank goodness they didn't kill anyone important,' Vic muttered as he watched the engraved murals self-etch across the pleasure barge's new armoured skin.

It was the only interesting thing that happened while they waited, though Vic kept checking for bounty ships.

It was two days before their turn came up. Two days was pretty quick. Again Vic marvelled at the resources behind this job. It was still, however, two days of being bathed in red. Two days of Scab lying naked and unmoving on the sofa. Some of the time Vic was pretty sure that he was data-mining, but not all the time. Fortunately Scab was using the smart chair's catheter and cleaning facilities. He was also smoking enough to make the ship smell despite otherwise excellent atmosphere scrubbers. Although furious with Scab, Vic eventually got bored and started talking to him, but Scab did not answer.

Bridging back into Real Space was cool relief.

With unaugmented vision Vic could make out the burn of the engines of other ships making for Pythia. Pythia itself was a disc of shadow deep in a cloud of particulate matter thought to come from one or more long-destroyed planets. The cloud glowed gold, illuminated by light refracting from the system's giant yellow sun. The star had a number, probably of interest to navigation systems and ship AIs, but nobody had ever named it. Pythia was the only thing that mattered in this system.

Closer to Pythia, the planet's long-range orbital defences let the *Basilisk* know that it was extensively covered. Scab 'faced his privacy bid over. Privacy was like everything else: you either fought or paid for it. When a mote of dust could spy on you, then those with the best tech and the most money got the best privacy. Vic had been told of a time where privacy was a right, before the Loss. He suspected that it was as mythical as the Naga. If there were people around to make money from it, he couldn't understand why they wouldn't exploit it. One of Pythia's hospitality contractors got back to them. The contractors were one of the lesser-known branches of the mystery cult, but they seemed competent and had accepted their bid. Scab changed course and made for their habitat after clearing it with the defence systems.

'So are you going to put some clothes on?' Vic asked. Scab still ignored him. *For fuck's sake*, the 'sect thought, *I'm supposed to be angry with him and he's the one doing the ignoring.* At the back of his head he knew this was because Scab didn't care. They weren't friends or even partners really; he was a resource, like the ship.

Space was more and more crowded the closer they got to Pythia. Vic could see the various habitats in orbit run by the subcontracted cult of Pythia employees. They went from garish, over-the-top, neon-lit luxury hotels to zero-G coffin stacks. Shuttlecraft and heavy maintenance automatons flew between the habitats and the heavily armed orbital fortresses with their rings of weapons satellites and static AG smart munitions. Vast fields of orbital solar panels absorbed light from the star, and along with various massive power-generating stations, dipped tethers into Pythia's cloudy upper atmosphere. Occasionally ghost fire could be seen flitting around the far end of the tethers. The tethers were the only thing other than sacrifices allowed through the atmosphere.

Scab banked the *Basilisk* over one of the super-hotel habitats. Vic looked down through the commercial holography displays, through the ornate transparent hull designed to look like crystal with iron supports, at the sculpted island landscape of the pool area. As they passed, the hotel's weapons batteries tracked them across its territory. The habitat they were making for was supposed to be mid-level and anonymous. Scab hadn't paid for luxury; he had paid for secrecy and security.

An incoming comms warning was 'faced from the *Basilisk* to Vic and then promptly disappeared as if it had never existed. Vic checked the *Basilisk*'s systems. The message had disappeared from there as well. Vic turned to look at Scab in his chair.

'What was that?' he demanded. At first Vic didn't think Scab was going to say anything. He was lying perfectly still, a long head of ash on the cigarette held in his fingers. Finally Scab turned to look at him. The ash didn't fall.

'If I tell you, do you promise not to go on at length?' The vibrations of his voice sent the ash tumbling to the floor, which quickly absorbed the waste.

'It's the *St Brendan's Fire*, isn't it?' Vic asked, referring to the Church frigate that had tried to accost them as they were leaving Arclight. Vic crossed all four of his arms. Scab just sighed. 'Did they say what they want?'

'They want us to stop searching for a way to break their bridge monopoly.'

'Which I'm comfortable with.'

'See, I just didn't want to have the same conversation again.'

'Well, I'll just do as I'm told then.' Despite the angry clattering of his mandibles, Vic was sure he nailed the intonation of human sarcasm.

'Good,' Scab said. Vic was a little annoyed that Scab appeared to have missed it.

Scab put a hat and sunglasses on. In the centre of the lounge a holographic picture of an augmented, heavyset feline male appeared. Vic looked over the feline. He wore utilitarian clothes that looked heavy enough to have significant built-in armour and an energy dissipation weave. The weapons he wore on display were similarly functional – no show, just utility.

'That Jide?' Vic asked, and then increased the magnification of the image, paying attention to the striping on the feline's fur. 'I didn't realise he was a Rakshasa.'

Scab nodded. The Rakshasa were an aristocratic warrior elite found on some of the more hidebound feline planets. As individual combatants they were very dangerous because of their warrior philosophy. As soldiers they were difficult to lead.

More detailed holographic images were appearing in the air. Rotating images showed. A human half-and-half whose slender androgynous beauty even Vic was able to admire. S/he was their kick-murder specialist, their silent killer.

Two humans, over-muscled man-plusses. They were either genuine twins, genetically altered to become twins or just cut to look the same. Obvious conflict-resolution world veterans, both of them sported significant levels of hard-tech augment. The twins were all scar tissue, metal and hardened composite. *Either one of them could give me a run for my money if they know what they are doing,* Vic thought.

The fifth and final member of the team was also significantly hard-tech augmented, though with some interesting soft-tech enhancements as well. The lizard was obviously a berserker. Their close-in specialist. Once berserk, he would be little more than an unpredictable scaled weapon.

'Seeder's sake, that's a heavy crew,' Vic said, wishing he could whistle through his mandibles. The 'sect 'faced to local comms and found that Jide's crew weren't much below Vic and Scab in the bounty-killer ratings. They specialised in taking down heavy high-profile targets. 'Wonder who they're here for?' But Vic already had a sinking feeling. Scab turned to look at his partner. Scab's milky eyes were hidden behind the lenses of his sunglasses. Vic looked at the holography and then back at Scab. He thought he detected the ghost of a smile on the human's face. 'They could actually do it!'

'Then I'll be dead and you'll be free,' Scab said and turned back to stare at the transparent ceiling. All around was the light and metal of busy high orbit. With a thought Scab rolled the *Basilisk* until their subjective up was looking down at the cloudy planet.

Vic didn't need to download any information on Pythia; everyone knew the story. It hadn't been called Pythia originally. It had been one of the first planets to be colonised by lost humanity. Overcrowded, its environment and resources were exhausted after centuries of habitation. Unrestricted nanite use led to overwhelming nano-pollution which first became a health risk and then a global pandemic. The solution was more nanites, a tailored viral nano-swarm designed to eat all the others and then destroy itself. However, the design team of the consumption swarm had been infiltrated by a nanite rights terrorist organisation. Instead of consuming the planet-wide nano-epidemic, it became its operating system and united it as one god-like swarm. The first thing the Pythia virus did was become a wind that blew across the planet, eating layer after layer of the planet's inhabitants' flesh. Flaying them down to picked-clean polished bone and then eating the bone as well. Pythia simultaneously became the planet's only sentient inhabitant and a civilisation in its own right made up of uncountable millions of tiny individuals.

This caused panic in the Consortium systems. Pythia had made it quickly into orbit, its unparalleled processing power allowing it to hack even the most secure military systems if they were 'faced. If they weren't 'faced then they could still be hacked, assuming a self-replicating mote of dust could get close enough to them.

The Consortium navy blockaded the bridge points. The navy sent entire battle groups after ships containing Pythia, and hired veritable fleets of bounty ships to do the same. Pythia was tracked down and destroyed, all except for the original planet. There was a battle between Pythian-held orbital weapon systems, the Consortium navy and at least one member of the Consortium Elite at the time. Pythia was eventually eradicated from orbit.

Nobody was quite sure what to do about the planet. Destroying it was a risky proposition because nobody could guarantee that wouldn't just spread the nanites across system space. Blockading was another possibility, but people would always try and find a way back for whatever crazy reason they thought they had. Tailored seek-and-destroy nano-swarm bombing was the only real option, but that had not worked well the first time.

Then Pythia surprised the Consortium by offering to negotiate. Pythia felt it was no different to the uplifted races. Its expansion was viral in nature, it needed to consume matter to procreate, and like all living things it wished to do so. Its attempt at expansion was just an attempt to secure such material.

Eventually a deal was brokered whereby Pythia was given free access to Known Space's comms networks. Its signal, in the form of intelligent search programs, was carried from beacon to beacon throughout Red Space. Pythia agreed not to attempt to control systems and allowed that to be written into sophisticated comms filters that any communication from the surface had to go through. All the search programs did was try to find every last bit of information. Ever. Then bring it back to Pythia. Pythia would then sift through the information, data mining on an enormous scale, piecing together tiny disparate bits of information to make astonishingly accurate predictions. It did this without ever violating secure systems, though some of the more sophisticated AI search routines were not beyond bribing people for information.

Meanwhile, Pythia ate. It ate every building and machine on the planet, everything made by uplifted hand. It made more and more of itself. Its processing power increased. Then it started eating the surface of the planet, stripping it away.

The information supplicants paid in matter. Either the debt relief they paid went into buying more matter or they just sacrificed the biggest item they could for what they wanted to know. Each sacrifice made Pythia more capable.

The clouds in Pythia's atmosphere were thick swarms of nanites. Breaching the atmosphere was a death sentence. The swarms would consume anything before it got close to what was left of the surface. There was some concern as to what would happen when the swarm consumed enough of the planet to destroy the magnetosphere.

Vic was looking subjectively up at the whorls of cloud in the atmosphere beneath him. Much of it looked violent. Ionisation made lightning play across the data storms that composed the think tanks for the more difficult questions that had been asked.

'Look,' Scab said, and part of the *Basilisk*'s transparent hull magnified. Vic watched as explosive bolts on orbital tethers released the carcass of a stripped parasite ship from a sacrificial orbital ship cradle. The massive ship with its insectile legs was designed to latch on to an asteroid and process the matter into carbon, which then filled the ship's inflatable cargo bladders.

Automated tug engines flared in the night, pushing the craft towards the planet at a perilously steep entry angle. Once manoeuvred into the correct trajectory, the engines separated and started their return to the orbital cradle. Scab slowed the *Basilisk* to watch the ponderous ballet of the parasite ship's last voyage. *Ever a keen witness of destruction*, Vic thought. As it hit the atmosphere the flare lit up one whole side of the planet's sky. *There's an element of show to this*, Vic decided. Looking around, he realised that some of the more luxurious habitats had gently tipped themselves, manoeuvring engines glowing as they did so, to allow better views for their wealthy patrons.

The ship died in fire, becoming a rain of flaming debris. The clouds swarmed across that debris, consuming it. From Vic's perspective the clouds seemed to be lit with their own internal fire across to the planetary horizon.

'That was our sacrifice,' Scab told him. Vic was no longer surprised by how ludicrous their sponsorship was.

'How long?' Vic asked.

To an extent, time was meaningless. Everyone had their own standards depending on their home planet, and most people tailored their physiology to the planet's day/night cycle, assuming it had one, regardless of their species' original home. In space, people either used Consortium or Monarchist standard time.

Consortium standard time was based on a twenty-six-hour standard cycle that was apparently human basic from before the Loss. Most felines felt it was unreasonable to be expected to stay awake for two thirds of such a long period of time.

Vic had felt the familiar sense of entrapment when he heard the solid metal-on-metal sound of the *Basilisk* being grabbed by the high-security habitat's docking arm. Then they had walked through anonymous corridors that could have belonged to any cleanish mid-range hotel anywhere in Known Space. His own room was small but blessedly designed for 'sects. More to the point, he could pretend he had privacy from Scab – who knew, maybe he actually did. Though that thought made him itch in the back of his skull.

They had been extensively checked for weapons. Most of their day-to-day stuff was fine. Illegal S-tech was completely out, so Scab left his energy javelin and the Scorpion on the ship. Both of them had had to divest themselves of some of their nastier virals and modify their nano-screens to be less abrasive. Their P-sats were fine, but they had to downgrade some of their systems a little. Scab had had to drain some of his more advanced liquid software out of his skull as well.

All this had been just over six standard cycles ago. The room that had initially been a welcome change from the *Basilisk* was now another small prison. Vic had exhausted most of the room's entertainment suite's options. After all, 'sect-on-human porn immersion was a niche market.

Vic was lying on the transforming piece of furniture that was the only place to sit, lie or sleep in the room, staring at the ceiling through his multi-faceted eyes. He had experienced reading a text file in a colonial immersion and had tracked down and tried reading one for entertainment. It had been exhausting. He couldn't get his head round having to create the images with his own mind. Now he was just wondering if it was possible to die from boredom and self-abuse.

It took a while for Vic to realise what the tapping sound was. He only realised that it meant that someone was hitting his door wanting to enter because he'd experienced this phenomenon in the same historical immersion that he'd seen the text file in.

Vic deleted the ability to read from his current neunonic applications and 'faced an order to the room for the door to open. Scab was standing there. Vic was relieved to see that he was fully clothed in brown suit and raincoat.

'I'm bored!' Vic shouted at him. Scab nodded and lit a cigarette.

'I can see that.'

'Have they finished cogitating?' the 'sect asked, trying out the taste of a new word. Scab almost raised an eyebrow but instead shook his head.

'Coming?' he asked.

The *Basilisk* was still docked back at the high-security habitat. Scab had reconfigured the smart-matter hull and hacked the ID code. It wouldn't be enough to hide from the Church as they could sense the bridge-drive signature, but it might help against some of the less-than-thorough bounty killers.

They had taken one of the shuttles to a more interesting entertainment-based habitat. Vic should have been a more than a little nervous about this, but boredom had turned his mental capacities into a kind of grey-coloured slush, and a week of immersion porn made him want to touch real human flesh.

They were in a multi-level mall. The smart matter was designed to look like dark-green, white-veined marble with arched iron bridges over a vast atrium and food court. Some of the food concessions even had automaton service rather than just assembler-dispensing nipples. One of them even had sentient staff, but Vic had decided that was a little sick and demeaning for the employees, particularly when they could have found employment in one of the real-flesh brothels.

The ceiling was transparent and the habitat was tipped to look down at the planet. Looking up made you feel like you were about to fall towards the cloudy nano-swarms.

Vic was looking up, using his antenna sensors to avoid colliding with other pedestrians. His P-sat bobbed along above him, augmenting the sensor data, not that this was required for anything other than simple obstacle navigation as most of the other patrons were giving the seven-foot, hard-tech-augmented 'sect a wide berth.

Vic felt Scab stop. His P-sat had transmitted the reason why before he lowered his head and saw for himself through his multifaceted eyes. It was inevitable, Vic decided. After all, their job was to track people. Obviously they were going to find them, even if it was by random chance. Vic decided that he was not what the humans called lucky.

Jide was standing in front of Scab. There was a flicker of something on the feline's game face. Later, Vic would run it through various analytical routines. He came to the conclusion that it was a moment of surprise. Then Jide read the situation.

The man-plus twins let go of each other's hands and continued walking around Jide towards Vic. The lizard and the human half-and-half held back. Seven P-sats rose towards the transparent ceiling. It was only because the reactions of everyone involved were so wired that these moments stretched out, Vic thought as he backed away from the muscle-bound twins.

Jide was close to Scab, so close it looked like they had been about to bump into each other. Vic couldn't understand why that would have happened. He also didn't understand why his own sensors and those of his P-sat hadn't picked up the other bounty killing team. Things weren't making sense.

The twins closed on him. He knew that bid and counter-bid with Pythian subcontractors would be going on. Jide would presumably be asking permission for violence and Scab counter-bidding to avoid it. Vic hoped. Vic's hand was close to the butts of his pistols but the twins were closing too fast. They wanted to mix it up with him. Vic knew that if he drew before they had permission, the habitat's security systems would vaporise him, at best.

Vic and Scab's P-sats were engaged in an electronic cold war with Jide's crew's P-sats. So far they were holding their own, as jamming signals confused sensors and countermeasures fought shutdown and control hacks.

Media P-sats came zipping across the mall towards them. A number dropped from the air as rival media providers engaged in their own electronics warfare for ratings.

The habitat's security systems granted carte blanche permission for violence. No restrictions within current capabilities.

Jide swung at Scab. Scab placed his hands on Jide's furry head and shoulders and jumped over the feline's muscular arm, landing just behind a surprised Jide, face to face with the lizard berserker. The berserker was swelling, internal carbon reservoirs rapidly being converted to muscle mass as natural and artificial rage and speed-enhancing chemicals flooded its body.

Scab fast-drew his tumbler pistol and shot all six rounds into Jide's back at point-blank range. Jide's armour and hardened flesh just about coped with the first four shots but the spinning rounds were designed to penetrate armour. The final two penetrated; secondary charges detonated inside Jide, sending the bullets spinning and fragmenting through the Rakshasa's body.

Scab rammed his synthetic diamond-tipped smart blade metalforma knife through hardened armoured flesh and soft-machine-augmented muscle into the back of Jide's neck, then sent the blade a neunonic command to widen and grow in the wound, the small carbon reservoir in the hilt providing the necessary matter. Scab forgot about Jide.

The twins charged. Vic's triple-barrelled shotgun pistol appeared in the hands of his lower limbs. 'Sect knees bent in the opposite direction to the rest of the uplifted races' knees. He bent his left leg, balancing on the right, bringing the foot up to the bottom of his abdomen. He let the twins close with him and then emptied all three barrels into the left twin's face at point-blank range. The explosive-cored flechette penetrators turned it into a red ruin. He staggered back.

Vic's left foot then shot out. Humans never expected kicks like this. The power-assisted prehensile claw that was his foot hit the right twin's knee and tore through it, leaving a mangled mess of metal, hardened plastic and carbon fibre. Right twin did not scream but his leg shot out from underneath him and he face-planted into the mock marble. Vic knew that all he had done was buy himself time.

The P-sat's cold war went hot. It turned into a strobing red shooting war as they zipped around the bridges, using them for cover while they continued screaming their electronic war across 'face connections.

Scab ducked under the blade of the berserker's smart sickle, stepping to the side and giving his opponent the slightest push in just the right place to keep him off balance.

The half-and-half was doing a backward one-handed cartwheel, the other hand throwing explosive burrowing knives. Keyed to Scab's EM signature, the knives' guidance systems would take them round the lizard berserker.

Above them, one of the twins' P-sat's energy dissipation grids was overwhelmed. It glowed red and then exploded.

Jide just stood still.

An electronic warfare burst from Scab's P-sat jammed the burrowing knives thrown by the half-and-half, and Scab ducked under them as the berserker turned back towards him.

Scab dropped the tumbler pistol and raised his right arm. Razor-sharp discs flew from the lizard-made disc projector strapped to his arm. Like the knives, the discs were keyed to their target's EM signature.

As the discs opened up the tumbling half-and-half's face and side, Scab drew his spit gun with his left hand, the gun's ergonomic grip moulding to the contours of his hand. He jammed it into the side of the berserker's head and with a thought started firing. The weapon's solid-state bullpup magazine was eaten up, disappearing into the weapon's barrel quickly, used up by the spit gun's ferocious rate of fire. The flechette penetrators buried themselves inside the berserker's skull, the envenomed needles fragmenting. The berserker howled and grabbed the back of his head. It would give Scab moments, but that was all.

Vic's lower right hand flicked the triple-barrelled shotgun open. His lower left hand snatched the lizard-made power disc from its clip in the small of his back and threw it in a wide arc, transmitting target data from both himself and his P-sat. His lower left hand then slid three rounds into the shotgun. As he did this, he leaned forward and used power-assisted metal to dig his two upper arms into right twin's flesh.

Right twin screamed as bladed fingers pushed through armour and into flesh. Vic straightened up and threw his opponent into the air. Then the bloodied hands on his upper limbs drew both his double-barrelled laser pistols. With rapid disciplined thoughts he neunonically transmitted orders to fire to the semi-automatic pistols. Right twin's energy dissipation grid lit up, turning him into a red neon silhouette flying through the air.

Vic's energy dissipation grid lit up as he started taking fire from one of the P-sats. Keeping one pistol on the twin, he moved the other to fire at the P-sat.

Despite his ruined face, left twin was trying to bring a short-barrelled disc gun to bear. Vic's lower right hand snapped the shotgun pistol closed. His abdomen rotated slightly for a better shot and he fired. The three rounds left the barrels of the shotgun pistol. The sabots fell away and the miniature ramjets on the micro-missiles ignited.

Left twin got off a wild shot from the disc gun. A few of the discs hit Vic's arm – he felt them beat armour and damage flesh and internal components. The force spun him round.

The micro-missiles from Vic's shotgun caught left twin in the chest. Their armour-piercing heads penetrated the man-plus's armour. The glow of their jet engines momentarily illuminated his chest cavity before exploding. It was little more than wet meat and muscle enhancement that fell to the cold hard marble.

Scab's metalforma blade had widened enough to sever the Rakshasa's neck and Jide's head fell off. Scab reached behind him and caught the falling metalforma blade as it was retracting back to its normal size. The feline's head bounced off the marble as the body toppled forward.

Scab backed away, trying to keep the wounded and angry berserker between him and the half-and-half. The berserker's smart sickles flew out at him, the black blades moving like liquid as they reached for his flesh to cut him open. The lizard's attacks were half overwhelming ferocity and half hard-wired randomised routines designed to make it difficult for opponents to predict them. The lizard was shredding Scab's coat; blood had been drawn and dripped, smoking, to the cold marble. Scab drove the metalforma blade up into one of the lizard's arms and then the other. Each time he neunonically instructed the blade to branch out to cause the maximum amount of damage, to render the limb useless. The berserker didn't feel it. The half-and-half continued trying to circle around behind Scab.

While fighting for his life, Scab reviewed the sensor data from his P-sat. Through the fog of electronic warfare and the red glow of a rapidly overheating energy dissipation grid, it provided him with the wider picture he needed.

There was an explosion in the laser red light show above them. Vic swore as his P-sat exploded. He was firing up into the air at two of the remaining P-sats. Both were returning fire, making the 'sect's energy dissipation grid glow bright red. Right twin was sitting up again, but Vic was pretty sure his power disc would take care of him. Then his disc changed direction.

Scab hacked the disc and gave it a new target. The flowing black blades of the berserker's smart sickles opened him up, biting deep. Pain was just another sensation, Scab thought, one that he would have liked to be able to embrace. Getting badly cut doing it, Scab stabbed the metalforma blades up through the berserker's reptilian maw, the blade branched out, growing inside the berserker's flesh, hooking into it. Then Scab yanked the blade out, tearing a hole in the flesh of its maw. The berserker didn't even feel it.

Scab screamed out as twin thermal oscillating blades cut through his armoured clothes, hardened skin and into real flesh and soft-machine augments. The half-and-half had got behind him. Scab's altered neuro-chemistry and internal narcotics deadened pain, leaving only the strange sensation of the knives moving through his flesh like it was water, and the smell of burning flesh.

Vic's power disc, which Scab had hacked, cut through both the berserker's legs. As the lizard tumbled to the floor, Scab jammed the metalforma blade into his neck and then spun, trying to elbow the half-and-half. S/he ducked the elbow, but at least the blades had come out of his flesh now. Scab's nanite and biotech medical applications tried to cope with the massive internal damage: biological systems shut down as redundant tech ones came online. Scab turned the elbow into a spin, bringing his leg up into a rear turning kick. The half-and-half flipped back out of the way.

Scab threw himself forward into a roll to get out of the way of the crippled berserker's floor-bound attacks. The berserker continued pulling himself after Scab even as the metalforma knife grew to shovel-head size in his neck.

Another P-sat exploded in the air above them. Scab turned into a strobing neon-red grid as the half-and-half fired burst after burst from a folding laser carbine. Scab rapidly reloaded the spit gun and covered his face with his arm to protect it.

Vic sprinted towards right twin, firing one laser pistol at the man-plus, the other at one of the remaining P-sats. Right twin sat up glowing red as he fired the cut-down disc gun. Discs impacted Vic's hard-tech armour, some making their way through. The 'sect felt no pain. He was too much machine. He just had the odd sensation of things moving inside him. Each shot sent him staggering, but he continued running forward, firing. The P-sat Vic was firing at exploded. Vic brought both pistols to bear on right twin. At the same time he finished reloading the shotgun pistol with his lower limbs and aimed the triple-barrelled weapon to the left under his outstretched upper arms and fired all three barrels. The sabots fell away as their mini-missile payloads locked on to one of the P-sats. The P-sat tried to flee, using the bridges and stanchions as cover. The micro-missiles' miniature ram jets ignited. The electronic warfare transmissions from Scab's P-sat prevented the targeted and locked P-sat from jamming the incoming micro-missile's guidance systems.

Scab stalked towards the half-and-half, emptying the clip from the spit gun into him/her. The berserker crawled rapidly after him. Penetrator flechettes from the spit gun pierced the half-and-half's armour and exploded. Those that hit flesh fragmented in the wound. Each fragment was coated in neurotoxin. Not enough to overwhelm the hermaphrodite's internal systems but enough to keep them busy and slow him/her down.

The battery on the half-and-half's folding laser carbine ran down as Scab tossed the empty spit gun away with a flourish. The hermaphrodite staggered as s/he tried to cope with the toxins. Scab, still glowing and smoking from the laser fire, leaped high into the air. He hit him/her in the chest with both knees, riding him/her to the ground as he repeatedly struck him/her in the face with sharpened envenomed fingernails. Fingers pierced armour and a combination of trauma and venom killed the half-and-half before s/he hit the ground. The berserker was still crawling towards Scab, reaching for him as the metalforma blade finished growing in the lizard's neck and its head fell off. The headless corpse slumped to the cold marble.

With bloody fingers, Scab reached into his suit jacket and took out his cigarette case. He removed a cigarette and lit it.

Vic reached right twin and kicked him hard. His power-assisted leg shattered the disc gun, and his clawed foot tore off half of right twin's face.

The micro-missiles caught the P-sat just below the transparent ceiling. The P-sat exploded.

Mandibles wide open and making a hissing clicking noise, Vic fired both pistols point-blank. Right twin's face became red steam.

Vic looked around. He was sure there were more P-sats, but he guessed they were following dead-owner protocols. The collateral damage wasn't too bad. Some stray beams, flechettes and discs had caught passers-by, but anyone who was dead probably had clone insurance.

Scab stood up. His coat had stopped glowing but was still smoking. He kicked the lizard berserker's corpse. The headless body had still been trying to crawl. He found the metalforma knife and picked it up. He jammed the blade into the half-and-half's neck, neunonically 'facing instructions to sever the hermaphrodite's head.

'Take their heads,' Scab said. Vic ignored him. He was running cooling cycles on his pistols, recharging them from his internal energy supplies through the matrices in his palms. He reloaded the shotgun, though he'd used the last of his saboted micro-missile loads. At the same time he was using his neunonics to buy, and have upgraded to his spec, a new P-sat.

Scab retrieved his spit gun and the tumbler pistol. Then once the metalforma knife had finished doing its job, he picked that up and collected the three severed heads, holding them by hair, fur and crest in one hand while he licked the blood off the fingers of the other.

Some bounty killers, particularly high-profile ones, made immersions of their jobs to augment their income. Vic wondered if Jide and his crew's experience of being killed at their hands was currently being auctioned to help cover their resurrection expenses. Neither Scab nor Vic, however, sold their experiences as immersions. The only recordings of them were audiovisual or other people's, normally fatal, immersion experiences of them.

Scab used the metalforma knife on both the twins, decapitating them. He held all five severed heads up to show the remote cameras. The message to other bounty crews was clear. Come looking for them, you'll end up having to get cloned.

*

Vic stared at Scab. Something wasn't sitting right with him. Scab was ignoring him.

'They'll come after us properly prepared,' Vic finally said, making his tone neutral, but he couldn't shake the feeling that his suspicions were written all over his insectile face and in his pheromone secretions.

Scab shook his head.

'Why not? The bounty from the cartel's got to be pretty big.'

They were in the private medical facility on their own habitat. The habitat had stepped up their security in light of what had happened. Scab had done his own medical work and was in the process of purging the local systems of all medical information on himself. Vic was lying on one of the couches as his damaged internal organs and components were speedily being regrown, and his armour and hardened skin were knitted back together. The featureless white room that was the medical facility transmitted progress straight to his neuronics.

'They won't be cloned,' Scab said. He made it sound like an afterthought.

'You transmitted a scramble code for the personality and memory uplink?' Vic asked, trying to keep his voice even. Scab just nodded. It was an expensive viral program. The uplinks were very heavily protected and had multiple redundant systems to prevent this sort of thing. 'That's pretty illegal stuff for Pythia.' Personality/memory-uplink scrambling software had been on the list of proscribed ware.

'Nothing's illegal with enough debt relief,' Scab said, still distracted. Then he turned to look directly at Vic with his dead eyes. 'They had to know.' Vic tried to meet the look but turned away. 'It's time for an answer.'

Scab headed towards one of the white walls. The smears of blood they had left when they first entered had long ago been eaten by nano-cleaners. Part of the wall opened for them.

The transparent piece of hull was shaped like an eye and lined with actual wood panelling. In front of it was a circular sofa upholstered in something that had once been alive and it was in no way smart. Vic was struggling to find a comfortable way to sit on it. Scab was slumped in it, smoking a cigarette, dried blood all the way up the arm of his suit jacket and raincoat.

The eye looked down on the planet. The view was either just wide enough, or had been compressed, to show the curvature of the planet against the golden light of the orange giant refracting on the particulate clouds. As Vic and Scab sat there waiting for the business acolyte to be possessed, they watched asteroids being dropped into the atmosphere. The fire of their atmospheric entry lit up part of their view.

The business acolyte was standing in the centre of the circle made by the leather sofa. He wore a collarless suit that buttoned up to the neck. His physiology suggested human, and the little skin that they could see looked human, or perhaps an oddly fashion-augmented feline. It was difficult to be sure because of the hood on the suit jacket and the featureless convex-mirrored, full-face mask.

Holography of the nano-swarm clouds in Pythia's atmosphere appeared in the centre of the room. The acolyte was stood in the apparent storm front as lightning played across it. It was difficult to gauge the scale of it, but Vic had the feeling that the storm front was anything up to hundreds of miles across. He pursed his mandibles, not sure what he was watching.

'I think that's the think tank they've had working on our problem,' Scab said.

The business acolyte collapsed onto all fours, shaking and gyrating in front of them. Vic couldn't shake the feeling that he was about to experience Known Space's oddest lap dance.

'That is correct.' The voice sounded like it was being agonisingly pulled from the acolyte's larynx. Pythia had overrun the willing aco-lyte's neunonic systems and was in control. 'Trillions of tiny bits of information, the fall of entire markets to the movement of a single molecule, the—'

'I don't care,' Scab said. 'Where is it?'

The acolyte moved his head, apparently to stare at Scab. Scab's reflection on the convex mask somehow didn't seem all that distorted to Vic.

'The end of the Art Wars left the Absolute in control of the Monarchist Elite,' came the strained reply.

'Weird fucking war,' Scab said, frowning. Vic looked up at him sharply. He was surprised that Scab had offered an opinion, let alone seemed to have mild emotion connected to the conflict. 'But we know this.'

'The safest place to hold the cocoon would be at the Citadel. If Fallen Angel told you the truth, then the cocoon is on Game, prob-ably deep below the Black Leaves as the Absolute's sanctum is the second most secure place in the Monarchist sector. Also, according to our psych evaluation of the Absolute, he will wish to keep the cocoon close enough to play with.'

'So it can't be done. Only pieces are allowed on Game, and they have to have experiential augments. They'd know who and what we are the moment we left orbit,' Vic said. 'Can we leave it now?' Scab just looked thoughtful. Vic shook his head. He could see what was coming.

There was a kind of quiet screeching from the acolyte. Vic stared at him. Blood ran out from under the mask. The acolyte's body twisted and contorted further. Vic gave Scab a questioning look.

'There is no love lost between the Absolute and the masters of the Living Cities on Pangea. They were the biggest losers of the Art Wars. They wanted to see their model of society permeate the entire Monarchist sector. If the Elder will consent to speak to you, they may aid you.'

Scab nodded. 'How long?'

'If you exhaust the slush fund you have access to, then that will buy you a one-week info lock. After that the information will be available at an exorbitant price to everyone.'

Scab nodded. Vic assumed he was spending the rest of whatever slush fund he had access to.

The acolyte collapsed to the floor. There was bloody froth bubbling out from under the mask.

'Is that it?' Vic asked.

The smart-matter floor engulfed the acolyte, presumably taking him to somewhere nearby for medical attention. Scab got up and left. Vic watched him go, irritation and a feeling of helplessness combining into impotent anger. He realised it was completely psychosomatic, but he struggled to control his breathing for a moment until his augmented systems took over and administered a mild sedative. He stood up and followed Scab. There was nothing else he could really do except 'face his own bid to Pythia for information. It wiped out three quarters of his debt relief in an instant.

Vic was immersed. He had no control so he decided to lose himself in narcotic-enhanced fantasy. His only-'sect-at-a-human-orgy fantasy dissolved around him as the *Basilisk* managed to send him a warning signal before powering down.

Vic sat up on his unmoving bed. The door to his room was open but the ship was dark. The walls were solid. There were no areas of transparency.

He stood up and walked out into the lounge. His optical enhancements ignored the darkness. Scab was standing in the centre of the lounge, still. Vic could feel the anger. It seemed to be coming off Scab in waves. He actually took a step back. Blood dripped from Scab's clenched fists. He had pierced the hardened skin of his palms with his fingernails.

Vic checked back over the last information from the *Basilisk*. They had been approaching the Pythia bridge point. It looked like someone had hacked the ship. Shut it down completely. Vic knew that wasn't supposed to be easy. The *Basilisk* had the best system security they could afford and it had been extensively and often illegally augmented by the privacy-obsessed control freak that was Scab.

'Elite ...?' Vic ventured.

The transmission had to be pretty powerful to reach their internal comms through the thick skin of the dead *Basilisk*. Vic actually screamed, then staggered, holding his head. Scab didn't move, but a drop of blood leaked from his nostril and made a smoking trail through his white make-up.

'To Woodbine Scab and Vic Matto, this is the *St Brendan's Fire*. We only wish to talk. Prepare for boarding.' The woman whose flickering image appeared in their minds was the same shaven-headed and tattooed Church monk they had seen on Arclight.

Vic felt the fear building. Scab couldn't allow this to happen. It wasn't in his nature. He would do something suicidal and make sure that he took Vic with him. He couldn't abrogate control of the situation like that.

'Scab ...' Vic started, searching for a way to talk his partner into being reasonable, but he knew that there was nothing he could say that would help.

'*Basilisk* to *St Brendan's Fire*.' Scab sounded calm. He was talking out loud; only someone who knew him as well as Vic could hear the barely controlled rage in his voice. 'Immediately return control of the *Basilisk* to us. If you do not, then you will find that information on the whereabouts of the bridge technology you are trying to suppress will be transmitted throughout Known Space.'

There was silence. Was it a bluff? Vic had no idea. Scab did bluff, but he also made sure that he did enough extreme shit that all his bluffs were believable.

'*St Brendan's Fire* to *Basilisk*. You're bluffing. That would screw up your own agenda,' the Monk said.

No, Vic silently screamed at her. *Look at your psych profile! He will destroy it for you even it means he fails.*

'Besides,' the Monk continued, 'how would you transmit the information? You're dead in the water.'

'We made a contingency arrangement with Pythia,' Scab transmitted.

It was the sort of thing that Scab would do, Vic decided. He planned ahead in that way.

'We just want to talk,' the Monk said after what seemed like a very long time. She had either bought the story or she just wasn't prepared to risk even the slightest chance of proliferation. Scab ignored her.

At any moment Vic expected to hear the metallic *clang* of a docking arm reverberate through the *Basilisk*, but instead the systems came back up.

Scab kept the hull dark but brought up scans of the *St Brendan's Fire*. The *Basilisk*'s weapon systems provided targeting solutions as Scab turned the ship back towards the bridge point. The *Basilisk*'s engines glowed as the bridge drive made a red tear in space.

17

Northern Britain, a Long Time Ago

They came out of the plains in the west, warriors who slept in mounds next to the rotting bones of their ancestors. The peoples from the lands surrounding theirs sacrificed food to them so they wouldn't be dragged down to Annwn, the land of the dead. Riding or running tirelessly, they headed north-east and then turned south.

Their keening drove the animals before them. Prey fell quickly, slaughtered and partially consumed, their blood splattering limed faces. The lucky people in their path made it to the hill forts. Those less lucky died quickly; the Corpse People didn't have time for anything else. All those in the hill forts could do was watch from the palisades as the Corpse People left a landscape spotted with carcasses behind them.

On the isles of madness, the wretched and the broken-minded ignored the exhortations of their priests and made their way to the water's edge. They could hear her sleeping song. The Corpse People stopped at the top of the hill overlooking the isles. Still, silent, they truly thought themselves dead. Animals were caught in the spell of the Mother's song. They ran towards her, into the marsh, into the water, into her slithering, somnambulant grasp.

There had been a battle here. The fort was on a high promontory that overlooked the entrance to the harbour. The fort showed signs of extensive damage. Britha reckoned it had been the giants who had done most of the damage by pulling down the timber-latticed, dry-stone walls. Parts of the rock beneath the fort's walls were blackened and scorched – by burning oil, the *ban draoi* reckoned.

It looked like the Goddodin had made their stand there. Judging by the dead being fed on by crab and seagull in the harbour, they had fought hard. The fact that tattooed, moustached, shaven-headed warriors still prowled the fort's palisade walls suggested they had succeeded in fighting Bress's forces off.

'It's not that they couldn't do it,' Fachtna said. 'I reckon they just didn't think taking the fort was worth the time.'

Britha turned to look at the warrior. The sight of the wry smile on his face further angered her. She was still less than happy after his so-called boat skills and instinctive understanding of the Black River had all but got them swept out to sea. The three of them had had to paddle so hard that Britha had felt her arms were close to coming off. She wasn't sure where she had found the reserves to carry on, but by the time they made it to shore, too tired to beat Fachtna with the butt of her spear, she was sure that she had significantly lost weight and she had been ravenously hungry again.

At the back of her mind Britha wondered if it hadn't been Fachtna's doing; perhaps the sea god of the Goddodin had carried them out to sea. She preferred to blame Fachtna, however. Being swept out into the fog-shrouded choppy sea had scared her. There was nothing you could do against the sea.

They had walked down the coast looking for horses to steal but had found only devastated or abandoned fishing villages. Even without horses, Teardrop and Fachtna had set an exhausting pace.

It was the kneelers that were making her angry, many of them naked, some of them with the blue-scaled tattoos of Goddodin warriors. Those that were clothed wore white. They lined the shore of the small bay on all fours, swaying from side to side, singing in some non-language that she didn't understand but found deeply unnerving.

'Look at their throats,' Teardrop said. They were standing among them. So far they had been ignored. The kneelers all looked deformed in the same way, as if their mouths and throats had had to change to make the words of the strange keening chant. Britha wasn't sure why and hated the thought, but somehow they reminded her of Cliodna.

'Is this Bress's doing?' Fachtna asked. 'Do they worship a new god?'

'This looks more like a sickness,' Teardrop said, distaste and more than a little worry evident in his voice. 'If Bress is the cause, I don't think he knew or meant to do this. People are frightened when they witness such power, and there is little they can do about it.'

'Aye, people follow power,' Fachtna said, nodding in agreement.

Britha spat and kicked one of them over. The thin elderly man looked up at her, his eyes managing to look both dead and ecstatic.

'How can people live so weak?' she demanded to no one in particular except perhaps the spirits of the air.

'They won't. Look,' Fachtna said, pointing to the promontory cliffs. Some of the kneelers were clambering up to the scorched rocks where the palisade had been destroyed. Britha shaded her eyes from the bright sun and watched.

'I knew fire would have worked,' she said to herself as she looked at the scorched rocks.

The climbers pulled themselves over the rock.

'All fire does is set them to burning. They wouldn't have felt it. When they noticed, they would have just dropped back into the water,' Fachtna told her to her further irritation.

'If they used the fire oil from the southern traders across the sea, then they would have seen the creature burning under the water. What must they have thought?' Teardrop said mostly to himself.

By now there were worried-looking spearmen standing in the breach in the palisade wall as the climbers approached.

The keening stopped. The swaying stopped. All eyes were on the climbers now, though all the kneelers remained on all fours.

'Why won't you stand up?' Britha demanded of them. 'You're not animals!' Teardrop laid an arm on her shoulder, shaking his head.

'They can't hear you,' he said.

Britha actually let out a cry of shock despite herself when the first one jumped. Her vision was now so keen that she saw the red splash he made on the sharp rocks just above the waterline.

Teardrop's face was etched with sadness as he looked down, shaking his head.

Fachtna stared at them, unable to understand what was happening. 'But he chose to—'

The next climber jumped. Britha turned towards the shoreline, though she had no idea what she was going to do.

'Stop them!' she shouted in a language she was pretty sure was theirs. Her voice carried across the harbour but the warriors in the fort gave no indication that they had even heard her. Her hand went to her mouth as the third one hit the rocks, the waves now moving the broken bodies of his two friends.

'Why—'

'There is only death or the sickness of the moon,' a voice said. It sounded strange – somehow gravelly and wet at the same time. She turned to see the emaciated man she had kicked over staring at her. 'The sickness of the moon is better. It is a blessing from the Dark Man, but some cannot wait. Some want the gifts he offers in our dreams too soon.'

Britha stared at him, trying to marshal her thoughts, thinking about the visions that the demon-tainted flesh she had eaten had given her. She thought of the dark man, the figure of nothing and the feeling that there was something terrible beyond him. She started to feel cold. The emaciated man narrowed his eyes, studying her.

'You know,' he said. 'You've felt his touch.'

'How could you give in like this?' Britha demanded. She had not liked his words. 'You have slain yourself, what you are, for dreams. Who willingly allows themself to be conquered?'

The old man shook his head sadly. 'You can no more fight the moon sickness or death than you can the sea. We followed false gods. Now all of Ynys Prydein belongs to death and madness. Can you not feel it?' It was the first time she had ever heard of Ynys Prydein. She could not, however, deny that something inside her but not of her was pulling her to the south. The man was smiling at her knowingly. She turned from him and started towards the fort.

Fachtna and Teardrop had built a fire. They were on the shores of the bay trying to keep as far from the kneelers as they could. Fachtna was cooking the last of the salted deer meat, with some wild vegetables that Teardrop had found. They would have to forage and hunt again soon, particularly if they kept eating as much as they had been. That would slow them down more. The black ships and Britha's people would slip further from them.

Britha was sitting away from them, hugging her knees, not really feeling the cold from the fresh clear windy night. Her spear was next to her on the ground. She was looking up at the hill fort. She could see the flickering glow of fires. There were roundhouses behind the palisade walls. Some of them had been damaged, but the intact ones looked very welcoming to her at the moment.

They had gone up to the hill fort but the Goddodin would not let them in. There had been a shouted conversation through the gate while slingers and warriors with casting spears covered them. Fachtna had not helped by cursing them for cowards who were too afraid to offer hospitality. Teardrop had sent the warrior away.

They'd had the bare bones of it. The black curraghs had come and with them giant demons from the sea. They had landed warriors further up the beach. The giants had climbed the cliffs while the warriors had attacked in a disciplined formation the likes of which the frightened warriors in the hill fort had never seen before. To hear them tell it, they had bravely fought off the Lochlannach, but Britha agreed with Fachtna: had Bress wanted the fort he could have taken it. Still, she had to admit these god-slaves had done better than her and her people, though she saw no Lochlannach bodies.

Without hospitality they had the choice of moving on, though it was growing late, or risking a camp close to the kneelers. Their keening and chanting were an annoyance, and their continued murder of themselves was shocking. A few had tried to speak to them. Britha had become so angry that she had set about them with the haft of her spear until she realised that they would have welcomed death at her hands. When Teardrop had threatened to curse them with everlasting life, they had fled.

'You wish you were up there, warm?' Fachtna asked. Britha had only just heard the warrior's approach. She sighed to herself – she could guess what was coming.

'I don't relish the company of cowards and fools who cannot tell friend from foe and break that which should never be broken,' she said, referring to the law of hospitality, without which there could be no trade, no diplomacy and peace could not be brokered after war. 'But I would welcome a roof above me and a fire near,' she conceded. 'Of course it doesn't help that your friend looks so strange. Where is he from?' she asked, not caring but trying to forestall the inevitable.

'From very far away, like me.'

'You are from very different people,' Britha said for want of anything else.

Fachtna nodded but Britha wasn't looking. 'I could keep you warm and tell you tales of the Otherworld,' he said. Neither of them noticed Teardrop over by the fire turn to look at them.

'No,' Britha said.

'You will not lie with me for knowledge?' Fachtna asked. She could hear the smile in his voice. 'Then it will just have to be for the pleasure of it.'

'If I was going to lie with someone for power and knowledge, it would be with your friend,' Britha said, still not looking at Fachtna because she was pretty sure that she would have to hit him if she did. She did not see Teardrop smiling as he turned away from them to look back into the flames. 'As for pleasure, you already bore me. That is not a good start.'

'I like a woman with spirit,' Fachtna said.

And I'd like a man who could sing a different song, Britha thought. She tried not to think about Bress. She was not blind to his evil but there was something there, a sadness that had somehow touched her. And he was beautiful.

Fachtna broke her from her reverie by grabbing her arm and pulling her to her feet. 'Let's find pleasure together!'

'Look, I'm sure this works with young landswomen—'

Fachtna covered her mouth with his. Britha was momentarily

surprised. Then she felt his tongue against her lips. She opened her mouth.

Fachtna cried out and staggered away from Britha, his mouth bloody. He looked up at her, anger in his eyes. Britha spat his blood into those eyes. Momentarily blinded, Fachtna did not see the punch coming.

His nose felt much harder than she was expecting, but he was from the Otherworld, she reminded herself. She was, however, both surprised and satisfied by the strength of her punch. She heard the *crack* of the nose giving under her knuckles. The force of the blow picked Fachtna off his feet and he hit the ground by the shoreline hard.

Britha jumped on him. Landing sideways, she jammed a knee into his throat and tore her sickle out of her rope belt. Fachtna was starting to move, to counter, when he felt the blade of the sickle against his nether regions.

'You are no warrior!' Britha spat through bloody lips. 'You are a childling grown large and I have gelded men for less! I lay this geas on you: if you ever touch a woman again without her words of permission, what little manhood you have will shrivel up and roll down the legs of your trews to be eaten by worms from the earth! Do you understand me, boy?!'

Fachtna opened his mouth.

'That's enough,' Teardrop said quietly. Britha turned to look at the swollen-headed man, his skin reminding her of smooth varnished wood. 'Britha, please.' Something in his tone made her anger subside. She got to her feet and grabbed her spear, stalking past Teardrop. 'He would not have—' Teardrop started.

'He touches me again, and I'll cut the fingers off that did it and then the cock that made him want to.'

Fachtna watched her go. Teardrop moved to his prone friend and stood over him, leaning on his staff.

'She is quite a woman,' Fachtna said through a mouthful of blood, seemingly ignoring the pain. Teardrop just nodded. 'I think I'm in love.'

'You're not in love. You can't have her, and that makes you moonstruck.'

'No, it's love,' Fachtna said, relishing the thought of the pursuit.

'We've been friends for a long time now,' Teardrop said. Fachtna nodded. Teardrop rammed the butt of his staff into Fachtna's groin.

Fachtna howled in agony.

'Don't touch her again,' Teardrop said, leaning down towards Fachtna as he rolled from side to side clutching his groin.

Britha heard the cry of pain, she suspected everyone in the harbour had. She did not look back but she did smile.

Teardrop stared over at the fort on the promontory. Beyond the gap in the rocks all he could see was darkness, a black sea and a black night. This country had beauty, there was no denying it, but he missed his home. He missed the wide-open plains, the thick woods teaming with game, but after his wife and his four children it was the sun that he missed the most.

He touched his head. He could feel its weight pressing down. He tried to block out what the crystal wanted to show him. It felt like there were thousands of screaming spirits somehow just out of sight, hiding. Those that didn't scream whispered obscene things to him in impossible tongues. He squeezed his eyes shut and tried to remember the words of the chant. He let it run through his head over and over again. A string of simple syllables but with power, sometimes the words were enough for peace.

'Are you here because you want to be? Or to anger Fachtna?' Teardrop asked with his eyes closed.

'Do you think I care about Fachtna?'

Teardrop thought on the question. 'No. No, I don't,' he conceded. 'But I think you want something.'

'I do,' Britha replied.

Teardrop opened his eyes and turned to look at her. Since he had tasted of her blood and she of the crystal, he could see the demon blood burning inside her, and if he concentrated enough he could make out the thin strand of the Muileartach's gift as well.

'I want your power.'

'Do you not have enough power?'

'It's not for me; it's for my tribe. I will trade for it.'

'What would you trade?' Teardrop asked wearily.

'What do you want?'

'The secrets of the *dryw*?' he asked, going through the motions.

Britha gave this some thought. The knowledge and the magics that had been passed down to her in the groves were secret. There was a powerful prohibition against telling them to outsiders. On the other hand, this man undoubtedly had power. Britha reasoned that she would be able to add what she learned from Teardrop to the power and knowledge of the groves. She was also prepared to face whatever punishment she would incur for betraying them. After all, she had failed her people; she had to do whatever it took to bring them back.

Besides, when she had obtained what she wanted of Teardrop, he could always be dealt with.

'Perhaps,' she answered. Teardrop turned to look at her. She wasn't sure what she saw in his face, his strange features were so difficult to read. Sadness, perhaps, disappointment.

'The secret of woman's magics?' he asked, trying to keep his voice neutral.

Britha went cold. That was another matter altogether. Betraying the magic of women to a man was everything the other *ban draoi* had taught her to guard against. Men were simpler creatures than women and there were just some things they could not and should not know, and if Britha angered the other *ban draoi*, nobody could wreak vengeance on someone like a woman could. Their magic was darkness, life and blood. They were connected to the moon and the land itself in the same way that men were connected to the sky. The consequences of betraying the *dryw* would be dire but she feared the *ban draoi* more.

She moved closer to him, took his free hand and placed it against her groin, and looked him straight in the eyes.

'That would depend on which secrets you meant.'

Teardrop could feel the heat of her, ever through her robe. Her smell filled his nostrils. He wasn't blind to her. He felt the stirrings of lust, but that just made him feel further from home. He wondered how much younger than him she was as he wrenched his hand free.

'A seduction? You would pay for mere power with your body?'

'It's my body. I use it how it pleases me. There's little payment involved it if pleases both of us,' Britha said fiercely. Sex was an intrinsic part of her rites as well as a pleasure. There were many different reasons for having sex.

Teardrop turned away from her and looked out past the rocks at the darkness. The squirming in his head made the darkness come alive for him. This place was so strange and distant.

'I have a family, and a wife I miss so much,' he said.

Britha nodded. She could hear the sadness behind his words. She could also hear the honesty, and it sounded raw to her.

He turned to look at her. 'And I think your heart – no, not your heart, maybe somewhere lower – wants another.'

Britha blinked at him. She was trying to think what she had said or done to give herself away. Was she under the control of magic? Had Bress done something to her and Teardrop could sense it?

'We weren't talking of hearts ...' she started.

'We were talking of desire. Love Bress or help your people. Trying to do both is folly.'

'I don't lo— I have to have that power.'

Teardrop rubbed his eyes. He could feel it moving in his head. At times the pain was close to unbearable. Just after he had joined with it he had screamed and screamed, trying to claw it out with his fingernails. Now he just felt so tired.

'You don't know what you're talking about. The price is too much. It would consume you. What you think of as you would cease to be.'

'So who did you use to be?' she asked.

Teardrop looked back at her, anger in his expression. *You told her too much, old man*, he thought. *You gave her enough to hurt you*. There was no triumph in her eyes.

The figure exploded out of the water, crossing the narrow strip of shore on all fours to where they stood. Pale skin in the moonlight as the figure leaped at Britha. Caught completely by surprise, she was carried to the ground, the figure on top of her. Britha was appalled to feel fingers under her robe, on her sex. A mouth on hers, a kiss that tasted of the sea, familiar except for needle-like teeth and the taste of blood and meat.

Teardrop was moving towards them, staff in his hand.

Britha fumbled for the iron-bladed knife in her rope belt. She grabbed her attacker by its long dark hair, yanked it back, and brought her head up and its head down at the same time. Britha's attacker's nose crashed into her forehead. There was a satisfying *crunch* and Britha felt something warm on her head. She stabbed at the figure with the blade but it had rolled away.

Teardrop reached them and raised his staff. Britha was also aware of the sound of someone sprinting towards them along the shore. The attacker leaped high into the air, legs curled tight under its body. Long, thin but powerful pale fingers ending in black claws grabbed the staff in mid-air. Both legs straightened into a double kick that caught Teardrop in the face and chest. He went flying, hitting the ground hard enough to wind him.

The figure landed on the ground just as Fachtna charged, his gently singing silver-bladed sword held high. The figure rolled towards Fachtna with incredible speed, closing the gap, grabbing the surprised warrior and then rolling back, using his momentum to throw him. Fachtna hit the ground face first.

Britha was on her feet, slashing with the knife at her attacker. The figure was bent low, hair covering its face, naked, obviously female. She hissed, backing away from the iron blade. Blood pouring from his face, Fachtna was back on his feet, angry, sword in hand and looking to hurt someone.

Teardrop, more cautiously, was trying to flank their attacker. His jaw hadn't just been broken, it had been powdered and was hanging loose from his face. He'd heard and felt ribs crack and found himself short of breath. He felt bones grinding together in his chest as they healed rapidly. It hurt. A lot.

The attacker flicked her hair back and Britha saw Cliodna, almost. Britha stepped back, shocked by the changes wrought in her lover's flesh. Her features were drawn back, angular, predatory. Lips opened to reveal rows of needle-like teeth. The gills on her neck sucked down air. Her body was leaner, there was something about it that made Britha think of a sword or a spear, with spikes of bone sticking out of newly formed fins on her forearms and lower legs, a spur of bone sticking out of each heel. She looked like a weapon now.

Teardrop also took a step back. In a language she was sure she shouldn't understand, Britha heard him beg a many-faced god for protection. Even Fachtna, as his damaged features rearranged themselves back to their original positions, looked unsure.

'Teeth and claws, and you won't look so pretty, sword-slave,' Cliodna spat at Fachtna. The warrior was ready to attack but his normal arrogance was absent.

'Is this a festival of rapine?' Britha demanded, furious at the attempted violation and appalled at what had become of her lover.

'I wasn't trying to—' Fachtna started.

'Quiet,' Teardrop told him.

'You spread your legs for him.' Cliodna jerked her head at Fachtna. 'And him!' She jerked her head at Teardrop.

'I didn't!' Britha protested.

'Not for want of trying!'

Fachtna spared a moment to glance at Teardrop. Teardrop was aware of it, rather than saw it. That was a future conversation he wasn't looking forward to.

'You left me!' Britha practically screamed, furious at herself for the tears that came unwanted to her eyes. Fachtna, while readying himself to attack Cliodna, was also listening hard to what was being said.

Realisation spread across his face like a sunrise. 'Oh really?' he said.

'Be quiet, Fachtna,' Teardrop said.

'And what of Bress?' Cliodna hissed, her face a mask of malice. Britha felt like she'd been slapped. Both Fachtna and Teardrop turned to look at her. She could feel the judgement in their glares without having to look at them. 'Just can't keep your legs closed for the Otherworld, can you?'

'It would seem that—' Fachtna started.

'Fachtna!' Teardrop shouted.

But that was it for Britha. The words were little more than magics woven to wound. She could see the intent. Anger overcame hurt.

'What, you spurn me so you can follow me and then throw my actions back in my face? Do what you please. Look what you've done to yourself! You are nothing in my eyes.' Cliodna was not the only one who could weave those magics.

'You swived Bress?' Fachtna demanded.

'No. Now be quiet, boy,' Britha answered in the voice she used on arrogant warriors. Fachtna's conditioning to obey whatever passed for the *dryw* where he came from silenced him.

Cliodna was suddenly in front of Britha. She tried not to flinch, tried to meet her eyes. The black pools that she had once found deep and beautiful now seemed alien and hard.

'Then why can I smell his stench in here?' she asked, pointing at Britha's head. 'And hear him here?' She pointed at Britha's heart.

Britha had no answer for herself, let alone her former lover. Tears were trickling down her cheek now. She flinched as Cliodna moistened her fingertip on the tears. There was something obscene about Cliodna's long tongue as it protruded between her teeth to lick at the tears, seeming to savour them.

'You're a pure-blood servant of the Muileartach, aren't you?' Teardrop asked quietly. There was fear in his voice.

'Not so pure now, witch-boy. Tell me, does it hurt, slowly being eaten from the inside?'

Teardrop swallowed hard but said nothing. Fachtna was resisting the urge to look at his friend.

Cliodna turned to stare at Britha. 'The Dark Man comes. Water and earth mean nothing. All women must feel the boots of the sky gods on their necks. It has been this way since Marduk struck down Tiamat. Run and hide while you can. I am only a weapon from this time on, nothing more.'

Cliodna turned, practically running on all fours, and leaped into the water, her sleek form making a minimal splash as she disappeared into its blackness.

'She seemed nice,' Fachtna said. Teardrop silenced him with a glare and looked at Britha. She turned away from him to wipe her tears. With one eye on the water, Fachtna moved across to her.

'Look, I know—' he started as he went to put an arm around her.

The iron-bladed knife was in her hand before he could finish. She opened his face from temple to cheek. Fachtna cried out and staggered back, holding the gash closed as he reached for his sword. Teardrop started towards them. Britha licked his blood off the blade, smearing her mouth red. The singing sword was half out of its scabbard when Teardrop reached Fachtna and grabbed his arm. He looked him in the eye, shaking his head. Fachtna was trying to control his breathing as the wound healed before Britha's eyes.

There is much rage in him, Britha thought. She found it less than frightening. 'I have tasted you and found you wanting, boy. Touch me again and I will curse you and your line. After I've gelded you.' She turned and walked away from them.

'You don't have any power!' Fachtna screamed at her.

'Fachtna, that's enough,' Teardrop told the furious warrior.

'Your power's a lie! You hear me? Nothing more than a jest!'

Teardrop wrenched the warrior around with surprising strength. He said nothing but the look he gave Fachtna shamed the other man into silence.

She had wanted to hear the sound of wind in the branches of the trees; the sound of the water lapping against the shore just reminded her of Cliodna. Instead she got the moaning sound that the god-slaves made as they appealed to their deity.

She had to lock it away, all of it. Her feelings were too close to the surface, too ready to burst out. Revealing them weakened her in Teardrop and Fachtna's eyes, and if she meant to use them against Bress, to help her people, then she could not allow that.

Cliodna was gone from her. Driven mad by her apparent mother, the Muileartach. Britha had to accept that she was not the same person and be prepared to fight her. Bress was pretty, and sad, and not like other warlords and warriors, but that was all. His reasons for doing what he did, his enslavement, sounded like weakness to Britha, and she could not hesitate when the time came to kill him.

The only person she could have any interest in was Teardrop, and that was only in terms of ritually taking his power.

These thoughts rampaged angrily through her mind until she used some of the techniques she had been taught in the groves to quieten her head. Britha slipped into a restless unquiet sleep to the sound of people offering themselves to an unnamed god.

She had nestled into a small cleft of earth between some stones. The moon, high and full overhead, shone a path of light across the otherwise dark water. What clouds there were, were little more than wisps. In her sleep she was aware of the light changing. Her eyes flickered to see the silhouette of a tall dark man standing over her, reaching towards her.

Then she woke up. Teardrop stood over her, leaning on his staff. The silhouette of his oddly shaped head was picked out by the light of the moon.

'I mislike people watching me sleep, and I mislike the kind of man who would do so.'

'Your sleep looked troubled,' he said, his face in shadow. Britha sat up, moving errant hair away from her face.

'Any reason it shouldn't be? What is it?'

'Bress?'

'I am going to kill him,' she said, and she meant it. Teardrop could read this from her but he could also see the song of her heart and the song of her mind conflicting in her face. However, he was prepared to take her at her word.

'What did she mean when she asked you how it felt to be eaten?' Britha demanded, still angry at how she had been woken. It had obviously been meant to put her on the back foot, to intimidate her. An answer was a long time coming.

'Power consumes you eventually,' he said, his voice flat, his face still in shadow, making him difficult to read, but she could tell there was more to it than that.

'That depends on the—'

'Always.'

There were cries from the fort. Britha caught the look on Teardrop's face as he turned. He looked troubled. Britha got to her feet, rearranging her robe. Through the break in the cliffs she could see a ship approaching, its prow crashing through the rough white water between the rocks.

Britha grabbed her spear and headed towards the shore. The god-slaves had picked up their pitch. They seemed to feel that the ship was an answer to their prayers.

Even in the darkness and with the distance, Britha found herself able to make out the details of the ship clearly. The vessel was huge and made from planks of wood that looked to have been both painted and varnished. It looked like a southern trading vessel. She knew that the crew would have skin darkened by the hot suns of the south.

She had only seen their like once before, though she had heard stories from others of the Pecht who had dealt with the strange traders from the hot lands far across the seas. She found herself awed by the strange craft. It made the wood and skin boats of her people look so rudimentary and primitive.

The oars had been raised to prevent them from being splintered by the rocks on either side of the narrow entrance. The ship moved only by its gaily coloured sail, though even without the oars it was a close fit for the large vessel.

In the stern of the ship Britha could see hugely muscled men and women in kilts made of bronze-tipped strips of leather, labouring at the huge lever of the ship's rudder. The navigator looked like those who worked the rudder, but older, gone to seed, though still powerful. He wore a *blaidth*-like garment but shorter and with no trews, and his footwear was a complicated series of leather straps. His eyelids and the skin around them were painted black, his head shorn, his beard trimmed short. He shouted instructions at the rudder-men and -women. Again, Britha wondered at how she could make out so much from so far away.

All of the crew looked so different to Britha's tall, pale, hairy people. With skin colours in various dark hues and bizarre clothing and ornamentation, the crew of the ship looked very strange to the *ban draoi*'s eyes.

'From your world?' Britha asked suspiciously as she and Teardrop walked down to the shore. The ram prow of the ship splashed through the water of the harbour, the sinister-looking eyes painted on it disappearing in the white foam.

Teardrop shook his head. 'Carthaginians, at a guess.'

A large, powerfully built man was holding on to the rail at the front of the ship. He wore a boiled leather jerkin over another *blaidth*-like piece of clothing. The light brown fur of some beast formed a small cloak. The man's trews seemed overlarge to Britha. She could also make out the hilts of a sword and dirk on a belt. He had a necklace from the teeth of some mighty beast around his neck and wore a studded leather band on his head. His hair was neatly trimmed to the shoulder except for two long braids. His beard and hair were dyed and lacquered. Part of his face was white, limed, Britha assumed, like some of the southron tribes did. More black dye traced out a pattern across his face, all of it running due to the salt spray. To her eyes the ship's master looked decadent, his face paint an extravagance that should only have been used for war or ceremony.

The Goddodin in the fort above raced along the stone palisades, keeping pace with the ship. Britha saw braziers placed for fire arrows. She wondered if they had any of the oil left. *Would it look like a waterfall of flame pouring down on the ship if they used it?* she wondered. It was something she almost wanted to see.

The man was shouting and laughing. He seemed to be by turns exhorting the sea, daring it to do its worst and crying out to a god named Dagon. Britha had no idea how she knew the language, she just did, it seemed.

Next to the master was a wiry man with the darkest skin she had ever seen, a deep rich brown colour. He was nearly as tall as Bress. He was stripped to the waist, though also wearing very large trews and leaning on a long-hafted great axe, the heads of which were two massive crescent-shaped bronze blades.

With a final crash the ship made it through into the natural harbour. The white-clad god-slaves on the shore seemed ecstatic, and were crying their thanks to the Dark Man.

The ship struck its sails. The oars came down to back row and slow the ship down. Stone anchors were slung overboard.

Britha was angrily shoving the god-slaves out of her way. Fachtna was following her, watching the ship manoeuvre closer to the shore. The injuries Britha had given him were gone. The man in the leather jerkin and the face paint was shouting up to the fort in a broken version of the Goddodin's language, which Britha was still able to understand, assuring them that he was here for trade as he had been before.

'So you'll ride your fish woman, you'll ride Teardrop, you'll even ride Bress, despite him killing half your people and enslaving the other half, before you'd ride me?' Fachtna asked.

'It's my right, the right of every woman to take their pleasure where they want and with whom they want. And it's not before, it's instead of, and frankly I would ride the Cirig's entire herd of beasties and the wolves in the wood before I got near you.'

'I'll have to warn them you're coming,' Fachtna told her. Britha turned to face him, her irritation with the Goidel warrior overcoming her fascination with the strange ship and its even stranger crew.

'Decide what it's going to take to get you to stop talking to me and decide now.'

Fachtna's retort was cut off by a ramp being dropped onto the shore from the ship. The master strode down it followed by the tall brown-skinned man, who seemed to be his bodyguard.

The quality of the master's clothing and his slight paunch marked him as wealthy. His bearing, however, was more that of a warrior than a merchant, but there was a definite intelligence behind his brown eyes.

The emaciated old man, who had spoken to Britha before, approached the ship's master. Britha again shoved him out of the way, sending him sprawling.

'This is not a fitting welcome,' the ship's master managed in the Goddodin tongue.

'We speak the language of Carthage,' Fachtna said. The ship's master looked thoughtful. His guard, bronze axe at the ready, was studying Teardrop with suspicion.

'And what would a northern barbarian know of the might and splendour of Carthage?' the master asked.

'Enough to recognise its tongue shouted across these waters.'

'You speak it well.' The ship's master looked at Teardrop then back to Fachtna. 'Did your demon whisper it? Pour it into your ear like honey?'

Britha was confused. 'We don't pour honey in ears.' She was surprised to find herself apparently speaking Carthaginian. 'We eat it.'

'And I am no demon,' Teardrop said.

'A sorcerer then?' the brown-skinned guard asked. Teardrop gazed at the man but said nothing. The guard met Teardrop's look and held it.

'My friend asked you a question,' the ship's master said.

'I heard,' Teardrop told him.

'Who is he to ask it?' Britha demanded.

'Where I come from the women let the men speak,' the Carthaginian answered.

'Where I come from it is courteous to introduce yourself, and where I come from we geld men for discourtesy. Since we're closer to where I come from than where you come from, which one of my ways would you like to respect?' Britha asked. Fachtna was staring at her with a raised eyebrow.

The Carthaginian gave it some thought; the guard shifted, ready to strike.

'The introduction, I think!' he finally said, his face splitting into a wide grin.

'Good choice,' Fachtna muttered.

Men, Britha thought, shaking her head. *Just another pissing contest.* Still, at least she seemed to have won.

'People call me Hanno, or Hanno of Carthage if there are more than one of my name here. My friend here has the honour of being Kush – once a slave, then a gladiator and now a close friend who keeps me safe from my enemies, though I have few of those.'

'Must you always mention me being a slave once?' Kush asked, sounding less than happy.

'It is a great thing to rise from being a slave to a free man!' Hanno cried.

Kush leaned in towards Britha, Fachtna and Teardrop. It was all Britha could do to stop herself from pulling away from him. 'I was not a slave for very long, you understand?' The three of them nodded. 'And it is an ill thing to keep a slave.'

'Oh, I agree,' Fachtna said. Britha couldn't help but glance down at the white-clad kneelers all around them. Hanno was looking a little uncomfortable.

'I am Fachtna, a Gael of the line of Mael Duin.' He stepped forward and grasped Hanno by the arm. The Carthaginian reciprocated. Fachtna turned to Kush but the bodyguard would not relinquish his hold on his axe.

'He means no offence but he likes always to be ready to use it,' Hanno said.

Fachtna shrugged, choosing not to take offence, for which both Britha and Teardrop were relieved.

'I am Teardrop on Fire of the Croatan.' He moved towards Hanno, offering his hand. Hanno looked to Kush, not taking the proffered arm immediately. Kush studied Teardrop and then Fachtna in turn.

'I think we walk with gods and demons,' he finally said.

'My friend has the nose for this,' Hanno said.

'And we will treat you as you treat us,' Britha told them. Hanno glanced at Kush again, who nodded. Hanno took Teardrop's arm.

'And I am Britha, *ban draoi* of the Cirig,' Britha said, offering her arm. Hanno regarded it coolly but took it.

'I do not know this word, *ban draoi*.' Hanno admitted.

'She is priestess, blessed by their gods or touched by their demons,' Kush said.

Britha turned on him. 'My power is my own and we do not make ourselves slaves to men or gods,' she told him angrily.

'You speak her language?' Teardrop asked, hoping to ease the tension.

'Anyone can see what she is for the looking,' Kush told them. Teardrop was looking at him with interest.

'You are not with these cravens who cower behind their wall?' Hanno asked, turning towards the fort. 'Without even so much the offer of a drink!' His voice echoed around the harbour.

'They were attacked,' Teardrop told them, 'by black ships.'

Kush and Hanno exchanged another knowing glance.

'You've seen them?' Britha asked.

Hanno shook his head. 'Kush here smelled them,' the Carthaginian said.

'There was something evil and unnatural on the seas in the south,' the tall axeman said. 'We wanted none of it.'

'We are traders, that is all. We will fight to protect ourselves but ...'

'Only a fool picks a fight with demons,' Kush finished and looked at Teardrop again.

'Good luck getting them to come out to trade,' Fachtna said as he nodded towards the fort.

Hanno spat. 'I told you we came too far north. There is nothing up here but sharp rocks, cold seas and colder women.' Britha stared at him. 'See!'

'We need passage south,' Britha said.

'Aye,' Fachtna agreed.

Hanno turned to regard them with a calculating expression on his face.

'Where the demons are?' Kush demanded.

'They will be moving faster than you and they are also heading south,' Teardrop said.

'The *Will of Dagon* is one of the fastest—'

'We know,' Britha said. She had met merchants before. They were always very proud of their ships.

'They are demon ships,' Kush said. 'Their unnatural power will move faster than even the *Will of Dagon*.'

'Take us as far south as your nerve will allow you,' Britha said.

Hanno glared at her. 'My nerve, woman, was tried in battle when you were still an infant wriggling in your own shit, and not against the likes of the savages you have on your small cold island.'

'Well argued,' Britha said, smiling. 'So you'll have no problem taking us.'

'If you can pay,' he said, crossing his arms.

Britha cursed herself for not taking any of the Cirig's gold. They had died on the red beach wearing their torcs, silver for the *cateran* and gold for the *mormaer*. She had not taken it because she had not earned it. Such gifts were for those who had proved themselves in battle as warriors. When they were defeated they belonged to the victors. The Cirig expected nothing less when they met enemies in battle. That said, these considerations seemed foolish in the face of practical requirements, but if they let their ways go, what was left of them? It was her job to keep, even enforce, their ways no matter how hard or inconvenient it was. She felt shame at wanting to barter away gold and silver bought with skill, strength and blood.

Britha had not noticed Teardrop staring at Fachtna. He sighed and took off a finely wrought silver torc wrapped around his left arm. It was in the style of the Goidel, not as chunky and chain-like as those worn by the Pecht.

'I will cut off a piece of this for you,' Fachtna told Hanno.

'Then you will spoil it for us, as we will soon own all of it if you wish passage south,' Hanno said.

'That is a gift worthy of a mighty *mormaer*,' Britha said angrily. 'One that you have not earned with mere trade.'

'So haughty, walk if you prefer. I'm sure your demons will wait.'

'This is not a good way to behave,' Britha told the merchant. 'You are taking advantage of us.' People just didn't act like this; they asked a fair price for the service rendered. They did not steal from you just because they knew you needed what they had to offer.

'Britha,' Teardrop said softly. She lapsed into a fuming silence. Fachtna reluctantly gave Hanno the torc.

'We would also like to seek passage,' the old man from the kneelers said.

'All seem to seek the demons this night,' Hanno said as he turned to the man. 'But can you pay?'

18
Now

Du Bois was hungry. He was hungry because he had been on the go for the better part of three days and his body's augmentations wouldn't let him become tired, or indeed ever operate at anything other than heightened peak performance. He was sitting in the mess at Fort Southwick eating as much high-calorie food as he could, as quickly as possible. His body processed the food with near-total efficiency and turned it into energy.

Portsmouth had been locked down. Police and military blockaded the three bridges onto the island. Du Bois didn't think it would help much and was largely of the opinion that it had been done to be *seen* to be done in what was being portrayed as a terrorist incident. He had, however, quietly circulated a picture of Natalie Luckwicke to those manning the blockades but he couldn't imagine getting that lucky. The press were on to what they thought was a suspect, and Control had D-noticed the press to make sure that her picture didn't get out.

Du Bois had come to the conclusion that Natalie had indirectly been the cause of what had happened in the nightclub and that somehow someone must have imbibed her blood. He wasn't even sure where to start with that – drug dealers, blood clinics or just some mixed-up kids with syringes of blood, and if that was the case did it mean that Natalie was dead?

He knew the DAYP were in the city but was wondering if someone or something else was involved. Judging by the interrogation and mutilation of Arbogast, they were after the same thing as he was, though he hoped that they did not understand its significance. However, when he seeded the rats and the insects and set up AI monitoring of the imagery looking for traces of Natalie, he discovered that there were parts of the city that the rats just simply did not go, mostly in the southern part of Portsea Island towards the Solent. The seeded insects just disappeared when they went far enough south, as if they were encountering some kind of blood-screen. *One problem at a time*, du Bois decided, unless that was where she was hiding. A manual search of the seafront was rapidly becoming the only option. He would not like to be Control having to explain that to the Home Office. Their influence was incredibly strong but not total. The people of Portsmouth and Southsea were not going to like having their homes searched by soldiers and police regardless of the reason.

'Excuse me, sir.' Du Bois looked up at the soldier. To his eyes he seemed far too young to be in uniform, though he himself had been much younger when he had first joined the order as a squire. 'There's a woman here to see you, sir.'

Du Bois wasn't sure what irritated him more, the mere presence of his brother here while he was working, or the fact that he had ridden his motorcycle. He decided it was the riding of his motorbike. The 1949 C series Vincent Black Shadow gleamed black and silver in the sun. The bike, along with his piano, were the possessions he prized most, the two things that gave him genuine pleasure.

Alexander, though it was difficult to think of him with that name looking at his distinctly female body, was leaning against the bike wearing leathers. His jacket was lying over the bike, and the tight black strapped top was causing a number of the soldiers on guard at the gate to stare. Knowing his brother, he had been flirting with them before du Bois arrived.

Alexander was taller than him, his long hair dark where du Bois's was light, finely featured, his cheekbones were V-shaped slashes that could either make him look like a goddess or completely wicked. They had the same blue eyes though. Alexander's body was full and statuesque. He would not have been out of place on a catwalk.

Even as a child, Alexander had been effeminate; du Bois had to protect him. He remembered his lack of comprehension when he discovered that Alexander liked to dress up in female servants' clothes. He remembered nightmarish times travelling across Europe, Alexander disguised as a woman, fear of his brother's proclivities being discovered, du Bois down on his knees morning and night praying for forgiveness for himself and deliverance for Alexander.

He had sought a cure for him, so he would not be damned to hell; instead he had found the Circle. Their access to L- and S-tech meant that Alexander could be whatever he wanted. Alexander had finally become a woman in the early nineteenth century. Du Bois had tried to accept it, envious of the way his younger bother could embrace each new age, disapproving of how he could embrace the excesses of each age as well. During a particularly bad argument in Marrakesh in the 1970s, Alexander had screamed at him that he was a fully functioning hermaphrodite. It had been too much for him. Du Bois had fled the argument, the Red City and North Africa.

Fully functioning hermaphrodite or not, Alexander was female-identifying now and wanted to be regarded as a woman. In this age nobody seemed to care, and even du Bois with his background could not see the harm and felt that God had greater sins to judge than Alexander's. His own, for example.

'Malcolm!' Alexander cried happily and threw herself into her brother's arms for a hug. Du Bois returned the hug uncomfortably.

'What are you doing here, Alexander?' he whispered. He was not pleased that she had even been able to find him. Someone in the Circle must have told her. He didn't like the security ramifications of that. It smacked of a loss of hope.

Du Bois had become the good servant; Alexander had reaped the rewards. His service had been on the condition that they look after Alexander. She had access to all the benefits and none of the draw-backs, as far as du Bois could see. She had thrown herself at immortal life with a strong appetite. Du Bois both admired and resented her for that.

'Alexia, I've told you.' There was just the slightest flash of anger in her eyes as she released him from the hug, a reminder of countless arguments in the past. Even du Bois had eventually been forced to admit that she was happier as a woman.

'What are you doing here, Alex?'

'I brought your bike.'

'You stole my bike and then I'm guessing you had it transported.' There was no way du Bois could see his sister riding the bike all the way from their family home, a castle perched precariously on the edge of the stormy west coast of Scotland.

'I know how bad it is,' she said.

Du Bois just shook his head. He didn't want to think about how she had found out. It was a cold but sunny day. The sky was bright blue and cloudless. A brisk wind caught Alexia's long hair. Looking at the day, it all seemed so ridiculous, but he couldn't help wonder how much longer they had.

'Want to go to Brighton and get fucked up?' Alexia asked brightly.

'I really don't,' he answered.

'Want to flagellate yourself and worry about the weight of the world on your shoulders?' Alexia asked with mock seriousness.

He had to laugh. It worried him how much her suggestion appealed. Actually he wanted to smoke, drink whisky and brood.

'I'm working.'

'Will it do any good or are you just going through the motions?' she asked, concern in her voice. He had to think about that. He genuinely wasn't sure. He was grasping at straws but anything was better than nothing. 'We lived longer than we should have, much longer. We've seen and done extraordinary things – well, that was mostly me; you've been consistently maudlin, grumpy, too serious and sarcastic – and it's all right to let go.'

'I'm the sarcastic one?' he asked, but the humour was gone and she was just looking at him with concern. 'It's not for us. You're right – we've lived too long – but if there's even the slightest—'

'Okay fine. Is there anything that you can do at this moment?'

He thought about that. He had arrived at a dead end. Natalie was almost certainly dead. He had no idea how her blood was being circulated but it wouldn't be enough anyway: they needed her, or at least a reasonable amount of her blood or a significant genetic sample. He shook his head reluctantly and then looked at his bike.

Across the South Downs, taking the bike as fast as it would go with the two of them, leaning low on the bends, du Bois was actually smiling. He heard the sound of Alexia's laughter snatched away by the wind.

They were somewhere north of Winchester, du Bois knew. They were on a hilltop outside an Iron Age fort. He had ignored the signs on the way. He could find out exactly where he was if he accessed his systems but he had decided to pretend to be human today. He was trying to remember what that was like.

Alexia had produced a picnic lunch from the bike's saddlebags, and having eaten that they were now leaning against a tree as they sipped champagne, sitting in high grass looking at a small herd of sheep. Du Bois would neutralise the alcohol in his system before he got back on the bike. He knew that Alexia wouldn't. The day was cold, though that didn't bother them, and a school day, so the only other people they saw were the occasional dog walkers.

Most of lunch had been Alexia talking about things he either couldn't relate to or was trying not to be judgemental about.

'Have you been here before?' she asked out of the blue. He had drifted off, not concentrating on what she was saying. He looked around as if seeing the place for the first time, trying to take it in.

'I don't think so. It's difficult to be sure.' They were quiet.

'Thank you,' she said after a while.

'For what?' du Bois asked, surprised.

'For taking me to Outremer. I know what you did and what it meant.'

Du Bois thought back. He had taken her there because he had heard that the rules that governed Europe at the time were not as strict there. That you could reinvent yourself. That you could lose your past. Or at least Alexander could. They had been one step in front of the Church authorities that had wanted to burn Alexander as an abomination in the eyes of God. He wondered about a god that would do that, except that now he knew there was no god. Though somehow that had never stopped him praying.

'Where are you staying?' he finally asked. The thank you was sounding too much like a goodbye.

'Brighton.'

That made sense to du Bois. Even he was aware that Brighton was a party town; the judgemental side of him wanted to call it decadent. Alexia liked it there and felt that she fitted in.

'So what are you doing here?'

'We have a gig in Portsmouth in a few days, on the pier.'

Du Bois had lost count of how many times Alexia had reinvented herself. Her current reinvention was as the front person for a band playing a type of music that du Bois found very difficult to listen to.

'And you need me to get onto the island?' Alexia grinned at him. 'You don't change, do you?'

'You could come.'

'You know I don't—'

'You like some of it, and you have to admit we're good musicians.' She was right about that. Alexia had always excelled at music – all the courtly arts, in fact. He had excelled in the arts martial.

'I'll get you into the city.'

'And I was worried about you.'

'I'll be fine.'

'That's a lie. None of us will.' She looked sad. Even after all the trouble she had put him through, all the chaos she left in her wake that he inevitably had to sort out, he hated to see her sad.

'You know I can't talk about it.'

'Everything comes to an end. You can rest now if you want.' Du Bois looked away and said nothing. 'But you won't; you'll rage against the sea and the heavens and the hateful uncaring gods themselves.'

Du Bois frowned. 'Are you quoting your own lyrics to me?'

Alexia's smile brightened her face.

'I knew you listened to us.' Then she became serious again. 'I wrote that for you. You're a bad servant, Malcolm. You always have been.'

'It's all I've ever known.'

They lapsed into silence again.

'You know,' Alexia started, 'I will be deeply disappointed if the apocalypse starts in Portsmouth.'

Du Bois had to laugh. Then he wondered if she just wanted to see the end. He looked around. There was nobody else on the hill. He wasn't sure what made him look over to the mound that had been the hill fort. Relaxed as he was, he had not let his guard down. She had appeared unnoticed through his blood-screen and even now seemed invisible to it. Something was spoofing the tiny machines somehow. The level of tech involved was frightening. On the other hand, she was there in plain sight. He cursed himself for being so reliant on technology.

'Malcolm?' He could hear the fear in her voice. Fear was an emotion they both should have been able to put aside a long time ago. They were not used to it. 'It's her, isn't it? The traitor?'

Malcolm's mind wandered back to a night in an earthen root-lined chamber. He remembered the flickering firelight, painted faces, fire dancing and the feeling that he had left his faith far behind him. The chalice full of molten red gold. He remembered how it burned inside. No way of surviving, it had been his death. He remembered her standing over him. Not the shambolic mess she was now, but strong, powerful, impossibly old and so very sad.

'Alexia, go back to the bike and get away from here.'

'But—'

'Alexia, please. She won't be here for you. I can't worry about you ...' *And fight her*, he left unsaid.

'I don't want her to kill you,' Alexia said fiercely. She meant it, but even now, after all these centuries, he could still hear the voice of the child who just wanted things to be better.

'Please.' He was all but begging her now. Alexia gathered their picnic stuff and headed back towards the bike. Du Bois waited until she was out of sight. He thought about contacting Control but assumed that Alexia would somehow deal with that. He wondered how the woman was hiding from the network of micro-satellites they had orbiting the world as he made his way towards her. He drew the .45 and swapped the magazine for one with nanite-tipped bullets. Somehow he didn't think it would help.

*

She was standing on what had once been the ramparts, looking out over trees at the patchwork of fields under the cold blue sky.

'It wasn't that different. All farmland. Of course, the trees were not here, but I like them. I like trees.'

'Good farmland's good farmland,' du Bois said warily. Even standing as far away as he was, he could smell her. She stank of urine and sweat. Her clothes were basically layers of filthy rags, her face obscured by grime, her hair a matted mess. She leaned heavily on a gnarled wooden staff. In her other hand she gripped a plastic bag full of what looked like rubbish.

'No wonder we can't find you,' he said.

'They wouldn't think to look where I hide.'

'They say that you're no longer real.'

'It's easier to be a legend than it is to be a person.'

'That you're a nano-form. That you live in the earth now.'

'They say a lot.'

'They certainly do.'

She hadn't looked at him yet. If anything she seemed to be enjoying the view, her mind somewhere else. Du Bois was content to let her be, though he himself was wound up like a spring, waiting for her to attack, assuming that it would be over soon. She laughed. It was a very dry-sounding noise.

'I'm not going to kill you, Malcolm. I like you. I always have done. You're so terribly earnest, to the point of parody.'

'So what do you want?'

'Would you believe me if I told you it was going to be okay?'

'I'd want to see some evidence of that. For example, access to your bloodline.'

'Me? No, I poisoned that knowledge a long time ago. I pissed in my own DNA when I saw what the Circle was becoming. I couldn't risk it falling into their hands.'

She sounds bitter, du Bois thought.

'You're protecting the prodigal.' It wasn't a question.

'Am I?'

'Did you help the Brass City kill the other children?'

She turned on him. The look of fury in her face made him step back, his hand reaching for the holstered .45.

'I don't kill children!' she hissed and then seemed to master her anger. 'Unless I have to. I disagree with their methods but the Brass City were right. This corruption that the Circle has become cannot choose the shape of the future of mankind. They will only

255

feed destruction. They will only teach people not to care. They will only teach them that they are helpless. These are lies.'

'Do you serve the angels now?'

She looked more exasperated than angry. 'What is it with you? Despite all the killing, somehow after all this time you still know right from wrong and always did. If only you would think for yourself. Alexia –' she nodded towards the car park '– is all appetite; you are all duty. Both of you could learn a little from the other.'

'She is a deviant.' The words were out of his mouth before he could even think.

'Don't call her that! You know it's not true and always have done! You just listen to all this bullshit you're fed. Religion's like anything else. Take the good stuff, ignore the hate.'

Du Bois wasn't sure if she was angry or just frustrated. She was, however, making him feel like a child.

'You didn't answer my question,' he demanded, as much to cover up the shame of what he had said.

'Have you ever even met an agent of the Eggshell?' He did not answer, but thinking back he hadn't. It had always been the Brass City and then smaller groups or individual madmen who had stumbled onto the technology. 'They are your legends, your myths. Fools, but at least they were honest fools.' *She either doesn't realise that she's contradicting herself or doesn't care*, du Bois thought. 'But no, I'm not serving them.'

'Then why are you here?'

'The key is for everyone. It is not for the rich and powerful to enslave humanity. The Circle has betrayed all that it was set up to do. It is a tool of tyranny and empire in whatever guise those nasty little ideas have now become.'

'It's not practical to save everyone – you know that. We're taking what we can, the genetic material to—'

'A slave race.' Her look was daring him to deny it.

'That's not true.'

'I founded the Circle. Who would know better than I?'

'Even if what you say is true, we're the only ones who have the resources to do anything, unless you believe in the Brass City's paradise.'

'A half-life.'

'They claim you wouldn't know the difference.'

'The problem is the same.'

Du Bois knew she was right. The processing power they had had access to for centuries, maybe longer, was still limited to a degree.

Recording functional human consciousness in its totality required massive amounts of storage, as every molecule in the human brain was the equivalent of a powerful computer in its own right. In order to store a single human consciousness, the structure and function of trillions upon trillions of molecules needed to be simulated, as well as all the rules that governed how they interact. It was the interaction that took up the real space. The random complexities of the human mind ran into thousands of petabytes.

'And that's assuming the flesh isn't corrupt and insane,' she added. 'Don't help them write their filth across the skies, Malcolm. It's beneath you.'

'I think it's the only chance we have.'

'And I think you're just too used to following orders. It's so much easier when other people make our decisions for us, isn't it?' She sounded sad. Du Bois didn't know what to say. It had never seemed easy to him. 'Do you know when I left?' Du Bois said nothing, just watched her warily. 'It was the artists. They kept the great minds, the scientists – though I suspect they will be modified, redesigned to toe the party line – but they wiped out so many of the great artists. Their future doesn't have any room for beauty and thought, I think.'

'That's a lie!' Du Bois said angrily, but the conversation with Hamad played over in his head.

'Some of them were my friends. They replaced them with the venal and the petty who happened to be the rich and powerful. They'll leave the best minds because they don't make good slaves.'

'What do you want?' Du Bois demanded again. He was trying to armour himself with anger. Convince himself that she was lying. The Circle was the grand plan. The best hope for humanity.

'You to join me,' she said evenly. Du Bois looked her up and down.

'Look what you've done to yourself!' he all but spat at her. He was feeling more secure in his convictions now. Comforted in the familiar surroundings of his belief. She was an external threat again.

'Don't be so stupid!' she snapped. Her anger would make it easier. 'I'm not joining you; you betrayed the Circle.'

'They have betrayed all of us!'

'Words.'

'Fine. You wish to remain nothing more than a violent slave, then so be it. Stop looking for the key or I will kill you. Do you understand me? Don't make your sister weep for you.'

Du Bois understood her perfectly. The key was in Portsmouth and alive, but she did not know where, otherwise she would have moved her. There was hope.

'You can go now,' she told him. 'I'm not going to sink into the earth or anything like that.'

'I still don't know your name.'

'You never will.'

Du Bois turned and walked away. He glanced over his shoulder. She was still there looking out over the land. There was something about the way she stood that made him think that she was so very tired.

Du Bois made his way quickly back to the bike. Alexia was there, of course. She had not abandoned him and was so relieved to see him. It was only then he realised how terrified he had been.

The amusements were closed, a neon beacon of wasted electricity garishly lighting up the night sky. Beth had done most of her work and was sitting on the sea wall again, watching two armed police officers walk along the front. Nobody wanted to come out and play with all the police around and the island blocked off from the mainland.

'Excuse me, love.'

Beth was slowly getting used to the mangled cockney of the Pompey accent. With her broad West Yorkshire vowels, sometimes conversations sounded like they were being held in two different languages. This voice was the most Pompey she had ever heard: she had to play it back in her head to decipher it.

'Yeah?' she finally said. She didn't like the look of him. Weasel-faced, lank, shoulder-length blond hair, looped earrings. He looked thin but she was guessing that under the shell suit was a wiry frame. He was leaning on a bizarre-looking cane that looked like it was made out of leather. His mouth moved with the constant chewing movement of the habitual speed freak. It was the eyes, though. She'd seen them before, working the doors. This was a man who didn't feel anything and so liked violence. A proper psycho.

Two large men dressed much more smartly, in suits and overcoats, flanked the weasel-faced man. Massively built, their pronounced jaws suggested steroid abuse. Beth had seen their like before in the gym.

'You looking for me?' the thin man asked. Alarm bells were ringing.

'Don't think so.'

'Sure? Jaime said you was. So did William. You do that to his fingers?' he asked, sounding casual. If there was anger there, it was because someone was playing with his toys, not because someone had hurt his people.

Beth got off the wall. 'You know my sister?'

'Probably be better if we asked the questions, love.'

'Who are you?'

'You're not very bright up north, are you? We're going to go for a bit of a ride. Have a bit of a chat, okay?'

'I'm a bit old to get into a car with strange men.' Beth turned to walk away.

'I don't think you want to do that.'

Beth made the mistake of glancing behind her. The big guy on the psycho's right had opened his coat to show the pistol stuffed in his waistband. Beth knew she should have kept walking but stopped. The man with the gun was trying to look hard but he had to be scared. The city was crawling with armed police and even soldiers. Battery Row was pretty open and he was carrying a shooter.

'You going to use that here?' Beth asked. She tried to sound casual, but her hand went into the pocket of her leather jacket, fingers curling around her brass knuckles. She didn't fancy her chances of crossing the distance before he drew the gun. These guys being mown down by trigger-happy police was little consolation if she was dead.

'What are you doing?' Ted was behind her, staring at the psycho.

Beth swore to herself. She didn't doubt that to run an arcade you needed to be hard, but she didn't think Ted was anywhere near this psycho's league, and he was old, fat and really unhealthy. The last thing she needed was to drag him into this, particularly with a gun involved. 'I asked you a fucking question, McGurk. You know better. You don't fucking come down here and hassle my people.'

Beth turned to stare at Ted. He was an easy-going guy. This was a new side of him. Fat or not, he suddenly came across as more than capable of defending himself. She wondered how many other people had underestimated him in the past.

'Hello, Ted, and watch your fucking mouth. That agreement was made a long time ago, and you're not quite the Jack the Lad you once were, if you know what I mean.'

'I stay out of your business; you stay out of mine.'

'I'm thinking of renegotiating. Besides, little missy here has been messing in my business. Beat up one of my boys, cut another. Something has to be done. You know that, Ted.'

Ted turned to Beth looking less than pleased.

'Do I look like a fucking little missy to you?' Beth demanded.

McGurk looked her up and down, an expression of exaggerated distaste on his features. 'You're too fucking ugly to rape. Your sister, on the other hand, she was proper rape material.'

Beth went for him. Ted, moving surprisingly quickly, grabbed her and managed to hold her back. McGurk just laughed.

'Enough ... Beth, not here ... That's enough!' Somehow the words got through, made their way through the red, and Beth started to calm down. 'Isn't that what they call overcompensation, McGurk? Didn't think you liked the ladies.' He glanced at McGurk's two minders.

'What the fuck's that supposed to mean?! What are you trying to say, you cunt?!'

'Just hear you like to break your boys in,' Ted said, still holding on to Beth. Ted looked at the minders one after another. Neither of them would meet his eyes. McGurk's face was red and furious. Ted whispered to Beth, 'I've got to let you go. You go for him and you're on your own. Understand? Now get a grip.' Beth nodded and he let go of her.

'They need to know who's boss, that's all! It just establishes, you know ...'

'Dominance?' Ted asked innocently.

'Yeah, like a wolf! You're not a fucking faggot if you're doing it to them!' McGurk screamed. 'I'm happily married and plenty on the side! You go around saying things like that and you could get yourself badly hurt. Know what I mean?! Now give us the bitch.'

'That's not going to happen, and this isn't a good time to be doing this. The city's crawling with plod.'

'Either she's one of yours, in which case we come back mob-handed, or she's not and you give her over. Save yourself the fucking trouble.' McGurk moved closer to Ted, leaning in towards him. 'Look, I get it. You were a big man when I was coming up, a hard man. I had to show respect. But look at you now. Too many fags, too many doughnuts, you got high on your own supply. Well, fat anyway. We can just take her now – you know that – but I'm still trying to show you some respect, okay? Let you get out of this with a bit of dignity.'

Beth looked at Ted. She was about to go with McGurk. This wasn't Ted's problem; she'd brought this down on him. Then she saw how angry he was. The big man was shaking with rage.

'For a piece of shit like you to think you can even talk to me like that ...' he managed. McGurk backed up. Shifting posture. Beth decided she was going to go for the guy with the gun first. Ted didn't know about the gun.

Then they came, everyone who worked at the amusements. Many were not physically impressive but some of them were. A lot of it was hard physical work. Men and women. The youngest to the oldest, a lot of them carrying whatever makeshift weapon they could lay their hands on.

'That supposed to scare me?' McGurk asked, sneering at the show people's approach.

'Go now while you still can,' Ted managed, his voice shaky, that of a man barely controlling his temper.

'I will fucking deal with you, you fat cunt,' McGurk told him, and then he and his two muscle-bound minders turned and headed back towards Old Portsmouth.

Ted turned to Beth. 'You need to go home now.'

At first Beth thought he was angry with her. Then she realised. 'What, do you think he ...?'

'Go now!'

She turned and ran, so intent on getting back to the flat that she didn't hear what McGurk was shouting after her.

Beth sprinted across the common, cursing herself for not getting to know the city better. Her lungs felt on fire by the time she crossed on to Osborne Road, making a car brake suddenly, heading for the centre of Southsea. She turned into Palmerston Road, the ugly concrete shopping precinct. She wasn't sure how she was breathing. She just didn't seem to be getting enough oxygen but she didn't stop. Past the church, the cafes on Marmion Road and right into Victoria Road South, wishing she owned a mobile phone. She had passed a number of roads she was convinced would get her there quicker but couldn't risk getting lost. People got out of the way of the powerfully built woman sprinting down the pavement. Beth's chest was agony now. Nearly there. Crossing Albert Road, she ended up on the bonnet of a skidding car, providing the terrified occupants with a freeze-frame image before she slid off. On to Campbell Road. She was amazed her run hadn't resulted in police interest.

As ever, Campbell Road was lined with parked cars. She tried looking for ones that didn't fit. A waste of time. Gasping down air as she fumbled with the lock. She was seeing stars in front of her eyes now. Into the hall. Up the stairs. Heart sinking as she saw the door to the flat was open.

Beth looked into the lounge. Maude was curled up on the sofa looking terrified. Uday was next to her, arms around her. Even in the moment that Beth had to take it in, Uday's look said it all. *You brought this down on us.*

McGurk was in the armchair playing with his cane. One of his minders stood next to him; the other was towering over Uday and Maude.

'Now where were we? Oh yes. Trevor, give this fucking mouthy bitch a bit of a slap, will you?'

Trevor was the one standing next to McGurk. He was across the living room with surprising speed, although if she hadn't just sprinted two miles he probably wouldn't have connected. He caught Beth in the jaw and she hit the carpet.

Beth reached under the sofa and grabbed the bayonet from its hiding place with her left hand. As she moved, she saw the look of surprise on Maude's face. Trevor cried out, surprise first, then pain and fear. It was an awkward left-handed stab, but she left the blade in his leg as she pulled the brass knuckles out of the pocket of her leather and hit him hard in the chin and then again with less force on the nose. Trevor's nose broke, blood spurting down his face, but he was already on his way down to the floor.

Uday flung himself at the other piece of muscle. He might as well have thrown himself at a concrete wall. He was easily batted aside. To Beth's amazement, Maude was trying to hit him as well. It didn't look like much of a contact but he cried out and grabbed his eye as Uday picked himself up and grabbed the big man's legs.

'Come on then, you southern cunt!' Beth screamed at McGurk. But he had a gun now. It was pointed at Uday's head.

'Now if we're all through playing silly fucking buggers,' McGurk said.

Uday was looking furious. Glaring between Beth and McGurk. Maude seemed appalled by what she had done. The minder had blood pouring out from under his eye. As Beth watched, he pulled the nail file that Maude had stabbed him with out of the wound. Beth couldn't believe that both of them had had the courage to fight.

Trevor was moaning, one leg of his trousers dark with blood. Beth stood on his leg so he couldn't move and tore the bayonet out. He screamed.

'Here! Any more of your nonsense and you'll get to see your two little friends make a very special film. Do you understand me? Now drop the shiv.'

'What the fuck's wrong with you?' Beth asked as she dropped the bayonet.

'Never you mind what's wrong with me, you cheeky slag. You just do as you're fucking told.'

'Where's my sister?' Beth demanded. Maude looked up at her, shock all over her face.

'You see the gun, yes?' He turned to the muscle that Maude had stabbed. 'Are you all right, Markus?'

'Yes, Mr McGurk.'

'Right. Well why don't you cuff her, take her downstairs and put her in the boot of the Beamer.'

'Yes, Mr McGurk.'

'I can't see that happening,' Beth said.

'Then I break both your arms and legs and you get to watch me rape your friends to death.'

It was too much for Maude. She broke down. Uday looked angry enough to charge a gun.

As subtly as she could, Beth dropped her knuckles back into the pocket of her leather. Markus cuffed her and then put his overcoat over the cuffs to hide them.

McGurk stood up. He looked down at Trevor with disgust and delivered a vicious kick to his wound. Trevor screamed. Then he turned to the furious Uday and sobbing Maude.

'I can find you any time I want. You understand me.'

Beth saw Uday swallow hard, bite back what he was going to say and nod. Then the three of them left, leaving the bleeding Trevor on the carpet.

19

A Long Time After the Loss

Scab had described it as an anal tract but Vic had put that down to his partner's natural unpleasantness. Vic preferred to think of it as walking down a massive bioluminescent artery. The translucent nature of the flesh of the floating city allowed him to see its internal workings, which looked like muscle, tissue and organs on a massive scale. He understood that felines, hairless monkeys and to a lesser extent some lizards could find this sort of thing uncomfortable, but he'd grown up in the chitinous environments of star hives which prepared him for this sort of biomechanics writ large.

They were moving along the artery/sphincter on the edge of one of the Living Cities. They did not know which one. They did not know how to differentiate or indeed if they could be differentiated.

The Living Cities were one of the most celebrated sights of the Monarchist systems and indeed Known Space, considered a triumph of bioengineering, though it was suspected that they had been built using illegal – under Church law – applications of Seeder tech.

Vic reached out to touch the flesh-like wall of the artery, running one of his upper hands down it, enjoying the sensation fed back from the tactile sensor on the mechanical appendage. Through the glowing translucent wall he could look down through the cloudless sky to the scarred grey rock of Pangea's surface.

Tendrils hung out of the bottom of the city as it floated on massive gasbags supported by redundant AG systems. The tendrils burrowed into the surface of the ruined planet like parasitical insects. Vic knew that the tendrils would be breaking down and sucking up the very surface of the planet itself for conversion and processing as raw material. Deeper burrowing tendrils would be harnessing geothermal energy from the planet's core. Frequent tectonic events would sever tendrils, spraying rock, heat or even lava into the sky, but the living city could always call on its massive carbon reservoirs harvested from the very matter of the planet and grow more.

Eventually Pangea would be exhausted and the Living Cities would either somehow have to move to another world or die. Other worlds were in short supply due to the limited number of systems that the Church allowed access to with their bridge technology, and the rapacious, exponential, almost viral level of expansion and colonisation of the sentient races. In other words, space was crowded, and almost every bit of it was claimed. On the other hand, even with Vic's limited knowledge of geospatial politics, and allowing for his near-total lack of interest in the subject, he realised that breaking the Church's monopoly could lead to the opening-up of more space to colonise.

The artery rose in a helix towards the living dome-like roof of this particular city, where massive cells photosynthesised the weak light of Pangea's main-sequence G-type star. Some effect of the planet's wrecked atmosphere made the star look white.

Much of the trip from Pythia to Pangea had been taken up with Scab trying to work out what the Church frigate had done to the *Basilisk* and upgrading the ship's security. Elements of Pangea's not inconsiderable navy were on the *Basilisk* the moment they opened the bridge from Red Space into Real Space. Security for Pangea was run by one of the largest private military contractors. *Basilisk* had been told to power down all weapon systems or be destroyed. Scab had done it without too much attitude – to Vic's surprise. They had then been escorted through orbital defences comparable to Pythia's. All of this was paid for through the export of biotech developed in the cities. Many of Scab's soft-machine augments were derived from Living City technology. There were rumours that the Living Cities' wealth came, in part, from illegal technology derived from their use of banned Seeder tech.

They had been extensively disarmed, much to Scab's disapproval. There had been no chance to bid for weapons, just a blanket refusal, and it was made clear that any attempt to bring virals into the city would result in immediate death. Scab had undergone a complete blood transfusion with less than good grace. He had even cleaned under his fingernails, removing all the neurotoxins. During the docking and decontamination procedures, Scab had his cigarettes and old-school syringes of opiates removed.

They had also had to shut down their external 'face links. Any communication was going to have to be done the old-fashioned way. Their nano-screens had to be extensively reprogrammed and internalised. In short, they both felt naked, though Vic was just enjoying being in the city. The warm wind blowing through the artery somehow reminded him of a human womb immersion he had once done. It had left him wondering why the little hairless monkeys ever left.

P-sats had obviously not been allowed. Instead they were being guided to a meeting place by one of the inhabitants of the city. They all looked the same. Neutral-gendered, Vic believed they were actually grown from the city. It was nominally human, as most of the inhabitants of the Monarchist systems were, and naked, which made sense. Vic was starting to find something artistic and aesthetically pleasing about the translucent skin, the internal organs on display and the glowing violet-coloured blood that provided them with their own bioluminescence. Looking around through the arteries and the flesh of the massive city, he could see them moving around doing various tasks. It made Vic think of the nanites that suffused his own body. Scab, presumably still grumpy at being disarmed, had wondered out loud why people would want to turn themselves into glowing bowel parasites.

The helical artery brought them to the highest level of the city. Vic looked down on it. From the top the city looked like a roughly circular plain. It was constantly moving, constantly rippling. The chamber they had arrived at was the first bit of opaque flesh they had come across. The sphincter-like door opened with a distinctly organic sucking noise. Vic and Scab followed their guide through.

The boardroom table looked as if it was made from sculpted tooth enamel. The chairs had been grown from the floor and were covered in a moss-like substance.

There were two other people in the room. One of them seemed to be clothed in black glass, and was leaning against the transparent flesh of what passed for a window in the outer wall. The other was the hairless tattooed Monk from the *St Brendan's Fire*. She was lounging on one of the chairs, feet up on the bone-white table.

The guide moved to one side, pushing himself against the flesh wall of the room. Scab was already moving towards the Monk. It looked like she was trying to say something.

Scab was in the air over the table. The Monk just leaned back and used one hand to flip off the chair and onto her feet. Vic sighed internally. He couldn't be bothered.

A series of short fast strikes with clawed hands opened up a cut on her porcelain skin. Normally, neurotoxins on his filed and hardened nails would be enough to slow the Monk down and give Scab the edge, but they had been removed.

Scab stepped to the side to avoid a powerful front kick. He turned the sidestep into a sweep, which the Monk leaped over. In mid-air she straightened her leg and caught Scab a solid blow in the face, sending him staggering back across the living boardroom.

She's good, Vic thought. Then he decided to look at the figure in black glass again.

'Oh shit,' Vic muttered as Scab and the Monk danced their violent dance. The figure in black glass was an Elite. Vic didn't think it was Fallen Angel but he couldn't be sure; with the exception of Ludwig they all kind of looked the same to him.

The Monk had closed with Scab, swinging at him with a series of vicious hooks. Scab threw himself back towards the floor. Landing with his weight on one hand, he kicked from the ground, catching the Monk on the side of the head with the toe of his spats. She staggered back but recovered quickly. Scab tried to hook his leg around her neck, but she moved with it and did a one-handed cartwheel out of the lock, landing crouched to face him.

Vic was caught between watching the Elite, who Scab would have also noticed but was ignoring in favour of violence that had a better chance of success, and the ongoing fight. The Monk was genuinely skilled rather than having augmented fighting abilities. She was experienced as well. Vic assumed she had the best soft-machine augments that debt, or in the Church's case actual credit, could possibly buy. He was able to read where and what she was going to do because she was a very efficient and skilled fighter. Scab, on the other hand, fought chaotically. The Monk had to deal with Scab moving to where he shouldn't, doing moves he shouldn't and fighting with a ferocity she couldn't match. He had a genuine desire to hurt his opponent.

Scab closed in and locked the Monk's arm. Grinning with savage joy, Scab kneed the Monk in the head and then repeatedly struck her in the face with his fingers. He was trying to push his filed-down fingernails through her armoured skull.

It was all over now. Scab's fingers had found her eyes. Any moment now membranes would pop and he would force the fingers into her brain, and his reputation would increase as he added a dead monk to his list of kills.

Then the Monk lost her temper. It was like a berserk rage without the augments, Vic thought. She lost an eye tearing his finger out. She headbutted Scab hard enough to break the reinforced cartilage of his nose. Then she somersaulted out of the lock. The sound of her arm spiral fracturing and dislocating simultaneously was loud enough to make Vic flinch. She screamed in pain, landed and kicked Scab in the chest.

Scab flew back across the room. The Monk leaped after him. Scab hit the wall. The Monk kicked him in the head. His skull cracked under the force of the blow. A look of fury on her face, the Monk repeatedly kicked him in the head, pulping his face and skull as he slid down the wall.

Vic was hoping this was freedom at last, but somehow Scab managed to leg-sweep her from the ground while she was too intent on turning his head to pulped meat. The Monk hit the floor and Scab axe-kicked her in the head.

'Stop this or I will destroy them both,' the guide said quietly to Vic. He only picked it up because his aural augments were able to filter out the sound of the fight.

'What? If you've got some skills as well, then jump in, have some fun,' Vic told the guide.

'I will simply ask the city to flex. Everyone in the room will be crushed.'

Vic sighed. A power-assisted leap carried him easily over the table. The tall 'sect landed softly behind his partner. Scab currently had the upper hand and was standing on one of the Monk's legs, fending off kicks from the other while trying to break her knee by punching it. He was aware of Vic behind him but had assumed that his partner had come to help.

There were a number of ways Vic could have handled trying to break up the fight, but he was feeling reckless. He grabbed Scab by the shoulders of his raincoat with his upper two arms and then flung Scab backwards.

Scab flew across the boardroom again and hit the wall. Behind Vic the Monk skipped to her feet. One of her arms hung limp at her side but she assumed a defensive stance. Scab was straight back onto his feet. Even through the pulped meat of his face, Scab's rage was plain to see. Vic actually staggered back a few steps. *This is it*, he thought, but he made himself big, stretching to his full height, all four arms outstretched.

'Are you out of your fucking mind!' Scab screamed. Vic had never seen him lose control like this.

'They'll kill us all if you don't stop,' Vic said. He couldn't quite keep the tremor out of his voice. His pheromone excretions told the rest of the story about how frightened he was.

Scab's face was contorting and he was gasping for air as he tried to control himself. The humourless and very familiar laughter wasn't helping matters, Vic decided. Both he and Scab turned to look at the Elite. What they saw were warped reflections of themselves in the glass armour.

'Something funny?' Scab asked in a tone that suggested to Vic more impending violence. *Good. You just kill yourself attacking an Elite, then Known Space will be fucking rid of you and I can enjoy the sights of the Living Cities while waiting for a bounty crew to catch up with me.*

'It's like watching a bad actor try to play you in a low-budget immersion.'

The black armour became liquid and was sucked into the Elite's skin. He was an Elite version of Scab. He looked healthier, less gaunt. He was wearing a skin-tight, long-sleeved black top and black trousers, and his lips were stained black. The thing that unnerved Vic most about Elite Scab was that his eyes looked alive, but there was a malignancy in their life, a hatred and a madness. Vic wondered if Elite Scab had had the same neurosurgery to remove some of his more unpleasant predilections as his partner. He wasn't optimistic about the chances of that.

'Bollocks,' the Monk said. It seemed to be a pre-Loss word for testicles, according to Vic's neunonics. He couldn't imagine why she'd choose to bring that up now. She was, however, looking nervously between Scab and Elite Scab.

'Could I arrange refreshments for everyone?' the guide asked, his tone neutral.

'As soon as we have killed the copy. I have no need to subject myself to the insult of his further existence,' Elite Scab said. Vic almost thanked him for his help in resolving the situation peacefully.

'I thought you were the original,' Vic said carefully. He knew he was taking his life in his hands and half-expected a thorough killing from Scab.

'I am,' Scab answered. There was something of the cornered animal about him at the moment, Vic thought. Scab clearly wanted to kill everyone in the room, but unusually for him – as Scab was prepared to pick fights with entire habitats – found himself horribly outgunned.

'You're little more than a biological machine. You were programmed to think what we wanted you to think. You're a pale imitation, nothing more. If this wasn't the case you'd still be able to make art,' Elite Scab told Scab.

'Art?' the Monk asked incredulously.

'Kill people in creative ways,' Vic told her. She looked unimpressed.

'You know what you are, messenger boy?' Scab asked once he'd managed to stop shaking with rage. 'Motivation, nothing more.' Vic couldn't read Elite Scab at all. He also didn't understand what Scab was saying. He was missing part of the conversation. He was also sure that Elite Scab would have to be one of the Consortium Elite, and if he and Scab were about covert Consortium business then he didn't understand why Elite Scab would be allowed to kill Scab or even what he was doing here in Monarchist space, the Living Cities' enmity with the Game notwithstanding.

Elite Scab turned to the guide, who was speaking.

'Since you all arrived here at the same time, we thought you might all benefit from a conversation. We can only assume that you will all have plenty of opportunities to kill each other once you are far away from Pangea, but for now there will be no more killing.'

Elite Scab nodded as if he was taking this in, but Vic recognised the signs that he was preparing to do something awful – he'd seen similar behaviour in his own Scab. There was little they could do. It was pointless attacking an Elite at the best of times, let alone unarmed. He respected the guide for standing up to Elite Scab, but it had seemed foolish to let him into the city in the first place.

'Look, can everyone called Woodbine Scab, clone or not, please just be reasonable for a moment,' Vic ventured.

Elite Scab looked a little bit exasperated at this, as he reached out and touched the wall of the Living City. It had taken years of research and untold amounts of debt relief to develop the Seeder-tech-derived programmable virus that coated Elite Scab's hand, but he still made its application look casual.

The guide screamed. The City shook, convulsed; there was a palpable feeling of pain and distress that even Vic picked up on. Through the transparent flesh they saw a helical artery crushed by a convulsion of muscle, the people in it reduced to squirts of luminescent flesh and blood. The guide sank to his knees in pain. The Monk moved around the table to help him to his feet despite her ruined arm.

'Apparently not,' Vic said.

'Mr Scab,' the guide, who Vic was beginning to think was a bit more than just a guide, said to Elite Scab as the Monk helped him to a seat, 'we of course respect your power, and you could cause us great harm, perhaps even destroy this city, but we would live on. What I don't think you could do is destroy this city before we kill you. I wonder if you have ever been this close to destruction before?'

'You think I care? I've razed planets, I've been worshipped as a god. I'm bored and I could kill my copy with a thought.'

'I'm not the copy,' Scab said quietly, dangerously.

'I don't think that harming us or killing your copy was what you were instructed to do,' the guide said to Elite Scab evenly. 'Though I confess I'm not sure of the purpose of your presence here.'

Vic could see his Scab bridle at this. There it was, the problem with

270

being a killer god: you had to do someone else's bidding. It was hard-wired into the Elite. It had to be or they would rule Known Space or simply run amok to see if they could grow bored with the killing. Elite Scab's features were still unreadable, but Vic guessed he didn't like being reminded that he was a servant either.

'You are both an unreasonable pair of fucktards!' Vic was surprised to find himself shouting. He was less than pleased to find that his involuntary outburst now had the attention of two of the most dangerous professional arseholes in Known Space. 'I mean really! I know we're all well armed and Known Space is a dangerous place, but there are other fucking means of conflict resolution where mutually assured destruction isn't a fucking certainty! I mean, what? Will your heads explode if we have a conversation, or will you find yourself unable to sustain an erection for the next five fucking years because an hour went by and you didn't manage to kill something?! I mean really! Grow! The! Fuck! Up!' Vic finally managed to get control of himself and waited for the inevitable killing.

'I'd clap if I had use of both arms,' said the Monk, who Vic was beginning to like and think of in relation to his egg-fertilising wand.

'We want the bridge tech,' Elite Scab said.

'Who wouldn't?' the guide said. 'But we do not have it.'

'That's not going to happen,' the Monk said.

'We would be prepared to offer Pangea membership in the Consortium, a senior seat on the board.'

'We are not interested,' the guide said. 'And we have not acquired bridge technology since you last mentioned it a moment ago.'

This is weird, Vic thought. It was as if the Consortium was showing its hand. They had sent an Elite out with little to negotiate with. It was almost as if the Elite had been sent here to be humiliated.

'You realise that if Pangea gains unrestricted access to bridge tech then there will have to be a military response from the Consortium systems.'

'Well yes, and we still don't have access to it.'

'Don't you get tired of being prisoners of the Church?' Elite Scab asked.

'You are asking the wrong people. We have all we need here.'

'Until you've sucked this world dry.'

The guide said nothing.

'You're the Elder, aren't you?' Vic asked the translucent glowing man. He smiled.

'The essence of the Lord of Pangea is contained within the cities and we are all linked. We are one.'

'So everyone on Pangea is aware of this conversation?' Scab and Elite Scab asked at the same time. The Elder nodded. Both looked less than pleased.

'Fucking amateurs,' Elite Scab muttered.

'You're thinking of it in terms of millions of individuals knowing your secrets, but we are as one and can be discreet when we choose. Now, you have delivered your message, though I'm not sure what it was. Please leave.'

Elite Scab's features were unreadable as he walked to the wall, Scab following every move. Elite Scab started to vibrate – it looked like he went out of phase – and then he just pushed through the wall and out into the freezing skies of Pangea. The Elder cried out again, and the room seemed to flinch. Elite Scab was hovering outside the transparent flesh. He turned to look at them, then the exotic matter of his armour leaked through his skin like oil. The black glass material formed into its coffin-like configuration and he disappeared into the sky.

'Well, he seemed nice,' Vic muttered. When he looked up he found Scab looking at him. Both were then distracted by a cracking noise and a shout of pain. They turned to the Monk, who had just put her arm back into place. It looked like it was starting to heal. Scab's face was returning to its normal dimensions as well, though it was still covered in drying blood.

'I'm a little confused as to who you're working for,' the Elder said to Scab. 'Because if you're not working for Consortium interests ...'

'Then you would be the next most likely client,' the Monk said as she sat down, grimacing slightly.

'Though there are competing interests in the Consortium,' the Elder said.

'Not for something like this,' Scab pointed out.

'Do you have a name?' Vic asked the Monk, feeling slightly smitten.

'Yes. Who doesn't?' she answered irritably.

'What are you doing?' Scab asked her.

'What does it look like?' There was pain written across her face, presumably from the healing process. 'I've worked quite hard to get to the point where I can have a reasonable conversation with you.'

'How did you find us? I put a week-long block on the information we got from Pythia.'

'I guessed,' the Monk said.

'You're lying,' Scab said with certainty.

'Well, let me just explain to you all the secrets of my trade,' she offered sarcastically.

'We have business to discuss with the Elder here. We can't do it with you here. Either leave or ...'

'What?' Vic asked. 'Get scolded by petulant psychopaths? The Living Cities have made it clear that not even Elite arseholes, no offence, are getting to push people around.'

'Mr Matto is right. It seems to require a great deal of effort and indeed the death of some of our people just to get you to have a reasonable discussion.'

'There's nothing to discuss, surely?' Scab said irritably, wishing that he could smoke. 'We want whatever is in the cocoon because it could break the Church's monopoly on bridge travel, and they want to stop us from doing that.'

'Actually, we want to help you steal it,' the Monk said. She was smiling. The Elder let out a sigh.

'You're very pretty,' Vic said. 'How do you feel about 'sects?'

'Sex?'

''Sects, insects. Cross-species copulation?'

'Why?' Scab asked.

'Because the Absolute having access to the cocoon is as abhorrent to us as it is to you. So once we've stolen it, *then* we can start screwing each other over to see who ends up with it.'

'Bit of a risk for you?' Scab said, but Vic could tell he was warming to the plan. There was even the trace of a smile in the slightly upturned corner of his mouth, though Vic had to magnify his optics to see that.

'Less of a risk than the Absolute having it. Besides, you're over-confident to the point of having a god complex; I don't see any huge problem in screwing you over.'

Now Scab was smiling.

'Back off, Scab. I saw her first,' Vic said, much to everyone's confusion, before turning to the Monk. 'You're very pretty. We should totally have sex.'

'And with reasonable conversation comes romance,' the Elder said.

'I've never had sex with an insect before. I wouldn't even know where to begin,' the Monk said, sounding a little surprised. She turned back to Scab. 'Unless you want to be reasonable. We'll pay you twice what your current employer is. You might even end up in credit.'

'The money's abstract now.'

'Let's not be too hasty,' Vic said. 'And it's okay. I have immersions which would help explain,' he said to the Monk.

'Explain what?' the Monk asked, confused.

'Sex with insects.' Vic was a little hurt that she didn't seem to be paying attention.

'Well, romance of a sort,' the Elder observed.

'Why didn't you open with that?' Scab asked.

'Offers of insect sex?' the Monk asked, more confused

'I would be up for that,' Vic said. The Monk glanced at him distractedly.

'The offer to work together and then I kill you and take what I want anyway,' Scab said, explaining the deal from his perspective.

'Like she had time!' Vic cried, trying to appear gallant in front of his new interest. 'Every time she, or the other guy, the one on Arclight, tried to talk to you, you responded with attempted and actual murder!'

'So you're not interested in the money then?' the Monk asked Scab.

'You can't pay me what I've been offered,' Scab said.

The Monk studied him. 'I believe you. On Arclight we had hoped that familiarity and a biological link would be enough to open negotiations with you.'

'What are you talking about?' Vic asked suspiciously. 'Scab, what's she talking about?' But Scab ignored the question and just stared at the Monk. She seemed surprised.

'Did he not tell you that it was his son he killed in the Polyhedron?' the Monk asked Vic.

Vic turned to stare at Scab, whose face was impassive underneath the crust of dried blood.

'Did you not even upload my file?' Scab asked.

'We had hoped that murdering your offspring was as much a phase as propagating them had been in the first place.'

'When did you kill your children?' Vic asked.

'Be quiet, Vic.' Then to the Monk: 'Stop cloning him, destroy the genetic material and his personality and memory uploads.'

'Is that a condition of your cooperation?'

'Was that when you killed me the last time and the ship got damaged?!' Vic demanded.

'Shut up, Vic. And yes, it is a condition of my cooperation.'

The Monk gave this some consideration.

'Agreed,' she finally said, somewhat reluctantly. Scab studied her for a while.

'You're good. The only reason I know you're lying is because you agreed too quickly to kill a member of the Church. But there were no tells whatsoever.'

The Monk looked less than pleased. She shifted in her seat and leaned towards Scab.

'I think you underestimate the importance of this.'

'Your monopoly. I think we understand the motivations of power and greed in the Seeder Church,' the Elder said. Vic was fascinated by the display of bioelectric energy that played through his internal organs as he said this. The Monk said nothing but Vic noticed that she swallowed.

'What?' Scab said suspiciously. Apparently he had noticed it as well. 'You don't feel it's about that?'

The Monk shook her head, a degree of defiance in the set of her mouth.

'You actually believe the shit you peddle?' Scab asked.

'Did you when you were the leader of a heretical street sect on Cyst?' she asked – somewhat combatively, Vic thought.

'What are you bringing to the table?' Scab asked her, changing the subject.

Instead of answering, the Monk turned to the Elder.

'We have access to the biotechnology and enough intelligence as well as experience from the Art Wars to enable you to infiltrate the Game and hopefully get you close to the cocoon you're after,' the Elder told them

'What's in this for you?' Scab asked.

'The Absolute, despite his power, is a very immature lord. He is playing games of control and empire that many of us have left behind. He has too much influence over what you call the Monarchist systems as it is. With his control of the Elite, access to bridge technology would give him the power to remake the entirety of the Monarchist systems in his image. He wants it all because he will never realise that it won't make him happy.'

'The Absolute's a man then?' the Monk asked. 'I find myself unsurprised.'

The Elder actually laughed at this. 'You've no idea how much of a male he is.'

'Are you sure you don't just want to fuck him over for your humiliating defeat in the Art Wars?' Scab asked.

'Would it make any difference to you if it was?'

'No, but I respect honesty.'

'This has considerably more to do with self-preservation.'

Scab nodded and turned back to the Monk.

'So why do we need to take the risk of working with people who don't have our best interests at heart?'

'Because they can get you in –' the Monk pointed at the Elder '– but only I can get you out.'

The plan was suicidal, Vic thought as he inspected a food bladder and watched a bioelectric charge arc from one organ, designed to store harnessed energy, to another. Despite sometimes making him feel like he was being digested, Vic loved the Living City. The Elder, who was basically just an avatar representation of the city, had given him the freedom to roam around and look at the biotechnological wonder. He was standing on an artery that curved underneath the roughly saucer-shaped domed city. Far below he saw the windswept and scarred rock of the planet's surface, the skirt of tendrils trailing towards it.

Vic reviewed the information he'd bid for from Pythia. He would have to erase it and trust to the remaining meat in his head to remember it. If he didn't then Scab would find it the next time he neurally audited him. It would be enough for Scab to cause Vic pain but not enough to kill him.

Jide and his crew had been on Pythia to buy information on a completely separate case. To Pythia's knowledge there was no bounty being offered for Scab and Vic, despite what Scab had done on Arclight. Scab had found who the most dangerous crew in the area were and had picked a fight with them to make an example. He had then paid bribes to manipulate the media so it looked like Jide had come after them.

Arguably the example could have been made without destroying Jide and his crew's chance at being cloned. Vic guessed that Scab had decided that it wouldn't be enough. He wanted other crews to know that if they came after him it was permanent death. He didn't want any distractions on this job.

It was too much for Vic though. Even if they got the cocoon, he still had no idea what it was about or how it connected to bridge technology. They also had the three most powerful organisations in Known Space about to squash them like bugs. They would probably let them experience the cutting edge of prolonged torture immersions first.

All of this contributed to Vic's decision. He felt that it was the only rational thing to do, though he giggled a little, his mandibles clattered together and he got a little aroused when he thought about it.

He was going to kill Scab.

The Elite was a photographic negative, a human-shaped shadow after a nuclear explosion in the all-encompassing light.

'Well?' the man behind the desk asked.

'I delivered your message,' the Elite said somewhat belligerently. 'Though I don't think I understood it.'

The man behind the desk just smiled.

20

Southern Britain, a Long Time Ago

She felt his weight on her. His skin on her flesh was hot, almost feverish. The tang of copper in his mouth, he tasted like the air just before a spring storm. Her fingers traced down his skin. She saw the dark pools of his somehow sad eyes before he entered her and she closed her eyes, back arching as she cried out. Strong fingers against her skin, his arms wrapped around her as she opened herself to him.

But there was something else in the room, something just out of sight, little more than a shadow that whispered to her. Promised her this and so much more, if only she'd give in.

Britha sat up straight, flushed, hot, covered in sweat and gasping for breath. She had wrapped her robes around herself to go to sleep as she always did, but they were in disarray now. The intensity of the dream had shocked her. An intense heat burned through her body.

'Britha?' Her head shot round to stare at the deformed man. She narrowed her eyes. She could see perfectly even in the depths of the night. Something had changed in Teardrop's eye: there was something in it now, a tiny glint of silver. 'Bad dream?'

Anything but, she thought. That was the problem.

There was a dry chuckle from the other side of Teardrop where Fachtna lay wrapped in his cloak.

'It didn't sound like a bad dream,' Fachtna said.

'That's what pleasure sounds like, boy. You're unlikely to ever hear it as the result of anything you do,' Britha spat.

The deck of the ship moved with the gentle lapping of the waves. They were anchored off a sandy beach below towering cliffs that should have been little more than shadows in this light, but she could make out every detail of them clearly.

'Perhaps if you had the real thing, you wouldn't need dreams to make you sigh?' Fachtna suggested.

The sound of the waves against the wood of the ship was drowned out by the prayers of the god-slaves that had come aboard with them at the harbour beneath the Goddodin hill fort.

Their presence discomfited her. The ship was a strange place, peopled by stranger people. More than ever she was becoming aware of how small her world had been. It had been one thing to deal with traders not unlike these on her own terms, in her own territory; it was quite another to be thrown in among them. On the one hand she recognised them as folk like any other – they breathed, ate, drank, shat, fucked and had the same needs and wants; on the other hand she found so little similarity between how they acted and how her own people behaved that she struggled to find any common ground. Even Teardrop seemed less bizarre than the Carthaginians. All of this, along with her new capabilities, hungers, feelings and the dreams that haunted her sleep, left Britha wondering if she hadn't somehow walked into the Otherworld.

It was obvious the experience was strange to Fachtna and Teardrop as well, but if they didn't have any more experience of life aboard a Carthaginian ship then they certainly seemed to have more knowledge. Both of the visitors from the Otherworld seemed to be enjoying the experience regardless of how strange it was for them.

Britha was annoyed by the presence of the god-slaves on board. She was sure they hadn't paid as much as Fachtna had for their passage. She also thought Hanno had since had cause to regret the deal as all they did was pray. It seemed they required little sleep. Their prayers sounded like nonsense even with her new-found understanding of languages. Teardrop said that they tried to talk in a tongue that their mouths were not made for. What she did understand sounded like appeals for secrets or knowledge or madness or death, perhaps all at the same time.

They had exhorted the crew to join in their worship but the sailors thought them all northern madmen, believing that the cold air had driven them insane. This was a belief held particularly strongly by Germelqart, the quiet navigator. A life at sea meant that he understood bits of many languages, but Britha only ever heard him speak the language of Carthage, which she now found herself able to understand. When he spoke it was tersely, his voice carrying to give orders to the two banks of thirty rowers. The rowers were all free men with massive upper bodies, from all over the known southern world. The colour of their skin went from light brown to almost black like Kush. Hanno said that free men cost just as much to feed but were more likely to outrun pirates if they had a share of the cargo.

Germelqart had made it clear that he felt the god-slaves were a curse, that he felt it was madness to invite onto the boat those who wished only destruction for themselves. Britha agreed with the navigator, whose magic was to direct them from one place to the next even though the next was far and out of sight. It was strong magic that to Britha's mind required a great deal of skill, Hanno's sacrifices to their god, Dagon, notwithstanding. Britha knew that the god-slaves' prayers to their Dark Man in the south would interfere with Germelquart's own workings.

Even if they hadn't seen what they had seen as they left the harbour, she still would not have wished to travel with them. Her last glimpse of the field of the dead haunted her. She could see them dressed in white or naked, swaying backwards and forwards like barley in the wind, while one of their number, once a warrior judging by his size, walked among them cutting throats. Harvesting them. Leaving them slumped together, their life's blood turning the sea red at the edge of the shore. She could not conceive of why, harsh as it was, people would not want to cling to life for all they were worth, as beyond this life they were at the mercy of gods who only cared for themselves.

They had been at sea for weeks now, hugging the coast. They had seen river mouths and massive inlets. Britha thought they had been travelling for so long that they must have reached another land, but Hanno, laughing, had assured her that it was still the same island that she had grown up on.

They had passed cliffs. On some of them they had seen beacon fires burning, warning of their passing. On others they had seen henges, some of stone, more of wood. There had been other wooden henges, half submerged, on some of the beaches they had passed.

Much of the land was heavily wooded, a lot of it very flat and nearly always marshy near inlets or the mouths of rivers that rivalled the size of the Tatha or the Black River. What few villages they passed were either abandoned or destroyed. The black curraghs were so far ahead of them now that the remains were not even still smouldering.

All but the most inaccessible of the clifftop forts had suffered the same fate. They had either been abandoned by their shrewd, if cowardly – in Britha and Fachtna's eyes – defenders, or they too had been destroyed, their walls pulled down, presumably by the giants.

At the larger settlements Hanno, Kush and some of the oarsmen went ashore for supplies and goods to trade back in their homeland. Britha was not happy with this and had told Hanno that this was not a good way to behave. Hanno had told her that had the people been there they would have traded, but they were not and he would be ruined if he returned with nothing to show for his voyage. Not to mention they needed supplies if they wanted to eat. He scoffed at the idea of leaving goods as payment. Sometimes Fachtna would go with them. Not to loot but to get a feel for the land.

They saw people very occasionally. Here and there they would see a warrior on horseback. The southrons were a tall, well-made people with no beards to speak of, but their dark hair was long, as were their moustaches, which they braided. Their mail and weapons looked fine from a distance, and their horses were much larger than the ponies they used in the north. Britha understood that their appearances were a futile show of force. These were chiefs, princes and champions who had come too late to save their people from Bress's depredations. It looked like a rich land but in the wake of the black curraghs the land seemed almost dead, populated mainly by ghosts.

At other times Britha had the sense that there were people keeping pace with the Carthaginian ship beyond a coastal treeline or hidden in the marshes. They were most likely a warband shadowing them in case they were raiders. She was sure that Teardrop sensed this too.

Fachtna was restless. It was all happening too slowly for him. He wanted, needed, to confront Bress. Britha wondered how much of that was fear of Bress and wanting to get it over and done with. He spent most of the time standing by the prow of the ship, getting soaked as the ram prow ploughed through wave after wave as sail and oar carried them south. Whenever he had the chance, he went ashore. Britha was sure that the nonsense of the god-slaves bothered him as well.

Britha had thought Teardrop ill. He had seemed in pain. She had seen him mouthing words in what she thought were the clipped syllables of his own language. At first, with disdain, she had thought him praying in a servile manner to his gods – it looked a little too much like begging. Then she had started to get the feeling that he was talking to someone that she couldn't see. This disconcerting feeling grew.

Fachtna had told her that pain was the price of Teardrop's power. This she could believe: it looked like the strange man was being tormented. Teardrop became colder, more distant, as if he was resigned to something. She was not sure if she was imagining things, but it looked to her like the veins in his head were bulging more. More than once she had thought something was moving under his skin. The flecks of silver in his eyes were not of her imagining. When she focused she saw that each one looked like a tiny shard of frozen quicksilver. The god-slaves were the least of Teardrop's worries.

The ship was eighty feet long by ten feet wide. They slept on deck with those rowers who did not sleep below, all of them crushed to-gether, sweating, farting and, in the god-slaves' case, puking when the wave sickness was upon them. The wave sickness did not bother Britha, Teardrop or Fachtna.

'Is it getting stronger the closer we get?' Teardrop asked with urgency in his voice. Meaning her dream. It was, but she neither wished to admit that to Teardrop nor think about what it meant. She was frightened by the intensity of her experience, embarrassed that it had been so public, tired of being in the cramped stinking confines of the ship and thoroughly sick of listening to meaningless jabbering and incessant praying.

'Enough,' she said quietly to herself. She got to her feet, not even bothering to adjust her robe, grabbed her sickle and made her way over the sea of sleeping and half-awake rowers towards where the god-slaves were kneeling by the stern of the ship.

'Britha!' Teardrop hissed, but she ignored him.

'Don't want your life?' she demanded. The god-slaves turned at the sound of her voice. She was no longer sure what language she was talking but they seemed to understand it. 'Fine. I'll have it.'

She started the words of the chant in the language of the Pecht, the language of her people. She saw the battle on the beach, the ruins of Ardestie, the destroyed broch empty, her people gone. Her people had fought until Bress's magics, the demon magics – she had to not forget that – had enslaved them. The warriors fought, the landspeople fought, the old folk would have fought, the children would have fought, and here were people, victims of the Lochlannach like her people had been, and they wanted to embrace it.

The words of the working were not familiar to her. They were old and cold, taught to her a long time ago in veiled whispers by the black-robed sacrificers. Dark magics, every bit as dark as the consumption of the flesh of your enemies to know their secrets.

She grabbed the first one by the hair. He did not resist. Her pleas-ure at the hot salt splash of blood on her face was a pale echo of what she felt when she made love to Bress and the Dark Man whispered to her. She kicked the corpse over the side of the boat. She had taken what she needed from it with powerful words. Let Dagon consume the flesh now, or the cowardly gods of the Goddodin. Carrion gods.

Fachtna was sitting up now. His face neutral, he translated what she was saying so the crew could understand who she was, what she was. Someone had run screaming for Hanno. He came on deck, pull-ing his *blaidth* on. Kush was next to him, naked but for a loincloth, carrying his bronze axe. The rowers were scrabbling away from Britha now. Hanno and Kush exchanged a look and Kush started forward. Fachtna stood up, still translating Britha's words as another god-slave died with no cry of pain, nor had she begged for her life. Britha used her sickle to paint the planks of the ship with the god-slave's blood. It ran into the gaps and dripped into the hold below.

Fachtna stood between Kush and Britha. He was leaning on his sword, which was still in its scabbard, but his message, as he continued with the translation, was clear. There was not a moment of hesitation from the tall axeman, who stepped forward, but Hanno placed a hand on Kush's shoulder and nodded towards Germelqart. The navigator was shaking his head.

Teardrop was on his feet, but Fachtna put a hand on his shoulder and shook his head. Teardrop, not long ago, would have stopped her, would have ignored Fachtna. He watched another of the god-slaves die and get kicked overboard. Then he knew he was just as culpable as Fachtna, as Britha. He found he didn't care about their lives.

Britha cared about their lives because she wanted them. She wanted what was left of their lives. She wanted what would have been. She would take their weak and meagre spirits. She would deny the Dark Man even the paltry strength of their weakness. She only hoped that by saying the words that stole their spirits, she would not taint herself with their weakness.

It was only after she had sawn through the final god-slave's throat, only after her robe was soaked with their blood, only after her skin was hot and red, that she realised how grateful each of them had looked.

She turned around to face the rest of the ship. The rowers cowered away from her even as blood trickled towards them. Hanno stared at her with horror, Kush with distaste, and Teardrop's expression was cold. Fachtna had an unpleasant-looking half-smile on his face, and the navigator, Germelqart, looked at her with approval and nodded his thanks.

Britha sat down on one of the benches with her back against the rail and hugged her legs. She could ignore the corpses in the dark water behind her but she still knew they were there. Britha did not sleep again that night, but that meant that she did not dream again either. When morning came, it brought raucous gulls to feed on the flesh of the floating dead behind them, the sun to dry the blood on wool and skin, and wind to carry them further south.

'This is not a good place to be,' Germelqart said. They had gone into the mouth of a river. It was not as large as the Tatha or the Black

River but it had looked a reasonable size. Hanno had said that he knew the river and that the people there called it the Tamesas, meaning Grey Father, who was apparently the god of the river.

Either side was marshland. Britha could not understand how people lived here, but apparently they did or had. They knew this because they could see smoke rising from what used to be their villages.

'This makes no sense to me,' Hanno said. 'These people were careful, clever people. They built their villages on mounds of dry earth in the marshes, and only those who had a guide who knew the secret ways could take you there.'

'They would have made one of the guides drink from their chalice,' Britha said. She still wore the blood of her victims. Flies from the marshes buzzed around her. The *Will of Dagon* was hidden from the main waterway of the Tamesas between a sparsely wooded island and the swampy mainland.

'It would be easy to get trapped here,' Germelqart said. Kush nodded in agreement.

'You are a timid people,' Fachtna observed dryly. Teardrop did not even admonish him for baiting the Carthaginians; he was staring to the north into the marsh at the rising smoke.

'This happened recently, I think,' Kush said. Hanno nodded. Britha stared west. Following the snaking line of the river they could see more columns of smoke. It was definitely the work of Bress.

'I think now we sail east to the land of the Gaul,' Hanno started. 'Then we hug the coast and head south regardless of how stormy it is. Their god Taranis hates and fears me, I think.' There was a snort of derision from Fachtna. 'Through the pillars of Hercules and back to my beloved Carthage.'

Germelqart nodded his agreement.

'No,' Britha said. 'They are not on the river any more.' She was certain of this. She had been feeling much stronger since she had taken the lives of the kneelers.

'And the Grey Father told you this himself, did he?' Hanno asked. His tone was derisive, but she smiled when she heard the fear there as well. They thought her a moonstruck witch now. It was a part she could play. It might even have been true.

'We go south,' she insisted. Hanno opened his mouth to protest.

'We're being watched,' Teardrop said.

'Frightened survivors,' Kush said.

Teardrop pointed into the swamp. 'And there's something in there ... power of some sort. It hides from me every time I reach for it.'

284

Fachtna turned to look at his friend with interest.

'Madmen, demons and witches.' Hanno spat over the side of the ship and touched an amulet that he had taken to wearing. It was a tiny effigy of Dagon carved from driftwood.

'If Teardrop says he feels something then he feels something,' Fachtna told them. Britha had turned to look at the man who claimed to be from a tribe called the Croatan.

'What is it?' she asked.

Teardrop shook his head as if concentrating. 'Something ancient and slippery, it coils away from me every time I reach for it.' He turned to look at Britha, then seemed surprised as if he was only now seeing her covered in drying blood. 'I think we should go ashore.'

'Yes, go ashore, die in the swamp and we can sail away before the black ships find us,' Hanno said.

'Hanno of Carthage,' Britha said, 'I don't think your god lives here. You leave us, and the corpses of those I slew will climb onto your deck as you sleep and slay you and your men. Do you understand me?'

Hanno looked furious. Kush looked close to swinging his axe. It didn't matter what either of them believed. Britha wasn't sure if she had the power to make good her threat, but enough of the crew believed her that they wouldn't let Hanno abandon them.

'Enough threats,' Kush told her. 'I mean it.'

Fachtna opened his mouth to say something but Britha cut him off.

'You were well paid, trader; all we ask is that you honour it.'

'I should have asked for more,' Hanno muttered, eyeing the torcs around Fachtna's neck and his left arm. 'You make this quick. If you have not returned by tomorrow morning then we will leave you because the evil spirits that burn the night with their demon fire will have taken you. This is known by the people who live in this evil place.'

Britha nodded.

'And we will flee the black ships if we sight them,' the normally quiet Germelqart said.

Fachtna opened his mouth. 'Agreed,' Britha said before the warrior uttered something insulting. 'You cannot fight them.'

'I only hope you can outrun them,' Fachtna said. 'But I doubt it.'

Trial and error left them soaked and covered with thick foul-smelling mud, but eventually they managed to find a trail over what passed for dry ground. Or at least ground that didn't want to pull them down into sucking mud.

'So we just walk into the swamp and hope we find someone?' Fachtna demanded angrily.

He's like most warriors, Britha thought. He liked being covered in blood, glory or fine things, but not mud.

'They know we are here,' Britha said. She could feel the eyes on her. The birds, the insects, reptiles and amphibians moving through the water or over the mud, the constant movement of the under-growth; it was easy to imagine the whole place as a living being.

'She's right,' Teardrop said. 'I can hear the mindsong here. But it is distant, far away somehow.' This got Fachtna's attention, Britha's too, but she chose not to show it, hoping that Teardrop would reveal more of his magics if she showed less interest.

'Why don't they show themselves?!' Fachtna cried to the skies. Nearby gulls took to the air, showing their displeasure in raucous squawking. Britha watched them and then moved off the trail and into the rushes. Almost immediately she was standing in water, though the spirits in the mud hadn't started dragging her down yet. Using the butt of her spear for support, she made her way to where the gulls had been.

Fachtna sighed, looked down in disgust at the mud coating his boots, greaves and trews, but followed her. Teardrop remained on the path, looking out over the rushes blowing in the gentle breeze. Perhaps he was listening for the mindsong, Fachtna thought, but more likely he just didn't want to get further covered in mud. Cursing, Fachtna pushed through the rushes until he found Britha leaning against an earthen bank, standing in a red pool of bodies.

'They died in battle,' he said. The pictures that swords and spears drew on flesh were plain enough to see.

Britha nodded.

'Someone brought them here?' There were some twenty bodies but this was not a place to fight a pitched battle.

'I think they are being given back to the land,' she said. 'Perhaps left in sacrifice because they could not protect their people.'

'But they died well.'

Britha looked up at the warrior, surprised to hear the emotion in his voice. *Is this what you fear, Goidel?* No tomb, no one to remember your deeds.

'Their ways are not your own,' Britha said simply. 'What I want to know is why the gulls will eat their flesh and bury them in the sky but the insects stay away.'

That got Fachtna's attention. He jumped into the pool and waded towards the bodies. They were a small pale people, though death and immersion would always make a body pale. There were traces of paint on their bodies but no tattoos. Whatever weapons and armour they might have owned had been stripped from them.

Fachtna cut into the flesh of one of the bodies.

'That is an ill thing,' Britha said angrily.

'It is an augury,' Fachtna said, distracted.

'And who are you to augur on the bones of people not yours, who have been left to rest in their own way?' she demanded.

'These wounds, they make channels in the flesh, like the roots of the tree,' he told her.

'These are Bress's weapons. We know this.'

Fachtna took some of the flesh into his mouth and tasted it.

'What are you doing?!'

Fachtna spat the flesh out. 'These are kin of yours,' he told her.

'These are not kin of mine, fool!'

'And yet in part your blood is the same as theirs.'

'Then they were corrupted by the demons and left here when they turned on their own people.'

'They died fighting Bress's band, and I mean the blood you share with Cliodna and the Muileartach.'

Britha considered this. 'The insects know that their blood is un-natural.' Fachtna said nothing. 'I thought the power you had was in your arms and legs and the weapons you bear.'

'Don't forget my cock.'

'You are a fool and I do not believe you,' Britha said in exasperation.

'Then I will have Teardrop tell you.'

Fachtna waded across the pool. He had reached the bank and was about to step up when he stopped.

'Why did you kill them?' he asked, not quite turning to look at her directly.

Britha spent some time deciding whether to dignify his question with an answer. 'Because they didn't care about themselves so I ate their spirits,' she finally said.

He nodded. 'Have you ever done the like before?'

'I've never met people like that before, and who are you to question me?'

'Would you have done the same in the past?'

Britha said nothing. The silence seemed to go on and on before Fachtna stepped out of the pool and started back towards where they had left Teardrop. Britha watched the warrior's back until the tall breeze-blown rushes swallowed him. What she didn't tell him was that she had not felt even a trace of remorse for what she had done. In fact, it had left her feeling stronger. She tried to ignore the sense of how far away she was from home and what she had been. She looked at the corpses and wondered if they had known Cliodna.

Fachtna made his way along a tiny game trail. He could see Teardrop just ahead of him. He was facing towards where the smoke was coming from. Fachtna held the bloody knife in one hand; the other held the strap of his shield, which was slung over his shoulder.

He stopped. Despite the blood, he pushed his dirk back into its scabbard. He was half convinced that his mind was playing tricks with him. Then, assuming a low stance, he swung the shield into his hand, the feel of the leather over wood familiar where he gripped it. His sword whispered from the scabbard. He soothed its song with a thought. It was hungry. It had been drawn and not used too often recently.

They were good. He did not understand how he had not known they were there – his senses being expanded far beyond the normal – but they moved with the direction of the wind in the rushes and they moved quickly. They were like wild animals.

He listened. Keeping still. Britha's footsteps on the trail behind him seemed thunderous. He had not paid close enough attention to Teardrop. He had not read his body like the weapons masters in the younglings' camp had taught him. The tension in Teardrop's stance told Fachtna that they had him.

Behind him he heard Britha stop. She had seen Fachtna's sword and shield at the ready. Fachtna heard her change her position, presumably readying her spear. *Now have the good sense to be quiet*, Fachtna thought. Then he heard the mindsong.

Britha had her back to Fachtna. She was still, her spear ready. She was not sure what was her awareness of someone or something in the gently swaying reeds around her and what was her mind playing tricks. All she heard was the wind and the water from the nearby river. She glanced over towards it. She could just about make out the *Will of Dagon*. There would be no help from that quarter. Quite the opposite: they would be pleased to see them gone.

She became aware of the music. It sounded simple, ancient and beautiful. It was a song without words. It was open, baring all. She started when she realised that she could understand it on a level much deeper than mere words, though she was not hearing it. She was listening to it some other way. She heard it inside her head, felt it through her body; her blood responded to it.

They came out of the reeds on all sides. They wore armour made of panels of boiled leather sewn onto skin to make it easier for them to move. Their spears were odd, made of wood, the ends carved into blades and then fire-hardened. Their shields were small and round, leather over wood, all painted with the same design. What could be seen of their skin was covered in mud. Over the top of the dried mud the same symbol was repeated. They wore full head coverings, not unlike the dog masks worn by the Cirig, except these were unmistakably in the shape of a serpent's head. The serpent was the symbol painted over the mud and present on their shields.

'Fachtna, I think I've made a mistake,' Teardrop said quietly, but his voice carried.

Britha saw Fachtna move imperceptibly. He was getting ready to attack. He, like her and Teardrop, was surrounded. It looked like death to her. She heard him spit out an unfamiliar word through gritted teeth: 'Naga.'

'Fachtna, wait,' Teardrop said, his voice carrying over the breeze, through the rushes.

'Better to die,' Fachtna said.

'It may not be as we think. Bress raided them,' Teardrop said. The warriors surrounding them said nothing.

'Look at them. This is typical. They have set themselves up a god.'

'Our god sees through our eyes and you are from elsewhere,' one of the warriors in the snake masks said.

'Isn't everyone?' Fachtna responded.

Britha could hear the warrior talking to Fachtna. The warriors around her were absolutely still, not even responding to any movements she made. Calm, yet she could feel their anger. She wondered how many people they had lost when the black curraghs came.

'I don't even want to know your name,' Fachtna said, an insult. It was not the ritual insult of a challenge but disgust at what the warrior was, letting the man know that he was beneath him.

The man said nothing; he just watched Fachtna.

'Fachtna, I need you to wait,' Teardrop said.

'It serves us nothing,' Fachtna said. 'Let's get on with it.'

Britha wasn't sure what was going on but she had never heard of Naga and so was sure that this tribe was no enemy of hers. *They may become such, but there's time for that later*, she thought.

'How will you face Bress if you are dead?' Britha asked.

'Better to die fighting than to come into their power. There is nothing left of you when they are finished anyway. It makes slavery under Bress look desirable.'

This chilled Britha, but the warrior was given to exaggeration, as all warriors and most men were.

'But this does not look like that,' Teardrop said. 'There are magics here but they are weak.' Britha could only just hear Teardrop, spread out as they were.

'Why aren't they attacking?' Britha wondered out loud.

'Because their god is watching us,' Fachtna growled.

'And wants you to know that the poison we coat our blades with is made from his blood. Our spears will pierce armour and flesh and rupture bowels. You will smell the filth of your own death.' It was the same warrior who had spoken before.

'Enough!' Teardrop cried. His stance relaxed but his staff stayed at the ready. The warriors shifted slightly, keeping their spears levelled at them. 'Either fight or take me to your god,' Teardrop demanded. Fachtna looked less than pleased.

The village was a series of roundhouses not too dissimilar to those of Britha's own people, although smaller. They were set on a number of low islands of hard-packed dirt that rose out of the surrounding marsh. They called themselves the Pobl Neidr, the People of the Snake, and were part of the much larger Catuvellauni, whose name meant Leaders of Battle. They had burned their own village, taken what supplies they could and fled into the marshes before Bress's raiders. They had tried to fight them using cunning and their greater knowledge of the land, or so Tangwen, the warrior who had been doing all the talking, told them. Tangwen was a woman but apparently found it useful to impersonate a man in order to get other warriors to take her seriously. This didn't make any sense at all to Britha, who also found it odd that they showed no reaction to Teardrop's swollen and deformed head

Fachtna was clearly not happy. He treated the snake-masked warriors with contempt and was obviously itching for a fight despite near-constant warnings from Teardrop. Leaving the village, they were taken deep into the marshes by hidden trails and sunken causeways. The People of the Snake moved with an easy grace through the marsh, but more than once Fachtna, Britha or Teardrop missed their footing and ended up soaked or covered in mud.

'We are going to find this thing and kill it, root out the centre of the corruption, yes?' Fachtna demanded.

'We are going to see what it is. Things are not as they should be here.'

Beyond realising that the Naga were a hated enemy of Fachtna, Britha could not make out what was happening.

She did not realise that there was a large island in the marsh until she stepped from a sunken causeway and onto it. It just blended with the rest of the marsh. There, staying low beneath the height of the rushes, she saw the rest of the People of the Snake. They did not have the fearsome countenance of the mud-covered, painted and masked warriors. They were landsfolk, or more likely fisherfolk and those who hunted birds, judging by the wooden frames with hanging fish and fowl. They regarded the newcomers with apprehension and would not look directly at their own warriors. This Britha understood: the warriors had taken on aspects of the serpents that they looked like. Dangerous spirits would possess them when they wore the snake masks. They were no longer kin to these folks but fearsome animalistic warriors.

In the centre of the island was what initially looked to Britha like a stone-lined well, but as she got closer she realised that it was a series of wooden steps lodged between the rocks of a dry-stone shaft going down into the island itself. Fachtna was shaking his head.

'What are you frightened of?' Britha asked, goading him.

'I am to keep Teardrop safe. Go down there yourself if you want.'

'You are safe if you do not wish ill on us and our father,' Tangwen said. She nodded to some of the folk nearby. They shrank from the serpent visage of her mask, and just for a moment Britha caught the look of discomfort on the other woman's face through the mud. They were brought food, a stew made from fish and fowl in bread trenchers, and wooden mugs of something ale-like. As a child offered Fachtna his food, he slapped it out of her hands. The little girl looked shocked and then very angry.

'I'll not accept hospitality from the likes of you,' Fachtna told Tangwen. Teardrop look pained. Britha watched Tangwen's expression darken and saw the look of anger on the other warriors' faces.

The blow landed so solidly because Fachtna had not been expecting Britha to hit him. His nose flattened itself against his face and squirted blood down over his mouth and bearded chin.

'What was that for?' the genuinely aggrieved Fachtna demanded.

'I don't care who these people are to you,' Britha told him, using her left-handed voice, the sinister tone, the one designed to frighten and curse. 'If you don't want their hospitality, then refuse it. If you want to fight, then challenge them. What you do not do is behave with the manners of a diseased dog in my presence, because what you do affects Teardrop and myself as well. They do not fear our swords or spears so you should not fear their food and drink! Do you understand me, boy!'

Fachtna looked furious. Britha was sure that he would at least strike her, perhaps even draw his sword. She was prepared to use the spear. The warriors of the People of the Snake and the folk under their protection watched. Chagrin replaced anger on Fachtna's face. Whatever he might have been, he did know how to behave with respect, and he knew that he was in the wrong, much to Britha's relief.

Fachtna knelt by the little girl.

'I am sorry,' he told her in her own language. Like all other languages he could speak it, and like all others Britha found herself able to understand it. Fachtna picked the bread from the ground, found bits of meat, barley and vegetables and put them back into the trencher. Then he ate it all. He handed the girl the wooden cup. 'If you would be prepared to get me another drink, I would drink it and with thanks. I would understand if you did not.' The little girl stared at him fiercely. He met her look, but she fetched him another drink. Fachtna thanked her and then stood up.

'I apologise. Please do not judge my companions on my behaviour. I will meet you over meat or metal as you prefer,' he said to Tangwen, who nodded her acceptance. Finally he turned to Teardrop and Britha. 'I apologise to you both.'

Teardrop shook his head, looking bemused. Britha nodded, accepting the apology though still angry. It was clear to her that the Naga, whoever they were, had done Fachtna a great wrong in the past. She had gratefully accepted her trencher and cup. It was good to taste normal food again, not the strange stuff they had given her on the *Will of Dagon*, which had done terrible things to her bowels.

'We are safe now,' she said as they accepted the protection of the law of hospitality by sharing food and drink with the People of the Snake. Perhaps Fachtna was right: perhaps these people were the lowest of the low, oath-breakers who would break the law of hospitality, but she knew that for her part she would not reject it.

Britha now understood why Fachtna had wanted to fight. This was neither natural nor right. She too felt the urge to drive her spear through the abomination of their hosts' living god.

Her people respected the serpent. It was a powerful animal. They invoked it on stone, in paint and in their woad tattoos. It was the symbol of the *ban draoi*, the female symbol of power, which was why it was tattooed across her back. What she saw before her, however, was nothing more than a mockery of the serpent she respected.

The chamber was large and lined with stone. They had entered from the shaft through a crawl space following a shallow stream. There was a dirt mound in the centre. The shallow stream surrounded the mound. Some kind of silver-coloured crystals covered the dry-stone walls. They crystals had formed in similar patterns to that made by wax as it melts down the side of a candle.

Set back further in the chamber, in the shadows thrown by the free-standing bronze braziers that lit the room, was the entrance to another chamber. Through the darkness Britha could make out the second, much smaller chamber. It was also lined with the crystal. There was a strange-looking sleeping pallet on the floor of the room. Something about it made Britha think of a nest. The air was thick with the smell that she had always associated with animals. As *ban draoi* she shared in the meat and milk provided by the livestock kept by the rest of the tribe. Her roundhouse had to be kept as a ritual space, however, and as such she had never had to share it with cows, sheep, goats or chickens.

On the mound was a handsomely carved wooden chair. The designs on it were strange to Britha's eyes. They seemed to flow and run into each other, hinting at some story that was beyond her ken. Next to it was a similarly designed table; it too looked ancient and strange. On the table were little tear-shaped fragments of crystal. Teardrop was looking at them with interest. They looked different to the crystals on the wall, more refined, or made from a different material.

Fachtna's face was made of stone. Britha could respect the effort he was putting in to remaining calm. Tangwen had said that their god had wanted to see them on his own. She had left the warning of the consequences of harming him unsaid.

'You have met my people before, I see,' the creature said. The S wasn't as drawn-out as she had expected, but it was longer than she was used to.

It was the very human-looking robes that disturbed Britha the most. They were not of her people nor any of the tribes of this island, but they would not have been out of place on some of the more outlandish traders she had met in her time. They had been colour-ful, once, finely made of some thick material that Britha could not identify, and fur-lined. They were also old and very worn.

To see clothes worn by such a creature seemed like a mockery. Its head was elongated, almost like an arrowhead. Its eyes were verti-cal yellow and black slits. Its skin was a patchwork of scales, mostly an unhealthy off-white colour, though with black patterns running down them. Its legs and hands were wrapped in rags but even disguised they looked wrong, unnatural. Long black nails poked through the rags at the tips of its fingers and toes.

Strangest of all was the long tail, also wrapped in rags. This strange creature looked very, very old.

'Do you have a name?' Britha asked.

'A number – I have been alive for a long time. You would be capable of pronouncing few of them. The people of the swamp call me Father. I misliked it at first but have come to appreciate it. People as disparate as they and I coming to have such a close bond.' When it spoke its long forked tongue flickered out in a way that Britha found unsettling. Behind the tongue she could make out wicked-looking teeth that folded up into its mouth.

'I think not,' Fachtna spat.

'They call you a god,' Britha said.

'That is no doing of mine.'

'Are you a dragon?' Britha asked. The creature hissed at her. It took her a moment to realise that it was laughing. Teardrop was as well. That earned him an angry glare.

'Would you like me to be?'

'I'd like you not to make sport of me with your forked tongue.'

'Then I am not. I am as you are. We have the same mother.'

His explanation posed more questions than it answered.

Fachtna grunted derisively, a sneer on his face.

'Do you seek death?' the warrior demanded.

'I allowed you in here armed as a show of good faith, of trust, as a result of your friend's mindsong. You look like a warrior from here, but you are unscarred, as are your armour and shield, and I sense you carry weapons of –' it glanced at Britha and then back to Fachtna '– ancient power. You are not from here, though your people once were or may be again, I am not sure which.'

Teardrop was looking around the cave at the crystal, a look of intense concentration on his face.

'What do you want of us?' Britha asked, trying to mask the revulsion in her voice. As the creature swung to look at her, she had to resist the urge to shrink away from its gaze.

'To help you, I think. The raiders are no friends of yours and they are certainly no friends of ours.'

'You are hurt?' Fachtna said.

'I am old and weak,' the creature replied.

'Else you would have changed these people.'

The serpentine creature looked at Fachtna for a long time. Its eyes didn't blink. The warrior held the strange gaze as best he could.

'I am not as others of my kind you may have met,' it finally said. Despite the creature's disquieting appearance, Britha could not miss the loneliness in its voice.

'You did not fall,' Teardrop said finally. 'Something about this cave protected you. You are not insane and corrupt like the others.'

The weight of the creature's years was apparent as it shuffled to its chair and sat down. Despite the strangeness of its face, the sadness there was unmistakable.

'You served the Muileartach,' Teardrop added. The creature nodded its head. The gesture looked strange in something so inhuman.

'When the madness broke through, I fled with my mother, who I served even as the rest of them were infected. We fled as far as we could, through the seas, but this is a small world.'

Teardrop walked to the wall of the chamber and reached up to run his hand over the rough crystalline growths.

'The crystal protects you?'

'Or hides me. I've never been sure which.'

Fachtna was following this exchange with a look of confusion.

'What are you saying?' he demanded. He did not like it that a cornerstone belief of his seemed to be under threat.

'That this Naga is not your enemy,' Teardrop said.

'I am more than a weapon. I will not use your flesh or plant my warped children in you.'

Britha was still confused but relieved that this Naga creature did not seem to wish them ill, horrifying though it might look.

Fachtna muttered something about the Naga not having a chance to defile his flesh.

'We have met other servants – they are starting to fall,' said Teardrop.

'We were not her servants. We were her, or rather their, children, just like you.'

'You speak of the gods?' Britha asked, confused.

'I speak of your forebears,' the creature told her. It turned back to Teardrop. 'I hear them fight. I hear their song as they fall. My cave keeps me safe. So far.'

'So the Muileartach has fallen?' Teardrop asked, sounding worried.

The creature shook its head slowly. 'No, you would have felt it. She sleeps.'

'So what is Bress doing with my people?' Britha asked.

'Bress is a servant. I have heard his master at the ceremonies of the Corpse People from the west and the demon-ridden slaves that Bress keeps. I have heard this in my dreams. I have seen the Dark Man in their fires. He comes to give birth. The anti-birth. Instead of life there will be death and Ynys Prydein will become Ynys Annwn, the isle of the dead.'

'Who is the Dark Man?' Fachtna asked, his hatred gone now, drawn in by the Naga's story.

'The Corpse People of the west call him Crom Dhubh. He will kill a man, steal the secret of birth so all will be stillborn, and then the Muileartach will fall and from her poisoned womb will come Llwglyd Diddymder.'

'What does that mean?' Teardrop asked.

'I only know the songs they sing to their servants, nothing more. I do not know this Crom Dhubh, but he is old and has power.'

'Only one man must die for this to happen?' Fachtna asked. The Naga's head seemed to wrinkle. Britha guessed it was frowning or concentrating.

'This is what is sung,' it finally said.

Fachtna turned to Teardrop. 'Have you heard this?'

'I have not dared open myself. Even with what little I did today, I heard the murmur of madness in the background. It sounded like ten thousand voices all struck by the moon and wretched.'

'You must beware his followers, the Corpse People. They eat the flesh of heroes, kings and those touched by the gods. They harvest their power.' Britha noticed the meaningful look that the Naga gave Teardrop as if trying to convey something else.

Teardrop nodded as if he understood. 'Where is the Muileartach?' he asked.

'You cannot go there. The very land itself will fight you.'

'We have no choice,' Britha said. 'Bress has my people.'

'Then they are not yours any more.'

'There is no shame in dying even though it proves you right,' she replied.

'You will not die. Not at first anyway. Not in the flesh.'

'You know we will go,' Teardrop said. The creature gave this some thought.

'I will ask Tangwen to guide you. Do not go down the coast but instead travel the length of the Grey Father. I will tell her to take you to the lands of the Atrebates to my friend Rin, their *rhi*. That will take you closer. Do not get Tangwen killed. Her people need her strength.'

For a moment nobody said anything.

'Thank you,' Teardrop finally said. Britha nodded in agreement. Fachtna was quiet.

'I'm sorry,' the warrior finally said.

'It saddens me to say that I think your response is probably the wisest. When you meet one of my people, don't hesitate. Kill them. All that they were would thank you for your kindness.' There was so much sadness in its voice, but even so Britha was surprised to see the tear that rolled down Fachtna's cheek. The creature turned its head towards her. 'I wish I could have been your dragon.' She had no words for him. 'Instead all I am is a foolish old snake who pisses in a circle to hide from the bad folk.'

'Do you come from the Brass City?' the creature asked as they turned to leave. Teardrop looked back and shook his head. Fachtna looked confused. 'You carry weapons of the many-edged ones.' For a while neither of them answered.

'We are from the *Ubh Blaosc*,' Fachtna told him. 'When you sing, sing of us.'

The seeds were flung into dark rough waters. They spiralled to the seabed to burrow and grow. Strange roots dug deep into the earth, drinking energy from its heat and travelling far to take metal from its flesh. Slowly it began to rise through the silted depths.

The captives were quiet now. Ettin had taught them the value of silence when their screams were not wanted. The smell of fear still sickened him though, and he could feel eyes full of hate staring at his back. The black curragh held steady in the choppy sea as he watched its head slowly grow out of the water.

They were not quiet when they saw it, when they realised what it was, what they were to become. Ettin laid about them with his whip, his latest victim begging him and cursing him to stop from his shoulder as he did so.

21
Now

They had been driving for a while but Beth was sure that she was still on the island. For one thing she couldn't see them trying to smuggle her out past the roadblocks. They were clearly on a very rough road as she was getting kicked around in the boot of the car. She had struggled with the cuffs but they were solidly built and had been put on tightly. She still had her Balisong knife and her knuckledusters in her jacket – they hadn't searched her before they dumped her into the boot.

The car came to a halt. She heard a gate creak open, and the car moved over what felt like soft ground. The car stopped again.

The bright light after the darkness of the boot made her squint. Markus was just a large backlit shadow reaching for her and dragging her out. *Suppress the anger*, she told herself. *Wait for the right moment.*

Her eyes adjusted to the light. Markus was pulling her towards an old greyhound racing stadium. Dilapidated and gutted, the stands surrounding the sandy track looked like they were falling apart though there were people gathering in the stands closest to her. There was a throbbing bass noise that she recognised as a generator. She presumed it was providing the power for the lights aimed at a corner of the track.

Beyond the stadium Beth could make out the lights of the police roadblock on the M275 motorway bridge that led out of the city. She had seen this area on the way into Portsmouth. Just past the stadium was the scrapyard with the rusting hulks of amphibious vehicles, submarines, tanks and the like. She was pretty sure the area was called Tipner.

Anger warred with fear as she saw McGurk in front of her. The light was behind him so she had to squint. She might have done it this time, she thought, pushed too hard. It doesn't matter how much you can look after yourself, you're fucked when they've got guns and more muscle than you. Still, it seemed a little public for an execution, what with all the people watching.

'What do you know about my sister, you bastard?' she demanded.

'That she was a dirty little whore,' McGurk said, to the sound of a few sycophantic chuckles.

'Fuck you!' The struggling was as instinctive as it was pointless. Markus had too tight a grip on her. She spat at McGurk but had no idea if it hit him.

'I'm a fair man—'

'You're an arsehole wannabe who's watched too many gangster movies!' Beth interrupted. She was willing herself to be quiet but it just wasn't happening.

Movement from the other end of the track caught her attention. Next to a brown multi-storey building, the glass in all its windows long since gone, was another gate. She guessed the scrapyard was on the other side of it. Five people were coming through the gate. Four of them were clearly guards, escorting the fifth figure that was in the middle of them all. Their size said muscle. Their body language said that they were nervous of the person they were escorting. The figure in the middle was hunched over and covered in a blanket. Something about this made her even more wary.

She looked back to McGurk. His smile was predatory and more than a little bit smug. She moved towards him but the gun came up.

'Pussy,' she said, trying to look him straight in the eyes despite the light.

'Think you're hard, do you? Even on your best day, love ...' He shook his head.

'That what you need the stick for?'

'What, this?' he held it up, examining it. 'You know what this is? It's a bull cock.'

'I can imagine you'd want a replacement.'

Even in the light she could see him frown. The four muscle and the strange covered figure were getting closer. Beth was downwind and could smell something like low tide.

'It's just an external manifestation, like. A reminder. So people remember who's got the biggest swinging cock, so everything just jogs along fine. So we don't have to make too many examples like this.'

'Put the gun away and let's find out.'

'You're fucking entertainment. Get used to it.'

McGurk looked to Markus, the gun still levelled at Beth. Markus unlocked the cuffs and started to back away as Beth put her hand into the pocket of her jacket as she grabbed his collar. Markus tried to turn but Beth's hand came out wearing brass knuckles. She punched him in quick succession on the side of his head, all the while moving back, dragging him by his collar, keeping him off balance. By the second punch the tips of the knuckles were red, by the fourth or fifth so was the side of Markus' head. The sound of metal hitting bone and flesh resonated around the stadium.

'Hey!' McGurk shouted, brandishing his pistol. Beth let Markus fall to the sand. She rubbed her nose, smearing blood on her face as she turned to stare at McGurk.

'You're about to do something bad to me. I won't come after you because you're a pussy who hides behind a gun.' She saw McGurk's mouth tighten in anger. 'So either shoot me or get on with it.'

McGurk laughed. He looked down at Markus' unconscious body, blood reddening the sand around his head.

'Fuck him. Stupid cunt should've searched you.'

'Yeah, he might have found this.' Beth produced the Balisong knife from her other pocket and flipped it open. McGurk looked at the tempered blade as it caught the light and then back at Beth.

'I like you. For some northern sub-literate you've got a pair, but that won't help.'

'Fuck you,' Beth said mildly and then turned to look at the people milling in the stands. Some looked wealthy; others didn't. Some had hunger for whatever entertainment this was written all over their faces. Others seemed nervous. 'And fuck your parasite friends.' Then she turned away from him to watch the group heading towards her. She didn't realise it, but simply ignoring McGurk had been the biggest insult she'd paid him. She didn't even register McGurk striding towards one of the stands.

The four guards were each holding the end of a chain that led under the blanket. They got about fifteen feet away from Beth and stopped. The smell was unbearable. She saw they all wore surgical masks. She wished she had one.

They clicked some release on their ends of the chains and heard what she guessed were manacles springing open under the blanket. The escorts dragged the manacle-ended chains towards themselves and ran. Now Beth was really worried. She wondered if McGurk was crazy enough to make her fight a gorilla or a small bear.

She had expected some kind of growl. What she got was a low, wet, bubbly, rasping rattle.

The hands that grabbed the edge of the foul-looking blanket weren't right. The skin was pale, wet and large amounts of it were peeling. There were webs of skin between the fingers, and what little she could see of the forearms also suggested more flaps of skin. It was the fingers that unnerved her the most. Each of them ended in long black hooked nails.

The blanket was torn off. Beth found herself retreating. She was reasonably sure it had once been human. She was surer that human flesh shouldn't look like that.

Its flesh was pale to the point of being a faint blue colour, like a corpse left in water. It was hunched over as if the ragged long coat that it was wearing covered a multitude of twisted deformities. Its hair was a stringy dark mess, much of it missing, and its eyes were milky white with no irises or pupils to speak of. There were slits at its neck. The slits seemed to be moving. Beth couldn't shake the feeling that they were gills and suddenly she didn't like living so close to the sea.

She felt herself back into something. She had back-pedalled all the way to the stands. Someone shoved her forward. She turned to grab them, shove them between her and whatever the thing was, but she saw McGurk pointing the gun at her. She looked around for ways out, but McGurk had known what he was doing. There were people on each gate, and if she made it to a wall without being shot they'd catch her before she could climb over. Her only way out was through whatever this thing was.

She moved forward cautiously, showed it the blade.

'We don't have to do this, but if you come close I will fucking cut you, okay?' Beth found herself reminded of conversations she'd had in prison.

It didn't seem to be paying any attention to her. Its head was cocked to one side as if listening to something. The odd thing was, you took away the skin problems and deformities, she reckoned the thing would look like a very normal guy. It was difficult to gauge its age, but perhaps forties or fifties.

It didn't move like a middle-aged man, however. Suddenly it darted forward, clawing at her. Beth felt a tug as she danced out of its way, the hook-like nails tearing through her leather, ripping it as she pulled away. It had moved so fast.

'My jacket!'

Retaliation was more instinct than anything else. The knife was mostly for show, to frighten. She had killed someone once and was in no hurry to repeat that. However, the ferocity of its attack took her by surprise and before she knew it she was hammering the blade up into the side of its head. She stabbed three times in quick succession, felt the impacts down her arms, heard the sound of bone breaking under the blade, felt something wet on her hand as she struggled to hold on to it. She pulled the Balisong out and swung with the knuckles, catching it in the jaw with enough force to send it to its knees. Beth stepped back and kicked it hard in the chest, knocking it over.

'Fucker!' she screamed, fear and anger mixing.

It rolled back to its feet and flung itself at her, hooked claws outstretched. Beth tried to dodge the lunge but screamed as hooks pierced flesh and dragged her to the ground. She tried to roll it over but was desperate to hold on to the knife.

It was strong. It was on the top. She felt her skin tear, on her chest, her face, her head, as it clawed at her. At some subconscious level her brain acknowledged the sound of cheering and shouting. She stopped trying to push it off. Fingers still wearing knuckles grabbed its head. Her arm was clawed open. A mouth full of jagged, wicked-looking teeth opened and drooled on her before trying to bite her fingers.

The knife flashed out into its chest over and over again, viscous warm blood spraying her. Then she was stabbing its throat to the sound of booing. Then she was stabbing under its chin and into its mouth as it howled. Blood made the metal of the knife slippery and she lost her grip on it. The creature flinched away from the blade, not realising it was stuck in its flesh. Beth screamed and put all her force into punching it in the face. She felt bone crack under the blow from the knuckleduster. The thing's head snapped around and it spat blood into the night air. Beth bucked her hips, grabbed its hair and dragged its head down towards the sand, rolling at the same time. The creature made strange keening sounds and rolled off her.

Beth was lying on the bloody sand next to the stinking thing. The moment's respite let her body tell her just how much pain she was in. She had to suppress it. She swung her leg over herself, using the momentum to roll onto the creature, which was wriggling around on the sand in obvious agony. She straddled it and grabbed its slick head. Its blood looked thicker than she thought was normal and black, even in the light. She barely registered the ringing of a mobile phone as she powered her brass-knuckled fist repeatedly into its face, smashing and then powdering bone as she made the face look like something other than a face. It stopped moving. She didn't stop hitting it. She didn't notice McGurk leaving.

Eventually she stopped and looked up to see the crowd, silent, just staring at her. She got to her feet and staggered towards them. Some of them stepped back.

Beth heard the creature get up behind her. She swallowed hard and closed her eyes. She clenched her fist around the brass knuckles. She had no fight left in her but that didn't mean she was going to stop fighting. She heard a ripping sound as vicious spurs of bone shot through its coat from its elbows. Beth started to turn.

Then there was light everywhere, wind and noise, shouted voices telling her that they had guns and that she needed to get on the ground. Gunfire. It didn't sound like it did on the telly. Shot after shot. Beth sank to her knees and then toppled forward onto the sand. The creature fell close enough for her to see its dead eyes.

A shadow blocked out some of the light. There was more shouting. *Have to shout to be heard over the wind and the noise from the light in the sky,* she thought. There was a pretty man – sandy-blond hair, blue eyes, well dressed in dark clothes – way out of her league. And he had a gun. A man with a gun was telling her to let go of the brass knuckles. Beth was worried that if she started laughing she wouldn't stop. She was dead. She was sure of that. *What danger is a dead woman with brass knuckles against shouting men with guns?* she wondered.

She wasn't dead. The paramedics had done a good job. The painkillers had done a better one. She was still a mess but she could walk and most of her limbs still worked. They had wanted to take her to hospital. Apparently she needed to be there. The blond man who seemed to be in charge had said no. There had been an argument, which he'd won. She was in an interview room in the big police station on Kingston Crescent. They had outdone themselves in making the room look institutional.

She hurt, but anger was carrying her through. It had to because what she knew about the world, particularly a previously unquestioned faith in – no, knowledge of – the non-existence of monsters, had been challenged. She had anger to deal with this. The alternative was a shaking crying mess.

The door opened. *He was attractive,* Beth thought as the blond man she had seen at the stadium entered. He had a folder under one arm and was carrying two cups of tea. There was something military in his bearing, but an officer not a squaddie. She'd known enough squaddies to recognise them.

He put one of the mugs down in front of her.

'I made it myself,' he said. 'And put lots of sugar in it.'

It smelled good to Beth. It smelled familiar.

He opened the folder. The only thing in it was a black and white photograph of her sister. Beth looked at him and then the picture. It was a good picture. She'd been caught in an unguarded moment. The smile on her face was genuine. Beth had seen too few of those in her life, but you could truly see how beautiful Talia had been. She hadn't needed the make-up and the attitude.

'Where is she?' the man asked.

'Dead, died in a terrorist attack. You may have heard about it.'

The man watched her for a while. His face was the perfect example of an adult disappointed by a wayward young person. He had children or a younger sibling, Beth decided. She broke the gaze and took a sip of the tea. It was good.

'Then why are you looking for her?'

'What was that?' Beth asked, meaning the creature she had fought. The man looked at her again, seemingly coming to a decision.

'A very strong and dangerous man with a series of unfortunate genetic deformities and deep-seated psychological problems. He was probably high on PCP.'

Beth considered this, nodding as he was speaking.

'Bullshit.' More silence.

'Okay. What do you think it was?'

'I don't know. But I'm pretty sure you do.'

'We saw the lights from the bridge. We investigated.'

'Did I kill it?'

'No, I did.'

Beth nodded again. 'Good. I think you did it a favour.'

'Look, Elizabeth—'

'Beth. Who are you?'

'My name is Malcolm du Bois. I'm working with Special Branch. Would you like to see some ID?' Beth just shrugged. 'You're in more than a little bit of trouble. Particularly with your previous—'

'What is the sentence for gladiatorial fighting these days?'

Du Bois looked at her and smiled. 'Fine. I need some information. If I don't get it, I'll lock you up. This is an anti-terrorist investigation. I can make you disappear for a long time and then make sure that you get sentenced to the full extent of the law. If I do get the information I want then I'll let you go.' He tapped Talia's photo.

'You think my sister's alive?'

Du Bois leaned back in his chair. He was getting tired of being asked questions. He pulled his cigarette case out of the pocket of his tailored leather coat.

'Cigarette?' he asked.

She shook her head. 'I've been told they're bad for you.'

Du Bois lit one of the cigarettes and then took a mouthful of tea.

'Don't mind if I do?'

Beth shrugged. 'I'll overlook the abuse of my civil rights this time.'

'She's not your sister.'

Whatever Beth had thought he was going to say next, that hadn't been it. It took a moment to penetrate.

'I grew up with her,' she told him. 'This is a weird approach if you want something from me.'

'She looks nothing like you or any member of your family. Your mother was unable to have children due to complications during your birth. I can provide you with medical records if that's what you want. There's no birth certificate in her name: in fact, according to the government there's very little proof of Natalie Luckwicke's existence at all. I imagine the only reason she slipped through the cracks for so long is because she grew up in Bradford. However, she is of an age and looks like the parents of a baby girl who went missing from Helmsley in North Yorkshire a little over twenty years ago.'

Beth stared at him. She didn't want to believe him, but too much of what he said fitted. Too much of it made sense. If nothing else, it pointed to the reason why Talia was the focus of so much unspoken resentment for her.

'Why?' she asked, uncertainty in her voice.

Du Bois didn't answer.

Maybe this is good, Beth thought. *If it's true then it doesn't matter so much that Talia hated her.* She could give up this stupid search for her. Make it not her problem.

'Bullshit,' she said without much feeling.

'I can prove it if you want, or the next time you see your father just ask him. Now, if you tell me what I want to know, we won't press charges, and remember you are now an accessory after the fact. We just want to find her. It's not your problem any more, and by the looks of it you won't live too much longer if you keep looking. I'll give you some money and you can be back on your way home.'

It sounded so attractive. Let it go. Maybe not the part about going home, but she had to look in her father's eyes. She wanted the truth, deserved the truth, and then she wanted to know why they loved a child they had stolen better than their own. *Fuck them, fuck them all.* She didn't owe any of them anything.

'Is she alive?' du Bois asked.

'As far as I know, no.' He started to say something. 'Listen. I came here looking for her. Then I discovered she was in the house that got blown up. I was going to leave it at that, but then I decided to find out what happened to her, how she ended up like that. The more I looked into it, the more it looked like people didn't want me to know stuff. It felt like a ...'

'Conspiracy?'

She nodded. 'But I don't think it was. I think she was involved in some really dodgy stuff, and when she died the people she was involved with just wanted to make sure nobody found out about their part in it. Just arseholes covering their tracks is all.'

'Like who?'

'Somebody called William Arbogast.'

'The man you tortured?'

It took someone coming out and saying it. She had no illusions about what she had done but somehow du Bois driving it home like that made it worse. His blue eyes seemed relentless. She looked away but nodded.

'Anyone else?' he asked.

'That was as far as I got. The rest are below him on the ladder and ...'

'You're not a grass,' du Bois finished with a sigh.

'No more than I have been.'

'So who picked you up?'

'I don't know.' Du Bois opened his mouth to protest. 'Now wait. I don't know if it's to do with Talia or me rattling the wrong cage, but I got a sheet chucked over my head in the middle of the road, a bit of a kicking and chucked in the boot of a car.'

He dragged deep on his cigarette and then stubbed it out.

'Younger sisters are a pain in the arse, aren't they?' he said.

She looked away from him again and nodded. Then cursed herself as the tears came and the shaking started. Du Bois just watched her. He was impressed that she hadn't gone into shock. He let her get it out of her system.

Finally she looked up at him.

'What happened to her? Terrorists? A meth lab? The same people as hit the nightclub?' Beth remembered seeing him there now.

'The truth is, I honestly don't know.'

She looked miserable as she took a sip of the lukewarm sweet tea.

'I'm going to see about getting you released, okay?'

Beth nodded numbly.

Du Bois walked out of the interview room. She was lying. She knew who had taken her to Tipner. Following orders, he should have made her talk. He was more than capable and had done it in the past, but she didn't deserve it. She wasn't part of his world. She'd had a glimpse, and he was still wondering what the S-tech-augmented hybrid had been doing in a greyhound stadium in Tipner, but she wasn't playing in the same leagues. She was just doing the best she could for her father. She hadn't done anything wrong as far as he could see. He could respect that. She got to walk. He would get what he wanted another way.

DC Mossa had told him that Arbogast moved in circles that had little to do with traditional criminals so he had got away with pretty much operating on his own. Somewhere, however, there was a connection between Arbogast and S-tech but du Bois just couldn't see it at the moment.

Beth had been lucky. If he hadn't been parked at the pointless roadblock on the bridge. If he hadn't seen the lights at the greyhound stadium and checked on his phone and discovered it was supposed to have been deserted. If he hadn't had the authority to task the armed police on the roadblock to follow him and to task helicopter support, then Beth would have been dead. The girl was tough, du Bois had to give her that. She had held her own longer than most. But he had put two nano-bullets in the chest of the hybrid and another two in its head to make sure it was dead.

As Beth sat there sipping another tea, wiping away tears and snot with the arm of her shredded jumper, her feeling of unease grew. She looked around the room for some explanation but found nothing. The longer she sat there the more frightened she became, and the sense that she was not alone grew stronger.

She stood up. She was the sort of person who, when she heard a noise in a house that she couldn't explain, went looking for its cause. She moved as fast as she could, limping around the room.

The corner. The shadows in one of the corners of the room. They were just the result of the dim light in the interview room, she told herself. Nothing unusual there. But now the shadows in the corner seemed much darker than they had any right to be. Beth told herself that it was just her tired, pained and drugged mind playing tricks on her. That it was the result of the stress and the shock of the horrors that she had seen and experienced tonight. But the mounting certainty that there was someone there just wouldn't go away.

She forced herself to take a step towards the corner. The shadows seemed to coalesce, solidify, move of their own accord in the way that shadows just don't. Another step. She could see the dark shape of a figure now. She looked around for a weapon, her brain desperately trying to understand what was going on. Adrenaline flowed. Fight won over flight in the locked room. But the chair was bolted to the floor.

The figure lunged out of the darkness. The bag lady. Except she was something ancient, primal, ferocious. She smelled of the earth. Sharp teeth, too many sharp teeth, ragged nails outstretched. The hag-like creature bit her own tongue and spat the blood all over Beth's face.

Beth could feel the blood move. Push itself into her face, through her skin. She opened her mouth to scream and hit the floor. She thought she heard someone whisper, 'It'll be okay.'

22
A Long Time After the Loss

Vic knew that there was no reason for the beacon to be all the way out here. It wasn't on any navigational chart. The information as to its whereabouts had recently been added to the nav systems by Scab. Vic liked nothing about this, but then he hadn't liked anything for some time now.

The bridge drive made a cut in Red Space. The *Basilisk* emerged into blackness.

'Where are we and where are the all the stars?' Vic asked. Scab ignored him.

There was something wrong with the blackness. Vic couldn't shake the feeling that the infinity of space was somehow closing in on him. He didn't like the way space seemed to move in the periphery of his multifaceted vision. He didn't like the feeling that somehow space was squirming.

'Is that a monastery?' Vic might as well have been talking to himself. He was receiving the image from the *Basilisk*'s sensors straight into his neunonics. It showed an ancient-looking habitat built into an asteroid. It had the look of a Church habitat but a very old one. A search of his neunonics found nothing that matched it.

The sensors showed indications of life but no weapon locks from defensive systems. That wasn't right. Vic couldn't think of another habitat that had no defensive systems.

'I don't want to go there,' Vic said firmly and crossed all four of his arms. 'I mean—' he started.

'Can you not want to go there silently?' Scab demanded, turning on Vic. This made Vic even more nervous as Scab seemed a little on edge.

The familiar *clang* of docking was followed by a grinding noise as the ancient docking arm tried to make a seal.

'Maybe we'll just be sucked out into space when we open the

airlock,' Vic said hopefully, but the docking arm finally made its seal. Scab 'faced opening instructions to the *Basilisk* and after decontamination procedures the wall opened. Vic didn't like what he saw. It was difficult to tell their race or sex, but they were probably human or feline, as they were wearing voluminous red-hooded robes that covered their features.

Between the two red-clad monks was an ornate cylinder floating on an AG drive. The cylinder was a nano-fabricated tank designed to look like wood, brass and glass. A thick black fluid swirled around inside another clear liquid, seemingly with a life of its own.

It was with dawning horror that Vic realised what these people were.

'This is a heretical cult!' he cried, only to be ignored yet again. Were these his real employers? Surely they were too poor for the sort of resources that Scab had been throwing at this thing.

'Night draws in,' one of the monks said. Human, male, working hard to impart as little emotion as possible.

'We have little time,' the other said. Vic couldn't be sure of its race, let alone gender.

'I need a message delivering,' Scab told them. 'Tell him that we're going to need a diversion.'

The monks nodded. Vic was coming to the conclusion that if he could work out a way to commit suicide without being cloned by Scab, it might be easier than this insanity.

The chimera reared on its cloven-hoofed rear legs, striking out with its claws as it surged forward, opening rents of red in the sculpted flesh of the tank-bred biomechanoid it was fighting. There was cheering from the various boxes grown out of the root-like wood that formed the arena.

Zabilla Haq turned away from the arena, distaste written all over her face. The bloodshed did not bother her. The biomechanoid was unimpressive in its modernity; she liked the classical elegance of the three-headed chimera, but then it had taken her a great deal of time and effort to grow it. Adapting and splicing pre-Loss genetic material from a goat, lion and snake had been the easy part. The dragon head had been difficult. It had meant the creation of an entirely new template, as she had not been prepared simply to modify an existing lizard template. Instead, using reptile DNA as a guide, she had written her own code. She was pleased with the result. The difficult part had been making the three heads co-operate while retaining a degree of individual function.

The chimera butted the biomechanoid and horns tore more flesh.

The lion head ripped another chunk of meat away as the staggering biomechanoid tried to bring its weapon gauntlet to bear. The hooded serpent tail darted over the chimera's body; fangs pierced mottled armour, and venom emptied into the biomechanoid's flesh. The chimera all but climbed up its opponent, using its claws, rearing high. Despite being the creature's creator, Zabilla couldn't help but admire the haughty and proud set to the creature's draconic middle head.

'I like it,' Gilbert Scoular said, sounding like he meant the opposite. 'But it's not terribly original, is it?' the fat, ostentatiously dressed, self-proclaimed genetic artist said from his chaise longue. He was heavily made up, sweating and being fanned by a licensed and chipped morlock servant that, it was whispered, he had grown himself and used as a sex toy. 'Good thing you didn't give it wings after all. I shouldn't like to see one of those nesting in the upper branches.'

Her inability to get it to fly had proved extremely frustrating. Scoular's attempts at biological espionage must have revealed this. Nearly every utterance was a passive-aggressive attack. Zabilla was too good at the Game to show a response, though her grip on the wine glass tightened. She felt her consort Dracup tense next to her. He was working his way towards a second name in the eyes of the Absolute and not as used to the constant barbed attacks of life in society as she was. He was reaching across his emerald-green, handsomely cut, knee-length padded silk tunic for the bone blade sheathed at his hip. He would scar Scoular's fat face and then call him out.

She stopped him with a glance, hoping that Scoular hadn't noticed her paramour's rashness. More to the point, she hoped that the Absolute wasn't tuned into her own experiential headware at the moment. Though that was likely, as they were now in the semi-final round of the hastily called audition for a chance to run the Absolute's secret 'grand project'. Calling the artist out in a duel would be tantamount to admitting that Scoular was not only a better genetic designer but witty enough to elicit a physical response with mere words. He wasn't. Dracup, on the other hand, had held her as she had cried tears of frustration when she was unable to make the creature fly.

'As ever, I bow to your greater knowledge of such things,' Zabilla said. She left the fact that her unoriginal creature was tearing apart his own creation unsaid. 'After all, you are the artist; I am a mere biophysicist. My studies mean that my interest can never be anything more than amateur.'

'Whereas your armoured spider with weapon-tipped limbs is an inspired idea,' Dracup told Scoular dryly. *Better*, Zabilla thought. *A little too obvious but better than drawing a blade.*

Their faces were bathed in a warm but less than comforting red glow.

'Oh, a hard-tech cheat. How ... special,' Scoular said.

Getting the dragon's head to breathe fire naturally had been very difficult. The crowd went wild. The bloodshed didn't bother her, but she found the cheering of the crowd a trifle gauche. Under her distaste she was trying not to smile. Scoular could not have failed to know that the flame was an application of biotech. His comment was so petty that Dracup even ignored the easy opportunity to challenge him to a duel.

The chimera paced around the sand of the arena, parts of which were on fire now. Firefighting drones remained hovering above on their AG motors. Zabilla uncharitably hoped that the dragon's fire had caught some of the bystanders. The arachnid biomechanoid was burning and badly damaged, trying to stand on limbs that were being consumed.

'No voice to your creature's suffering?' Zabilla asked.

Scoular said nothing. He had been overconfident. He had spied on her and created a creature to win. There was no pain reaction because he hadn't thought he would need one. Like many who played, he understood the pleasure part of the Game, he didn't understand the pain. It was not just about indulging appetites.

'I hear the heads found two dead wiped pieces,' Carinne Serano, Scoular's fashionable arm-piece, said. She was trying, somewhat desperately in Zabilla's opinion, to ease the conversation away from her financial paramour's humiliation.

The wiped pieces were once people, actual players of the Game. They had been taken and all trace of their identities, from distinguishing features to personalities and memories, had been nano-virally destroyed before they were killed. It was one of the most horrific deaths a player could experience. All their triumphs would count for nothing as they were reduced to their original vat-grown templates.

Despite the fact that everyone playing the Game was sculpted with the same basic features, a template designed to reflect the Absolute's original beauteous form before he ascended, Zabilla always found herself surprised by how much that template could differ from person to person.

Carinne, for example, was petite and pretty, while she herself was tall and striking. They both had high cheekbones, sharp features and narrow angular faces, yet Zabilla could look commanding and at times cruelly beautiful, whereas Carinne looked insipid to Zabilla's eyes.

The same was true of Dracup and Scoular. Scoular's obese body proudly bore the ravages of his excesses in the same way the Rakshasa bore their scars. Scoular was obese to the point where he had to use expensive miniaturised AG motors to help support his layers of fat so that he could move more easily. Whereas Dracup was whip-thin and looked like a weapon poised to strike, or some sort of not-so-patient predatory insect – but in an attractive way, Zabilla thought.

'It's an outrage,' Dracup said, not without feeling. 'It'll be morlock rights activists. I hear they're campaigning for sight now. It's as if they think they have the right to as many senses as we do. I mean, what do they need them for beneath the Black Leaves? Sight would be a hindrance in the dark.'

The chimera charged through flame. Horns gouged vat-grown flesh and teeth sank into the same. The charge turned the wounded, burning, multi-limbed biomechanoid onto its back. Zabilla found herself liking the warmth of the flames on her face. She found herself liking the colour red.

'They're basically the same as us, you know? The morlocks, I mean,' Scoular said somewhat distractedly as the chimera feasted upon his creation. 'It'll be outside forces. If it wasn't, then the Absolute would know.'

Dracup was trying to mask his contempt for Scoular and said nothing. Zabilla watched the dragon and lion bury their heads up to their necks in the dead biomechanoid. The lion head appeared again, red, and roared.

Can you feel that, Absolute? Zabilla wondered. 'It's part of the Game,' she said quietly, still transfixed by the gory display playing out on the arena floor.

Even Dracup looked shocked.

'The Absolute said that he would never wipe players,' Carinne stammered.

'It's heresy to even suggest so!' Scoular all but shouted. Zabilla was sure that there was a degree of triumph in his voice. He didn't understand pain and he didn't understand daring. Zabilla allowed herself a small smile before turning to face them both.

'What's heresy? To suggest that the Absolute can't change the rules of his own game or to suggest that for some reason the Absolute would have to inform you both first?' she demanded, allowing just a hint of anger into her voice. She saw their doubt and fear, the insecurity that came from realising that the rules were not as they had thought. None of them wanted to face up to this possibility. Scoular glanced back down into the arena, his creation now just a feast for the victorious vat-grown myth.

'Of course, you realise there's a lot more to it than winning the battle, don't you?' he asked Zabilla, who nodded. 'Elegance of design, aesthetics, things that a mere copy can't allow for. It's about impressing the Absolute with the skill of your design.'

'As I said,' Zabilla was smiling, 'I am a mere amateur.'

He didn't understand the Game. Scoular was right: it wasn't about winning the fight, but it wasn't about impressing either. It was about sensation. The bit of her design that would win the audition wasn't the creature's ability to vanquish its foes or the elegance and potency of the design. She would win because of the sophistication of the experiential biofeedbackware that would allow the Absolute to experience every moment of the fight from the chimera's perspective. The taste of flesh, the feeling of breathing fire, the animalistic triumph at the kill: the Absolute drank sensation. Scoular knew that on one level but he made the mistake of thinking that the Absolute was just a bigger and much more powerful version of himself. He would never understand the simplicity of the thirst for pure sensation.

'You should let me kill him,' Dracup said as they made their way along a gnarled narrow branch, grown into a walkway, towards the air jetty. They were in the upper branches so the sides of the walkway had been grown into handsome abstract patterns.

'According to you, I should let you kill everyone. Have you ever thought that you haven't yet earned your second name because, in the unlikely event that the Absolute focuses on you, he is party to these feelings? Subtlety, my dear, subtlety and sensation.'

'The Absolute enjoys violence,' Dracup said with a certainty that only the young could have. He was right. The early parts of Game history, immediately after the terraforming, were basically an orgy of violence. Despite the elegance and sophistication of the terraforming design, the roots of the arboreal arcologies were soaked in blood. Bodies had hung from some of the branches like particularly fecund fruit.

Zabilla sighed and looked out at the massive arcology trees reaching up to pierce the atmosphere. All of them were studded with dots of bioluminescence. Each dot was a window. Game had been an experiment in Seeder-derived, nano-technological terraforming. Game's size, its 0.75G, geological stability and the abundant energy of a large, nearby main-sequence G-type star had all pointed towards the viability of growing starscraper arcologies. The wish to harness solar energy suggested to the nano-architects that trees grown from an engineered wood-analogous substance would be both practical and aesthetically pleasing.

The roots grew deep into the planet to provide stability. The roots sought out Game's natural resources and harnessed its geothermal energy. Leaf structures in the upper branches harnessed solar energy. The black leaves in the lower sectors harnessed infrared energy from both above and from heat escaping below. The biotech machinery that provided for the needs of the inhabitants – sewage and sanitation, water recycling, food creation, etcetera – was housed in the darkness below the black leaves. The vat-grown, blind subhuman morlock servitors oversaw this machinery. Other servitor creatures, designed to look like attractive birds or small arboreal mammals, saw to maintenance and sanitation requirements in the upper branches.

The upper branches divided the light from the artificial moons into competing beams that shone through the membranous translucent energy-gathering leaf canopy. Game's moistness meant that mist was often present, further refracting the artificial moonlight. The effect was atmospheric and to Zabilla pleasantly eerie. She saw one of the larger avian servitors take off and flap through the misty night air. Dracup came and leaned on the rail of the walkway, looking at Zabilla intensely even as she stared out into the forest of city-sized trees.

'The Absolute enjoys originality; violence can be a short cut. If you were to duel Scoular or assassinate him, both of which are beneath you, then you would need to do so in an original way.' Even to Dracup she would not admit how she had distilled her views of what the Absolute wanted down to pure sensation – after all, he was another player. She had no doubt that the Absolute enjoyed good gamesmanship, but he/she/it must have seen it all now in the thousands of years of Game's existence.

'I ... I am trying to learn,' he said haltingly.

She turned to look at him. 'There's nothing attractive to either the Absolute or myself about weakness, do you understand?'

Dracup nodded. Like everything in the Game, she felt like she was playing out a scene, but she had worked hard enough for the Absolute this night. She wanted something for herself just now. *Do you hear that, Absolute? Ride me if you will, but I need to let go. Maybe this is what he wanted, less artifice, more feeling.* No, she didn't want to think like that.

It was bad form to reward an underling with something he wanted after he had disappointed you. The problem came when you wanted the same thing. Zabilla grabbed the back of Dracup's head and pulled him closer into her, exchanging a long kiss that became more urgent as it went on. She felt his hands sliding her skirt up and she jumped up onto him, wrapping her long legs around his waist.

With a thought, the baroque luxury G-car rose into view at the end of the jetty. It bobbed slightly on the four ball-mounted AG motors at each of its corners before docking. With another thought, the doors to the car split open. Another thought turned the plush interior red like her thoughts in the arena.

Dracup carried her, mostly blind, mouths meshed together, to the G-car, falling onto the soft carpet. The door closed behind them as the G-car took off, the AI pilot banking the vehicle towards Zabilla's abode.

Zabilla wriggled out from underneath. Dracup's hand snagged her underwear and dragged it down. She pushed herself onto one of the seats, spreading her legs, hunger written over her normally emotionless face. This was for her, to forget herself, the Game, the Absolute, the audition. This was for her only. Later she would test the limits of the heightened nerve endings she'd had grown in Dracup. Later she would feed the Absolute, later she would play the Game, lose herself in it, but not now.

In a distant chamber something started to pay attention to one of its favourites. Again.

The ride home had been sublime – dangerous but sublime. She had let herself go when her Game play was about control. She knew that many were good at feeding the Absolute sensation with abandon. Zabilla had always found the need to work at it.

When they arrived home they had worked at it, each little act designed to maximise either pain or pleasure, the whole thing designed as a beacon for the Absolute. She thought she had felt it in her experiential ware but the scientist in her knew that was her imagination. The Absolute was a silent ghost in their pain and pleasure centres. If people knew when the Absolute was present, then the heads would not be as effective as they were at rooting out the anti-social losers who played against the Game itself.

Like most players she'd had her rebellious phase when she had been a student. She had sworn that she was never going to play the Game, engage with it, never earn her second name, and like everyone she found herself inexorably drawn into it. Then she found that she understood it, found that she was good at it. Now she realised that rejection of the Game was just an excuse that losers made.

Zabilla had studied biophysics, specialising in Seeder biotech, how it interacted with Quantum phenomena and how it applied to Red Space and exotic entanglement. Though she had to be careful studying Red Space applications because anything that even remotely looked like research into bridge technology was heretical. The Church audited her research on a regular basis and she had received more than one censure. On one occasion a line of research she believed had been encouraged by the Absolute his/her/itself had resulted in a threat of excommunication. It was a serious threat. She had wondered why the Church felt they needed the Seeders as a religion. Progenitors they might have been, but their time was gone, and now they had the Game and the Absolute. The Absolute had the powers of a god, and after victory in the Art Wars the Absolute even had god-like killer angels to do his/her/its bidding.

Zabilla's apartment was a handsomely appointed three-storey nook high enough for her to make out stars through the canopy of bio-engineered leaves. The bottom level was her lab, steel and glass, the wood grown around it and redesigned to be non-porous and support a sterile surface. The upper two storeys were open plan, a catwalk running around the top floor. Through the large window opening in the wall she could see the light-speckled shadows of the other trees. The bed was on a raised plinth that grew from the floor and the wall. A small waterfall and pool provided a water feature/bath/shower combination. Discreet sound-dampening projectors took care of the constant noise of water.

They experimented. They gave her apartment's sound-dampening properties a run for its money as they pushed Dracup's heightened nerve endings to their limits. Afterwards, exhausted, Zabilla had to carry Dracup up the wooden steps to her bed. She laid him down trying to decide how she felt about him. Was he anything more than just a handsome, if severe, game piece? More to the point, what was she to him? A lover? A mentor? A stepping-stone to a better thing for an ambitious player? If so, then he was a much cleverer player than she had so far given him credit for. When she was younger it had been easier to differentiate between Zabilla the person and Zabilla the player.

She looked down at him. He looked peaceful, more innocent, when asleep. She wondered if that was the only time they could be themselves. It wasn't the first time she had thought this. But dreams contained sensation as well. Even when they slept they were not alone. There was something in the back of her mind. Some sense of disgust at this violation of her sleeping mind, an alien feeling that she hadn't felt in so long. She tried to suppress it. She had no idea why she was feeling this way. Not when she was so close to winning the audition.

She released a potent anti-anxiety drug into her bloodstream, then a less potent sedative. She had time to climb into bed and roll next to Dracup, feel his warmth, before fatigue and the sedative overwhelmed her and took her where she could be herself.

It was like a sting, a tiny pinprick but it felt deep. She shouldn't have felt it, but she was a light sleeper and had paranoia routines written into her neunonics. Even then she probably wouldn't have felt it if it hadn't been for her heightened nerve endings. She had forgotten to send a chemical signal to dull them before she fell asleep.

She sat up in bed feeling vulnerable and frightened, dragging the sheets around her. She hadn't felt like this since she was a child. *Where was all the fear coming from?* she asked herself.

Almost immediately she turned to look at Dracup. He was deeply asleep in a way that was difficult to fake. She confirmed this with physiological readings provided by the medical applications of her nano-screen. Her first thought had been that Dracup was playing some kind of gambit.

She checked her internal systems. There was nothing as far as she could tell, no biological or nano-agent. She checked her nano-screen and the apartment's security systems. Neither of the systems had detected any kind of foreign presence in the room.

Zabilla was beginning to convince herself that she had been dreaming when the banging on the door started. She jumped and turned to stare at the closed aperture in the wood. Her security systems should have warned her the moment somebody turned into the corridor that led to the door to her apartment. The fact they hadn't meant that they had been overridden. That and the sound, that particular knock, the sound from a thousand immersions and a million newscasts, meant that it was the heads outside.

Feed from the door sensors to her neunonics confirmed this. Outside, two of the powerful automatons with the enlarged smiling face of the Absolute, pre-ascension, were waiting at her door. The grin on their massive faces looked more obscene and frightening to her now than ever before.

The knock came again. Her mind raced. What had she done? Had Scoular managed to frame her? A bold and clever move if he had, but it had better be watertight or else she would destroy him. Then she thought back to her feeling of disgust, of violation from having the Absolute see inside her mind. She had committed treason. She had gone from being a player to being a loser. The thoughts had come unbidden! It was so unfair.

'What?' Dracup sat up, quickly going from rudely woken to

completely alert. He turned to look at her. There was no fear in his expression; instead there was a questioning look on his face. It was just short of accusation.

The knock came again. They never knocked more than three times. Now they would override the apartment's security. The aperture opened. Zabilla's neunonics told her that Dracup had sent the command. She couldn't shake the feeling of teeth closing in around her.

The two heavily armoured automatons stepped into the apartment, looking up at the bed. They looked like walking statues, their faces twisted, agonised somehow, sinisterly clownish parodies of the pre-ascension Absolute.

'Can I help you?' Dracup asked.

Zabilla wondered when he had become assertive. She controlled the fear. She put on her Game face, quite literally. 'What do you want and why are you disturbing me at this hour?' she demanded.

Dracup turned to look at her, raising an eyebrow. On the other hand it was the question of a completely innocent person.

Neither of the heads said anything. Zabilla had pulled her nano-screen in as the heads expanded theirs. There was sparring at a nano-level as their nanites interrogated hers and Dracup's.

'What just happened?' the voice, modulated for psychological impact, asked. She wasn't sure which of them had spoken.

'Explain yourself,' she told the heads.

'For a moment there was something not of the Game in here,' the voice answered. She felt coldness creeping through her. The pinprick. The strange thing was that she thought she had heard something that she had never heard before from a head. It sounded like it was unsure of itself.

'Well, have you found anything?' she asked.

'Why were you reviewing your physiological readings and security systems?' the voice asked, suspicious now. Dracup turned to look at her. He looked suspicious as well.

'I thought I felt something. A pinprick, but it was nothing, a dream or some half-waking sensation, nothing more. What made you think there was something else here?'

'It came from the Absolute,' the voice said.

So the Absolute had been monitoring her as she slept. Again the cold clammy feeling of violation rose inside her. She tried to force it down. Both the heads seemed to be staring at her with the dead black holes in their mask-like faces where eyes should have been.

'Perhaps the Absolute only felt what I felt?' she said.

'Have you found anything?' Dracup asked impatiently.

'No,' the voice answered.

'Will you be taking any further action?'

There was a pause.

'Not at the moment.'

The heads turned and left the apartment, the aperture door shutting behind them. Dracup gave her that questioning look again. She wanted to talk to him, to hold him, to take comfort from him, but this would only leave her more vulnerable, and her paranoia, one of the most important qualities of the professional player, would not allow her to show that weakness.

The massive chamber was arched like a Seeder cathedral. The wood had been grown into detailed ornamental patterns. Parts of it were friezes showing the history and mythology of the Game and the Absolute. It showed the Absolute's journey from a world of toil to the world of leisure and pleasure that was the Game. In which you didn't have to work unless you chose to. All you had to do was play the most involving game that had ever been created.

The hall had been grown out of the main trunk, its back wall a series of stained-glass windows. Sun shone through, illuminating the dust motes and larger nanite clusters in the air. Zabilla stood next to Dracup, her installation, her gift, in front of her in a covered glass box about the size of a large cupboard. Scoular was to her right, with Carinne and a similar covered box in front of him. He didn't look confident; in fact, he looked ill.

Zabilla recognised most of the crowd. They were the top players from the arcology within the fields of genetics, biology and biophysics, as well as a number of art critics.

Shallow stairs led to a raised area in front of the stained-glass windows. On that platform stood the avatar, an automaton with an idealised body of brass complete with suitably intimidating phallus. Its face was a mask of beaten platinum and gold. The Absolute as a pre-Loss God. The sun made the polished metal gleam and sparkle to the point where it was difficult to look directly at the automaton. It was like a genuine religious experience, Zabilla thought. All her doubts of last night were forgotten. The avatars were direct representatives of the Absolute, and this one was here to judge the final part of the audition.

The avatar's musical tones were still ringing around the hall from its opening address. There had been polite applause, then all eyes turned to Scoular, who was sweating heavily, and Zabilla. She tried to suppress her awe as the avatar turned its imperious gaze on them.

She bowed slightly and held out a hand towards Scoular. It would, of course, appear like the gracious gesture of someone allowing their opponent to go first. It was not; it was calculated. She wanted the impact of going last. Scoular probably would have done the same thing, but he looked too sweaty, sick and nervous. When he realised what she'd done, he glared at her.

With as much of a flourish as he could manage, Scoular tore off the sheet covering the glass box. The glass box then disintegrated in front of their eyes, allowing a better look at its contents.

Lying in a nutrient bath were what looked like the torsos of a male and female human, though sex was difficult to tell because they were completely fused together. The semi-human chimerical organism almost rippled against itself in never-ending, distinctly sexual gyrations. Pleasure seemed to be written in a series of artistic blushes on its skin.

There was a degree of art to it, Zabilla had to admit, particularly the blushes and the suggestion of different genders, but at the end of the day it was little more than a pleasure generator. She wasn't even annoyed that Scoular had upped its output by using heightened nerve endings gained from his espionage directed at her own research.

There was hushed conversation among the crowd. Zabilla felt her contempt for them. Nobody wanted to be the first to compliment or criticise; they wanted to see what others would do first. They lacked boldness, which was why they would never be truly great players.

She looked down as if politely trying to hide a smile. Dracup was less subtle. She gave them time to take in Scoular's work. He was looking sicker by the moment, particularly as applause seemed less than forthcoming.

Finally, after she felt expectations had been raised enough, she nodded to Dracup, who without a flourish removed the sheet as Zabilla's glass box began to disintegrate.

The most difficult thing had been to combine the scream with musical tones to make something beautiful out of agony.

Like Scoular's design, it was little more than head and torso. There was to be nothing that was unnecessary. Like Scoular's design, it utilised her heightened nerve-ending biotechnology. Other than skin and mouth it had no sensory organs, but those were the only two it needed. Its body existed only as a conduit for pain and music. A metal clamp fused with its spine held it up. In the nutrient bath opposite it was a tree. Purposefully designed to look like an arcology tree, its branches moved like tendrils. Its leaves were monomolecular razors that dug into the musically screaming torso's flesh.

People stared at it. Genuinely moved by the beauty of the music of her creation's screams, Zabilla allowed a tear to run down her cheek. Dracup, who had tears streaming down his, would later tell her that many in the audience were similarly moved.

The sound of metal clanging against metal over and over again caught everyone's attention. Zabilla looked up to see the avatar, seemingly staring at her with the unmoving mask of its face, applauding with its large brass hands.

'This is mere pornography!' Scoular disgraced himself by shouting. His voice sounded weak and was barely heard as applause broke out around the hall. Scoular sank to his knees. Nobody noticed. Carinne went to him, trying to help him up, but even with the tiny AG motors that helped support his fat he was too heavy for her. 'What've you done?' he screamed at Zabilla.

She turned to look at him. *I introduced a very new, very subtle, very difficult to detect and trace, very deadly and particularly well-timed virus into your system when we shook hands earlier,* she didn't tell him. She hoped the smile communicated it all. His public execution for little more than opposing her and having poor taste was part of the audition as far as she was concerned.

Scoular collapsed onto the wooden floor. His last living act was to meat-hack Carrine, activate the upmarket combat abilities that all good consorts had written into their neunonics and augmentations, and send her after Zabilla.

Which was what Dracup had been waiting for. He interposed himself between Zabilla and Carinne and moved forward to meet the other consort. Carinne's face was a contorted mask of hate and anger. There had obviously been a powerful emotional element to the hack. Carinne suddenly crouched, her leg swinging out to sweep Dracup's. Dracup flipped back. Carinne was already back up, advancing on him, drawing her own bone knife. Dracup landed on his hands and kicked up from the ground, surprising Carinne. The blow caught the other consort just under her sternum. There was an audible *crack* as Carinne was lifted off the ground by the force of the blow. She staggered as she landed but immediately started towards Zabilla again.

There were shocked gasps from the crowd as Dracup threw his bone knife. Carinne blocked the flying blade at the last moment with her own, sending Dracup's blade skittering across the floor. Thinking him unarmed, she went to finish the job, but Dracup had used the minute distraction of the flying blade to close with Carinne. He grabbed the elbow and wrist of her blade arm and twisted the knife round. Before Carinne had a chance to resist, her own blade was stabbed up through her mouth and into her brain, where it released its deadly payload of neurotoxin. Carinne shook; blood frothed from her mouth, and she tumbled to the ground.

Dracup smoothed down his tunic and retrieved his blade.

Zabilla found it hard not to smile. She tried to control her face as she heard the sound of metal footsteps resonating off wood. She turned to look at the gleaming avatar.

'Will you come with me, please?'

To call this vehicle a G-car was to do it a disservice, Zabilla thought; it was like a luxurious flying fortress. The inverted cauldron shapes of AG motors ran up either side of the vehicle. The destination, however, took her by surprise.

They sank beneath the Black Leaves into the roots. She needed her augments to see into the outside, where darkness prevailed. She saw the huge machinery of the roots and was even able to make out a degree of movement as the root structure steadied the arcologies they supported.

As they got closer to the roots themselves, she started to make out the morlock servitors maintaining the machinery. They lived in squalor in tiny shanty towns made out of what they could scavenge from the waste of the world above the black-leaf canopy. She saw morlocks in cast-off finery clambering over mountains of once-fine furniture, ornamentation, artwork and other bits and pieces of assembler detritus from the world above. Rubbish that people had for one reason or another never got around to disassembling. Dracup was unable to conceal his distaste. Zabilla was less sure it was the morlocks' own fault.

All through the journey the avatar had said nothing, and Zabilla, wanting to show poise and calm, had also remained silent.

They sank into the planet itself. Spiralling slowly around massive roots that dug into crust and then mantle. Finally they flew through a network of airlock-like heavily armoured doors that shut behind them one after another.

The luxury G-car landed in a huge open space. There were other more utilitarian and military vehicles present. The structure might have been the first construction that Zabilla had ever seen that was not made of wood. She had to search her neunonics to find references to nano-bonded reinforced concrete.

Still without saying anything, the avatar, now looking as ostentatious and out of place as Zabilla felt, led her through a heavily defended series of chambers to a very secure laboratory, which, unlike her own laboratory, seemed to be all substance and no style.

Lying on a metal table in the centre of the lab, surrounded by very visible sensors of every conceivable type and a ring of automated weapon systems, was a strange, roughly coffin-shaped cocoon structure made of a white substance that Zabilla did not recognise.

'Congratulations. You have got the job,' the avatar said.

23

Southern Britain, a Long Time Ago

'Why are they here?' It was unusual for Bress to hear nervousness in Ettin's voice.'

At Crom Dhubh's behest. They harvested the crystal,' Bress said emotionlessly.

'But then why does the dragon remain?'

'It feeds from her while poisoning her like a parasite. It wants to ride her corruption when it comes. Besides, it is a little added security.'

'These primitives are no threat to us.'

'Some of these primitives have the blood of the gods in them.'

Ettin stared at Bress for a moment, trying to fathom him. 'Watered down,' the two-headed creature said, turning away.

'Not all.'

'Your woman. The one you spared.'

'She is not my woman, but she is coming south with two others.'

'As I said, primitives.'

'They are from the Eggshell.'

Ettin turned to Bress again. 'That is a myth.'

Bress could not be bothered to respond. If it was a myth then where had the warrior and the swollen-headed demon come from? He looked at what they had grown. It towered high above the ships and the wading giants. He tried to ignore the smell, the screams. They were allowed to scream now as they were feeding her. He thought of the dragon burrowing into her flesh like a venomous tick and he tried to ignore the feeling that he had just betrayed his entire species.

Dead men writhed on the ground before the fire. They looked like worms, grubs, their movements a mockery of dance. The dead men averted their eyes and cowered as a figure formed in the fire. Formed of flickering black flame, the figure was warped, twisted and difficult to see, as if parts of its shape made no sense. The horses whickered, whinnied and stamped nervously where they had been tethered. It was not the sight and smells of the corpse-studded ground that made them nervous.

Those prostrate on the ground felt the power of this mere shadow of their charnel god. The Dark Man in the flames, Crom Dhubh, the man the witch folk fire-danced with, was just a more powerful messenger of oblivion than they themselves.

'Carrion warriors, continue to drive the weak before you, take your fill of their flesh and drive the rest to the sacrifice.'

Cadwr was nervous, but the young warrior knew he had led his small part of the warband well. They had ranged along the south-western banks of the river of the Grey Father. They killed those they caught, let the rest flee to be herded to the south by the larger bands led by Ysgawyn. They burned the land and slaughtered the cattle. There would be famine when winter came. Only the dead gods would feast, as would their servants, those who ate the flesh of heroes blessed by the gods themselves.

'What would you have us do?'

The warped, living black flame turned to look at the young warrior covered in lime and blood.

'When you meet Ysgawyn, go to the Crown. Slay this Rin; he is old and weak like the blood of the god within him. Bring the rest of his people to my servant, the tall man. I will send beasts from the Otherworld to aid you.'

Britha stood in the darkness just beyond the light of the fire and the circle of lime- and gore-crusted warriors. She knew that simply by being still they would not see her for looking. It was movement that gave away the hidden.

The figure in the fire was making her sick. She could feel it in the air somehow. She felt the violation of the natural order of things, a connection between the living fire and wherever this dark figure actually stood. The Cirig knew that you never looked too hard into a fire as you risked attracting the attention of callous gods who lived in burning places.

As sick as it made her, she felt its call. *Was this shadow Bress's master?* she wondered. The figure spoke to the same parts of her that the dreams of Bress did. The dreams were more frequent and intense now. But perhaps it was just the thought of battle that was making her wet.

They were in the northern lands of the Atrebates, the tribe whose king they sought. What the black curraghs had left, the Corpse People had despoiled. Tangwen said that the Corpse People had been one of the many tribes that made up the Durotriges, a confederation of peoples from the far west. They had been expelled from the confederation for their dark practices. They lived on the plain where many of the other tribes placed their dead in barrows or left them for the crows to carry to the Otherworld. The plain bordered Annwn, the land of the dead, and the Corpse People were thought to have strayed too close to that border.

They had been travelling for ten days now. The last Britha had seen of the People of the Snake had been the little girl holding one of Fachtna's arm torcs. The *Will of Dagon* had carried them west up the river until Hanno had finally refused to take them further despite there being plenty of loot for the Carthaginians from deserted and destroyed villages. Tangwen had led them on foot from there. The young hunter and warrior had taken them deeper into the ruined landscape. They had gone west first, skirting areas that had been raided, trying to avoid bands of warriors from further north seeking to protect their lands. Then they headed south. Britha did not trust the land here – its flatness seemed unnatural – but she had to admit that before its despoliation it must have been very rich.

'What have you brought for me?' the warped figure in the living flame asked. Its inhuman voice made Britha's skin crawl. Bress must be his slave. This monster must have forced him to drink from the chalice she had seen. She had to push down these thoughts, focus, forget about Bress. All that mattered was her tribe. Regardless of this thing's hold on Bress and her attraction to him. Bress still had to die.

The boy they brought forward was too terrified to cry. Pale and naked, there were cuts on his head and face where hair and eyebrows had been shaved off. The smile on the face of the warrior who'd asked about Rhi Rin told Britha that he took pleasure from this. She'd seen the look before on the face of blood-drunk warriors and black-robed sacrificers who relished what should have been no more than their duty. The boy shook like a leaf. *They were not a strong people*, Britha thought.

They made the boy kneel before the fire. Cadwr crawled behind him, averting his eyes. He put the stone blade into the small of the captive's back. He would destroy the bone there so the boy could not move and then feed him to the fire so the Dark Man could drink the weakling's suffering. The smiling lime-covered warrior wanted the smell of blood boiling in blackening skin so that Crom Dhubh would know his devotion. He was looking forward to the ragged feel of the rough stone blade tearing through soft skin and hard bone. He savoured the boy's fear as stone touched flesh.

An arrow grew from Cadwr's head. He felt the impact. Knew something was wrong.

Across the fire he saw Edern staring at him. Behind Edern the darkness parted, revealing a strange man with skin like wood and a swollen head. Not a man but a demon! The demon had a black knife in his hand. The blade had somehow captured the flames from the fire within it. A red smile appeared on Edern's neck as the demon drew the blade across limed flesh with no more effort than a man slicing butter. Then the darkness came for Cadwr. Confused that he could die again, he hoped he was travelling to his reward.

Two of their number were dead before the Corpse People even started to reach for spears and swords and climb to their feet. Even hardened warriors who thought themselves dead jumped at the horrible keening noise. Britha seemed to fall from the sky. After all, they hadn't seen her leap off a nearby moss-covered boulder. Her face contorted as she made fear magics with her voice. She landed behind one of the Corpse People; the head of her spear exploded out of the man's chest. Part of the haft followed as Britha's momentum pushed it through and rammed the point into the ground. Rather than try and tear the spear out, Britha pulled her sickle from her belt and turned to face the closest warrior.

Teardrop had insisted that their weapons, including Tangwen's arrowheads, were first soaked in the blood of either himself, a reluctant Fachtna or Britha. Teardrop had then burned some kind of sweet-smelling plant to make smoke and chanted at the weapons. He said that he was telling them what to do. Britha thought this nonsense. Iron knew how to kill before it was forged. The heat in the pregnant metal of the belly of the forge was just the pain of birth.

The warrior had drawn his sword. The pitted blade shone in the firelight. Southron warriors polished their blades rather than leaving them blue from the forge as they did in the north. He swung the sword two-handed at Britha, who parried, also using both hands, catching the blade in the curve of the sickle. Surprise flashed across the warrior's face. He had not been expecting Britha to be strong enough to stop the force of his blow.

Behind Britha another of the Corpse People swung a carved stone and bone club at the back of her hooded skull. Fachtna emerged out of the darkness behind him. His angry-sounding, singing, ghost-bladed sword made a cut through the warrior from shoulder to deep in the man's stomach.

Britha kicked the swordsman back, again surprising him with her strength and staggering him. Then she swung the sickle two-handed up into the warrior's groin. A long way from dead, he collapsed to the ground clutching his ruined manhood. This time she used his high-pitched screams to cast her fear magics. Her first victim was still sliding down the haft of her spear.

Two warriors charged Fachtna's back. Two arrows appeared in the back of one, Tangwen firing from the trees, her snake mask high up on her head to give a clear view as she shot. The man hit the ground, sliding in the dirt as Fachtna spun around, lifting his leg over the fallen man. The second warrior had been going for a low strike with his spear, hoping to push it into Fachtna's bowels. The Gael brought down his leg with incredible speed and stamped on the haft of the spear, splintering it. He swung the large oval shield strapped to his left arm into the charging spearman, lifting him off his feet and then slamming him to the ground. Fachtna pulled the shield up and then drove his sword through the man's chest and deep into the earth beneath him.

Tangwen sprinted through the woods illuminated by the beams of moonlight the thick branches of the burned trees let through. She kept the flames from the campfire to her left, trying not to look directly at it as she changed position. She knelt down, dropping the two arrows she had already taken from her quiver to the ashen earth next to her. She watched as three warriors advanced on Teardrop, two with spears and one with an axe. The swollen-headed man was holding his own, parrying the spears with his crystal-tipped staff, but the axeman had his weapon held high and was waiting for just the right moment to strike.

It didn't matter that he had trained as a warrior as well as a shaman. It didn't matter that he had been in battles before. Whenever he was attacked, Teardrop was always aware that he was fighting for his life. Fachtna never let the thought of defeat enter his mind, so he said, but Teardrop always felt he was one mistake from death. He always felt the rise of panic within him and had to fight not to succumb to it.

The axeman was cagey, biding his moment as the spearmen pressed him. The sound of wood and metal on wood filled the air. Both spearmen thrust at once. Teardrop swept both spearheads to the side but they pushed against the staff, trying to force his guard down. Then the axeman charged.

Tangwen had one of the arrows nocked. She loosed and then grabbed the other arrow, nocked and loosed that before the first arrow had even reached its target.

The arrow caught the axeman in the side of the head with sufficient force that the arrowhead burst out of his skull on the opposite side. The momentum of his charge kept him moving forward even as he collapsed to the ground. Another arrow appeared in the back of the neck of one of the spearmen. He hit the ground before he was aware of what had killed him. The final spearman made the mistake of glancing towards his dead friend. When he looked back at Teardrop he saw the butt of Teardrop's staff flying towards him.

Tangwen heard the *crunch* of Teardrop's staff caving in the final spearman's face. He turned and raised a hand to her in thanks.

'Oh, Teardrop!' Tangwen moaned as one of the lime-covered, gore-streaked Corpse People charged him, sword raised high. Tangwen nocked another arrow but she had her own problems. Three of the enemy were sprinting into the burned forest heading straight for her. How they could see her so well she did not know, and they were running in with the fire directly behind them, which would affect her aim.

Teardrop only just managed to spin out of the way of the swordsman's blow. He continued to spin in a full circle, and his staff caught the man in the back of his head with sufficient force to lift him off his feet. Teardrop quickly closed with the swordsman as he rolled over. All but standing over him, Teardrop slammed the butt down towards the warrior's head. The swordsman parried the blow two-handed. Teardrop slammed it down again. The swordsman rolled to the side and then smacked the staff out of the way, knocking Teardrop off balance. The man rolled to his feet and grinned at Teardrop, drooling. Teardrop knew he was outclassed.

Teardrop pointed the staff at the swordsman and called upon the crystal. He felt it creep further into his head. He screamed as it went directly to the pain receptors in the soft matter of his brain. Suddenly he saw things in a different way, in a way that mere humans were not meant to see. He reached out with impossibly long limbs only notionally attached to him and made a tiny change before he snapped back into his own body with its agony-filled mind. The swordsman's scream drowned out Teardrop's. It looked as if the hilt of the enemy warrior's sword had slipped through his hand to fuse itself into the man's arm. Fighting the pain and the seemingly inexorable advance of the crystal tendrils in his mind, Teardrop spun again, using his staff to sweep the man's legs out from underneath him. The agonised warrior hit the ground. Teardrop stood over him, raised his staff and put the man out of his misery.

An arrow flew through the fire-blackened wood. It took the first man in the throat. Tangwen loosed the second arrow from a standing position in a hurry. She barely had time to curse as it hit the man in the leg. The third was almost on her. She tried to distract the charging warrior by throwing the bow at him. This gave her time to grab the hatchet from her belt as the man batted the bow to one side and charged. Tangwen had long ago learned the pointlessness of trying to fight much larger opponents head on. As he reached her she sank to one knee and swung her hatchet hard at the side of his knee. She felt the blade bite deep into flesh and hit bone. The man screamed even as his sword sliced into her wood and wicker snake's head helm and opened the side of her head. She lost hold of the hatchet as the man barrelled into her.

Tangwen found herself lying on the floor fighting pain, nausea and unconsciousness, the side of her head wet, sticky and covered in dirt. She managed to push herself up as the man rolled towards her. She threw herself on him, grabbing the stone dagger from his belt and ramming it into his mouth, breaking teeth and, with a scream, pushing it up into his brain. The corpse bucked under her and then was still. She caught her breath.

The kick caught Tangwen in the side of her chest, picked her up off the body of the man and slammed her into a tree, burned bark crumbling under the impact. Then he was on her, hands around her throat, bestial look on his face as he squeezed the life out of her. It was the one she had shot in the leg. She dimly wondered why he hadn't run her through with sword or spear. As things got darker, as she lost the fight for breath, as she clawed at him, she was horribly aware of his stench – of decay and the corpses he tried so hard to emulate.

The blade of the sickle dug deep into the warrior's stomach as Britha wrenched it upwards. His war cry choked out and was replaced by the screams of the eviscerated. Britha yanked the sickle out. She staggered back as another of the Corpse People seemingly appeared out of nowhere, charging her, axe held high. Sidestepping, she fish-hooked the axeman in the face with the sickle and used his momentum to guide him into the fire. There was an explosion of sparks as the screaming man rolled around in the flames, his hair and trews catching fire. It looked like he was writhing around in the shadow of the Dark Man. As if his own god was consuming him. *Good*, Britha thought.

Wetness sprayed her face and the fingers around her throat fell away. Tangwen opened her eyes and saw Teardrop standing over her. The black-bladed knife he held in his hand was dripping. He raised a foot to kick the now-dead strangler off her.

Fachtna moved the shield rapidly between the blades of the two swordsmen. The shield shook with each impact. A third warrior stabbed at him with a spear. He turned the point with his sword and then swung to counter-attack. The spearman brought the haft of his weapon up to block. The singing sword cut through the wood and sliced the warrior open diagonally from hip to shoulder. Fachtna sidestepped rapidly, knocking the falling man towards the swordsmen. Fachtna bisected one of the warriors' heads as he tried to move out of the way of his dead companion. As the other one charged him, Fachtna ducked behind his shield and rammed it forward, putting all his force behind it, battering the man's sword strike out of the way and knocking him back. Fachtna reached around the front of the shield with his sword and slashed the blade across the man's legs. Flesh just seemed to open up at the touch of the ghostly blade. The man fell into Fachtna's shield and the Gael braced as he slid down it. Fachtna finished him by running the blade through the back of his neck.

Britha's blood was up. Breathing hard and covered in blood, she wanted to fight more. Kill more. She looked around. All were still or almost dead, their fight long gone. Disappointed, she let the dripping blade of her sickle hang at her side. The burning man launched himself out of the fire, axe held high. Britha started to turn. Something passed her face, brushing against it. An arrow appeared in the burning axeman's mouth, and he fell to the ground. Britha became aware of the smell of burning flesh mixed with the coppery tang of blood and the smell of ruptured bowels. She turned and looked into the woods. Tangwen was lowering her bow. The blood that caked the other woman's face looked black in the moonlight. Teardrop was standing next to her. Britha could make out both perfectly despite the darkness. She nodded to the hunter.

The figure was still there watching them from the fire. 'I know you,' it said. Somehow Britha could feel the words in her blood. She did not want to look at the figure. There was something wrong with it. It hurt her head to look. His shape, though the shape of a man, did not make sense at some fundamental level.

'Get up!' she snapped at the blood-splattered and terrified boy the Corpse People had been about to sacrifice.

'You are close to being one of us,' the figure continued. Impossibly deep, its voice seemed to reverberate inside her. She tried not to stumble. She reached for the boy, who was shaking uncontrollably, and after several attempts she managed to pull him to his feet.

'You have to go to your people,' she told him. It was useless. The boy did not understand her words.

'He has no people,' the voice said. There was no maliciousness there: it was a simple statement of fact. It earned the figure a glare from Britha despite the nausea-inducing pain that lanced through her head as she did so.

'Is your power to mock us through the flames?' she demanded.

'I have no power. None of us do. Our mistake is to believe that we are something when we are less than nothing.'

'Crawl on your stomach if you will, but do not try to drag us down there with you,' Britha shouted.

'I apologise. I have misled you. I am not talking of my beliefs. This is knowledge, simply a case of understanding my place in things and yours.'

Teardrop was striding towards the fire, the hood of his cloak pulled up.

'Release my people and you can do what you will. We will trouble you no more.' Britha sensed and tried to ignore Fachtna glaring at her.

'I don't know or care who your people are. I want to know you better. Bress wants to know you better. Death wants to know you better. I can promise you the fulfilment of every desire you have and those you do not know before the end comes.'

Britha tried to suppress the images of Bress that came to her mind, how they made her feel. The Dark Man was there as well, watching, his presence not unwanted.

'I desire my people released.'

Teardrop stared into the fire. Fachtna joined him, sword in hand. The warrior had put his cloak back on and pulled the hood up.

333

'Can you see it?' Fachtna asked.

'I see it,' Teardrop said quietly. Fachtna swung his blade into the fire. There was an explosion of sparks. The figure warped and then was gone. Glowing embers filled the night air. Britha turned to look at the pair.

'What were you looking for?' she demanded.

'A crystal blackened by the fire,' Teardrop muttered. 'And you know better than to talk to them.'

'Not if she's swiving them,' Fachtna muttered.

Britha bit back an angry retort. 'If you saw it,' she said to Teardrop instead and then pointed at Fachtna, 'how did he know where to strike?'

Neither of them answered. There was the wet sound of iron hitting flesh and the sound of bones breaking. All of them turned to look at Tangwen as she struck again and again at a corpse. Finally satisfied, she moved on to the next one and repeated the process. Feeling their eyes on her, she looked up. One whole side of her head was covered in blood.

'We break their bones so when they rise again all they can do is crawl,' she told them and then sat down hard, holding the side of her head. Teardrop moved quickly to her and knelt down to examine the wound. As far as Britha could make out, the serpent had given some of its people the blood magic, but it was not as strong as hers and certainly not as strong as Teardrop and Fachtna's.

Fachtna looked out over the trees. They were heading down into a plain where there was little in the way of woods. It looked like many of the trees had been cleared long ago to make way for farmland. Britha had glimpsed the once-fertile plain earlier in the day when they had been in the trees trying to find a way past the patrols of Corpse People. She had never seen anything like the scale of the farming here. *It must be able to feed thousands,* she had thought.

Far to the south there was a line of hills. She could make them out only because her night sight was suddenly so good. That, and the crown of one of the hills seemed to be on fire, while flames from campfires and torches spotted one of the other nearby hills.

'Wolves,' Fachtna said, looking out over the plain. 'They are the size of lions, white in colour with red feet and maws.' The warrior did not sound happy. He glanced at the frightened boy.

Teardrop's head whipped round. He had been making a poultice and dressing for the side of Tangwen's head. Britha was watching him closely enough to notice that he'd added a silver tear squeezed form the corner of his eye to the dressing. She would have his secrets yet, she thought.

'From the Otherworld?' Britha asked, meaning the wolves, still watching Teardrop. White-furred animals with red eyes and maws were known to come from there.

'At least changed by Otherworldly powers,' Teardrop muttered. Something in his tone made Britha bristle. It was as if he was trying to appease her somehow.

'We cannot leave the boy,' Fachtna said. Teardrop was nodding. Tangwen looked up at Teardrop, an incredulous expression on her face.

'If he will not go to his people or others that will help him, then he will die,' Britha said, giving word to Tangwen's thought. Not for the first time she wondered how comfortable things must be in Fachtna and Teardrop's Otherworldly home that they could afford to think such things.

'We may as well kill him ourselves then,' Fachtna snapped. Their reliance on magic made them soft, Britha decided as she moved over to the swordsman Teardrop had killed. She saw that the sword had embedded itself in the man's forearm, fusing with the flesh somehow. She glanced over at the swollen-headed sorcerer.

'It would be a kindness,' Britha said.

'He comes with us,' Fachtna said firmly. He looked to Teardrop for support. Britha could see that Teardrop desperately wanted to agree with him but understood the practicalities of their situation. The boy's courage was spent. He would be insensate for the foreseeable future. 'The boy is under my protection,' Fachtna announced.

Britha decided to make the decision easier for the rest of them. She stalked over to the boy. Fachtna, realising what she was about to do, ran towards her. Britha grabbed the unseeing drooling boy and opened his throat with her sickle.

'No!' A heartbeat later Fachtna had yanked her away from the boy. Letting go of her, he grabbed the child, trying to will life back into his body.

'Are you out of your mind?!' Britha screamed at him, furious. 'Laying your hands on a *dryw*!'

Fachtna was back on his feet, the shimmering, singing ghost sword sliding from its scabbard. His features seethed in fury.

'No!' Teardrop shouted, putting as much authority into his voice as he could. He knew his friend well and was certain he would kill Britha. Fachtna hesitated, staring at Britha with unbridled hatred. She met his gaze defiantly. Teardrop could see her own anger at the breaking of the ban on touching a *dryw*, but it was as nothing compared to the rage that was close to pouring out of Fachtna.

'Fachtna, please.' Teardrop poured the magic of reason and old friendship into his words.

'If we baulk at the first hard decision then we will not succeed,' Britha told the seething warrior. Teardrop cursed her, wishing she would keep her tongue still behind her teeth.

'If we become our enemy then we are already lost,' Teardrop countered calmly. Britha turned to look at him.

'The boy was weak.'

'So were you when we first found you,' Teardrop said.

'I would have survived.'

'Not if we'd cut your throat,' Fachtna spat and turned away into the darkness.

Britha watched him go, trying to mask her contempt. She looked back down at the dead boy. Then what she had done hit her, and she almost retched. Teardrop watched the stricken expression crawl across Britha's face.

'It's getting worse the closer you get, isn't it?' he asked as he returned to dressing Tangwen's head wound. The hunter from the People of the Snake had chosen to remain quiet. She was not sure that she would have done what the *ban draoi* had done but she had recognised the need for it. If Britha hadn't killed the boy then he would have been torn apart by wolves or tortured to death by the next band of Corpse People that came through here.

'I'm not—' Britha started and then looked from the dead boy back to Teardrop. All the colour had drained from her skin now. 'For my people ...' she started. They were all that mattered, she thought, but traces of doubt were creeping in.

'Freeing your people will mean nothing if this madness remains unopposed,' Teardrop told her as he tried to control the harshness in his voice.

It wasn't just the responsibility to her people that was making her doubt. A kingdom of desire was not an unattractive idea.

Britha had lapsed into a feverish sleep lying in a wet ditch listening to Fachtna and Tangwen having sex. Fachtna was making most of the noise.

It was like the time that Cliodna had taken her far out into the sea and then pulled her down with her as she had dived deep. After Britha had conquered her fear, once she had understood how much time she had under the water on one deep breath, she had found that she liked it. She had liked looking up at the sun through the water. Except that this was cold and dark and she felt the weight of the water pressing on her. She heard the songs of the mighty fish that Cliodna had claimed were not fish, but their singing was wrong, twisted, as if both pained and malignant somehow. Yet these songs were familiar from long ago. From before she was born, before any of them had been born. It was welcoming in a disconcerting, bordering-on-obscene way, like returning to a once-familiar place after a hideous crime had been committed there. And she burned, Britha burned from within. She felt like she contained the pregnant fire of a forge within her, but the pain and the heat were not unwelcome.

She could go deeper. There was something beneath her through the cold murk of the water, something huge and old.

Britha's eyes flickered open. She was immediately aware. She was uncomfortable and cold but not to the degree she should be. The normal aches and pains she would expect from spending the night in a cold wet ditch just weren't present. She knew the wind had changed; she could smell wood smoke on it. She could hear the sound of distant hoof beats. She could smell the metal, leather, wood and sweat of her companions. She had not liked the dream, least of all her response to it.

She could smell the cake made from flour and ground tansy leaves that Tangwen was eating. Britha sat up to look at the other woman. The lean hunter was younger than Britha had first thought, her hair cropped very short. Tangwen realised she was being watched and looked over at Britha.

'I do not wish to bear his children,' she said, gesturing with the tansy cake. She turned away from the *ban draoi*. 'They would be stupid.' Britha tried to suppress a smile. All warriors wanted children, well, sons anyway, so part of them would carry on and probably grow up to repeat their father's short brutish life.

Fachtna was kneeling in the ditch some distance away looking to the south. It was late afternoon, Britha guessed. She had slept a long time and woken ravenous. They had decided that night was the best time to travel, though the Corpse People seemed to fight and patrol as much at night as they did during the day.

'They have seen more of the white-furred animals from the Otherworld. Teardrop has a potion that helps disguise our scent,' Tangwen told her quietly. 'It seems there is little natural left here.' And it was true. The Corpse People seemed more interested in burning, killing and destroying for the sake of destruction than looting or taking slaves. Crop-rich fields had been burned and even salted in some cases.

Teardrop came crawling along the ditch. Britha risked a peep over the top. The line of hills seemed closer now. Three of the hills were topped with wood-walled forts surrounded by defensive ditches: the Crown of Andraste. Two were besieged; the third had fallen last night. The gentle breeze brought the screams of the defenders of the fallen hill fort, their torturous executions a portent for the other two garrisons.

Teardrop sat down next to her, keeping his head well below the lip of the ditch.

'What are we doing here?' Britha asked

'If we are to fight Bress, we will need help.'

'Those forts are about to fall; these people cannot help us.'

'They were strong enough to last this long.' But Teardrop didn't sound like he believed it himself. 'We will see if we can make it to the forts during the night.'

'And then we will be trapped in there like the defenders until these people break the gates or come over the wall and kill us all.'

'Do you have a better idea?' Suddenly an angry Fachtna was right next to her. 'Can you summon an army of dead heroes to fight with us?' He was right: she had nothing. 'It's very easy to come up with reasons not to act.'

It had started to rain heavily, making the dark night darker and colder. The torches and the campfires were dimmed but did not go out. Fire arrows still left arcs of light in the night sky as they flew into the hill forts. The thatched roof of more than one roundhouse was ablaze behind the forts' walls. They could hear the cries of the defenders, screams of anger or pain. The attacking Corpse People were strangely quiet, however.

They kept their heads down and approached where they saw the fewest attackers. They were the least of the Corpse People's problems. After all, who would be stupid enough to join the besieged during a siege? The problem was that the Atrebates inside the walls had no reason to trust them and every reason to think that anyone wanting to gain entrance was part of a ruse.

This was how they found themselves running along the second-innermost defensive ditch. Those Corpse People they had encountered had ignored them, though more than one had glanced in their direction, wondering who the warriors and the *dryw* not covered in lime were, but then they knew that Crom Dhubh had other allies in the south.

Teardrop skidded to a halt and sank into a crouch. Fachtna stopped and backed towards him, keeping an eye out all around. Tangwen did likewise, an arrow nocked, though she did not like using her bow in the rain.

'This is pointless,' Teardrop said. 'They will not let us in during this.' Fachtna said nothing. Despite what he had said earlier, he had to agree with Teardrop. Had he been a defender he would not have let them in. 'We have to retreat, hide and then come back when there is a lull and treat with those inside.'

'Ware!' was all Tangwen had time to say. The Corpse warrior did not even cry out as Tangwen's arrow took him in the chest, the arrowhead easily penetrating his boiled leather breastplate and silencing his heart. The enemy warrior slumped to the ground and slid to the bottom of the ditch in the mud.

Realising that Britha and her companions were not allies, more warriors were running down the muddy slope towards them. Tangwen was nocking, drawing and loosing arrows as quickly as she could. Fachtna raised his shield high and swung his sword low. He took a blow on the shield but the shimmering sword blade sliced through the skin, flesh, muscle and bone of his attackers' legs. More of the Corpse People charged him. Almost every blow of his sword killed or incapacitated one of them.

Orange flame blossomed to the east where they knew the main gate was. There were shouts of victory and cries from the wounded. The air was rent with the sound of bellowing. Britha recognised the sound. It was the roaring of an angry and pained bear, a large one by the sound of it.

'The Crown falls!' Teardrop cried.

Britha grabbed him. 'Come on!' Pulling him with her, she started running towards the gate.

They killed any who got too close as they ran, but now all the Corpse People knew they were not friends. Britha had taken an arrow in her arm, but after snapping off the haft she found she was able to ignore the pain. Fachtna was running and killing with a spearhead in his leg and an arrow sticking out of his shoulder. More and more Corpse People, eerily quiet, were turning to attack them, charging down into the ditch. As they ran around a bend they could see the flames from the burning gate. It seemed the fort was about to fall. The defenders and attackers were frenetic violent shadows against the orange glow.

339

The four skidded to a halt as one of the largest shadows rose up onto its hind legs and roared in pain and fury. Fachtna spat and made the sign against evil. The others just stood and stared. It was the largest bear that Britha had ever seen, fully twenty-five feet tall. Its Otherworldly heritage was obvious in the white of its fur and the red of its eyes, which seemed to glow in the firelight. The red on its paws and maw were more likely from the blood of its victims than signs of Otherworld origins. Parts of its flesh were covered in a crusty, almost spiked, stone-like material, but the most terrifying thing about it were the six animated tendrils that grew out of its back. As they watched, the tendrils dragged screaming defenders from the wall and crushed them, or brought them to the bear's paws for the creature to tear apart, or offered them to the bear's maw for its huge teeth to shred. Britha was both frightened and offended by this violation of nature.

Arrows, sling stones and casting spears filled the air, studding the creature's white fur, but it ignored them as it lumbered on its rear legs towards the gate. Britha was running, a cold anger controlling her movements. She sprinted up to the top of the bank closest to the wooden wall. The track that led to the gate zigzagged between the defensive banks along the ditches that divided them to make it more difficult for attacking forces. The bear was on that track. But on its hind legs it towered about ten feet above the bank that Britha was sprinting along. She was oblivious to the arrows and casting spears from both defenders and attackers flying past her. She was unaware of Fachtna running after her, killing anyone who got close. She was unaware of Tangwen putting arrows into those that Fachtna could not deal with. She was focused on running and whispering to the demon that lived in her spear, feeling its heat through the haft.

Britha leaped with a power she had never known she had. She curled her legs up underneath her as she sailed though the night air and the pouring rain, almost untouched by the hail of spears and arrows. She didn't even feel the defender's arrow as it pierced her leg. The bear turned ponderously, some instinct warning it. She screamed as she stabbed the spear two-handed through the creature's skull. The weapon bit, cracked armoured skull and was forced by nearly in- human strength into the creature's brain, where unseen branches of metal shot out from the spearhead. Britha stood for a moment on the creature's shoulder, then twisted the spear and tore it out in an explo- sion of gore that spattered her frenzied features. The head of the spear was still waving tendrils of metal, the spearhead slowly reforming to a point. Britha turned and leaped off the bear as it started to topple.

The Corpse People ran as the massive malformed creature toppled to the ground with a resounding *thud* in an explosion of mud. Britha landed easily on the soft ground, knees bent to take the impact. Teardrop stalked to the top of the second ridge in the knowledge that he had a role to play now. He sent the magic of fear ahead of him through the air despite the cost. The Corpse People recoiled, though he felt the protection that had been given to them by Crom Dhubh.

'All those who oppose the will of the true gods will die!' he screamed. Then, steeling himself, almost weeping with expectation of the pain, he closed his eyes. Inside, more of him died as he felt the other burrow deep into what was him and consume it. He saw the other, watched it reach out through places that shouldn't be, and he watched the changes it made. Too long, too much, too soon. There was too little left of him now. Teardrop hit the ground. In a large semicircle around him the warriors of the Corpse People went down like wheat mown with a sickle. Reshaped bones had burst through flesh, killing them before they'd even had the chance to scream.

Fachtna strode out of the ditch and onto the track. He was heading straight towards the remaining Corpse People.

'Come and die!' he screamed. 'Come and die with me!' Steam poured off him. He seemed to glow from within. A haze surrounded him, and where he stepped the mud hissed and more steam rose. Britha followed Fachtna, but only as close as the waves of heat would allow her to get. The two of them marched at the transfixed Corpse People backlit by the burning gate. As one the Corpse People took a step back. Any who raised a casting spear or a bow found themself with an arrow sticking out of somewhere vital as Tangwen covered Fachtna and Britha from the shadows.

The Corpse People decided that they were not as ready for death as they thought. They found that there were still things to be afraid of. They turned and ran.

Ysgawyn watched his army, with victory in its grasp, break and run. He could see perfectly in the night from where he stood before the other besieged hill fort. He could see what the two men and the two women had done.

He turned to his second, Gwydyon. The older man was massively built, balding and wore a sheepskin cloak over his limed skin. His body was a patchwork of scar tissue earned from hundreds of hard-won battles and one-to-one challenges. He had been a tribal champion before he had become a leader.

'I want examples made. We are dead. The dead do not fear the living. If they choose to be afraid again then let them fear me.' Gwydyon nodded. Ysgawyn knew that Gwydyon would turn enough of the cowards over to the tribe's most talented torturers to make his point. 'This is good,' he said. 'I had thought all the heroes and those blessed by the gods gone, that we had killed them all, but these are powerful. We will feast on their flesh and steal that power.'

Gwydyon did not answer.

24
Now

Du Bois opened the door to the interrogation room.

'I've got your—' Then he saw Beth sprawled on the floor. He dropped her brass knuckles and the Balisong knife on the table and knelt by her. Working quickly, he checked for signs of life. Satisfied that she was just unconscious, he rolled her onto her back. His nano-screen was picking up trace signs of something else just having been in the room, but its attempts to find out more were being frustrated.

Consciousness returned to Beth with an immediacy she had never felt before when waking up. She was not surprised to find herself lying with du Bois kneeling over her. She was aware of her surroundings with a new totality. She was also conscious of the pain from her injuries receding, aware of the wounds healing. Something was very different about her. Her hand reaching up to her face was a reflex action, nothing more. She knew that the blood the strange earth-smelling figure had spat at her was gone.

'What happened?' du Bois asked, looking at her strangely.

'I think I must have passed out,' Beth answered, her hard-earned suspicion of authority figures kicking in. 'Bit embarrassing really. I guess I took more of a kicking than I thought I did.' She stood up. She felt better than she had in a long time, but there was something strange, a heat under her skin. It didn't feel wrong but it was certainly different. Du Bois was watching her carefully. Beth noticed her knife and knuckles on the table. 'You're giving me them back?'

Du Bois seemed lost in thought for a moment before answering. 'Everyone should be able to defend themselves.' He took his wallet out of his pocket and removed a handful of twenty-pound notes. 'Go home, Beth, before this city kills you.' *Because it'll be time soon enough,* he added silently. Beth would have loved to be able to refuse the money but she didn't. She needed to look her father in the eyes one more time.

'Am I free to go?' she asked. Du Bois nodded.

The noise that Inflictor Doorstep was making with the corpse of the dead dealer was beginning to get on King Jeremy's nerves. As well as turning his body into grey armoured flesh inscribed with spirals, Inflictor had also rewired his own brain to mimic the more bestial of his favourite villains from various media sources. Even Jeremy was wondering if he'd gone too far.

'Well?' Baron Albedo asked.

King Jeremy was looking at what seemed to be a tab of acid, a little red stain on a piece of blotting paper. He touched a lost-tech-modified glove against the stain. The molecule-sized machinery that infused the glove took a sample of the red smear and the result of the diagnostic appeared in Jeremy's vision.

'It's blood.'

'Nanites?'

Jeremy just nodded, trying to ignore the wet ripping noises. He would leave part of his nano-screen behind to replicate itself and then seek out any forensic evidence they had left and destroy it.

'Biological or machine?'

There were thought to be two distinct forms of the lost tech. Jeremy believed they were from two disparate, ancient and probably long-dead alien civilisations. One technology was biological, the other seemed to be machine-based.

'Biological,' King Jeremy said. 'It's her blood. Some fucking simpleton can't see beyond their own petty drug dealing.'

'There's a hunger ...' Dracimus said. He was lying in a pool of blood on the filthy floor next to the corpse Inflictor was shredding. He had adopted a different diagnostic approach and just taken some of the Red Rapture. Given that it might open gates, that had been a bit rash, Jeremy thought. ' ... behind the sky ... waiting for us.'

'Inflictor?'

The demon-headed boy swung round to face Jeremy, his face and arms red. Hard to believe that he had once been a weedy kid from Iowa with an off-the-chart IQ and a distinct lack of empathy. *Still, now he could be more than the next school shooter,* Jeremy thought. 'I hope you've left the brain, mouth and larynx attached.'

Inflictor nodded.

Albedo pulled a syringe from a hardened case on his belt. The blue glow from the material inside the syringe was nothing more than an affectation. Dracimus leaned down and pushed the syringe into the dead dealer's eye.

'Run a current through him,' Jeremy said.

It felt like a static shock, only more so. Then it was constant. Something wasn't right. Was he being electrocuted? Then there was the feeling of drifting away from himself. Like good ketamine. Dissociation.

The previous few moments came back to him as a red memory. The knock on the door. The four guys in hoodies. American accents. One of them had been a demon. Jaime panicked. His instinct was to flail about, but he couldn't feel his body.

Jaime opened his eyes. They were still there. There were two guys leaning over him. Both with handsome chiselled features. Cross-breeds of American high-school alpha males and Greek gods, Jaime decided.

Jaime opened his mouth.

'I don't care,' the one on the left said. 'You'll try to reason, bargain and then beg. I don't care. I just need to know who gave you the Red Rapture and where I can find them.'

'Look, you don't understand. I'm scared of you, I really fucking am. I think you've put some horrible shit in me, but this guy ... this guy ... he does things, y'know?' Jaime didn't like the way his voice sounded. It seemed to lack depth, resonance.

The one on the left looked saddened. It was mockery.

'Albedo, can you provide some perspective, please?'

The one on the right reached down and Jaime felt fingers grab his hair.

'Hey, what the fuck!' He felt himself being lifted, very light. There was something wrong with his neck, as if there was something hanging from it. Jaime looked down on his decapitated body. He started to scream. He screamed until they unplugged him.

Du Bois pushed open the door to the coroner's examination room.

'Out,' he told the assembled people gawping at the corpse of the creature he'd shot in the old dog stadium. One older man, presumably the coroner, opened his mouth to complain. 'Either get out or I'll have you arrested under the anti-terrorism laws and hold you indefinitely just to prove what a dick I am.'

Something in his tone, or the rumours which had been flying around Kingston Crescent about who he was and what he did, must have convinced them that he was serious. They left with as much dignity as they could manage. Du Bois didn't fully understand democracy. It seemed pointless to give people the right to self-determination when so few had any interest in it. Now that humanity had reached a certain level of comfort and people didn't really seem to want to think for themselves, he believed it was better that they just did what they were told. Then everyone would be happy. Hence he saw the far-reaching powers of the anti-terrorism laws as a step in the right direction, though why they had to be dressed up with the excuse of terrorism he had no idea.

The sheets had already been pulled back from the corpse. It had definitely been human once and probably not that long ago. The changes would have been brought on by thousands of tiny machines capable of reproducing and then rewriting the basic building blocks of life.

Du Bois held his phone over the body and shot footage of it from every conceivable angle. The base human had been modified to be aquatic by the look of it, and then overdesigned with claw-like nails, shark-like teeth and retractable spurs of bone to be someone's idea of a weapon.

He took out a small leather case, unzipped it and pulled out a small vial. He neurally transmitted an order to the smart matter the vial was made from, and a needle grew out of its base. Du Bois stabbed the needle into the body with some force to break through the over-lapping plates of exoskeleton. The blood that filled the vial looked normal enough. The needle retracted as du Bois attached the vial to the bottom of his phone. The screen of the phone showed the results of the blood analysis. It was filled with tiny nanites – an ancient design, the biotech of the Seeders. The worrying thing was that this particular strain of nanites was very rare. They had not come from the Pacific Source. He had only seen this type once before.

Du Bois thought of the secret deep below the family seat on the stormy coast of western Scotland, and transmitted the information from the blood and the footage he had shot to Control. He ran the footage of the creature through an intelligent forensic image program, which reconstructed what it would have looked like the last time it was human. Finally he took the reconstructed images and ran them through facial recognition software against every database currently on the Internet.

He sat down, lit a cigarette and gazed at the body, thinking about Beth going toe to toe with what was effectively a killing machine. It took the software just over twenty minutes to find some matches. This was due to Internet speeds and the slowness of the systems it had invaded, not the software itself. Du Bois looked at the possibilities, discounting them until he found one that seemed to match. Matthew Bryant had lived in one of the nicer parts of Portchester, near the castle, and worked at a large computer company in senior management. He had two kids in their teens, the eldest at a good university. His life story was a list of the successful, sensible and responsible choices you made in life if you wanted a happy one – from a conventional perspective anyway. He had also been a keen scuba diver. It had been during a dive in the Solent that he had gone missing. It was assumed that he had had some sort of mishap, and his body had been washed away by one of the nastier tides in the channel.

Things were starting to click into place for du Bois. He began to understand why he was struggling to seed the city. There were still pieces missing, however. He switched applications on the phone and checked the trace. The missing pieces would have to wait. There was still some unfinished business to take care of.

It took more courage for Beth to push open the door to the flat than it had to fight the monster. What made it worse was that Maude was so relieved to see her still alive. It didn't occur to her to be angry with her new friend. Her reaction nearly overwhelmed Beth. She had grown up in a very cold environment. She wasn't used to this. The tears came again.

It wasn't lost on Uday, however, that Beth had brought violence into their home. He glared at her angrily.

The explanations had been difficult. How could she tell them what had happened? She settled for saying that she had just got a bit of a kicking. She found out that the muscle she'd knifed in the leg was called Trevor. They had bound up his legs as best they could, given him lots of painkillers, some vodka and, astonishingly, made him a cup of cocoa. Eventually he had thanked them and with some difficulty limped away, telling them he was going to A & E but he'd keep them out of it.

'My bayonet?' Beth asked. Uday and Maude looked confused. 'The knife.'

'Oh,' Maude said in a small voice. Uday gave Beth a look of disgust. 'It's in the bathroom sink. It's still … dirty.'

'It's an heirloom, my great-grandfather's,' Beth told them by way of an explanation. She didn't think it had appeased Uday in any way, shape or form.

'I told you.' It was all he had to say. She'd brought it down on them. She was just a different flavour of trouble from Talia.

'I'm sorry.' It wasn't nearly enough. 'I'm gone now.'

'You don't have to,' Maude said, but Beth had been speaking to Uday, and his face was made of stone.

'Will they come back here looking for you?' he asked. Beth considered. She didn't want to lie to them, not after this.

'They might,' she finally said. 'Can you get out of Portsmouth?'

'Yeah, we'll just leave our degrees, drop everything and go into hiding, or maybe we can return to our families, thousands of pounds in debt with nothing to show for it,' Uday suggested acidly, every word hitting home. 'I take it we can't go to the police?' Beth wasn't sure how to answer that.

'We're staying,' Maude said firmly. Both of them turned to look at her. 'I don't care how scared we are, I'm not going to drop my life for these ... bullies!' The small goth was angry. Beth guessed it was this resolve that had stopped her from leaving university when evidence of her fledgling porn career had surfaced.

'I'll sort it,' Beth said. She said it almost out of desperation and then realised that she meant it. She just didn't know how to go about it. 'I have to go up north then I'll come back and sort it.'

'Yeah?' Uday demanded sarcastically. 'You going to go up against some Pompey hood? Just like in a film? I've a better idea. Why don't you just fuck off back to Bradford and stay there? In fact, leave us your address just in case any more arseholes come looking for you.'

'Uday—' Maude began.

'No. She's no better than her fucking sister. Worse. Talia brought drugs and exploitation with her; at least she didn't bring violence! Didn't have us taken hostage in our own house!'

Maude looked like she was about to cry. Beth knew that if Maude cried, she would.

She turned and left the lounge. In the bathroom, the sink looked like it belonged in a slaughterhouse. Beth cleaned the blood off her great-grandfather's bayonet. She had a train to catch.

Du Bois parked the Range Rover outside Fort Widley on Portsdown Hill, another of the Victorian structures built to defend Portsmouth from a French invasion that had never come. A massive red-brick edifice built into the chalk of the hillside, the fort provided a commanding view of the suburbia and commercial estates below, then Portsmouth, the Solent, the Isle of Wight and beyond, though much was obscured in the murk of low cloud on the grey morning.

He checked the trace again. It was almost irrelevant now that they had an address. It was more a question of timing rather than anything else. He still had more than enough time to make the drive.

Du Bois climbed out of the four-by-four. It had been too late to make enquiries last night after he had let Beth go, but this morning he had rung around Mr Bryant's friends and family, particularly other members of the Solent Sub-Aqua Exploration Club based at Fort Widley. He had discovered some interesting things. Anna Bryant was scared of something, something that she was not prepared to go into over the phone. When he'd tried to speak to friends of Bryant from the diving club he discovered a lot of the numbers were disconnected. Entire families had disappeared with only a few missing-persons reports filed.

Du Bois finally got hold of a spouse. Through tears and anger he was told that all the members of the club had begun to act strangely. They were spending more and more time either diving or at the fort, though they had become very secretive about what they were doing. The woman's husband had become less communicative. He had been nasty, even with his children. His diet had changed. He had started to 'smell funny'. Eventually he had announced that he was leaving his job and his family. The estranged spouse hadn't used the word cult, but it sounded a bit like that.

The club had a large lock-up at the fort behind a huge arched doorway with two iron-reinforced doors. The padlock proved no challenge for du Bois, and he pulled one of the doors open. Inside was a dark cavernous space and the stench was overwhelming. It was the reek of people living rough, using the place as a toilet, and the smell of the sea at low tide.

Du Bois moved cautiously. The place was a mess. Most of the equipment hadn't been touched in months. His eyes cut through the darkness, amplifying the light from outside. The crates of diving equipment made it somewhat labyrinthine, but he could see no signs of life. There was a scattering of bedding and camping equipment, but something about their arrangement made them look more like nests than an area where people were sleeping rough.

Du Bois stopped and looked up. Dangling from one of the exposed roof beams, suspended on a chain with a meathook through its lower leg, was a body. It had clearly been there, rotting, for a while. Du Bois knew what a partially eaten corpse looked like.

Behind it was a large tank of murky green water containing a dark shape. Du Bois approached cautiously. He had the urge to draw the .45 but resisted. He still had the sense that there was nobody else in here, an intuition confirmed in part by his blood-screen. He magnified his vision and improved the resolution. It was an effigy made of scavenged bits of driftwood and marine detritus, and looked like a Sheela-na-gig, a fertility statue, an exaggerated and swollen pregnant female form. But there was something warped and wrong about the figure. All around the tank were the bodies of rats, birds, dogs, cats, various other small animals and even two sheep, a pig and a cow. None of them showed signs of having been eaten.

Du Bois had had enough. It was clear the place had been abandoned long ago. With a thought he linked to his phone and texted a request to Control for a clean-up crew. Normal people couldn't be allowed to know how weird the world actually was. Then with another thought he started a search on material relating to Fort Widley, putting it through various filters to harvest the information he was looking for, though he wasn't sure quite what that was.

Walking out into the murky morning light away from the stench was a blessed relief. The result of the search came back. Despite a mild feeling of being violated by information, du Bois sifted through the material in his mind rather than externally on the phone. The closest he came to what he was looking for were unsubstantiated urban myths about tunnels that led from the Palmerston forts on Portsdown Hill, down into the city and even as far as the sea defences on the front at Southsea.

Du Bois thought tunnels unlikely in engineering terms. He double-checked against online Ministry of Defence files. According to documents from the Victorian era, they had looked at tunnels but found them to be 'unfeasible'. He didn't have time to go searching for legendary tunnels. He added a search request to the clean-up crew request and then climbed into the Range Rover. He headed north.

The train pulled into the grey stone and concrete valley that was Bradford in the late afternoon. Never pretty, the murky weather had leached all the colour from the city. Beth had the money for a bus but felt better than she ever had before, her wounds all but healed during the journey. She almost ran up the Otley Road, past the cemetery where she'd spent many hours either with friends or alone, and turned into the familiar street of rain-slick-grey, stone terraced housing. It was only when she put the key in the lock that she knew this was for the last time.

After all the life and movement in Portsmouth, after feeling content, however briefly, for the first time, after the possibility of an actual life and then the screaming red violence, the dusty dirty house where cigarette smoke hung constantly in the atmosphere seemed so still and dead. The smell of a human being rotting away added to the feeling. The thing was, Beth couldn't remember a time when that hadn't been the case.

Her father was in the lounge, as ever, his oxygen mask hanging down as he sucked on a cigarette. The glow of the cigarette tip was the only point of light in the room.

'Hello, Dad.'

'Did you find her?' he asked, his voice little more than a rasp. Beth shook her head and watched disappointment spread across his face. She tried to muster sympathy for him, even pity. All she could do was try not to be any crueller than she had to. He had made his choices. He had to live with them.

'Who is she?' She watched her father swallow hard. Saw the fear replace disappointment.

'I ...' he started. It would have been easier if he had been a better liar. Then he could have told her that he loved her as much as Talia, or even just loved her at all.

'I'll go back and look ... I'll find her, but you have to not lie to me. If you lie, I swear you'll never see either of us again and I'll go to the police.' It was a gamble, a bluff, but prison had made her a better liar than her dad.

'The police will be the least of our problems.'

'You're dying. It doesn't matter now.' It wasn't said unkindly. The saddest thing, for Beth anyway, was that there was just no feeling there at all. 'You stole her, didn't you? You took her from some nice people, destroyed their lives and brought her to this dead place?'

'You don't know what you're talking about!' Beth was surprised by the anger in his voice, though it quickly subsided into a hacking cough.

She watched him for a while and then realised that this was the cruelty she was trying to avoid. She stood up, took the cigarette from his yellow-stained fingers and stubbed it out in the overflowing ashtray. She was careful to make sure there were no sparks from the cigarette left before she put the mask over her father's face and spun the wheel on the oxygen tank. She went and sat down, letting her father recover, until he took the mask off and spoke.

'When you were born, you were too big, odd-looking. You did something to your mother, tore her up inside so she could never have children again, and we'd wanted to have a big family. It was you that killed her in the end, you know? Complications from your birth.'

And there it was, Beth thought, the reason for all the resentment she'd endured growing up. A crime she'd committed while she was being born. She said nothing.

'And we were left with this strange little girl who didn't look like other little girls, didn't want to be like other little girls.' He put the mask back over his face and took more gasping breaths. *Wasn't treated like other little girls*, Beth added silently, *wasn't loved like other children*.

'So you stole a child?'

Her father shook his head and removed the mask from his face.

'No! We're not monsters, not kidnappers. We saved that child. Saved Talia. And because we did something good, we got the daughter we deserved.'

He put the mask back on. What Beth realised then was that he wasn't actually trying to hurt her. He never had been. As far as he was concerned, this was just the way that things happened.

'It was a friend of your mother's from school. Not a close one, mind. She picked us because there was little connection between her and us. Beautiful woman, bright too, very intelligent and good at sports.'

Not like us then.

'She'd heard that we wanted kids but were having trouble. You know how small this town is. Someone had offered her a lot of money to get pregnant with a view to adopting the child when it was born. Rich people. But she found out that wasn't what they had in mind. They were some kind of cult. They thought she was important some-how – something to do with genealogy, bloodlines, selective breeding, all that nonsense. They had a place high up on the moors. She told us they were breeding children to be sacrificed.'

Beth was shaking her head.

'No, it's true! I didn't believe it at first either, but she was scared, really scared. Not for her – she knew she was dead – but for the baby.'

What was clear was that her father believed this stuff. A week ago she would have dismissed it as nonsense, but it had been a busy week.

'She had arranged to take the baby out – to Helmsley – and they'd let her, though they'd sent someone with her. We left you with your gran and actually disguised ourselves. We took a carrycot the same as Natalie's and put a doll in it. Then in a tearoom we made the swap – in the bathroom. Scariest thing I've ever done in my life.'

And then you got your proper little girl. But she'd known, somehow she'd always known, and she'd resented us for it. It occurred to Beth that they'd got away with it probably because they were so inconsequential.

'They killed her, you know,' he said between rasping gasps of oxygen. 'Ran her down up on the moors shortly after we got Talia.'

Beth just nodded. She thought about saying all the things that she wanted to say. That it wasn't her fault her mum couldn't have children. That it shouldn't have mattered that she was big. That she wasn't actually ugly. That she had loved them unconditionally. That she missed her mum as well. That Talia was a horrible person who didn't care about anyone but herself. But she knew it wouldn't help. He genuinely wouldn't understand. He was just a stupid, selfish, dying old man. He might as well have been a stranger. She stood up.

'Where's Talia?' he demanded.

Your perfect little girl's been doing porn, turning tricks and is very probably dead. Beth very nearly said it.

'I don't know.'

'Where are you going? I need help. Looking after.'

Beth's laugh was without bitterness, but was devoid of humour as well.

'I'm going upstairs to get my records and then I'm going back to Portsmouth to find my bitch of a sister and get her out of whatever shit she's in, and then that's it for me and this family.' Beth thought about it for a moment or two. 'I went to prison because I killed Talia's boyfriend. I caught him beating her. It looked like he was going to murder her. She testified against me, and none of you even came and saw me, let alone said thank you.'

'You helped put your mother in the grave!'

'I don't think I did. I don't think this family deserves me.'

Beth turned away from her father for the last time. She went upstairs to get her records. It was so sad that they were the only things left for her in this house.

He heard the front door pulled shut. It was the sound of finality, an end. Tears rolled down his cheeks. It wasn't that Beth was gone. She had never done anything but bring pain to the family. It was just that she had been the last faint hope he'd had of seeing his little girl Talia again. After all Beth had done, he still found himself surprised by her selfishness.

'That's a fine young woman you have there, Mr Luckwicke,' du Bois said from the corner.

'I knew you'd come.' He closed his eyes. From the moment they had taken Talia from the tearoom in Helmsley, he'd been living in fear, waiting for this moment.

Du Bois stepped into view. Twenty years gone, and Natalie's bodyguard hadn't aged a day.

'Oh, how we looked for you,' the blue-eyed, blond-haired killer told him.

'Nobody ever thinks to look here. We're not needed any more.'

Du Bois nodded.

'Talia?'

'Is not your daughter. Your daughter just left.'

353

'You're going to kill her?'

'Beth? I hope not.'

'Talia.'

'I'm going to kill you, but I've known that for more than twenty years. I'm relieved that you're not a pervert. I think you probably did the best you could for Natalie, but after the little exchange I just overheard, I don't think I'm going to feel very bad about it.'

'You don't know—'

'No, *you* don't know how hard Beth has been fighting for her sister. Now do you want me to make it look like murder, suicide, natural causes or an accident?' Du Bois hadn't asked the question unkindly.

The old man looked at du Bois, appalled. 'I'm not going to choose!'

'It's your last chance for a bit of control in your life.'

The two men stared at each other for a while.

'Suicide.'

Du Bois nodded. 'Your guilty conscience does you some credit at the end.'

To Mr Luckwicke's surprise, in his last moments he thought of Beth. He remembered her smiling and laughing when she was very young.

As du Bois walked across Peel Park to where he had left the Range Rover, he set his phone to checking mobile-phone call logs. When that didn't work, he started cross-referencing traffic through cellular-phone masts.

He would have to drive quickly if he wanted to see any of Alexia's concert. *Gigs, she calls them gigs*, he reminded himself. He had already arranged for her, the band and the gaggle of lackeys, parasites, sycophants and would-be lovers who followed her around to gain entry to Portsea Island through the roadblocks.

The Range Rover unlocked itself as du Bois approached, pulling off his leather gloves.

Du Bois had been right to bring his own whisky. The stuff they had behind the bar on South Parade Pier was horrible. Fortunately the bouncers had left him alone after he had shown them one of the warrant cards he habitually carried with him.

The venue was packed. He had made it back for the second half of the gig, though his driving hadn't been terribly legal. Clearly Alexia's band – Light – had something of a following, locally anyway. To du Bois's eyes the audience all looked like they had gone out of their way to look either grotesque or as if they had next to no moral standards. The dancing looked more like the melee at the base of a castle wall during a siege. He watched as dancer after dancer scrambled onto the stage and then threw themselves back into the crowd, and wondered what the point was.

The music could have been worse. Du Bois could not deny the technical skill of both his sister and the musicians who played with her, and they definitely seemed to put feeling into their music. Their songs were much longer than the pop music he had come to expect in the last sixty or so years, but at ten to fifteen minutes were still much shorter than what du Bois considered to be proper music. There were moments of quiet melody and clean vocals that du Bois had to admit were quite beautiful. Alexia's voice was still clear and pure but he struggled to listen to the incredibly heavy bits and all the screaming. Though he had to admit, in terms of endurance alone, the screaming was an extraordinary vocal performance, but if you were just going to scream like that he couldn't see the point in writing any lyrics.

By the time he finished the whisky, he had overcome the guilt at taking the night off. Perhaps it was the darkness of the music making him pessimistic but it almost certainly didn't matter now. He had a selection of possible numbers, all pay-as-you-go phones with no credit cards registered to them. He had phoned them en route from Bradford and managed to rule out four of the seven. The other three he had set his phone to ring on a regular basis, but they were all currently turned off. If there was an answer, it would connect through to him immediately and trace programs would triangulate the signal. There wasn't much else he could do.

He waited until the venue was empty before he lit up a cigarette while he waited for Alexia. He assumed there were still staff from the pier somewhere, but the band had gone on and most of the venue had been swept up. The bouncers had left long ago.

'Well?' Alexia asked. After all these years he still struggled to find something honest to say that wouldn't hurt her feelings. 'You hated it, didn't you?' She was laughing.

'I liked bits of it. You know, the bits with melody and form.' She laughed at him again. 'You knew I wasn't going to like it. All the roaring and screaming.'

'You are so old,' she said, laughing at him some more. She leaned over and kissed him on the cheek. 'Thank you for making this possible, and thank you for subjecting yourself to it.' Du Bois looked pained. 'No, really it means a lot.' She straightened up. 'Just let me clean up a bit ...'

'Are you still not ready? Everyone else has gone.'

'Hush now. I'll change and then we'll find a deliciously sleazy club somewhere. Perhaps we can find some muscle-bound young stud who can help pull the stick out of your arse and maybe, then, we might be able to get you laid.' Du Bois looked less than happy at this.

'Is sex your answer to everything?' he asked disapprovingly.

'It seems a healthy response to the impending end of the world.' Alexia was suddenly very serious. She turned and wandered back towards the changing room.

Du Bois stood up and headed for the stage. One of the keyboards hadn't been put away. He sat down in front of it and pressed a few keys. Nothing happened. He had to download the instructions straight into his mind before he was able to plug it in, turn it on, get it to make noise and find a setting that made the instrument sound vaguely like a piano.

Long steely fingers started with the opening strains of Debussy's 'Clair de Lune'. It didn't feel the same as a real piano: there was something lacking in the personality of the instrument, no sense of exploration like you had every time you sat down at a new piano. However, he had to admit, as his fingers danced across the keys, that it sounded good. Quickly he was lost, playing the piece from memory. He remembered the first time he'd heard it – in a bar in Paris, played on a badly tuned upright as Europe headed inexorably towards its most ruinous war to date.

'You're much better than you give yourself credit for,' Alexia said as he finished. He had known she was there and glanced over at her. She wore her long straight hair loose and had on a pair of tight jeans, ridiculously oversized boots and a sleeveless T-shirt with some horrible design on it that du Bois found difficult to approve of.

'I'm not sure how much is me and how much is the blood,' he said. Alexia came over and laid a hand on his shoulder. Du Bois could still remember the first time he had heard her – him, then – sing, the first time he/she had played the harp, in what seemed like a fleeting moment when their parents had been alive.

It got darker for a moment. A shadow had passed in front of one of the lights on the pier outside. It was a warning. Du Bois stood up, hand going into his jacket.

'Malcolm?' Alexia sounded worried. Outside the shadows seethed, coming to life like a swarm of black flies. Then the swarm was pouring in under the main doors to the venue.

'Go!' du Bois said.

'But—'

'Now!' The .45 was in his hand as the swarm started to form into something resembling a solid shape. Du Bois ejected the magazine and replaced it with a magazine of nano-tipped bullets.

'I'm not going to lea—'

Du Bois turned to her. 'Alexia, please. I can't fight and worry about you as well,' he pleaded. The form was beginning to look like the bag lady they had seen at the hill fort.

'It's her, isn't it?'

'Go! Please.'

Reluctantly, Alexia left the stage. Du Bois moved towards the bag lady, the .45 held securely in a two-handed combat grip. She was a nano-form now, though he doubted she understood it in those terms. She probably thought she was some ancient thing of the earth.

'So you're not going to leave it alone then?' she asked, her voice a gravelly rasp.

'I can't. Not until I hear a better plan.'

'Stop trying to find the girl. Her mother is the sea. They tried to wake her once before and left only old night and chaos in their wake.'

Du Bois had no idea what she was talking about.

'Are you here to kill ...' He began and then fired the pistol three times in quick succession, hoping to catch her off guard. His internal targeting systems showed him where each bullet was going to hit. Centre-mass, nearly perfect shots. She darted forward, turning into an animated cloud of black. Solid again, she lashed out with her stick even as it was elongating and starting to resemble something more like a spear. The .45 flew from numb fingers as the spear butt caught his hand. She brought the butt around again in a long but frighteningly fast sweep. Du Bois felt bones break in his leg as he was swept off his feet. It was more like the ground rushing up to hit him than him falling to the ground.

'A gun!' She was angry now. Fingers tearing through his flesh, even as it hardened. Fingers grasping ribs, rupturing internal organs. Happening too quickly. He felt himself picked up by his ribcage and flung through the air. The moment she let go, flesh started growing back, bones began to re-knit. He crashed through a window, thudding onto the wooden boards of the pier outside the venue.

She was a cloud again. Fortunately du Bois had the presence of mind to roll away as she solidified over him. She brought the spear down, breaking the railway-sleeper-thick beams of the pier's walkway.

Du Bois rolled to his feet, the bones in his leg re-knitting just enough to support his weight again. He grabbed the punch dagger from his belt buckle and transmitted a desperate instruction to the assembler contained in its hilt.

The bag lady stalked after him and thrust out with the spear. Du Bois rammed the punch blade into some iron railings and jumped, grabbed one of the lamp posts on the edge of the pier and swung out over the water. The lamp post was bending dangerously, close to breaking. The spearhead just missed as she stabbed at where his back had been. He swung back round to the pier and let go, catching the bag lady with a kick to the head that sent her staggering back. She recovered quickly and delivered a stepping kick that drove him to the floor, then stabbed the spear down towards him. Du Bois rolled out of the way, using the momentum to bring him up into a crouch. The beams beneath where he had been exploded as the spear went through them.

Du Bois leaped as she swung one-handed at him with the spear, powerful augmented legs taking him high over her head. He knew that he needed to keep out of her reach until he had a weapon.

All along the pier the lights on the lamp posts flickered out. In the amusement arcade the fruit machines died. The surrounding streets and houses went dark. Lightning played across the white-painted iron railings of the pier. The assembler in the hilt of the punch blade was rewriting the surrounding matter at a molecular level, using a pre-programmed template to create something useful. It needed power to do that, and the weapon it was creating would need power as well.

Du Bois landed and twisted like a serpent, the head of the spear just missing him. He rolled forward and then back up onto his feet, sprinting for the wooden wall of a building. She chased. He jumped, put a foot against the wall and then kicked back into a somersault over the bag lady's head. She stabbed out with the spear again, the head splintering panels in the wall. She raked it back, tearing through the wall like it was paper, trying to get at du Bois, but he was running back to where he had left his knife.

Du Bois tore the new form free of the railing, leaving a large hole where the assembler had utilised and subsequently transformed the surrounding molecules. When du Bois thought about such things, which was rarely, he considered it some kind of alien alchemy. The process hadn't quite finished, but what he was holding looked like a broadsword of the type he had first used in the twelfth century. Except that it was shimmering, indistinct and making a humming noise. The blade was a millimetre thick, very sharp, very hard, oscillating at a furious rate and white hot. A super-efficient, solid-state battery, which had just drained half the power from Southsea, powered the sword.

Du Bois turned to face the bag lady, who immediately became a swarm and engulfed him. He felt his flesh open everywhere. She painted him red as he screamed. He felt like little more than meat as he hit the ground again. These were wounds that his internal systems would not heal quickly. The nanites that made them would war with his as they tried to fix the wound. It was over. He could not fight this. He was wondering why she was bothering with the spear.

She reformed a few metres away. Looking down at him.

'I think you would have made the right decision given time, but there isn't any. I think you're just too weak.'

Du Bois pushed himself up onto all fours and then to his feet. He looked like he had been scribbled on with a razor.

'If you're going to do that,' he managed, 'then you can't complain about me using a gun.' He started shutting down his pain receivers. It would mean he would not know his limits. He would probably be dead before he was aware of it, but he knew he had to die on his feet fighting.

'A fair fight?' she asked. He nodded, though both knew it would never be fair. 'A good death.'

'I've lived long enough,' he said quietly. Du Bois knew that she would hack the cloning process and he would not be coming back. He knew he would miss this world and the people in it. He would miss Alexia.

He brought the sword up into a two-handed guard. She came at him with a bewildering number of rapid spear strikes: she swung and stabbed at him, two-handed strikes, one-handed thrusts, the spear moving towards him as if it wanted his flesh. He parried and dodged, moving sinuously, always trying to be where she least expected him to be. Ancient moves taught to him deep in the rock. He moved around the spear and her blows but never gained the upper hand. His sword and her spear cut through or destroyed any part of the pier they touched.

He ducked, dancing sideways under the spearhead, a blow meant for the side of his head just missing him. She reversed the movement of the spear and tried a back swing. Du Bois moved forward, for the first time in the fight on the offensive. He blocked the haft of the spear with his left hand, reaching across his body. The force of the blow broke every bone in his hand, but he did not feel it and the bones quickly started to heal again.

He was close enough now, inside her reach. He spat blood in her face. The nanites in the blood immediately attacked her nano-defences. She cried out, although even momentarily distracted she still had the presence of mind to reverse the spear and hit him in the stomach with the butt. She hit him so hard that the blunt force trauma burst the skin and broke three of his ribs, sending splinters of bone into his internal organs. The force of the blow took him off his feet, and he landed on one knee.

Du Bois swung the sword. It was as near a perfect blow as he had ever landed. He cut easily through the haft of the wooden-bladed spear to slice her open from her hip, up her torso and across her face. Then he stood up, reversed his grip, and with all the strength he could muster brought the sword down straight through her, practically bisecting her head and torso. She staggered back. Somehow she didn't split in two. In the horrific wound all du Bois could see was blackness. The wound started to seal itself like a zip.

He smiled.

'I win,' he told her and then lowered the shimmering, humming sword to his side. His phone told him that he had just received a text.

The bag lady spun the two halves of the spear around and jammed them together. The spear immediately healed itself. Then she stalked towards him and stabbed the spear into his foot. He felt the spear blade branch out and start growing up through his flesh, breaking out of and then back through his skin, climbing inexorably towards his heart, lungs and finally his brain to kill him.

Behind them, the wooden building they had wrecked collapsed.

The five distinct reports rolled across the water like thunder. The bag lady was solid when the bullets hit. The nanites infected her nanoform as powerful defences tried to track down each little machine and consume it.

'Die, you fucking bitch! Die!' There was more anger there than fear. Alexia attacked with more frenzy than skill with the two long-bladed Japanese fighting knives du Bois had had custom-made for her a long time ago. The weapons were balanced to contain tiny reservoirs in the hilt, the nanites delivered via grooves down the folded steel blades. The nanite virus that had cost Alexia a small fortune to obtain, helped the bullets to overwhelm the bag lady's defences. It didn't look like she died so much as turned to smoke.

As the roots retracted from du Bois's leg, he collapsed to the ground. Alexia dropped her knives and ran across to him.

'Thank you,' he managed through a mouthful of blood, as she burst into tears.

Part of the pier collapsed into the sea. Alexia and du Bois were on that part. Alexia had to pull him out of the water. He found himself lying on the pebbled beach looking at the night sky, his view spoilt by the constant blue strobing from the lights of the multitude of emergency vehicles that had turned up.

There had been a heated discussion with paramedics. Du Bois could not afford to have them examine his body. In the end he'd had to show his special-forces warrant card to some high-ranking police officers and have them threaten to arrest the paramedics if they didn't leave him alone. All the while, Alexia had fiercely stood guard over her brother.

Du Bois lit a cigarette. He'd managed to get a packet from one of the police officers. He reckoned he'd got the cigarettes because they thought he was about to die. Instead he was lying on the pebbles wondering how long it would take for his internal systems to repair themselves.

He pulled out his phone.

'You know you can do that internally, with your systems? The phone's just an external security filter and storage device,' Alexia told him.

'I got a text during the fight, but the phone's systems quarantined it and didn't pass it on.'

'Someone was trying to hack you?' Alexia asked and sat down next to him.

'It's from her,' du Bois said, sounding confused. It had been sent moments before the bag lady had died.

The bag lady's jamming during the fight had confused du Bois's blood-screen but even through the jamming he had been aware of Alexia. The bag lady's systems were more sophisticated than his; she too must have been aware of Alexia sneaking up on her with his gun.

Du Bois ran a security diagnostic on the quarantined message. There was nothing there as far as he could see. More to the point, the file was tiny. He opened the message.

'I hope a good death is enough,' Alexia read. 'I don't deserve a good death. I am a coward. I am too connected to leave. No, that is a lie. I am too frightened to leave and I do not want to become a ghost frozen in brass. There are so few of us left now. You must do the right thing. I have faith in you.' Alexia stared at the screen and then at du Bois. The message was signed with an unfamiliar name.

'Do you suppose that's her real name?' he wondered.

'Couldn't she just have committed suicide?'

'She had to die in battle. She was a lot older than us.'

He took another drag on the cigarette. It was a long time since he had been this badly hurt, perhaps even back when he was just a normal human. He noticed one of the pay-as-you go phones he had been checking was switched on and his mobile had automatically called it.

He heard a ringing from behind him. Coincidence, surely. He craned his neck. Every movement hurt. Further up the beach he saw a figure he vaguely recognised. Du Bois magnified his vision, and DC Mossa, the detective who had first told him about Natalie, came into sharp focus. She was frowning as she looked at a ringing mobile. She pressed and held down a button. The ringing stopped and du Bois saw that the phone he had been calling had just been switched off.

'Have you still got my pistol?' he asked. Alexia handed him the .45. Water dribbled out of the barrel. He would have to strip it down and clean everything later. He dried it as best he could on the coat a paramedic had lent him and stood up, shrugging off the coat. He limped towards Mossa.

'Malcolm?' Alexia got up to follow him.

Mossa looked up as he approached.

'You look like shit.' she said. Then she noticed the gun in his hand. 'What's ... What the fuck?!' Du Bois pointed the gun at her. Mossa had been loud enough to draw attention to herself. People saw the gun and came running. There were firearms officers present. They knew Mossa. They didn't know du Bois, who found himself with MP5 sub-machine guns levelled at him. After the beating he'd just taken, they didn't seem all that frightening.

'I don't care,' he told her earnestly. 'I just want a name, and it won't get taken any further. You don't give me a name and I'll blow your head all over the beach.' After all, she didn't know that the gun was empty.

There was lots of shouting. Du Bois frowned. He wanted to hear what Mossa had to say.

'It was you on the phone?' she asked. He nodded. She looked at the gun and saw the resolve in du Bois's face.

'When I phoned in to re-task the police working the roadblock to help me raid the dog stadium, someone made a call from Kingston Crescent on your phone to another pay-as-you-go in the Tipner area, as close to the old dog stadium as triangulation could make out. You tipped someone off. I want to know who. Tell me and I'll make sure that you don't get prosecuted and you get to retire on full pension. Don't tell me, and I blow your head off and find out anyway.'

There was more shouting. The only reason du Bois hadn't been shot was that some of the senior officers on the scene thought they knew what he was.

'McGurk,' Mossa finally said. It was obvious from the reaction of some of the officers around them that what she had said made her dirty. Guns were lowered. Du Bois's .45 wasn't.

'Where can I find him?'

25

A Long Time After the Loss

Even with the window polarised, the light pollution spilling into the large sparsely furnished marble office turned the two figures into shadows, like the negative of an old photograph.

'You know what you are asking me?' the Elite demanded.

'I'm not asking you,' the tall figure behind the desk said.

'Because my copy demands it?'

'No, because slavery is the price of great power.'

The Elite turned and walked to the window looking out into brightly-lit orbital space. Inter-starscraper vehicles looked like tiny black bugs lost in the sea of light.

'This is a waste,' the Elite said, and then sought his way through the glass. There was pain. His master was well defended.

A grotesque, an outlander, reaching for her, the needle in his hand, and she knew he was going to wipe her. Kill all her achievements in the Game, make the Absolute lose interest, deny her communion. Why was she helpless? She had her bone knife, a discreet thorn pistol, her body was laced with elegant and deadly virals; but the needle got closer until it filled her vision.

'Zabilla?' Dracup said gently. Her eyes flickered open. Internal narcotics dealt quickly and efficiently with the rising panic. Dracup was gazing down at her, but there was some vestige of paranoia from the dream that had her mistrusting how he looked at her. Beneath the concern, she thought she saw something new – towards her, anyway. A callousness. She bit back the anger. He was a fool if he was growing tired of her now while she was so close to such a major triumph in the Game.

More worrying was that the Absolute could not have failed to monitor the dream now that she was so important to the research into the cocoon. She wondered if the dream was a warning, the price of failure. Then she wondered if such thoughts were treasonous, if for no other reason than not being entertaining enough. Besides, she could not imagine that the punishment for failure would be so mundane, so private and over so quickly. She would surely become a public spectacle, entertainment, and the most galling thing would be that all those she had beaten to get where she was today would be there to enjoy her fall.

The fear was gone now, thanks to the drugs, and had been replaced with irritation.

'A dream, nothing more,' she told Dracup as she got up. She missed her old apartment. A not unattractive sculpted root structure made up two walls of their well-appointed apartment in the bunker down among the roots, but it could not make up for the loss of the view. She could not see the other atmosphere-piercing arcology trees. There was not that green quality to the light as the sun shone down through the translucent leaf canopy above, nor the bioluminescent glow at night. There was little of the Game to amuse her, just research. Down below the black leaves, she might as well have been one of the morlocks who served her. She got up and made her way towards the shower nook. The roots shifted, opening at her approach.

'Be careful that your subconscious does not betray you,' Dracup said.

Zabilla spun to face him. 'What's that supposed to mean?'

He was immediately conciliatory. 'Just that we are being monitored closely ...'

'Do you not think I know that?' *Why are you saying this out loud?* she left unspoken.

'And now is not the time for a treasonous subconscious.'

'And what exactly would you like me to do about it?'

'More drugs?' he suggested. Again he sounded reasonable, but again his suggestion just irritated her. Like everyone in the Game, she was used to altering her mood with chemicals, whether to enhance sensation, as a less controllable alternative to immersion theatre, to enhance performance, or just to remain seemingly calm in the face of other players' moves. But other than performance enhancers, which would eventually make her crash, she needed to be able to focus without distraction. Mood-changing drugs dulled her wits.

Now she was wishing for a calming agent, a way to slow her racing brain as she strode rapidly towards her lab. Dracup was next to her, and they were flanked by two heavily armed human guards, four security satellites – S-sats, better-armed and larger versions of the P-sats that some of the more modern and gauche players favoured as familiars – and their two morlock retainers/assistants. The morlocks were frighteningly human-looking, Zabilla had to say. Dressed in what were apparently fabricated copies of pre-Loss servant finery, they looked like small pale people with skin where their eyes should be. Despite their blindness, they never seemed to have any problem finding their way or assisting with often quite delicate procedures.

She was getting nowhere. The cocoon was resisting all but the most invasive means of investigation, and the most invasive means seemed to threaten some sort of self-destruct impulse or were simply so ruinous that they would harm it. What they were not doing was getting any closer to discovering the secret of bridging to Red Space.

It didn't help that an avatar was there daily. She could feel its hollow, empty eyes on her as she worked, somehow disapproving. Her reports went directly to the Absolute.

They went through one security checkpoint after another, each more thorough and invasive than the last. Zabilla reflected that all her research was being conducted against a backdrop of one security breach after another. There had been a number of breaches – electronic, nano and, most worrying and the most effective so far, biotechnological. It was whispered that the Consortium almost certainly had people on the ground, and it seemed unlikely that the Church was not making some attempt to secure its bridge monopoly. The sophistication of the biotech attempts, however, pointed to the Living Cities on Pangea. The avatar had told her that more than one of the Monarchist systems' Elites was within response distance if anything happened.

Zabilla and Dracup walked through the final security and anti-infection field. They had to retract and lock down their nano-screens before they were allowed in and then were assigned S-sats designed to project a sterile field around them. The lab was as nanite-free as any place could be made.

The airlock system to the lab opened. They cycled through and Zabilla once again found herself looking at the cocoon with the realisation that she was starting to hate the thing. The avatar was already there. If indeed it had ever left.

'There was another security breach last night. An attempt was made to gain access to the genetic files kept on base personnel,' the avatar neunonically 'faced to them both. Dracup looked up, interested.

Zabilla wondered what possible interest security matters could have for her. Too late she realised that any conversation with an avatar was almost certainly monitored through its experiential ware by the Absolute. The automaton with the fixed face of beaten gold seemed to be staring at her. She should have said something loyal, explained her thoughts. Instead she was thinking that they should know that all she was interested in was solving the puzzle of the cocoon.

She knew that it had come from some sort of recently functioning Seeder craft. She knew that it was made from an incredibly tough biological material that shared characteristics with both bone and enamel. Initially she had thought that the name cocoon was misleading and that what she was dealing with was a kind of biological computer laced through the incredibly strong material, but one of the more invasive scanning procedures had pointed to it having a cavity of some sort inside. That was before they had to shut the procedure down, as according to the more passive scans they seemed to be adversely affecting the cocoon.

Brilliant, she congratulated herself. In more than a month of research, all she had managed to do was confirm that the cocoon was hollow. Though they also knew that it had some sort of internal power supply or store, again laced throughout the cocoon. If it was capable of drawing power from elsewhere then it was probably due to the complex entanglement effect that they had seen with other pieces of S-tech. If this was the case, then who knew what it was capable of?

They had tried introducing other forms of S-tech in attempts to interface with it. They had tried uplifted races' versions of technology derived from S-tech, 'sect derivatives of Seeder tech from the Hive Worlds being the most sophisticated, and actual S-tech itself from the small collection of working xeno-archaeological finds present on Game. Even the smallest S-tech find was enough to turn a planet into a conflict-resolution world. There were graveyards of ships in some sectors of space that had come about due to similar space-borne finds. It was all to no avail. Like most modern nano- and smart-matter-based technology, S-tech was designed to be adaptable and have more than one use, but for some reason what they had did not seem compatible. Perhaps, like the Church, the Seeders had wanted to limit bridge capability. That suggested that the cocoon, or whatever was inside it, was a highly specialised application of S-tech.

Zabilla wished that she had a Church bridge-tech expert to torture but knew they were rarely allowed to leave the Cathedral, and when they did they were heavily protected. An Elite probably could have extracted one, but the Church had made it clear that any attempt to do so would lead to an immediate ban on the provision of bridge technology to the faction in question. There were rumours that one had escaped from the Cathedral but that its knowledge of bridge tech had been protected by some very dangerous and deeply implanted suicide routines. Any attempt to extract the information would result in the wiping of the tech's mind followed by their death.

In short, she was attempting to reverse engineer something from a position of near-total ignorance. In fact, the clearest thing about her research so far was that the ability to create nth-level perversions was not going to help her.

The avatar was watching her again. She had been aware that Dracup and the avatar had been discussing the security of the facility over the secure 'face link. She had been standing there staring at the cocoon for ten minutes now.

'Perhaps some kind of stimulus will help?' the avatar suggested.

'It would be a distraction,' Zabilla answered in a more testy tone of voice than was generally considered wise when talking to a direct conduit to the Absolute.

An idea was beginning to form, but as ever the problem would be interfacing the cocoon with other forms of technology. What she hoped was that the cocoon understood its own purpose and would act accordingly. It was tenuous, but there was precedent for it with S-tech applications, particularly with biotech. There was a degree of intelligence in the alien flesh. Most likely nothing would happen, but the worst-case scenarios for what she had planned were catastrophic.

'I have an idea,' she told the avatar. 'We need a ship with a bridge drive.'

Dracup turned to stare at her.

'That is a bold request,' the avatar said. 'You are intending to try and interface a ship's nav systems with the cocoon?'

'If this cocoon holds the secret to bridge tech, then a nav computer is designed to interface with it.'

'Except that ship nav systems have anti-tamper systems just like bridge drives.' The Church provided both the nav systems and the drives. Both were intrinsic parts of the stranglehold the Church had on Red Space.

'Yes, but if this is pure S-tech unmodified by the Church, then it shouldn't have their countermeasures against tampering.' Though it had remained pretty tamper-proof so far, she thought, but that could just be down to the nature of the forces it needed to survive to fulfil its purpose. 'We won't be tampering with the nav comp, just offering it another connection. The worst that can happen is we junk a bridge drive and a nav comp.'

'No, the worst that can happen is that you succeed and open a bridge to Red Space, and the gravitational forces involved tear Pangea apart. Or perhaps you just decompress the entire planet and collapse the atmosphere.'

Zabilla looked pained. She had to admit that opening a bridge was her greatest fear due to the unknown interplay between the gravitational forces at play when opening a wormhole, and how that would interact with Pangea's own gravity. All bridge drives had a fail-safe against bridging too close to planets. This was also the reason bridge points were always so far from planetary and stellar bodies. The Church had always warned of the catastrophic results of planetary bridge points. The comment about decompressing the planet, however, was sheer ignorance. Sadly, she thought that before she realised the Absolute would be monitoring her.

'Would it perhaps be better to do it in space?' she suggested.

'Too much of a security risk. We would make ourselves vulnerable to attack by Consortium Elite.'

'Seeder tech tends to be intuitive. I don't think it would allow catastrophe.'

'It is a lot to gamble on a guess.'

'There's some evidential basis for my guess, but I'll be honest with you, I'm out of ideas. If you don't want to do this then you may as well get Gilbert Scoular down here – perhaps he can make the cocoon look prettier.' *Assuming that Scoular had been cloned since I killed him, that is,* Zabilla thought.

The avatar stared at her. Dracup did a good job of hiding his concern.

'Very well,' the avatar finally said. 'The Absolute says that you play this Game well.'

Zabilla nodded. She didn't even feel relief. If anything, she was more worried than she had been before. It was a desperate move to stay in the Game rather than anything approaching scientific method. She tried to suppress the feeling at the back of her mind that this was a searing indictment of just how irresponsible the Absolute was. It was willing to risk everything, all its people, the Game and itself on some pretty wild speculation.

The security was mostly human, as interlopers had hacked the heads in the past. They were some elite unit of the Absolute's Toy Soldiers and there were a lot of them. Not to mention S-sats, though Zabilla could not understand why they would be any more secure than the heads. Perhaps they were on some kind of isolated control 'face. They were in the large open space where the G-car had first landed, a hangar made of poured reinforced concrete. The reinforcement in the concrete was a nano-process that bonded the individual molecules more tightly together. They were also protected or watched by the bunker's automated weapon systems: turret-mounted strobe guns, smart munitions batteries, infrasonics, attack nano-swarms and virals. Zabilla didn't see any Elite but assumed they could be there quickly if anything went wrong. It felt like overkill, but Zabilla was aware, intellectually anyway, that it was not.

She had watched the craft come down on the elevator platform. It was an old Rapier-class, three-person, long-range strike craft. The fighter/bomber was a decommissioned antique from the Art Wars that had been in the collection of one of the more successful players, though the truly great players frowned upon interests outside the Game. Zabilla thought the three nacelle-mounted Real Space engines made the craft look a little like the tridents she'd seen used by gladiators in the murder arcades. The Rapier fighter/bomber was one of the smallest classes of craft that had a bridge drive.

The cocoon was brought in on small AG motors and guided over towards the craft. Zabilla, with Dracup's aid, had been using the full extent of her S-tech knowledge to repurpose and reprogram some of the Absolute's S-tech collection. She also had a length of tendril-like biotech cable, the best money could buy, grown in a 'sect Hive habitat, to act as a connection. The avatar, who was there watching, did not want the cocoon going inside or even getting too close to the ship.

In theory, it was as simple as attaching the nav comp to the cabling, to the S-tech interface and then to the cocoon. That was the easy bit. Then they had to somehow make the nav comp give them diagnostic information on the cocoon. By this point Zabilla wasn't even sure where this ridiculous plan had come from. She must have been desperate when she thought of it, though she was struggling to remember the genesis of the idea. It was now apparent that it was pointless. It wouldn't work. She'd been clutching at straws.

The avatar turned to look at her.

'Self-doubt is not an attractive quality, let alone in a player of your calibre.'

'I ... I'm ... sorry,' she said. Images were coming to the fore in her mind. Not images, memories that had been hidden from her. *They had worn some sort of camo suits. The grotesques had seemingly come from nowhere. At first she had thought they were morlock-rights activists or even losers. She saw the needle and knew she was about to be wiped.*

'This is tremendous waste of resources, not to mention a security risk,' the avatar continued.

'There's something wrong ...' Zabilla started.

Dracup turned to look at her. 'Shit,' he said. 'Too soon.'

The Absolute actually shifted in its nutrient bath. More then fifty feet long and around ten feet thick, the Absolute resembled something between a slug made of human flesh and a giant phallus. What passed for its mind and its nerve endings were laced throughout the organism's entire form. Once human, it had redesigned itself to take signals from hundreds of thousands of experiential broadcasts at any one time – the ultimate receptor of sensation. A creature designed specifically as a sensualist. It now realised that something was wrong. Something was terribly, terribly wrong.

It could feel its avatar neunonically give instructions to the AG motors suspending the cocoon to return it to the secure lab, to the automated defences to open fire and to the S-sats to do the same. All of them were ignored.

The Absolute itself tried to take control of Zabilla and Dracup if for no other reason than to find out what was happening. Even if they had been meat-hacked it would make an example of them. Instead it found that the experiential link was simply missing.

The Absolute squirmed and splashed around in its tank. This was exciting but it couldn't be allowed to lose. It wasn't what the Game was about. It was about pleasuring itself. The Absolute used the experiential link to take control of ten thousand of the best electronic security and warfare specialists on Game and in orbit. It opened the most secure computer system on the planet to all of them and had them move in unison to retake control of the bunker's automated systems.

All the while it was playing back one of Dracup's hidden memories before the experiential link had been severed. It saw Dracup programming diagnostic routines into the lab's equipment. Even deep in his subconscious Dracup hadn't been aware of writing the code after he had examined the bunker's electronic security, also subconsciously. The sophisticated security hack had been laced throughout the new diagnostic routines that Dracup had been developing consciously.

It was a shame they hadn't been players, the Absolute thought. They played well. Just as long as they didn't win. It had to win. That was the only rule of the Game.

Dracup took control of the automated weapon systems and the S-sats. The avatar became a prism of light as every strobe gun targeted it. The rotating barrels of the fast-cycling lasers filled the air with lines of red and threatened to overwhelm the avatar's energy dissipation grid.

Then every AG-driven smart munition hit the avatar. The powerful automaton ceased to exist and was replaced with a sizeable crater.

The force of the explosion knocked Dracup and Zabilla to the ground. It only staggered the nearby armoured and augmented Toy Soldiers.

The Absolute felt the excitement rising. This was the most alive it had felt in centuries. There was a genuine threat here to something it wanted, but it was going to win. It took control of every Toy Soldier in the bunker complex. All of them were now rushing towards the hangar area with the purpose of killing Dracup and Zabilla and securing the cocoon.

As one, the remaining Toy Soldiers turned to look at the prone forms of Zabilla and Dracup. The strobe guns and anti-personnel weapons from the S-sats were cutting swathes through them, but all the smart munitions had been used on the avatar. They would be vaccinated against the virals, their own nano-screens would be programmed to fend off the nano-swarms, and the infrasonic would do him and Zabilla more harm than good, Dracup thought.

It was sickening. What remained of Zabilla was only just starting to realise what she'd done, even as her personality started to recede, screaming in this new and alien mind. The Zabilla fragment remembered releasing the program into the system bit by bit. The intelligent program had been developed by the Living Cities from code sold to them by Pythia by way of the Consortium's intelligence agencies. The idea was that it was nearly undetectable. Released in discrete parts, it then formed briefly to find and record information. It had been partially detected and part of it destroyed, but not before it had managed to record the genetic files of every person serving in the bunker. Zabilla had retrieved the information in a set of results from one of her apparently failed diagnostics. She had put it together in her deep subconscious. The information had then gone to the implanted targeted viral factory that ran through her small intestine.

Dracup grabbed one of the Toy Soldiers, its ornate armour giving him lot of purchase. He rammed the bone knife into the top of the soldier's neck just below his jaw line. Neurotoxins flooded the soldier's system. They probably wouldn't be enough to kill an augmented soldier, but they wouldn't help. He backed away, still holding on to the knife and the soldier, using him as a shield as the others all started firing at once. Dracup threw himself back over the cocoon as the Soldier he'd been using as a shield exploded into chunks of steaming superheated meat.

Dracup landed next to Zabilla behind the cocoon, finding he had the Toy Soldier's aesthetically overdesigned, double-barrelled laser rifle in his hands. Dracup's augmented hearing filtered sounds, so he could make out Zabilla farting very audibly, which explained the look of concentration on her face, he thought, as she released the virals into the air. Almost immediately the bunker 'faced viral warnings to their neunonics.

'Send the signal,' Dracup 'faced to her.

'Not yet. We need a diversion,' she replied.

Dracup popped up from behind the cocoon and fired several double-barrelled bursts of red light at the closest Toy Soldiers. The pitiful energy dissipation grid on his armoured clothing went neon and threatened to overload. Half the flesh on his face superheated and blew off down to the bone from a hit, but it gave the tactical software in his neunonics the time it needed to assess the situation. He started firing grenades from the underslung launcher, shifting aim, firing again. Each grenade was programmed with timed air-burst commands fed from the tactical software to explode where they would cause the most damage. Another moment's glance showed the automated strobe guns cutting swathes through the Toy Soldiers.

Dracup ducked back behind the cocoon next to Zabilla. Half his face was just hot armoured bone now and still smoking. The problem with virals was that they took too long to kill. Dracup put together a fast and messy hack. The idea was to use the bunker's defence nano-swarms as carriers for the targeted virals to speed things up. He wasn't sure how useful they would be but it was worth a try.

When his Toy Soldiers started to die, the Absolute decided that he didn't like this any more. They might well be trapped but perhaps they would be content with simply destroying the cocoon. Particularly if they were working for – or had been co-opted by – the Church. He sent one of his favourite toys. He sent Fallen Angel.

They were mostly cowering behind the cocoon now. They had kept low, crawled towards a wall and sandwiched themselves there. The Absolute didn't dare fire on the cocoon, though Zabilla was reasonably sure it was more than capable of taking laser fire. The beams from the strobe guns looked like a near-solid wall of red as they repeatedly stabbed down into the Toy Soldiers. Dracup had S-sats firing from concealed locations at any Toy Soldiers that tried to charge their position. Zabilla had a thorn pistol in each hand; Dracup still had the laser rifle; now all they had to do was watch either side of the cocoon for Toy Soldiers trying to flank them. They were helped by visual feeds from the S-sat and the bunker's systems. The feeds also showed that the Toy Soldiers were starting to fall. The virals were taking effect as Dracup and Zabilla started to remember who they really were.

Scab and the Monk had smuggled themselves onto Game in the stomach of an imported piece of livestock, some kind of large grazing lizard from a Rakshasa-held feline park world.. They had then spent two days completely still, clinging to a mostly deserted part of one of the arcology trees close to where their targets lived, waiting for the results of some very subtle and well-programmed trace nanites.

They had already had themselves modified to look like their prey, and copies of the Game's experiential ware had been implanted into them. They had also had some very interesting subconscious neunonics routines put into their systems. These were designed to be very well hidden, as the Absolute, by its nature, had some of the most sophisticated mental auditing systems in Known Space. All of this had been provided by the Living Cities, who had a lot of experience in finding ways to infiltrate the Game.

Sophisticated trace nanites had allowed Monk and Scab to plot a time when their targets would be most vulnerable and – more importantly – when they would be relatively lightly monitored.

The targets had put up a fight. Both might well have been experienced duellists, but neither were born killers or Church-trained monks. Their virals had caused a bit more trouble, however. Scab and the Monk had wiped them and junked their DNA. Their personal belongings had either been taken or disassembled. Scab and the Monk had then used a customised anti-forensic nano-swarm to destroy other traces of their identity. They had downloaded all the information from Zabilla and Dracup's neunonics and then wiped them as well.

Then came the really clever stuff, the stuff that the Living Cities had been working on. Using a highly illegal application of S-tech, Scab and the Monk rewrote their own genetic codes to not only resemble Dracup and Zabilla's, respectively, but at a given chemical signal to mutate back to their original forms. Then, using an intuitive AI program, they overwrote the information on their own neunonics with the information from Dracup and Zabilla's neunonics. The intuitive program filled in the blanks as best it could and then, based on that information, used an adapted meat-hack program to overwrite Scab and the Monk's personality. To all extents and purposes they had become Zabilla and Dracup.

Scab had liked none of this, but he hadn't seen another way. Their subconscious minds had subtly been doing all the work during their infiltration, waiting for the correct set of circumstances to signal their resurgent personalities.

There was no feed from the bunker. Fallen Angel couldn't be bothered to hack his way in to find out the tactical situation as he dropped through the branches of the arcology trees. He was feeling lazy today, not at all creative, positively bored. He was just going to turn up and destroy everything that wasn't a cocoon. The Absolute might command him, but even it would never dare put experiential ware in an Elite so the phallic slug would have to find another way to enjoy the experience.

Targeting information on the ware told the Monk where to aim the thorn pistols, going for the exposed flesh in the Toy Soldiers' ridiculously impractical armour. Even so, it was taking too long for the virals on the splinter bullets to kill the soldiers. Things were getting more and more hairy. She played her penultimate trick.

One of the things about players was that they never paid any attention to morlocks. The Monk didn't control them, though Zabilla had had the biotechnical know-how to do so. She just released them from their programmed bonds. They didn't need any encouragement to fall upon the Toy Soldiers from where they had previously been cowering. Their rage was a thing to behold.

Scab continued to fire at the Toy Soldiers with the laser even as they were dying. He just liked shooting people.

'Now?' Scab 'faced. He was unable to talk as half his face was still a red smoking mess.

The Monk shook her head. Scab was beginning to wonder if all the talk of getting them out was just nonsense. He was pretty sure that any moment now Ludwig or one of the Angels was going to turn up and destroy them at a fundamental level.

It was a melancholy act of destruction. Not his best, but he was looking at destruction himself. Still, it was more than enough to herald his arrival after his coffin had bridged in all but unnoticed.

The focused particle beam cut through the entirety of the top of the arcology tree. It was one of the smaller ones: only thirty or so storeys breached the atmosphere. Then he hit it like a meteorite. The force destroyed about half of it but sent the rest tumbling through the branches of other arcology trees towards the surface of Game far below.

'Look upon my works,' he muttered to himself as he watched the wreckage tumble down through the thick branches of the arboreal cities. It was carnage, but only abstract to him. It was so quiet where he was. He liked it up here in orbit. He liked looking down on the planet, seeing the branches spread out below him like a spider's web.

He shot up into high orbit. The beam stabbing out from his weapon – it was in a rifle configuration at the moment – was almost an afterthought as he cut one of the planetary defence battle cruisers in two. High above Game, the two halves of the cruiser slowly drifted apart.

'Notice me,' Elite Scab whispered to himself.

He set the weapon to a wide-burst D-beam and played it up and down the top branches of one of the taller atmosphere-piercing arcology trees. The network of primordial black holes fed the weapon power via a form of complex entanglement. The D-beam rewrote the genetic codes of anything the signal hit and cancerous mutations appeared all over the outside of the tree. Inside, the inhabitants were reduced to protoplasmic slime or mutated into forms that weren't conducive to survival in this reality. Some became super-efficient alien predatory life forms. Others might even have evolved into higher forms, though they were probably destroyed by destructive slimes and super-predators before they had time to appreciate their enlightened nature.

The Absolute flopped around violently in its nutrient bath. Ludwig was still out drinking suns, whatever that meant. Both the Angels were close but a Consortium Elite had just attacked them. He would need both of them to protect the Game. He sent the order to Fallen Angel. The attacking Elite was the priority.

Planetary attack warnings appeared in their neunonics. Scab and the Monk stood up from behind the cocoon. The hangar area was carnage. Scab sent an instruction to the AG motors on each corner of the cocoon. The cocoon rose unsteadily into the air as one of the motors had been destroyed. They made their way quickly through the carnage and red steam, shooting anything that moved, though they tried to leave the morlocks alone as they were finishing off the wounded Toy Soldiers.

The hatch to the Rapier fighter/bomber opened at a neunonic

command as they approached. The Monk reached in and ferreted around for a bit. She came back with two rather vintage-looking emergency spacesuits.

'Really?' Scab asked, becoming more and more suspicious of the escape plan.

'You don't have to wear it if you don't want to.'

Reluctantly Scab put his hands into the black bubble of the suit and let it grow over him before fixing the visor to it. His neunonics interrogated the suit. It was old but functional, so he dropped some updated 'ware into its systems. The Monk did the same. As she did, she hacked the Rapier's systems and started them up, running rapid diagnostics on those that she needed.

'You'll do,' she muttered to herself.

'What, you're going to fly us out of here?' Scab asked, both confused and mildly interested, which was arguably more emotional than he'd been for a good long while, not counting his time as Dracup, and he was trying to forget about that. He was deeply uncomfortable with the emotional dependency Dracup had on Zabilla.

The Monk sent the heavily coded and very secure override command. Immediately after, she sent a time-bomb self-destruct routine. She was determined to leave as little trace as possible.

'Fuck!' Scab was unused to genuine surprise and had only just sealed the spacesuit as reality tore open and revealed the red beneath. The Rapier had just opened a bridge point. Even Elites couldn't do that. Scab turned to look at the Monk.

'Its all bullshit, isn't it, about not being able to open in a planetary gravitational field?'

'There's a fail-safe device on every bridge drive. Any attempt to open a bridge point in a strong gravity field junks the drive.'

'But you have an override for the fail-safe?'

'Obviously. Imagine the carnage if people knew they could pop in and out of Red Space, sneak up on their enemies. Also, we're genuinely not sure of the effects of repeated openings of wormholes in gravitational fields on the fabric of space-time. You coming?'

The Monk stepped forward, the cocoon floating behind her.

'But it's all right for the Church to have the knowledge?'

'Which we can't use because then people would know. You won't tell anyone, will you?' She was heading straight for the rip. Scab grabbed another laser rifle, a bandolier of grenades and some spare batteries and followed.

'No, I'll keep the information and use it for myself.'

'I like the way you volunteer for death, or at least total personality erasure,' the Monk said. 'Or maybe it's too late for that.'

The Monk climbed over bodies to step through the tear. Scab followed her into the red.

26
Southern Britain, a Long Time Ago

There was screaming, the *thrum* of a bowstring, and the screaming stopped. Tangwen lowered the bow. She stood on the rampart looking out down the hill and over the vast fertile plain, so different from the sea of swaying reeds in which she had grown up. The morning mists mingled with dirty smoke from the campfires, from the smouldering remnants of the third hill fort, and smoke from the pyres the Corpse People were using to burn their captives in plain view. *If they'd wanted them to suffer, they should have tried burning them out of bow range*, Tangwen thought. There were four Corpse People around the pyres. They had died with arrows in them trying to light the fires, but Tangwen was running short of arrows coated with the poison that was Fachtna's blood.

The defenders had said little as the four had entered the fort the previous night. Fachtna was still steaming, too hot to approach, Britha, a blood-soaked nightmare, carrying Teardrop. They had thought them gods or perhaps demons and had sunk to their knees – much to Britha's contempt. Tangwen was afraid that they would let these people down, that they were not what the Atrebates believed them to be, but then she had spent her whole life in the presence of a living god and knew how helpless and how much like everyone else they could be, child of the Great Mother or no.

'Fools,' Britha said as she appeared at Tangwen's side. She used that word a lot, Tangwen thought, but said nothing. The defenders either showed Britha great deference or gave her a wide berth. The warriors who wore stripes of black and blood vertically down their faces and braided crow and raven feathers into their hair, thought her a messenger from their bloody warrior goddess. 'A man called Feroth taught me to fight and he taught me about battles as well. If you want an enemy to surrender then you show mercy, you give them a reason to. If they think that surrendering will lead to burning then they will fight to the last.'

'They say that they kill and eat the warriors, those blessed by the Great Mother, but that the rest they take south towards the sea.'

'I think that is where my people are,' Britha said grimly and then lapsed into silence. The wounds she had taken last night had all but healed. The Atrebates had left the corpse of the bear at the gate. It would be another obstacle for the attackers. Tangwen had noticed how the carrion eaters, even the flies, stayed away from the corpse. 'They are just children playing at being dead,' Britha finally said. 'They are liars.'

'I think they believe it,' Tangwen said. Though they hadn't last night when the four of them had driven the corpse people away, but then she herself had wanted to flee when she had seen Fachtna and Teardrop's magics, and Britha's bloodlust.

'You have done what was asked of you. Will you return to your people? I think a hunter of your ability would be able to sneak past them.'

Tangwen wasn't sure.

'I think ...' She searched for the right words. She remembered the time before the black ships had come. They would hunt, they would raid or even more rarely they would go to war with another tribe. Things were hard, but looking back they seemed simpler: she had been much more carefree, even if she might not have appreciated it at the time. ' ... that it will not matter if I go back to my people. These –' she nodded towards the Corpse People '– or the ones in the black ships, they want everything, like the tribes the traders tell lies of, who they say cover many lands across the seas.'

'You'll come with us?' Britha asked. Tangwen wasn't sure but she thought she heard something like gratitude buried deep in Britha's words.

'Where?'

'This place is a trap. We stay here, we die. We must know what lies to the south and we must take an army.'

'I do not think that the warriors of the Atrebates will—'

'The king will see us now.' Neither of them had heard Fachtna's approach and Tangwen jumped at his words. They turned to look at the warrior who looked like a Goidel to Britha and claimed to be something called a Gael. He was not carrying his shield, but his armour, which Tangwen knew had turned many a spearhead, arrowhead and sword, looked almost good as new. The singing ghost sword was sheathed at his hip. Tangwen noticed that Britha was staring at the leather case strapped to his back. It was about half the length of a spear and Tangwen was sure she had seen it move as if something was struggling to get out. She knew that if Britha was interested in it, it was because she smelled power there, magics that she could use to help her people.

Fachtna bore no scars, though he was walking with a slight limp. He had said the Corpse People must have painted their weapons with blood blessed by their gods. Like Britha he looked pale, gaunt and hungry. This was a siege. Regardless of how grateful the Atrebates were for their brief respite, or the awe in which they held the four of them, they could not allow Britha and Fachtna to gorge themselves. *It must be the magic*, Tangwen thought. *It feeds on them when they use it.*

'How is Teardrop?' the young hunter asked.

'Dead,' Fachtna said. He did not look at Tangwen, he just glared at Britha.

Tangwen felt her stomach lurch and tasted bile in the back of her throat. She had liked Teardrop despite his strange appearance and outlandish dress. Fachtna might be a fine warrior, handsome, well made and worth a tumble, but she could talk to Teardrop and they had a bond of blood – they had saved each other's lives. She reached up to touch the dressing on the side of her head. When one of the *dryw* had checked the wound this morning, they had told her that it was all but healed.

'His power will be missed. It is much needed. Can it be taken from his body after death?' Britha asked. Tangwen turned to look at the other woman. The hunter was offended but knew that the *dryw* tended to be a lot more practical than warriors.

'He had a family, you know?' Fachtna said with a voice full of contempt and anger.

'The proper rituals will be honoured.'

'A wife.'

'Fachtna, I'm sorry, but people still live who can be helped.'

'Three daughters.' Britha sighed and looked impatient. 'A fine young son, and all you care about is stealing power from his still-warm body?'

Tangwen watched anger spread like fire across Britha's face. Her knuckles whitened as she gripped the haft of her spear more tightly. This had been coming since Britha had killed the boy. Tangwen understood why she had done it – it was kinder – but Britha had done it so coldly.

'What I care about—'

'A cruel jest, Fachtna.'

Britha and Tangwen looked towards the now familiar, strangely accented voice of Teardrop. Tangwen turned angrily on Fachtna.

'Why would you say that?!' she demanded.

'Because its true. My friend Teardrop is no more.'

Tangwen was confused by Fachtna's words. Was he in another impassioned warrior sulk? She turned to Britha, who was staring at Teardrop suspiciously.

'Who are you?' she demanded. Tangwen turned back to look at Teardrop and noticed his eyes. They were a silver colour and multifaceted like the gems the richest of the traders from across the sea wore on their fingers. All the veins on his head stood out as if they were gripping his head tightly. 'What are you, for you are no man?'

Tangwen took a step back. Holding her bow in her right, her left hand moved to the quiver that hung from her hip. Teardrop turned to look at her. There was nothing of Teardrop there, only something strange and monstrous.

'Still want my power?' Teardrop asked, looking back to Britha.

'I want weapons to fight Bress and this Crom Dhubh,' she said more cautiously.

'This is the price,' Fachtna said. Teardrop looked at him but said nothing.

'Will he stand with us?' Britha asked. Fachtna just nodded. 'Then let us go and see this king.' Britha walked past Fachtna, heading deeper into the hill fort. Teardrop looked between Fachtna and Tangwen as if examining them both, as if he had never seen either of them before, then turned and followed Britha.

Tangwen and Fachtna were left. The silence grew.

'It's difficult to mourn your friend when his body still stands among you,' the warrior finally managed. Tangwen was shocked to see tears streaming down Fachtna's face. The warrior sank to the mud. Tangwen knelt next to him. She wrapped her arms around him and held him as sobs racked his body. She felt tears come to her own eyes, though she wondered how either of them could cry among all this madness.

The track branched into three and the middle path branched into two more routes further up. One of the two central tracks led to a gate in the west wall that had been blocked up. Britha and Teardrop took the other. They walked past granaries raised on stilts to keep out vermin. There were guards on the granaries. Not the professional warriors of the Cigfran Teulu, the Family of the Raven, the Atrebates *cateran*, but rather doughty landsmen with staves. The landsmen here did not seem to carry spears, Britha noticed with disdain. *This must be a soft land*, she thought.

To their left were a number of roundhouses little different from those Britha had left in Ardestie. The people watched the two strangers pass, women, children and men. They looked gaunt, haggard and more than a little frightened. They stared, but when Britha stared back they did anything to avoid looking her in the eyes. There were still some sheep, pigs, a few cows and chickens, so the siege had not gone on too long, but just looking at the animals reminded her of the hunger that gnawed away at her. She felt like she was being eaten from the inside and her blood burned. *I am as much monster as you now, Cliodna*, Britha thought.

'A fine salmon leap,' the creature that was trying to contain itself in Teardrop's body said, referring to her killing of the bear creature.

'What are you?' Britha demanded. She had seen the thing sprouting out like a vast crystalline plant from his body, reaching to places that didn't make sense to her. It hurt for her to look at him, pain through her skull so bad it made her feel sick.

'An explanation would do you no good.'

'Why don't the others see you as you are?'

'Fachtna can, obviously. The rest do not have the potency in their blood that you do. Blessed by the Muileartach and Crom Dhubh, by life and death. That is why you can see, but sadly you will never understand.' Britha felt like she was being insulted but chose not to rise to the provocation. This thing was unknown but seemingly powerful, and she did not wish to provoke it. 'Because of your slaying of the bear, they think that you are one of us.' Britha realised that he was talking in the language of the Pecht, her language. It had similarities to what was spoken by the southron tribes, languages which she now somehow instinctively understood, but was different enough so that any of the Atrebates who were listening would not understand.

'They think I am from the Otherworld?'

'They will.'

Britha was about to ask more but they had arrived at a large circular stone structure in the north-west corner of the fort. It was raised on a mound and its walls were about eight feet high, though with regular square gaps in the stones. There was a large opening in the southern part of the wall.

'What is this?' Britha asked.

'A holy place.'

'I don't understand.'

'A place dedicated to their gods.'

'But it's huge. They could build many roundhouses here, or granaries, graze animals or train warriors.' Britha could just about understand why god-slaves would have small shrines in their round-houses to bargain with their gods for favours, but this extravagance seemed like insanity.

'They are a rich tribe.'

'They are moonstruck.' Britha would have said more but they had passed through the gap into the circular structure. Inside was a large stone pool of what looked like very stagnant water. In the centre of it was a stone statue of an exaggeratedly pregnant female figure with an oversized vagina.

'The Muileartach,' Britha whispered.

'Here they call her Andraste,' the thing that wore Teardrop told her. Though he spoke the language of the Pecht, Andraste was a southron word, and as he said it one of three figures turned to look at them. The figure was tall and thin and wore the brown robe of a *dryw*. Britha found his stare more disconcerting than she would have otherwise as he wore an *enchendach*, a feathered bird mask, in the shape of a raven's head. Britha pointed at him.

'That is ill done. What has this one to hide?' she said, mistrusting the mask.

'Eurawg does not hide; he honours the gods,' the second figure said, stroking a thin black moustache streaked with white. He looked old and grizzled, and had gone to seed, but it was clear to Britha that not long ago he had been fit and physically powerful. His clothes were of fine quality, the dirk at his hip even had some kind of precious trade stone embedded in its pommel. His voice had sounded reasonable enough in tone but she could hear the pain in it. He was sitting on a pallet of straw but was clearly not comfortable, the result of the two mangled legs that stretched out in front of him. His eyes spoke of intelligence; his scars spoke of a willingness to fight; and the expression on his face was one of interest and bemusement. *This is no fool,* Britha thought. She also thought she could see the faintest trace of fire running through his blood.

'I honour the goddess and I honour her daughter.' The voice from the mask was little more than a whisper. Britha did not like the voice and did not understand the reference to the daughter of the goddess. She glanced at Teardrop suspiciously.

'This is Rin, *rhi* of the Atrebates.'

Britha nodded to the man on the pallet.

'So this is the daughter of Andraste?' the third figure asked scornfully. She spoke with a voice obviously used to wielding authority. At first Britha had taken the figure in battle-scarred armour to be a man. On closer inspection it was obvious that the powerfully built woman had once been handsome, though never beautiful. Now she was all hard edges, scar tissue and broken teeth. One of her eyes was a white mass surrounded by scarring; her left ear was missing; no hair grew around the wound, which was still raw, though it had obviously happened many years ago.

Britha was about to deny that she had any connection to any god when Teardrop said, 'That is correct. Britha is the daughter of Andraste, and I am her herald.'

Britha turned to Teardrop, but his features remained impassive and he did not look at her. With the silver crystalline eyes he looked more Otherworldly than ever before. It was hard to imagine he had ever been just a man.

'You'll forgive me if I do not immediately accept this,' the woman said.

I don't blame you, Britha thought, but decided to remain silent, waiting to see what Teardrop was going to do next.

'Morfudd!' the *dryw* in the *enchendach* hissed. 'You would deny the word of your goddess!'

'Shut up, Eurawg,' the woman said.

'You cannot speak to one of my rank like—'

'Shut up, Eurawg.'

'What would you have of us?' Teardrop asked.

'Proof,' Morfudd said. Britha had to admit that she liked the warrior.

'You do not demand—' Eurawg started but Morfudd turned on him.

'I will not blindly follow anyone who turns up claiming to be the daughter of Andraste, and stop trying to sound sinister, Eurawg. You're not fooling anyone.'

'They're family,' Rin told them by way of explanation and apology.

'Morfudd leads the Cigfran Teulu,' Teardrop told Britha. 'The warband is sacred to your mother, hence their leader must always be a woman.'

'The Cigfran Teulu is only sacred to Andraste in her aspect as the hag,' Morfudd said. 'But then as her daughter you would know that.'

The *dryw* all but tore off his *enchendach*. He was young: he could not have left the colleges in the groves all that long ago. Britha wondered why there was no older or more experienced *dryw* to treat with them, particularly as she was the daughter of a goddess, apparently.

'Rhi Rin, I must protest. We have—'

'Enough,' Rin said quietly. 'There is no denying that you have power and we thank you for coming to our aid last ni—'

'The fort would have surely fallen—' Eurawg began.

'It is not for you to judge military mat—' Morfudd began.

'Don't talk over your king,' Britha said quietly. Both of them fell silent.

'Will you stay and fight with us?' Rin asked.

'What news from the south?' Britha responded.

Morfudd and Rin exchanged looks.

'I—' Rin started.

'Do not poison your words; speak truthfully,' Britha told him, but it was Eurawg who spoke.

'To the south-east there is a stretch of water between three islands. That stretch of water is sacred to your mother, Andraste. We take those of the Atrebates who have been touched by the moon to the two islands closest to the shore. The Regni to the east do the same.'

'*Did* the same,' Morfudd corrected him. 'They have been attacked from the sea, perhaps destroyed.'

'The black ships?' Britha asked.

'What do you know of the—' Morfudd started suspiciously.

'Let the boy finish,' Rin said gently. 'I mean the *dryw*.'

Eurawg looked less than happy as he continued with his story. 'There is a special order of the *dryw* who care for those afflicted by the moon. One morning, not more than ten days hence, we found one of them, a young man, a foundling, a child of the mad who had been raised by the *dryw* on the island. He was bloody, exhausted, near dead and nearer madness. He told of the black ships. He said that they came from the Otherworld and that they were planning something.'

'What?' Britha asked.

'The waters are sacred. The border between this world and the other is weak there. They would pervert what is sacred to your mother and they intend a summoning.'

'A summoning of what?'

'He did not know, but he said they intended a great sacrifice.'

She had known – at some level she had known – but it still rocked her. During the worst times, the times when mere survival meant a payment of blood to the land, the black-robed *dryw* were capable of sacrificing many, but this beggared belief. *They must have hundreds on both boats by now.*

'The Llwglyd Diddymder,' Teardrop said. Britha translated the words into her own tongue: the Hungry Nothingness. She wanted to ask him what it meant but didn't dare show ignorance in front of Rin and his people.

'What is this?' Rin asked.

'An ancient evil from the darkness beyond the stars,' Teardrop pronounced in tones that made Britha want to laugh.

'Can it be fought?' the crippled *rhi* asked.

'Not by us, not here. You need to stop it before it is summoned,' Teardrop explained.

'Well, she is the daughter of Andraste,' Morfudd said, gesturing dismissively at Britha. 'It should not be difficult for her to lay waste to the Corpse People and the demons on these black ships.'

'I am not the only servant of the gods abroad right now,' Britha said. She cared little for the deception but she was not willing to break it either. 'Where is this shepherd of the moonstruck? May we speak with him?'

Eurawg answered: 'Whatever he had seen had driven him mad. He spoke of demons in the flesh, dead gods in his head, hearing singing from the night sky and that the sea wanted him. It was too much for him, and he died trying to cut his own face off.'

'Tell them the rest,' Rin said quietly.

'Essyllt, my predecessor, she went to the Isles of the Moon—'

'With ten of the Teulu as escort, ten we sorely need right now,' Morfudd interjected.

'And you have not seen them since?' Britha asked, almost knowing the answer. It explained why a *dryw* so obviously young and inexperienced was here to treat with them.

'Oh, we've seen their faces,' Morfudd answered, her voice bitter and angry.

'When the Corpse People attacked, they used the moonstruck from the island like the living use hunting dogs. The mad wore the flayed faces of Essyllt and her escort.' It was Rin who spoke. Britha could hear the sadness in his voice. This was no tyrant. This was a king who cared for his people. He must be frustrated by his affliction, she thought. It would make what they had to try and convince him to do all the harder. 'So what would you have of us?'

'Your fight is not here, it is in the south,' Teardrop told him.

'They would corrupt the sacred waters of Andraste. This must be stopped!' Eurawg said. Britha found herself wishing he'd put the mask back on and just stand there looking sinister, but doing so quietly.

'And yet I have a fort full of people that I must protect,' Rin said. Morfudd was nodding.

'Which will not matter if this summoning succeeds,' Teardrop argued.

'The people here cannot come with us – they are not warriors. I take the warriors away, they will be massacred. The Corpse People do not care for captives or pillage. All they care about is destruction. Some say they even eat the dead. They are cannibal spirits, the restless dead of Annwn sent by Rhi Arawn to plague us,' Rin said bitterly.

'They are men – we proved that to you last night,' Britha told the king.

'You have not seen them pluck arrow and spear from their dead flesh; you have not seen their wounds heal in front of your eyes,' Morfudd said angrily.

'Which served them naught last night,' Britha said.

'We are not all the children of the gods!' Morfudd roared. Eurawg glared at her.

'Yes, you are,' Teardrop said with the sort of quiet authority Britha connected to the *dryw*. It was how you made warriors and kings listen. 'The magic is weak in your blood, but you have been touched by the gods.'

Rin looked at the strange man with the swollen head and the silver eyes, trying to decide what to admit to.

'It was true in my youth I could do things that others couldn't before ...'

'In battle?' Britha asked.

'A cart, would you believe. I may be favoured of Andraste in battle, but not when I'm helping bring the harvest in.' Britha was impressed despite herself. Few *mormaer* would lower themselves to help with the harvest. 'But this does not matter. If we leave the fort the people here will be massacred. In fact, if we leave the protection of the walls then we will all be massacred. If you have the means to fight the Corpse People then share them, and once we have defeated them we will go south with all haste.'

'There is not the time,' Teardrop said.

'And you know this?' Rin asked.

'If both ships are there—' Britha started.

'Both?' Rin looked to Eurawg.

'The *dryw* from the Isles of the Moon said that there were more than two ships. Many more.'

'How many do they plan to sacrifice?' Britha asked Teardrop.

'As many of the people of Ynys Prydein as they can find. They will make it Ynys Annwn,' Eurawg said.

'You must sneak out of here, no horses, no metal armour—' Teardrop began.

'If you are simply moonstruck, then you have our leave to go to the isles!' Morfudd shouted.

'There will be nothing left!' Britha shouted, silencing them all.

'I cannot and will not leave my people. It is pointless even talking about this any more.'

'If you stay here the Corpse People will overrun you. They nearly wiped you out last night.'

'Not if you share with us your ability to harm them,' Rin said.

'Which we won't,' Teardrop said with finality.

'We cannot defy the will of the gods,' Eurawg said. 'We should do what they ask.'

'Eurawg, shut up,' Rin said. 'So you would leave us here to die?'

'You're dead anyway,' Teardrop answered.

'We have no choice. The gods, our gods have spoken.' Eurawg was pleading.

'Eurawg, *shut up*! Have we not sacrificed enough, shed enough blood, drunk for you, feasted for you enough?' Morfudd shouted at Britha, though it was clear that she did not entirely believe she was the daughter of their goddess. 'You repay us by leaving us to die!'

'How many times must I say it,' Teardrop asked, letting anger creep into his voice, though something told Britha that was for show as well. 'The people here are dead anyway. The only question is whether or not your warband dies at the same time or confronts your real enemy.'

'The Cigfran Teulu serves the people. We have no choice but to stay,' Morfudd said with finality.

'Then you are cowards who may as well beg Crom Dhubh for death,' Britha said.

'And you will fare even less well without the blessings of your goddess,' Teardrop added.

'We have seen nothing from you to suggest you are who you say you are,' Morfudd said.

'Were you not at the gates last night? Did you not see their power?!' Eurawg screamed at the warband leader.

'And if we heal your king and make your warriors stronger and faster, and if we empower their weapons to wound those from the Otherworld, then will you summon your courage to stand with us?' Teardrop demanded.

'It would go some way to proving you are who you say you are,' Morfudd said.

'You are thinking that once we have done all this, you will simply take our power and cower behind these walls,' Britha said. 'It's what I would think,' she added.

'If we give our word, we will do what we have promised,' Rin said.

He looked troubled, deep in thought.

'How will you do this thing?' Eurawg asked, his hunger for power and knowledge written all over his face. Teardrop stared at the boy, who cringed under his inhuman eyes.

'Blood magic,' Teardrop pronounced.

Morfudd snorted in derision. 'You would turn us into little more than Goidel blood-drinkers! You would make us Baobhan Sith.'

'Enough,' Rin said quietly.

'You can't be—' Morfudd began.

'Then what?' the king asked her. 'We know that the Corpse People are connected to what is happening on the Isles of the Moon. We cannot harm them. The only reason our walls did not fall last night was because of these strangers' display of power. What would you have me do? If they do not aid us tonight then we are dead.'

'But abandon our people?'

'Your landsmen must wear the armour that the warriors do not take with them, and must man the gate and the walls. They must try and hold out as long as possible,' Britha told them

'While we sneak away,' Morfudd said bitterly. 'Will you at least arm them with weapons that will harm the Corpse People?' Britha hated to hear the tone of pleading in the proud, strong woman's voice.

'No,' Teardrop said emotionlessly.

'Why?!' Now desperation.

'Because there is only so much magic, and it always comes at a cost.' Teardrop had a faraway look on his face as he said this.

'Swear to me that this is the only chance that any of my people have of living,' Rin said. Teardrop opened his mouth. 'Not you, demon, her.' He nodded at Britha.

'The warband are probably all dead as well, but they will die trying to protect everything there is. I swear this by blood and bone and all I value,' Britha said. She meant it, but it was an easy oath to swear. It cost her little but the king seemed to believe her.

'There is one other thing.' The silver-eyed man continued. 'You must hold a feast in honour of the goddess.'

'This is too much!' Morfudd would have said more but Rin held up his hand.

'I feel sore used by Andraste, for whom I have taken many a head,' the king told them. 'We will feast, we will feast in the face of death so that our enemies know that though our iron will not kill them, we do not fear them, but to Annwn with your goddess.'

*

390

'What is the Hungry Nothingness?' Britha demanded as they walked away from the circular stone temple.

'Just play your part if you ever want to see any of your people again,' Teardrop told her. Britha bit back an angry retort. Something told her that it would do no good and that Teardrop, or whatever he was now, was serious.

As they started preparing for the feast, Tangwen saw the argument. Britha remained quiet while Teardrop spoke in a low voice to Fachtna, who raged. He raged in his language, the language of the Goidel traders who claimed they came from an island in the west. She did not speak the tongue but she knew some words. One word she had learned because it was useful when dealing with traders was that for falsehood. Fachtna shouted it a lot.

Tangwen watched as the three walked along the track to the circular building that the hunter knew to be a temple. Then they were gone for a long time. Tangwen wondered what the Corpse People must be thinking as the smell of beef, pork, mutton and chicken started to fill the air. The feast was going to be mightier than any she had ever been to before. *So this is how rich tribes ready themselves for death*, she thought.

Some time later, bored with watching the Corpse People swarm over the opposite hillside like maggots, she went looking for the others. If they didn't want her in their temple then the *dryw* could chase her away.

Tangwen walked into the temple to see Fachtna and Britha hanging upside down from a drying frame. Both of them were naked, both of them pale. Both had been cut and bled. Underneath, cauldrons collected their blood. Teardrop was sitting next to them.

Teardrop looked up as she entered and stared at her impassively. Tangwen could not take his staring eyes on her. She turned and fled.

After the warband had drunk their fill, reddening their chins on Fachtna and Britha's blood. After Teardrop had worked his magic. After weapons had been washed in the blood until there was no more of it. After the king had drunk of the blood and then been dipped into the cauldron and they had watched the blood disappear into his skin. After ruined legs had been healed and the king walked again. After all that, Britha's eyes flickered open. He had not taken all her blood. There was still some left inside her, but so little. She was so hungry, so weak. It had felt like death and there had been nothing there.

*

Tangwen watched as they carried Fachtna and Britha to where the feast was laid out. Weak though they were, they grabbed for the food, coming close to knocking over trestles as they gorged themselves on whatever they could shovel into their mouths. Many watched them in disgust. They ate so much it shamed Tangwen to be associated with them, but as they ate she saw their colour come back and meat return to their bones in front of her eyes. She found herself making a sign to protect herself against evil.

The warband did not attend the feast; they ate sparingly and drank little. Instead they walked the walls. This was for the folk. Rin spared nothing in terms of drink. There was a desperation to the drinking. The feast had seemed forced, but soon there was singing and dancing. *Good*, Tangwen thought, glancing over the walls. *Throw it in their faces.* But there were tears and embraces as well. Few had any doubts as to what was happening, but Rin wanted everybody to be drunk when they met their end.

Morfudd had asked to stay. She had been told no. Eurawg had asked to go. He had been told no. When the Corpse People came it would be his job to kill the youngest children so they did not fall into the hands of fiends.

The tears and the fear only kicked in when the warband gave away their armour and shields and it became apparent they were to leave the fort. Shame was written all over the tear-stained faces of the men and women of the Cigfran Teulu. They could not even look at those they had sworn to serve.

There would have been panic among the folk except for their king. They loved their king. It surprised nobody when he refused to leave.

Before they sneaked into the night, Rin spat in Britha's face. Anger coursed through her – she came close to running him through with a spear – but in the face of her anger, despite the demonstrations of power that he'd witnessed, Rin held his ground. 'That's for your mother,' he told her. Britha managed to control her anger.

They slipped over the darkest part of the walls at dusk before the Corpse People closed on the fort. A long drop by rope into the ditch, down to the treeline and then they crept away. Every one of them bar Britha, Teardrop, Tangwen and Fachtna felt like the basest betrayer and coward. Though Fachtna understood them and felt a little of what they felt.

They pushed hard, skirting west to avoid the Corpse People's pickets. Then they turned south-east. They pushed hard because they did not want to hear the sounds of battle, though there wouldn't be much of one. They weren't quick enough to escape the screams.

They saw its head first. Morfudd told them that she had never seen such a thing before and that it had not been there when last she had been this way.

'It's too big,' Britha said, appalled.

'Things of that size cannot be built,' Morfudd said firmly. It had to be more than five hundred feet tall and stood in the channel between two smallish islands close to the coast. Much further out was a third and considerably larger island. They had been cresting a large hill that ran parallel to the coast for some time now, walking through acres of what had once been woodland. Most of the trees had been felled. Britha couldn't imagine how many people it must have taken to remove this many trees. But the trees were quickly forgotten when she saw the small fleet of black curraghs surrounding the structure in the water.

'And yet ...' Teardrop said. Britha did not like the sly smile on the face of the stranger wearing her friend's form.

'It's a wicker man,' Fachtna said, no life in his voice.

27
Now

Beth spent the night on the streets just outside Waterloo Station. She woke up the following morning feeling fine, no aches, no pains and aware of her surrounding to a surprising degree. She wasn't sure what was happening, but she felt different. She was worried that the insane old woman in the interrogation room had infected her with something. Or maybe du Bois had, and the bag lady spitting blood was a hallucination. Whatever it was made her feel stronger, faster, much more aware and very, very hungry. Of the money that du Bois had given her, she'd spent a surprising amount on food.

On the train from London to Portsmouth, Beth was impatient. She wanted to deal with McGurk. If he knew anything about her sister he was going to tell her this time. After all, how many monsters could he have?

She walked quickly from Portsmouth Central across the common to the garish plastic and concrete of the amusements. Without all the light and the noise there was something distinctly depressing about them, even on a fresh and sunny day like today. She waited. It was still early. It would be a while before anyone turned up. She watched a ferry make its way through the Solent's mild chop, the wind blowing her hair. The Isle of Wight looked far away today.

The main thing on Ted's mind as he cursed the old key refusing to turn in an old lock was having a nice sweet cup of tea. He didn't feel like he could face the day, and he certainly couldn't cope with punters, until he'd had his second cup of tea.

'Ted?'

The voice made him jump, and he didn't like the way his heart felt in his chest at the fright. He'd been on edge since McGurk had come to visit. McGurk had been right: it was a long time since Ted had been someone in this city. He turned to look at her.

'Thought we'd seen the last of you.'

'I need to know something,' Beth said.

'Be a love and pick that up, will you?' He nodded to where he'd spat his cigarette. Beth bent down and gave it to him. He took another drag. 'Well, you'd better come in and have a cup of tea.'

They sat up in the concrete saucer above the arcades. The cafe might have been nice in the 60s. Still, it looked out over the Solent towards the Isle of Wight. She watched as the hovercraft left its nearby terminal and headed out over the water.

Ted shuffled over to the table and gave her a cup of tea with far too much sugar in it and a chocolate bar that she devoured almost immediately.

'Hungry?' She just nodded. 'So? You looking for your old job back? Because I know I don't pay much, but I need reliable people.'

'I'm sorry,' she said through a mouthful of chocolate.

'You had trouble?' She nodded. 'McGurk?' She nodded again. He sighed. 'Maybe this ain't a good city to live in?' Beth finished her chocolate and took a sip of the tea. It was so sweet she was mildly worried about getting diabetes if she drank it all.

'I need to know where I can find him.'

Ted gave a short bark of laughter devoid of humour. 'You fancy yourself as someone who can look after themselves, don't you? For a bird, I mean.'

Beth could see where this was going. He was going to try and impart some chivalrous for-her-own-good, street knowledge to her.

'Look, I know how it looks, but I know what I'm do—'

'No! You really fucking don't. Beth, he runs the drugs and prostitution in this town. He's supposed to have his grubby little fingers in human trafficking, dog fighting, bare-knuckle boxing. He rapes anyone who comes to work for him so they know the score.'

'He thinks I'm too ugly to rape.'

'Then he'll carve you up, and if he doesn't he's got boys with fists, big boots, clubs, knives and even shooters. Stay the fuck away from him.'

'He's got my sister,' Beth said quietly.

Ted stared at her. 'Shit,' he finally said and looked down. Suddenly he wished he was thirty years younger or even had just looked after himself properly. You messed people up, you had to if you wanted to carve a piece for you and yours, but McGurk didn't know when to stop – no decency, too greedy. The hard girl in the leather looking at him from across the table, eyes full of emotion, made him feel guilty. 'He got her hooking?'

'I don't know.'

Ted leaned in close, not quite willing to believe what he was about to say, pleased that nobody else was there. 'Look, you ever say that I told you this then I'll deny it, but go to the plod.'

'They get close to him, he'll cut his losses, deny it. They can't do the things that I'll do to him to find out where she is. Besides, I think there's someone else after her, someone bad, fucked-in-the-head bad.'

'Beth, before you even get close to him he'll have one of his lads shoot you. And they'll do it and go inside for him without even mentioning his name. I'm sorry for your sister. I can make enquiries – see if she's on the streets – but I'm not having your death on my conscience.'

She sat back in her chair. He could see how desperate she was.

'Ted, pick three of the hardest guys here and I'll fight them …' He jumped when she slammed an antique bayonet down on the table. 'He's fucking tried carving me up before. It got him nothing. They've got shooters, they best use them quick, and frankly I don't give a fuck if they do. I went inside for beating some cunt to death for what he did to my sister. I nearly did it again to … some monster he chose to do for me. I fucking promise you, Ted, it's him who's got to be scared now.'

It took Ted a while to realise that the prickling sensation he was feeling in his spine was fear. He put off saying anything by lighting another cigarette. She shook her head when he offered her one.

'What about me? He's a tasty geezer. Beth, I like you but I don't know you. We're not close and I don't owe you anything.' Beth stared at him. He saw her knuckles whiten around the hilt of her bayonet as disgust crept across her face. He sagged in his seat and told her what she wanted to know. Beth turned and looked out the window. It wasn't even far away.

Du Bois hated eating in the car. It wasn't just the crumbs; it made the car smell as well. He was parked on Broad Street in Old Portsmouth looking at the old defensive wall on the waterfront. It amused du Bois that this area, now so desirable, had once been known as Spice Island and been a hotbed of vice. Some things just didn't change that much, he decided, bearing in mind what he was here to do.

There was still a huge police and military presence in the city, though the latter had been played down. The roadblocks and some of the other more draconian precautions that had been taken had been relaxed. It seemed that the authorities knew they were little more than window-dressing.

He was still injured, slow and weak. There was new-growth skin where the bag lady had partially flayed him, hence the eating. He did not feel anything like at his peak.

He had reviewed McGurk's file. He seemed to be a particularly nasty version of your standard provincial UK gangster: small-minded, short-sighted and vicious. *So where had he got the servitor from?*

His ability to think was being severely hampered by loud bass-heavy music. On the other side of the road a little further up, a van was parked, its side door open, a large sound system pointing out of it. There were four men in hoodies and clown masks putting on what du Bois could only speculate was some kind of dance exhibition. Though what the gyrations, gymnastics and spinning on their backs had to do with dancing was beyond him. He'd only worked out it was supposed to be dancing by the music. A surprisingly large group of tourists had gathered around the dancers – so large they were starting to block the road to the most westerly point of Old Portsmouth. Du Bois felt like calling the police but decided that he was being petty.

Elizabeth Luckwicke passed along the walkway on the top of the wall. Du Bois was not pleased to see her and had hoped that she would stay in Bradford. What really surprised him was that she appeared to have a blood-screen, and a powerful one. He could make out the representation of augmentation in his vision. He could see fire burning through her veins.

He dropped the baguette he was eating and climbed out of the Range Rover. He didn't like where she was heading, either. He thought about calling out to her but decided against it. She was an unknown factor now. He wondered how much she'd pulled the wool over his eyes. Instead he headed after her.

Beth hurried along the wall ignoring the pounding beat of the break-dancing crew entertaining the tourists. Out of the corner of her eye she saw one of the clown-masked dancers, standing on top of the van, throw a handful of glitter into the air. They were dancing to a hip-hop tune that sampled the old 'Mr Sandman' song.

Looking along Broad Street, she could make out the pubs ahead, the water and then Gosport. To her left the white sail-like Spinnaker Tower rose above Gunwharf. Beth came to a squat square tower attached to the defensive wall. She took the narrow steps down to street level.

It was called the Lighthouse and it was on the waterfront on Tower Street, which ran parallel with Broad Street. Du Bois stood on the

Round Tower, which overlooked the Lighthouse. It was a large, four-storey, pseudo-art-deco luxury home with a small observation tower. A spiral staircase with large windows stuck out of the side of the house. He watched Beth hammer on the door at the bottom of the staircase. He watched a thug come out of the door to the third floor and head down the stairs.

The heavy opened the door an inch. Beth kicked it completely open with surprising strength, knocking him back, and then preceded to beat him with what looked like a pickaxe handle with a bike chain wrapped around it until he stopped moving.

Above Beth, du Bois watched another two of McGurk's thugs appear on the staircase, one from the second floor, another from the third carrying a snooker cue. Both were wearing suits. Du Bois had to admit that for a shell-suit-wearing toerag, McGurk seemed to expect surprisingly high levels of sartorial elegance from his lackeys.

Beth could already hear the feet on the stairs thundering towards her. She was pretty sure that the guy who had answered the door was still alive as she stepped over him. She sprinted up the stairs, meeting the first guy immediately. He kicked out at her head. She ducked and swung the pickaxe handle at his supporting leg. She had hoped to hurt him enough to knock him off balance. Instead she heard the *crack* as bones fractured under the surprising force of her blow. He cried out as his leg collapsed. Beth grabbed his hair, dragged him out of the way and then continued up the stairs.

She ducked as someone swung a snooker cue at her so hard it broke when it hit the wall. Moving quickly up the stairs, she punched with her left. She was surprised when he doubled over. Even though she was wearing her brass knuckles, her left hand had always been the weaker one. She dragged him forward so he fell face first on the stairs. There was shouting above her. The heavy was still moving. She turned around, grabbed the railings for support and put the boot in until he lost interest in fighting.

First floor, open-plan kitchen, empty. Second floor, lounge area, nice view of a passing ferry, empty. Third floor, games room, snooker table, bar, another big window and McGurk with two of his boys on either side of him pointing guns at her. There were three more muscle in there: one had a snooker cue, one was using his thumb to open a folding knife, the third was unarmed. The black holes of the gun barrels brought her up short.

'My fucking house! You come into my fucking home!' The only

emotion Beth could muster was disgust. McGurk was screaming so loudly he was drooling.

'You came into mine,' Beth told him, angry he was hiding behind guns.

'I'm allowed to. I can do what I want in Pompey! You are fucking nothing!'

It seemed to Beth that people had been saying something similar to her all her life. She was starting to think it had more to do with them than her.

'Where's my sister?' she said, quietly but unable to mask her distaste.

'Do you know what I'm going to do?!' he screamed.

'Make an outlandish threat that you'll never live up to?' du Bois asked as he stepped into the room.

'Shit!' Beth said quietly and then moved to the side. The guns were suddenly pointed at du Bois, who raised his arms.

'I'm just here to talk.'

McGurk looked du Bois up and down, taking in the raw patches of skin.

'What happened to you? Disagreement with a strimmer?' The laughter from McGurk's cronies was forced. They knew their cues well. Du Bois looked a little apologetic. 'You're the plod that talked to Arbogast?' McGurk said suspiciously. Du Bois nodded. 'You armed?' Du Bois nodded. 'We'll be having that, then. Markus.' The unarmed guy that Beth recognised from her kidnapping, the one she'd stabbed in the leg, went over to search du Bois, who held his arms up higher to make it easier for the bodyguard to search him. Markus took the .45 and the tanto off him.

'Careful with that,' du Bois said, nodding at the .45. 'Gift from a very grateful lieutenant in Delta Force.'

'That supposed to impress us?' McGurk demanded.

'Apologies if you feel I'm name-dropping.'

'What do you want?' McGurk demanded.

'Natalie Luckwicke.'

'Don't give her to him!' Beth shouted. McGurk and du Bois were equally surprised by her outburst.

'Shut up,' McGurk told her. 'Don't know what you're talking about. Now can you think of any terribly compelling reason why I shouldn't beat you both to death with my cane?'

'Is that a bull's cock cane?' du Bois enquired.

'Why, yes it is,' McGurk said sarcastically.

'You're going to beat us to death with your cock substitute? Given your propensity for sodomising your employees –' du Bois looked around at the five men with McGurk, none of whom would meet his eyes '– has it occurred to you that you're a repressed homosexual and that you'll be much happier if you admit it and just leave all this misguided rage behind?'

Beth was trying hard not to laugh.

'Fuck you!' There was more drool. 'I've fucked every whore in this city, especially this cunt's dead sister!' Beth bristled, but one of the guns turned back towards her. She controlled herself with difficulty. The rage wasn't red in colour any more; it was blue, cold, and seethed under her skin.

'How admirable,' du Bois said.

'Do you think I won't off plod?' McGurk demanded. His men were looking a little nervous. After all, it would be one of them who pulled the trigger, and this was a large room with lots of glass in it. Another ferry was going past the window.

'I don't think he's a repressed homosexual. I think he's just a frightened little man,' Beth said.

'Fuck you, bitch!'

'Where'd you get the servitor from?' du Bois asked.

'What? That fucked-up mutant thing?'

Du Bois sighed theatrically. 'It's as if Oscar Wilde never died for our sins.'

'"With slouch and swing around the ring/ We trod the Fools' Parade!/ We did not care: we knew we were/ The Devils' Own Brigade:/ And shaven head and feet of lead/ Make a merry masquerade." And fuck you, you patronising public-schoolboy wanker,' McGurk said.

'Good choice. Where'd you hear it?' There was not trace of humour in du Bois's voice.

'Who the fuck d'you think you're—'

The two shrouded, snub-nosed, suppressed .38 revolvers slid quickly out of the sleeves of du Bois's finely tailored leather coat on forearm hoppers. Du Bois lowered his arm. The shots were barely louder than coughs. Neat red holes appeared in the centre of the foreheads of the three men holding guns. All of them stood there for a moment and then toppled to the ground. Nobody moved. Beth looked appalled at the people she had just seen die in front of her. She looked down at Markus, feeling faintly nauseous that she actually knew the guy's name. It wasn't like when she'd killed Davey; there was only cold calculation from du Bois. He shifted his position to cover McGurk with one revolver. The other vaguely covering his two remaining men.

'Beth, would you mind getting my pistol and my knife?' du Bois asked. Beth glanced at him and then bent down and picked up the .45 from the floor near where Markus had dropped it. She did not give it back to du Bois.

'You know how to use that?' he asked. Beth ignored him and put the gun in the pocket of her battered leather.

'What do you guys want?' McGurk asked cautiously.

'The same thing we wanted before I shot your friends. Obviously,' du Bois said.

'As far as I know, the girl's dead. She died when her house blew up. You must have seen it on the telly. The mutant thing, a friend of mine found it in a basement.'

'Where?'

'I don't know, down near the front in Southsea.'

'Now where's the girl?'

'I told you: she's fucking dead and causing me no end of grief while she's at it.'

'I have considerably less compunction in shooting low-rate rapist plastic gangsters than you do police officers. It would behove you to answer my question or I'll start with your kneecaps.'

'You can't get all of us—'

Beth walked forward, grabbed the cane out of McGurk's hand and laid into him with a ferocity that made du Bois take a step back.

'WHERE'S MY SISTER?! WHERE'S MY SISTER?! WHERE'S MY SISTER?! WHERE'S MY SISTER?!'

McGurk was battered, bleeding, sobbing in pain and fear and had wet himself a long time before Beth realised that he now really wanted to tell her where Talia was. She stopped beating him. She was still shaking with rage. Curled up in a foetal position, he told her. One of the muscle gave them directions.

'Remember everything he's ever done to you,' Beth told the two thugs. 'Who wants the stick?' Then she threw the bloodstained bull penis on the floor, turned and walked out.

With a thought the two .38s slid back up du Bois's sleeves on their hoppers. He picked up his tanto, sheathed it and followed Beth.

She was waiting for him around the corner just past the second floor, pointing his own .45 at him. Du Bois was moving to the side as soon as he saw the gun. As he was higher than her he risked a kick, sending the .45 spinning from her fingers. Beth didn't hesitate either. She was as surprised as du Bois was at how fast she ripped her great-grandfather's bayonet from her inside pocket and stabbed it up through du Bois's arm as he reached for her.

Du Bois screamed as the force of her blow pushed the tip of the bayonet through his nano-fabric-armoured leather coat and then through his hardening skin. He kicked out forward, hard. His foot caught Beth centre mass in the chest, lifted her up off her feet and sent her flying the rest of the way down the stairs and into the wall at the bottom. She slumped to the floor but started moving again almost immediately. Du Bois was appalled at how highly augmented she was. He did not understand how he could have missed this. He leaped down the stairs, his foot smashing her in the head so hard it cracked the plaster behind it. She was still moving towards him despite the blood oozing from her head. In desperation he triggered the hopper on his left arm, pointing the .38 that slid out at her.

'Girl, I have been killing for centuries!' Either this or the gun made Beth stop. That made no sense either. If he shot her the bullets would hurt, they might even incapacitate her, but unless they were coated with nanites or carried a nanite payload that counteracted how quickly her own obviously high-level nanite augmentation could heal her, then she would be fine. It was as if she didn't know this. 'Why attack me? Broadly speaking, I'm on your side.' He wondered if she knew that less than twenty-four hours ago he'd killed her father. Yesterday he would have said no, but then yesterday he had been sure that Beth was a normal girl – for a violent ex-con from Bradford.

Beth glared at him. Du Bois tried to ignore the sound of bad things happening to McGurk above. She wondered if anyone had called the police yet.

'Seriously, talk to me. I don't want to hurt you or your sister, quite the opposite really.' Then it hit him. 'Are you from the Brass City?' He didn't think her look of confusion was faked. She had no idea what he was talking about. 'The Eggshell?' More confusion.

'My father told me what you are,' she told him.

He didn't happen to mention what you *are*, du Bois thought. 'And what's that?'

'You're in some kind of cult. You bred her for sacrifice.'

Du Bois stared at her. Then he started laughing. Then he sat down on the stairs but kept the gun on her.

'And you believed that?' he asked, still laughing.

'Everything's a bit fucking weird!' Beth snapped at him, less than happy that he was laughing at her, and her head hurt, quite a lot, she could feel it moving of its own accord, mending itself, though she was starting to feel really hungry again.

Du Bois thought about it. The truth was arguably odder.

'Do you know, I almost see where he got that from,' du Bois admitted.

'Well, what do you want her for?'

'It's true she was part of a selective breeding and genetic manipulation programme. She and many other children were born to have their genetic material harvested, but we weren't going to kill them, just take samples while they lived privileged lives.'

'And where are these children now?' Beth asked. Du Bois thought about lying. Instead he lit a cigarette and tried to ignore the horrific noises from upstairs.

'They're all dead.' Beth started to say something. 'No, we didn't do it. To all intents and purposes they were wiped out in a terrorist attack. That's why we need your sister.'

Beth wanted to believe him. Her instincts were to trust him, but she didn't feel she could risk it, not when she was so close.

'I'm taking my sister and we're going,' she told him.

'Something's coming. Talia is very important, and you'd both be better off coming with me.'

'I don't think so.'

'I don't have to have this discussion, Beth. I can take her any time I want. You don't even know how to kill me. Trust me.'

'Would sawing your head off with a World War One bayonet do it?' she asked.

It might, du Bois thought. 'I don't think you've got that in you.'

'You get between me and Talia, we'll find out,' she told him evenly.

Du Bois looked at her through the pall of his cigarette smoke. He took another drag. He made his decision. Beth just would not stop going after her sister. She had more will and courage than the entire ruling council of the Circle put together.

'Fine, but they'll send others like me after you,' he told her. *To hell with the Circle.* 'And I'm taking some samples from her before we go our separate ways.' Beth opened her mouth to object. 'I'm probably going to get killed for this, so no more arguments.' He stood up and downloaded the route to where McGurk had said Talia was directly into his mind. It was very close. Du Bois supposed McGurk had wanted to keep her nearby. 'And give me my gun back. It really was a present.'

'No.'

Du Bois was not sure why he was surprised it was a lock-up. His ability to quote Wilde notwithstanding, McGurk had been a small-minded man. Du Bois let Beth handle the man guarding her sister. He heard bones crack under her fist. He was a little worried that she'd hit him so hard she'd killed him.

Talia was lying on a hospital trolley being fed with a drip and apparently giving blood. She was no longer a pale waif-like beauty; she looked gaunt and near-dead.

Beth rushed to the side of the trolley.

'Talia!' Her sister was unconscious.

Du Bois immediately began checking her vitals. She was okay but suffering from constant sedation and enforced bed rest. Her breathing was a little shallow and she was probably malnourished, but her pulse was fine.

'What are they doing to her?' Beth demanded, more distraught than he'd heard her so far.

'At a guess, they're using her blood as some kind of hallucinogenic narcotic.' Beth looked at him like he was mad. He left out that he thought her blood coming into contact with some kind of sensitive mind was probably the reason Talia's house had been destroyed and all those people had died in the nightclub.

He produced a leather case from his jacket and removed a number of vials from it. He placed a few against her skin and two in her mouth.

'What are you doing?' Beth demanded, reaching for the gun as the vials grew needles and started drawing blood. The ones in her mouth took scrapings. Talia was starting to stir. 'Don't you think she's lost enough blood?'

'This is our agreement,' du Bois said in a tone that did not invite argument. 'I'll be out of your life soon.'

Beth looked like she was going to object again as he rolled Talia onto her side. She moaned and then cried out in pain as du Bois pressed one of the vials into the base of her spine.

'She's going to need medical help,' du Bois told her. *Which is probably where the next person the Circle send will find you,* he left unsaid. 'I can drop you where you choose. Then you'll never see me again.' *Because I'll be dead,* he thought as he took the final vial away and let Talia drop down onto her back.

'Beth?' Talia said woozily. Beth looked at her, tears springing into her eyes. Du Bois wished that they had more of a future, but he wasn't sure that any of them did. 'I've been having really bad dreams, Beth.'

Beth looked at du Bois, who moved to pick Talia up. Beth grabbed him by the arm to stop him. She wrapped the sheets around Talia and then lifted her light form off the trolley herself. Du Bois unhooked her from the drip.

Beth carried Talia, who was fading in and out of consciousness, as du Bois led the way across Broad Street past the break-dancing crew. As they passed the dancers, the music changed to that of some pop song that du Bois vaguely remembered from the 80s. As it did, he heard the sound of many people stamping their feet on the ground in unison. It was a sound that wouldn't have been out of place on a parade ground. Du Bois and Beth both glanced behind them. They were surprised to see all the tourists standing to attention in neat rows and staring at them. Then, in time with the music, old and young alike started dancing towards them, clicking their fingers. The break-dancers in the clown masks were nowhere to be seen.

'Run!' du Bois shouted. Both .38s slid out of his sleeves, though he knew they would not be sufficient.

'What? They're just dancing,' Beth said, more bemused than any-thing, and was then appalled when du Bois started firing both pistols as he backed off.

'They've been slaved!' du Bois shouted. Beth looked confused. Du Bois struggled to find something to say that would make her under-stand. 'They're zombies!' he shouted as the crowd broke into a run at them. Beth finally seemed to get it and ran for the Range Rover.

'Welcome to the douchepocalypse, motherfuckers!' one of the clowns shouted from behind the van, and started firing. The sound of the automatic weapon was monstrously loud in the street, echoing back from the walls and across the water. Du Bois had a moment to wonder at someone using such a big-bore round in an automatic weapon when a shot caught him in the shoulder. His armoured coat hardened, his skin hardened, but the force of the .50 Beowulf bullet spun him round and he hit the ground, his shoulder almost certainly broken. The closest of the slaved tourists was reaching for him. Du Bois put the final two rounds from the right hand .38 into the slave's legs. The man went sprawling across the ground.

Beth reached the Range Rover. Its lights were blinking to suggest that the doors had been unlocked. It took her a moment to connect the sparks flying off the vehicle's armoured body with the thunderous roar of gunfire. With that came the realisation that she was being shot at. Even then it seemed unreal, something so far removed from her experience as not to be taken seriously. Beyond the four-by-four she saw passers-by scattering, running towards the closest cover or even freezing.

Hindered by Talia, Beth nevertheless managed to yank open one of the back doors. A burst of fire caught the door, which slammed shut. She felt something hot fly past her ear and instinctively she cowered away, but then she grabbed the door, pulling it open again.

From his position on the ground, du Bois found himself surrounded. Slaved tourists reached down for him. He kicked out and scrabbled backwards as his shoulder healed painfully.

'Cover! Cover! Beth, shoot them!' They were snagging his clothes now, clawing at his exposed skin. It wouldn't be difficult for them, en masse, to hold him down, augmented or not.

Beth heard du Bois as she threw Talia onto the Range Rover's back seat. More firing. The car was haloed by sparks, some of its bullet-resistant glass starting to crack under multiple impacts from heavy-calibre fire.

She looked back to see him surrounded by 'zombies'. Beth grabbed du Bois's .45 from her jacket pocket, leaned across the bonnet of the Range Rover like she'd seen in films and tried to pull the trigger. Nothing happened.

Lots more gunfire now, more than one shooter, perhaps as many as three or four. The slaved tourists were dying silently and uncomplaining, hydrostatic shock from heavy weapons blowing limbs off. They were shooting at him through the slaves.

He kicked out at the knee of one of the tourists, grabbed his tanto and hamstrung another before managing to get to his feet and break free of them.

As he sprinted for the Range Rover he saw Beth struggling with the .45.

'The safety! The bloody safety!' he all but screamed. Then he tried something. He sent her the knowledge of firearms imprinted on his neural nanonics. He had no idea if it would work.

Beth had no idea what was happening. There was a strange feeling in her head like creeping warmth – it lasted a moment – then a shooting pain so intense that she collapsed to the ground behind the Range Rover. She could feel blood trickling from her eyes, nose and ears, but suddenly she knew how to use the cold piece of metal in her hand.

From the ground she saw one of the clown-masked gunmen sprint from behind the van, heading for cover behind a car on the same side of the street as the Range Rover. Beth took aim.

*

406

It's fucking amazing, King Jeremy thought. The problem with shooting people for real was that it was never as spectacular as it was in the movies or games: there was never as much blood. So the four of them had overlaid VR graphics filters on their real vision. Everything happening in the real world they could see, but the filters added much more splatter and made it look as if they were living out their favourite first-person shooter. Him and Baron Albedo unloading at that guy the zombies were trying to bring down had looked awesome. The zombies had all but exploded in front of their eyes. You could even change the environment. He knew that Dracimus had placed himself in some environment where he was a supervillain mowing down superheroes, and he was pretty sure that Inflictor had simulated some sort of hell environment.

Albedo's dancing-zombies idea had been inspired as well. He would, however, have to talk to Dracimus about shouting 'Welcome to the douchepocalypse'. Major uncoolness.

King Jeremy aimed the AR-15 – converted to fire the massive .50 Beowulf rounds on full automatic – at the blond guy sprinting for the Range Rover. As he did so, Inflictor made a run for the opposite side of the street.

Du Bois threw himself across the front of the Range Rover as Beth fired the .45 repeatedly from her position on the ground. The running gunman dived behind the car he was making for, though she was sure she had hit him.

Du Bois rolled into a crouch, ignoring the painful jarring in his still-healing shoulder. He snatched the pouch clipped to his belt which contained four magazines for the .45 and slid it along the ground to Beth. He didn't give her the nanite-tipped bullets.

He spun, keeping low as the Range Rover rocked from hit after hit. He saw some of the slaved tourists running towards the back of the car. The .38 on his right arm slid out on its hopper at a thought. He flipped the cylinder open and emptied the spent cartridges, then, grabbing a speed loader from his pocket, slid the new rounds home and flipped the cylinder shut.

On the opposite side of the road he saw one of the masked gunmen running towards cover behind a car. Du Bois made for the rear of the Range Rover. As he did, a fat tourist in a loud shirt came around the back of the vehicle. Du Bois shot him three times in the face at near point-blank range. Each round was a glaser, a hollow-point bullet filled with number-12 shotgun pellets. The pellets spread out inside the victim after impact. Du Bois strode around the back of the Range

Rover, where another one of the slaved tourists charged him. He fired the suppressed revolver another three times and then with a thought the hopper slid the still-hot .38 back up into his sleeve.

Du Bois yanked the rear door of the Range Rover open, catching another one of the slaved tourists under the chin. Yet another appeared. Du Bois pulled the tanto and cut him across the throat, bringing up his leg to front-kick him for good measure. It gave him a moment. He hit the quick release on the storage compartment in the floor of the Range Rover. The top slid back and he had time to grab the SA58 FAL carbine before four hands grabbed him from behind and wrenched him out of the car. He kicked back, sending all three of them to the ground. Over the road he saw the clown rise from behind the car and bring the massive barrel of the modified AR-15 to bear.

Beth scuttled back, keeping low as round after round sparked off the armoured Range Rover. The gunman she was sure she had hit appeared over the roof of the car he'd dived behind and fired. Beth opened the front passenger door of the Range Rover and took cover behind it. More rounds sparked off it, battering the door into her. She fired three quick shots through the gap between the open door and the body of the vehicle. Instinctively she seemed to know just where to place the shots. She expected the guy to take cover. Instead she saw bits fly off his hood as he staggered back, and rather than falling over he just took aim again and fired.

'Beth!' du Bois shouted from the back of the Range Rover.

With his left he battered at the slaved tourists clawing at him, with his right he loosed a long burst from the FAL carbine at the clown on the opposite side of the road. He walked the rounds down the body of the car, the armour-piercing tips punching through the vehicle's body. There was a spray of blood, and the gunman jumped back from the car. He then disappeared behind it.

Du Bois cried out as teeth bit into his ear. His skin hardened and the teeth broke, but not before drawing blood. Beth appeared over him, pointing his own .45 at him. She fired once, shifted the pistol and fired again, executing the two zombies attacking du Bois.

'Get the shotgun,' du Bois told her as he rolled to his feet. Using the back of the Range Rover as cover, he fired short bursts at the van, trying to suppress the clowns still using the van as cover. He was disappointed to see that the van seemed to be armoured as well. He was more pleased when a stray round killed the sound system.

*

Shoving the .45 in her waistband, Beth grabbed the shotgun. Somehow she knew it was a Benelli M4 semi-automatic. She grabbed a bandolier of cartridges and slung them over her shoulder. Behind her, du Bois had retreated behind the Range Rover's rear door as he changed magazines. Another slaved tourist rushed in. Beth fired under the door, taking the zombie's legs out from under her. The zombie's head bounced off the door before she hit the ground.

Beth moved back around to the side of the Range Rover closest to the wall. There were zombies charging in from that direction as well.

The slaved tourist whose legs Beth had blown off was grabbing at du Bois's legs. It was annoying, and as he stamped down, breaking fingers, he knew he'd feel teeth biting into him soon.

They needed some respite. He turned back to the rear of the Range Rover and grabbed the M320 grenade launcher. He opened it, removed the grenade inside and replaced it with another type. He stamped down again as he felt teeth bite into his leg.

He moved around and fired the grenade at the remaining slaved tourists charging towards his side of the Range Rover. Flechettes filled the air briefly and turned the slaved tourists into so much meat. He would do penance for murdering the innocent later. It would not be the first time.

'Awesome,' King Jeremy whispered as, in his augmented vision, the blond guy's grenade turned the zombies into a blood storm. Remembering himself, he pushed another magazine home. He was aiming, he told himself, but really he just liked firing the gun.

The first zombie slammed the passenger door shut as they charged in. The shotgun blast took him in the stomach. He was still running, dead, when the one behind shoved him out of the way. Beth shot him. The third hurdled the bodies of the others and Beth shot him at point-blank range, taking most of his face off.

The clown on their side of the road, behind the car, was firing with a clear line. Big-bore rounds tore through the other zombies charging Beth. She let the Benelli drop on its sling, grabbed the .45 from her waistband and walked forward, firing one-handed at charging zombies and then the gunman. She grabbed the front passenger door just as the .45's magazine ran dry, and yanked it open to crouch behind it to reload as the clown behind the car fired on her again.

Du Bois appeared next to her. At first she thought that he was holding some kind of huge pistol, but her new-found knowledge corrected her as he fired the grenade launcher.

King Jeremy actually had the foresight and was quick enough to slow everything down. He watched the 40-millimetre high-explosive grenade fly from the launcher, hit the car that Inflictor was hiding behind and explode. The car was lifted into the air. Inflictor was flung back hard enough to dent the car he hit. He slumped to the ground.

'Cool,' King Jeremy said. He had to give the blond guy credit. He had skills.

Despite knowing their own capabilities, even King Jeremy was surprised when Inflictor got to his feet. He watched his co-member of the DAYP throw away the AR-15 – the explosion had buckled the rifle – and draw his massive .50 Desert Eagle pistol.

'Yes! You fucking mad man!' Then he had to duck behind the van as bullets sparked off the armour all around him. At the other end of the van, Baron Albedo was firing at the Range Rover, laughing like a lunatic. *What a fucking high*, King Jeremy thought.

Du Bois had returned to the rear corner of the Range Rover and was exchanging fire with the two clowns in cover at either end of the armoured van.

Beth was mostly keeping her head down as neither the pistol nor the shotgun were ideal weapons for engaging the clowns at that range. She was using the time to reload the Benelli.

He emerged out of the smoke and flame, running over the top of the car that du Bois had blown up, heading towards the Range Rover. Most of the clown mask was gone; underneath was some monstrous face out of a TV show but somehow rendered horribly real. He was coming straight at Beth. She levelled the .45 through the gap between the door and the car, the door battering into her legs with each impact from the running monster's massive handgun. Beth fired the .45 rapidly, emptying the pistol into him. He staggered with every shot but kept coming.

King Jeremy hunkered down behind the van as the blond guy fired at him. From his position he could see Dracimus cowering behind a car further along the road.

'Get up and shoot!' King Jeremy shouted over their internal link.

'I'm shot!' Dracimus answered.

'Don't be such a fucking pussy; it can't kill you.'

'You haven't been shot. It really hurts!'

King Jeremy turned to point the modified AR-15 at Dracimus.
'Stand up and fucking shoot!'

Inflictor barrelled into the door of the Range Rover, slamming it so hard into Beth that it knocked her insensible for a moment. He opened the door and grabbed her, turning as he threw her through the air. Beth hit the ground some eight feet away. Dazed for a moment, she was quickly scrabbling for the shotgun still on its sling.

Du Bois turned to see the clown lift the massive Desert Eagle and point it at Beth.
    He moved wide to get a shot, bringing the FAL carbine to his shoulder. Behind him the gun clown who'd taken cover, the one du Bois was sure he'd shot, rose from behind the car. Too late du Bois realised his mistake and turned back to face him.

Dracimus fired. His first shots were a long undisciplined burst, but then the skills they'd hard-wired into themselves kicked in. He brought the gun under control and fired a short burst and then another. He grinned as he made the blond guy – who in his augmented view of things was his most hated goody-two-shoes superhero – dance in the middle of huge explosions of blood.

As the monstrous clown brought the Desert Eagle up, Beth knew that she'd never bring the shotgun to bear in time. The flame from the pistol's muzzle looked enormous, and she actually saw its slide shoot back and the ejected cartridge fly out the side. Then again, but the slide stayed back this time. *Good.* He couldn't shoot her any more.
    She was dead before her head hit the ground.

King Jeremy and Baron Albedo moved across the street in a low crouch, weapons at the ready like they'd seen in films. King Jeremy went around the front of the Range Rover, Baron Albedo the back.
    King Jeremy found Inflictor standing over the woman's body. There were two massive entry wounds in her chest.
    'That was fucking insane, man!' King Jeremy said, checking she was dead and clapping his friend on the back. Inflictor turned to look at him. *He's probably seeing a fellow demon*, King Jeremy thought.
    'Let's hurt it,' he said, meaning the dead woman.
    'Er ... she's dead, dude.' King Jeremy could hear sirens now.
    'Did you see that?! Did you see me fucking kill him?!' Dracimus

said as he ran across the road. He stopped to stand over the blond guy's body. 'Oh yeah! He's all kinds of fucked up!'

King Jeremy resisted the urge to shoot Dracimus. He was pissed off that Dracimus, who'd been a pussy throughout the gunfight, had got the kill shot on the guy.

'Check them for tech!' King Jeremy barked.

'Why, man?' Dracimus said. Baron Albedo was already searching the blond guy.

'Because I fucking said so. Inflictor? Inflictor!'

The demon-faced boy turned to look at King Jeremy.

'Get the girl out of the back of the car and put her in the van.'

Inflictor nodded and went to do as he was bid.

'King J?' Baron Albedo said. He was holding up a small leather case. King Jeremy went over to look at it. Albedo had unzipped it by the time he got there. Inside were some vials, blood, a white fluid and some other bits and pieces that Jeremy didn't immediately recognise. He shrugged but took the case.

'Anything else?'

'Not without looking harder.'

The sirens were getting louder. Across the road, Inflictor was tossing the heavy speakers of the sound system out of the van one-handed.

'No time.'

King Jeremy, Dracimus and Baron Albedo ran across the street back to the van.

28
A Long Time After the Loss

The top of the arcology tree falling towards the planet had become so many burning meteorites. It was quite beautiful, Elite Scab thought as he watched the flaming matter crash through the inhabited branches far below. *People who thought themselves good lied to themselves. When you'd seen it, done it, you could not deny the beauty of destruction on this scale, of mass murder, the music of screaming.*

He was keeping his systems stealthed. He wasn't going to make it easy for them when his death came, but not too hard either. They would be able to find him if they looked.

He felt calm, tranquil. He had always resisted the idea of fate. He liked to believe that he had made his own path, but he had been a slave too long, he now realised. He had thought that the inevitability of his death would feel like a trap, but it was quite the opposite. He felt liberated.

He watched the ponderous yet somehow strangely balletic approach of the massive capital ship over the planetary horizon of Game. It didn't eclipse the G-type sun but its outline obscured a significant part of the bright star.

Thick fingers of light reached out for him, bending slightly due to the gravity well. Kinetic projectiles burned as they were shot through the bubble of the atmosphere. According to his suit's scanners, or rather its instinctual understanding of space and the information contained in his neunonics, the capital ship had just fired every one of its AG-driven smart munitions. The munitions were accelerating to the limit of material science.

He knew the ship. It was called the *Necronaught*, a childish name to Elite Scab's mind. A powerful AI helped run it. The AI had bonded with the crew, making the ship almost alive to them. They had a relationship with it. The *Necronaught* had wreaked havoc on the Pangean fleet during the Art Wars. It had been among the first ships through the planetary blockade and the ship most significantly responsible for the death of one of the Living Cities.

What a waste, Elite Scab thought. He was in a different physical state by the time the first beams reached him, too different for them to harm him. He took his time making his way towards the craft. He wanted to appreciate the display of firepower. He could make out the burn of other smaller faster ships making their way towards him.

He remembered the last time that he had seen a display of the *Necronaught*'s firepower, huddled in a crowded mercenary carrier broadcasting constant cries of surrender and pleas of clemency for independent contractors. He saw the bright lances reaching down from high orbit. Watched the sky become a canopy of fire as the kinetic payloads hit the atmosphere. Slowed down in his neunonics, he watched the AG smart munitions blossom into multiple sub-munitions and the wreckage of escaping craft start to rain down on the scarred rock surface. Scab, as he'd been then, had picked his escape craft based on the strength of its defences.

At some level all of them had felt the death of the Living City. Scab had disliked the violation, the suggestion that at some fundamental level there was an empathic connection between all living things. Instead he wondered if the crew of the *Necronaught* felt like gods. He wanted what they had.

He was not going to take revenge on the *Necronaught*. Those memories belonged to a different person, who should have been long dead. His ghost had been resurrected in the pathetic clone copy that even now he knew was down on the surface.

Some of the more exotic payloads tugged at him, harmed him, he supposed, as he made his way towards the ship. The shields, what most people thought were S-tech but what Elite Scab knew were L-tech, were more problematic. There was actual pain and loss. He was diminished, but he did not scream as he pulled his way through them. He was breathing hard, covered in sweat as he fell through the armour and hit the ship's cold hard deck.

With less than a thought he sucked the sweat back into his skin. He would use the salt and water for something more useful. He stood up. To the terrified-looking crewman standing in front of him, it looked like he was clothed in black liquid glass. The crewman, a tall human, base male in gender, had seen the Elite in a moment of weakness. He died immediately.

Elite Scab released the virals and the nano-swarms, all S- and L-tech derivatives. They would be too much for the *Necronaught*'s countermeasures. He gained access to the ship's systems through the dead crewman's neunonics and downloaded multiple crack and control AI programs based on a template of his own personality. Each of them had an inbuilt self-destruct code but they would overwhelm the *Necronaught*'s security, possess the host AI and effectively sequester the ship.

While this happened, Elite Scab walked through the ship killing the old-fashioned way. Every time he ran an extruded blade through a crew member or legionnaire, he thought about their souls. He knew that the soul did not exist. It was an ancient idea from before the Loss that he had come across. So much more information was available to you when you became an Elite. He knew that ultimately they were all little more than biological automatons created by the Seeders, but as he watched the screaming faces of his victims appear momentarily in the animated exotic matter of his armour, it was difficult not to think that the living material of the armour was consuming their souls. What he felt sure of was that the exotic matter wanted to consume life.

He took control of the ship. He 'faced with the ship's nano-field for an external view. The *Necronaught* was belying its dark name. It looked like it was made of light as every other ship in the vicinity fired on it. The carbon reservoirs struggled to remake the ship's reactive armour quickly enough to cope with the multiple impacts of sub-munitions and kinetic shots. In the centre of the ship, as faces screamed out from all over his armour, Elite Scab was barely feeling the hits.

Scab ignored the rest of the fleet; instead he aimed the *Necronaught* at the surface of Game and fired all its beam weapons and the kinetic shots that the carbon reservoirs had managed to regrow at the planet's surface.

'Notice me,' he whispered.

He felt the rip in time/space. *I should feel exalted*, he told himself. Angels were coming especially for him.

It was quite tranquil floating upwards in the red light through what looked like the roots of the arcology trees, except here everything, all matter, was black and skeletal with oddly exaggerated angles. The frameworks of the arcology trees looked like expressionist sculptures rendered in blackened bone. The only matter here was the trees. It seemed that you had to be of a certain size to be remembered in this red-world copy. None of the smaller details – G-vehicles, piles of assembler debris, extraneous buildings – seemed to be present, and there were certainly no other life forms, not even ghosts. With the exception of the two of them riding the cocoon, their flight capability provided by the three working AG motors, everything was still. It was like a dead world. Scab found himself liking it.

They were sitting opposite each other on the cocoon. Scab's end was listing a little, as it was the end with the destroyed AG motor on one of the corners. He had held on to the ornate double-barrelled laser rifle he'd taken off the Toy Soldier. The Monk still had a thorn pistol in each hand.

'So, should we be pointing guns at each other in some extended Mexican stand-off?' she asked.

Scab gave this some thought. 'I know what a stand-off is. What's a Mexican?'

'Never mind.'

'If it helps, I'll kill you with a blade when the time comes.'

'Thanks.'

'No thanks needed.' He turned and looked her up and down. 'It just seems like it would suit you more.'

The Monk resisted the urge to thank him again. Sardonic just didn't seem to register with him. 'So your double-cross is in place then?' she asked instead. Scab looked at her. He'd left the visor of the spacesuit clear but his expression was unreadable.

'The Game exists here,' Scab said, meaning the planet. This was after a period of silence as they rose through the red light towards the black leaf canopy covering the lower levels – or that's what they would be in Real Space anyway. 'There's gravity?'

'We don't know why. It's some kind of simulacra, a smaller echo of our universe with different physical laws and coterminous points. Perhaps the ghost planets exist as navigation aids.'

'Navigation aids?'

'Red Space is constructed space – it's artificial.'

It took a long time for what she had said to sink in. Scab's view of Red Space had just been radically altered, if he chose to believe what she had said.

'Constructed by who?' he finally asked.

The Monk shrugged. Scab resisted the urge to kill her for making a gesture so significantly lacking in grandeur after what she had just told him. Later he would come to the conclusion that he did not cope well with having his universe altered at such a radical level.

'We're not sure, Seeders would be our best guess. Perhaps the Lloigor.'

'Who're the Lloigor?'

There was no answer. Instead the Monk smiled in a way that

416

infuriated Scab so much his finger inched towards the bone blade still at his hip.

'These are Church secrets, right?' Scab asked suspiciously. The Monk nodded. 'Why are you telling me this? You must be pretty confident that you're going to come out on top of our double-cross.'

'How are you going to get out?' the Monk asked, meaning from Red Space. She had a good point. She gave him some time to think on this. 'Churchman likes you,' she finally said.

So that's it, Scab thought. He was being given a taste. It was an obvious manipulation but it still angered him. 'The Consortium thought I could be used as well, when I was Elite.'

'You still are,' the Monk said.

'A copy is.'

'I don't mean to be offensive, Mr Scab, but on the other hand I'm not afraid of you, so fuck it, right? But it seems a lot more likely that you're the clone.' She caught his face hardening. He wasn't a tolerant man, and she'd pushed what little tolerance he had beyond his normal limits. 'Now you can try and kill me, maybe even succeed, but I assure you it's mutually assured destruction. Or you can listen to me.'

'Everybody wants their own pet psychopath, someone to frighten the other children with. It's a sad state of affairs for Known Space,' Scab said through gritted teeth, controlling his anger, barely.

'We don't want you because you have a head full of rabid squirrels, and frankly if the Church Militia and the monks don't scare people then our ability to embargo bridge technology should. Churchman wants you because you have an enquiring mind. You question. Have you any idea how rare that is?'

'A head full of what?'

'See?'

'Who is Churchman? Your leader?' The Monk didn't answer, but Scab knew the name-drop had been carefully calculated. 'So let me see if I understand you properly. You're trying to avoid the double-cross by recruiting me?' Very few people had ever heard Scab laugh. There was genuine humour in the laughter, but no warmth. The Monk found the noise grated on her. She didn't like it.

Suddenly they were in the shade. They looked up to see huge chunks of wreckage plummeting towards them from high above. Both tried to neuronically order the AG motors to take what was going to be very languid evasive action. Eventually the Monk desisted, realising that Scab was stubborn enough to get them both killed if he didn't have his way.

The wreckage rained down around them. Where it hit, the tree broke like delicate ceramic. The wreckage that hit them just seemed to shatter, causing the cocoon to bob slightly on its motors.

'What's happening?' Scab asked, though he was beginning to guess.

'I think it's your diversion. The Game is being attacked.'

'That's happening in Real Space?'

'I would imagine it's considerably worse in Real Space.'

'And it has an effect here?'

The Monk didn't bother to answer.

You had to understand things on a quantum level to see the particle beam cutting through the *Necronaught*. Elite Scab knew that to penetrate the heavily armoured hull of a capital ship, even as it was breaking its back as it hit the atmosphere belly up, would be taking the Monarchist Elite's weapon close to the exotic material's tolerance levels, as it drew energy from a network of micro-black holes. A network harnessed by civilisations long dead.

Elite Scab closed his eyes, savouring this, standing on the lip of the split in the ship as impacts made the two parts of the ship fall away from each other. There was fire all around. Beneath, he knew there would be lightning as the atmosphere ionised around the debris. He had created an extinction-level event plummeting towards the day side of the planet. *Is this the diversion I want?* Elite Scab wondered.

He felt rather than saw the black wings. Heard the screaming. There would be no electronic warfare. This was no silent duel of nanites and biologicals. Elite Scab smiled. They would light up the skies.

He lifted his feet and flew down through the ship, wreathing himself in flames as he pierced the atmosphere. He was sure it was Horrible Angel after him. She was always the furious one. Tearing through burning wreckage after him, Fallen Angel would be setting an ambush, calculating trillions of possibilities to make the best shot and then leaving it to chance and chaos.

Down through the branches of the arcology trees at hypersonic speeds. Through the black leaves. Pulling up and flying through dark canyons of massive roots. Angel's wings spread out wide high above him, the particle beam a near-constant lance stabbing through branch and leaf, creating waves of destruction running parallel with his erratic flight path as he wove in and out of the city-sized trees, wishing he had time to play genocidal lumberjack.

Far behind them the sky went black as the first wreckage hit the ground and thousands of tonnes of debris were thrown into the air.

Through the black cloud the fires were almost invisible. The ground shook, Elite Scab only registering this through the shaking of the massive arcology trees.

He turned corkscrew at speed, letting his own particle beam lash out, carving scars on trees, cutting chunks out of them. He knew that Horrible Angel would be running a completely randomised set of evasive manoeuvres designed to not be where any sane mind would assume she was.

Crystalline receivers embedded deep inside Elite Scab detected the first attempts at sorcery. Imported higher-dimensional physics designed to block the complex entanglement effect, or in other words cut him off from his energy and ammunition.

It angered him. He wanted the Game as his funeral pyre. This was not how it should be done, but he knew she would be concentrating on the higher-dimensional physics. He used his own sorcery, rode the carrier beam back to find her. Angling all coherent energy shields forward, he aimed for her and accelerated. He went straight through one of the arcology trees, exploded out the other side and hit Horrible Angel. Materials that probably shouldn't touch, touched, and physics struggled to catch up.

The other Elite recovered instantly. Blades extruded from both their armours, appearing and disappearing where they needed them as they fought at bewildering speeds. The debris cloud engulfed them, but it meant less than nothing to these people, with their heightened senses and their instinctive understanding of everything around them.

Horrible Angel broke contact first. She was vulnerable for a moment. Elite Scab risked a shot. His weapon became a rifle in an instant in his hands, and he fired a subtle DNA beam, hoping the low-energy beam on the strange frequency would sneak past her shield and armour to rewrite her genetic code into something less god-like.

It was a fire-and-hope because he knew what was going to happen next. He had felt Fallen Angel take control of the orbital defence platforms above Elite Scab's area. He knew they had been fired.

The wing display made Horrible Angel's flight look almost graceful. The orbital weapons platforms fired, reaching into the atmosphere, destroying anything in their line of fire as, like angry gods, they reached for Elite Scab.

Elite Scab had a moment to think that it had been perfectly timed. Then the force of many impacts drove him deep into the crust of the planet beneath him. And he remembered pain again.

*

The Red Space echo of Game seemed to be coming down all around them. They tried to avoid the worst of the falling debris as the expressionistic simulacra trees crumbled, but much of the debris had the consistency of ash by the time it reached them.

'I don't suppose you want to share your exfiltration plan with me?' Scab asked. The Monk didn't dignify the question with an answer. Instead she watched him almost curiously as it rained ash out of a red sky.

'You know that Vic's dead by now, don't you? I'm sorry, but he was probably your best weapon,' she told him with the same searching expression. Scab just nodded. 'Will you even miss him?'

'Who are you to ask me that?' He wasn't angry. It was another question he didn't quite understand. It was almost as if he expected her to answer it somehow.

'I was just curious, I guess. Vic was the only life form you regularly and closely associated with. I just wondered if you'd developed some kind of connection to him.'

'Do you want me to take revenge now?'

The Monk looked down at the small cocoon they were riding.

'If you want. Or you could mourn.'

'Do you find emotions help being a killer?' This time there was genuine interest in his voice.

'No. No, I really don't.' The Monk seemed lost in thought for a while. 'Having something to believe in does.'

There was more laughter, and the Monk didn't like it any better this time.

'I think that makes you more dangerous than me, certainly madder.'

'Maybe just less cynical.'

They rode up again for a while, watching the echo of a world being destroyed by unseen forces. Scab was wondering if there was an exfiltration plan. Perhaps she was hoping to fly the thing all the way to the H-space beacon. After all, she had said that Red Space was smaller and governed by different physical laws.

'While we're sharing, where's the Cathedral?' Scab asked. The Monk ignored him yet again.

Scab looked around. He was starting to get bored. The slow ascent. Nothing to see but crumbling black skeletal trees and ashen-rain-obscured red sky. It took a while, but then he realised there was movement among the branches. There were indeterminate forms that seemed to be made out of some kind of deeper blackness than their surroundings. Faceless and roughly humanoid in shape, they had large bat-like wings and what looked like stinger-tipped tails. They crawled over the trees in a way that looked less like a flock and more like a swarm. They seemed somehow parasitical to him.

The other movement was more difficult to pin down: a suggestion of a quadruped, an off-kilter, almost canine lope to it, but whatever it was – or they were – it seemed to come from places where there shouldn't be anything. It hurt Scab when he caught the movement and actually tried to look at it. He had the idea that it was formed of tiny multifaceted crystals that moved together like a machine doing an impression of biological life.

Scab brought the laser rifle up to bear. Targeting graphics appeared in his vision as he tried to understand what he was seeing through the cross hairs. The Monk was watching him with an expression of bemusement on her face.

'What are they?' he asked eventually, lowering the rifle. They didn't seem any threat, and although he fancied killing something that he'd never killed before, particularly the crystalline things that made his head hurt, there were too many unknowns.

The Monk shrugged. 'We don't know. Aliens maybe. Real ones, not just uplifted animals like you and me. Maybe they're technology or weapons or ghosts. Maybe just some Red-Space-imprinted manifestation of what we have up here,' she said, tapping her head. 'Maybe we should think better thoughts?'

Scab stared at her, trying to decide if she was making fun of him or not. He had not found her answer particularly satisfying.

It wasn't enough. It hurt, it hurt so much. He imagined that every one of his cells was undergoing the white-light pain of a nuclear birth. There was no him, only agony. Suddenly he felt a connection. Something out of sight. Something appalling. For the first time he felt kinship, a connection, an empathy. He was a messenger, a herald, a harbinger.

The armour's integrity had held. Much of the energy had been sent elsewhere, a light show bleeding out into empty space. His shields were down, but he was being fed the energy to rebuild them.

It happened in moments – Elite Scab rebuilt himself – but moments were a long time for people like them. They must have assumed he'd been destroyed. Which meant for moments they weren't aware of him. Had he gone somewhere else? The contact had made him feel dirty. It made him feel alive and wish for death. He wondered if this was what having a purpose felt like.

He hit the atmosphere like a comet. There was flame to the horizon.

He bathed in energy-weapons fire from a surprised orbital defence network. He rose into space, looking like he was made from a vast spectrum of light, a humanoid prism. Space felt cool to him.

He heard Horrible Angel screaming. It was an infrasound weapon for mortals in an atmosphere. Here it was a special effect. He liked it. It was suitably dramatic. The electronic warfare attacks were a disappointment, a silent duel, a distraction beneath them. They did, however, mean that for the first time he became fully aware of Fallen Angel's presence. He was manipulating the forces of higher-dimensional physics in an attempt to cut off the complex entanglement effect. The amount of energy they were using must have been putting an enormous strain on the carrier signal from the primordial black hole network. Scab fought back. A conceptual sword-and-shield battle fought through other dimensions. It was science that only the ancients who had developed the technology understood. Fortunately their technology had been user-friendly.

Horrible Angel flew at him, cycling rapidly through her weapon's various flavours of attack. Focused particle beam, DNA hack beam, ghost bullets fed to her through the entanglement effect from vast magazines in the Monarchist's Citadel. Fired at a cyclic rate far in excess of anything a mechanical device could manage, the intangible bullets sought his flesh. They wanted to become tangible inside him. Elite Scab flickered through the frequencies of his coherent energy shields unimaginably fast to stop the bullets, as each one was keyed to a different vibration. He changed physical state at the same time, drawing on vast amounts of energy to do so, always trying to be in a different state from the bullet that was passing through where his body should be.

He knew something now. He sent a command back through the entanglement link. He knew that in the Citadel alarms would sound as his override code gave him access to a weapon that required full board permission to use. There would be a silent panic as those who supposedly could make that decision neuonically sought to stop his override signal. It had never been used. It was a massive escalation that if used they could never walk away from. *Fuck them*, Scab thought. He could see his death from here. This would be his goodbye.

Circling around distant suns, networks of orbiting crucibles made of ancient alien technology came alive and drank their respective suns. He became the triangulation point for the energy of three suns sucked dry in an instant.

He saw her wings. She was beautiful, her armour made her look like she was encased in living obsidian. He would miss her scream.

The rifle-shaped weapon in his hands was a focus point. Nothing more. He fired. For a moment her flesh became an event horizon.

She was staring at the cocoon. Had been for a while. Scab studied her. She was soon to be a victim but despite himself Scab was starting to find her intriguing. Suddenly it occurred to him that this was important to her, personally. This almost automatically meant that Scab would struggle to understand the reasoning. He understood wants but only really in terms of the id. This was something else. It clearly wasn't just a job to the Monk.

'Does monopoly mean that much to you?' Scab asked.

'Any degree of control is a possibly misguided attempt to stop the uplifted races from tearing themselves apart,' she told him distractedly. It was obviously something that she'd heard before.

'Fuck it. Let them.'

The Monk sighed and looked up at him.

'What a wonderfully constructed facade of nihilistic luxury,' she said. For some reason Scab thought she sounded a little uncomfortable with the words.

'Huh?' he asked.

'You have neunonics. Don't pretend that you didn't understand what I said.'

'I know what the words mean. I'm just not sure of their relevance.'

'There's too much beauty and wonder in Known Space for there not to be people there to bear witness.'

Scab nearly laughed in her face.

'Leaving aside that nobody cares enough to stop and look beyond whatever their next personal fix is, that's just narcissism. Stop trying to convince yourself you matter. It'll be there long after we're gone.'

'We're not so sure.'

Scab stared at her hard. She wouldn't meet his look. That hadn't seemed quite such a calculated thing to say, unless she was getting better at faking it. It was also clear that short of killing her and interrogating her neunonics, he wasn't going to get any more. He didn't want to kill her, yet. He wanted to see her way out, because he certainly didn't have one. They lapsed into silence again.

'What is this?' Scab finally asked, tapping the cocoon. She looked up at him. Suddenly she was guarded. It was like watching someone slam a polarised visor down.

'It's what you think it is. Money, power, chaos.'

'What's it to you?' he said evenly.

'The fall of the Church.'

'No, really.' The Monk did not answer. 'I know that Church neu-nonics are good and that you'll have a time bomb in there to wipe them when you die, but we ... I've been pretty well resourced for this. I wonder if it'll still be there when I interrogate your corpse's neunonics. The answer, I mean.'

'And if I told you it didn't matter, or rather it wouldn't matter to you or anyone else involved?'

'Then I'd say you'd have no reason not to tell me.'

Scab hadn't been expecting the smile.

'You're right.' But she said nothing more, to Scab's slight irritation.

Then behind them the red sky went black. The planet shook and everything around them came apart, a silent explosion of ash.

It was a slow bullet, a magic bullet that killed him. Fallen Angel had fired it seconds ago, a ghost bullet on a discrete carrier wave. He'd not so much fired at Elite Scab as seeded space with them. Each bullet fired at his weapon's impossibly fast cyclic rate was a mixture of L- and S-tech. The bullets carried a payload of high-end nanites and virals designed, at great expense, with one purpose in mind: kill the other guy's Elite.

Fallen Angel had linked his weapon's aiming system to a chaos fact/probability targeting routine. The bullets travelled through vectors where Elite Scab could be. The bullet hadn't hit Elite Scab. He'd moved into its path. It was fate's bullet. It was the inevitable bullet.

There was literally no room for tear ducts in the redesigned physiology of an Elite. When he got back to the Citadel he would try and weep for Horrible Angel. He knew that the black exotic matter would leak out of him like black tears only to be absorbed back in through his pale skin. There was, of course, less than no body. Her armour was gone as well. They were down one Elite.

Elite Scab had a body, though. Fallen Angel moved gracefully through the debris, heading for Elite Scab's corpse as his own systems came back online. Even though his systems were hardened with ancient alien technology, they had still been knocked out. His wings expanded out of his back again.

The planet below was dead now. It looked like an apple someone had taken a bite out of. Some of the orbital platforms and ships on the other side of the planet might have survived. He couldn't hear them yet. They were probably desperately trying to get their systems online as the dead planet pulled them down towards its surface. He couldn't hear the Absolute either. He hoped it was dead. It had repelled him.

It had not been a worthy master for them. It had turned an entire planet into a form of masturbation.

He found him. Elite Scab hung there in space. His armour looked undamaged. Soon his coffin would form around him. Fallen Angel would try and stop it, capture the tech, but it would be for nothing. The coffin would open a bridge at the beacon and start its autopilot funeral procession through Red Space back to the Consortium Citadel.

Hate and wishful thinking conflicted within Fallen Angel. All he could have asked for was a body to mourn. Like him, she hadn't backed herself up. It was a cheat for light that burned as brightly as they had. And hate. He could never kill Scab enough.

They had felt the force of whatever had happened as it passed through them. It was a sensation rather than something real, an echo with only slightly more physical presence than a hologram, and now they were floating up through a blizzard of ash. Through the gentle blizzard Scab could make out the expression of worry on the Monk's face.

'Did your diversion just destroy a planet?' she demanded.

It seemed unlikely, Scab thought, even for an Elite. On the other hand, there was nothing but ash now.

'Why do you look so worried?' he asked.

'What, the apparent destruction of a planet and the death of billions is not a sufficient cause for worry?' she demanded. It occurred to her that human emotions couldn't handle this sort of atrocity as anything more than an abstract. At least that was what she told herself, because she couldn't deal with the thought that she'd had a part to play in this crime. Scab shrugged. 'Red Space navigation isn't a precise science, well, at least not without a nav comp. Landmarks would have helped,' she finally told him.

'Maybe if you tell me what you're looking for?'

The Monk 'faced a command from her neunonics to stop the cocoon's rise. Scab could see it now through the gentle ash storm. The *St Brendan's Fire* was perfectly still in the black blizzard. His neunonics showed multiple weapons locks.

'Going to kill me with a blade now?' the Monk asked.

'Shit,' Scab said.

29

Southern Britain, a Long Time Ago

'It can't be done,' Morfudd said. Britha had to admit that she was probably right. They didn't have nearly enough people. They would need ships and they had no way to kill giants.

'We have to try,' Fachtna said grimly, but Britha could see that he did not hold out much hope. *To have come this far*, she thought helplessly.

'We are all going to die,' Teardrop said, matter of fact. 'Come to terms with that.'

'For nothing?' Morfudd asked.

'Stay here if you want,' Fachtna said.

Tangwen was leading the way. Behind them, riders crested the hill. They were Corpse People. The horses they rode were large and well built, their coats white in colour, their mouths and lower legs red – steeds from the Otherworld.

Ahead between the two islands they could see the massive wicker man rising from the waters, though Britha knew it was not made of wicker. Despite being several miles away she could make out its iron and wood framework. Above the line of the water its legs were filled with what looked like firewood. Its torso had different levels, each containing people. Her eyesight was now good enough to make out the arms of the frightened people inside the structure. After having the little crystal seeds pushed into their skulls they might have been docile enough, but now the seeds' magics seemed to have worn off. What was worse was that somehow she could feel their fear. It was like a background noise to her thoughts. Worse still, she knew that there was something in those waters, something that called to her. She wanted nothing more than to wade in and let the dark waters cover her. She knew they would not be cold, somehow.

Teardrop came to stand next to her.

'They hope this will bring their god? This Llwglyd Diddymder?' she asked.

426

'What we call the Muileartach and what the Atrebates worship as an aspect of Andraste is the last goddess who has not been corrupted by the sky gods. They will use the pain and fear of the sacrifice to drive her mad.'

'How?'

'She would feel it anyway. The goddess is not unkind, but the crystal seeds you saw in your dream are magics that will carry the suffering directly to her. Already what is happening will be affecting the goddess's servants.'

To Britha this seemed like cruelty for the sake of cruelty. Like those warriors who enjoyed hurting people more than victory, like the *mormaers* who abused their position. It was not the way to act, and it was the job of those with responsibility, the *dryw*, the *cateran*, to stop such things. As she watched the black curraghs around the wicker man and the giants wading in waist-high water close to the shores, she wondered how they could take all this on with only fifty warriors.

'This.' She nodded at the wicker man. 'This is the man that Crom Dhubh must kill as the Serpent Father said?' Teardrop nodded. It was foolish and weak to worship the gods, she knew, but she found herself feeling sympathy for the Muileartach. 'Why do this to her?' They were talking in the language of the Pecht, so Morfudd would not understand and realise that she was not the daughter of Andraste, though the warrior was watching them suspiciously.

'Because they are low men,' Teardrop said. Was there a hint of anger in his voice? 'And because as a goddess, the one we call the Muileartach has magics far more powerful than anything you or I could imagine. She can open the way for this Llwglyd Diddymder.'

'That name was not taught in the groves,' Britha told him.

'I do not know of it either.'

'It is not a good name.'

'Agreed.'

Tangwen came running back, keeping low.

'I have found a causeway onto the island and hopefully through the marsh.' The east side of the western island looked boggy.

They could hear the sound of hoof beats behind them. Britha glanced over her shoulder. The Corpse People had made their way down and were now galloping towards them but were still some distance away.

Tangwen turned and headed off. Britha went to follow. Morfudd stayed still and her people did likewise.

'This is a poor place to fight warriors on horseback,' Teardrop told her. 'On the causeway they can only come at you a few abreast.'

'Though if you run you may live longer as a craven,' Britha said impatiently. She was sick of having to coax them every step of the way. Morfudd stared at her. Britha realised then that the other woman hated her and would quite like to kill her.

'Your people are dead; your *rhi* is dead,' Fachtna said grimly. 'All any of us have left is to sell our lives dearly to the monsters that did this.'

Morfudd turned to Fachtna. The warrior had been getting steadily grimmer. The choices they had made, the sacrifices, Britha's killing of the boy and the changes in Teardrop had all taken their toll. The swaggering bravado was gone.

Finally Morfudd nodded and they all made their way down onto the causeway.

'I think they know we are here,' Tangwen said nervously.

'I don't think those that matter care,' Britha told her. The hunter had been scouting ahead. She had now decided to stay closer to the main group.

They had crossed the causeway to the east side of the western island and were now following it past channels of water and reed-choked islands of viscous mud. It smelled of low tide and decay. The shore of the eastern island was hundreds of feet away but they could still make out the bodies tied to poles. They were above the waterline now, but at high tide the poles would be partially submerged. Each of the corpses tied to the poles was a red ruin below the waist. They had also had their faces cut off. Gulls picked at the cadavers.

All along the shore of the eastern island the mad had come to jeer and scream at them. Clad in rags or naked, many of them bearing self-inflicted wounds, they looked wretched. Britha didn't like it and it was clear they were making the Cigfran Teulu nervous. They spat and made signs to protect themselves from evil. They saw their future on those poles.

Standing among the army of the wretched were what Britha guessed were their *dryw*. They wore soiled robes that might have once been white. Leaning on grisly decorated staffs, each of them wore a flayed skin mask of someone's face over their own features. If once they had cared for the unwanted, moonstruck or other unfortunates, then that time was long gone.

Some of the mad ran across the mud, threw themselves into what was now quite a small channel between the two islands and swam towards them. Some of the warriors readied their casting spears.

'Save your spears!' Fachtna's voice rang out over the mud. The authority in it had them hesitating. Fachtna was at the front of the column with Britha, Tangwen and Teardrop. Morfudd was at the rear because that was where they were expecting to be attacked first. Morfudd glared at Fachtna, who cursed himself. The Cigfran Teulu glanced at Morfudd. She motioned them to lower their spears.

'Horsemen!' Morfudd's voice carried to the front of the column. Britha, Tangwen, Teardrop and Fachtna turned to look. Sure enough, Corpse People on horseback were approaching three abreast along the causeway.

It was an interesting choice, Britha thought. She would have dismounted to attack. The back three rows of the column formed up. Their longspears became a wall of pointed metal enchanted with Fachtna and Britha's blood magics.

'Make way! Move!' Fachtna was pushing his way through the men and women of the Cigfran Teulu towards the rear of the column.

Ysgawyn rode in the third rank of horsemen on the causeway. Under normal circumstances he would have attacked on foot, but the horses they rode were from the Otherworld. They would not shy from iron spearheads like normal horses and he was impatient to taste the meat of the last of the Atrebates. The slaughter at the Crown of Andraste had been a fine thing, but there had been no challenge, no warriors. They had sneaked away like cowards, and he wanted the power of the four who had defied his army at the gate.

Ahead they could see the three lines of Atrebates. Six abreast, they had levelled their longspears but had no armour or shields. Gwydyon rode in the second rank. The squat, massively built, scarred war leader held up his hand to bring the column to a halt.

'Sound the *carnyx*,' Ysgawyn whispered to the man next to him, who lifted the long curved brass instrument to his lips. The head of the *carnyx* was in the form of a horse's skull in bronze. Normally they would not sound the horn. Normally they were as quiet as the dead when they attacked.

The deep bass note of the *carnyx* sounded out over mud, marsh and water. Bress moved to the side of the curragh and looked north towards the two islands and the mainland. Ettin joined him. Bress noted that he now carried a great axe with a double head made of two crescents of bronze. On his shoulder Ettin's second head, that of a painted man with a lacquered beard and dark hair, remained silent. The tall pale man glanced at his second with distaste.

'If he has told you all he can, let him die,' Bress said.

'There,' Ettin said pointing. Though some miles away yet, they could make out the horses on the causeway.

'Cowards! Your king begged for mercy while we ate his flesh, raped the corpses of your women and fed your children to our wolves!' one of the Corpse People shouted, a rider in the front rank. He opened his mouth to shout again. The casting spear broke his teeth on its way through his head. Fachtna kept moving through the ranks of the Cigfran Teulu borrowing another two casting spears as he went. He stopped just behind the last three ranks.

'They will charge,' he said.

'Horsemen will not charge a wall of spears,' one of the warband replied.

'They *will* charge. You must not break. You must hold. Those of you not in the front three rows, lend your strength and push. Put your spears in the horses. Push them deep and up – make them rear – you understand me?'

The warriors around him did not look happy but they nodded. Morfudd was otherwise occupied in the rearmost rank preparing to receive the charge.

'First give me some room.' Fachtna had seen who had given the order to halt the horses and the man behind him who had given the order for the *carnyx* to be blown, presumably to warn the black curraghs. Across the channel on the other island the mad jeered and called for their blood.

With a simple gesture Gwydyon ordered the advance. The three horses in the front rank, one of them now ridden by a truly dead man with a casting spear through his head, charged. The line of horses behind them moved forward at a slower pace.

Hands changed their grips on the hafts of longspears. Feet shifted for better purchase on the causeway. Despite Fachtna's words, they expected the horses to shy from the spears at the last moment. Closer, the horses becoming larger, their colouration told of their heritage, known from dark tales told around the campfire or late at night when the warriors were children. Those they had thought, until recently, to be unkillable dead rode the Otherworldly steeds.

As the horses reached the spearheads they all but leaped into them. Spears pierced horseflesh. Horses screamed. The spears soaked in the blood of the daughter of their goddess and her champion held, somehow, and did not splinter. Men and women slid back on the causeway; those behind them pushed, stopping the slide, adding their strength to the three rows of spears, giving them the strength to hold their ground.

One of the horses, the one with the dead rider, a longspear nearly all the way through its body, opened its mouth impossibly wide. Its teeth were those of a predator. It bit the face off the spearman who'd run it through. The dead man, his face a bloody ruin, did not fall. The press of the melee held him up. A warrior in the third rank, who'd just seen her lover's face bitten off, screamed and despite the press lifted her spear and pushed herself forward to run the weapon through the horse's skull.

'And step!' Morfudd cried. And somehow they did. The two remaining horses reared. Spears forced them back. One of the riders fell off his steed, impaling himself on three spears, but they did not drop due to the press of bodies.

The other horseman in the front row stabbed out with his longspear as his shield caught blow after blow. His spearhead ran through the head of the woman next to Morfudd.

'And step!' Morfudd screamed, furious now as her friend's hot blood splattered her face. And again they did, holding their dead up in the press of bodies as they went.

Fachtna had pulled his boots off. He climbed up onto the shoulders of the spearmen and -women and ran from shoulder to shoulder over the warband, his bare feet giving him more purchase. Then he leaped. Powerful leg muscles, infused with what Britha would have thought of as the magics of his people, carried him over the heads of the first rank of horsemen as the spears in their flesh forced the rearing horses over and into the mud of the marsh.

Fachtna threw both his casting spears in mid-air. The rider next to Gwydyon died, a spear in his chest. Gwydyon raised his shield just in time, the spear meant for his head hitting the shield, its point piercing the wood.

Fachtna tore his sword out of its scabbard. His spear had made Gwydyon raise his shield so that his face was covered. Fachtna swung as he came in. The ghostly singing blade cut straight through Gwydyon's shield and then continued its path through his body and then through his screaming horse's flanks.

Ysgawyn watched the warrior he had seen from afar the other night land in front of him as his warband leader's torso slid diagonally off the rest of his body. The man spun and sliced upwards with his sword, held two-handed. Ysgawyn threw himself back off his horse as it was decapitated. The warrior kicked at the horse as it toppled and came straight for him. Ysgawyn lost interest in the fight and leaped from the causeway onto an island in the marsh.

None of the horsemen near Fachtna seemed interested in fighting him. He watched the Corpse People's king flee across the marsh as he tried to recover his breath.

Behind him the Cigfran Teulu charged the second rank, butchering the horses and killing the last remaining rider. Soon they were killing the third-rank riders as they tried to turn their horses. Morfudd was next to him now.

The rest of the horsemen were turning their horses as best they could to make their escape. Those close to the front were in disarray. Horses reared; others jumped into the marsh and got bogged down or broke their legs. There was no battle now, just killing. It could have gone very differently. The Corpse People could have ridden straight through them, but the Cigfran Teulu had held.

There was a savage grin on Morfudd's blood-spattered face. The warband's blood was up. They were feeling the rush of combat.

They had lost three fighters. Fachtna had respectfully suggested to Morfudd that they recover all the weapons that had been blessed with the blood magics. He, along with some of the warband, took discarded Corpse People's shields. Unfortunately they did not have time to strip the dead of their armour.

Fachtna was impatient to get going. Tangwen had scouted ahead a little. The hunter could see that one of the curraghs had come close to the shore and warriors, the tips of their spearheads glinting in the sunlight, were making their way across sandbanks to the island. The giants were moving too, but none were approaching them.

Morfudd and Fachtna joined Britha and Teardrop at the front as Britha moved ahead to keep an eye on Tangwen. Some of the moon-struck wretches had made it to this side of the channel and more were following, but they seemed happy to wade around in the mud, occasionally throwing it at the warband but not getting any closer.

'We need to move more quickly,' Teardrop told Morfudd, who nodded and turned to hurry her warriors.

Britha was coming to the conclusion that she hated beaches, or indeed any body of sand close to water. She wished for night. She wished for enough woad to cover herself and the warband, and she wished for a warband who would fight naked.

Instead what she saw was a line two deep of a hundred demon-ridden Lochlannach spearmen standing on a sandbank, a curragh in the water behind them and behind that two of the horribly misshapen giants towering over the ship. She remembered broken chariots and horseflesh and the mangled bodies of the warriors of the Cirig. What were they thinking? They could fight the spearmen, just, with the help of blood magic, but the giants?

'Each one of us only has to kill two of them,' Morfudd said. 'With your help we will triumph.' But she was looking uncomfortably at the giants. They knew them to be excellent swimmers despite their deformed limbs and the horrific growths that sprouted from their rough skins.

'We will not fight with you,' Teardrop told her. To Britha's surprise this seemed to come as a relief to the warband leader.

'You will fight the giants then?' she asked. The Cigfran Teulu had acquitted themselves well, but the giants were something else. The dead looked like people and subsequently were found to be so, and fighting them had been comparable to what they had done in the past. The giants, however, were things that should not be, things from stories told by the bards out of their colleges to the west beyond the plains of the dead. Giants were thought to be long dead.

'No.'

Fachtna frowned at Teardrop, who had been staring at the giants as if searching for a way to kill them. The warband had spilt onto the sand at the end of the causeway, and the two forces were eyeing each other. There had been no point in hiding.

Morfudd turned on Teardrop. She did not flinch away from his strange eyes. 'Then I call you craven, demon!' she spat.

'We need you to carry the fight as close to the water as you can, and indeed into the water if possible,' Teardrop told her.

'And then what?' Morfudd asked.

'Die well.'

Morfudd stared at him. Then she started laughing.

'Your sacrifice will not be so that we can escape.'

'I will fight with you, at the start,' Fachtna told her. Teardrop opened his mouth to object. 'Don't worry. I will meet you in the water.'

'The water?' Tangwen said. 'Did you see the people tied to the poles?'

As the discussion went back and forth around her, Britha could not shake the feeling that the water was her home. Where she should be. She knew that beneath its surface she would hear a song calling her back.

'What about stealing a boat?' Tangwen asked.

'We don't have time to break the magics that control them,' Fachtna told her.

'We'll be fine in the water,' Britha said. 'I'll protect you.'

Teardrop was looking at her, almost smiling. Britha did not see what they had to smile about. From here the wind carried the smell of hundreds, possibly thousands, of people kept in close captivity, the cries, their pleas. From here they could better appreciate the sheer size of the wicker man as it towered above them.

Britha stripped off her robe and cut her rope belt in two with her sickle. Half of it she tied to her spear as a sling. The other half of the rope she tied to the sickle, which she slung over her shoulder. Tangwen took off her trews but tied the long rough-spun shirt she was wearing between her legs. She had left the bow and looked sad to see it go. Teardrop used some thong to make a sling for his staff, but both he and Fachtna assured the others that they could swim fully clothed and in Fachtna's case armoured, though both removed their boots.

The Atrebates marched out, their shield wall a little sparse as they only had the shields they had taken from the dead Corpse People. The Lochlannach stood between them and the water. At first it looked like the Cigfran Teulu would close in the usual style, but they then picked up the pace a little, though Fachtna dropped back and then stopped. The warband charged. As they did, they screamed the name of their dead king. Morfudd had reminded them of everything they had lost. She had told them how all those who had died by the hand of the invaders were watching them now from Annwn. She had reminded them that the Cigfran Teulu were not the pretend dead of the Corpse People; they were walking dead and the only thing left was the formality of actually dying. She told them that they did not have to care about their lives any more.

As they charged, many of them with wide smiles on their faces, few with any fear, their feet kicking up wet sand as they ran, they shifted direction to concentrate on the left flank of the Lochlannach line, as they looked at it. Because they were outnumbered, this meant that the Lochlannach could wheel around and hit them in the flank and eventually the rear, but that did not matter today.

*

He would need more matter. Fachtna felt the sand beneath his feet as his flesh grew roots and started sucking it in, cycling the sand through conduits in his flesh to the implanted assembler in his stomach. The assembler converted it at a molecular level to L-tech nanite-augmented flesh. He would only be able to handle the vast increase in mass and the large amounts of energy needed to sustain it and still move for a very short period of time. Already as he grew, his flesh warping and becoming monstrous, the heat bleeding from him was turning the sand around his feet to glass. The pain was becoming unbearable. That was the reason for the berserk fury. If not for the *riasterthae* frenzy, no warrior would be able to survive. He started to glow from within. Fortunately his armour was designed to shift with his warped *riasterthae* form and was able to deal with the extremes of temperature. His last action before the agony forced him to lose himself to the frenzy was to draw his rapidly oscillating thermal blade. His last thought was, *Kill the giants.*

The thing that was once Teardrop became aware of the glow first. He turned and saw what Fachtna had become. The warrior was huge now, a mountain of unsustainable muscle mass that glowed from within, contorted, no longer human, features that told of the agony of his flesh, steam shooting from a blow hole in his head. There was a look of horror on Teardrop's face.

'Too soon!' he shouted. Britha turned and glanced behind her. She had a moment to see what Fachtna had become. The glance was not nearly long enough for her to understand.

The warband threw their casting spears at the last moment. Few hit their mark; that wasn't the point. They aimed high, then, still running, swapped the longspears or swords that they had in their free hands into the hands they would wield them with just as they hit the Lochlannach line. The casting spears made the Lochlannach raise their shields high.

Morfudd led the charge. She closed only slightly ahead of the rest of her people. Her shield got her past the spear point on one side. She held her spear vertically and slid it down the spears on the other side, pushing them away from her. She kicked up the shield of the one she had hit. Couldn't get her spear to bear, so she let go of it and dragged her sword out of its scabbard and opened up his chest. Her shield was stuck so she let go of it. She kicked out against the Lochlannach spearman in front of her, knocking him back into the second line. Since she had drunk the blood of the newcomers she had felt stronger, faster and more powerful than ever before. She held her sword two-handed, and as the already wounded Lochlannach was pushed back towards her, she cleaved him open with a cut from shoulder to hip. She then became furious that she could not get the corpse out of the way quickly enough to get at the second rank. The force of the charge had carried them forwards. Morfudd was standing in water now. She had not noticed.

It was hard not to get caught up in it. Inside her, the urge to disappear into the water and the burning in her blood that wanted to kill competed. Whispers from her spear – even now its haft was burning – agreed with the lust for violence that burned inside her.

She ran at the line, wet sand under her bare feet, the salt smell of the sea strong in her nostrils despite the stink from the wicker man, the screams and pleas of the captives now drowned out by battle cries and iron and wood meeting flesh and bone.

The Cigfran Teulu line hit the Lochlannach just ahead of her. Spears slid under shields, searching for bodies to bury themselves in. As the enemy spearmen lifted their shields, Atrebates leaped onto them, riding them as they threw themselves sword and spear first into the Lochlannach's second rank.

Britha leaped high and far. For her there was a moment's tranquillity. She heard nothing, the din of battle lost for a moment. There was just the sea and the bright blue sky as her salmon leap carried her over the heads of the Cigfran Teulu and the Lochlannach. Then the bloodlust was back as she stabbed down with the spear in mid-air. She felt the spear's craving for flesh as it was driven home into the chest of one of the Lochlannach in the second row. Britha almost lost her grip on the spear but managed to hold onto it as the weapon's head split into branches and grew through its victim's ribcage. The path of her flight pulled the spearman over backwards into the water. Britha landed with a splash. The spearhead reformed and she wrenched it out of the dead man's chest.

Screaming as she hewed her sword from one side to the other into anyone foolish enough to get close to her, Morfudd suddenly found herself knee deep in bloody red water with no enemies in front of here. They had fought their way through, she thought exultantly.

She turned. The ferocity of their attack had demolished the two lines of Lochlannach on the flank they had hit, but the other was wheeling to hit them in the back, presumably in response to some unheard order from some unseen leader.

Suddenly, on a sunny cloudless day, Morfudd found herself in the shade. She turned and looked up.

The giant reached down and grabbed Morfudd. Lifted her up, its fingers curving around her to make a fist and punched that fist into the shallow water. She was dead instantly. The giant threw her broken body at her own people and lifted up a foot to stamp. Lochlannach or Atrebates, it made no difference.

The stamping giant splashed everyone with bloody water and was close enough to Britha for the impact to knock her off her feet. She was underwater for a moment and for that moment heard the song. There was a sadness to it. The Muileartach knew pain on this day.

Britha sat up in the red water, fighting all around her. To her right something monstrous and glowing with an inner light hit the Lochlannach line. Enemy warriors went flying. The *ban draoi* knew that had this been a mortal army they would have broken and fled. There was an explosion of steam. Lochlannach and Atrebates alike fell away from the massive creature, their exposed skin red and blistering from the heat.

The monstrous thing that Fachtna had become barrelled into a giant's leg, swinging the ghost blade at it again and again, hacking at it, each cut going deeper. The giant reached down for Fachtna, its skin seeming to melt and run as it did so. It grabbed him apparently oblivious to the pain, but then staggered and finally fell into the water.

Fachtna leaped high out of the steaming water and landed on the giant's chest. He hacked with his sword and tore with bare burning hands at the thing's chest as if he was burrowing into it. The giant grabbed at him, but the heat had sunk Fachtna's monstrous form into the creature's flesh. Strange fluids squirted out of the giant's chest – Britha guessed it was blood – and lumps of its flesh were flung out. Some of it floated, other bits sank. There was an explosion of red liquid, much of it turning to steam as it sprayed close to Fachtna's deformed glowing body. This looked more like the blood Britha was used to seeing.

Distracted by the death of the giant, she didn't notice the Lochlannach moving towards her until she felt his foot on her chest pushing her down as he raised his spear. She reached for hers, but a shape rose out of the red water behind him. Teardrop grabbed the man's head and pulled it back as he stroked his black-bladed knife across the man's throat. A red smile appeared on the man's neck and he fell. Britha realised that she knew him. His name was Dubthalorc.

He was one of her people, a landsman. He had been known for raising the best sheep and his wife had been very good with a loom. Britha watched him slide into the water sadly.

Another Lochlannach charged but suddenly fell, yanked under the water. Tangwen appeared. She was red from head to foot, like the dirk she'd just rammed through the Lochlannach's leg. She pushed his helmet forward and then repeatedly hit him in the back of his head with her hand axe until he stopped moving.

'We have to go!' Teardrop shouted over the din of battle and glanced angrily at Fachtna, who was wading through the Lochlannach, breaking them like toys. Just then there was the unmistakable sound of a large fire catching. Britha glanced behind her. Both the legs of the wicker man were in flames. Now the screams of the captives over the water far exceeded the sounds of the battle. Teardrop grabbed Britha and dragged her into deeper water.

They dived. It felt like home to Britha. She could hear the mind-song. It took every shred of willpower that she had not to turn and swim to the west.

Fachtna dived into the water in an explosion of steam. All around him the water boiled as he bled off heat and excess matter. He was tired, bone-weary, pained and hungry. He swam as fast and hard as he could. Surfaced to take a breath, long enough to see flames and hear screams, then beneath the surface again. He did not look behind him. He knew that the Cigfran Teulu would fight as long as they could.

With its legs on fire, Britha was wondering how they would climb up into the wicker man, but as she surfaced for another deep breath she saw a rope hanging from it. Presumably it had been used to hoist people or materials up. A casting spear hit the water close by. She glanced to her right to see one of the black curraghs. She dived again and watched more spears quickly lose their speed in the water. Teardrop was level with her but they were leaving Tangwen behind. She had no idea where Fachtna was. The water here was much deeper. As she swam she was aware of dark shapes darting through the water beneath her.

An exhausted Fachtna reached the wicker man first. The water above him looked orange as a result of the flames licking up the legs of the giant figure. He could hear the screams even under the water now. Worse still, when he surfaced he could smell burning flesh. Anger overwhelmed fatigue and the despair he felt as he looked up at the climb he had to do. He surged out of the water, grabbed the rope and started pulling himself hand over hand, not using his legs.

The climb was always going to leave them exposed. As he pulled himself up, Fachtna saw one of the black curraghs surging through the water towards him. The Lochlannach on board started throwing spears, but the wind that carried the wicker man's stench and the screams of its prisoners also blew smoke around him. He still felt some spears pass close by him, making eddies in the smoke, but soon he was too high for thrown spears to hit him. Fachtna knew that the wicker man would not collapse. The metal drawn from the earth would have been seeded with smart matter designed to stand up to the heat. The wood would burn and so would the people.

Britha did not want to leave the water. It was better down here, safer. She certainly did not want to climb hundreds of feet into the air on a rope. Teardrop shamed her by grabbing the rope and pulling himself out of the water and up into the smoke. She quickly lost sight of him. Before the magic entered her blood, she would not have been capable of this. She surged out of the water, grasped the rope and started to pull herself up.

Fachtna felt others on the rope beneath him. As he reached the metal framework and the thick wooden planks at the base of the wicker man's torso, he saw other ropes. His shoulders and arms were just extensions of pain. He had little idea how he was still hanging on, but he knew that he had to collect as many of the ropes as possible so that people could use them to climb down. *For what?* he asked himself as he swung hand over hand around the framework, excrement and urine dripping down on him through the cracks between the planks above. *So that they can be massacred by the spearmen in the black curraghs, so they can be hacked to pieces by mad men, so they can be swept out to sea?* Fachtna was a strong swimmer and augmented, but even he'd had trouble with the currents. It felt hopeless, but he didn't have any better ideas, and the flames were rising quickly up both legs of the wicker man. Above him the screaming and pleas for help were starting to be replaced with the sound of coughing. He himself was covered in soot but the smoke would not affect him.

Pulling a handful of ropes with him, Fachtna climbed over the lip of the torso's base. Soot-blackened arms stuck out through the metal framework, reaching for him.

'Back!' he shouted. Eventually a large man pushed a circle clear on the inside. He did so not without difficulty, they were packed in so tightly. Leaning back, Fachtna drew his sword and easily cut through the frame. There was a surge towards him that threatened to knock him off the framework. He brought the singing burning blade forward. 'Back!' he shouted again before turning to the large man. 'Listen to me.' He handed the man the bundle of ropes he had collected. 'Tie these off against the framework so they don't swing back under. There are people coming up behind me. Don't climb down this rope; let them up. The strong have to carry the weak and any children too small to climb themselves. When you think you can jump, do so. The moment you hit the water, swim away from the ropes or others will land on you. You have to stay here and make sure this is done. If we give into fear then everyone will die. Do you understand me?' The man was staring at him. Then he turned and started climbing down the rope. *Good. I need an example,* Fachtna thought. He kicked the man in the face. The man flew backwards off the rope and disappeared into the smoke. A hand grabbed his arm. He turned to see an elderly but formidable-looking woman.

'It will be done as you say,' she told him, and then immediately began organising people. The smell of the people was so overwhelming that it brought tears to Fachtna's eyes as he pushed his way through them, but to their credit they did not panic as word spread of what was happening.

The wooden steps that led to the next level were gated and barred. His sword cut through the gates with ease. At each level he appointed gatekeepers and told them what they had to do, that they had to try and keep the calm or all would die. In as much as he could judge, he chose the strongest personalities. Examples were made. He didn't want to do it – they'd suffered enough – but panic would kill them all.

Tangwen was exhausted when she reached the rope dangling down from the wicker man. She had grown up in a marsh and close to the Grey Father. If you wanted to survive then you had to be a good swimmer, but the currents in the channel between the two islands were vicious. She was not chosen of the gods like her companions, and it had taken every last bit of her strength to stop herself from being swept out to sea. As she looked up at the rope, tears in her eyes, she knew that she could not make the climb. She'd let Fachtna, Teardrop, Britha and all the people in the wicker man down.

Tangwen felt something bump against her from below. She looked into the water and saw a dark shape darting away. The large man plummeting into the water from above startled her. The surprising thing was he didn't come back up, but nearby the water turned red.

'Move now!' Teardrop said in a voice that brooked no argument, and people backed out of the way for the swollen-headed creature with the bulging veins and crystalline eyes. He was followed moments later by a naked soot- and bloodstained woman with a spear slung over her back. Britha sat down on the soiled planks, her upper body a mass of pain. She didn't think she could move her arms and she was so hungry. She looked at the wretches around her, collected herself and then stood up and painfully slipped the spear off her back and readied it. A woman was organising the captives' escape on the ropes, savagely berating anyone who tried to push ahead while the strong took the frail and the smallest children down. The woman was doing this through fits of coughing. Britha could feel the smoke in her lungs but somehow still found herself able to breathe. She was not surprised to find that Teardrop was unaffected by the smoke as well.

Britha looked questioningly at Teardrop. The creature that used to be a man had taken his crystal-topped staff off his back. Teardrop turned and headed towards the steps.

With a thought Bress brought one of the black curraghs in as close as he dared to the wicker man. The craft might be able to fit between its legs but he didn't want to risk the fire and he had a feeling that it would be raining captives soon. Ettin stood next to him as both of them stared into the smoke. They could see the ropes hanging down.

Ettin went first. He backed up and then ran along the deck and leaped into the smoke, his second head berating him as he did so. Then Bress did the same, his cloak trailing out behind him as he ran and then leaped, the smoke swallowing him.

Long, strong fingers grabbed the rope, cloak billowing as he started to pull himself up, following Ettin. There were captives climbing down the rope as they ascended. Ettin told them to jump. Most did, plummeting past them. For those that didn't, Ettin grabbed one of the bronze torture blades from the front of his apron and slashed at them until they let go.

As he climbed, Bress woke the dragon with a thought.

Seven levels. Each level packed with captives taken from many different tribes. Fachtna rushed up, cutting through bars and metal gates. Spoke to the people, told them how to help themselves.

It was selfish, he knew. He should be down there helping keep the calm, helping people climb down. Or he should seek out Teardrop and watch over him, but he wanted a moment. He climbed onto the head, standing up on it, his bare feet gripping the metal framework. Just a moment above the stench. Just a moment free of the smoke. Just a moment with the clear blue sky. Looking out over the two islands, the third behind him. The long ridge of the hill on the mainland, much of it wooded except for the ugly clear scar where they had taken material to build this abomination and the fuel to fire it.

He did not want to look down to see the curraghs, to see the fate of the captives who had managed to climb down. He did look down, however, when he heard the sound of huge amounts of water pouring off something. He watched the dragon rise out of the water.

Britha was amazed by how orderly it was. While most were terrified, they were holding themselves together long enough to act in their own best interests and those of the people around them.

They had found a place on the fourth level clear enough for Teardrop to sit down cross-legged, his staff across his lap, and close his eyes.

Then she heard the panic start, the screams, the sounds of struggling, cries of pain mingling with fear. Britha ran to the edge and looked down. As the dragon rose up level with her, water still pouring off it, she nearly soiled herself.

Behind her, Teardrop had started to beg and gibber, talking nonsense rapidly and pathetically. He was weeping openly. Britha forced herself to turn away from the monstrous form of the rising dragon and back to Teardrop. She watched in horror as blood leaked out of his clothes and wounds appeared all over his face, his skin blackening and blistering as if it was being burned. Some of the cuts on his face and head, the lower ones, leaked blood. Ghostly tendrils of what looked like crystal emerged from the cuts higher up. His features were racked with agony of the like Britha had never seen before. It was with mounting horror that she realised what Teardrop had come here to do. All the pain and suffering that Bress and his master were trying to use to drive a goddess insane, Teardrop was going to take unto himself.

Tears sprang into her eyes.

It was easy to mistake it for a dragon. The Naga craft had its membranous wings extended for atmospheric operations. It had a main body, which housed the craft's biotech drive and the other organs that provided life support, and a long neck, which led to the craft's brain and the Naga who ostensibly melded with it to act as overseers as much as pilots for the brute organism.

Fachtna watched it rise from the water, almost oblivious to the screams of panic from below. It was overkill. After all, what could one warrior do against such power. He felt gratified that Bress or his master felt that he warranted such a grand death.

Then he smiled and reached for the case on his back as his internal targeting systems locked on to the dragon, plotting targeting solutions and preparing to transmit them. He took the case and opened it. It was heavily shielded and constantly transmitting narcotic, soporific programs to the spear inside.

Fachtna lifted the drowsy spear out of its case. A demonic face formed in the smart matter of the lower part of the weapon's long bladed head. The haft of the weapon extended to over six feet. He felt the psychotic AI in the weapon start to wake. The Lloigor had always felt that function followed form. If you were to make a weapon, then the weapon, to fully fulfil its purpose, should hate because its purpose was carnage. Even allowing for that, the AI in the spear, which some called Lug, had far exceeded its initial programmed hate and gone into the realms of near-uncontrollable madness on battlefields eternities ago. If some of the stories were true, then the weapon – like its makers – could have been older than this universe. Fachtna himself was nearly overwhelmed by the weapon's hunger for slaughter. He almost lost himself in its myriad rage-filled psychoses.

The dragon breathed and engulfed the top of the wicker man's head in fire. Superheated plasma turned the smart-matter-seeded metal into a melted and fused mess.

Fachtna's leap took him high above the wicker man just as where he had been standing moments before was turned to slag. Fachtna was aiming for the wicker man's shoulder. He almost overshot. His bare feet failed to grip as he slipped painfully onto his arse and started to slide off. He grabbed the framework of the wicker man with his left hand and used it to swing around until he was facing the dragon again. The Naga ship tilted to one side as it circled the wicker man, looking for another shot.

Fachtna pulled his right arm back and threw the spear at the dragon. He transmitted his targeting ware's firing solutions to the insane AI at the same time. The spear's AG drive kicked in, accelerating it to hypersonic speeds, the resultant boom deafening the screaming captives below. The thermal head superheated to white hot as it hit the Naga craft in an explosion of burning biotechnological armoured skin and flesh.

Through conduits and corridors that had more in common with veins and arteries, the spear sought out the Naga symbiotically fused with the craft and the other semi-autonomous organisms/weapons that lived within it and killed them all.

Fachtna drew his sword again, cut through the framework and dived into the now-empty seventh level of the wicker man. He rolled forward onto his feet and ran. The dragon breathed once more. Fachtna felt the heat on his back; his hair caught fire as the shoulder of the wicker man was turned to slag.

Through the layers of psychoses, the spear recognised the craft as a manifestation of its ancient enemy. It sought out the craft/organism's beating heart and slew the dragon.

Fachtna glanced behind him. The Naga craft was listing badly to one side. Then the disruption in the air at its tail, caused by the craft's Real Space drive, simply stopped, and it plummeted towards the sea.

Fachtna stopped running and headed back to the edge of the fused area of the wicker man's seventh level, patting out the flames in his hair as he went. He ignored the burning sensation from his feet and the smell of flesh cooking as he looked out and watched the dragon crash through one of the curraghs below. Even frightened, even deafened, the captives still managed to cheer.

Now comes the hard part, Fachtna thought. The program had taken up an enormous part of the memory within his internal nanite headware. The program was complex, intelligent, ancient and had its own personality. It was designed to do just one thing: soothe the spear enough for it to return and be replaced in its case. To the spear this would feel like the betrayal of a lover played out in moments that for the AI stretched out for lifetimes.

Possession by the spear was a definite threat. Fachtna activated protective programs, mystic sigils that would look after his internal systems; he dropped calming narcotics into his augmented systems to try to suppress the psychotic rage spillover into his consciousness. He ran through calming mental and physical exercises taught at warrior camp and later by the technomantic *dryw*.

The spear returned to Fachtna's hand, its haft receding. Fachtna tried not to hurry as he sent the various codes designed to make the AI sleep. He placed it in the case and with a pronounced sigh of relief closed it.

The foot caught him dead centre in the back with a force that would have snapped a non-augmented spine. Instead it sent him sprawling across the soiled boards.

Bress let go of the framework he'd used to swing in and dropped down onto the floor behind the prostrate Fachtna. Behind him the framework that had opened for him with a thought was growing shut.

'You're a long way from your Eggshell, little man,' he said evenly. Fachtna rolled over to face him. He felt a little thrill of fear. He wished he hadn't used the *riasterthae* frenzy to kill the giant. He couldn't withstand another frenzy today. He wished his arms and shoulders weren't still in agony despite the best efforts of his augmentations to repair them.

'I thought we were a myth to the likes of you?' he asked for the sake of something to say.

'Long gone perhaps, but Crom has a long memory.'

Besides fear, Fachtna also felt excitement. He really wanted to kill this man. He was less happy when Bress leaned down and picked up the case with the spear in it.

'What's this?' he asked.

Fachtna skipped up onto his feet, sword in hand.

It was warm in here. Her internal breath felt like the dry desert wind from a hundred lives ago. Except in her breath was moisture. He stood in a cave of bone and flesh, his hands and the side of his head sunk into the wall. He shared the thoughts and feelings of a creator. He was perverting them. He had fed her pain and fear and hatred, and she had given that form. From her womb they had grown like blisters through her skin. Skin that was strong enough to survive the deepest abysses the oceans had to offer. Slowly she was waking. Unlike her sisters, her creator had not driven her irrevocably insane, but the pain of the sacrifices would be enough to harm her mind. That would allow him to influence her to open the way.

The pain and the fear lessened significantly. She could still feel it, even asleep, but it was not being fed directly to her via the transmissions of crystal parasites. He had felt the interference but thought nothing of it. Small people with small minds. They could not be allowed to stop the sending, however.

Smoke poured up through the planks in the floor of the fourth level, obscuring most of their view and the people waiting by the steps. They were just coughing, sobbing shadows now, cursing those who moved so slowly beneath them.

Teardrop was a bleeding mess, still sitting cross-legged, his arms held out, no part of him unwounded. If his skin was not cut then it was burned. His gibbering had long ago ceased to be language, and blood came from his mouth as crystal oozed from his eyes. He was now just making a rasping rattling noise.

The first thing she noticed was that the cursing, sobbing and coughing had stopped. The captives came through the smoke towards them, arms outstretched, enslaved by the magic of the crystal seeds in their heads again. Britha moved in front of Teardrop. She heard him coughing and spitting out blood behind her. Crom apparently wanted Teardrop and Britha dead more than he needed the captives' fear.

Fachtna and Bress stared at each other. Fachtna held his sword two-handed in a mid-guard; Bress, his bastard sword in one hand, the spear's case in the other, was much more relaxed.

'You have done a lot of damage by coming here,' Fachtna said. Bress's laughter was devoid of humour.

'Have you painted yourself the hero here?'

'I'm not trying to kill thousands of people.'

'Not here perhaps, but tell me how you live outside the laws of causality. Because you have decided that you are a good man? Your actions as much as ours, well maybe not as much as ours, have re-written the future. What you left is no longer there, not that either of us would ever remember what has been.'

'Assuming that time/space does not crack.'

'Time/space is more rugged than you give it credit for, believe me.'

'What you're doing is monstrous.'

'Only from a very limited and selfish perspective. What we are doing is speeding up the inevitable. If you had really wanted to stop us, then you should have sent more than two.'

'Limited resources,' Fachtna told him. 'Are we going to fight?'

'This isn't a fight, it's a murder.'

The tiny part of Teardrop's psyche that was alive no longer resembled anything even remotely like a sane human mind. The crystal parasite was a kaleidoscopic spider's web, straddling planes of existence and non-existence, trapping the suffering of the vessels of pain and feeding it back down into the electric signals that surged through biological existence.

Then the pain stopped. What had been Teardrop struggled like a broken thing in his own fractured and hellish mindscapes filled with impossible things that humanity had not evolved enough to perceive without their minds shattering.

The crystal network reached out for an instinctive understanding. What it found instead was darkness surging back, feeding down to the pain vessels, controlling them, enslaving them. The darkness was a tiny part of something immense, but its power nearly overwhelmed the parasite's web. Then the parasite shifted until it found the right path and started to tentatively taste the dark thing.

Crom Dhubh could not even remember pain. He savoured a sensation that to him was as new, but he still screamed as he tore his hands and face from her flesh. He could destroy the parasite, he knew that. After all it was the creature's unfertilised eggs, or at least what they could make of the eggs in three-dimensional space, that they had at great expense harvested to put in the heads of the pain vessels.

He could destroy the parasite, of that he had no doubt, but he needed his power and he did not want to give it any more access than it already had. Let him block the fear. There was blood in the water now. It would mean expending more of his power than he had wanted, but he could force her to open the way now. He could induce the horrible birth.

Blades flickered out at a bewildering speed: strike, parry and counter-strike. Bress had a bad mixture of speed and strength; his blade had more reach, and he defended himself too well for Fachtna to get inside that reach without losing significant amounts of flesh.

Smoke billowed up through the planks as if they were over a volcanic vent. Every swing of a blade caused eddies in the smoke. No blood had been drawn, but Fachtna was the one being forced back. He felt his back hit the framework of the wicker man. Bress swung. Fachtna ducked under the blade and threw himself into a forward roll. He felt Bress slice a layer of flesh off his back, the other man's sword going straight through his armour. Bress's sword cut through the wicker man's framework and swung through the smoke-filled air outside the cage.

Fachtna rolled to his feet. He knew that the wound on his back would not be healing any time soon, as the nanites that impregnated Bress's blade attacked the nanites that would normally knit his flesh together again.

Bress hit Fachtna with a back kick that he had no business trying in a sword fight where incredibly sharp implements were being waved around at speed. The kick took Fachtna off his feet and sent him flying over the planks. Bress stalked after him. Fachtna scrabbled to his feet and turned just in time to parry a powerful strike.

'I could make the metal come alive and hold you down,' Bress told Fachtna.

The massive two-handed strike that almost forced him to his knees shouldn't have been so fast, Fachtna thought. With just enough strength to hold Bress's blade away from him, Fachtna kneed the taller man. Bress showed no sign of having felt it. He threw Fachtna back and kicked him in the stomach, causing him to stumble. The arc of Bress's sword somehow looked lazy to Fachtna but he knew that he could not get his blade up to parry it. Bress opened up Fachtna's thigh but did not sever anything vital. That was when Fachtna realised that he was being played with.

It had gone quiet below but then the screams restarted. Sounds of true panic. Moments later, the smell of human flesh cooking. Fachtna knew that the bottom level had caught fire.

Britha fought like she had never fought before, her spear striking at any that got too close. Then there had been too many and they had pulled the spear from her. Then she had fought with the sickle. Then she had fought with her hands, feet and forehead, and finally nails and teeth, desperately trying to keep them away from Teardrop. But they were all over her. They were going to tear her apart with their bare hands and they were going to do the same to Teardrop.

Then it was over. Then they were people again, not demon-ridden slaves. They dropped her, confused and frightened, many of them wounded. They dropped her onto the soiled planks and she curled up into a ball, sobbing. They backed away from her.

'*Ban draoi?*' The words spoken in her own language, the familiarity of the voice, made her open her eyes. She recognised the child despite her soot-covered face and red-raw eyes. A girl from Ardestie, a daughter of one of the landsfolk families. What made her cry harder than anything was that she could not remember her name.

Through the grief and the panic, the girl's concern made her remember why she was there. A monstrous force was fostering fear and pain in her people and drinking it to poison a goddess. She sat up and looked over at Teardrop. His mouth was moving but he was beyond language now.

Panic. Screams from below as the lowest level of the wicker man's torso caught fire.

The massive bronze crescent of one of the great axe's blades bisected Teardrop's skull. He collapsed sideways, well and truly dead.

'You fucking whore!' Hanno screamed at her in Carthaginian. 'You did this to me! You soiled my luck with your blood sacrifices on a ship holy to Dagon!' His was the second head on Ettin's lopsided and broad shoulders.

'I'll mount you up here so you can watch me rape your corpse,' Ettin told her. 'You'll learn to stay dead when I kill you.'

Grief and fear was gone. Ettin swung Kush's axe down at her. Britha rolled away, grabbing her hungry spear as she came up onto her feet. Cold anger had replaced everything.

'Come and die,' she told the monster. He stalked through the smoke towards her.

Fachtna was grinning, laughing. It was easy now. He knew he was going to die. He stopped caring about winning, stopped caring about getting hurt. Any blow that didn't look like it was going to kill him immediately, he took.

Bress opened up his upper left arm from shoulder to elbow, severing tendons, making it useless. Fachtna spat blood at him and laughed as he screamed in pain and made a reckless backhanded upwards cut. The hot ghost-like blade cut through Bress's armour, piercing flesh and carrying on up to cut into his face.

Bress lurched back. Fachtna side-kicked him, staggering the tall thin man, though he lost some of his right leg doing it. He moved forward after Bress, but his leg gave out under him. That didn't matter. He left himself open as he chopped down at his opponent's head. Bress got his blade up barely in time to parry, but the force of Fachtna's blow brought the tip of his blade down onto Bress's head, opening it up. Blood poured down his pale face. Bress had finished humouring Fachtna.

She felt the force of the axe blow reverberate down her arms as she blocked it with the haft. Had the spear not been Lochlannach magic, the axe would have cut straight through. Britha kicked out under the spear. It was a solid blow, but Ettin barely felt it. Instead he brought the axe back for a two-handed sideways blow. Britha hit him with the butt of the spear in the face. Except it was Hanno's face. The Carthaginian's eyes rolled up into his head but he did not lose consciousness. Instead he drooled blood as he continued screaming obscenities at her.

She needed to put distance between her and Ettin so she could use the spear. Ettin swung at her. Britha leaped, bringing her knees up.

The axe swished under them. She landed and moved to the side and away from Ettin, through the smoke.

The captives were trying to give them as much room as they could, though from the screams they knew that all that waited for them below was fire and death.

Britha stabbed out with her spear. Ettin parried it with the haft of his axe, knocking it away so hard Britha almost lost her grip on it. She went with the momentum of the parry and swung the spear around her head as she backed away from Ettin's approach. She turned the circular movement of the spear into a thrust. He was ready for her. He caught the spear with the axe and, one-handed, yanked it out of her grip, dragging her forward. He dropped the spear and punched her in the face, sending her staggering back to the sound of Hanno's cheers. Britha grabbed for the sickle still hanging from her side by the remains of her rope belt. Ettin side-kicked her and took her off her feet. She hit the floor hard as he raised the axe above his head to Hanno's exultant shouting.

Bress caught Fachtna's sword hand at the wrist. He smashed the warrior in the face with the hilt of his sword, then brought the blade down on Fachtna's sword arm, severing tendons. Fachtna's sword fell away from unfeeling fingers. Fachtna spat at his foe, and Bress flung the Gael away from him. Fachtna landed on the edge of the still-hot area that had been destroyed by the dragon. He tried to get to a kneeling position but now both his arms were useless. Bress helped him to kneel by pulling Fachtna up by his hair. Bress took several steps back. The wind caught the smoke and Fachtna saw clear blue sky. *It's a really nice day*, he thought, *and I have accomplished much.*

Bress swung his sword.

The two halves of Fachtna's body tumbled out of the wicker man into clear blue sky, only to be swallowed by smoke.

Even as she grabbed for the sickle, she knew it was too late. The axe fell. Ettin was yanked back, the head of the axe biting into the planks just in front of Britha. Kush and Germelqart each had one of Ettin's arms and were dragging him away from her. Hanno screamed at them to stop.

With one arm, Ettin threw Kush off, sending the large powerful man flying into the framework. Kush bounced off and hit the floor. Ettin grabbed Germelqart with the other hand, lifted the Carthaginian off the floor by his head and then started to squeeze. The navigator screamed.

Britha was searching around desperately for her spear.

Tangwen jumped high into the air behind Ettin and buried her dirk deep into his real head. Ettin roared and tossed Germelqart away. He turned. Tangwen was backing away. Ettin cuffed the hunter so hard that she too was flung into and bounced off the wicker man's framework.

Ettin turned back to Britha, who rammed her spear into his fat stomach and drove it up into his ribcage, all the while staring straight into his eyes. She wanted to watch the light go out.

With a roar Kush brought his axe down on Ettin's shoulder, driving the bronze blade diagonally into his chest, where it met the metal branches growing out her spear's head.

'It's my axe!' he screamed.

As Ettin sank to the floor, Britha knelt down with him to watch death come to his eyes.

Satisfied, she stood up and went to check on Tangwen. Kush put his foot on Ettin's body and wrenched his axe free. Then he lifted it high and cut off Hanno's head.

'I'm sorry, old friend. You deserved better.' Then he decapitated Ettin just to be on the safe side.

Tangwen was in tears.

'I'm so sorry. The swim, the climb ...' She stared at Teardrop's body, guilt all over her face.

'It's okay,' Britha said.

Germelqart was getting unsteadily to his feet, aided by Kush. Both of them bore the ravages of their captivity.

'I told you I heard Hanno,' Kush told the navigator.

'Do you still want my power?' Teardrop asked, though his voice sounded wrong. All of them turned to stare. His lips were moving; the rest of his body looked very dead. The muscles on his face were slack, making the movements of his mouth all the more obscene, particularly as his head had been cut in half and one set of lips was slightly out of synch with the other. Inside his swollen skull they could see the crystal moving like it was alive, or rather like it was many living things.

'That should not be happening,' the normally taciturn Germelqart said. 'I do not like Ynys Prydein and will not come back here.'

It took Britha a moment or two to realise that the odd rasping noise was Teardrop's laughter. Kush raised his axe.

'The dead should be still,' the tall black man insisted.

'Wait,' Britha said, though she almost completely agreed with him.

'You so wanted my power,' Teardrop said. He was right. Now she could not think of anything she wanted less. 'It's a heavy price. You have no idea, but you are not done yet.'

Britha felt tears spring into her eyes but knelt down by Teardrop. The crystal tendrils that reached for her from his ears, nose, mouth, eyes, that flowed from the grisly split in his head, did not look wholly real.

As they pushed into her head, touched her mind, shattered it, rebuilt it so she could at least perceive – though never understand – she screamed until her throat bled, then they felt very real.

She became a border. She saw the rest of everything that was this tiny space. She drooled blood as the meat part of her mind tried to shut down. Her mind grew beyond the stinking sweet prison of her flesh into other space beyond the ken of the people around her, who cowered away as her cranium bulged and the crystal parasite consumed the meat of her brain and forced its tendrils into her veins and arteries, making them swell.

It wasn't just Britha who opened mercury eyes.

Bress stalked out of the smoke, bloody sword in hand. Kush raised his axe; Tangwen, her dirk still in Ettin's skull, grabbed her hand axe from her belt.

Bress glanced down at Ettin's body. There was a slight smile on his lips. The smile disappeared as he looked at Britha's inhuman eyes. She stood to face him.

'It's still me,' she told him.

'For now. Your friend is dead,' he told them, and then, so there was no confusion, 'I killed him.' He nodded outside. Kush, Germelqart and Tangwen turned to look. Britha did not; she had felt the violation opening. Circles of blue pulsing light, and through it living, squirming, black, bacteria-like nothings, reached for its antithesis. To what was left of Britha it was like the sky was being eaten by maggots. It sought to touch the Muileartach and make her the same as her sisters, to corrupt the last progenitor.

'No,' Germelqart said and sat down hard. Kush was praying to the gods of his childhood, forgotten until now. Tangwen started to weep again.

Blister-like growths broke the surface of the water to the west and vomited forth monstrosities into the water and onto the land, the fruits of a womb poisoned by Crom Dhubh.

Beneath the wicker man the water was a red froth as the captives from it were attacked from beneath the surface.

Britha could not bear to turn to look at their failure just yet.

'Will you make me kill you?' Bress asked.

'We will take our chances in the water,' Britha told him as quick-silver tears rolled down her face.

'Go lower. I have opened the way for you,' he told her.

Britha stepped forward, wrapped her arms around his neck and kissed him.

'I must kill you,' she told him when they had finished, though she was still holding him, looking up at him. He nodded. She noticed that he was carrying the case that Fachtna had borne since he'd known her.

Bress turned and walked into smoke and flame.

30
Now

A huge gun, shining and silver, held by a monster. Muzzle flash, slide going back in slow motion, used cartridge being ejected. Then the same again. Like getting punched in the chest, hard, except you don't die when you get punched in the chest.

Beth gasped for breath and sat upright. She'd been killed. There was an afterlife. It looked like a motorway being negotiated at speed in a bloodstained Range Rover with spiderweb cracks in the windscreen.

'Not professional. It was strange – they had skills but they acted like it was a school shooting spree.' There was a pause. 'Yes, download the satellite footage.' Another pause. She was trying to recognise the voice. She'd been in a gunfight. No, that was ridiculous. She didn't know the first thing about guns. Even as she thought that, all her knowledge about firearms became apparent to her. 'I have the possibles. Yes, it's likely they've changed the vehicle's colour and plates.' Another pause. His name was du Bois. He'd killed people in front of her. He wanted her sister. 'We need to stop it. Police involvement worries me because the van's armoured and they're heavily armed. They'll walk through the police but it could get Natalie hurt. That said, we need to stop them and a roadblock is the best idea I have.' Another pause. 'They are very resistant to damage. We need more nanite-tipped rounds.'

Beth turned to look at du Bois. He was driving like a lunatic, weaving the Range Rover in and out of the angry traffic. He was covered in drying blood.

'Understood.' This seemed to signal the end of the conversation though he wore no headset and she hadn't heard the other side of the conversation from the Range Rover's speakers.

'What?' Beth managed. She didn't feel hurt, just weak and hungry.

'You have no idea, do you?'

'What?' she managed again.

'Someone's put a lot of tiny machines called nanites in you. They're very advanced. It's technology derived from one or more ancient alien civilisations.'

'What?' Beth wondered why he would make this nonsense up.

'You'll have to cope with the denial later. Suffice to say, unless the damage is too much or there's too little left of your body, they will put you back together.' He slewed the Range Rover off the hard shoulder, up the slope at the side of the road and then back down onto the motorway in front of a furious driver who was liberally using his horn to critique du Bois's driving.

'Where?' she asked, thinking this would be easier.

'On the way to Southampton airport to stop the very nasty gentlemen who have kidnapped your sister from getting onto a private jet and flying somewhere even less convenient than Hampshire.' Du Bois drifted the Range Rover across three lanes as they headed up a hill. Beth glanced behind her to see Portsmouth disappearing from view.

'Those people ...'

'Who? The gunmen? They're up ahead. Their van has changed colour and they're driving carefully. I have a satellite link feeding me footage. At least I think it's them. There are a couple of possibilities.'

'I don't understand.'

'The footage? It's being fed directly into my head. Remember those tiny machines we discussed.' He was clearly mad. She still had her great-grandfather's bayonet and suddenly she was hell on wheels in a gunfight and could survive being shot. She saw the faces of the zombies one after another as she'd shot them almost instinctively.

'No, not the gunmen. The zombies.' Du Bois didn't say anything, just concentrated on weaving in and out of the traffic. 'They were dead, weren't they?'

'They were slaved. Normal people who had been infected with a specific type of nanite that allows someone else to control them.'

'Innocent people?'

'Yes.'

Beth started to shake.

'Could they have been helped?'

'Given time and resources.' After he had answered honestly, it did occur to him that it would have been better to lie.

Beth was not prone to hysteria, or panic, or tears, but she felt a pressure in her chest and was finding it difficult to catch her breath. She was also shaking like a leaf. Du Bois spared a glance at her. He could see how pale she was, even covered in dry blood. He wished he could have this sort of response, a normal healthy response, to having just killed a lot of people who largely didn't deserve it. Instead for him it was a very cold and clinical, some would say cynical, equation. He would kill tens and many thousands would survive.

'Okay, Beth. If you concentrate you can control this.'

'Control this? Control this! I've just committed mass murder with some fucking madman! I don't want to control this!'

'We had no choice. The death of those people was the fault of the men who have your sister. I need to know if you want your sister back.' They were on the hard shoulder now, undertaking car after car.

'You bastard.'

Manipulative or not, he needed her help.

'Undoubtedly. I need you to handle a gun. Are you with me?' She said nothing but he noticed that the shaking had stopped.

'Why didn't we just drive away with Talia? This thing's armoured, right?' Beth asked, though in the heat of the gunfight it hadn't occurred to her.

'We were armed to the teeth and very difficult to kill. It never occurred to me that we'd lose.'

'So they can't be killed either?'

'There are ways, and I'm carrying two now.' He had his .45 back. It was loaded with the only magazine of nanite-tipped bullets he had. He also had the punch dagger on his belt buckle. Beth didn't say anything.

King Jeremy glanced in the side mirrors again. It was definitely the same Range Rover and it was closing on them fast. They must have been augmented somehow, which worried him. He'd heard rumours of other agencies that knew about the lost tech. He'd heard names like the City of Brass and the Circle but nothing more than that. If the goth girl was living tech, it could explain why others would be interested. He assumed they hadn't fallen for the cosmetic changes they'd made to the van. The gunfight had been fun but he didn't relish another.

Dracimus was next to him in the van's cab. He hadn't stopped talking about the fight and shooting the blond guy. Baron Albedo was in the back looking after the girl and stopping Inflictor from doing anything to her. Jeremy was trying to decide whether or not to try and bluff it or put some more of his uploaded skills into use and drive like he was playing Fire and Gasoline. British cars were boring. He had a pretty good visual overlay to make the whole thing look cooler if he went for it. He wanted to, but getting out of the country stealthily would make life easier.

Inflictor made the decision for him. King Jeremy heard one of the hatches on the rear window being popped.

'Inflictor!' King Jeremy screamed. His voice was drowned out by the thunder of big-bore rounds.

Du Bois was trying to make up his mind if it was them or not. The muzzle flashes, the roar of automatic fire and the sparks on the road helped. It looked like an entire magazine was fired. Du Bois was yanking the steering wheel from side to side, braking hard and then accelerating even harder as he tried to dodge the cars screaming to a halt or that had been hit. The cars that braked got rear-ended. One crashed into the central reservation, flipping into the lanes on the other side of the motorway. A tumbling, airborne car sideswiped the Range Rover. Du Bois fought with the vehicle, feeling two of its wheels leave the ground. He wrestled it back down onto all four.

Inflictor ejected one magazine and rammed home another. This one had red tape around the bottom of it. He poked it out through the firing hatch and pulled the trigger.

'King J?' Baron Albedo called.

'Go ahead!' Jeremy had to shout over the roar of the gunfire. Baron Albedo moved to the firing port in the other rear window.

Tracer fire filled the air, drawing lines of phosphorescent light between the van and the Range Rover, the lines continuing onwards as the rounds bounced off armour. There were two guns firing out the back of the van now. The second was accurate. Round after round impacted. The first was all over the place, firing at anything that moved, even cars on the opposite side of the road, causing more crashes as cars tumbled and flew through the air.

Du Bois accelerated, trying to get between the van and other vehicles. Their side of the road was mostly clear. The opening salvo had caused a pile-up that had effectively blocked the road behind them.

'This many rounds, they must be Americans,' du Bois muttered.

'What now?' Beth demanded over the sound of bullets impacting and the vehicle's screaming engine.

'We find a way to stop it without getting your sister killed!' he shouted back. He hoped that the roadblock would work.

Then the ground started to shake. It shook so much that du Bois had to slow down to maintain control. He noticed that the van did the same. A crack in the motorway went shooting past – Du Bois almost crashed in astonishment. Something shot up out of the ground and grabbed the underside of the van.

For a moment he thought they'd run over someone. Which would have been cool. They'd just leave a red smear on the concrete, King Jeremy thought. Then the van stopped.

Seat belts bit into Dracimus and King Jeremy's torsos. Talia had been laid on the floor and was slowly being buried in hot shell casings, her head towards the back of the van. Now her legs bent and she almost stood upright against the back of Dracimus' seat. Baron Albedo hit her hard as Inflictor flew into the back of King Jeremy's seat.

There was the tinkling of spent cartridges falling to the floor. Then nothing.

Jeremy recovered first. 'Is she all right?' he demanded. 'Is she fucking broken?!' *This could not be for nothing*, he thought wildly.

'She's banged up but fine,' a dazed Baron Albedo told him.

Du Bois had both feet on the brake as he tried to stop the Range Rover. The four-by-four left a lot of rubber on the road but stopped twenty feet short of the van.

Beth and du Bois looked in amazement at the tentacle sticking out of the road.

'Is this normal?' she asked in a small voice.

'It's really not,' du Bois said, his eight hundred or so years of experience proving useless now.

There was the sound of more automotive carnage. On the opposite side of the road a large articulated lorry had jack-knifed in the road, blocking all four lanes of traffic. To du Bois's eyes it looked like it had been done on purpose. A car swerved and shot up the bank into the air and then turned over. More and more cars hit the truck. One came straight through the lorry's trailer. In front of the lorry a Portsmouth city bus was coming to a halt.

Something burst out of the side of the bus. It was moving too quickly to make out clearly, but it had a wedge-shaped head, looked armoured, moved like a predatory animal but was vaguely humanoid in shape, though with entirely too many limbs. Landing on the road, it leaped at the van.

Something hit the side of the van.

'Hey!' Baron Albedo said as Inflictor grabbed his Desert Eagle while drawing his own so he had one in each hand.

The side of the van was torn open.

Beth opened the passenger door of the Range Rover, climbed out and aimed the FAL carbine through the gap between the door and the vehicle. Du Bois was out of the other side, the Benelli shotgun in his hands.

Men and women poured out of the bus at a shambling run. There was something wrong with them. With horror, Beth realised that they all looked like the thing that she had fought in the greyhound stadium. Du Bois fired the shotgun again and again and again at them. The shotgun blasts were knocking them down but not killing them, but du Bois needed the nanite-tipped bullets in the .45 for the gunmen in the van. He was pretty sure they were the DAYP.

There was the sound of gunfire from the van. The six-limbed armoured creature staggered back but did not fall. There were cries of panic from inside.

The sliding door on the van's passenger side slid open. Beth watched as the big one stumbled backwards out, firing a pistol in each hand back into the van. She started firing. Aim. Short burst. Correct. Short burst. Repeat. Round after round hit the big one with the inhuman face. She turned him red, firing so quickly that although they were controlled bursts it was almost like she'd emptied the entire magazine into him at once. He stumbled with every impact, bringing one of the Desert Eagles up to fire at her ineffectively. She ducked behind the door, reloaded quickly and then fired another thirty rounds in short bursts at him until he fell over.

Then the door on the other side of the Range Rover was ripped off.

Too many. The shotgun was the wrong weapon. He heard the rapid firing of the carbine from the other side of the Range Rover – Beth was holding up her side of things. He fired the last round from the shotgun and let it drop on its sling. By now some of them had made it to the van. He could make them out crowding around the van and dragging someone, presumably Talia, out.

The six-limbed thing turned and looked at him as if noticing him for the first time. At least du Bois assumed it was looking; he could see no eyes on the bony, ridged, fan-like head. It bounded straight at him with surprising speed. He only just got out of the way as the door where he'd been standing moments before was ripped off its hinges. Du Bois fast-drew the .45 and at point-blank range fired again, and again, and again. The entire magazine was gone in moments. It sprawled across the tarmac, leaking some kind of violet fluid. The .45

was smoking, its slide back. Du Bois stared at the thing. He'd used all the nano-tipped rounds he had.

Two more of them clambered out of the passenger side of the van's cab. Unerringly Beth poured fire onto them as they tried to bring their weapons to bear. Driven by a cold rage, she was giving some thought to going over there and sawing their heads off with her bayonet when she had finished shooting them.

Du Bois ejected the magazine from the .45 and slammed in another. Firing from one knee, he started putting two rounds into each of the mutated people carrying Talia. They staggered and some fell, but there were too many and he had to be careful not to shoot the girl.

He stood up, ejected the magazine, reloaded and fired again, walking towards the bus, using a different approach now – shooting them until they went down. Two more hit the ground, but they were still moving. He suspected he was putting a lot of rounds into members of the Solent Sub-Aqua Exploration Club. Another magazine hit the tarmac as a new one was slammed home. He'd grabbed more magazines from the compartment in the back of the Range Rover after the gunfight in Old Portsmouth, but after this one he only had one more left.

The shot caught him in the shoulder, spinning him around. The ragged nano-fabric woven into the rags of his leather coat hardened, as did his skin. Had he been a normal man, the hydrostatic shock would have blown the limb off. One of the gunmen was firing through the rip in the side of the van. Du Bois turned on him, firing one-handed as he advanced, his left arm rapidly healing. Few of the shots were hitting but they had the desired effect of making the shooter keep his head down. When his left hand could move again, he pulled a fragmentation grenade out of his pocket and yanked the pin out with his right. He let the spoon flip off, his internal systems counting for him. Baron Albedo was firing as the grenade flew into the van.

The second was down but the third had made it to cover in front of the van and was returning fire. Beth was switching between suppressing him and putting more rounds in the two on the ground to prevent them from healing.

The van exploded. Beth prayed her sister hadn't still been in there.

Du Bois had already turned and was sliding his last magazine home into the .45. The bus was beginning to pull away. He started running, trying to get an angle to fire on the driver. He risked two shots but they went wide. He fired the remaining six into what he was pretty sure was the engine block, but the bus kept on going.

He heard and his blood-screen told him that there was someone coming up behind him. He turned to see a man staggering across the tarmac, skin and flesh regrowing as he made his way towards him. Du Bois grabbed the punch dagger from his belt buckle and rammed it into Baron Albedo's throat. The blade of the dagger disintegrated into nanites that surged through Albedo's systems, quickly overcoming the young man's own nanite defences as they sought ways to kill him.

Baron Albedo, aka Clifford Sharman, had once been a nice kid from a little town in north-western Idaho who got picked on for being clever. He died on a stretch of motorway a long way from home.

Du Bois holstered the .45, ran back to the Range Rover and jumped into the driver's seat, throwing the shotgun in the back. A lot of the mutated people he'd shot were starting to get up. He could hear sirens and there was a helicopter in the air above them. Du Bois prayed it was police and not media.

'Beth!' he shouted. Beth jumped in. 'They've got Talia.'

'What the fuck were you doing?' she demanded. He put the Range Rover into gear and gunned it forward. Du Bois ran over Inflictor Doorstep and Dracimus. King Jeremy ran for cover around the other side of the smoking van as they passed. Beth glared at du Bois. He felt her stare but did not acknowledge it. He'd failed her.

There was no door on du Bois's side. He reached over and pulled his seat belt on as he drove. Beth did likewise and then loaded another magazine into the hot-barrelled FAL. Neither of them noticed that the tentacle that had exploded out of the earth to bring the van to a halt had gone.

Du Bois took the Range Rover up the bank at the side of the motorway and into farmland, taking it across country to a road that would get them heading back in the general direction of Portsmouth. As soon as they were on the road he had another one-sided conversation with himself, requesting that the police stay off his back. Then he was requesting more satellite footage.

'Do you know where they are taking her?' Beth asked. Du Bois nodded and then asked her to get something from the gun compartment in the back of the car.

Passing over the M27, they got a chance to see the carnage they'd help create, two severe pile-ups, one each side of the motorway. The emergency services were struggling to respond. It had happened so

461

quickly and much of Portsmouth's fire, ambulance and police personnel would be at the site of the gunfight in Old Portsmouth. Circle influence or not, du Bois didn't think that he'd be able to get out of this one. Someone would be hung out to dry, and publicly. You couldn't keep blaming the Muslims. On the other hand, Europeans had been doing that since the Crusades – he of all people should know that.

Up onto Portsdown Hill, looking down on Portsmouth and Hayling Island next to it, on the other side of the Solent the Isle of Wight, a beautiful fresh sunny day with barely a cloud in the sky. *They were in a bus*, he thought. *How much further ahead could they be?*

Past Fort Southwick, Control started sending the satellite footage directly into his skull. Not dodgy low-resolution, spy-satellite footage, but footage from the Circle's own satellites, though they pre-dated the Circle; in fact, they pre-dated humanity. He saw the bus pulling into the lock-up at Fort Widley from high above.

There was no subtlety or stealth involved. Du Bois drove the Range Rover through the rickety wooden door of the lock-up in the Victorian fort, narrowly missing being impaled by splintering chunks of wood. He slammed on the brakes to avoid hitting the rear of the bus.

Beth and du Bois were out of the Range Rover. Checking all around them. Where their eyes went the barrels of their guns did as well. Beth still had the FAL carbine; du Bois carried the .45 calibre Heckler & Koch UMP sub-machine gun that Beth had got from the gun compartment in the back of the car.

The lock-up had the same feeling as it had the first time he had been there. Cavernous and empty. They moved through it quickly, searching. Beth found the sacrifices.

'Is this what they want her—'

'I very much doubt it. Focus.'

Beth shook herself out of it. Du Bois knew that she was very much playing a part at the moment. He'd dropped some high-end skills into her head, and her natural talents and level of fitness had allowed her to keep up and integrate them quickly, but she would pay for it later with migraines that would make her wish for death, and probably with internal bleeding as well.

He spotted misshapen footprints in the grime on the floor. He cursed himself. He should have checked this place more thoroughly. He should have been more emphatic to Control about the importance of following this up and dealing with it, regardless of whether Control needed every last resource at the moment. The footprints led him deeper into the racks of equipment and down into the tunnels that ran through the fort. He signalled Beth and she joined him. They followed the prints.

They found the entrance in a storeroom. The passage was seven feet high and five wide. It looked recently dug. The walls looked fused somehow, which to du Bois's mind wasn't structurally sound. He glanced at Beth.

'What dug this?' she asked. Something didn't look right. There was something more animal than human about this. On the other hand, it might have been her imagination playing tricks, what with all the strangeness of the last week.

'At a guess, the same thing that drove a tentacle through solid ground to stop a van.'

'Everyone wants Talia,' Beth muttered.

'Stay behind me and watch your shots. The rounds in your carbine will rip straight through people and into your sister; the ones in mine won't. Any doubts, grab the automatic from the holster at my hip and use that instead, okay?'

Beth nodded and tried not to think about how many rounds she had put into the air during the fight on the motorway.

Du Bois didn't say that if they encountered any more of the armoured six-limbed servitors they were in trouble because he had no more nanite-tipped bullets.

They crept into the tunnel. Moving swiftly, weapons ready. Du Bois was sure he could hear noises from further down.

It was a bump in the tunnel floor that gave it away. The walls of the tunnel, the roof and the rest of the floor were so smooth. It looked like someone had kicked up a bit of the floor on purpose. He stopped.

'What?' she asked.

He could hear her nervousness. Most of the rest of what had happened today had happened suddenly. Her system had been flooded with adrenaline, which her new augments would know how to use very efficiently if they were anything like his. But this walk into the tunnel was giving her a chance to think. Getting her scared. Giving her mind a chance to trip her up.

'Malcolm?' Nobody called him Malcolm except his sister.

'Turn back. We need to get out of here right now.'

'What? But—'

'Now!' They turned and sprinted back to the storeroom and then back out into the lock-up.

'What's going on?' Beth demanded.

'I think the tunnel was booby-trapped.'

'You think?'

'Would you prefer it if we were down there when it went off?'

463

'What about Talia?'

It wasn't so much that Beth was wearing him down – she had acquitted herself well, much better than most – it was more the day itself. It had been pretty intense, particularly for an operation on mainland Britain.

'I just thought, perhaps unreasonably, that looking for your sister WOULD BE EASIER WITHOUT THOUSANDS OF TONNES OF RUBBLE ON TOP OF US!' he screamed, finally losing it. Beth held her ground and looked like she was about to shout back. Du Bois was trying to work out how unprofessional it would be to have a cigarette. Meanwhile, he searched through the available information on the Solent Sub-Aqua Exploration Club via the liquid memory of his neuralware.

The tunnel blew. The door to the storeroom blew off its hinges; the collapsing tunnel squirted rubble out into the lock-up. Beth and du Bois were covered in dust.

'Andrew Coulson, a member of the diving club and a demolition engineer,' du Bois said, though he couldn't really see Beth through the thick cloud of dust.

'Did they have any lorry or bus drivers in the club?' Beth asked. Du Bois thought she sounded a little sheepish.

'Helen Smith, another member, had a full HGV licence, and Brian Wilcox was a retired bus driver.'

'Maybe we should get out of here?' Beth said.

'What an excellent idea.'

They walked back to the Range Rover.

'Do you know where they were going?'

'I have some ideas. McGurk said that Matthew Bryant, the one you fought, was found in a cellar in a house close to the front. If there's enough left of McGurk I'll ask him which house.' Beth looked at him sceptically. 'I don't know who or whatever they are, but they have their own access to S-tech.'

'S-tech?' Beth asked.

'I'll explain later.' *Or more likely it won't matter, because you'll be on a Circle operating table being vivisected, your nanites harvested,* he thought bitterly, knowing she really didn't deserve that. 'But basically, seeding the local vermin didn't work. And there's a city in the way of accurate satellite thermographics, and that's assuming they can't counter thermographics anyway, which seems unlikely.'

Beth was staring at him blankly. 'Are you just a madman?'

'I'm not. Sorry.'

She watched an idea dawn on his face and raised an eyebrow.

'When I spoke to Bryant's wife, she seemed to be hiding something, or holding something back,' he said.

They climbed back into the Range Rover as he instantly recalled Bryant's wife's address from his memory.

Down the hill through Cosham, onto the Southampton Road, under the motorway, Port Solent Marina and then Portsmouth Harbour proper on their left-hand side. Across the harbour they could see the grey stones of Portchester Castle. Beth noted that du Bois was driving less like a psycho now. Admittedly the roads were busy but she knew it meant less urgency. Less urgency meant less hope.

Du Bois turned the battered four-by-four, which was getting some stares – particularly as it was missing a door – into Castle Street. Beth noticed the nice houses down by the castle. She couldn't even begin to imagine living here or what that world was like. It was more alien to her, almost, than the madness of the last few days.

The air was full of the sounds of sirens. There were now several helicopters in the air. She could see one close to the Spinnaker Tower at Gun Wharf. She guessed that was over the scene of the gunfight in Old Portsmouth. The others were to the west over the carnage on the motorway.

Some kids pointed at the Range Rover as they drove by. Beth stared back because she was too numb to think about turning away.

Everything about the house looked nicely suburban. Beth tried to suppress her contempt. She knew this was based on envy. Right now she would have given anything to live there and be oblivious to the madness that hid under the surface of the real world.

There was an estate agent's For Sale sign stuck in the lawn with a big Sold sticker across it. The house looked empty. Du Bois didn't curse, he just seemed to sag in the driving seat. Then the door opened. The woman coming out looked like she had been attractive when she was younger and had tried to hold on to her looks by using too much make-up and hair dye. She glanced at the Range Rover and put the box she was carrying into the back of a Volvo estate. She glanced at them again and headed back to the house.

Du Bois concentrated momentarily.

'That's her.' He got out of the car and walked towards her. 'Anna Bryant?' She turned and stared at him. Apparently she didn't like what she saw and backed towards the house. Beth got out of the jeep as well. 'Mrs Bryant, I know we look a sight – it's been a pretty rough day – but my name is Malcolm du Bois and I'm with Special Branch.

We spoke over the phone.' He reached inside his torn and battered leather coat and pulled out his warrant card and held it up for her. She stopped but still looked like she might bolt at any moment.

'Is this to do with that?' she inclined her head towards the noise of the sirens.

'I'm afraid so. Can we talk in the house?'

She looked terrified but swallowed hard and then nodded. She must have worked out that it was something to do with her husband. Suddenly Beth felt absurdly guilty for the part she had played in his death.

'I'm afraid I can't offer you tea or coffee. We're moving ...' she said, embracing platitudes to put off a difficult situation just a little longer. Du Bois assured her that was fine with a degree of impatience in his voice. 'Why wouldn't they let me identify his body?' she suddenly demanded.

'A possible biohazard issue,' du Bois lied smoothly. It was the official cover story so the lie came easily. Mrs Bryant looked stricken. 'When we spoke on the phone I was sure that you were holding something back. We need to know what that is, and we need to know now, I'm afraid.' She had started shaking her head before he had finished talking.

'I don't know what you're talking about.' The lie and guilt were obvious.

Du Bois looked angry. Even so, Beth was shocked when a knife appeared in his hand and he rammed Anna Bryant back into the wall, putting the blade up against her throat.

'Look we don't have—'

Du Bois was astonished when Beth grabbed him by the back of his coat, spun him round and slammed him into the door frame so hard he fell to the floor.

Beth stood over him. 'What the fuck?' she demanded. Du Bois looked apoplectic. 'Not everything's about bloody murder! Do you understand me?! Now you fucking stay down there and think about what you've done!' she continued before turning to the terrified Mrs Bryant.

Beth managed to calm her down and get the story from her. After she had reported him missing, after they had waited the requisite amount of time, after she had had him legally declared dead, she had seen him in the street, but he had looked odd. She had been too frightened to report it because it would have meant losing the insurance money and calling into question the house sale. She had not said anything because she assumed that he had abandoned her and the children.

Mrs Bryant had seen him go into a house on Alhambra Road opposite South Parade Pier.

There was silence as they climbed into the Range Rover.

'You angry with me?' Beth asked.

'Yes.'

'Good. I'm really fucking angry with you. Want to take it out on somebody else?'

'Yes, I do.' Du Bois started the Range Rover, put it into gear and drove off.

31

A Long Time After the Loss

The death of the *Basilisk* had been brutal. As soon as the bulk freighter carrying the Monk and Scab – hidden in the stomach of livestock – left Pangean space, the Church frigate opened fire on the *Basilisk*.

There was no way Scab could receive any form of communication during the infiltration, but even so the name of the game was to hit the *Basilisk* so hard its comms wouldn't have time to do anything. All the beam batteries on the port side of the frigate fired, drawing lines of light and spatial distortion to the converted Corsair-class ship. At the same time all the kinetic shot racks were also emptied. The *Basilisk*'s energy dissipation grid flared briefly before the ship burst and, to all intents and purposes, ceased to be.

More than a little of the Pangean orbital station the *Basilisk* was docked with was also damaged. Weapon systems locked onto the *St Brendan's Fire* as Pangean naval craft sought to reach firing positions in higher orbits. The Living Cities immediately lodged protests both with the frigate and with Church authorities on Pangea. The Church apologised, explained it was a Church sanction and offered to pay compensation, but behind all their apologies was the unuttered threat of sanctions. The Pangean authorities let it go.

None of which mattered to Vic. Disguised as wreckage, he was being propelled by a jet of gas towards the *St Brendan's Fire*. He was wearing the finest power-assisted combat armour that debt could buy, with some illegal upgrade modifications done by Scab and himself. They had put every bit of naughty stealth technology they could find into the armour, and he was running it with minimal systems.

He watched the *St Brendan's Fire* get bigger and bigger. If it moved, he, no they, were screwed, Vic thought. He'd then have to activate his P-sat, currently attached to the back of his armour in a heavy combat chassis, make his way back to a Pangean orbital habitat and try to disappear. Which would be difficult if the Church was after him.

The Church frigate didn't move. Vic did get a little worried when the frigate started breaking up bits of rubble with its laser batteries. Fortunately he seemed to be too small for them to go after. They stopped firing on the rubble when an automated Pangean weapons platform put a warning shot across their bows.

Minute jets of gas adjusted his course. He was aiming for a weak spot in the frigate's external surveillance, but he knew that his trajectory would have to be just right or he would be detected. Fortunately they did not have a coherent energy shield up. It was just too expensive to keep running constantly, and few people were prepared to attack the Church, let alone on their own. Once again Vic reflected on his own stupidity and cursed the existence of Scab.

Contact. The glove on his armour stuck itself to the composite hull of the religious warship. He pulled himself down onto the hull. Close by he could make out friezes of alien cityscapes designed to represent the Seeder civilisation picked out on the craft's hull. He was pretty sure the friezes showed the fall of the Naga. Pulling himself down behind an extruded statue of one of the six-armed, wedge-headed Seeders on its cross, Vic adhered himself properly to the ship. He activated various low-power stealth systems and down-powered himself into a death-like trance, as close to suspended animation as he could get.

Vic woke. There was just a moment of disorientation and then surprise that they were in Red Space. Then fear as he saw the blackened skeletons of trees. He risked looking around. The strange and massive tree-like skeletons were everywhere. He had heard stories of places in Red Space, xeno-archaeological digs in ancient ruins, some said ruins that predated the existence of Real Space, but he had thought them just stories. He didn't think such stories being real boded well for him.

This would be the most dangerous part of the operation, he thought. *Well, this and trying to wrangle Scab's vicious little pet.* He placed a blob of a putty-like substance against the hull. It didn't look like much but its cost must have been astronomical. After all, you're not meant to hack the matter of armoured spaceship hulls, even if the armour is reactive smart matter.

Vic didn't like the feeling of sinking through liquid carbon. Everything was black around him. It was like a very slow free fall following the putty, which had spread out into a thin blanket. As he fell, the liquid carbon became solid explosive-infused reactive armour above him. He had nightmarish thoughts of fusing with the armour, to be ejected when a kinetic shot hit as the armour exploded out to counter the shot's impact. On the other hand, if the frigate's crew detected anything, all they would see was a glitch in the armour that would need to be checked the next time they were in dry dock, presumably at the Cathedral.

Vic felt himself hit the hull proper of the frigate. He spent some time in total blackness that neither his nor the suit's optics could pierce, working via pre-programmed touch to place a circle of very powerful thermal seeds against the hull. He used the putty sheet of programmable smart matter to act as tamping and to isolate the thermal seeds from the liquid carbon, because if anyone had ever done this before then they hadn't bothered to record the results of any chemical reaction. Even so, there was a moment of fear after Vic 'faced the detonation code to the thermal seeds when he thought he saw a faint glow though the blackness.

Vic and the sheet of programmable smart matter fell through the hole in the hull of the ship in a rain of liquid carbon. Vic landed agilely and, for someone in full combat armour, reasonably quietly, on all six limbs. No alarms went off because there was no need for alarms. Ships couldn't be penetrated in this way. Above his head the carbon immediately started to harden into more useful armour.

Vic's biggest problem now was the surveillance aspect of the ship's internal nano-screen. His nano-screen had been augmented with the best stealth nanites that money could buy on the free market, but the Church had infinitely more resources than he and Scab did, even with the pair's mysterious and obviously wealthy backer. Scab had sampled some of the Church Militia's nano-screens during the fight at Arclight, and in theory Vic's screen was supposed to belong to one of them, but he knew it wouldn't last for long. *Best get on with it then,* he thought.

His nano-screen picked up someone's approach. Vic backed into a doorway. He saw a feline in the uniform of a lay Church crew member come into the corridor, stop and then advance more cautiously as he saw the hole.

Vic, despite his current bulk, moved nearly silently behind the feline. The first the crewman knew was when Vic extended all four sword-like blades from his arms as he towered over the feline and then stabbed them into his flesh in the right places to kill him instantly.

Vic retracted the blades. He felt no real remorse for killing the feline – he wasn't really wired up that way – he just sort of knew it was a waste and wondered if a crew member on a Church frigate had good clone insurance. The blades had held up the feline and the body started to fall when they came out of his flesh. Vic caught and then easily picked up the corpse and took it with him. No point spending time trying to hide it. He only had so much time before the ship's nano-screen detected him.

Vic detached the P-sat in its combat chassis, a heavier and more armoured weapons platform with increased targeting and sensor capabilities. Vic immediately started receiving feed from the P-sat 'faced directly to his neuonics.

Vic went one way at a corner, the P-sat the other. Vic reached his destination first. He was standing before a plain metal door in a plain metal corridor. The door opened somewhat unexpectedly. The Church Militiaman, thankfully without armour on, stared at Vic in his full combat armour. Vic didn't hesitate. He threw the dead feline at the human male. The Militiaman staggered back.

Vic was aware via the 'face feed from the P-sat that it had launched tiny AG-driven, hunter-killer smart rounds. They were designed to seek out and kill automatons and other autonomous weapon systems like ship-controlled P-sats.

Vic had to do as much damage to the ship's company as he could in as little time as possible before the security systems caught up with him. He stepped into the bunk area. Everything seemed to slow down. Men and women, mostly human, mostly base gender, raced for their personal weapons. Vic drew his triple-barrelled shotgun pistol with his top left arm. With his lower right he pulled the six-barrelled rotary strobe gun from its clips on his back and swung it forward, assisted by low-powered AG motors designed to help with its weight.

The head of the guy he'd thrown the feline at disappeared as a 12-gauge slug entered it and then exploded. Another slug took a Militiawoman behind the dead guy trying to bring her ACR to bear. He moved his upper torso to the left and fired the final barrel of the shotgun. A reptile Militiawoman dived out of the way as her bunk exploded.

With a thought he triggered the strobe gun, bathing the bunk room in a flickering hellish red glow. The sound of superheated air molecules exploding ran together in a constant staccato. The rotating barrels allowed for them to cool, which meant a higher rate of fire than single- or double-barrelled laser weapons. It looked like a constant red line bisecting the room.

Red steam from boiling blood turned the room humid as the laser all but sawed people in two. Vic holstered the now empty shotgun pistol with his upper left arm while his upper right grabbed the reptile disc from its holder over his shoulder and threw it, activating its autonomous hunter-killer program. A 'face feed from his tactical neuonics would keep the disc out of the way of his other ordnance.

His top limbs grabbed his advanced combat rifle from his back as he dropped the strobe gun. The gun's four-legged spipod unfolded and the weapon went looking for more victims.

Meanwhile, the P-sat had taken out two crewmen it had met in the corridor with neurotoxin-coated flechettes fired from a suppressed spit gun. It had just attached a thermal seed frame to the reinforced door that led to Command and Control in the centre of the frigate.

The strobe gun was advancing, its barrels swinging back and forth, firing nearly constantly, its targeting systems finding victims sometimes with the help of info 'faced from Vic's own neunonics.

Vic fired the six grenades from the ACR's under-barrel launcher. The first one was a controlled-replication, flesh-eating nano-swarm. The second was a viral grenade. Both were high end for the black market, but Vic had suspected when loading them that the *St Brendan's Fire's* countermeasures would be able to cope with them. The remaining four were flechette grenades which filled the air with high-velocity needles.

Vic's two lower limbs drew his double-barrelled laser pistols. His upper and lower torsos counter-rotated as the ACR and the lasers fired, mopping up whatever the heavier ordnance had missed.

Through the 'face feed from his P-sat Vic was aware that it was now in C and C. The command crew died quickly, taken out by the P-sat's swivel-mounted auto-shotgun firing frangible fragmentation rounds designed not to harm any of the instruments. A measured laser killed those the shotgun didn't. The P-sat left one crew member alive in C and C.

The ACR's magazine was solid-state, each bullet assembled in the barrel. Its bullpup magazine looked like it was being eaten as the weapon was fired. The last of the magazine disappeared up into the weapon. Vic slid another magazine home almost immediately but didn't fire.

A Militiaman died as the strobe gun cut the bunk he was using as cover in half and then near enough did likewise to him. Another almost got his ACR to bear on Vic, but the disc cut his throat.

More than fifty were dead now. Everything was red. They hadn't fired a single shot. Then Vic's sensors warned him that the ship's alarms had started to broadcast to the crew's neunonics. Any remaining passive security systems were now active.

With a command from Vic, the spipod leaped up onto one of the few remaining bunks and fired into all the bodies to ensure they were dead. It was little more than red-light butchery.

Vic caught his returning disc and clipped it back onto its shoulder mount. He left the bunk room and made for C and C, his ACR at the ready, his lower torso swivelled so his bottom limbs could cover his rear. A few crew members showed their faces in the corridors, but bursts of bullets and beams discouraged them from getting involved. Only one fired back. Small-calibre spit pistol bullets flattened against Vic's armour. Vic killed him to make a point. If the guy got cloned then maybe next time he would be able to work out the difference between bravery and stupidity.

As he approached C and C, Vic started getting armour integrity warnings 'faced from the suit to his tactical neunonics. It appeared that the armour was slowly being eaten away by a weaponised nano-screen turned nano-swarm. Vic sped up. He stepped over the still-glowing hole in the door to C and C, and turned to look at the tank.

The navigator looked through the green water and transparent tank wall at Vic. The dolphin had been extensively augmented with hard and soft tech. Most people also assumed that Church navigators had a degree of S-tech in them as well.

Vic's armour was seriously malfunctioning now. He could see part of it dissolving. Soon the nanites would find a weak point in the armour, break through and start eating him.

'I don't have much time. Surrender control of all systems to me now,' he 'faced on an open channel.

'Just a moment and I think it'll be over,' the navigator told him.

Vic was already moving. He liked to think that he'd given the dolphin the chance to be reasonable. He opened the airlocked delivery tray, unclipped the case that Scab had given him and, steeling himself, opened it. The Scorpion was already up, its sting arched, its body language that of impending violence. The Scorpion scared Vic and always had. It was unpredictable and hateful S-tech. It could just as well decide to murder him.

'Don't do that. Let's talk about this!' Even modulated and 'faced, Vic could hear the fear in the dolphin's voice. The nanites were through his armour. Vic screamed as they started to eat him alive. Vic dropped the Scorpion into the tray and slid it shut.

The navigator thrashed around so much that he injured himself and red clouds appeared in the water. Vic fell to the ground, his armour now all but dissolving, his exoskeleton starting to do the same.

The thrashing from the tank stopped. The *St Brendan's Fire's* systems opened themselves to him. He only just had the presence of mind to deactivate the nano-swarm while he still had flesh and components. The pain stopped almost immediately as his own systems flooded his few remaining biological organs and his mind with numbing narcotics.

His systems were starting to rebuild. He would find some more raw materials in the frigate's med bay to help him rebuild himself before the rendezvous.

It was a blissed Vic who managed to sit on one of the couches and let it grow to envelope his awkward and now partially eaten 'sect frame. Blissed or not, the sight of the Scorpion dug into flesh just behind the dolphin's artificial gill, sting buried deep in the navigator's skin, was horrific. Its legs had grown to form what looked like a skin-tight cage clamped into the cetacean's flesh. The navigator was still alive, his eyes full of pain.

Vic shut down the ship. There were still people in there. Those he couldn't trap, he turned the ship's remaining security systems on. The rest Scab could kill. Vic didn't mind killing, but Scab actually liked to be a monster. Scab liked hide-and-seek. Vic stationed the P-sat outside the hole in the door to C and C to watch his back.

Open access showed him the *St Brendan's Fire*'s rendezvous point in planetary Red Space with the Monk.

'You're not supposed to be able to do that,' Vic mused. But then you weren't supposed to be able to take a Church frigate on your own, no matter how good you were. You also weren't supposed to be able to break a Church navigator's conditioning so easily. You certainly weren't supposed to get away with it, and he didn't imagine he would.

Scab stared at the frigate. He got a very good look at the ship's batteries, most of which were pointed at him.

'And of course you know how to navigate in planetary Red Space,' he said grimly.

'It's over. I'm sorry. It's up to you: we can put you back into Real Space if you want, but you should know we had to destroy your ship and kill Vic. Your employer will be after you. It might be better if we kill you now.'

Scab looked down with a half-smile on his lips. 'You have to earn the right to kill me,' he said, and then looked at her, grinning savagely.

'I think we've just done that. I'm talking about what's best for you. We harbour no ill will towards you, but you're a very dangerous person to leave in play as an enemy.'

'Even for the Church?'

'Even for the Church.'

'I'm not your enemy.'

Vic was holding the ship in a blizzard of black ash in a red sky. He wasn't sure what was happening, but he was reasonably sure that he was in some kind of Red Space simulacrum or echo of the planet Game. He had watched the massive blackened skeletal trees collapse like they were made of burned paper.

In his neunonics he could see Scab in his disguised form and the Monk in hers sitting on the strange coffin-shaped cocoon thing. Somehow Scab's face behind his visor dominated the image from the ship's external visual sensors. Vic locked weapon system after weapon system onto Scab as he counted the ways in which he hated that man. There would never be a better time than now. There was no way Scab would survive and he did not have clone insurance. Scab wanted to die – he was daring everyone in Known Space to do it – but nobody had the balls. Now with a thought Vic could kill him. No comebacks. Except. Vic glanced over at the Scorpion in the tank. The navigator that the Scorpion appeared to have fused with was staring at him.

'Leave me something of her,' Scab 'faced over their secure link.

He wanted to scream, weep, tear at what little remained of his flesh, thrash around, engage in all the human melodrama he'd experienced in immersions. Instead he just sagged in the couch and cursed himself for a coward. He heard the Monk 'face the *St Brendan's Fire*, wondering what was taking so long.

'I'm sorry,' Vic 'faced her back.

The Monk's head whipped around to look at Scab. She was moving for her bone blade. Scab grabbed her wrist. A laser cannon on one of the beam batteries fired. The Monk's torso turned to red steam which then promptly froze. Scab was still holding her upper arm.

He stared at the *St Brendan's Fire* until the forward airlock ramp lowered from the head of the craft like a mouth. With a thought Scab commanded the three AG motors to take him into the airlock.

Scab cut the fused flesh off the Monk's severed hand and attached the warmer to it, returning it to simulated life. He stared at Vic all the while. Vic would not look at him, could not meet his murky lifeless eyes. He didn't need to look at him to feel the disdain.

'Why were the weapons on me?' Scab finally asked.

'Dramatic irony?' Vic suggested.

Scab was not disdainful of Vic for wanting to kill him. He was disdainful of Vic for not going through with it.

Scab stripped the spacesuit gauntlet off the reanimated hand, then he put the hand on the cocoon. It was warm, and he cut the flesh to let some blood leak out onto the cocoon's strange shell. Slowly the cocoon started to dissolve. Vic stared at it in horror.

32

Southern Britain, a Long Time Ago

Falling through smoke. Falling through a clear blue sky, the churning red water of a feeding frenzy below her. Britha told herself that she couldn't hear all the screaming. That she couldn't hear how much she had failed these people. The thing crawling through her head recoiled from the violation of the sky hanging above them like an angry living black sun.

The water hit her hard, tasting of salt, copper and meat. Shapes writhed over each other like a basket full of eels. The sea seemed full. The force of her impact carried her down. To part of her the ocean seemed home, to another part the bloodlust seemed right and proper. The thing in her head howled and sent unimaginable pain lancing through her.

Something grabbed her arm. She did not fight. It pulled her deeper. What was left of her real mind told her that she was not of the sea as the pressure mounted, but somehow she did not die.

It was there, through silted water, down under the mud, something huge, ancient, alive and suffering. Something trying to wake but waking into a world of fear, pain, burning and slaughter. It was so large as to be difficult to comprehend, like a mountain, a living mountain.

The energy in the water was palpable. Patches of its flesh glowed through the murky water, making patterns, lightning playing across those patterns. Britha knew somehow that this was the energy that violated the sky, letting the Hungry Nothingness in.

Someone, something, took her deeper. She should be drowning now. Britha felt the touch of the living mountain's hard flesh. It felt like rock or a shell but then it opened to softer flesh. She was not being consumed, she told herself. It was more like the births she had helped with over the years. It was like going home. It was not just the blood, the blood which had granted Britha power and magics, that called to this creature. Something at a much more primal level recognised the creator of life.

Now falling again. Britha landed on something warm, wet and alive. She felt a hot wind, like breath, on her skin. She tried to cope with the pain, tried to ignore the horror of what she had just done. She felt feverish. Her body was fighting itself, it wanted her to give in to fury and destroy life, but she was home and would be safe.

Britha opened her eyes and tried to make sense of things. It looked like a tunnel but she knew that she was in a living thing. Living stalactites of translucent white flesh dangled from the ceiling, giving off a faint glow and moving with the warm wind and of their own accord. The long corridor had regular arches of bone. The walls and floor remind her of the dimpled flesh on the inside of a mouth. The flesh rippled with movement.

And Cliodna stood over her. She too seemed to sway with the warm wind. Crouched over like a predatory animal, she did not look like her lover any more. She was all armour and hard edges. She looked like a warrior. No, Britha corrected herself, she looked like a weapon. The other woman seemed to seethe somehow.

Cliodna reached down and ran a sharp black claw across Britha's skin. Britha did not cry out. Her head wanted to burst and the claw wound seemed like nothing. Even through the war in her body and the agony in her head, even though she was slowly beginning to realise that some of the thoughts in her head were not her own, the thought that Cliodna would hurt her made all the strength that had carried her this far evaporate. She wanted to curl up and end it. If Cliodna wanted to then let her kill her.

Instead Britha got up unsteadily.

Cliodna threw Britha's spear at her feet. 'Kill me,' she said quietly.

Quicksilver tears sprang from Britha's eyes but she didn't move. Cliodna darted forward and more slashes appeared in Britha's flesh. The blood ran down her, dripped onto the flesh of the floor and was instantly absorbed.

'Kill me,' Cliodna said more loudly and licked her bloodied nails. Britha knew that the Otherworldly woman couldn't help herself and shook her head.

Cliodna embraced Britha. Her skin was course and rough now, she felt jagged and sharp. She grabbed Britha's hair and yanked her head back. 'Kill me!' Cliodna screamed in her face, breath smelling of meat, before sinking rows of teeth into the other woman's shoulder and pushing sharp nails through her skin.

This time Britha screamed and pulled away, Cliodna's fingers and teeth tearing her flesh.

Britha staggered back, sobbing. 'I can't!' she screamed.

'I can smell that monster's scent on you,' Cliodna growled. 'Either kill me or I will kill you.'

'You pushed me away!' Britha screamed at her. She knew it wasn't fair. Now more than ever it was evident that Cliodna had done it for Britha's safety. Not only that, it would seem that Bress was more than a little responsible for Cliodna's transformation.

'I don't want to live like this,' Cliodna told her. 'I only destroy. I am hanging on to what little is left of me. My nails are bloodied by the meat of my younger brothers and sisters!' Britha knew she meant her and the other peoples of Ynys Prydein and beyond. 'Soon I will be gone. I would rather I be killed by someone I loved, when I was capable of that. Better that than I become a terror to your people.'

'I'm sorry but—'

'Then I will kill you and forget my name and all that came with it.'

'I can't ...' Britha was begging Cliodna to understand.

'You have no choice. It is your responsibility to stand between your people, all people, and the likes of me. Isn't that what they taught you in the groves? I'm holding on as long as I can, but there is a red tide inside me.' Britha was sure she could see tears mingling with the remaining drops of water on her lover's face. 'Please.'

The only way she could do it was to give in to the fire part of her that lived in her blood. To let the demon that lived in the spear have its way as her hand closed around its haft. Later she could tell herself that it wasn't even her who wielded the spear that she pushed through her lover.

Britha finally managed to throw the red-tipped spear away from herself. The demon in the spear laughed as it showed her Cliodna's death at her hands. She sank to her knees. She screamed as the pain returned. She could feel the thing crawling through the rip in the sky like it was a hole in the back of her mind.

She was in the same cave of flesh, with the same warm wind and rib-like arches of bone. She did not know how or why she had come back from the red rage. Behind her there were rents in the Muileartach's flesh that she had dug with the spear in her frenzy.

Then she remembered the other voice. *No*, she decided, *voice wasn't the right word*. Despite her magics allowing her to understand all other languages, there was no common language between her and the thoughts that she felt rather than understood, that had soothed her, called her back, though they themselves were filled with pain.

She reached for the Mother's mind. The pain in there almost killed her immediately. It had already turned the Mother's elder children insane. Sent them into the water to slay her younger children, to put them out of their misery. To her massive and very alien intellect it seemed the most merciful thing to do. Then the Mother was there in Britha's mind, through the link in the blood given to her by Cliodna. The Mother tried to protect her from the pain and the suffering being sent to her by Crom Dhubh, but Britha was crawling across the floor of the cavern, screaming, wounds appearing on her flesh.

'I can make it stop.' The voice was like silk, low and mellifluous, somehow breaking through all the pain. Seductive, the voice offered what she needed.

He was so very tall. His skin was black. Not the very dark brown of Kush and his compatriots from the kingdoms across the sea far to the south. He looked like a tall and beautiful member of a long-forgotten race. His skin was the absence of light and colour. Naked, he knelt next to her.

She almost asked him to do it, to take the pain. Then the parasite in her mind recoiled from his power. Her mind, struggling to understand what the crystal was showing her, visualised it as lines of black energy crackling into him, which he turned into poison that bled into the Mother. The man did not just exist here and now, but stretched into other places which, although Britha could now see, she had no way of understanding. Crom Dhubh was not there. He was a man-shaped hole in the world. The nothingness inside that hole squirmed like maggots writhing over each other. Britha threw up.

'It's nearly over,' he told her. She wanted to surrender to the voice but the crystal would not let her turn away from what he really was. Britha concentrated on the stray threads of his outline. She reached out to another place. It hurt. Like she had been snapped. She took a thread and pulled.

Crom Dhubh's head rotated, breaking his neck. Bones splintered, piercing organs, flesh and skin. He fell to the ground, his body a wreck. He looked like a broken doll.

The energy stopped. The poison seeping from him stopped. Begrudgingly the crystal showed her the little part of Teardrop that it had jealously kept. Britha touched the Mother's mind. Suddenly Britha could feel the pain and the terror of all those in the water. Being attacked and fed on by the Muileartach's predatory elder children, by poisoned creatures released from corrupted wombs. It threatened to overwhelm her, but she held on to the mind of the Muileartach and the fragment of Teardrop as he taught her the mindsong.

Teardrop knew it as something else, some kind of instruction, but

Britha recognised it for what it was. A complex and beautiful magical working designed to lull a god back to sleep.

She could feel the Muileartach reach out and call her elder children back home, sing her own song as she tried to soothe their fractured minds. As the pain receded, Britha started to feel her anger. Britha felt rather than saw writhing tentacles flick out and destroy black ships like a reflexive response to pain.

The organs that ran through her, organs possessing magics that Britha could barely understand, which could draw power from the stars in the night sky, glowing organs, which had opened the way for the Hungry Nothingness – they closed the way as the Mother fell asleep. The way collapsed. The tear closed and was gone, as if it had never existed. There was no sense of it at all, and the wound in her mind closed.

Only the connection with the sleeping god allowed her to cope with the pain.

There was a sound like dry twigs snapping. He did not so much seem to stand as rise before her. Britha looked up at Crom Dhubh.

'I was dead and dry, full of dust when your people were brute animals,' he said quietly, his impossibly deep voice carrying. She wondered if any of her people had lived.

'That sounds like no way to be. I think you should go now,' she told him through the pain.

'Would that I could.' He turned and walked away.

Britha was surprised that she was still alive. She did not think she had the strength left to fight anyone, let alone someone with his power.

'This must seem like a victory to you, but I am eternal. The parasite in your head will consume you. You are already dead,' he said, answering her thoughts.

'Why?' she asked.

He stopped but did not turn around. 'The pain.' He sounded sad.

She was being consumed. Joining. Going back, becoming one. The comfort of something else's flesh all around you. Her Mother wanting her to hide something deep inside. A secret that the Hungry Nothingness could never know again. Her Mother had to sleep before her insane sisters found her. Already they were reaching for her.

The coldness and the weight of the sea again. It felt like death after where she had been.

*

She had washed up on a beach in the company of twisted monstrosities that crawled, slithered and flew and recognised her as kin.

She had no idea how long she had been wandering. It seemed like an age. Her throat was bloody from screaming due to the pain in her skull. She did not understand how there could be so much pain when there was so little of her left.

The crystal grew from her skull in a way that no other could see, to places that could not exist. The paths to these places only made her hurt more when she looked at them.

The circle of stones was far vaster than any cairn she had seen. Some part of her which used to be Britha recognised it as the time between times, either dusk or dawn, she wasn't sure which. The time when the borders between this world and the Otherworld were at their weakest. The southrons had not inscribed symbols of power on the stones to protect against the influence of the gods.

Shapes all around the stones. People? No, the dead. Spirits. Her people. She sank to her knees in the centre and somehow found it in herself to scream with her ruined voice.

Something moved deep in the earth.

Britha was more aware of, than actually saw, a star going out in the sky.

Pulsing blue and white light.

The light faded. The stones again. More people. Shouting, running, readying weapons. All of them like Fachtna, well made and richly appointed with armour and fine weapons. No, they were different stones. Teardrop had told the truth. The earth was the sky and the sky was the earth.

In the Otherworld they showed their power. They caged her in light and destroyed her with fire. Just before the fire consumed her, she saw the dead. Fachtna was watching her from beyond the circle of stones.

33
Now

Beth sat in the Range Rover at the bottom of Alhambra Road, picking dried blood off herself and looking at the wreckage of South Parade Pier. Knowing what she knew now, it was difficult not to think that this was the apocalypse – but happening here in Portsmouth? A back-alley apocalypse largely unnoticed maybe, seen out of the corner of the eye. The helicopters in the sky, the light and the sirens meant that people knew something was happening, but they talked a little louder, the laughter was more forced and they pretended it wasn't. Or maybe this wasn't the apocalypse. Maybe this happened all the time in the secret world Beth seemed to have been inducted into. Perhaps every terrorist atrocity or disaster was actually brought about by this hidden conflict of monsters, strange technology and madmen.

'There's a house down there with its windows painted black and it smells bad,' the chief madman said. Beth looked over at du Bois. He wasn't looking at her; he was glancing over at the partially destroyed pier. Another piece of collateral damage in this hidden war. She wondered if she was on the right side. She would think about that once she got her sister back.

Beth felt something wet coming out of her ear. She touched it and her fingers came away bloody. Indescribable pain lanced through her head and her vision went red. Beth found herself in the passenger footwell of the Range Rover, curled up as if trying to hide from the pain. It had lessened, but her head still felt white hot and was throbbing. Du Bois was looking at her with a degree of sympathy, though no surprise.

'What's happening?' she managed before screaming again. There were very few people on the streets. The city had been told that it had been the target of multiple terrorist attacks. Home might not feel safe at the moment but it felt safer than outside. However, Beth's screams, the badly damaged Range Rover and their ragged and bloodstained clothing were drawing attention. Du Bois watched people get out their phones and press one button three times. That didn't matter.

They were covered on that front. They were supposed to be special forces combating a particularly bloody group of terrorists. The local police were kicking up a storm but were holding off. Du Bois knew that helicopters filled with Special Boat Service commandos were en route to Portsmouth.

'I dumped a lot of information into your head at once.'

'All the gun stuff?' Beth said and then suddenly looked out to the choppy Solent under the bright blue sky.

Why did she do that? he wondered. 'Small-unit tactics and … yes, all the gun stuff. Normally the information would be assimilated in a much more careful manner, but there wasn't time. Whatever you have inside you coped admirably but there was always going to be bleeding and pain. I'm sorry.'

'I almost certainly wouldn't be alive if you hadn't.' *Assuming I believe you*, Beth thought. 'I would have been trying to fight those things with a bayonet.'

'You have a bayonet?' du Bois asked, a little confused.

'That's it? That's what we're going on? Blacked-out windows and a bad smell?' Beth asked, holding her head, the pain having subsided a little.

'The smell's really bad. And it seems to have its own naturally occurring blood-screen.'

'I don't know what that means.'

'They have access to technology like … It means it's the people who took your sister, okay?' du Bois said, sounding exasperated.

Beth looked up the Alhambra Road. It was a road of white-painted terraced houses which had seen better days, like much of the seafront in Southsea. Most of the houses were four or five storeys high.

'What's the plan?' she asked.

'I do this, and you sit here and try to cope with the pain.' Beth stared at him. She didn't realise her eyes were full of blood. 'No? That's what I thought. Has it occurred to you that if the pain distracts you, it could get us both killed? Not to mention, I don't have anything that could even kill hybrids. The best I can hope for is to debilitate them for a while. When they heal they'll also be very angry about having just been shot.'

'Really?' Beth glanced towards the gun compartment in the back of the Range Rover. 'With all the guns you've got?'

'It's not about the guns; it's about how quickly their internal nanites can knit them back together again. I don't have anything that can stop that from happening, I've used them all, and all the guns have a different purpose,' he said somewhat defensively.

'Look, I won't let you down, but if I have to I'm going in there on my own,' Beth said. Du Bois sighed. 'So, what's the plan?'

'Well, when I was having a look at the house I just happened to attach some frame charges to the bay window ...'

Du Bois backed the Range Rover up the narrow road at speed, clipping more than one car. He then yanked the wheel and reversed the four-by-four up against the wall of the house with the blacked-out windows, not quite braking in time, letting the wall of the house stop the car.

With a thought he sent the command to the radio detonators on the frame charges. The bay windows on the front of the house exploded inwards.

Beth was out of the car running at the front door, the Benelli M4 at the ready. Du Bois was on the bonnet of the Range Rover, the H & K UMP in his hands.

Beth fired lock-breaker rounds into the door's hinges and then the lock, looking away as she fired so she didn't get blinded by splinters. Du Bois leaped through the hole where the black-painted panes of glass had been.

Beth checked the hall quickly but saw nothing. She raced up the stairs as she heard du Bois kicking in doors on the ground floor. Quickly she checked the rooms on the first floor. There were signs of lots of people having lived there recently. The place stank like sewage. Discarded food, most of it meat, had been left to rot, but there were no flies.

Du Bois ran by her on the landing as he headed up to check the second floor. Moments later Beth was on the stairs heading to the third as du Bois searched below.

On the third floor Beth kicked in the door to the first room she came to, a back bedroom. The same soiled mattresses, the same rotting food, the same smell of sewage. She tried not to gag as she heard du Bois on the stairs to the fourth and final floor.

Beth came out of the back bedroom and moved to the front, kicking it open. This was not quite as bad, perhaps because the blackout curtains that had covered the windows had fallen down, making it less usable.

If her senses hadn't been quite as acute as they had become recently, Beth wasn't sure she would have heard the burst of suppressed sub-machine gun fire from upstairs. She probably would have heard du Bois's cry of surprise, however, and definitely the sound of glass smashing above her. She saw a shape, much larger than du Bois on his own, plummet past the window. She heard the impact and a scream. Beth rushed to the filthy window and looked out. Du Bois was lying mostly on the roof of the Range Rover. Something not unlike what she had fought in the dog stadium was crouched over him, repeatedly slashing at him with an extended spur of bone.

Beth ran out of the room, leaped over the landing banister and landed on the stairs close to the second-floor landing. She ran down the few remaining steps and charged at the landing window. The black-painted single pane exploded outwards as she hit it. It felt like she had a long time to think about what a stupid move this had been on the twenty-five-foot drop to the ground.

Knees bent, Beth landed fine, pleased that the bones in her legs hadn't exploded. She moved quickly to where the hybrid thing was savaging du Bois's face. Beth put the shotgun barrel next to the thing's head and pulled the trigger. Its head disappeared in a spray of blood and bone.

'Are you okay?' Beth asked.

'Of course I'm not fucking okay! I think I've broken my spine, and you just about blew my face off!' Beth glanced down at him and had to admit some of the cuts on his face looked a little like pellet wounds.

'Sorry?' she ventured. Du Bois lay there glaring, but at the sky, not at her. 'Well, get up then,' Beth finally said.

'I don't suppose it's occurred to you that a forty-foot fall onto my back may have caused some damage?' he asked testily.

'Oh,' Beth said. 'Will it heal?'

'Given time.'

'Were there more up there?'

'I don't think so.'

'So she's not in there?'

'I saw what looked like a basement door. I wanted to clear up first, so if we went in we wouldn't get any nasty surprises from behind.' Du Bois screamed as Beth jarred his broken spine taking the UMP from him. She already had his .45 and his spare clips. She relieved him of his ammunition for the UMP as well.

'You said yourself that we didn't have much time.' Beth glanced down the street again. Despite the clear blue sky, the Solent was looking choppier and choppier. Waves were coming over the beach and onto the road. Some of the seawater was even washing up to where they were.

'I don't think –'

'I'll be fine.'

'– that leaving me here this exposed is a good idea and you will not be fine; you will almost certainly be eaten.'

'Then see you and thanks.' She turned, UMP at the ready, and headed back into the house.

Beth had found that whenever things happened quickly she was fine. It was when she had time to think that things became tricky. She stood at the door down to the basement for a long time trying to make herself reach out and touch the handle. She knew there was something on the other side of the door. Felt it.

Beth opened the door, barely realising that she was doing it. She was at the top of a set of concrete steps looking down. The smell was strong but it was the smell of the sea and not altogether unpleasant. It was carried on a warm wind. Beth found that she could see perfectly in the darkness. She moved down the stairs. The fear was gone. It had to be her imagination but she felt as if something was calling her.

It wasn't a basement. It was a crossroads. Tunnels of fused stone and earth met there. *It was a wonder the whole street didn't collapse,* Beth thought. The passage going south was alive. It looked like an empty vein and it was where the warm wind was coming from.

At some level Beth knew this was all wrong, fundamentally so. This was part of something that should not be, that didn't exist in the world as she understood it. But another part, perhaps the part that had been sprayed with blood by something old and strange, understood. It was that part that was being called to by a huge, alien and sleeping mind.

Pushing the calling aside, Beth brought the suppressed Heckler & Koch up in front of her, the folding stock secure against her shoulder, and moved ahead with the weapon at the ready.

The tunnel took her down. She didn't have to walk far before she knew she was under the sea. She even felt the tube sway with the water and the sound of pebbles sliding up and down.

Beth knew that she should be freaking out. She was clearly walking through something that was alive in some way. She knew first hand how dangerous the things she was following were, but somehow, instinctively, she knew this was okay. She all but felt welcome.

It was pitch dark but her eyes had no problem seeing ahead of her, though everything looked grey. Then there was a glowing. It looked like the chemical light she had seen some animals make on nature documentaries. The word bioluminescence suddenly popped into her head. She wasn't sure where it had come from – another part of her 'gift' from the mad old woman?

The pain in her head was still there but it was now a dull ache. With rising disquiet she realised that she was being soothed by something. She had a sense of enormous scale, a mind all around her and not like her own but familiar. A mind that slept but was close to waking.

The light was growing brighter. Beth decided to abandon caution. She knew that if she didn't go straight in then fear would freeze her. Keeping low, moving rapidly, the UMP sweeping left, right, up and down with her movements, she entered a cavern.

The warm wind was stronger here, like moist breath on her skin but still not unpleasant. She was wading through water. No, not water; it felt more viscous. It put Beth in mind of amniotic fluid. It was a massive space, arched with a bone-like material, the flesh walls reminding Beth of the inside of a mouth. Islands of a bone-like material stuck out of the fluid. Beth's vision magnified, and at the end of the cavern she could make out what looked like massive internal organs pulsing with life.

They were there, of course: the twisted, once-human, mutated hybrid servants. They moved like ambulatory patches of darkness, blocking the glow in places. Edging towards her. There were a lot of them. *How big was this fucking diving club anyway?* Beth wondered.

'May as well get this over and done with,' Beth muttered. She advanced, firing a three-round burst. A head shot, a hybrid went down. Shift the weapon, her instinct – or some ancient technology if du Bois was to be believed – telling her where to put the shots each time. The sub-machine gun's kick against her shoulder felt comfortable. The muzzle flashes lit up the cave, making the dark shapes of the hybrids look as if they were moving under a strobe light.

They dived into the fluid with barely a splash. Beth had a moment to think about how graceful they looked as the dark shapes darted towards her through the water. She lowered the weapon to fire into the fluid. It cost her a moment before she 'remembered' how useless bullets were underwater. She had to get out of the liquid.

Running slowly through the water, churning it up, still firing short controlled bursts as she moved. Black sprays of backlit blood flew from every target she aimed at. So many of the shadows in the dimly lit cavern seemed to be moving. In shades of grey she saw them charging, swimming towards her. She didn't think of them as people; they were ... The word antibodies was supplied to her.

Boots touched dry bone as she raced up an outcrop. One of the hybrids exploded out of the water nearby. He fell back into the water with three rounds, fired from the UMP, in his skull. More of them were leaping onto the outcrop as Beth ran up it, firing. The way they came out of the water and landed made her think absurdly of penguins.

The clip ran out in the UMP.

'You all right there, mate?' a voice with the warped cockney accent of Portsmouth asked. Du Bois had a moment to reflect on how having your spine broken encouraged people to ask stupid questions.

'Oh yes, I'm perfectly fucking fine,' du Bois snapped from his position atop the Range Rover.

'Really? You look a little fucked up.'

'You have peerless observation skills.'

'What? Oh what, are you being a smart cunt?'

'Actually I'm just trying to find the requisite level of stupidity so we can converse in a meaningful manner.'

'Posh cunt.'

'Indeed.'

Spinal injuries were complicated and challenged the healing abilities of his nanites. They had to pull a lot of matter from other places in the body and adjust it at a molecular level. They took longer to heal, but despite the discomfort, du Bois could feel his spine knitting together again.

A sallow pockmarked face with bloodshot eyes, greasy hair and rotting teeth appeared in his line of vision. Du Bois was aware rather than felt the man searching inside the remains of his jacket.

'Nice phone, mate. That's mine now. Ooo, some money. What's this then? You've got more than one warrant card here, mate.'

'Really? You haven't noticed the body of the sea creature lying next to the Range Rover?' He heard splashing. It seemed like the water had risen higher while he'd been lying there.

'Yeah, he's all kinds of messed up.'

'And that's English, is it?'

'What?'

'Never mind.'

'Did you shoot him?'

'No. The person who did is a very angry lady from Bradford with an exceptionally large gun. Why don't you put my wallet and phone back and run away, and she probably won't kill you.'

'Why don't I take them and run away?' he asked. Du Bois had to admit that he had a point. Some other operatives had powerful electrical charges in their phones and other items which could be set off by transmitting a command from their internal nano-systems. Du

488

Bois had always eschewed that upgrade, assuming he'd never get into a situation like this.

'The harder you make it for us to recover those items, the more you'll suffer,' du Bois assured the man.

'You're pretty scary for a paraplegic,' the thief told him.

'Now you get a vocabulary?'

The case! du Bois suddenly thought. *Did the man have the case?* He tried to make contact with the smart systems on the vials inside the cases containing the blood and genetic samples from Talia. They were out of range.

'Shit!' du Bois shouted.

'You all right, mate?' The thief's apparent concern wrong-footed du Bois for a moment.

'Brilliant! Not only is my spine no longer broken, but thankfully I'm no longer being robbed.'

'No, you are, really.'

'Sarcasm not your thing then?'

'Oh, I get it. Good one. You won't mind if I look in the car then?'

'No. Go ahead. Take your time.'

'That's all fucked up as well, by the way.'

'Oh is it? Well thank you for letting me know, and please do keep me up to date.'

The Range Rover shifted underneath him as the thief climbed in, sending pain shooting through du Bois's spine. He was trying to remember the last time he'd truly been aware of the case while entertaining complex revenge fantasies involving the man in his Range Rover.

'Fuck me! Is this a shooter?' Du Bois thought that the world must hold constant surprises for this individual, every moment a new experience.

'If by that you mean is it a gun, then no, it's a teapot.'

'Sarcastic cunt.'

'Well quite. I don't suppose it's occurred to you not to say and do things worthy of sarcasm?'

'What?'

'Never mind.'

'So what are you, a copper or something?'

'Look, I don't mean to be rude, but I'm trying to concentrate here. If you absolutely must rob me then could we have a little more robbery and a little less chat?'

'You're the boss.'

The gunfight in Old Portsmouth was the last time he knew for sure that he had had the case. It was the only time he'd lost consciousness. He didn't think that he'd just lost it, which meant that the DAYP must have it. He closed his eyes. This was unimaginably bad, particularly if, as du Bois imagined, Beth was about to get herself killed and not retrieve Talia.

When du Bois opened his eyes he saw that the thief was holding his FAL carbine.

'All right if I take this, yeah?'

'Oh please do. After all, I understand there's a world shortage of sub-literate morons with automatic weapons.'

'You know, you're really not very nice.' The thief actually sounded hurt.

'Having my back broken and being robbed has brought out the worst in me. I'm normally a sweetheart.'

'You don't have to be so nasty about it,' the thief said, and then pointed du Bois's own carbine at him. Du Bois had a moment to ponder how he'd basically talked the man into shooting him with his own gun. Perhaps he should be nicer to people, he reflected. He heard the man start to squeeze the trigger.

Beth let the UMP drop on its sling. She swung the shotgun round, bringing it to bear. The muzzle flash was that much brighter as a nearby face disintegrated. The loud report of the weapon compared to the suppressed whispers of the H & K seemed like a violation of the place.

They were so close that Beth barely needed to aim now. Just shift the shotgun slightly and fire, and another one flew off the outcrop and into the now bloody fluid. Beth knew that she had not killed them, though several were floating face down in the liquid.

In the periphery of her vision she saw two of the six-limbed, bone-crested creatures that du Bois had killed on the motorway climb up onto nearby outcrops. She knew she had nothing that could even harm them.

The shotgun was empty. She drew the accursed .45 smoothly from the holster at her hip, pulling the hammer back on an already chambered round as she did so.

'Stop!'

Beth heard the cry in the momentary lapse in the gunfire. Thinking back, she had heard the cry during the fight, but she'd been busy. It was a male voice. The hybrids around her stopped their advance but swayed, many of them baring their teeth in silent growls and drooling horribly. Beth levelled the pistol at the closest one but did not fire.

'Please stop!' the man's voice said. It was a strong voice but sounded odd, like the man had something stuck in his throat. There was movement and a figure, more human-like than the rest, moved to the top of an outcrop to stand next to one of the servitors.

In the greys of her vision she could make out eyes that were dark pools. His skin was pale and scaled. His neck seemed to palpate slightly and his head was utterly hairless. Webbed fingers with sharp-looking black nails were wrapped around a staff which appeared to be made of the same bone material as the outcrops. He was clad in soaking rags which hung off him and revealed much of his pale skin.

'You can lower your weapon. We will not attack you if you do not attack us,' he told her. 'I am Ezard.'

Beth nodded to him and holstered the .45. She quickly reloaded the UMP and then started pushing shells into the M4's tubular magazine.

'Look, I don't give a fuck about any of this. You can have your secret war. I just want my sister.'

'I am afraid that won't be possible.' He sounded apologetic.

'Then a lot more of you are going to get shot.' Though Beth was reasonably sure that all the ones she'd shot earlier were already starting to heal. She was also sure that she recognised a few more from the motorway. She'd last seen them lying on the ground after du Bois had shot them, a lot.

'She has to leave here with us,' Ezard said.

Beth just nodded, finished reloading the M4 and let it drop on its strap. She swung the UMP up and aimed it at Ezard. The hybrids stopped swaying and hunched ready to attack. The servitor next to Ezard looked about to pounce. Beth was pretty sure it could make it to her in one leap.

'I will fucking shoot you,' she told him.

'Then I will heal, and you will die for a meaningless gesture. She has to come with us.'

'Why? Why is she so important to every fucking freak in this city?'

'This is not the Divine Mother; this is her seed,' Ezard said. 'All the shit in the city, the violence, the abuse, the pain, hatred, fear – all of this is pollution. The Divine Mother feels it all, and over the years it has slowly driven her insane as she sleeps. She must wake, give birth to the seed and leave this place for somewhere where there is no hatred.'

'You'll have to go pretty far to find that,' Beth muttered, playing for time.

'We are going very far away,' Ezard told her seriously. His meaning sank in.

'Seriously? You people are more deluded than I thought. Why her anyway?'

'She is of the Divine Mother's line, part of her. Within her is the code that opens the way.' This didn't mean anything to Beth.

'And you know this how?'

'The Divine Mother speaks to me in my dreams, and then I speak those dreams.'

'Assuming I believe this, and everything's a bit weird at the moment so why not, the problem is a little thing called consent. Whatever you think you're doing, you can't just go around kidnapping goths. She's had a rough enough time recently without being held prisoner by some kind of crazy star cult.'

'It's okay, Beth. I am loved here.' Talia: wan, pale, tired-looking but even in the grey light still beautiful, Beth had to admit. She was in the same hospital-like gown they'd found her wearing in the lock-up. She stepped up onto the outcrop and patted the servitor like it was a pet. Beth sighed, felt her heart drop and lowered the UMP. She saw what was coming. 'I am to be their ship queen.' Beth suddenly felt so very tired. The adrenaline bled from her, and she felt close to collapse and very, very hungry.

'Talia, come on. Please, let's just go,' Beth managed.

'I can't; they need me.'

'You have no idea what I have gone through ...'

'Can't you just be happy for me? I have found my place. You will too one day.'

Shooting Talia was only a passing thought, Beth told herself as she tried to remain calm.

'You've really outdone yourself this time, haven't you? Not satisfied with abusive boyfriends who nearly beat you to death, with pimps and mobsters ... no, you have to go and find a cult of fucking sea monsters? How are you going to top this? Date Satan?'

'I don't think Satan is re—'

'The thing is, Talia, you are loved. I don't know why you don't think you are – maybe we aren't as interesting as some cult living in a weird thing in the fucking Solent – but every time you do something like this it causes pain, and then we have to come and sort it out for you.'

'I never asked you for anything,' Talia said. Beth could still hear the petulance and wondered if this lot knew what they had let themselves in for.

'We're sisters.'

'You know that's not true, and I've always known.'

'We're sisters in every way that matters. Now, please ... I'm tired and I want to go home, and your dad would probably like to hear from you before he dies.'

Tears sprang up in Talia's eyes. 'Why are you doing this to me?'

That was it. 'To you!' Beth was incredulous. 'To you?' Now angry. 'Think beyond yourself for just one moment!'

'Do you know what's fucking happened to me?!'

Ezard and the hybrids were just listening. There was that air of discomfort that comes from outsiders witnessing a domestic row.

Beth took a step forward, jabbing her finger at Talia, the hybrids moving out of her way. It all came back to her. Talia's unconscious body as she went after Davey. Seeing her own sister testify against her. Dad in his chair, the look of disappointment in his eyes. Flashes of the violence across Portsmouth to try and get her back. The people hurt or terrorised along the way.

'You selfish fucking bitch! I keep waiting for you to grow up, to realise that there are other people in the world! That we're not all here just to play roles in your next fucking self-destructive drama! Where ... where ... you try and cause as much pain as you fucking can because that's the only way you think that you can matter to other people! You fucking victim!' As she finished her rage bled out of her.

Talia's face was a mask of cold fury.

'Flush her and shit her out,' she said imperiously.

Something like a sphincter opened above her. Hybrids dived from the bony outcrop as liquid hit her, blasting her off the outcrop like a riot cannon.

The feeling of connection to something overwhelmed her. The connection in her blood, the same shared flesh that was technology, made her feel the wakening of a massive and ancient intellect. It overwhelmed her thoughts as she was consumed.

Somewhere else.

They felt their sister through red dreams in monstrous, corrupted and insane minds. They reached for her, to make her like them. Now all could wake and grow and spore. They felt something in their seeds, some parasitical life.

The sound of metal on metal.

''Ere, it's not firing. Is it broken?'

493

'How can I be of assistance in my robbery and murder?' du Bois asked as he turned to look at the man.

'Oh, the safety's on.' There was another metallic click. 'Should you be moving your head like that with a spinal injury?'

It was agony, but du Bois brought his right arm across his body so his hand was aimed at the thief.

'Seriously mate, you'll do yourself a mischief.'

'You are about to shoot me with my own carbine, yes?'

'True,' the thief conceded and aimed the weapon at du Bois again. The shrouded snub-nosed .38 slid out of his sleeve on the hopper with a thought. He fired the revolver twice. Even the tiny recoil of the .38 was enough to cause him agony. The thief disappeared from view. Du Bois knew he had hit him. In the face and the upper right arm. The face could have been a graze though. He heard the *splash* as the thief hit the water, and then thrashing and what sounded like the mewling of a wounded animal.

'You shot me,' the thief squealed.

'Funny, that,' du Bois said from the top of the Range Rover. He was now putting all the effort he could into moving. It was agonising. 'What do you think caused me to do that?' he managed through gritted teeth.

Du Bois slid off the roof of the Range Rover and landed in about a foot of water. Pain lanced through him and he blacked out for a moment. He came to next to the thief. His right arm was a mess and looked like it was hanging on by only a tendon or two. The face shot was just a graze or the glaser round would have killed him.

'You shot me!' the thief said again between piteous cries.

'You can go into shock, you know,' du Bois told him. 'Oh, never mind.' He managed to get both arms up. The two .38s slid out and Du Bois shot the man ten times. He was dead after the first. Du Bois stared at the man with undisguised contempt. Then he slumped against the Range Rover in the water. Soon he'd be able to walk. Waves were coming up Alhambra Road now. He'd left his mark on this city. The Solent was muddy and stormy-looking under a clear blue sky.

Du Bois looked back at the dead man. Had it always been this easy for him to kill, he wondered? He had murdered the thief in a fit of temper and he knew it. Was it just a case of asking a god he knew did not exist for forgiveness and then getting on with the rest of his day?

Du Bois reloaded the .38s, not so much feeling guilty as worried by the absence of guilt. They slid back up his sleeves and he grabbed the FAL. Du Bois forced himself painfully to his feet. He managed to lean into the Range Rover and grab some more ammunition for the carbine before turning and limping towards the sea.

Gone. Separated from it. For a moment she'd felt its mind; for a moment she'd touched her sister's mind. Then she was outside. She was in the cold and the dark, the weight of the water pressing down on her. She was too tired to fight as violent current after violent current kicked her around.

Suddenly she was sucked upwards, the force inescapable. Her lungs felt like they were being crushed. Soon it would be time to try and breathe water.

Then she was in the air but still in the water. Then falling.

Du Bois was standing nearly waist-deep in the sea, with much bigger waves on the way. The beach was covered now and the waves were over the ruined pier as he watched it rise, water pouring off it, concealing its true shape, that of a biomechanical, vaguely Piscean-shaped seed pod, larger than the largest aircraft carrier.

A hidden Seeder, here of all places, du Bois thought. The signs had pointed towards it, but even sleeping it beggared belief that the Circle had not known. He thought back to the presence beneath the family home. His family's own secret. Had he known?

The sky was slashed open with a blade of pulsing blue light. There was the sound of air escaping on a massive scale as it was sucked through the wound in the sky. Du Bois had thought he would be asleep and never witness this himself.

The water seethed. Writhing tentacles of all sizes breached the surface. Du Bois didn't even flinch as one lashed out and destroyed a building on the corner of Alhambra Road.

She was awake. It wouldn't be long before her sisters realised this. Then they would wake. Their corruption, whatever had caused the fall of the Seeders, driven them mad, would pollute the one here. When they awoke, fully, then it was over.

Beth found herself in seething water, tentacles whipping all around her. Inside her head was a roaring, a near-deafening white noise that made her want to clasp her hands over her ears, though she knew that it would give her no respite.

Fully clothed, in rough water, weapons weighing her down – she just wanted to give in and sink.

Had the frigate been patrolling in the Solent because of the so-called terrorist activity? du Bois wondered. *Or did the Circle have a hand in its presence?* It was a Type 23, HMS *Leicester*, he thought. He saw the smoke and moments later heard the booming echo of the ship's fore-mounted 4.5-inch gun. It fired again before the first shell had even hit.

The water exploded near her. The shock wave bounced her through the water, threatening to powder bone as the liquid magnified the force. Then again. She was not sure why she did, but she discarded the UMP, the Benelli and all her remaining ammo and started to swim. Above her part of the sky was red.

'Fools,' du Bois muttered to himself.

The frigate fired two Sea Wolf surface-to-air missiles. They shot out of their vertical launch tubes and headed for the seed as it rose towards the red wound in the sky. From the front of the ship two Sting Ray torpedoes sped through the water towards the flailing tentacles. From the pad at the rear of the ship, a Sea Lynx helicopter took off. It was an impressive display, du Bois thought as he shook his head.

Everything around her was fire and force. Her body was repeatedly battered, flung through the air and then driven under by successive explosions. Overpressure burst her eardrums and her bones were powdered.

The tentacle flicked out reflexively, responding to pain. It caught the frigate amidships, breaking its back, cleaving it in two with such force that the two halves crashed against each other before they started to sink, sliding rapidly beneath the muddied churning water.

The surface-to-air missiles hit the seed, battering it around in the sky, blackening and bloodying flesh designed to withstand the rigours of deep space, but it continued to rise. The energy matrices on its skin crackled with bioelectricity as it rose through the wound in the sky. Then the wound was gone.

The Lynx pilot was clearly having problems: the destruction of the *Leicester*, the strange air currents as a result of the wound in the sky and, du Bois guessed, probably just the strangeness of the whole thing. The pilot managed to steady the craft, and moments later the helicopter fired two Sea Skua missiles one after another. They impacted among the greatest concentration of tentacles. A huge amount of water was thrown upwards and some of the smaller tentacles were destroyed or severed and blown into the air. The response was inevitable, the whip-like tentacle flicking out with such force that the helicopter had disintegrated before it was driven down into the water.

Du Bois did not need the biohazard warnings he was receiving from his blood-screen. If the Seeder had woken then she was sporing. Suddenly every phone within earshot started to ring.

'Well, it had to start somewhere,' he said.

It had taken a lot of hacking. He had not even known what the RAF was at the beginning of the day. They'd shut down supposedly secure phone networks. They'd intercepted electronic communications, introduced viruses into air-traffic-control computers and sent fake commands.

They'd been up against someone else as well, someone with know-how and access to lost tech. It hadn't been as simple as fucking with the puny human computer systems, like normal.

And Baron Albedo was dead. Properly dead. Killed by the blond guy who wouldn't die himself, and his bitch had shot Inflictor and Dracimus a lot. That shit was not supposed to happen, King Jeremy thought. And they hadn't even got the goth bitch with the trippy blood.

'Bad day,' Jeremy said quietly as he toyed with the case that Baron Albedo had taken off the blond guy. The thing about bad days, King Jeremy reflected, was that they weren't supposed to happen to him. Someone would have to pay for this.

34

A Long Time After the Loss

'What are you doing?' Vic demanded as he watched the cocoon slowly dissolve. Vic was reasonably sure that he had nailed a very human-sounding borderline hysteria in his voice. If not, he knew that Scab would pick up on his panicky pheromone secretions. 'We've got no idea what's in there. It could be viral; it could be dangerous Seeder tech – anything, something worse than the Scorpion. You can't open it.'

'And yet ...' Scab said. He hadn't taken his eyes off the cocoon. He was getting dressed. He had injected himself with a chemical, given to them on the Living Cities, which was slowly returning Scab to his normal self, reversing the DNA process that had allowed him to disguise himself on Game. Vic had brought some of Scab's stuff with him: his suit, hat, hand weapons, the energy javelin, his P-sat – though not the heavy combat chassis – a case of cigarettes, ear crystals with his music and the case for his works. The important stuff, Vic had guessed. Scab's internal repair systems were still trying to regrow part of his face.

'Look. Let's just deliver it to your employer and retire, separately, rich, or at least almost out of debt, to a life of luxury, and wait for the Church, or some of these Monarchist crazies to, at best, assassinate us. If you're bored you can hunt down the surviving crew members. You'll enjoy that.' He glanced up at Scab.

'I'm tired of being a nightmare. You don't have much imagination, do you?'

'That's really not true. I have lots of it, and all it's being used for is to imagine the bad shit that's going to happen to us as a result of this. Much of it involves very powerful people using a remarkable amount of resources to make me suffer.'

'We're not turning it over,' Scab said. He was still staring at the cocoon as he pushed the javelin back into its hidden sheath in his right arm. The coherent energy blade glowed under his flesh for a moment. Once the shock of Scab's statement had worn off, Vic realised that Scab actually had an expression on his face. Curiosity.

'W-w-why not?' Vic managed. He wasn't sure he'd ever been so frightened, not even after he'd had his brain modified to be more human and he'd experienced his first dream. Apparently foreign images in his head while he slept – it had been terrifying.

'What do you mean why not?' An insect gaping is basically an insect with all its mandibles open. Scab looked up at Vic as if noticing him for the first time. 'Everyone wants this.'

'Yes, I've noticed that,' Vic said, sounding a lot calmer than he felt. 'I think the being killed by an Elite drove it home. So what – and I want to know the answer to this question less than any question I've ever asked before – do you intend to do with it?'

'Well, to get the best price, we should auction it,' Scab said as he ensured that all his weapons were sitting properly in holsters and sheaths.

Vic nodded, shutting down certain of his mental faculties and transferring their running to his neunonics, while he drowned himself in tranquillisers so he wasn't utterly overwhelmed by hysteria.

'And who do you envision coming to this auction?'

'I'd imagine the main bidders will be the Church, the Consortium and representatives from the Monarchist systems, but anyone who can meet my price is welcome.' Everything in place, Scab lit up a cigarette. His neunonics were cycling through his collection of pre-Loss music trying to find something appropriate for the cocoon's big reveal.

'Please, Scab, don't misunderstand me. I have delusions of ruling Known Space as well, but we don't have the power to back it up. We're just a couple of guys with guns is all.'

'It'll be difficult, but I'll find a way to make it easier for them to just give me what I want.'

'They'll track us down and kill us afterwards.'

'I'd welcome that.'

'What about me? I don't have a fucking death wish.'

'What about you?'

'They'll kill me.'

'At best.'

'That's what I said!'

'So?'

Vic stared at him for a moment. He saw this was going to be problematic.

'You can understand why I don't want to be killed, right?'

'I guess. I just don't see what it's got to do with the plan.' Scab was getting angry.

'Fuck you, Scab.' It might have been one of the bravest things he'd ever done. Scab looked at him like he was studying some kind of new phenomenon.

'What do you think our arrangement is?'

'Slave.'

'Don't give me that. You are very well paid.'

'Can I leave now?'

'Obviously not. You are a resource, a very well-paid resource. Don't ever forget that. You have had a good run and been well paid for it, but nothing is for ever.'

'Motivating.'

'Would you prefer to be slaved?'

'What are you asking for from the three most powerful groups in Known Space?'

'Would you prefer to be slaved?'

'I deserve an answer.'

'You deserve what I choose.'

'The problem with you, Scab, is you don't leave people with anything. It's all very well being the most hard-arsed cunt in Known Space, but you've left me with nothing to lose, so either kill me, slave me, go fuck yourself or answer the fucking question.' Vic was pretty sure he had killed himself.

Scab was staring at him. His face seemed impassive again but Vic knew the human well enough to recognise the anger.

'Nobody's spoken to me like that since the Legion.'

Vic just spread out all his limbs, palms up, fingers open in a kind of multi-limbed 'sect, I-don't-care shrug.

'If I tell you, will you stop whining and be useful again?'

'Oh, I apologise that my impending death is making me whiny.'

The look that Scab then gave Vic let him know that the human was being indulgent. Vic guessed that retrieving the cocoon and double-crossing the Church had put his 'partner' in what passed for a good mood in Scab world.

'Fine. Yes, then. I'll stop "whining".'

'I want the surgery they did when they made me join the Legion undone. I know they have a full copy of my personality in the Psycho Banks. I want to be as I was, full and hole, not this weakened version of me.'

'A monster?' You had to work hard for that word to mean anything among the casual cruel brutalities of Known Space.

'Whole.'

'King Shit of Cyst?'

'I'm missing something.'

'That's not much to ask.'

'Then I want to be Elite again.' Something cold ran through Vic as Scab said this. It was a very human feeling.

'That will just put you under the control of whichever power agrees.'

'Not if I don't undergo the conditioning.'

Vic stared at him. He thought he had known it was coming. He had heard stories about Scab: the street sect on Cyst, his kingdom of agony, the mountain of bones, from gang leader to world ruler under the Consortium's nose. As an Elite with no control over him, he could do the same to star systems, perhaps even more than that.

It wasn't bravery. It was instinct. Vic was moving before he had even thought it through. If he had, he would have been too frightened to do anything, or he might have killed himself and hoped for the best.

His top right limb drew the triple-barrelled shotgun pistol. The left was going for the reptile power disc. His lower limbs were drawing both double-barrelled laser pistols.

Scab threw himself over the cocoon, the metalforma knife palmed into his left hand. He threw it as he rolled. His clothes turned into a red neon grid as four beams hit. The tripled-barrelled blast caught him in the back. The explosive rounds penetrated his armoured clothing and hit his hardening skin and then exploded, taking a chunk out of his back.

The knife hit Vic in the throat. It didn't penetrate his armour but stuck there, the smart-matter blade digging through the armour for flesh. Scab's P-sat rose behind Vic and lit up his energy dissipation grid with laser fire.

Scab was on one knee, filling the air with flechettes from the spit gun in his right hand. The flechettes would do little but irritate and distract Vic. Scab emptied the reptile mini-disc launcher on his upper left arm. The hundreds of tiny discs were keyed to track Vic's electromagnetic signature. Scab was a bright neon figure now, his energy dissipation grid glowing, about to succumb to Vic's laser fire which would cook his flesh.

Dropping the empty shotgun pistol, Vic leaped into the air, extending the blades on his top two limbs, still firing the laser pistols with his lower limbs. The leap took him over the cocoon. Scab drew his tumbler pistol and had time to fire twice. The slow bullets would burrow through Vic's armoured exoskeleton and then fragment, spinning inside him. Vic sent an incredibly illegal post-mortem kill instruction to his neunonics, which would in turn control his hard-tech systems that made up the majority of his body and keep his weapons firing.

Vic landed in front of Scab already dead. The metalforma blade had pushed through his neck armour and fanned out, killing him.

Vic's blades scissored in on Scab, the 'sect's lasers still firing. Scab stepped inside the reach of the blades. His right forearm glowed momentarily, and the spit gun he was holding exploded as the energy javelin shot through it and Scab drove it into Vic's chest cavity. The S-tech coherent energy-field weapon cut through Vic's armoured skeleton, Scab moving it around inside his partner's chest until the post-mortem attack was beyond the corpse's capability.

Vic's body stopped moving. Scab, bloody and burned, stepped out of Vic's bladed embrace and looked at him, shaking his head. Vic was probably the finest resource he'd had. If he had had to choose between Vic and the Scorpion, he was not sure which one he would have picked.

On the other hand, the cocoon was almost gone. What was in it was starting to take form. Still smoking, Scab wandered over to stand beside it. The last remaining bits of the cocoon seemed to dissipate. Scab was quite surprised to find himself looking down at a slender, pale, dark-haired, apparently natural human female. She opened her eyes and then immediately started to die.

'That fucking bastard!' the Monk shouted. Or would have if she hadn't been in a nutrient tank having her body regrown. Instead she had 'faced it vigorously.

'Is that any way for a woman of the cloth to talk?' Churchman asked mildly. The Monk thrashed around in the tank to glare at him through the gel with natural eyes. 'It's not the first time you've died,' he said.

'It's the first time I've had to be cloned, and I can't say I'm enjoying the experience.' Through the gel she could make out the general outline of Churchman, or rather the technological form that gave what was left of him a semblance of being alive.

'I haven't seen you this angry in a long time.'

'I'm going to kill him.'

'He's been in touch.'

Epilogue
The Walker

One foot in front of the other. One foot in front of the other. Under a bloody sky the walker moved through a blackened living landscape of ghosts and remnants. The last city was just over the horizon.

Acknowledgements

Thank you to Dr David Luke for taking some time out to answer questions on DMT, altered states and the 'Machine Elves of Hyperspace'.
And thanks to Jo Luke for typing those notes up.

To Kath Anderton who took the time to comment on early parts of the novel despite having a great deal going on in her own life at the time.

Thank you to Nicola and Simon Bates for their hospitality whilst researching Portsmouth and thanks to Fay Brown for her company and help in doing the same.

Thank you very much to everyone who took part in Other Great Uses for Gavin Smith Novels.

Thank you to Chloe Isherwood of Chloe Isherwood Photography, not only for organising the Other Great Uses for Gavin Smith Novels but also for the Age of Scorpio photo shoot, or Three Hysterical Days in Wales as I've come to think of it.

Also for the photo shoot, thank you to Rachel Nicholson (make-up), Matt Karma Bryant (editing), Yvonne Cunningham (location and AD), Stephanie Lindley (Tangwen), Kiera Gould (Cliodna) and Gabriella Howson (Britha).
And thanks to Evenlode Studio and Number 15 Leather and Costume for providing props and costumes for the shoot.

To my fellow authors for support and advice: Stephen and Michaela Deas, MD Lachlan, Chris Wooding and Anthony Jones.

Thanks again to the gaming community for their support, particularly to Namon, the Charioteers and the Lords of Barry.

Thank you to my agent Sam Copeland at RCW Ltd.

Thanks to my editor Simon Spanton and to Jon Weir, Charlie Panayiotou, Gillian Redfearn and Marcus Gipps at Gollancz. And to Hugh Davis for the copy edit.

To my family and friends for their patience, support and enthusiasm (and particularly my dad this time for an amusing afternoon of wondering around the Angus countryside failing miserably to find the ruins of a Broch).
And to Yvonne for her evil brand of patience.

Finally I'm thankful to everyone who buys a copy of anything I write and I would particularly like to thank those who take the time to comment on websites, Facebook, Twitter and/or write reviews, good or bad, your interest is greatly appreciated.

Gavin G. Smith, Leicester, 2012
www.gavingsmith.com